Across the tempestuous tapestry of the South as it rises from the ashes after the shattering Civil War—against the turbulent backdrop of the emerging Westward movement, the best-selling Windhaven Saga continues. . . .

Beginning with the first *Windhaven Plantation* novel, which told of the proud and passionate Lucien Bouchard—the builder of a plantation, the patriarch of a family dynasty, the founder of a legacy that is the embodiment of the American tradition, *Windhaven's Peril* continues his story. It is his plantation, his dynasty and his legacy that is stamped across the hearts and minds of his children—and his children's children who carry on. . . .

At Windhaven Plantation Luke Bouchard, his beautiful young wife, Laure, and their children plan to launch a new life. But the past catches up with Luke and unresolved disputes re-emerge. . . .

At Windhaven Range, while Luke's son, Lucien Edmond Bouchard, oversees a spring cattle drive to Abilene, bushwhackers storm the ranch. And later, Lucien Edmond himself confronts land swindlers who have the audacity to take on Windhaven Range. Love and romance bloom as well between the young and desirable Felicidad, a vivacious Mexican orphan, and Lucas, Djamba's proud and handsome son. And another unforgettable love story unfolds—that of Pablo Casares, the lonely and heartsick *vaquero*, who rescues a widow and her children from proverty and sorrow. . . .

From the first *Windhaven Plantation* to *Storm Over Windhaven*, from *Legacy of Windhaven* to *Return to Windhaven*, the explosive tale of the private passions and the public triumphs of the Bouchard family continues to unfold . . . in *Windhaven's Peril.*

OVER TWO MILLION COPIES SOLD

The Windhaven Saga:

Windhaven Plantation
Storm Over Windhaven
Legacy of Windhaven
Return to Windhaven
Windhaven's Peril

WINDHAVEN'S PERIL

Marie de Jourlet

PINNACLE BOOKS   **LOS ANGELES**

WINDHAVEN'S PERIL

Copyright © 1979 by Book Creations, Inc.

An original Pinnacle Books edition, published for the first time anywhere.

Produced by Lyle Kenyon Engel

First printing, June 1979
Second printing, June 1979
Third printing, July 1979
Fourth printing, October 1979

ISBN: 0-523-40499-9

Cover illustration by Bruce Minney

Printed in the United States of America

PINNACLE BOOKS, INC.
2029 Century Park East
Los Angeles, California 90067

Gratefully dedicated to the Book Creations, Inc. team of Lyle and Marla Engel, Philip and Leslie Rich, and Rebecca Rubin, whose painstaking aid and encouragement lend inspiration and guidance to reward an author's labors.

Acknowledgments

The novelist who deals with the history of the past has a double challenge: first, of course, that of recreating the atmosphere and setting of an epoch. Yet in so doing, he or she may lose sight of documented historical accuracy in projecting the story and the involvement of characters. That is why I must express my indebtedness to the following for verifying important facts in this book and suggesting many helpful ideas which made it still more logical: Joseph Milton Nance, Professor of History, Texas A&M University; Mrs. Evelyn M. King, Assistant Director of Special Research, Sterling C. Evans Library, Texas A&M University; Rosanne McCaffrey, Research Coordinator, New Orleans Historic Collections; James R. Travis, University of Alabama Press at Tuscaloosa; and Kevin Bell, Curator of Birds, Lincoln Park Zoo, Chicago.

In addition, a grateful accolade to Fay Bergstrom, who transcribed and typed the manuscript so painstakingly, herself suggesting rephrasing at rough spots and contributing suggestions which greatly accelerated the creation of the work.

Marie de Jourlet

Luke Bouchard

Laure Prindeville Brunton

The
Bouchard

Edwina
Bouchard
1868~

Hugo
Bouchard
1861~

Kenneth
Douglas
1865~

Joy
Hunter V
1869~

Arthur
Douglas
1863~

Howard
Douglas
1863~

Andrew
Hunter
1854~

Melinda
Hunter
1852

Charles
Douglas
1835~

Jimmy
Belcher
1853~

Connie
Belcher
1855~

Laurette
Bouchard
1837~

Sybella
Wilson
1868~

Millie
(deceased)

Maybelle
Williamson
1820~

Mark
Bouchard
1819~1864

James
Hunter
1822~

Arabella
Bouchard
1844~

Henry
Belcher
1821~

I Windhaven Plantation
II Storm Over Windhaven
III Legacy of Windhaven
IV Return to Windhaven
V Windhaven's Peril

RON TOELKE 1978 Op. IX

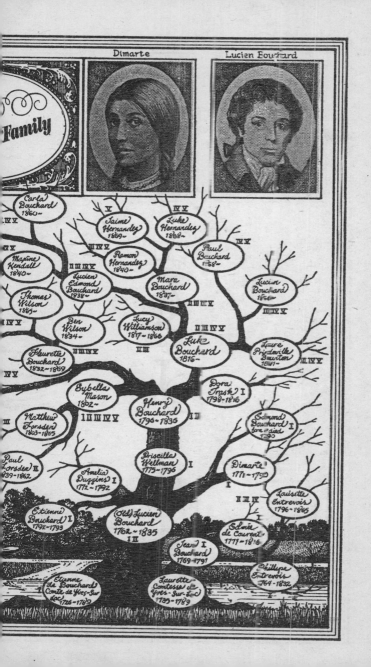

Dimarte

Lucien Bouchard

Family

Carla
Bouchard
1860~

Jaime
Hernandez
1859~

Luke
Hernandez
1868~

Paul
Bouchard
1868~

Maxine
Kendall
1840~

Ramon
Hernandez
1840~

Lucien
Bouchard
1866~

Thomas
Wilson
1865~

Lucien
Edmond
Bouchard
1938~

Mare
Bouchard
1837~

Ben
Wilson
1834~

Lucy
Williamson
1817~1866

Fleurette
Bouchard
1832~1869

Luke
Bouchard
1816~

Claire
Pidgeon Hall
Brewton
1841~

Sybella
Mason
1802~

Henry
Bouchard
1796~1836

Dora
Trask I
1798~1846

Matthew
Forsden
1803~1865

Edmond
Bouchard
born & died
1790

Paul
Forsden II
1839~1862

Amelia
Duggins I
1772~1792

Priscilla
Wellman
1775~1796

Dimarte
1771~1792

Louisette
Entrevois
1796~1865

Etienne
Bouchard I
1792~1793

(Old) Lucien
Bouchard
1762~1835

Selita
de Couront
1777~1816

Jean I
Bouchard
1769~1791

Phillipe
Entrevois
1764~1832

Etienne
de Bouchard
Comte de Yves-Sur-
Lac 1726~1789

Laurette
Comtesse de
Yves-Sur-Lac
1739~1789

WINDHAVEN'S
PERIL

PROLOGUE

It was mid-January 1869. Almost four years had passed since Appomattox and the end of the bloody Civil War. Yet those four years had not brought about President Lincoln's hoped-for peace, "with malice toward none with charity for all." The South was still torn asunder by the retaliatory "punishment" imposed upon it by the victorious North—by the Carpetbaggers' regime which had given power, through the Union League, to the Radical Republicans and the freed blacks.

Not always had this part of the country been the scene of strife. In earlier times the mighty Creek Indians had roamed and hunted. They had thrived then, and built their villages, knowing that there was no enemy strong enough to force them from the land which had been their birthright for generations.

The Creeks had, however, long since been driven by the white man to the Far West. Only the old men, sitting in rocking chairs on the verandas of frame houses, could remember the Indians. When the wind rustled against the branches of cedar and cypress trees along the Alabama River, the old men heard moans in the night. These were allegedly the spirits of the once all-powerful Creeks, returning to the lands which they could never forget.

But in reality the sounds were far more ominous. They symbolized the oppression of the Northern conquerors, not mournful ghosts seeking to return to where once they had ruled. They were made by vindictive men who disguised themselves as ghosts, men who brought to the haunting shadows of the night the grim echoes of the whip and the gun. The light of the friendly moon was

1

dimmed by the glare of flaming torches that lit up a sinister cross.

Eighty years before, young Lucien Bouchard had left his father's estate in Normandy, France, and after crossing the Atlantic he landed in Mobile, Alabama, and journeyed upriver. There he had met Tunkamara, *mico* of Econchate, married the *mico*'s daughter, Dimarte, and lived among the Creeks. Now the village of Econchate had become Montgomery, the flourishing capital of Alabama, which had been readmitted to the Union the previous June.

Now it was Luke Bouchard, Lucien's grandson, who had returned to the land which Tunkamara had given to his grandfather long ago as a bond of brotherhood.

Old Lucien had believed strongly in the universal brotherhood of man. He had shared his profits with the Indians and freed the black slaves who had been given to him by Tunkamara. Now Luke Bouchard, at fifty-two, had returned to the land of his birth, where his grandfather before him had begun a new life in a strange new world.

While in his late teens, Luke had helped to build Windhaven, the red-brick château that was a replica of his grandfather's birthplace in Normandy. During that time, he had fallen in love with Lucy Williamson, who lived on a neighboring plantation. They married and had two children—a son, Lucien Edmond, and a daughter, Mara.

Luke's own father, Henry (Lucien Bouchard's only son), had driven his young wife, Dora, to fling herself into the river in order to escape her husband's cruelty. When Henry Bouchard took a second wife, Sybella Mason, and his dissolute son Mark was born, it had always been Mark whom Henry preferred over Luke.

Luke, like his grandfather, had a philosophy of life that was tempered by the books he read and by a genuine respect for the land on which he worked, rather than for its immediate profits. His brother Mark, on the other hand, had married Lucy's younger sister, Maybelle, and deserted her after their daughter, Laurette, was born. He was killed smuggling contraband during the Civil War.

It was his stepmother, valiant Sybella, then, who became a true mother to Luke. She nurtured his ambitions to work the land of Windhaven Plantation in such a way that it would not be ruined by the endless growing of cotton—a crop with which the South seemed obsessed. She had enthusiastically supported Luke's desire to manumit all their slaves, long before the advent of the Emancipation Proclamation. And when Yankee troops, at the very end of the war, burned Windhaven and killed Sybella's second husband, Matthew Forsden, Sybella had stood courageously beside Luke, urging the rest of the family to follow them to Texas, to found Windhaven Range.

The Bouchards had traveled first to New Orleans, to buy supplies and to have wagons made for a journey across the Texas plains that would lead them to Carrizo Springs. There they would find good grazing land in a valley near the life-giving waters of the Nueces River.

Old Lucien had put aside, in an English bank, a valuable legacy in gold for his grandson—a legacy that would allow the Bouchards a new stake in their new life, since all Confederate money had become useless. Luke had given his half-brother, Mark, a third of that legacy as the latter's share of Windhaven Plantation, so that Mark could make no further demands upon a family he had so ruthlessly abandoned.

While in New Orleans, Luke had met John Brunton, head of the bank which had handled old Lucien's accounts for so many years. There, too, he had met the golden-haired Laure Prindeville, John Brunton's fiancée. She had flirted with Luke so outrageously that he yielded to her seductive powers for one heedless hour, only to be stricken afterward with remorse over his infidelity.

The Bouchards had taken a steamboat to Galveston, Texas, where Sybella's daughter, Arabella, had disembarked with her husband, James Hunter, and their two children, Andrew and Melinda. James would go to work for his cousin as a factor of a cotton mill there. The rest of them had gone on to Corpus Christi, and then traveled by wagon to find what would become Windhaven Range.

In this new life Luke Bouchard had learned, through his own experiences, something of the hardships which his grandfather had faced. He defended the ranch against marauding bandits, and made an ally of the powerful Comanche chief, Sangrodo. During one terrifying bandit

3

raid, Lucy was killed while trying to save Lucien Edmond's two children. After her death, Luke decided to place Windhaven Range in Lucien Edmond's hands, return to New Orleans, and then pursue his plan to regain Windhaven Plantation.

John Brunton, who had succumbed to yellow fever shortly after Lucy's death, had arranged for a black freedman to buy Windhaven, along with the original fifty acres of land which had been part of the *mico's* gift to Luke's grandfather.

Once again, Luke had begun a new life, this time as a banker. He took over John Brunton's bank in the latter's name, to fulfill his pledge of friendship. And he had courted and married John's widow, Laure, whose child Luke knew in fact to be his own. He had fought a duel to the death with Armand Cournier, a cousin of the man who had attempted, years before, to woo and win Arabella in order to gain control of Windhaven Plantation. And then Luke had gone back to Alabama, to the charred remains of the red-brick château near Lowndesboro, that plantation which fronted the Alabama River, with its winding turns and its tall bluffs and its glades of trees.

Luke bought back the fifty acres and what was left of the château from Phineas Atbury and his wife, Hannah—the black couple who, at John Brunton's direction, had acquired old Lucien's holdings. The Klu Klux Klan dragged Phineas and Hannah Atbury out to the forest and flogged them mercilessly. They were warned to abandon the château and the land if they wished to live. But Luke and his workers defied the Klan, and one of Luke's loyal black workers killed the leader, Hurley Parmenter.

Now Luke Bouchard, advanced in years yet young in spirit, was ready to begin still another new life—this time at Windhaven Plantation with his beloved Laure and their two small children. His youngest son, Paul, had been born only a few weeks before. Now, just as he had dreamed of doing for so long, Luke was determined to live up to his grandfather's concept of equality. White and black workers would toil side by side upon the rich land. The crops would be varied. There would be none of the poverty and monotony of the subsistence farming that had already be-

4

come a widespread practice throughout much of the enfeebled South.

Best of all, there would be a homecoming, a time to know love and to share it, a young wife and two children who would be a part of whatever fortune might lie ahead for the Bouchard family.

CHAPTER ONE

On this Friday evening, there was no thought of the mournful and sinister sounds of the night or what they might portend. In the red-brick château, there was the brightness of candlelight and the hum of happy voices as the young black foreman, Marius Thornton, directed the volunteer workers. They were busy restoring the rooms of the château so that the next day Laure Bouchard might be made welcome. Luke himself, his smiling face and wiry body belying his age, had pitched in along with the others to polish the floors and clean the walls.

Dan Munroe, one of the volunteers, had beamed with pleasure at Luke's grateful thanks, when he surprised him with a cradle and a crib which he himself had built during his spare time. They would go into the bedroom in the right wing of the first floor that would belong to little Lucien and the baby, Paul. The charming soubrette, Mitzi, would sleep in the same room and look after the children, since she had insisted on accompanying her beloved former employer, Laure, to Alabama.

At eleven o'clock the next morning, the steamboat *Alabama Belle* would drop anchor at the remodeled wharf from which Lucien Bouchard had once shipped his cotton to Mobile, and Luke would be reunited with his adored young wife and little Lucien and Paul. It was the thought of this reunion which made him seem far younger than his years. Admiringly, he ran his hands over the smooth wood of the crib and the cradle, and again thanked Dan Munroe for his thoughtfulness.

Luke turned to watch Marius Thornton standing beside his lovely young wife, Clementine, who was sitting on an ottoman and crooning to her six-week-old son. His smile deepened to see the adoring look which the young black

6

exchanged with the attractive mulatto. Marius reached out and put his forefinger against the baby's tiny hand. He chuckled happily as the baby at once clenched it and made a cooing sound.

Luke was anxious to see little Paul. It would be the very first time he had seen his youngest son. He remembered his pledge, up there on the towering bluff, that Windhaven would again resound with the happy laughter of children and young people, with the voices of blacks and whites working together in an amity and understanding which would transcend bigotry, fear, and hatred, three evils which had, like a slow incendiary, burst into the pyre of the Civil War. Yet, Luke reflected, with people like Dan and Marius around him, people who shared his dream and believed in the integrity of work and its own satisfying reward, there would be no thought of North and South, only of a united fellowship. That had been Lucien Bouchard's credo, and it was his as well.

As Luke vicariously shared Marius's joy in his family, he thought of his own plans. Windhaven Plantation would be a kind of cooperative enterprise. Many of the freed blacks, who had originally purchased their allotted fifty acres, fled when the Klan had come calling on the Atburys. He could legally acquire those abandoned acres now. And he would hire, at good wages, both whites and blacks who felt about the land as he did and who showed a skill for developing its potential.

Hannah Atbury would be the cook for the plantation. Her husband Phineas, who was still not completely recovered from his flogging by the Klan, would act as steward. It would be a post that would restore his dignity and let him share the responsibility for the rebuilding of Windhaven, without taxing him too much, physically.

Then there was Moses Turner who, despite his fifty years and arthritis, could still do a good day's work in the fields. His ailing wife Mary was much better now, and Luke had suggested that she sew and clean the clothes of the other workers on the land It would be a responsibility which, as she herself had gratefully declared, would give her both pleasure and pride of accomplishment.

Over in the other corner was Hughie Mendicott, a middle-aged widower. His lanky, hard-working sons, Davie

7

and Louis, worked beside their father in the fields furrowing and tilling, preparing the rich earth for yams and fruits and vegetables. There, chatting animatedly with him, was plump, good-natured Buford Phelps. Phelps's very presence proved the validity of old Lucien's and Luke's theories about entrusting men with responsibility and letting them stand on their own two feet.

Just two weeks before, Phelps, a representative of the Freedmen's Bureau, had called upon Luke Bouchard to make sure no discrimination was being practiced, or reprisals being taken, against the black workers on this land, now that a former Southern plantation owner had returned to it. Pompous and self-important at first, he had inspected the carefully planned acreage and listened to Luke's explanation of his plans for raising cattle and a variety of crops. Afterward, Buford Phelps had uttered a sigh and shaken his head.

Then he had apologetically declared, " 'Scuse me, Mister Bouchard, sir, I didn't 'spect to find anything like this here at all. Seems to me like there's goin' t'be lots o' work for people and a good livin' to make. I'd like it fine if you'd give me a chance to work on some land right along with these other folks." Luke had immediately invited Phelps to move into one of the abandoned shacks and see what he could do with the acreage alloted to the former owner. Now, the formerly boastful advocate of black superiority was working as hard as any of the others and thoroughly enjoying himself.

Hannah Atbury moved toward Luke, softspoken and deferential. That deference was founded not on servility, but on respect and admiration for what he had done to save her and her frail husband from the ruthless Klan. "All the dishes are washed good, Mister Bouchard, sir," she announced, a smile on her lips. "Silverware, too. Everything's all ready for your sweet wife tomorrow."

"Thank you, Hannah. It'll be a wonderful homecoming. Why, just an hour ago I walked through all the rooms on the second floor, and you'd hardly know there had been a fire. Everybody's done wonders. I mean to tell them so, too, Hannah."

Hannah Atbury shook her head. "It's you that's done the wonders, mostly, Mister Bouchard. I told Phineas, there

8

you was up on the ladder helping put up that new portico and then sanding down those stone steps 'til they shone like a mirror."

"I know," Luke chuckled to himself, his eyes suddenly distant. "When I was just a boy, I remember helping grandfather build this beautiful place. I wanted to have a part in it, to do something all by myself that would suggest how much I loved him every time he saw it. I helped put up that first portico. In a way, Hannah, it's a sign of a new life and happy times coming."

"It sure is, Mister Bouchard. Every one of us wishes you and Miz Laure all the years of happiness the good God is sure to spell out for you both. And the babies too—that goes without saying."

Luke Bouchard did not trust himself to speak. He gripped Hannah's hand and nodded and smiled. Then, clearing his throat, he finally remarked, "If it isn't asking too much, maybe we ought to have some refreshments for all these overtime workers of ours, Hannah."

"I already thought of that, Mister Bouchard." Hannah Atbury forgot her dignity enough to giggle. "I've got some nice baked ham and sweet yams and as strong a coffee as I could get in the store over at Lowndesboro, and I 'specially made some biscuits, and there's honey and an apple cobbler, too."

"Well now, Hannah, for that sort of feast I think I could do some more work myself right now," Luke Bouchard declared, laughing.

But Hannah Atbury shook her head. "No sir, you aren't going to do another lick of work today, Mister Bouchard. Dan 'n Hughie 'n Moses, they told me this is their way of saying thank you for giving them all a chance and making us feel just like a family. Hard to believe now we were ever slaves, Mr. Bouchard."

Luke Bouchard's face sobered. "I think I understand how you feel, Hannah. And really, there never were slaves at Windhaven Plantation, from as far back as when grandfather was first given this land by the chief of the Creeks and dreamed of building this fine house on it to remind him of where he had been born and where he had been happy as a young man working on the land."

* * *

The *Alabama Belle* slowed its engines and the great paddle wheels churned the river water as white-haired old Captain Horace Tenby raised his hand to the stevedore in charge of the steamboat's whistle. Three long blasts resounded, and petite Mitzi Vourlay gasped and hugged little Paul closer to her as she stood at the rail beside golden-haired Laure who held tightly onto the hand of little Lucien.

"Sorry if I startled you nice ladies," Captain Tenby politely doffed his blue cap. "We're only a few miles away from Lowndesboro now, so I figured I'd let Mister Bouchard and his folks know you'll soon be at the dock."

"That's very thoughtful of you, Captain Tenby," Laure smiled. She had let her golden hair grow long, almost to her waist, and it was gathered in a fillet of white cloth. She wore a blue dress with long skirt and high neck, which was covered with a fur-lined cape to protect her from the chilly January winds. Little Lucien cooed and pointed at an oak tree that seemed to stand on the very edge of the riverbank. His mother nodded, bent over, and put her arms around him. "Yes, darling, a tree. Isn't it a big one? Just wait until you see all the wonderful trees and flowers at our new home. And Daddy will be there to say hello." Looking up, she saw that Mitzi was regarding her with almost tearful happiness, and she added softly, "It'll be the first time he's seen Paul too, *ma chérie.*"

"*Oui, c'est vrai,* Madame Laure," Mitzi agreed. Now twenty-one, Mitzi was even more beautiful than when Luke Bouchard saw her that first time he had called at the Union House to meet John Brunton. She, too, wore a fur-lined cape over a neat, black silk dress with a widely flaring skirt. She looked sedate and poised, quite unlike the charming soubrette who had acted as parlormaid in the elegant *maison de luxe.* John Brunton had established the house as a front, so that he might continue his banking activities without arousing the suspicions of Union officers who were then in control of New Orleans. From the way Mitzi held the baby Paul and never let Laure and little Lucien out of her sight, it was evident that she thoroughly relished her new status in life.

Majestically the three-decked steamboat, newly painted red, white, and blue, continued along the winding turns of the swiftly moving river. Mitzi observed the bluffs that rose on each side of the river and exclaimed, "*Quel beau paysage, n'est-ce pas?*" to which Laure readily agreed. "Yes, it's very beautiful. So peaceful and so many kinds of shrubs and trees and the red clay bluffs and the banks— what a paradise it must have been for the first people who came here."

"That's a fact, ma'am," Captain Tenby said, still hovering nearby and eager to be of help to his two lovely passengers. "Fact is, the war didn't touch this part of the South very much, and that's a blessing. Only now, well, feelings still run mighty high down here against the Yankees and the way they sent their niggers and Carpetbaggers to loot everything in sight. Now I don't hold with disloyalty to the Union, and I for one was sorry to see brother fighting brother like they did those four terrible years. All the same, I sort of understand why there's folks who band together and try to put a stop to some of the things the Yankees are doing."

"You mean the Ku Klux Klan? But I read in the *Times-Picayune* that it had been outlawed," Laure replied in surprise.

"That's true enough, ma'am, but they're still around, no mistake about it. You see, the real loyal Southerners know how to keep a secret, and they won't identify them to any of those Yankee law officers or soldiers trying to round them up. The way I see it," he dolefully shook his head, "is that the Yankees will just have to take it a mite easier now that they've got us where they want us, and maybe the Klan won't be so active."

"I sincerely hope so," Laure murmured, remembering Luke's letter last fall which had related how he had gone to the klavern in the woods to try to save Marius Thornton from a vengeful and terrible death. That letter had made her weep for concern over his well-being, just as she had over his duel with Armand Cournier. Her admiration and respect for him had turned to love that afternoon when, after the duel and heedless of his own danger, he had saved a little boy from a mad dog on a New Orleans street. Though she had lived all of her life in New Orleans, Laure knew now that she belonged to Luke Bouchard and that she would be his helpmate at Windhaven Plantation, now so new and unfamiliar to her. It would be her home, too, from this day forth.

Seeing the anxious look on Laure's face, Captain Tenby hastened to reassure her, aware that he had blundered in mentioning the Ku Klux Klan. "Mister Bouchard's just fine, ma'am, just fine. Brought him some supplies from Mobile just two weeks ago, I did, and he told me he's really looking forward to having you see how nice he's fixed up the old place where his grandfather lived. Wonderful family, the Bouchards, salt of the earth. I met old Mister Lucien many a time on this river when he was taking his cotton down to the countinghouse in Mobile. And I tell you this, ma'am, it makes me feel young again to know that Mister Luke Bouchard is going to use my old steamboat hauling his goods downriver again, just like in the old days."

"You're very kind, Captain Tenby. You know, my little boy here is named after my husband's grandfather. Lucien darling, this is Captain Horace Tenby." Laure bent down again with a feline movement, her lips wreathed in a loving smile, both hands around the little boy's waist as she turned him toward the white-haired captain of the *Alabama Belle*. The blond little boy smiled, shook both fists, and uttered a questioning, "Dada?"

"No, angel, it isn't your daddy, but this very nice man is bringing us to see him," Laure murmured. Captain Tenby took off his blue-visored cap with its faded gold braid and offered it to little Lucien, who reached for it with one hand, and turned it over and over, as if critically examining it.

"Takes to it, ma'am, just like it was made for him," Captain Tenby chuckled. "Maybe that's a sign he's going to grow up to run one of these big paddleboats up and down the old Alabama."

"It's a fine, needful trade, Captain Tenby, and if that's what little Lucien wants to do, I know he'll do it well," Laure declared with pride as she straightened up, clasping the little boy's hand in hers. "I see the château now —just beyond that tall bluff! How beautiful it is, how sturdily it stands all alone, as if on guard!"

"*C'est vraiment magnifique*," Mitzi Vourlay agreed as the steamboat passed the towering red bluff where Lucien

Bouchard and Dimarte shared their eternal reunion. It moved slowly toward the rebuilt wharf just beyond the red-brick château with its twin towers.

"It's been an honor and a pleasure to have brought you and Miss Mitzi and the children back home, ma'am," Captain Tenby said, beaming as he doffed his cap again and inclined his head toward both Laure and Mitzi. "Now you be sure to give my best wishes to Mister Bouchard, and tell him I'll be looking forward to seeing all of you again real soon."

"Of course I'll do that, Captain Tenby. Thank you so much for all your kindness. I'd best go get my baggage now." Laure looked eagerly at the château, then moved away from the rail, nodding at Mitzi to follow her.

"I've taken the liberty of having the boys get your luggage ready, and they'll carry it down the gangplank ahead of you, ma'am. We'll drop anchor in another minute or two. It's been an easy passage. Sometimes this old river gets a mite skittish, but it's been good as gold today, in your honor."

"You're very sweet, Captain Tenby. I shall certainly tell my husband what wonderful care you've taken of us. And I, too, look forward to seeing you again." Laure extended her hand and, his face reddening like that of a schoolboy, Captain Horace Tenby bowed his head and raised Laure's hand to his lips. Mitzi Vourlay, cradling little Paul, found it hard to suppress a giggle of amusement at this thoroughly Gallic gesture.

"There he is, Mitzi, see?" Laure pointed to the tall gray-haired man standing beside Marius Thornton on the wharf, as the *Alabama Belle* edged toward the landing place and dropped its anchor. "Let's hurry, Mitzi, I can't wait to see him."

"*Moi aussi,*" Mitzi confided in a scarcely audible whisper. She had been infatuated with Luke Bouchard since their very first meeting. The gracious courtesy with which he had always treated her had served to intensify that emotion. Indeed, on the journey from New Orleans, she had falteringly admitted to Laure that in her loyalty to her golden-haired mistress, she had decided to come to Windhaven Plantation without thinking of the potential hazard which her proximity to Luke might cause. And Laure, un-

13

derstandingly, had kissed her and told her, "*Chérie*, even though you worked in the house, you were never more than a maid and I know you're still a virgin. I myself shall see to it that you meet a nice, considerate man who will love you the way Luke loves me. So set your mind at rest, *ma petite*, you're much too honorable and idealistic ever to come between the two of us."

Two sturdy, grinning stevedores carried Laure's and Mitzi's trunks and valises off the boat, then doffed their caps and stepped to either side of the gangplank as the two young women descended, carrying the children. Luke Bouchard uttered a cry of joy and came forward to take little Lucien in his arms as he turned to Laure and kissed her ardently. Mitzi watched, holding little Paul, and could not help uttering a faint sigh of envy at the ecstatic way in which they looked at each other. Then she blushed as Luke turned to her, kissed her on the cheek, and setting little Lucien down, eagerly asked, "May I take Paul from you, *ma chérie*?"

The baby was now almost six weeks old, thriving, black-haired with large, blue eyes. As Luke held him, little Paul opened his eyes and uttered a gurgling little cry.

"He's inherited my father's black hair, Laure. What a fine, strong boy he is!" Luke Bouchard exclaimed.

Then, handing Paul back to Mitzi, he again lifted little Lucien up in his arms, smiling down at the blond little boy, who reached up and touched his chin with both tiny hands. There were tears in Mitzi's eyes as she watched, but these were tears of joy to see the emotion so transparently engraved on the incisive features of this man to whom she had been so compellingly drawn.

"Everything is in order for you, my darling," Luke told Laure as he turned to the smiling group of blacks who had gathered to welcome her. "You know Marius, of course. He's done wonders, as have all these others, in putting things to rights in grandfather's château so that you may see why we were always so proud of it."

"It's good to see you again, Marius," Laure exclaimed as she offered the handsome young black man her hand. With an embarrassed grin he shook it, and then stepped back, saying, "It's going to be an even lovelier place now that you're here to live in it, Miz Bouchard."

"Thank you so much, Marius."

"Laure, this is Hannah Atbury, who's going to be our cook, and Phineas, her husband, who's going to be our steward. You remember, John Brunton had the Atburys buy this house and the fifty acres of land on which it stands. They've been extremely courageous, and I owe them a great deal."

"Then so do I. It's good to meet you, Hannah, Phineas." Laure graciously acknowledged the introduction, stepping forward to shake hands with both of them.

"And here we have Moses Turner and his wife, Mary," Luke continued. The tall, arthritic black man came forward a bit sheepishly to shake Laure's hand, as did his frail, slender wife. "Mary is a wonderful seamstress, Laure," Luke added, "so if you've brought along any clothes that need stitching or hemming, she'll be happy to look after them for you."

"Why, to tell the truth," Laure confessed, "I bought a new dress that needs taking in at the waist."

"You just give it to me, Miz Bouchard, ma'am, I'll have it done in a jiffy," Mary Turner promised.

"And now I want you to meet Dan Munroe and his wife, Katie, and their children, Tom and Elsie." Luke turned to the wiry middle-aged man and his attractive mulatto wife. "It was Dan who put the Klan to rout last fall when they caught Marius and tried to make me join their lawless society."

"Thank you, Dan, for what you did for my husband and Marius," Laure said softly as she grasped the tall black's hand, then turned and smilingly shook hands with Katie and their two children.

"And now I want you to meet Hughie Mendicott and his boys, Davie and Louis," Luke concluded. "You wouldn't believe how much work those boys can do in the fields. They're grown men already."

At this, both David and Louis glanced with embarrassment at the ground as Laure, first shaking hands with their father, gave them each a maternal hug.

"Clementine, it's time now," Marius Thornton called to his lovely young wife, who hurried forward with a bouquet of wild flowers and handed them to Laure, saying, "All of us helped pick them, Miz Bouchard, ma'am,

15

but they're nowhere near as pretty as you are, that's for certain!"

Laure took the bouquet and, tears glinting in her green eyes, turned to Luke and tremulously said, "It's the most beautiful homecoming a wife could wish for. And now, darling, let's take our sons in to see their new home."

CHAPTER TWO

Luke Bouchard's enthusiastic black tenants had indeed done wonders to erase the ugly smirch of smoke and of charred wood which the fire of the Union troops had left in its wake. Laure exclaimed with delight over her spacious bedroom. Mitzi was installed in the room adjoining hers, with a comfortable bed and the hand-carved crib and the cradle in opposite corners of her equally spacious room. Luke had taken his grandfather's bedroom, and in the study adjoining it had placed a handsome new escritoire which he had brought with him from New Orleans. It was almost an exact duplicate of the one at which Lucien had composed his letters and had drawn up his accounts of Windhaven Plantation.

Clementine had assigned herself the role of Laure's maid and brought with her from the kitchen a lovely porcelain vase in which to put the wild flowers she had presented to her mistress. She lingered a moment, making certain that everything was in order, and then volunteered, "Hannah will have lunch ready in about an hour, Miz Bouchard, and I'll call you then. Or maybe you'd like me to bring it to you on a tray?"

"Oh, no, Clementine," Laure declined. "You mustn't go to all this fuss, really you mustn't. I'm not used to being pampered, and just as soon as I've had a chance to get my bearings I want to help as much as I can with the household. Now that I've left New Orleans for good, it's only proper that I should do all I can to make things comfortable here for my husband. But thank you anyway. You and everyone else have been so very kind."

"Well, Miz Bouchard," Clementine replied, blushing, "the folks around here think an awful lot of Mister Luke,

17

and now that we've met you, we think he's a mighty lucky man."

Then it was Laure's turn to blush and, impulsively, to hug and kiss the attractive young woman.

After having freshened up from her journey, Laure nursed little Paul and then had Mitzi put him in his new crib for a nap. She then put on a simple muslin frock and followed Clementine downstairs to the dining room. She took her place at one end of the table, and Luke rose from his chair at the other end to bid her welcome. At the long, beautifully decorated walnut table, the black workers, their wives and children were seated. Luke had invited them to lunch not only to welcome his wife, but also as a sign that life at Windhaven Plantation would be based upon equality, respect, and sharing.

There was another surprise for Laure—a highchair for little Lucien, made by Dan Munroe. Hannah had prepared a nourishing, clear broth for the boy, which Mitzi fed to him. Luke, chatting with his workers, sent Laure many a loving glance as he watched his little son enjoying his first meal at Windhaven Plantation.

Hannah had surpassed herself for this, Laure's first meal at the red-brick château. Shortly after dawn, Dan Munroe had slaughtered two suckling pigs, and Hannah had baked the fresh pork along with a casserole of sweet yams and tasty apple slices. From her stock of autumnal fruits, carefully preserved in the dry cellar, she had used up all of her persimmons to make two large, juicy pies. There was real coffee, too, despite its outrageous price at the Lowndesboro store.

After lunch, Laure praised Hannah's cooking effusively, and expressed her sincere thanks to all the workers and their families for having thus welcomed her. Then, excusing herself, she went to her room for a much-needed nap, while Mitzi took charge of Lucien.

At about four-thirty Laure awakened, greatly refreshed, and went to her husband's study. She found him seated at the escritoire, writing a letter to his stepmother, Sybella.

"Come in, dearest. I was writing to mother—of course I'll add your very best wishes."

"Yes, by all means, Luke. I do hope I shall see her again one day."

"I've a feeling she's firmly established her new roots in Texas, and she'll be watching over my son Lucien Edmond and his wife Maxine, and their children Carla and Hugo. And of course, best of all, over her new grandchild, Edwina, Maxine Bouchard's daughter, born last October. That reminds me, Laure. It was so thoughtful of Fleurette to name her and Ben's first child Sybella, after my wonderful mother."

Laure came toward him slowly, put a hand on his shoulder and stared at him gravely, her green eyes soft and tender. "I understand you more and more each day, my darling," she murmured. "How could I ever have thought of you as just an old sobersides? I'm not even conscious of your age. You've made me yours so thoroughly, so profoundly. When I see how closely you are bound to all of the members of your family, no matter where they are, I begin to understand the great legacy you inherited from your grandfather."

"All of us owe much to him, Laure," Luke responded softly. He put his hand over hers as he smiled tenderly up at her.

"Would you mind if I visited his grave with little Lucien this afternoon . . . just the two of us, dearest?"

Luke's eyes widened, and then a joyous smile curved his lips. "I know grandfather would like that, my dear. I promised him and his beloved Dimarte that I would bring you there when you came—but I think he would like to be alone with you and to commune with you. I'll show you the easiest way up the steep bluff, and then I shall wait and be with you in spirit."

"I'd like that very much. And tomorrow I'll take Paul up there. He's still so little, he needs his sleep now. But I want him to feel the presence of your grandfather and Dimarte."

Luke rose and took her into his arms, gently kissing her eyelids. Then he murmured, "You, too, my beloved, reveal with each day of our lives together something new to cherish and to love." Then, bringing her hand to his lips, he kissed it as he might that of a queen and led

19

her first to her room, where she donned her fur-trimmed cape and then to Mitzi's.

Hearing the gentle knock at the door, Mitzi hurried to open it, putting a finger to her lips and gesturing toward the cradle where the baby slept. But Lucien stood in his crib, holding onto the wooden bars and, as he saw the smiling, gray-haired man approach, called out "Dada!"

Luke smiled at his son. Lucien, he thought, looked very much like his great grandfather. He had wispy, soft blond hair and large blue eyes, and there was a firmness to the line of his chin which, more than any other single physical trait, was reminiscent of old Lucien Bouchard. It seemed to symbolize the forthrightness and honesty which was so much a part of the Bouchard heritage.

"Yes, precious, you're right, it is your daddy. Come, now, my darling, I'm going to take you for a little walk. But I'll carry you, so you'll be safe and sound," Laure whispered as she lifted him from the crib. Mitzi hurried to fetch the child's tiny coat and, as Laure set him back down on the floor, buttoned it around him, then kissed him.

Luke glanced at his son with pride, then at Laure, who was holding tightly to little Lucien's hand to prevent his running ahead. They went out through the kitchen, and Hannah left her stove to come to the little boy, bent down and kissed the top of his head. She hastily wiped her tears with the hem of her apron as she watched Luke and Laure open the door and go out into the fields with Lucien.

Laure stooped to lift the little boy into her arms, soothingly murmuring, "Now you and mama will go visit your great-grandfather, darling." Turning to send Luke a look of unwavering trust, she added softly, "You were right, my darling. I knew it that afternoon when I teased you so shamefully and you took me—I knew I had conceived your child, not John's. And that's why today, my very first day at Windhaven Plantation, I want to tell your wonderful grandfather and his beloved wife how much I've learned about all the fine, unselfish things he did and the inheritance of abiding love he left to strengthen all those who followed after him."

"My very dearest." Luke was deeply moved as he

20

watched his son fidgeting in Laure's arms. "Yes, Laure darling, and now you're part of that heritage. I know that grandfather will praise my great good fortune in persuading you to share my life. You've courage and pride, just as his Dimarte had. And besides these two wonderful sons you've given me, you've given my life a new purpose and meaning. It will keep me young for the rest of my days so long as you share them with me."

When they reached the tall red bluff, Luke Bouchard pointed toward the path that led up the gradually rising eastern slope. Laure turned to face him. There was a long moment of silence, as he kissed her forehead and then bent to kiss the cheek of his son who blinked his eyes at the tall man who loomed above him. "God bless you both," Luke whispered and then stepped back.

Laure's eyes were full of tears as she turned from him and began to climb the path. Luke watched as she disappeared from view, among the trees and dense shrubbery which so abundantly embellished the bluff. The sun was low in the west, and the sky was touched here and there with shades of red and purple, heralding an early sunset. The air was still and, unseasonably, there was no chill to it this late January afternoon.

Luke looked out over the expansive acres that comprised the original plantation. Here and there he could see the dilapidated shacks of the freed blacks who had acquired the land after the war, only to abandon it in their terror of the Klan. Once again he promised himself that both white and black workers would share the rewards of that soil which would again be bountiful to those who worked side by side. The earth was timeless. It knew neither creed nor bigotry. And it would respond to the wisdom of men who understood how to bring forth its latent riches.

Laure reached the top of the bluff and walked unerringly toward the two massive hickory trees. She saw the clearing in front of them, where the waist-high grass had been uprooted to bare the sites of the graves of Lucien Bouchard, Dimarte, and their son, Edmond. She put Lucien down, and then knelt and contemplated the last resting-place of this heroic pioneer and of his beautiful Creek mate. Dimarte had given Luke's grandfather the joy of knowing himself to be no longer a stranger in an alien land. She had shown him how much he was loved and accepted by her and her proud, undaunted people.

Laure could not hear the murmuring of the Alabama River far below. The trees were still—there was no wind to move the branches. And it was too early for the night birds to commence their impatient gossip.

Laure spoke in a hushed, reverent voice, amid a kind of timeless silence. "I bring you your great-grandchild, Lucien Bouchard. Your dear friend John Brunton and I named him after you because of all the men he had ever known you were the most honorable and considerate. And I, who had no part in that long friendship save for what John so often told me, have now become a Bouchard myself—joyously, hopefully, thankfully."

There was no sign in the rich red earth that there had once been three separate graves. But, knowing from Luke where each was buried, Laure reached out her left hand to touch old Lucien's resting-place. With her other hand she held her son, who watched in solemn silence, as if he too understood the symbolic and profound meaning of this communion with the dead.

"I promise that you will be proud of your great-grandson, Lucien Bouchard, as proud as I who have borne him, as proud as I am to be the wife of him who helped conceive him. To make the bond even stronger between us, Lucien Bouchard, I have given Luke another son, Paul. Both of my children shall recall your bravery, your decency, and your unselfish life. Luke has told me so much about all the Bouchards that I truly feel I am one of you. May God give you and Dimarte and the child eternal peace and happiness in the knowledge that your grandson has come back to the land you loved so much, to which you gave your life so unstintingly, and which now holds you forever in its keeping."

She made the sign of the cross and repeated the gesture over the forehead of little Lucien. Then she lifted the little boy and moved to where Dimarte lay. "Beloved woman, sleep beside him who adored you and to whom you gave lifelong inspiration. May the passing years give me a small part of your wisdom and guide me in being a good wife. May I be able to give to Luke the same help and love which you gave to your Lucien. I respect you and understand in my way the life of the Creeks."

Once again she crossed herself and then made the sign of the cross on the little boy's forehead. Very slowly she turned and went down the path. Twilight had begun to fall upon the bluff, and she heard the night birds sing. As she went down to meet Luke Bouchard, there was the sound of a wakening owl's greeting through the gentle dark.

CHAPTER THREE

"Moses, wake up, please, man!" Mary Turner bent over her husband's bed, holding a lighted candle in one hand while she gently prodded his shoulder with the other. "Please, Moses, I'm mighty scared, there's someone moanin' out back past our garden patch!"

The sleeping man mumbled, then slowly rolled over onto his side away from Mary. Frantic now, she gripped his shoulder and shook him hard. "You just gotta wake up, Moses man! I'm mighty scared—sounds like one of them ghosts, the white-sheet kind that come 'round and make trouble for us poor niggers! Oh, please, Moses honey, wake up now!"

"Whazzat? Who—oh, Mary—what's the trouble, you feeling poorly?" He rolled over onto his back, blinking his eyes, staring uncomprehendingly up at her drawn face. Then he put a hand over his eyes to shield them from the flickering light of the candle she held above him.

"Thank God you done woke up, Moses. Sit up now 'n listen good. Maybe you can hear what I been hearin' the last hour or so, right after you went to sleep!"

"God, woman, must be well past midnight by now—"

"Sure is, but I just couldn't sleep, what with all the excitement of Miz Bouchard 'n those sweet babies comin' here to live with us 'n Mister Luke. I lay there thinkin' how kind she 'n Mister Luke was sittin' down at the same table to break bread with us. 'N then I heard this awful moanin', Moses."

"Hush, Mary, so's I can listen too. Maybe you just had a bad dream." Wincing from the twinges of his arthritis, Moses Turner slowly sat up in the crude bed, which was comprised of a large, irregular wooden rectangle over which a mattress of corn shucks and some threadbare blankets had been draped. Then his eyes narrowed and his face became taut. "Hey now, woman, I hear it too, plain as day. Sounds like it's comin' from that old shack Benjy Porter used to live in before the Klan came 'round here last year and treated poor old Phineas and Hannah so mean."

"I 'spect you're right, Moses. God, I'm sure scared—maybe the Klan done come back to drag us out and treat us the same way!" Mary began to sob.

"Come on now, woman, that ain't likely and you know it deep down inside." Moses Turner tried to comfort his wife as he rose and put an arm around her shoulders, then patted her cheek. "We all know that Mr. Luke drove the Klan away last fall 'n Dan shot that fellow who ran the store and was the head of it. Now just hush your cryin'. I'll go get Dan and we'll see what's what."

"All right, Moses, but please be careful—I don't want to lose you, you're all I've got left." Mary began to sob again.

"Lord's sakes, woman, you know I don't like that sort of unhappy talk. Now, didn't we all have a great time this evening and didn't Mister Luke tell us how he's goin' t' make this land produce like it never did before, and we're all gonna eat good and have money in our pockets? Now you 'n me we been through the worst of this, the war and all, yes, and the Klan, too. We ain't gonna be scared of a noise in the night. You go back to bed, and I'll go get Dan right now."

"All right, but I'm not gonna blow the candle out 'til you get back, Moses," Mary reluctantly agreed as she moved back to her bed, which Moses had made more comfortable by adding another two mattresses and the sturdiest blanket they possessed.

Mary propped herself up on one elbow and watched as Moses tugged on his blue denim trousers and then donned an old leather jacket and the muffler she had knitted him for protection against the cold night air. "You be careful now, Moses, real careful," she anxiously urged.

"I will, Mary honey. Now you try to go back to sleep. Dan 'n me'll take care of everything," he reassured her, and then hurried out of the shack.

Dan Munroe's cabin was several hundreds yards to the north, and Moses Turner knocked on the door and bawled out, "Dan, Dan, wake up, come quick, you gotta help me!"

The door was opened by Katie who clutched her robe around her with one hand and stared wonderingly at the arthritic black. "What's the matter, Moses?"

"Mary 'n me heard somebody carrying on real bad in that old shack of Benjy's. Is Dan up?"

"He is for fair now, with all that noise," Katie tartly retorted. "And the kids, too. Dan, it's Moses—he's heard some noise out in the fields and he's worried about it."

"What kind of noise, Moses?" Dan Munroe appeared, rubbing his knuckles over his eyes and yawning.

"It was Mary who heard it first, Dan. Seems like she said somebody was moanin', just like a ghost. I thought maybe it might be some of those Klansmen comin' back again, like last fall."

"I'll bring my pitchfork along. Katie, you go back to sleep. Make sure the kids do too. I'll be back in a jiffy, and don't you fret, you hear?"

"All right, Dan, if you say so. But you just be careful. You know, you shot that Hurley Parmenter and saved Marius from those mean white folks, so some one of them might just figure he wants to get even with you—I wish you'd take your gun instead of that old pitchfork." Katie's voice trembled with anxiety.

"Now you look here, woman," Dan told her firmly, "if there was real trouble we'd hear lots more noise by now, and from more than just one fellow. Maybe it's somebody sick. But if it relieves your mind any, the gun's loaded and set against the wall behind that barrel of flour. If Moses and me don't come back right away, you take it outside and fire it in the air. That'll bring Mister Luke and the others mighty fast."

"All right, then. Take care of yourself, Dan honey, please, for my sake." Katie hugged him and gave him a fiercely desperate kiss, then stepped away, biting her lips with apprehension.

"Let's go, Moses. You say it's Benjy's shack the noise is coming from?" Dan walked quickly to the farthest end of the fields, toward the high bluff.

"First I thought Mary was having a bad dream, Dan, only then I heard it plain as I hear you," Moses explained.

The ramshackle hovel which the freed black had abandoned after the first visit of the Klan stood like a doleful wraith in the lonely field, its warped door partly opened, its plank roof sagging. As the two men approached, the sound of moaning increased, and then there was an inarticulate gasp.

"Should'a brought along a lantern or a candle," Moses grumbled. "Hardly any moon and—hey, Dan, look there, there's somebody lyin' on the floor. Poor soul—must be real sick—"

Dan handed the pitchfork to Moses, entered the shack, and crouched down beside the inert form. Then he called out, "It's a woman, an old woman—she's been whipped awful bad. You go back to Mary and bring some water and see if you got any salve, like we used on Phineas and Hannah that time!"

"I'll be back in a jiffy," Moses exclaimed and, despite his arthritis, turned and ran back toward his own cabin.

"There now, you'll be all right. God, they whipped you something fierce," Dan muttered angrily. Very gently, he took hold of the woman and turned her onto her side, grimacing with anger as he saw the bloody streaks left by the whip. She was frail, white-haired, her faded calico dress ripped down to her hips at the back, and clinging only by a shred around the neck. "Can you talk, can you tell me who done this to you?" he urged gently.

The woman, her bony face contorted in agony, made a supreme effort, blinking her eyes and trying to form words with her thin, trembling lips. Finally there emerged in a husky whisper, "I'm Ellen from Attisburg way—it was the K—Klan that whipped me—"

"But why?"

"They didn't like what I said about their kind, I guess. They said I was—I was a conjure woman an' they was gonna teach me to keep my mouth shut—oh, I hurt so—"

"Sure you do, ma'am. It's a wonder you're not dead—they whipped you as hard as they would a man, the cowardly bastards!" Dan swore. Then, very gently, he asked, "Did they bring you here, Ellen?"

"No, they—they left me tied to a tree—'n I guess I must

have fainted—leastways, when I came 'round, I got loose and started coming upriver fast as I could—didn't want them to catch me again—then my strength gave out—where am I—who owns this place?"

"Now you save your strength, ma'am, don't try to talk anymore. You've stumbled onto Windhaven Plantation, and Mister Luke Bouchard runs it. He's a good fine man, and he hates the Klan just as much as we do. He'll see you're not turned out. Moses, hurry up with that water."

"Here it is, nice and cold as I could get it from the pump." Moses Turner knelt down with a pannikin of cool well water. Carefully he held it to the woman's lips as Dan gently eased her into a sitting position. Groaning softly but fighting her pain, she gratefully drank, then sighed, "That's mighty good, sweet and cool. I feel better now. Thanks, you're mighty good to poor old Ellen."

"We're goin' to lift you up and get you to bed and have one of the women rub the salve on, Ellen," Dan Munroe explained. "We'll try not to hurt you."

"I know, I know. You're good men, you couldn't hurt no one, 'cause you don't hate like those folks that wear white sheets and say they're spirits. God'll judge them and punish them in His good time for all the wrong they done us. That's what I told 'em, and that's why they whipped me so bad—said it was a warnin' to others not to get too uppity with their betters."

The two men gently lifted the frail old woman and carried her out of the shack, across the fields to the kitchen door of the château. There, by dint of loud knocking and calling, Dan roused Hannah Atbury, who exclaimed with horror when she saw the victim and at once led the way to one of the guest rooms. She took over then, upbraiding the two men for the way they were handling the old woman, helping to ease her down on the freshly made bed. Then, with many an angry imprecation at the evil-doers who had dared abuse an old woman in this brutal way, she herself rubbed on the soothing salve, bidding the two men leave the room so that they would not gaze upon the old woman's nakedness. "There's a pot of coffee on the stove, Dan, you just make yourself useful and heat some up for Ellen here," she directed testily. "Moses, you go look in the sideboard just off the pantry. There's a

28

bottle of old Madeira in there. Take one of the glasses and pour Ellen a stiff drink. It's the best medicine there is for her right now."

Half an hour later, Ellen lay on her side, her head propped up by two thick pillows. Hannah had draped a fresh sheet over her lacerated back. By this time, Luke Bouchard was awake and, having heard the noise, came to find out what was wrong. His face was grave with concern. He bent down toward the frail old woman and asked, "Do you know for certain that it was the Ku Klux Klan who did this dreadful thing to you, Ellen?"

"Yes, sir, I'm sure. They said that's what they was."

"And you walked here all the way from Attisburg—my God, what courage and strength you have!" he exclaimed in wonder.

Ellen smiled faintly. "They call me a wicked old conjure woman. But that ain't true, mister. I used to be Mr. Fawcett's slave a couple miles out of Attisburg. When the war come, he and his family cleared out—don't rightly know where they went. I stayed on in a little cabin and worked my garden so's I'd have enough to eat. And I helped other black folks who didn't know what to do after Mr. Lincoln set us free. But I don't hold with no voodoo or stuff like that, no sir! Only seems like I got the gift of seein' what might happen to all of us, and then I speak out—that's what they didn't like."

"So Hurley Parmenter's men didn't disband after his death," Luke Bouchard said softly to himself. Then, aloud, "Well, Ellen, I promise you no one will hurt you from now on. If you've a mind to, I'd like you to stay here until you're well. Then maybe we can find something for you to do. We've got vegetable gardens that need tending; and maybe you can help Hannah in the kitchen."

"I'd like that real fine, sir. The men that brought me here, they said you was kind and good to folks—I can see that now, just lookin' at your face."

"I try to be, Ellen. There's still too much hate in the world."

"Yes, sir," the old woman muttered, nodding with an effort. " 'N there's goin' to be lots more deaths before all of us is done. Oh God—" She stared intently at Luke, then shook her head and blinked her eyes, which had suddenly filled with tears. "I wish to God I never had the gift to see things—I feel so helpless, can't do nothin' 'bout what I see, only tell folks, maybe warn 'em."

"There's no need to blame yourself for that, Ellen," Luke said gently. "And if God has given you this gift, He knows the goodness of your heart, in trying to warn people of what you see."

"You're mighty kind to say that, mister. It eases my mind lots to hear you. Let me see your face clear now, look at me good and hard."

"You must get some rest, Ellen," Luke softly urged.

But she propped herself up on one elbow and stared intently at him, her lips moving silently, her eyes wide and searching. Then she sank back with a gasp. "Oh, Lord, I seen just now when I looked at you that there's a dark cloud comin' down over little ones mighty dear to you."

Hannah, who had been hovering nearby, stifled a gasp and made the sign of the cross as Luke Bouchard, a concerned expression crossing his face, knelt down and took the old woman's hand in his. "Go on, Ellen, I won't laugh or say I don't believe. There are many things none of us can explain. Perhaps you truly can see into the future, and I'm willing to listen."

"I know you mean what you say, mister. When I looked at you just then, I saw it plain as I saw your face. A big dark cloud coming down over little ones, like I said. One of them runs away and the other is swallowed up by the cloud and carried off."

"Little ones dear to me," Luke Bouchard softly repeated to himself, then started with anxiety. "Can it be little Lucien and the baby, Paul?" Unwittingly, his hand tightened over the old woman's as he leaned forward. "What else do you see, Ellen?"

She had closed her eyes now, and her voice was faint but still audible. "You must give them a sign, mark them so's you'll see them again and keep them close to you. An' I see that dark cloud disappearing and at its end is a rainbow in the west. You will sorrow, but you will then find the rainbow. . . ."

"Thank God for that," Luke Bouchard murmured to himself, pondering what the old woman prophesied. He rose, and gently said, "You must try to sleep now, Ellen. Hannah will look after you. I want you to feel welcome here. And I thank you for what you've told me. Perhaps it's a warning, and I mean to heed it. Yes, as I heeded the words of Sangrodo's old shaman and as grandfather heeded the words of the *windigo* of the Creeks so long ago."

Luke went outside into the cool night. He needed time and quiet to think. Ellen's words had troubled him more than he cared to admit, and his first reaction had been that her vision might concern Lucien and Paul.

What, indeed, would he do if his children were taken from him? And who could devise such a monstrous and inhuman scheme, much less find justification for it? Who was it that lurked in the shadows of the past or, perhaps, in the present, hating the Bouchards enough to want to strike at them by kidnapping helpless children?

Luke stared at the bluff where his grandfather and Dimarte were buried. For a moment he stood, silent and unmoving. Then he murmured, half-aloud, "Oh, God, watch over us. Protect my family and all those dear to me, both here at home and those who live far away. And especially, protect our children from evil."

Turning slowly, he headed back toward the château. He would not tell Laure about Ellen's vision. There was no need to worry her. He would take what precautions he could, and would write to his son from his first marriage, Lucien Edmond, at Windhaven Range, in case her prophecy should prove to include him and his family. Luke would be careful, vigilant, and perhaps Ellen's warning would prove false.

CHAPTER FOUR

By the first week of February, the sun was already warm and the mesquite had begun to bud near the Nueces River. There had been rain enough in the past month to make the grass thicken and grow in abundance along the valley of Windhaven Range. The longhorns grazed side by side with the Herefords, which Lucien Edmond Bouchard had bought for interbreeding, and already Ramón Hernandez had counted fifty new calves sired by the Hereford bulls.

Early in the morning, Mara's handsome young husband, Ramón, rode out on the range with Lucien Edmond, accompanied by Andy Haskins and Joe Duvray. They wanted to make a preliminary count of the herd they could expect to drive to the market in the spring. "Most likely it'll be Abilene again, Ramón," Lucien Edmond declared as he reined in his gray gelding and waited for Ramón to come up to him on his mare, Corita. "You know, just after we made that drive to Abilene last year, there was practically a national panic about Spanish fever and its effects on longhorns and Texas beef."

"I remember your telling me."

"Joseph McCoy didn't let that ruin his market, though. He hired several expert lassoers and reinforced a stockcar with good, sturdy planking. Then he loaded another car with some smart Texas cow ponies, hitched onto a Kansas Pacific work train, and headed west for the buffalo feeding grounds. They filled the car with buffalo bulls, which they had to drag aboard with rope and tackle. Then McCoy hung long canvas streamers on each side of the car, signs which told all about the wonderful healthy cattle bargains at Abilene and that Spanish fever in the Texas area was a myth. The buffalo train went all the way to

32

Chicago where they turned them into a grass plot in the Union Stockyards for public display."

"It sounds like a circus," Ramón Hernandez chuckled.

"Exactly. Luckily for McCoy, the stunt worked like magic. Chicago buyers came back on a special excursion train, and the market was revived. Now McCoy writes me that Texas cattle are very popular and in great demand. So this time we ought to get an even better price. Just look at some of those strong calves there—they have all the vitality of the longhorn combined with the endurance and resistance of the Hereford. There won't be any talk of Spanish fever with this herd when we drive it to market, Ramón!"

"*Es verdad, certamente,*" the young Mexican agreed, smiling. "But we'd better figure out how many vaqueros to take along on the drive and how many to leave here to defend the hacienda."

"Let's you and I sit down this evening after supper and work things out, Ramón. By the way, I've a pleasant little duty to perform, in the nature of a wedding gift."

"Oh?"

"Yes," Lucien Edmond replied. "Have you noticed how much time Djamba's son, Lucas, is spending around that pretty little orphan girl, Felicidad? It won't be long before they're ready for a wedding. Well, I'm going to give them a gift of twenty-five acres right near Henry Belcher's place, and I was thinking that some of the vaqueros who stay behind could help to build a house for them."

"You are the best *patrón* in all Texas, Lucien Edmond," Ramón Hernandez answered. "I shall never forget your kindness to me, and that of your father when my lovely Mara did me the honor of accepting me as her husband."

"It was a lucky day for all of us when you rode from Corpus Christi to warn us about Diego Macaras, Ramón. If it hadn't been for you, we might not have kept Windhaven Range. And my sister's happier than she's ever been before. That's your doing too, hombre. Now let's ride on to the end of our land and see just how many stray cattle we're going to have to round up and brand in the next few weeks."

"I think we'll have at least five hundred more in this spring's herd," Ramón Hernandez declared.

"And they'll command higher prices," Lucien Edmond replied. "But with a larger herd, there are always more dangers to be anticipated—stampedes, attacks by bushwhackers or hostile Indians. And there are always a few who are poisoned by reckless grazing before our vaqueros can see just what they're eating. Then too, I mean to stop by the Creek reservation as I did last year, and make Emataba a present of at least twenty steers and cows."

"That is a very good thing."

"Yes, and its effect will be long-lasting. In the first place, the Indian agent is extremely lax in that area, and I could see with my own eyes that many of Emataba's people were badly fed. And that's another thing—we might bring some extra blankets along. Those winters can be cold up north, and the agent isn't too concerned whether his charges are warm enough. Great-grandfather would be shocked if he could see the neglect and contempt with which the tribes are treated, just because their skins are red."

"But they are proud men, and I know how careful you are to avoid any suggestion of charity."

"That's true, Ramón. But you see also, Emataba has already spread the word that we come from Texas and that the men of Windhaven Range are generous to his people. The other Indians—the Kiowas and the Comanches —will know that we keep the faith which my father pledged to Sangrodo. But it won't be long before those tribes are driven out of Texas and herded like wretched animals into reservations which are no better than cattle pens. Perhaps it's as well great-grandfather didn't live to see what has happened to the people who lived on the land long before the white man came. But he did live to see the Creeks driven out of Alabama. And he was aware of how the greedy land speculators tricked them out of their land certificates, exchanging them for a bottle of whiskey or a ragged blanket or two during their arduous march West."

Lucien Edmond paused for a moment, then rose in his saddle and pointed. "Ah, just as I thought. See those five steers off behind that mesquite? Let's flush them out. A little exercise will do us both good!"

34

Both young men laughed and nodded to each other as they spurred their horses and rode toward the mesquite, shouting and waving their sombreros as the steers, bellowing in protest, rushed from their hiding place and loped out into the valley.

Celia, the cook, and Maybelle Belcher stood chatting in the kitchen, comparing recipes for a stew which they planned for the evening meal. Celia, who had gone along as chuck wagon cook on the drive last year, insisted that all the vaqueros preferred stew spiced only with chilis, while Maybelle emphatically maintained that abundant vegetables in good variety were far more nourishing.

Meanwhile, Felicidad Ramirez sat at a table in the corner, peeling potatoes. Felicidad had come to the ranch house at Carrizo Springs last June, through the sympathetic aid of the vaquero Vittorio Salancár. He had gone back to Nuevo Laredo for a week to visit his elder sister and had seen Felicidad leaning against the side of an old ramshackle hut and weeping bitterly. When he stopped to ask why she was crying, she had told him that she was an orphan who had been working for the lecherous owner of a *posada*. Her employer had given her an ultimatum—either become his mistress or be turned out into the street and be blacklisted as a whore. Vittorio had brought her to the ranch and Sybella had welcomed the unhappy girl with maternal solicitude and given her a job in the kitchen. Djamba's handsome son, Lucas, had fallen in love with Felicidad almost as soon as she arrived. Indeed, at this very moment, he entered the kitchen by the back porch, trundling a sack of potatoes. Celia whirled on him, exchanging a mischievous glance with Maybelle Belcher. "Now what's all this foolishness, Lucas boy? Can't you see that poor Felicidad hasn't even finished the last lot you brought her? Are you trying to make a slave out of her? I must say, that's a fine way to court a girl. Now, when your father was trying to get me to jump over the broomstick, he made sure that I didn't have any work at all to do, and he made a fuss over me."

At this, Felicidad covered her blushing face with her hands and turned toward the wall, while Lucas, his eyes widening, at first taking his mother's pretended harangue seriously, stood with his mouth open. Then, seeing the twinkle in her eyes and the conspiratorial wink which Maybelle Belcher returned, he burst into hearty laughter. "You had me scared there for a moment, ma. Well, I guess I might as well 'fess up to it. I just want an excuse to talk some with Felicidad."

"All right, you two lovebirds," Celia joked good-naturedly. "Go out in the backyard and do your mooning. Besides, looks to me as if we've got enough potatoes for the stew. You can just take that sack back to the storeroom off the bunkhouse until it's needed again, boy."

"Whatever you say, ma," Lucas grinned. "Howdy, Mrs. Belcher."

"Howdy yourself, Lucas. When are you two going to get married, anyhow? Everybody around here knows that the two of you were made for each other," Maybelle replied.

Lucas strode over to the table and bent down to whisper to Felicidad, "Come on, honey, they're just kidding us, they don't mean any harm. Anyhow, I want to talk to you about maybe building a little house for the two of us—for when we're married, of course."

"Oh, Lucas, *mi corazón!*" Felicidad murmured. She hastily rose from the table and, locking her fingers through his, hurried out into the yard.

"Well, it should be any day now," Maybelle Belcher told Celia.

"He's a good boy. He's been a wonderful son, couldn't ask for better. And she's such a sweet thing. When you think what a life she had until Vittorio found her, it's a blessing that she's got a chance to have a good life here and to have somebody like Lucas care for her. But you know, Mrs. Belcher," Celia's face sobered, "to tell the truth, I'd really like to see them married by a priest. I know there aren't any churches around here, any more than there were back in Alabama where we came from. But the Bouchards are Catholics, and I've read from time to time out of their prayer book and learned all about the Mass. It's a beautiful religion, and I'd like to see Felicidad and Lucas married in that faith."

"I know what you mean."

"Back in the old days, when we were slaves, we didn't

have any rights. A woman could be taken away from her man, and their children could be sold down the river. Thank God old Mr. Lucien and Mr. Luke never held with that. Just the same, even though we weren't treated like slaves at Windhaven Plantation, lots of us black folk prayed for the day when we could stand up and be counted. You know, marrying and having records made of births and maybe even own property."

"I can imagine how you must have felt, Celia dear," Maybelle Belcher agreed.

Outside the kitchen, Felicidad Ramirez glanced nervously around as Lucas, having led her to the protective cover of a giant oak tree, put his arms around her waist and kissed her ardently. "Oh my, *mi amor*," she stammered as waves of color surged over her olive-tinged cheeks. "Somebody might be watching. We shouldn't—"

"Now you hush, honey," Lucas murmured as he cupped her chin, tilted up her gentle, heart-shaped face, and repeated the kiss, this time more lingeringly. Felicidad made only a token struggle and then, with a happy little sigh, clung to him. When the kiss was over, she pressed her cheek against his chest and murmured, "*Querido*, God has been very good to me. He has given me a new home and now he has given me such a wonderful hombre who cares for me."

"Caring's not half the right word, honey," Lucas corrected with a smile. "I love you something fierce, and I want to marry you just as soon as I can—you know that, don't you?"

She nodded. Of medium height, Felicidad was slender and beautifully proportioned, her bosom high-perched and surprisingly opulent. Her glossy black hair tumbled nearly to her waist, and her expressive, dark-brown eyes were fringed with thick lashes through which she gazed adoringly up at Lucas. The owner of the *posada* for whom she had worked had taught her English, since many of his customers spoke that language. And here at Windhaven Range, Sybella Forsden had spent at least an hour every afternoon giving English lessons to the pretty orphan.

Now Felicidad murmured, her eyes closed and a dreamy expression on her lovely face. "I want that as much as you do, *mi corazón*. But it must be done properly, and I pray it will be in a church by a padre. Then I will truly feel that I belong to you, that I am no longer the orphan that Señor Gonzalez wanted to make into his *criatura*."

"You mustn't ever think of that again, sweetheart," Lucas urged as he bent down to kiss her again, stroking her thick, silky hair with his left hand. "We're not slaves anymore, honey, and none of the people who ever worked for the Bouchards, even way back when it all began in Alabama, were slaves either—not really. Before we get married, though, I've got to think of getting a house built and some land to put it on so you and I can settle down and have children—you do want children, don't you, sweetheart?"

Felicidad blushed furiously as she hid her face against Lucas's chest and nodded shyly.

His arms tightened around her as he stared back at the sprawling ranch house. "Our place won't be as big and fine as this, of course, but it'll be nice and cozy. When I build it, I'll see there's plenty of room for the babies we'll have. There'll be a boy I'll name after my daddy, and the girl's name you can pick yourself."

"It is so sweet to think of so much happiness. I never thought it would be like this for me," Felicidad whispered. Then, her eyes starry, she lifted her face to his and, standing on tiptoe, locked her arms around his shoulders and kissed him with increasing ardor, quite forgetting her earlier fears of being seen by any member of the household.

"You will be proud of me, I promise, when I am your *esposa*," she confided. "I have learned how to cook very well. One night, your nice mother says she will let me prepare the entire meal. Then you will see what good things I will be able to make for you when we are married, Lucas."

"That'll be just fine, sweetheart. Say, I just thought of something. You know, ma is getting on in years and she might not be able to go along as cook on our cattle drive to Abilene. I heard her saying just the other evening to Mrs. Belcher that she was hankering to visit my sister, Prissy, and her family. Like as not, Prissy's probably going to have another child. She told Daddy she wanted a big

38

family and so did Jicinte—that's the Comanche brave who married her. They're living in Mexico now, in Sangrodo's camp—"

"Oh, yes, Lucas. I respect him very much. He was such a good friend to the *patrón* and his family. But where I came from, everyone hated *los Indios* because they killed the men and took many of the women back to their villages to be their wives and their slaves."

"That may be, honey, but don't forget both the Mexicans and the white men did the same to them when they drove them off the land where they'd lived for hundreds of years. But we don't have to worry about Indians now, Felicidad. Sangrodo sent word to all of the tribes in Texas that the *patrón*, as you call him, is a good man and would never rob or cheat them."

"*Es verdad*, I know." Again she pressed her cheek against Lucas's chest and remained silent for a moment. Then, mischievously, she looked at him from beneath her thick lashes, and murmured, "If your mother does not feel strong enough to go on the drive, Lucas, and if I practice cooking very hard, maybe I could take her place. Then I could go with you to Abilene, couldn't I?"

"Sure, I guess you could. Only you know, I'm not going to make love to you until we get married. And it would be very hard to keep from making love to you if we were alone together all that long way and back, Felicidad."

Again she blushed and nodded. Then she whispered, "It would be just as hard for me, Lucas. But we will be very good until we are married by a padre, won't we? Because then, when you are my husband, it will make up for all the long waiting."

"Sweetheart, yes it will! Felicidad, you don't know how I wish we could be married right this minute. Now you'd best go back into the kitchen. I'll go see Daddy and tell him that you want to cook for the vaqueros on the drive."

CHAPTER FIVE

While Luke Bouchard was still at Windhaven Range, before he left for New Orleans to help Laure Brunton restore her husband's bank, he instructed Lucien Edmond to make a gift of land to Simata. This had been out of gratitude to the young half-Indian scout for having led Captain George Munson's troops into Sangrodo's ambush, thus bringing the ruthlessly ambitious officer to justice for the massacre of the helpless Comanche women, children, and old men of the stronghold.

A parcel of land had been sectioned off to the southwest of the hacienda and Simata, aided by Djamba and Lucas, had built a sturdy log cabin, somewhat like a dugout. The lower half was set well below ground level to provide a welcome coolness during the scorching summer months. It was also a kind of fortress, since it flanked the Bouchard ranch house on one side while Henry ·Belcher's place guarded the southern and left side. The dugouts in which Andy Haskins and Joe Duvray had lived during the building of the hacienda had been retained as sentry posts. Farther north, as Lucien Edmond well knew, there were many reports of horse thieves and bushwhackers. These men, lawless desperadoes, had sought out the central and sparsely populated region of Texas where they were immune to civil authority and free to pursue their marauding life. There was as yet no stable law throughout this newly readmitted state, except for troops at such distant points as Fort Griffin and the once-decimated Fort Inge.

Somewhat to the southeast, the house of Ramón and Mara Hernandez stood as a further sentinel against attack of Windhaven Range. And, several hundred yards away from that, would soon stand the house which Lucas would build for his beautiful young bride, Felicidad.

Thus, Windhaven Range was growing in size and strength along this isolated Texas border, where the land was rich enough to provide a good livelihood for those who brought to it purposeful ambition and hard work.

It was the first week of February, and Felicidad had wakened with the sun. After eating a hasty breakfast and finishing her kitchen chores, she decided to go for a walk. She thought of her plans for the new house and the land where she and Lucas would live after their marriage with eager anticipation. Of course there would be a garden, and she had noticed several tall elm trees which would provide a perfect shade from the blazing summer sun. There was a serene joy in her face, banishing all the wistfulness which Vittorio Salancár had seen in Neuvo Laredo. Last night, indulged by Celia and Maybelle, she had, by herself, prepared not only the food for the vaqueros in the bunkhouse, but also the meal for the Bouchards. Lucien Edmond had risen from his chair to compliment her effusively, making her blush with happiness. Then he had said to the others, "I think we have found our cook for the drive."

Felicidad had been so overjoyed that she had quite forgotten her shyness. Running to Luke's tall, handsome son, she had flung her arms around him and kissed him impulsively. Then, realizing her own daring, she had gasped and turned crimson, and retreated to the kitchen in confusion.

She could hardly wait to ride in the chuck wagon and to prepare the meals for the riders who would drive the cattle to Abilene. Just as soon as the drive was over, she and her dear Lucas would be one. Then they could move into their new house, love each other and have the children she wanted so much to bear him.

So this morning, walking around the elm trees and busily deciding where the rooms of the house would be, she turned at last to the south and began to walk toward the distant creek. From it, she would bring water for her husband-to-be, water to quench his thirst and for the cooking of his meals. Her soft lips turned up at the corners in a happy smile and, humming a Mexican folk song which dealt with undying love, Felicidad quickened her steps. In her dreams, she was a bride already. She had left the house while her husband was still asleep, her mind and flesh tingling with remembered ecstasy of their night together, as she began her wifely chores.

Suddenly she started, her eyes widening, at the sound of a shrill scream. It sounded like an animal in pain. Then she heard it again. She turned to look for the source and, cautiously advancing, followed for about fifty yards the direction from which the sound had come.

At first she was fearful that it might be a wild boar or wolf. She moved slowly southward, and when the cry came again, she perceived a large bird lying at the base of an oak tree, some distance from her. It was struggling, waving one wing, the other flapping uselessly. It lifted its head, its sharp beak opening to emit still another piercing cry of pain.

"*Pobrecito,*" Felicidad murmured as she came forward more resolutely. She could see now that it was an aplomado falcon, about eighteen inches long. Its coloring was predominantly blue with a dark band across the chest, a pure white throat, brown legs and a barred tail.

During her childhood, she had spent years as a kind of foster child to a family who had been friends of her parents. There she had met an elderly man whom everyone called Tío Jorge. He had known how to tame wild birds and trained falcons to hunt—falcons exactly like this one. She remembered, too, what he had told her about these hunting birds: when you first caught them, you must put a hood over their eyes so that they would not peck at you.

Hearing her approach, the young falcon again lifted its head, staring at her with fierce yellow eyes. Its pointed beak opened menacingly as it uttered still another strident cry. Its talons opened and closed, as if wanting to defend itself, and again it flapped its sound wing wildly.

"I will not hurt you, *pequeño halcón,*" she murmured. Reaching up, she unwound the bright red bandanna with which she had covered her head to shield herself from the already oppressive heat of the sun. She moved forward slowly so as not to frighten the wounded bird. As she approached, she spoke in Spanish in a soft voice, praising its courage and its beauty. Then, swiftly moving behind it, she crouched down and bound the bandanna over the falcon's eyes, avoiding the savage lunges of its beak. All the while, she continued to address soothing words to it in the gentlest tone of voice. Once the hood was in place, the young falcon's struggles diminished and it lay on its back, its talons clawing the air convulsively.

Remembering again what old Tío Jorge had told her, Felicidad looked around for a stick. Finding a broken branch, she returned to the blindfolded falcon and held the branch in both hands at its ends while she gently offered it to the gripping talons. At once the bird's claws closed tightly around it. "There we are, *pobrecito*," she said in her sweet clear voice, "I will find you a home and I will help you heal your broken wing. But where did you come from, *pequeño halcón?*" She looked up and saw a towering yucca tree some twenty feet away, and the outline of a nest. "Oh, it was from there. Your parents flew away—perhaps the good *Señor Dios* called them to Him just as He did mine. And then when you tried your wings, you fell out of the nest and flew against this big tree and broke your wing. That must be how it happened. But now you need have no more fear, little one. Felicidad will look after you, you will see."

She turned back toward the hacienda, holding the branch out in front of her at arm's length. The wounded falcon continued to hold it, now and then emitting a plaintive cry as she walked slowly and carefully. Its broken wing drooped, and she shook her head in commiseration, murmuring, "*Pobrecito*, soon you will feel better, have no fear."

Then she caught sight of Lucas, who was emerging from the bunkhouse, and called to him. "Lucas, come help me, por favor!"

Djamba's tall son uttered a startled cry and came running toward the pretty young girl as he realized what she was carrying. "Felicidad, what's happened to you? That's a falcon, I'm pretty sure —"

"Si, a young one that fell out of the nest and broke its wing. I heard it crying and I could not let it suffer so."

"But look at that beak, Felicidad, it might have hurt you," Lucas exclaimed, glancing warily at the hooded bird of prey.

"Oh no! I am not afraid of it. You see Lucas, when I

was a little girl, there was an old man who used to train birds like this to hunt for him. And he taught me how to cover its eyes and give it a stick to hold onto so that you could carry it. Do you see that poor broken wing? Can you not put a splint on it and make it well again, Lucas? You are so wise and strong—surely you can help this little bird."

"You mean you want to make a pet of it, honey? I don't know." Lucas scratched his head dubiously and squinted at the bird's sharp beak and tightly clenched talons. "It's a wild thing. I don't know if you could trust it."

"But of course I can! It is very young; it can be trained, you will see. Now that I am here and so happy, I am beginning to remember the nice things from when I was a little girl. Will you not help me, Lucas?"

"Of course I will, sweetheart." Lucas grinned sheepishly. "Here, let me take the branch. It will tire you to hold your arms out all this time. There, you see, I can do it, too," he declared as she let him take the branch in his two strong hands. "Tell you what, Felicidad, I'll try to fix its wing and then I'll build a big cage for it. You know, there's a little shed right off the bunkhouse, just a few tools in it. We could put the cage in there so it would be safe, and you could visit it when you want to."

"That would be wonderful! And I will make friends with it and gentle it so that it will not hurt you or me, I promise."

She opened the door to the shed and Lucas entered, carefully setting the bird down, still gripping its branch, atop a wide flour barrel. "I can see where the wing's broken, Felicidad," he announced as he carefully studied the falcon, which was lying on its back. It had uttered one shrill, fearful cry when he had set it down on the barrel, but now it lay passively, as if it sensed that its captors meant no harm. "Hold the branch a spell, honey, while I find something for a splint," Lucas said.

In the opposite corner, an old barrel stave lay on the floor. Lucas retrieved it, drew his well-honed hunting knife out of its leather scabbard, and began to whittle off a thin, sturdy piece to serve as a splint. This done, he opened another flour barrel and removed the top drawstring of one of the sacks to serve as cord. Approaching,

44

he whispered, "You'd better pinch the bird's beak shut with one hand, honey, this might hurt. I see just where the break is, it'll just take a jiffy to set it right."

"Be gentle, Lucas," Felicidad urged. Her eyes filled with tears as she stared down at the hooded young falcon. Crooning softly to it in Spanish, she shifted her left hand to compress the sharp beak between two fingers, while keeping her right hand on the middle of the branch to which the bird clung. Then, glancing at her fiancé, she nodded, holding her breath in anxiety and standing very still.

Deftly Lucas lifted the broken wing and set it quickly, while the falcon thrashed furiously, trying to open its beak and shrill its pain. A moment later, he had pressed the whittled piece of stave along the wing and bound the drawstring tightly round it, making a firm knot. "There, it's done. Now I think it's safe to leave him here, Felicidad. I'll go get Daddy and see if we can't fix up a big cage so that you can keep him here safe and sound while the wing heals."

"How brave you were, *pobrecito*," Felicidad murmured to the struggling falcon. "That is what I shall name you— *Coraje*—courage. How proud and fierce you will be one day when your wing heals and you can fly and hunt and have the freedom of the sky! You may be an orphan like me, but now you have someone to love you, just as I have my Lucas." Then, seeing that Djamba's son had already left the shed, she murmured, "Lie still and rest, the pain will be gone very soon, I promise it. I shall be back, then we will find you some food and you will have a home here until you are strong enough to try your wings again."

The young falcon made chittering noises, raising its blindfolded head several times. It seemed somehow to understand that the gentle voice it heard sought to assuage its terror of captivity. It held out the splinted wing, giving a loud shrill of pain; then it lay, its chest heaving, as Felicidad gently stroked the white throat. At first it started. Then, as her hand continued to caress it, the bird stopped struggling and lay still, clenching the branch which served as a finite support in this new world of darkness.

A few moments later, one of the vaqueros who had been hired the previous year, Pablo Casares, opened the door of the shed and entered. He inclined his head to Felicidad, holding a pan filled with water in one hand and a dead mouse in the other. He was nearly forty, had been born in Guadalupe, and had gone to work as a vaquero in a little village not far from Nuevo Laredo. He was a friend of Vittorio Salancár, who had urged Ramón Hernandez to hire him. Pablo's mother had been killed in a Comanche raid, and his father had been shot to death by the arrogant son of the aristocratic mineowner for whom he had worked. He was of medium height, slight of build, but remarkably wiry and expert at taming horses. Lucien Edmond Bouchard had already decided that he would ride one of the points on the forthcoming spring drive to Abilene.

Felicidad put a warning finger to her lips as she continued to stroke the young falcon's throat and gestured to Pablo to set the pan of water on the floor and then to hand her the mouse. As he did so, he whispered to her, "Señorita, they are already making a cage for the *halcón*."

"*Muy bueno, gracias,*" Felicidad whispered back as she gingerly accepted the mouse. Pablo removed his hat and watched, a fascinated smile on his weatherbeaten face. Secretly, he was infatuated with the lovely black-haired girl, who reminded him of his own young sweetheart Concepción Rivalda. Concepión had been a flirtatious young girl who had led Pablo to believe that she wished to wed him, only to jilt him for the son of a wealthy shopkeeper. Since then, the middle-aged vaquero had obstinately put the thought of women from his mind. But here, in the gracious and friendly atmosphere of Windhaven Range, his loneliness and his early romantic aspirations had been intensified by the presence of Felicidad Ramirez.

He stood, watching, as the girl held out the mouse toward the falcon's beak. It devoured the rodent rapaciously. Pablo shuddered and shook his head, amazed at Felicidad's fearlessness. He had seen hawks and falcons strike down doves and even rabbits, hurtling down from the skies to pounce upon their prey. The sharp beak of the young falcon made him afraid for Felicidad. Sensing this, she turned to him and whispered, "He will be fine, Señor Casares, he will not hurt me. It is good of you to want to help. I will stay with him until the cage is ready."

"*Bueno*, señorita, I will tell Señor Lucas. You are sure you do not wish me to stay here—"

"*Pero no, gracias.*"

"*De nada.*" He had replaced his sombrero, tipped it, and hesitantly backed out of the shed, not totally certain that he should leave her alone with the fierce-looking bird. Felicidad laughed softly, then began to stroke the falcon's dark-banded chest, speaking softly to it in her native tongue and reassuring it that there would be no danger here at Windhaven Range.

Djamba and Lucas quickly contrived a makeshift cage of sturdy wooden boards, about half the size of a chest of drawers. It had pegged slats which served as bars, and a round wooden wagon spoke, which fitted into hollows on each inner side, provided a perch for the falcon. When it was completed they brought it into the shed and set it down on one of the empty barrels. Felicidad was delighted. "But that is beautiful. Oh thank you, Lucas, and you too, Señor Djamba!" she exclaimed, clapping her hands with joy. "Lucas, *querido*, please put the pan of water inside and I will lift Coraje into his new home."

Lucas grinned sheepishly as his father winked and chuckled at him, and hastened to pick up the pan while Djamba removed several of the slats. Felicidad, still crooning reassuringly to the falcon, gently lifted the bird, still clinging to the branch, into the cage and toward the improvised perch. Feeling it, the falcon groped for the round wooden spoke with its talons. Felicidad swiftly untied the bandanna and stepped back, while Lucas hurriedly replaced the slat bars.

"There, I think that'll hold him," he declared, glancing at his lovely fiancée. "But I don't know, honey, I wouldn't want to get too close to him. Pablo told us how you fed him. That sharp beak could mark your pretty face or worse—I don't even want to think of it."

"Then don't," Felicidad retorted with a saucy moue as she approached the cage. "He is my pet, my *halcón*, and if you two strong men are afraid of him, you who have killed bandits and rattlesnakes and cruel things, then I must be braver than you, *no es verdad?*"

"I guess she's got us there, son." Djamba burst out laughing and clapped Lucas on the back. "Well, Felicidad, looks like you and my son are going to have a good, long, happy life, and I'm glad for both of you. He couldn't do any better, I'll tell you that."

"You are too kind, Señor Djamba," Felicidad murmured, as she moved toward Lucas and pressed her head against his chest, with a happy sigh. "I am the lucky one, not he."

"As long as you both feel that way, that's the meaning of love," Djamba said gravely. He thought to himself how he had secretly loved and deeply respected Sybella Forsden ever since he had become Henry Bouchard's slave, years before the Civil War. He added, "I pray that you'll both feel that way about each other for the rest of your lives. That would make Celia and me very proud and happy—to know that our son had discovered how strong and lasting love can be."

CHAPTER SIX

It had been a slow day at the Brunton and Associate Bank on Greenley Street, just below Canal in New Orleans. A driving rain had begun early this February morning and not ceased until well past noon. Consequently, many customers who were accustomed to doing their banking in the morning had postponed it. At about three o'clock, the sun at last emerged, its rays gleaming on the wet, wooden banquettes. An elegant carriage turned from Canal up Greenley Street and stopped in front of the bank. A black, top-hatted, elegantly liveried coachman descended, and with a great flourish, opened the door and stepped back to let his passenger emerge. The latter curtly nodded and directed, *"Attendez-moi ici, Cornelius. Ça sera peut-être quinze minutes au plus."*

"Bien, Monsieur Cournier." The elderly coachman doffed his silk hat. Then, thrusting his carriage whip back into its upright socket, he hurried to the door of the bank to open it for his master and bowed again before returning to his post at the reins of the carriage.

The man who entered the bank and made his way directly to the marble counter was slim, gray-haired, and in his early fifties. He had a pointed Van Dyke beard and a fastidiously waxed mustache. His face was bronzed by the sun, and he wore a frock coat and trousers of fancy white linen, with matching calfskin boots. In his right hand, he held an ivory-knobbed walking stick made of glossy teakwood. He wore a red cravat and a red carnation in the buttonhole of his coat lapel.

Charming Madelon Fortier, who had been the bank's official hostess since its opening day, had married a pastry-shop owner just recently. Her place had been taken by a stately young woman of twenty-five, Delia Markson.

Jason Barntry, who presided now as manager of the Brunton and Associate Bank, had himself engaged her. Delia's parents had died six months earlier from yellow fever, and what little they had managed to save from their small grocery store had been eaten up by medical bills and funeral expenses. Delia's father had been a customer of the bank, and so Jason Barntry had offered her this post as soon as he learned of her bereavement and the poverty which threatened her.

Delia approached the sun-bronzed Creole and said with a gracious smile, "May I serve you, monsieur?"

"I desire to see the manager of this bank, mademoiselle." He did not give her so much as a glance as he spoke, but stared appraisingly around the bank.

"If you will wait a moment, monsieur, I shall bring him to you," Delia Markson replied. Dropping a curtsy, she turned and went to the office of the middle-aged manager whom Laure and Luke Bouchard had promoted from the post of trust officer when they had decided to return to Windhaven Plantation.

Jason Barntry, a tall, gray-haired man with a self-effacing manner and a passion for hard work, had been employed by John Brunton until Benjamin Butler had closed all New Orleans banks arbitrarily and replaced their personnel with his own men. In order to survive, Barntry had been obliged to take a low-paying job as a greengrocer's clerk, and the war years had brought grave economic stress to his wife and himself. When Luke and Laure had rescued him from his dire straits, he had shown his gratitude by spending nearly all of his free time studying the financial policies of other city banks and reading as many books as he could find on the subject. Under his management, the Brunton and Associate Bank was flourishing, and now held an enviable financial position in New Orleans.

As he approached Cournier, Jason Barntry smiled in greeting. "May I be of service, monsieur? I was told that you wished to see me. I am Jason Barntry, manager of this bank."

"Then, Monsieur Barntry, you are precisely the man to take charge of this transaction. Allow me to introduce

50

myself. I am Henri Cournier. Armand Cournier was my brother."

"I understand. Permit me to offer my condolences, Monsieur Cournier."

"Thank you," the Creole replied coldly. "May we discuss this in your office? I have brought with me proof of my identity and also a copy of a document from the probate court of the city which entitles me, as his only survivor, to claim my poor brother's estate."

"Of course. If you will please come this way, Monsieur Cournier."

Once inside Jason Barntry's private office, Henri Cournier indolently reached into the inner pocket of his linen coat and produced the two documents. One of these established his identity; the other was a copy of the court order, ruling that Henri Cournier, by the terms of his late brother's will and as the only survivor of the family, might legally make claim upon any banking institution in which his brother's funds or the contents of his safe-deposit box were kept.

Jason Barntry examined the papers, then nodded. "These seem to be in order, Monsieur Cournier. I shall have our principal trust officer, Mr. Edgar Maxton, bring you a statement of your late brother's account."

"Thank you. I wish to conclude this business as quickly as possible. I may say that I intend to transfer whatever holdings my poor brother still retains here to the bank of Gabriel Mercier."

"I regret that you wish to make that change, Monsieur Cournier. Our bank is, as you may or may not know, considered quite sound and rated highly."

"I know of your bank's reputation Mr. Barntry. My decision remains as I have stated it," the Creole insolently declared.

"As you wish, of course." Jason Barntry rose, excused himself, and conferred with Edgar Maxton who, a few moments later, brought to his superior's office a current statement of the late Armand Cournier's account. Jason Barntry examined it, then handed it to the Creole.

"I see there is a savings account of $50,000, and an investment account in which my brother deposited

$25,000, as well as the proceeds from the sale of 450 shares of this bank's stock at $102 per share," the latter declared.

"That is correct, Monsieur Cournier. When your brother first opened his accounts at this bank, he specified there were to be two accounts, one of savings and the other of commercial investment. As you can see yourself, his deposit of $25,000 has netted him—or you, I should say—a profit of $3,000. As to the shares of stock, they were purchased at $100 per share, and the $2 represents the special dividend which these shares earned while on the market."

"Very good. It does appear that your bank has handled my poor brother's affairs commendably, all things considered. I shall therefore require a draft in the total amount of $123,900—if my addition is correct?"

"It is, sir. I shall have Mr. Maxton prepare the draft and I myself shall sign it."

"Thank you." The Creole curtly inclined his head, his face cold and disinterested. "I believe my brother had a safe-deposit box as well?"

"He did, Monsieur Cournier. Do you happen to have the key?"

"Yes, I brought it with me. I may tell you that I returned from a small plantation which I owned in Haiti only after the holidays, though of course I had had correspondence with the probate court of your city as soon as the news of my brother's death reached me last June. I have moved into the house known as Three Oaks, upriver from here, which my brother obtained some time ago."

"I know the property, Monsieur Cournier." Now it was Jason Barntry's turn to be coldly polite. "I myself shall escort you downstairs to our vault, and leave you to examine the box. May I have the key, please?"

With a shrug, Henri Cournier reached into his coat pocket and produced the key, then rose and followed the bank manager down the steps to the cellar of what had once been an old warehouse building and, after Luke Bouchard's acquisition of the property, had been converted into the bank, with shops occupying the front on the next street.

A young clerk straightened as he saw his superior come down the steps to the counter of the vault. He greeted him in his most unctuous manner. "Good afternoon, Mr. Barntry. And to you, sir, also."

"Thank you, Morton," Jason Barntry replied. "This is Henri Cournier, and he has a court order to take possession of the contents of his late brother's safe-deposit box. Here is the key. If you will give him the box, I should be obliged to you."

"At once, Mr. Barntry. Just a moment, Mr. Cournier." The young clerk stumbled over the French pronunciation of the Creole's name, and the latter scowled with irritation. "There's a private booth that may be convenient for you, sir. Come this way, please."

"I shall have the draft ready when you come upstairs, Monsieur Cournier," Jason Barntry declared. He nodded to the Creole, then went back up the steps to his office.

Henri Cournier waited until the young clerk had handed him the box, and then entered the private booth, closing the door behind him. The box contained only a few documents and a letter sealed with red wax, with the initials "A.C." impressed by an engraved ring. On its face, it bore an inscription: *For my brother Henri in the event of my death*.

The Creole had carefully placed his walking stick in a corner of the booth. Now he seated himself in the chair near it, so as to have it within reach, as if he feared the entry of some intruder during his perusal of this letter. Glancing suspiciously at the door, he broke the seal and opened the envelope. He took out several neatly folded sheets inscribed in an elegant script, and read them intently, his cold gray eyes narrowing and his thin lips tightening.

My dear brother Henri,

In the event of my death at the hands of Luke Bouchard in an honorable duel to which I have challenged him, I direct you, should he be the survivor, to keep your pledge to me which we made years ago to avenge our grandfather's dishonor and shame. I write these words on the afternoon before our fated encounter. As you remember, our grandfather was betrayed through the treachery of the woman who had married the Comte Jean de Bouchard and had accompanied the latter to Haiti. Auguste Cournier fell in love with this woman, who lied to him and induced him to believe that she wished to divorce her husband and become his wife. After her intrigue had been discovered by her husband's servant, she lied again and professed that our grandfather had forced her to yield carnally to him.

The consequences of that treachery and those lies left our grandfather a dying, hopelessly crippled man, dishonored in the eyes of all society. Thus, the name of Bouchard has become synonymous with infamy to all of us. You remember also what happened to our poor cousin, Edouard Villiers, when he tried to woo Arabella Bouchard.

I believe that my skill with either rapier or pistol should be sufficient to preserve my life. However, if by chance I fall victim, then remember again that infamous name of Bouchard. It must surely be by treachery that he kills me, if it is so ordained. And if he does, Henri, I call on you to avenge me. From afar, do all that you can and will to put obstacles in the path of this descendant of that evil Jean de Bouchard, to cause him pain and grief such as he and his forebears have caused all of us related to our beloved Auguste Cournier. In this solemn hour, I urge you, as brother of my own blood, to renew your pledge until it has been fulfilled to the letter.

Your affectionate brother,
Armand

Henri Cournier read the letter again, slowly folded it and thrust it into his waistcoat pocket. With a malevolent smile, he murmured as if to the spirit of his dead brother, "I take the oath here, and I will keep my pledge, Armand, never fear!"

A moment later, Henri Cournier ascended the steps to the floor of the bank and made his way back to Jason Barntry's office. There the requisite draft awaited him. Taking out a wallet of handsome Moroccan leather, he carefully folded the draft, thrust it inside, and pocketed the wallet. Then, with a brief nod, he declared, "Thank you for your punctilious handling of this transaction. I bid you good afternoon."

The white-columned mansion of Three Oaks, which had once belonged to the impoverished Horace Amberley (who had been forced to sell the estate to Armand Cournier for a pittance), lay forty miles upriver from New Orleans. There were great cypress trees and hedges of magnolia fronting it. The winding path from the road led through a magnificent lawn and garden to which its new owner had now added a newly painted picket fence on all sides. Henri Cournier had taken a chartered packet from New Orleans in the late afternoon, and was just finishing dinner in the sumptuous dining room, attended by a handsome quadroon named Rosabelle and a surly-looking, blond manservant named Roger Benson.

Cournier wore a red velvet dressing gown and slippers. He was completely at his ease as he sipped fastidiously from a crystal goblet filled with a vintage Bordeaux. When he had finished the *entrée* of roast ham with sweet yams and wild rice liberally sprinkled with pecan nutmeats— a dish of which he was inordinately fond—he summoned Roger Benson with a snap of his fingers.

"She is waiting in the antechamber, I presume, Benson?" he drawled.

The stocky valet, his pudgy face marked by thick sideburns, smirked and nodded. "Been waiting 'most an hour, Mr. Cournier."

"Very good. She can wait until I have finished my dessert. However, you may tell Rosabelle to take her a cup of coffee. At least that will show her that we are men here, *n'est-ce pas*, Benson?"

"That's right, Mr. Cournier," the valet snickered, his lewd grin revealing irregular, decaying yellow teeth.

"Really, Benson," Henri Cournier took another sip of his Bordeaux, "I must ask you not to come so close to me. You should really do something about those teeth of yours. And I should not take it amiss if you would bathe more often. Now then, have Rosabelle fetch Miss Harrison some café au lait."

Roger Benson scratched his head and looked uncomfortable. "You mean—" he hesitantly began.

"You idiot, you might also try to learn a little French from the rest of my household staff. Rosabelle will know what the term means. Just tell her to bring a cup of it to Miss Harrison directly. But first, have her bring in the trifle and the sweet port. And before you go, you may as well fill that snifter glass with brandy. You will find it in the crystal decanter on the sideboard."

"Very good, Mr. Cournier."

Henri Cournier watched his valet amble over to the sideboard. He grimaced with distaste as the latter nearly dropped the glass top of the decanter in his eagerness to execute his master's order. When Roger Benson set the snifter down beside his master, the Creole shook his head. "You have spilled several drops of this rare brandy on the outside of the glass. Decidedly, I shall have to teach you the finer arts of waiting upon your master. However, you are useful enough to me in other, more vulgar ways—as you may be tonight, by the way. So keep yourself in readiness."

"I get your meaning, Mr. Cournier." Roger Benson grinned again, then chuckled bawdily. "You're planning on a little fun with that fancy lady, I suspect?"

"That is none of your business. If I require your services, I shall summon you. Now go tell Rosabelle to serve the lady."

After he had eaten all of the trifle, helped himself to two glasses of port, and then sipped his own café au lait after pouring part of the contents of the snifter into the cup, Henri Cournier lit a Havana cigar and leaned back with a sigh. This evening was in a way a celebration, heralding his return to the city of his own birth. Haiti had been pleasant enough, but tedious and broilingly hot, though of course in summer New Orleans was intolerable. His brother had been well advised to buy this upriver mansion. Moreover, it was an excellent place from which to conduct his own affairs. He intended to take over the management of his brother's bordellos, gambling saloons, and other profitable enterprises. The bank draft had already been deposited in Gabriel Mercier's bank at the highest available rate of interest. And now that he had sold his own plantation in Haiti he could devote his advancing years to the full appeasement of his well-cultivated tastes and, best of all, to the pursuit of vengeance—in the name of his dead brother.

When at last he had finished his cigar, Cournier rose and made his way to the beautifully decorated antechamber off the foyer of the Amberley mansion. The young woman seated on a low, upholstered bench uttered a startled gasp and rose, color flooding her creamy cheeks. She was about five feet seven inches tall, twenty-five years old. Her radiant strawberry-blond hair was coiffed in an imposing pompadour which left her shapely neck bare. Her face was sensitive, a cameolike oval, with a delicate, small nose whose thin nostrils quivered with emotion as she confronted the Creole. She wore an elegant, brown-silk dress with puffed sleeves and a long, flounced skirt, which was obviously the work of a well-known New Orleans dressmaker, and fawn-colored slippers that buttoned high on her slim ankles. Henri Cournier appraised her, and then eyed the tabouret beside her, noticing that she had taken only a few swallows from the cup of café au lait. Amused at this, he permitted himself a faint, ironic smile as he declared, "I regret to have made you wait so long, Mademoiselle Harrison, but I have spent most of the day in the city—my affairs are pressing, you know—and I had to dine late. I trust you will forgive me."

"Please, Monsieur Cournier, may we come to the point? The letter which your manservant delivered yesterday told me that I was to come here to settle the matter of my brother's debt."

"Yes, Miss Harrison, that is true. Are you familiar with your poor brother's activities?"

The young woman drew herself up, her cheeks flaming as she felt his eyes upon her, and, setting her teeth, tersely replied, "I know about his gambling, yes."

"But perhaps you do not know that he lost $40,000 at the establishment named Bon Jeu, which belongs to me, Miss Harrison."

"Oh my God—but he couldn't have—he never had that sort of money! Father left us only a few thousand dollars when he died last year." Now her rich contralto voice trembled with anxiety.

"But I daresay he would have made no bones about picking up his winnings if fortune had favored him, Miss Harrison," Henri Cournier continued. "Also, I happen to know that your house is heavily mortgaged and hence can hardly serve as collateral to offset this heavy debt."

"My God, Monsieur Cournier . . ." She clasped her hands despairingly, twisting her long slim fingers as she stared imploringly at him. "Can't you be content with what Max did to himself? He put a bullet through his head last week, and left me a letter saying that it was the only way out. He just couldn't go on gambling anymore and losing the way he had."

"I am afraid, my dear Miss Harrison," Henri Cournier replied, his voice ironically suave, "that a gambling debt is one of honor which cannot be erased by suicide. And when I mentioned the mortgaged house, it was simply to acquaint you with the practical side of the matter. Obviously, I cannot levy any hold upon that house to satisfy the money your brother lost to my establishment."

"Do you mean—you can't be so heartless, Monsieur Cournier—there's nothing left, I must look for work. All my life I've been accustomed to money, and now there isn't any—even during the war we were able to live decently—oh God, what's to become of me?" the young woman groaned, her fingers twisting back and forth in her mounting anxiety.

"And I may also remind you," he calmly broke in, "that prior to the war, you could have been sold at auction like a slave. Now that that is no longer possible, I am prepared to employ you. But it is understood that you will do my bidding, until such time as I deem the debt completely settled."

"Employ me? I—I don't understand—"

"Oh, not as my mistress," he said contemptuously, "although you're extremely handsome and desirable. I have in mind certain other projects which your services may be of aid in furthering."

"Please explain what you mean, Monsieur Cournier. I'm at my wit's end. I don't know which way to turn, truly I don't. I—I'm ready to work, but I don't know what my talents are—my education—"

Impatiently, he shook his head. "I'm satisfied that you

are well-bred, a fine lady brought up, as most wealthy young girls are, to expect the best things in life. I may not require these services of yours for some time, but you will hold yourself in readiness, and you will be bound to me by the agreement we make tonight. Meanwhile I shall hold your brother's IOU, until such time as the debt has been cleared to my satisfaction by your cooperation. Is that understood?"

"I—I suppose so. But—but how am I to live in the meantime?"

"As to that," again he permitted himself a wry, thin-lipped smile, "you will move into Three Oaks. There is plenty of room here. Your lodging and meals will be provided, and at the same time you will be under my surveillance constantly so that I may assure myself of your good faith when I do require your real services."

She turned scarlet as she saw his eyes again sweep her from head to foot. His lingering scrutiny shamed her, for Amy Harrison was a virgin. She had been betrothed six months before to a wealthy young Creole, the son of a banker, who had broken off his engagement after he had learned of her brother's suicide. "But then I should be further indebted to you, Monsieur Cournier," she at last exclaimed, her high-perched bosom heaving with emotion. "You are playing a cat-and-mouse game with me, and it's cruel and heartless! I told you, I—I'm willing to work to pay off my brother's debt, if nothing else will satisfy you—but to tell me all this, that you'll keep me here until such time as you need my—my services—I don't understand!"

"Why, then, Mademoiselle Harrison," he chuckled dryly, "since you are so eager to begin paying off that debt, I shall make an immediate demand upon you. I shall credit your dead brother's account with, shall we say, $5,000 if you obey me at once."

"What—what do you mean by that?" She took a step backward, her dark-blue eyes very wide and moist with the hint of tears.

"You will strip naked before me, Mademoiselle Harrison. You will go down on your knees and promise faithfully to serve me, with no thought of evasion. You will not be permitted, for one thing, to escape the way your brother did, for my servants will see to it that you are well guarded while you live here—which will begin immediately, by the way."

"How dare you!"

"You are being unreasonable," he chuckled maliciously. "Not even the highest priced *fille de joie* could command so high a tariff for simply unveiling her loveliness."

"You—you wicked, heartless scoundrel—I'd never do a thing like that! And—and I'd never be your mistress, either!" she exclaimed defiantly, her voice breaking into sobs.

Cournier went to the door of the antechamber and beckoned. Roger Benson entered, grinning from ear to ear, holding in his hands a brown leather riding crop. "You want me, Mr. Cournier?" he asked with a sly wink.

"I do indeed, Benson. Miss Harrison is reluctant to undress. Perhaps you can serve her as a lady's maid."

"No! This is vile! I shall complain to the authorities—" Amy Harrison cried out hysterically as she backed toward the corner of the little antechamber.

The valet approached her, raising the riding crop, baring his yellow teeth in a lustful grin. "You'd best do as Mr. Cournier says, ma'am. I'd hate to use this on you, but I will if I have to. Come on, be a good girl and take your duds off."

"What a vulgar way you have of putting things, Benson," Henri Cournier observed with another grimace as he stood, arms folded across his chest, watching the trembling young woman whose eyes were fixed on the upraised crop.

"I tell you, I shall complain to the authorities! You can't treat a decent woman this way—" Amy Harrison mustered a last despairing attempt at bravado.

Roger Benson glanced back at his master, who gave him a barely perceptible nod. With a leer, the valet advanced and slashed the young woman across the shoulders with the flexible riding crop. Amy Harrison uttered a shriek of incredulous pain and horror. She stumbled back against the wall, lifting an arm to fend off the blows.

"I'm sorry, ma'am, but I've got my orders," the valet explained mockingly. Then he applied another stroke. The whip curled around Amy Harrison's slim waist. With a cry of pain, she tried to run toward the door, but Roger Benson thrust out his foot and tripped her, sending her sprawling onto the floor. Then, bending over her, he repeatedly lashed her back and shoulders, commanding her in a harsh voice. "You do what Mr. Cournier tells you to, you hear, you bitch? Get your clothes off fast or I'll whip them off you, understand?"

"Oh God—please—have mercy—I can't bear it—oh stop —stop—yes—yes—oh God, if only you'll stop—yes—I—I'll do it!"

Roger Benson stepped back, his face flushed. He was panting, but kept the crop upraised, ready to punish further resistance. Painfully, sobbing distractedly, the young woman stumbled to her feet. Tears ran down her crimson cheeks as she began to remove the brown silk dress.

"Hurry up with it, or I'll have to give you a few more licks, ma'am," Roger Benson urged hoarsely.

The dress fell to the floor, and Amy Harrison, blinded by her tears, removed her stays and camisole with fumbling fingers. At last she stood clad only in a pair of pink silk drawers decorated with lace bows at her knees and waistband, white silk stockings and her fawn-colored slippers. Her ivory breasts bore the ugly, darkening welts of the riding crop, as did her shoulders and upper back.

Now, head bowed, her pompadour disheveled and curls hanging down one tear-stained cheek, she huddled in a corner, clasping her arms over her naked breasts before the unbridled lubricity of her two tormentors.

"The pants, too, and be quick about it," Roger Benson urged in a thick voice. He playfully flicked the plaited tip of the leather whip against Amy Harrison's beautifully curved haunches.

With a cry of agonized despair, she unfastened the waistband of the drawers and began to tug at them until they slithered to her ankles. At once she clapped a hand over her thickly downed virgin mound, the other arm crossed over her bosom. Totally humiliated, she submitted herself to their scrutiny.

"Very well, Amy." Henri Cournier purposely used his victim's Christian name for the first time. "Now then, kneel down, kiss my slippers and swear that you will serve me faithfully until such time as the debt has been wiped

61

out. Quickly now, or else I fear that Benson will grow impatient."

Shuddering violently, half-fainting, the almost naked young woman sank down on her knees and bowed her head to Henri Cournier's slippered feet. She forced herself to press her trembling lips against each of his slippers and then, in a quivering voice, mumbled the formula of appeasement and submission.

"That will suffice, I think," Henri Cournier said after a long moment of ecstatic contemplation of his groveling victim. "I am a reasonably just man, Amy. I shall remit the $5,000 as I promised. However, since you saw fit to insult me, I must have some satisfaction. And since I do not care to consort with a mere servant, such as you now are, I shall ask Benson to satisfy himself. However, to show you again that I am fair in all my financial dealings, I shall remit a further $1,000 of your brother's debt for the temporary discomfort which I fear my valet is about to cause you." With this, turning to the delighted valet, he drawled, "After you've finished, take her upstairs to the east wing and lock her in the green room. Tell Jennifer to stay with her all night and watch her, in case she thinks of escaping her debt the way her silly brother did." With this, he opened the door of the antechamber and left, closing the door behind him.

Amy Harrison slowly raised her head. Her face was contorted. She did not fully understand what was going to happen to her. She saw Roger Benson unbuttoning his breeches, and then a stifled shriek of horrified comprehension was wrested from her. "Oh no!"

"Oh yes, bitch, you stirred me up something fierce—"

She tried to rise, but two brutal lashes from the riding crop kept her from getting to her feet. As she screamed in agony and tried to scramble away from him on all fours, the valet seized her by the hair, flung her down on her back, and then, with a brutal laugh, mounted her.

Outside, Henri Cournier had lit another cigar and was savoring its bouquet, quivering with erotic excitement at the screams and sobs that emanated from the little antechamber.

CHAPTER SEVEN

By the second week of February, the vaqueros of Windhaven Range had ridden out over Lucien Edmond's eight thousand acres to round up those cattle that had not yet been branded, as well as to keep a running tally of the total herd to be driven to Abilene by the beginning of March. Lucien Edmond had estimated that the cattle could be brought into Abilene by the end of June. He would have time to visit the Creek reservation where the courageous *mico*, Emataba, still ruled over those once-proud warriors who had dominated the old South for so many years.

Andy Haskins and Joe Duvray, as well as Simata, sometimes accompanied by the barking Jubal, rode out on their own mission to round up mild mustangs. They would be trained and perhaps incorporated into the large *remuda* which would accompany the herd on the long drive. They also rode along the perimeter of Windhaven Range, for although there were no neighbors on any side of his range as yet, Lucien Edmond had ordered that visible markers be set at intervals along the boundaries of his acreage. News had reached him of bushwhackers, cattle rustlers, and marauding Mexican bandits who occasionally came as close as Ugalde and might threaten the peace and security of the Bouchards.

Despite his handicap, one-armed Andy Haskins had proved already not only that he could handle weapons as well as any two-armed man, but also that he was an expert with the lasso. On the second day out his lariat looped around the neck of a superb black stallion. With the end of the lariat securely tied to the pommel of his saddle, the young Southerner dismounted and, seizing a shorter lariat from the other side of the saddle, hobbled the stallion and halted its frenzied attempts at flight. An hour later, he and Joe Duvray led it back to the corral and released it into a separate pen. There Joe Duvray blindfolded and saddled the restive stallion, and Andy Haskins was soon astride it, seizing the reins. A crowd of excited vaqueros watched him ride the bucking mustang and successfully master its violent struggles to dismount its unwanted rider. When at last the stallion acknowledged defeat, its head drooping, its flanks wet with lather, they burst into cheers and acclaimed him as *un muy gran vaquero*. Then Andy Haskins turned to the admiring Lucas and, with a sly chuckle, declared, "Lucas boy, that's going to be your mount on the drive. By the time we start off, he ought to be gentled enough for even Felicidad to ride him safely."

"That's a wonderful present, Mister Andy." Lucas' eyes shone with delight. "That's a horse with plenty of stamina for a long drive. It was mighty thoughtful of you to pick him for me."

"Think of it as a wedding present for the two of you." Andy Haskins grinned and extended his hand to Lucas, who shook it energetically and clapped the Southerner on the back.

During the past week, pretty Felicidad had visited the shed near the bunkhouse, whenever her chores allowed her free time, to tend the young falcon. After a few days, Coraje had begun to recognize the sound of her gentle voice. Dutifully, she replaced the water in the falcon's pan each day and several times, despite her natural squeamishness, caught and killed a mouse which she fed to Coraje. As she did this, she repeated the bird's name several times, stroking its head with her left hand. After the bird had been fed, she removed the improvised hood and stroked its head feathers.

Coraje's gleaming yellow eyes always fixed on her with an intensity that sometimes startled her. At the outset, Coraje had attempted to peck at her hand, and Felicidad quickly withdrew it, all the while continuing her gently soothing words. By the third day after its capture, however, the falcon only cocked its head. From time to time it would move its sharp beak toward her hand, but without pecking it. "That is good, my beautiful one," Felicidad murmured. "You and I shall be amigos, and when you are well enough to fly again, perhaps you will not go too far away from your friend. You have such courage, it will be good to have you here in case there is danger."

The falcon made a chittering sound and bobbed its head as if agreeing with her. She examined the splinted wing. Lucas had told her that within two or three weeks the splint could be removed, and that the falcon should be able then to make its first attempts at flight.

Sometimes two or three of the vaqueros, all of whom had fallen in love with her, came to watch Felicidad feed the captive bird, admiring the gentleness and fearlessness with which she always treated this usually savage predator. Pablo Casares was usually one of those in attendance, although he would have angrily fought any of his *compañeros* had they dared to accuse him of being in love with the attractive young orphan. The hardness and loneliness of his life after his fiancée had jilted him some twenty years before, had altered his temperament from that of a carefree young man to a dour and silent, although conscientious, hard-working vaquero. Yet, watching Felicidad, Pablo Casares was drawn out of himself to recall those almost forgotten hours of joy when he had believed his sweetheart was truly in love with him. But, being an honorable man who lived by the unwavering code of the vaquero, he pledged to himself that he would act toward Felicidad as a protector and never as a would-be suitor— no matter how much his own longing for her grew with each new day.

On this second Sunday of the month, Lucien Edmond Bouchard, Djamba, and Ramón Hernandez hitched teams of horses to three supply wagons and began the trip to San Antonio. There they would purchase ample stocks of flour, beans, coffee, and other staples for the drive to Abilene. While in San Antonio, Lucien Edmond would send a telegraph to a cattle breeder who lived on the outskirts of St. Louis. This breeder, he had learned from Joseph McCoy on last year's drive to Abilene, had imported a number of Brahma bulls and heifers because they seemed to be immune to "Texas fever." Lucien Edmond was convinced that the breeding of Brahmas like these with his Texas longhorns would do a great deal to eliminate the danger of spleen fever. The concern over "Texas fever" was one which extended throughout the Southwest and even the Midwest.

The word was that the enterprising Joseph McCoy and his associates, who had financed and constructed cattle pens, chutes, and scales and managed to obtain favorable shipping rates with the railroad, were lobbying to bypass the rule of quarantine which had been laid down to prevent longhorns from entering Dickinson County. From what he had learned thus far, Lucien Edmond felt that the sturdy, durable Brahmas seemed already to have resisted many of the ravages which beset other types of cattle and, through proper crossbreeding, would impart disease-resistance to his own herd. He was prepared to pay as much as $2,000 for a pedigreed bull and half again as much for a healthy Brahma heifer. If Windhaven Range was to prosper in the future, it would be done—just as old Lucien Bouchard had originally conceived—by entering into long-range projects which might sacrifice immediate profit in return for future gains.

There was still another reason, a sentimental one, for Lucien Edmond's trip to San Antonio. Ramón and Djamba could have brought back the necessary supplies by themselves. But Lucien Edmond intended to commemorate the tenth anniversary of his marriage to Maxine Kendall—on February fourteenth—by getting her a particularly memorable present, as well as gifts for their children, Carla and Hugo, and their four-month-old daughter, Edwina. That was why he had yoked an extra wagon behind the one he drove.

It was all he could do to keep from telling Maxine his reason for being absent on their tenth anniversary when he saw her reproachful look on the morning of the departure, just three days before that all-important day. That look had lingered as he climbed into the driver's seat of the lead wagon to which he had attached four of the strongest geldings in the *remuda*. Maxine, carrying little Edwina in her arms, with Carla and Hugo on each side of her, had come out to bid him Godspeed, and he could see that the corners of her mouth were quivering and that there was a suspicious mist in her eyes. But to tell her his real reason for going to San Antonio would spoil the secret and detract from her radiant pleasure when he returned. There would be other anniversaries in store for them, and perhaps they might visit some of the family in Pittsburgh or Chicago or back on Windhaven Plantation to make the next anniversary more than compensate for his current seeming neglect. So he contented himself with calling to her, "We'll be back by the end of the month for certain, darling. I've some very important business in San Antonio that can't wait, or I'd have stayed home, you know that. I love you, Maxine, and I'll miss you every moment of the time that I'm away."

"Be careful, dearest," she had called back, then bent her head to chide Hugo, who was pulling frantically at her skirts to attract her attention. Lucien Edmond could see that she had turned away to hide the tears in her eyes, and he was saddened by that. But the thought of what he would bring back cheered him. He called to the horses, and the wagon pulled out into open country, with Djamba and Ramón following in their wagons.

Mara Hernandez had been sorry to see Ramón go off to San Antonio with Djamba and Lucien Edmond. She knew that when he returned it would be only a few days before he would set forth again on the cattle drive to Abilene. The drive itself would take three months, and then another month would be needed for the return trip, once the herd had been sold. She had never believed that a man could be so gentle and tender and yet so very much a man as this Mexican vaquero whom she had once lashed and contemptuously called a greaser because he had warned her not to ride into renegade Comanche territory. Their son, Luke—a name chosen by Ramón to honor Luke Bouchard, his wife's father, who had given them this land on which to begin their life together—was now thirteen months old. He was black-haired like Ramón, and as healthy and sturdy as his father, yet with sensitive features inherited from his spirited mother. Luke Bouchard believed that this child born of Bouchard blood and the vigorous blood of a young Mexican who had many times proved his dignity and courage, would impart a legacy that would reach out into the future and strengthen this growing family.

Mara, like Maxine, had seen her husband off on the trip to San Antonio, holding little Luke in her arms and smiling tenderly as the young vaquero waved for a last time to her and the child. Her eyes, too, had been full of tears, but these were rather of a joyous, secret promise she made to herself. When Ramón returned and before he left on that long drive to Abilene, she was determined to ask him to give her another child, and this one, she hoped, would be a son, too. He would be named Jaime, after Ramón's father who had been brutally flogged to death by the rich silver-mine owner who had employed him. As a boy, Ramón had witnessed that dreadful execution. Mara well knew that he wished to have a son whom he could name after his father and thus perpetuate his memory. Yet, in his gratitude to Luke Bouchard, he had renounced that desire. Because she loved him so and because she now knew that there would never be another man for her, willful, iconoclastic Mara promised herself that she would fulfill his fondest dream.

About two weeks after Lucien Edmond, Ramón and Djamba had gone to San Antonio, Felicidad and Lucas visited the shed to inspect Coraje's splinted wing. To the girl's delight the wing seemed to have healed completely. The falcon flapped both wings as soon as it heard Felicidad's voice. "Take off the splint, Lucas, and I will hold Coraje's beak so that he will not peck you," Felicidad enjoined as they both approached the cage. Removing several of the vertical slats which served as bars, Lucas cautiously reached in while Felicidad, from the other side, soothed the falcon and reassured it. She grasped its beak between her right thumb and forefinger and stroked its proud head with her left palm. Deftly, Lucas disengaged the cord and splint, and nodded. "He's ready to test his wings for sure, Felicidad, honey. Do you want to try it?"

"Of course I do! Here, take that stick on the floor and touch his claws with it—that's it—see how he takes hold? Now we'll take him outside and let him fly a bit," the pretty young girl exclaimed.

She and Lucas walked slowly out through the open gate of the stockade which fenced in the sprawling hacienda of Windhaven Range, and stopped midway between it and the Belcher house near the creek. Removing the hood, the girl softly murmured, "Now, Coraje, try your wings, *querido halcón!*"

The falcon's fierce yellow eyes glared at Lucas, but it made no motion to attack him. Then it turned its head toward Felicidad and uttered a soft chittering sound. "You see, Lucas, he knows me!" the girl cried. "That's it, Coraje, Lucas is your friend, too. We will watch you fly, and then you must come back to us!"

With a great flapping of wings, the aplomado falcon rose from the stick and soared high above their heads. At first it flew hesitantly, without any pattern of flight, until, satisfied that its wings would respond to its demands, it rose higher and higher until it was almost out of sight.

"Oh no, I want him back," Felicidad sobbed. Then, cupping her mouth with her soft hands, she called, "Coraje, *vienes aqui, por favor!*"

Lucas shook his head dubiously, then glanced at his pretty sweetheart, sensing her disappointment. Again she called, this time more loudly.

Suddenly, with a great rush of wings, the young falcon swooped down from the sky and came to perch once again on the stick which Felicidad held out, cocking its head and looking defiantly at Lucas as if to say, "You did not think I would obey her, but you see I have done so."

"That's wonderful, Felicidad!" Lucas exclaimed.

"And now, we must teach Coraje to hunt. Sometimes, if you are working out on the range, you will not be here to help find food for Coraje. Oh dear—" A sudden thought made her face fall with disappointment. "If we both go on the drive, Lucas, who will look after Coraje?"

"Never mind, honey. Maybe one of the vaqueros will know what to do. He'll keep him safe for us until we get back," Lucas consoled her. He put out a hand to touch her, and then drew back with a gasp as the falcon's head darted forward and the sharp beak nipped his knuckle. "Ouch! That hurt!"

"You see?" Felicidad laughingly exclaimed. "Coraje is going to defend me. He doesn't know yet that you and I are going to be married. But he won't do it again if I tell him not to."

Then stroking the falcon's head, she explained that Lucas was her dear friend and that he meant no harm. The falcon regarded Lucas with a wary stare, and then seemed to settle back on the perch, as if satisfied with her explanation.

"Try again now. But put your hand out with the palm up, to show Coraje you are not going to strike him," Felicidad urged.

Somewhat reluctantly and sheepishly, Lucas obeyed. This time the falcon, a bit warily, permitted Lucas to touch the dark band across its chest.

On the following day, Lucas watched Felicidad release Coraje again. This time, noticing a little dove, the falcon swooped down, killing it upon impact, and flew with its kill to a perch near Felicidad. When Felicidad approached, Coraje made gurgling sounds as if to express pride. Although Felicidad winced to see the little dove, she nonetheless praised the falcon. Lucas again shook his head, saying, "It beats all—you'd think that bird had a human mind and could understand you, honey!"

Felicidad could not help giggling and audaciously whispered back, "So long as *you* understand me, dearest Lucas, I shall be *muy feliz!*"

One night there was a thunderstorm, and the sky remained overcast the next morning, with hardly a hint of sun. Felicidad hurried out to the shed to visit Coraje as soon as she finished washing and putting away the breakfast dishes. As was her wont, she greeted the falcon in the sweet, soothing tone which it at once recognized. Coraje emitted its customary sound of acknowledgment, preening its feathers and shaking its head. *"Buenas días,* Coraje! *Que pasa, mi halcón?"* she said as she approached the cage. "Oh, you have finished all your water. Never mind, I will go right to the creek and bring back a fresh panful for you." Adroitly removing some of the slats which served as bars to the cage, Felicidad drew out the pan and replaced the bars. There was, to be sure, water available in the kitchen in a barrel which one of the vaqueros filled each day. But Felicidad enjoyed the walk to the creek, with clumps of reeds and luxuriant foliage bordering it, as well as the sight of the yucca and the oak trees which served as protective shelter when the sun was at its zenith.

Pablo Casares had just come out of the bunkhouse and greeted Felicidad. She waved back to him with a happy smile, and continued toward the creek. The middle-aged vaquero sighed disconsolately, and shook his head. *Diablo*, it was high time he went back to his native Guadalupe and found himself a *novia*. How lonely this life was, and how much more lonely because he could see the joy of this charming young woman and her fiancé. He told himself he must be careful never to show how much he envied them their happiness, how he wished that Lucas had not already spoken for her hand in marriage. Under the influence of this thwarted yearning, Pablo decided to walk toward the creek to make certain that no harm befell Felicidad.

At the southern end of the creek, there was a small peninsulalike stretch of ground which extended from the base of the creek into the water. It was solid, covered with nearly waist-high weeds. Felicidad had often used it to squat down and thrust her pan well into the clear water. This morning, however, the water was murky from the heavy rain, and it lapped at the edges of the little spit of land as she moved, shoving aside the weeds with one hand, to find her usual place.

Bending over, Felicidad reached down into the water with the pan just as the ugly head of a grayish-black water moccasin emerged from the opaque surface. Felicidad uttered a cry of alarm and drew back her hand, but not in time. Viciously, the water moccasin sank its fangs into her wrist and, as she straightened, clung to her like a grisly decoration.

Her scream of terror brought Pablo Casares at a run. Quickly unholstering his Starr .44, he took careful aim and fired. The writhing snake jerked, then dangled inert as Felicidad, paralyzed with fear, stood staring at it. The pan had fallen into the water and sunk out of sight.

The vaquero ran to her, tore the dead snake's jaws from her wrist, and flung its body away. Then swiftly, while he consoled her in their native tongue, he seized his hunting knife and made two incisions directly across the ugly bluish punctures left by the snake's fangs. Making her sit down, he began to suck the blood from the wound until he was satisfied that the venom had been removed. Then he tore off a strip of his rough shirt and made as tight a tourniquet as he could above the wound, thrusting in a little twig to give it greater pressure and so halt the circulation of any remaining poison.

Felicidad gasped, her head falling back. She looked wan and pale, and a wave of nausea seized her right before she lost consciousness. Swearing under his breath and sweating with his own anxiety for the lovely victim, Pablo Casares carefully lifted her in his arms and carried her back to the bunkhouse. The vaqueros who were not out on the range clustered around her, each offering advice. Miguel Dondaro, one of the Mexican cattle drivers hired last year, was as close a friend to Pablo Casares as the latter permitted. He eagerly suggested that they give the girl whiskey; but Pablo shook his head. "That would be the worst thing you could do for her, amigo. Go to the kitchen and get her some hot milk. Whiskey stirs the blood, and if there is any poison left, it will speed that more quickly—*pobrecita!*"

An hour later, Felicidad was improved enough to sit up, while Lucas knelt beside the bunk, an arm around her waist, his eyes filled with tears, staring with anguish at her drawn face.

"She will be all right, Señor Lucas," Pablo Casares assured him. "I am glad I was there to be of help."

Lucas turned to the middle-aged vaquero. "May the good God bless you, Pablo. You saved my Felicidad for me. And I bless you myself for being so quick and knowing what to do." Then, to Felicidad, who had forced a wan little smile to her trembling lips, he declared, "Honey, I don't think you should go on the drive as our cook. You'd best take it easy. One of the vaqueros can cook for us. I'd feel better if you stayed home and rested, and got well and strong again. Because when I come back, I want us to be married just as quick as we can."

"I—I want that too, dearest Lucas." Felicidad put out an unsteady hand and touched his head. "But I'll be all right, truly I will. And I want to go along with you to Abilene and watch over you myself."

72

"No, darling, I won't let you. I'll tell Mr. Lucien Edmond —he ought to be back any time now from San Antonio— and I know he'll feel the way I do."

"Señor Lucas," Pablo Casares spoke up, twisting his sombrero between his strong lean hands, "I am not a bad cook. If you do not mind, I would like to volunteer for the work on the drive."

"Instead of riding point?" Lucas turned to him in surprise. "But everybody knows how much you look forward to that, Pablo."

The middle-aged vaquero shook his head, an apologetic smile brightening his homely face. "There are other vaqueros here who ride better than I do. There is Benito Aguilar and there is Sanchez Maderos. No, Señor Lucas, I wish to do it. If I had walked there with her, the snake might not have bitten her. I ask it of you, *por favor*."

CHAPTER EIGHT

Lucien Edmond Bouchard leaped down from the driver's seat of his wagon and strode toward his wife, Maxine. "We made good time getting home, darling," he commented, as he took little Edwina from her arms, and tenderly kissed the drowsy, curly-haired child. Then he bent down to greet Hugo and Carla, who had run out of the hacienda with shouts of glee at his arrival.

The vaqueros had already emerged from the bunkhouse, ready to haul the supplies from the wagons into the storage sheds. Djamba and Ramón, standing side by side and exchanging whispered comments, grinned as Lucien Edmond straightened, still carrying Edwina in his arms, kissed Maxine gently on each cheek and said, "A belated happy anniversary, my dearest wife. I hope you will forgive my neglect and absence, for I have brought back something from San Antonio that will give you constant pleasure when I am away. Djamba, Ramón, get two of the strongest vaqueros to help you carry my present in from the rear wagon."

"Oh my goodness, Lucien Edmond," Maxine gasped, her eyes widening, "a present that big? What can it be?"

He chuckled as he handed Edwina back to her and then went to the rear of the second wagon to supervise the unloading of the supplies. Two vaqueros hastened forward to aid Ramón and Djamba at the back of the rear wagon, while Maxine, her curiosity mounting by degrees, moved slightly forward to witness what was taking place. Then she uttered a gasp of astonished delight. "A piano—oh, Lucien Edmond, how wonderfully thoughtful of you!"

"It's a Beckendorfer," he explained casually. "Actually, it was a stroke of luck finding it in San Antonio. Just

74

before Christmas, I thought of getting you a piano, because I know how much you love music. But of course there wouldn't have been time to have sent a cable all the way to Hamburg and had it here in time for our anniversary. As it happened, when I was at the Citizens Bank, the manager mentioned that a German family was selling their household effects to raise money enough to get to California. So I called on them and found this spinet. Fortunately, they were including it in the sale. It's in wonderful condition, and I had it tuned just before I brought it back. Ramón and Djamba packed it securely enough so that I don't think it got too out of tune."

"Oh my darling, you don't know how I've longed for a piano!" Maxine beamed. She handed Edwina to a smiling white-haired Sybella, and flung herself into her husband's arms. Her eyes were brimming with tears of gratitude and love.

The spinet had been hand rubbed until the rich wood glowed, and Maxine followed the four men who lifted it carefully and carried it up the steps of the front porch and into the ranch house. "It will be just fine in that corner of the living room," she directed.

Lucien Edmond followed and took her arm as he smiled tenderly at her. "There's something else I brought along, not quite so heavy, and not at all secondhand."

"Oh my darling, please don't try to apologize for the spinet—it's so beautiful, and I'm sure the people who had it loved it as much as I shall!" Maxine told him.

Lucien Edmond had taken out of his waistcoat pocket a purple velvet jewel case, and now handed it to his wife. She uttered another gasp of delight, opened it and stood speechless for a moment, in admiration. "February was your birthday month as well as our anniversary, my darling. And amethyst is your birthstone, I know," he gently explained.

Maxine took out the necklace, looking up at him with adoring tenderness, and then handed it to him so that he might clasp it around her neck. Then her arms went around him and they kissed, oblivious of their delighted, attentive audience.

It was Lucien Edmond who at last disengaged himself

from Maxine's embrace. "And now, my dearest, I'm going to owe you another apology. We'll be starting our drive to Abilene in about a week, you know, so I'll be gone even longer this time. But I wanted you to know how much I've thought about you and how I'll be with you in spirit when I'm gone again."

Cradling Edwina in her left arm, she slipped her right hand into Lucien Edmond's left, squeezing it tightly. Djamba and Ramón exchanged a sympathetic, knowing look, and then Djamba headed for the kitchen to be reunited with Celia and Lucas. Ramón remounted Corita and energetically urged the mare on toward his own house, where Mara and little Luke awaited him.

Indeed, both were on the porch, Mara having seen the wagons drive in through the stockade gate. Her eyes were wet with tears as she watched her young husband dismount swiftly, tie Corita's reins to the post at the left side of the porch, and hurry toward her, his face aglow with pleasure.

"*Querida, mi corazón,* how I've missed you!" he exclaimed in a husky voice as he drew her to him. Then, bending down, he greeted his strapping little son who smiled and formed with his soft lips the word *Dada.*

Ramón looked up at Mara, his eyes wet with tears of happiness as he hugged his little son and kissed his forehead and cheeks. "What a strong boy," he murmured. Then, taking Mara's hands in his, he drew her to him again and whispered, "*Te quiero mucho, mi corazón.*"

"No more than I want you, Ramón, my husband, my lover, my very life," she whispered back as she clung to him. Little Luke glanced up at them, shyly smiling, then clapped his hands and again uttered, "Dada."

"And you're as good a father as you are a husband, my dearest one," she whispered softly, radiant through her tears. "But now you'll be gone from me again for four or five months, won't you?"

His face sobered. "*Sí, querida.* That's my job. And I'm proud of it, because if I hadn't come here and met your father I'd never have met you and had such joy. And now you've given me this strong son who will carry on my name."

"But I know something else, dearest," she confided as

her arms went around him again and she pressed herself closer to him. "I know how you revered your own father, how you wanted to keep his name alive. Before you go on the drive you must give me another son. And this one we'll name Jaime. This child will be an even stronger bond between us, Ramón."

"*Por todos los santos*," he said in a gruff voice to hide his nearly choking emotion, "let us go inside where we can be alone and not have people see how a vaquero acts when he is with his *mujer!*"

"Well, I should think so." Mara could not suppress a teasing giggle and her cheeks turned red as his dark eyes fixed ardently on her lovely face. "Let me put little Luke in his crib and give him the toy that Andy Haskins made for him. And then, my *gran vaquero*, do not wait until nightfall to make me yours again."

Ramón Hernandez trembled as he took her into his arms, and kissed her throat and cheeks and eyelids. Then, reluctantly releasing her, he murmured, "Then do what must be done and quickly, for I am burning for you, Mara, *mi mujer, mi corazón.*"

"I promise I won't keep you waiting long, dearest Ramón," she teased with a bold look that made him shiver in anticipation.

It was the day before the drive to Abilene, a bright, sunny day which was an augury of good fortune. Lucien Edmond had conferred with Ramón, Djamba, and Simata. Djamba had decided to remain behind to guard the hacienda—and most of all to protect Sybella, to whom he had long ago dedicated himself. Celia would understand, he knew, and since she had only recently recovered from a mild case of river fever, she would be happy to have him at home. He thought to himself how far they had come along the pathway of life, beginning as slaves on Windhaven Plantation. He, a former king of his people whose own brother had betrayed him into slavery, had been purchased by Henry Bouchard. And Celia, Djamba's mulatto wife, had been a slave, bought by Pierre Lourat and again by Henry Bouchard for his own secret lusts, to serve as his concubine. But Henry Bouchard had not been able to claim his coveted purchase of conquered human flesh: his own teenaged son, Mark, had ravished her that first night when she had been brought home stealthily and put in a room where Henry's wife, Sybella, would not find her. Yet it had been Sybella who had finally stood between Henry and the terrified mulatto slave, demanding that he free the girl, holding him at pistol point.

How well Djamba remembered the unexpected tragedy of that dreadful night. Henry Bouchard, stupefied at being gainsaid by his own wife, had suffered a fatal heart attack. Sybella had then freed Celia and later gently urged him, Djamba, to court and marry Celia.

Celia's first daughter, Prissy, had been Mark's child, but her next baby, Lucas, was the result of Djamba's and Celia's union. He loved Celia as a man loved a good, loyal wife and partner, but his love for Sybella Forsden was almost a sacred pledge, one in which there would never be consummation, but only the deepest respect and the most honorable, selfless love.

"I'm sorry to hear about Felicidad's misfortune," Lucien Edmond had said when Djamba explained why she would not take over the cooking duties on the chuck wagon. "And it's very self-sacrificing of Pablo Casares to offer to take her place."

Ramón spoke up. "Pablo Casares is quick, efficient, and he knows what to do. Of course," this with an amused chuckle, "he will have to get used to the vaqueros calling him María."

Lucien Edmond frowned, not quite understanding. "Why María?"

"It's a custom on the range, Lucien Edmond." Ramón had at last lost his earlier awe of Luke Bouchard's son. After Lucien Edmond had several times remonstrated with him for adding a "Señor" to the conversation, he finally dropped it. "Out here, they call the cooks Mary, and of course María is the Spanish for that. But Pablo has a sense of humor, he won't mind. You know, I believe he's really very much in love with Felicidad, but he'd never let anyone know it. I've talked to his *compañeros*, and I know that he had a disappointment when he was a young man. It soured him on women for a good many years, you see. But now that he's found a home here, it's only natural that he's beginning to mellow."

78

"It would be a good thing if we thought about finding a nice girl for Pablo, then," Lucien Edmond concluded.

Ramón changed the subject. "By the way, you were right about there being a good five hundred more cattle this year, Lucien Edmond. The tally comes to about thirty-three hundred. We can easily spare twenty heifers and steers, maybe even a bull if you're so inclined, for Emataba and the Creeks."

"Good, I want very much to do that. Well then, we had about two dozen vaqueros last year on the drive to Abilene. We'd probably best take a few more with these extra cattle."

"Yes. If we take thirty men including Lucas and Simata and myself, that should be sufficient."

"How many will that leave us to defend the house?" Lucien Edmond pursued.

"Andy and Joe will stay on guard, of course, and we'll have Ned, Dave, and Frank."

"And how many others?" asked Lucien Edmond.

"A good dozen vaqueros, Lucien Edmond. And all of them will be armed. You planned well when you bought those extra carbines and the new Starr .44's in San Antonio, as well as more ammunition. I think that should be sufficient to protect those left behind. The Macaras brothers are dead and that ends their threat. Thanks to Sangrodo's friendship with you and your father, most of the Indians in the territory are friendly. Those Kiowa Apaches who attacked us last year were renegades, and they've been driven farther west by now. And we'll leave good old Jubal who will bark and warn people if any intruders come visiting."

"Yes," Lucien Edmond laughed, "and we can count on Henry Belcher to take up arms if there's any evildoing around here. He's as good as any vaquero with that old Whitworth of his. And Maybelle's almost as good herself —remember how she killed Merle Kinnick to protect little Timmy and Connie?" His face sobered for a moment. "I've often thought that we are all like Job, whom God tests by confronting us with adversities to try our love, patience, and tolerance for one another. And when all these troubles are over, we thank God for His trial, and are humbly grateful that we have proved worthy of it."

"Amen to that." Ramón crossed himself and nodded gravely. "I have felt that way, too, many times, Lucien Edmond. Some of the men have said they wished there was a church to which they could go to make their confessions. Each man here is a devout *católico*, you know, Lucien Edmond."

"I do indeed, Ramón. As I myself am, as my father was, and as my great grandfather before him," Lucien replied. "In Alabama, there were no churches of the faith into which old Lucien Bouchard was born except at the Spanish garrison in Mobile. I have often thought it would be wonderful to have a chapel here, a place to which a man may go in solitude to commune with his God and feel closer to Him."

"Si. It would be good to have a priest here who could bless us as we begin this long drive to Abilene and give us strength and courage to face any dangers which we may meet along the trail," Ramón Hernandez mused.

"In the South," Lucien Edmond observed, "most churches are of the Protestant Baptist sect. I suppose it is because most of the people who settled there brought their faith with them, just as my great grandfather Lucien did when he came from Normandy. Yet he was able to keep it in his heart, and I am sure all good men of every religious denomination do the same when they are isolated on the land on which they live. Yet last year, Ramón, when we buried our good *compañeros* after that Indian raid, and when we lost men like Antonio Falzedo in the attack by Carlos Macaras and Pedro Tolivar in the stampede, I wished there had been a priest with us. I felt inadequate to perform what few simple last rites I could for the souls of those brave men. Perhaps, in years to come, as more settlers come to this part of Texas, there may be a church built. Then we will be able to go to make our peace with Him who watches over all of us."

Ramón Hernandez nodded. "I wish that with all my heart, Lucien Edmond. Have you decided who will ride the points and who will be at the back of the herd to round up stragglers?"

"Yes, Ramón. I will promote Manuel Rodriguez to one of the point posts, and Benito Aguilar will ride the other point. And Vittorio Salancár will ride at the back of the

herd, along with Jorge Feliz. We'll spend today and tomorrow making sure that all our cattle are branded and
that the young calves are able to travel. Those still too
young and weak should be left behind."

"I agree. I meant to tell you, Lucien Edmond, that the
boundary markers have been placed. Now you will be
able to ride from one end of your land to the other and always know where yours leaves off."

"That's good. If we ever have neighbors, having boundaries will prevent senseless disputes. This freedom is good
for the men as well as for the cattle, Ramón. I sincerely
hope we'll never have to put up fencing."

Ramón shook his head and frowned. "I too, Lucien
Edmond. A vaquero feels hemmed in when he sees a
fence. His easygoing freedom is disturbed, and then—"
He stopped suddenly and pointed westward. "Isn't that a
rider coming toward us, Lucien Edmond? He's not a vaquero or an Indian, I can make that much out. But he's
on an old piebald mare that has come a long way, unless
I am no longer a judge of horses."

"You are as good a judge of horses as you are of men,
Ramón. Don't belittle yourself," Lucien Edmond reassured
his brother-in-law. "Now let me see whether my eyesight
is as keen as yours. No, he is not a bandit, of that I am
certain, and not a vaquero either. He wears—now I can
just make it out—a brown robe, and he sits astride a very
old, worn saddle."

"The brown robe, Lucien Edmond, I recognize it—it
is worn by the order of the Franciscans." Ramón crossed
himself, his eyes aglow. "We were just now talking of how
wonderful it would be to have a good padre come among
us and bless the work we are about to do. See how God
has answered our prayers!"

"It is another proof that He watches over the good
fortunes of the Bouchards. Let us ride up to this good
man and welcome him to Windhaven Range." Spurring
his spirited gelding, Lucien Edmond Bouchard rode out
with Ramón Hernandez beside him.

CHAPTER NINE

As Lucien Edmond reined in his gelding, he gasped. "Friar Bartoloméo—I never thought to see you again so far from Santa Fe!"

The brown-robed Franciscan was a stout, jovial man in his mid-fifties, his pate bald, save for a whitening circular fringe around the top, his eyes a pale blue yet with a sparkle of humor to them. He blinked several times, passed a thickly calloused, pudgy hand over his shaggy brows and squinted at Lucien Edmond. "Why, I remember you, my son. You had driven your first herd to Santa Fe and the army fort. And you were accompanied by an escort of Comanche. When I saw them, my son, I said to myself that you truly had been inspired by our dear Savior to understand the brotherhood of man. And this fine ranch . . ." He rose in his saddle and looked around, an approving smile on his weatherbeaten face. "Is this where you live and work? Ah, now I remember how you told me that you had come from Alabama after that terrible war which turned brother against brother."

"Yes, Friar Bartoloméo. But you're tired and you've come a long way. Do accept my hospitality and come back to the ranch house. You'll be my guest for as long as you wish to stay."

"That's good of you, my son. Yes, I've come a long way and spent many months in doing so." Then he chuckled and patted the head of his piebald mare. "Poor Caridad will be grateful for a rest, too. She has carried my heavy weight uncomplainingly all the way from Santa Fe."

"We have plenty of horses in our *remuda*," Lucien Edmond replied, "and it would be my greatest pleasure to give you a fresh mount for the rest of your journey—which I hope you will delay for a time. And now I'd like to introduce you to my top wrangler who is also my brother-in-law, Ramón Hernandez."

The young Mexican respectfully inclined his head and murmured, "I ask your blessing, padre."

"You have it, my son. As to the gift of a horse, Señor Bouchard—you see, I remember your name, my son!—you are far too generous. And Caridad will be put out if she is replaced after having been so loyal and faithful to me. But we will talk of that later."

The three men turned their horses back toward the hacienda, and Lucien Edmond vouchsafed, "Ramón was married to my sister by a Franciscan like yourself, Friar Bartoloméo. He had the same first name as you, but he came from the mission of Dolores in San Antonio."

"Why, yes, I know him well. What a coincidence it is, my son, that my namesake should have united this fine vaquero to your sister! For he, like myself, is devoted to spreading the word of our Lord to the Indians—but not in the spirit of the *conquistadores*. We are somewhat more enlightened now, you see." Friar Bartoloméo sighed ruefully. "The difference between us, my son, is that my namesake in San Antonio began his missionary work with the Aiyuta Sioux and then the Ojibway, before he and two of his good brothers founded the mission in San Antonio. Now, he is content to spread the doctrine of good faith and respect for one's fellow man to the children who come to the mission school in San Antonio, whereas I am dedicated resolutely to helping my less fortunate brethren of the Indian tribes. That is why, indeed, I am an outcast in Santa Fe."

"An outcast, Friar Bartoloméo?" Lucien Edmond echoed with surprise. "How can that be? Here, Benito, take the good padre's mare and see that she has food and water, and a comfortable stall."

Lucien Edmond, followed by Ramón at the side of the friar, opened the door of the ranch house and said, "It is my pleasure to welcome you as my honored guest, Friar Bartoloméo. Do enter and make yourself comfortable. I'll bring you some cool water directly."

"You are very kind, my son." The Franciscan uttered a sigh of relief as he lowered himself onto the living room

83

couch. "I must take care not to overindulge myself, Señor Bouchard. It is never good to pamper oneself—then, when there is hard work to be done, the flesh may balk at doing what the spirit directs."

Lucien Edmond permitted himself an amused smile. "After a journey such as yours, Friar Bartoloméo, I do not think the recording angels will register any black marks if you ease yourself for a few moments. Let me bring you the water and have our cook prepare you a tasty luncheon."

"You must not go to any trouble for me, my son."

"It is no trouble at all. We rarely have visitors, and just before you arrived, Ramón and I were talking about the need of our men and our own families to have communication with a priest of our faith. My great-grandfather and my own father were good Catholics of French descent. Ramón and the other vaqueros on this ranch are Mexicans and, therefore, of the Spanish branch of the Church. We live in harmony and we believe in the same just and merciful God."

"And He exists for all men, no matter what the color of their skin or their politics may be."

"We believe that, too. When we came here there were no settlers within many hundreds of miles, only bandits and Indians. Through God's help we stood victoriously against the bandits, and the Indians befriended us because my father saved the life of the son of a chief of the Comanche. My great-grandfather, who came from France to Alabama, was the first to teach us all the lesson of brotherhood. He lived with the Creeks and married the daughter of a chief, and he learned that the God of the Creeks is much like Him whom all of us serve."

"It is such a simple thing that one wonders why mankind has not understood it through the centuries," the friar agreed. As Ramón returned with a crystal glass filled with cool water, his eyes brightened. "I hope that Caridad has been watered and fed by now," he said. "Her need is truly greater than mine. This last day and night of our journey were very trying. All afternoon the sun blazed down upon us, and at night there was a violent storm."

"I have just seen Benito in the kitchen, padre," Ramón

reassured him. "He says that Caridad is already at home in her stall."

"*Gracias*, my son." Friar Bartoloméo lifted the goblet to his lips, and forced himself to drink slowly but with evident relish. "How good it is! It reminds me of the parable at Cana, where our dear Lord changed the water into wine."

"I believe it was for a bridal feast, was it not, Friar Bartoloméo?" Lucien Edmond volunteered.

The Franciscan nodded. "Yes, my son. In the Holy Gospel according to Saint John, we are told that at the marriage in Cana of Galilee, Jesus said unto the servants, *Fill the six waterpots with water, and bear them unto the chief steward of the feast.* And it was this miracle of changing the water into wine which manifested His eternal glory and His disciples believed in Him."

"And then," Lucien Edmond continued, "He went up to Jerusalem and drove the moneylenders out of the temple as well as those who sold oxen and sheep and doves."

"That is true, my son." The friar nodded gravely. "And because of His zeal for the House of God, He was destined to suffer martyrdom to purge our frailties and sins."

At this moment, Celia entered the living room and, seeing the friar, also crossed herself before murmuring, "Lunch is ready, Mr. Bouchard, for you and your guest. Miz Sybella and your wife would like to join you, if it's all right."

"But of course, Celia," Lucien Edmond replied. "We shall all be a family here, and Friar Bartoloméo will bless the food which God has provided." Then, turning to the friar, he said, "It would please me greatly if you would sit at the head of the table and say grace for us."

"Thank you, my son. It will be a great joy for me."

As he entered the dining room with Ramón and Lucien Edmond on either side of him, the Franciscan smiled broadly at the sight of Carla and Hugo standing before their chairs, with Maxine behind them, an arm around the shoulders of each. "How good it is to see the faces of children!" he observed. "And this, my son, is their lovely mother? Truly I see in their faces the love they have for her and you. In all this house I feel it already."

Celia served a simple lunch of stew, biscuits and honey, coffee, and slices of newly baked spice cake. Friar Bartoloméo said grace, and then began to eat with obvious restraint. Only reluctantly did the friar accept a second helping of stew that Lucien Edmond urged on him, while saying, "During this past week, I have lived mainly on herbs and a little water, except some evenings ago when I stopped at the campfire of a group of Kiowa braves who had been hunting. They had not done well, but they were kind enough to share a very small deer with me. How tasty this is; yet I must not be greedy."

After lunch, Lucien Edmond and Ramón went back with Friar Bartoloméo to the living room. Intrigued by the friar's arduous journey, Lucien Edmond asked, "Are you on a mission, to have come so far?"

"My son, in a sense I am. In another, I am an outcast from Santa Fe."

"But how can that be?"

"It is a long story. I would not bore you with it."

"It will not bore me, Father."

"As you wish. You know, of course, that the order to which I belong was founded by Saint Francis of Assisi. He was a wealthy young man, self-indulgent and self-centered, until he learned the will of our dear Lord, whereupon he gave up all his wealth and led a life of poverty and charity. You recall his famous sermon to the birds?"

"I have read of this, yes," Lucien Edmond agreed.

"In one sense I was much like Saint Francis in his youth. And I sinned greatly against God. But He forgave me and gave me a chance at a new life, that I might relate His manifold blessings to those who, perhaps like myself, had sinned and believed themselves incapable of redemption."

"You, a sinner, padre? I find that hard to believe," Ramón Hernandez interposed.

"No, my son, for each of us is a sinner until he is taught the right way. But it is not enough to be taught, as to a schoolboy. One must apply the lesson to one's own soul—as I myself was made to do."

He sat back now, clasping his hands as if in prayer, his eyes closing for a moment as he reflected. "I was the son of a wealthy merchant in Madrid, and I knew that I would inherit wealth and that life would be easy for me. I was not a roisterer in taverns nor a frequenter of loose women, and yet what happened to me was perhaps far more terrible than had I been so profligate. I was in love with an innocent, God-fearing girl. Indeed, our banns had been read in the Holy Church. And then appeared my Satan, who was sent to try my supposedly virtuous nature."

Ramón and Lucien Edmond listened attentively, exchanging a sympathetic glance with each other.

The Franciscan regarded them, then closed his eyes again and resumed his story. "There was a swaggering captain of a ship named the *Santa Cruz*—and what a grim jest the name of his ship was, for he himself was the opposite of that precious, holy symbol. This ship was to sail to Cuba with supplies for the plantation owners, many of whose families had come from Madrid. And during his stay in port, he met the girl to whom I was promised. With his insinuating charm and his stories of his adventures upon the ocean, he so dazzled her that she yielded to his lusts. Oh, what an abomination—for my poor girl, realizing how she had been tricked and debauched, took her own life and thus risked the peril of eternal damnation."

"What a tragedy," Ramón murmured.

"When I heard of what my Conchita had done, I swore an oath of vengeance. I wished to play God's own executioner, and so I had murder in my heart. Following the code between gentlemen, I challenged this debaucher to a duel and killed him. Yes, it was a duel with witnesses, sanctioned by law and with all of the proper rules observed. And yet, when he lay dead at my feet, I knew that I had committed murder and that I was worse than he who had taken only his carnal pleasure of an innocent girl. I, instead, had taken a human life. So, my poor father having died a week before that duel, I gave my legacy to the poor and I took monastic vows. I spent ten years in the poorest provinces of Spain, tending the sick, helping the needy, laboring like a peasant to atone for my sin. And then at last I was sent to *Nuevo* Mexico."

"I would not presume to judge, Friar Bartoloméo," Lucien Edmond spoke up, "but I am certain that in His eyes you have done sufficient penance. My own father was

87

forced into a duel with an evil man who tried to kill him before he could turn to defend himself. I know that he was stricken at the thought of having taken a human life and I know that he prayed for salvation, as I for him."

"It is easy, my son, to justify one's actions by specious words and thoughts. For some of us, it is the scourge and sackcloth and the hair shirt of the Penitentes, just as in the Middle Ages when the terrible Black Death ravaged all of Europe. There were worshipers then who walked through the cities scourging themselves and covering themselves with ashes and confessing their terrible guilt. But what is most to be remembered is that a man's conscience nags at him constantly until he can be at peace with himself, and in one sense that is the voice of God demanding expiation and atonement. Or at least so it was with me."

"But why, then, after all this, do you say that you are an outcast from Santa Fe?" Lucien Edmond asked.

"When I first arrived in Santa Fe I tried to help the Pueblo Indians and to do what I could to ameliorate the greediness and the cruelty of my own people against their Indian brothers. After several years of this, the leading citizens of Santa Fe wrote to the Bishop of Madrid to demand that I be expelled. He, in turn, sent me a chiding letter bidding me look to my flock and not to go outside my station. Well, those poor Indians were my flock just as surely as were the children of the *ricos* who were being brought up to regard the Indians as their deadliest enemies. So I resigned my post and took a vow to dedicate the rest of my life to spreading the gospel of brotherhood among all the Indians of the Great Plains."

"And they, alas, are in danger of extermination, or at best of being driven out of Texas to reservations in the West," Lucien Edmond Bouchard observed.

"Yes, I fear that is true. Yet for the past year and a half I have lived among the Kiowa, the Comanche, even the Apache, as well as the Navaho, and I have shared their dangers and their hardships, and I have gone without food when their braves have found no buffalo on the hunt. I have tended the sick, I have washed their feet and their sores, I have tried to come to bickering man and wife with a message of love and kindness. For these, too, are the children of God as much as you both, my sons. They speak a different tongue but they are all in His image, and they respond as we do to kindness, honor, and courage, as well as to truthfulness. It is such a simple lesson that I wonder it has taken mankind so long to learn it." He made a fatalistic gesture with both hands, uttered a rueful sigh, and leaned back against the couch.

"Did you come by way of Fort Inge, Friar Bartoloméo?" Lucien Edmond asked.

"Why, yes, my son."

"Not quite three years ago my father met the Comanche chief, Sangrodo, whose stronghold was near that fort. The commander of it wished to gain glory by killing peaceful Indians, and he destroyed the stronghold. In turn, he and his men were led into an ambush and paid for their butchery with their own lives. So Sangrodo and his men fled across the border into Mexico. But because of his friendship for my father, he sent word to all the Indian tribes of this great territory to tell them that we were friends. I wonder if you stopped at the fort on your journey here, Friar Bartoloméo?"

"Yes, for an hour or two to fill my water sacks and to beg a little food. The present commander is a man of almost my age, I should say, a gentle man who reads the Bible. We spoke about the Indians, and he bears them no hatred. Yet he told me he had orders to patrol the territory and to drive away hostiles. That is his duty, but I think he is a good man and would not kill peaceful Indians such as this one of whom you have just told me."

"I am glad to hear that, Friar Bartoloméo. In two days we begin a cattle drive to Abilene, to sell our herd at the market where the railroad is. We are going to visit a Creek reservation and the chief, Emataba, is the son of the very man whom my grandfather knew back in Alabama. His people are poor they have little food and clothing, and the Indian agent there does not listen to their pleas."

"I should like to learn more about them, my son. I have never been among the Creeks, but I know of their history and how they ruled the South before the white man came. Perhaps—but no, I should not ask it—"

"Ask whatever you will, Friar Bartoloméo."

"Perhaps you would let me go with you to visit them? Perhaps I might be needed there."

"That would be a wonderful thing." Lucien Edmond's face lit up. "We shall talk of that tomorrow. But now I would like to ask a great favor of you, to marry an orphan girl to the son of my foreman. They are both of your faith."

"If they are truly in love and wish to share their lives, it would not matter, my son."

"And perhaps you would also bless the vaqueros before they leave on this long drive with all of its unknown dangers."

"That will also be a joy."

"I will have Lucas and Felicidad come to see you later. But I know you are tired, and I think that you should take a good siesta."

"You are very good to me, my son. And because you see me as I am, fat and old, I am weak and human enough to confess to you my human failings—it is comfortable here after my long journey, and I feel the love that is in this house everywhere."

Lucien Edmond put out his hand as the friar prepared to rise from the couch. "Stretch out there and enjoy your siesta. Thank you for coming to Windhaven Range, Friar Bartoloméo. God has surely answered our prayers by sending you to find us."

It was one of the most convivial evenings the Bouchards had known since their departure from the beloved château near Lowndesboro. Even Maybelle and Henry Belcher and the two children were in attendance. Friar Bartoloméo Alicante's round, weatherbeaten face was bright with joy as he sat at the head of the table and held forth to an attentive and eager audience. Even the children found his stories of his life among the Indian tribes fascinating. And when the supper dishes had been cleared away, Lucien Edmond led him to the kitchen where Felicidad stood, holding hands, like an infatuated schoolgirl, with Lucas.

Felicidad took the friar's hand and kissed it, stammering, "Padre, the *señor patrón* has said that you are going to marry us. You do not know how grateful I am. I—I would ask that you hear my confession first, to make sure that

I am worthy of my dear Lucas." Shyly, she glanced at Lucas, who put his arm around her waist and self-consciously held her close to him.

"Of course I will, my child. But you cannot have many sins to confess. I can read that in your eyes and in the happiness you already show with this fine young man beside you. May you both be blessed by our dear Lord," the Franciscan friar replied.

Thus it was that on the evening before the arduous drive to Abilene was to begin, Felicidad Ramirez and Lucas Forsden—for white-haired Sybella had graciously urged that Djamba's son assume her married name just as if he had been an adopted son—stood together in the living room of the Bouchard ranch house, hand in hand, to take the vows of holy matrimony. Maybelle Belcher had spent a week sewing a white muslin dress which was to be Felicidad's bridal gown, and, in keeping with the adage of "something borrowed and something blue," had lent her a pair of her own silk slippers and a pretty blue silk scarf to wind around her shapely neck.

When Friar Bartolomeo had pronounced them man and wife, Felicidad turned to Lucas, clinging to him, tendering him her sweet mouth in an ecstasy of loving communion. And this time, Lucas showed no shyness as he proudly and ardently returned his young wife's impassioned embrace.

Since the proposed house for the newlyweds had not yet been built, Andy Haskins came forward self-consciously. "Joe and I figured they ought to have a proper honeymoon. So tonight I'm going to move in with Joe, and Lucas and Felicidad can have my dugout. It's as private as anybody can get, and it's about the only present I can give them. I hope I'm not speaking out of turn."

Felicidad, blushing, hurried to the young Southerner and completely flustered him by kissing him. Laughing through her tears, she declared it the loveliest wedding present any girl could ever have.

Lucien Edmond had Celia and Djamba uncork his oldest bottles of Madeira and serve the wine in goblets to all of the wedding party. Lucas took his goblet and clinked it against Felicidad's, staring deeply into her eyes and murmuring, "I can't believe what a lucky man I am. And you don't know how glad I am we got married just before I had to go away, Felicidad darling."

At last they slipped away, and in the dark gentleness of the night with its quarter moon, made their way to Andy Haskins's dugout. The one-armed Southerner had a comfortable little house, however narrow. It was cool, and there was a sturdy bed with blankets. Lucas blew out the candle and then, trembling to hear Felicidad undress in the darkness, joined her. Shy yet ardent, she clung to him, kissing him, to kindle her own yearning which would overcome her virginal fears. And their mutual cries of rapture at discovering each other's bounty and love were heard by no one save themselves as the night of rapture began its exquisite course . . .

It was dawn, and the sky was a cloudless blue with bold tints of red and purple to banish the somber aura of the night. Very gently disengaging his arm from Felicidad's waist, Lucas eased himself from the narrow bunk that had been their nuptial bed and hastily tugged on his riding breeches and his cambric shirt. He bent to touch her cheeks with reverent fingertips, to brush her drowsy eyelids with his lips and to whisper her name. It meant "felicity," and she was truly named, for the night had brought him ecstasy beyond his dreams. She had clung to him trustingly, answering his passion with her own gentle caresses. And when her own desire had been wakened, she had wordlessly and gloriously urged him to take her with full force, to possess her so that she would know that she was truly his. Now she slept the dreamless, happy sleep of a fulfilled woman, wife, and lover still so young and innocent, yet wise beyond her years with the rapt communication of love fully granted and shared.

Lucas reached up to pull aside the tarpaulin flap that covered the dugout, as he ascended the narrow ladder, squirmed onto the ground, and then pulled the flap back so that no rude light should waken her before her sleep was fully ended.

Beyond the stockade, the vaqueros had brought their geldings, and Ramón, aided by two of his *compañeros*, had haltered all the horses of the *remuda* together to ride them at the rear.

Lucien Edmond Bouchard had already said his good-byes to Maxine. And Mara, holding sleeping little Luke in her arms, stood on the porch of their house to watch her husband fix the end of the halter of the *remuda* horses to the saddle horn of spirited Corita.

The blacks, the vaqueros, Andy Haskins and Joe Duvray, all of whom would remain behind to guard the ranch house and its occupants, had knelt. So, too, had the vaqueros of the drive. Friar Bartoloméo Alicante stood beyond them, making the sign of the cross and speaking first in Latin, then in Spanish, transmiting all their prayers into his own confident voice as he lifted his face to the brightening sky to invoke a blessing. There was a reverent hush, broken only by the snorting and mooing of the steers and heifers gathered just beyond in what seemed an endless, milling procession.

All of the vaqueros, as well as the workers who would remain behind, had previously visited one of the little storage sheds that Friar Bartoloméo had converted into a confessional. He spoke the last words of invocation, raising his face to the sky and holding up his arms as he sought a divine benediction. Then he nodded to Lucien Edmond Bouchard, who gave the signal.

Sanchez Maderos led up a roan gelding with a comfortable new saddle, and indicated to the Franciscan friar that it would be his to ride. At the same time, he murmured, "Your mare, padre, is resting and eating well. Have no fear, they will look after her while you are gone. And the *compañeros* who will stay behind have asked me to tell you that when you do return, they will have built a chapel where, if you stay with us again, you can say Mass and hear our prayers of thanks to God."

"*Gracias,* my son. The Lord will reward you and your *compañeros.* And I, who am only a poor, humble servant of Him who died upon the cross to save us all, thank you with all my heart for such news."

Then, rubbing his sleeve across his suddenly misty eyes, the friar mounted his gelding as Ramón Hernandez, waving to Mara and little Luke, called out, "*Adelante, muchachos!*"

CHAPTER TEN

On the same March morning when the drive to Abilene began from Windhaven Range, Arabella Hunter, Luke Bouchard's step-sister, was discovering that her breakfast had made her queasy. This was all the more surprising because, since her reconciliation with her husband James in June, she had been enjoying spectacularly good health. Even now, at forty-five, her luxuriant black hair showed not a trace of gray, and her buxom figure retained the voluptuous allure of her youth.

Arabella's flirtation with Durwood McCambridge, born out of her boredom with the monotonous life in Galveston, had boomeranged in the most exciting way. When she had discovered that her husband had helped an attractive red-haired widow find a situation as governess, she had angrily accused him of sparking. James Hunter had resorted to a method he had used with great effectiveness earlier in their marriage. He had turned her across his lap and resoundingly spanked her with a hairbrush, after which he had made passionate love to her.

Since then, Arabella had zealously tried to make herself more loving and appreciative than ever, secretly thrilled by his masterful evidence of real affection for her. And James Hunter, realizing that his wife had reached an age when both boredom and insecurity might affect the normal tenor of her ways, had devoted increasingly more time to Arabella. It had been, indeed, a kind of halcyon second honeymoon for them both. As a factor for his cousin's cotton mill, he had in the past six months expanded the sales outlets and been rewarded with a handsome salary increase. And Arabella knew herself to be loved and cherished, an exciting bounty to be granted a married woman with two children at her mature age.

So thorough and complete was her happiness that she could even be tolerant of the increasing beauty of her daughter, Melinda. Her earlier feeling that the slim, vivacious black-haired girl was her rival had been replaced by far more maternal solicitude. She wanted to make sure that Melinda did not become boy-crazy. The attractive girl, nearing her seventeenth birthday, had already drawn the respectful attention of eligible teenaged males among the Hunter acquaintances, and Melinda had quite abandoned her interest in the docile pony that had been one of the happy surprises the children had discovered when they had moved to Galveston. Only Andrew rode the pony, Toby, now, and his interests had begun to sway toward reading and collecting stamps.

Where Arabella once had subconsciously resented the girl's vivid beauty, she basked now in the comforting knowledge that her husband's passion for her had been deliciously revived. And since he was tall and generally solemn of manner, a dignified and quiet man by nature, his renewed conjugal attentiveness was all the more thrilling.

Yes, the children were maturing satisfactorily. The nervous tension of bringing them up was now fortunately a thing of the past, and thus it was that Arabella truly began to regard herself as blessed and fortunate in her thoroughly satisfying marriage.

All in all, she reflected, there were compensations for the insular life to which she had been forced to adapt when they moved to Galveston. James, always thrifty, was now earning a vastly improved salary and this had been translated into many comforts for their pleasant little house. He had even suggested that she hire a woman who would serve in the dual capacity of cook and maid. Jennie Cafferty had proved to be a treasure. Plump, dowdy, but tirelessly good-natured and a hard worker, in her mid-thirties and of Irish descent, she had come to work at the Hunter house after the first of the new year. It had been one of James's Christmas presents to Arabella.

Jennie had been widowed five years before when her army scout husband had been ambushed by a party of Osage braves. She had come to Galveston shortly afterward to live with her married cousin, but when the latter's husband died of pneumonia, the cousin decided to move to California to look up a former beau.

James Hunter had learned of Jennie's sudden economic plight and engaged her at a highly satisfactory wage. Moreover, since the wife of one of his mill hands operated a neat little boardinghouse about a mile away, he had been able to install Jennie there for the sum of twenty dollars a month, allowing her to feel she had her own place to live and was not a slavey in the Hunter house. That, too, had pleased Arabella—now, more than ever, she preferred to have her husband's undivided attention.

This morning, because of her sudden indisposition, Arabella had decided to remove her stays. Perhaps their pressure had caused the disconcerting feeling in the region of her middle. Also, the weather was unseasonably warm and humid. Wearing only her pink silk wrapper, she examined herself in the gilded mirror which hung on one side of her room. Then she caught her breath and her eyes widened as a sudden incredible thought came to her.

But no—it couldn't be; she was certainly past the age for *that*. Then she put a hand to her cheek and gasped aloud. Only last week had been her customary time, and nature's phenomenon had not occurred. They had been so busy going to the theater and then the opera that she hadn't paid any attention. But now there could be no doubt, considering the listless indifference she was feeling.

Openmouthed, she stared at her reflection in the mirror. Then again she put a hand to her cheek and turned a vivid scarlet in confusion. Whatever would the children think—to be a mother at her age, all of forty-five! Why, it was—it was indecent!

Flustered as she was, she did not hear James Hunter knock softly at her door and enter. He was going to take the steamboat after lunch to St. Louis to conclude another business deal for Cousin Jeremy. At the sight of her almost nude with the wrapper slightly open and with her back to him, he looked into her mirror and chuckled. "Even a mirror doesn't do you justice these days, Bella my dear."

"Ohhh! J—James—you—you startled me—oh my goodness—" Hastily she belted the wrapper, nearly scandalized at the thought of showing herself in such deshabille in broad daylight.

"Now then, Bella, there's no need to act like a prude with your own husband. The children are in school by now, and we've a full hour or so before I have to leave for the dock." He teased her as his fingers grasped her round, dimpled shoulders and drew her to him.

"Oh James—you don't know what's happened—oh my gracious, I—I'm almost ashamed to tell you—"

"To tell me what? That you've been a very obedient and loving wife? But I've known that for some time now, and I quite approve of the new Bella. Yes, that hairbrush worked wonders, didn't it?"

"James Hunter!" she gasped aloud, her blushes deepening, and she hid her face against his chest and clung to him.

"Well, it has," he chuckled. "I think some enterprising businessman might make a fortune by making a durable model and peddling it to husbands with skittish wives. As a matter of fact, if I weren't doing so well in Cousin Jeremy's business, I might even take a flyer at it myself."

"Oh, don't talk like that, James, you make me so ashamed—and I've just found out—you won't believe it—I can hardly believe it myself—"

"Now, now, Bella," he soothed, as his hands lowered to stroke her ample hips, "what's this guilty secret of yours? It isn't about a flirtation, I'm pretty sure of that. I've kept my eye on you, young lady, ever since the little episode with that young swindler, Durwood McCambridge. By the way, he left Galveston a few months ago. I've heard that he's onto some new scheme to get hold of good Texas land. Well, they'll catch up with him wherever he goes, just as they did here, mark my words."

"Of course you know I haven't flirted with anybody—except you, James darling," Arabella whispered as she snuggled closer to him. "But—but I'm going to have a child—and at my age, James. Whatever will Melinda and Andrew think?"

"They'll think they'll have a new brother or sister—or, who knows, maybe even both—to reckon with. Do you know, Bella, I find it a rather delightful notion, and it's certainly very flattering to both of us, I must say."

"Oh, J—James!" Her gasp was muffled as she hugged him more tightly, not daring to look up at his smiling face.

"Very flattering indeed, and I think it's most appropriate you've decided to receive me in this, shall we say, pre-maternity dress. Since I've at least an hour before I have to leave, let's put it to excellent use. It may even help ensure the blessed event we may now both contemplate," he murmured as he began to draw her toward her bed.

"James Hunter! Now, here, in broad daylight?" she gasped.

"If you find it irksome to have your husband still in love with you, then I shall apologize and withdraw—"

"Oh James Hunter, you—oh you're just wicked—but oh God, how I love you, darling—here, let me help you with your breeches—you musn't wrinkle your nice new frock coat—you're so handsome, it's no wonder everybody wants to buy Cousin Jeremy's cotton—"

Arabella, half-giggling, half-blushing, began to aid her husband in divesting himself of his clothes, A few moments later, eyes closed, head tilted back, her fingernails convulsively digging into him, she abetted his impetuous desire with tiny little cries and ardent kisses. And when he at last left her bed, she lay drowsily langourous, a dreamy smile curving her full red moist lips.

Durwood McCambridge, the unsuspecting cause of Arabella's passionate reconciliation with her husband, had not prospered during his foray in Galveston. The thirty-two-year-old Easterner had earned his living by his wits since he had been a boy of fourteen, when his parents had gone their separate ways. At the outbreak of the Civil War, he had escaped conscription in the Union forces. A wealthy Albany widow had given him $300 with which he had bought a substitute to go off to war for him, while he remained safely cooped up in her bedchamber.

A year before Appomattox, she had caught him visiting the dingy upstairs room of her Irish maid and in rage had dismissed them both from her service. During the rest of the war, he had teamed up with an unscrupulous munitions maker who sold defective ammunition to the War Office at a staggering profit. When Secretary of War Stanton discovered the fraud and sent an officer to arrest the munitions maker and his glib young salesman, Durwood McCambridge made his way to St. Louis where he briefly worked as a bouncer for the madam of an elegant bordello.

One of the patrons of this bordello was a land speculator who excited the young Easterner with his tales of huge overnight profits to be gained by buying up property on which the original owners had defaulted on taxes. Texas, his new friend pointed out, was virtually an untapped frontier for such enterprise. The population was sparse, and those Confederates who had settled there before the war might very well have received no clear title when they purchased their land, due to the legislative changes and the secession of Texas from the Union. Accordingly, McCambridge and his new associate, Jerome Bentham, set up an office in Galveston, and it was there that McCambridge met Arabella Hunter at the theater.

When Arabella Hunter had discovered that her flirtatiousness was likely to involve her more deeply than she had believed, she had rebuffed him. Undaunted, McCambridge turned his amorous attentions to the bored middle-aged wife of another potential victim of his intended land grabbing. She proved extremely helpful in introducing him to other citizens from whom he ingeniously attempted to extract investment funds for the purpose of acquiring defaulted properties at a pittance. But after he and his partner had collected over $25,000, one of his victims made a trip to the land office in Austin and discovered that the properties McCambridge had so glowingly described as available for a few hundred dollars did not even exist. The upshot was that Jerome Bentham and Durwood McCambridge hastily departed Galveston, each going his separate way.

From Galveston, McCambridge fled to San Antonio where he grew a Van Dyke and had the barber dye his curly hair brown, instead of its natural black. Having divided the $25,000 with Bentham on the eve of their hasty departure from Galveston, he banked his share under the name of Quentin Durwood, thus paraphrasing the title of one of Sir Walter Scott's most successful novels of which he was extremely fond. He rented a little house on the edge of town, bought himself a horse and carriage

99

and a new wardrobe, and waited for opportunity to present itself.

Early in 1869, what appeared to be a truly golden opportunity did present itself. Quentin Durwood—to give him his new name—was seated in a fashionable San Antonio restaurant. Since the restaurant was crowded, he found himself obliged to share his table with a suave, gray-haired man in his late forties who introduced himself as the Baron Rodrigo de Austencio. Despite the baron's Spanish Quentin Durwood was able to recognize a confidence man exceeding only himself in genius. By the time they had finished their dessert and coffee, they were fast friends and avowed future partners.

In reality, the baron was a shrewd land speculator, born Norman Cantrell forty-six years before in Pensacola, Florida. Just before the Civil War, he had tried to perpetrate a land swindle in Massachusetts and had been very nearly ridden out of town on a rail by the irate citizens who had invested in his nefarious scheme. He had spent most of the war years in New Orleans as a professional gambler, and the luck of the wheel and the cards had given him a sufficient stake to embark upon a grandiose project, the scope of which fairly took away Quentin Durwood's breath and won his unstinting admiration.

Once the alleged Baron de Austencio had ascertained that his companion at the table was a swindler like himself, he expansively explained, "Now you see, Quentin— if that's your real name—I can't take entire credit for this little idea of mine. It was really my daddy who gave it to me when he fought under Old Rough and Ready. He went in as a corporal at fifty, when they took Chapultepec, and they made him a sergeant when our boys marched into Mexico City. Then my daddy married a Spanish belle out of Pensacola and got me in the bargain. She used to tell him how the fine old families who came to the New World got land grants from the King of Spain."

The younger man leaned across the table, his eyes bright. "I begin to catch your drift, Baron. You figure if you can move in on the settlers around the border who aren't quite sure they've got clear title to their land, you can show them old documents signed by the King of Spain himself and oust them."

The gray-haired older man chuckled and nodded. "You catch on fast. Matter of fact, I've been looking for a partner, younger than myself, full of piss and vinegar—the sort of man who doesn't let obstacles stand in his way."

"You mean if the settlers don't want to honor your grant, you'll take the land anyway."

"I can see you and I are going to get along just fine. Do you speak Spanish at all?"

"A little," the former Durwood McCambridge admitted. "Just enough to get a meal and maybe to have a señorita share her bed with me."

"That's practical knowledge. But I'll see that you become as fluent as I am. With me, of course, it came easy, seeing that I had a Spanish mother. Now listen, I've been working on this for a couple of years, and I'm just about ready to move."

"Count me in," the Easterner excitedly exclaimed.

"First, you'll have a little homework to do. Aside from brushing up on your Spanish, you're also going to have to do some surveying."

"Surveying?" Quentin Durwood echoed.

The gray-haired man nodded. "I had a stroke of luck just about two years ago. In a saloon in Natchez, I ran into an old toper who had once worked in a library as an historian. He was crazy about old books, and when he couldn't copy them, sometimes he stole them. That's what got him thrown in jail and turned him to the cup that cheers, if you follow my meaning."

Quentin Durwood was breathless with excitement and could only nod. The baron continued. "The best part about old Theobald—that's his name, Theobald Arnison—is that he writes a beautiful hand and he's one of the cleverest forgers it's ever been my pleasure to meet. Now maybe you begin to see where all this is leading."

Quentin Durwood uttered a low whistle, then glanced around nervously to make sure that no one was eavesdropping on their conversation. "You mean he can actually take an old piece of paper and make it look like a genuine Spanish land grant?"

"He's done that already. I've had him practicing, and I dole out his whiskey ration when he shows progress, not before. He has sources for genuine old parchment, the

101

kind they used in Europe hundreds of years ago. If you were to study the originals, you wouldn't be able to spot the difference. When you figure that the people we're going to show these documents to can hardly read to begin with and don't know anything about this history, you can see the unlimited possibilities."

"Indeed! I tell you, Baron, fate sent me here to dine."

"Likewise, I'm sure. These documents from the King of Spain have to describe the property so that there's no doubt in the settler's mind that it's his land we're talking about. That means you've got to go look over some property, and the best place is near the Mexican border. There are plenty of ex-Confederates in Texas already. But there are also a lot of immigrants who couldn't get along on the Eastern Seaboard who are buying Texas land and settling down as far away from big towns as they can."

"Where do you think I should head?"

"A lot of these people came overland from Corpus Christi." The baron smiled patiently, as if he were explaining a lesson to a schoolboy. "They'd head along the Nueces River, but of course they'd want to be close enough to a good-sized town for their supplies. That would mean San Antonio—you can see yourself how many wagons come into the city every day to load up at the general stores. I figure you'd find a few settlers around what they call Ugalde. It makes sense to go after land along the Mexican border. Texas is still new as a readmitted state, and boundaries can easily be up for grabs. That's where these documents will come in mighty handy."

"Yes, I can see that," Quentin Durwood agreed.

"Seems to me there used to be a Comanche stronghold near Ugalde, but by now I'm pretty sure the soldiers have driven them west. The buffalo are disappearing too, and that means that the hostiles shouldn't give you too much trouble along the border. There may be a few renegade bands going over into Mexico and bringing back horses and women as they've always done, but by and large it's safer now than it's ever been."

"I can start tomorrow. But what's in it for me, Baron?"

"I'll cut you in for twenty-five percent of the value of any property we acquire and then sell. That's cash on the barrelhead, Quentin boy." The baron gave his new-found friend an appraising look. "From the way you're dressed, I suspect you've already acquired a little stake of your own. So there's no need to talk about giving you any advance. Tomorrow I'll introduce you to old Theobald and let you see some of the documents. Then you take yourself off to the Ugalde region and look over some likely pieces of land there. Make notes about physical landmarks that'll stand out and that can't be mistaken on a document, like maybe a deep canyon or a crooked little creek—you know what I mean."

"Sure! It sounds practically foolproof."

"The foolproof part of it is the sort of settlers we'll try to move off their land. If they're stupid, it'll be easy. If they're bullheaded, that's where you'll have to use a little physical persuasion. I take it you don't mind using firearms?"

The Easterner shook his head. "There's no law and order in Texas anyway, and a few grubby settlers won't be missed."

"Now that's the way I like to hear a man talk. Just to show you my heart's in the right place, I'll stand treat for supper tonight. Come over and see me about ten tomorrow morning. I'm at the Galvez Hotel, room two-oh-seven." The tall gray-haired man rose and extended his hand. "*Gracias*, Señor Durwood. I have a feeling we are about to make history."

CHAPTER ELEVEN

Even though a year had passed, the scenery along this first stretch from Windhaven Range northward had changed little. There were no habitations or other settlers, only a stretch of level land, marked here and there by mesquite and chaparral. There could be seen, occasionally, towering yucca trees with sword-shaped, evergreen leaves and dazzling clusters of large, white, lily-like flowers on tall stalks. And there were patches of cacti, some brownish, some green, and clumps of trees near the more verdant slopes of little hills that dotted the countryside.

"Look, Lucien Edmond." Ramón Hernandez pointed ahead as Luke's blond son rode back from the head of the herd to ascertain that all his riders were in place and that the cattle were moving readily and docilely. "There are still hoof marks left from our drive last year, a good sign."

"I agree, Ramón. We've more experience in fording rivers and we know what to do if bad weather makes the cattle restless. I mean to follow the same route we took to Abilene last spring. The men seem in good spirits."

"Yes, Lucien Edmond. And it amuses them to have Pablo Casares as their cook. They're calling him the 'old lady' as well as 'Maria,' just as I said they would. And it pleases him. He feels important now, and all the vaqueros are his friends."

"It's as well that he's busy with his new job as cook, so he'll forget Felicidad," Lucien Edmond reflected. "Sometimes loneliness and yearning can overcome a man's deepest sense of honor, or at least torture him into forgetting it for a time. I must try to find someone for him, as soon as the drive is over."

"I would not suggest, Lucien Edmond," Ramón countered, "that we look for pretty señoritas for our amigo Pablo in Abilene. The saloon girls there are ready to fleece a vaquero out of all his *dinero*. And there will be rustlers and bushwhackers as well, now that the market has grown so important."

Lucien Edmond's face was grave as he nodded assent. "We've taken along extra ammunition and most of the carbines. I left a few carbines and some of the best repeating rifles back home to defend against any attack—God grant there won't be any trouble. On a long drive like this, I regret the weeks were away from home, not knowing what's going on, with no way of communicating with them or they with us."

"I have a feeling that the good God is looking over us. Did He not send us the holy man to go with us on the drive and to bless the house and all those who stayed behind?" The young Mexican crossed himself and then waved a greeting to Friar Bartoloméo Alicante, who cheerily waved back from his place at the tail end of the herd, and vigorously nodded that all was well.

"Even the rains didn't wash out the ruts of our wagon wheels." Lucien Edmond glanced at the sunbaked earth as he turned his gelding away from the *remuda*. "From the looks of the sky, we should have a few days ahead of sunny weather. Let's see if we can't make good time, without driving the cattle too hard. There's a small creek up ahead—we'll let the cattle drink and rest a bit, and then push on until sundown."

As the sun began to set Pablo Casares was already busy in the chuck wagon, swearing under his breath at his own clumsiness. He, who had been one of the swiftest riders, whose lasso could unerringly bring down a galloping steer, and whose ability to hog-tie and brand a struggling, bawling calf or heifer had won him the plaudits of his companions, now prayed for a swift inspiration to satisfy the hunger of his friends and of the *patrón* who had placed such confidence in him. *Por Dios*, he told himself as he began to build a fire with dried buffalo chips and stalks, he would show them all, before they got to Abilene, that he was as good a cook as he was a vaquero. Then his face softened with a nostalgic memory of Felicidad. Maybe in Abilene there would be some strong and not-too-old *mujer* who would see that he could make a good husband, even at his age. A man should have a woman who would walk with him in the moonlight and talk of things to come and make plans for the good life ahead. How he envied that strong, young Señor Lucas!

When at last his stew was ready and the odor of beef, onions, and potatoes had drawn the vaqueros into an impatient, noisy line before the chuck wagon, he ladled out an extra-large portion and called, "First, *hombres*, we shall let the padre bless this good food that God has given us so that we shall enjoy it the more." And, staring down their impatient looks, he marched toward the stout friar. "Padre, this is for you. It is the first time I am a cook, and I hope it is good. But if you bless it, it will make it taste better."

"Certainly my son. But you should not have such little confidence in yourself, Pablo Casares. It looks and smells delicious, I tell you this in advance." Then, raising his voice, Friar Bartoloméo Alicante invoked a prayer of thanks for the food, and prayed also for those honest men who would eat of it this night.

Pablo Casares hurried back to the chuck wagon and began to ladle out the stew, his homely face aglow. No longer did he feel the slightest sense of loss at having given up his post as a point rider to take on this task. And when he produced a dessert of biscuits, sugar, and berries, and heard the loud praise of his *compañeros*, he would not have changed places with Lucien Edmond himself.

Lucien Edmond sat down beside one of the little campfires and greeted the Indian scout, Simata, who had already begun to eat the savory supper. "You agree that it was a good idea to start a month earlier than we did last year, Simata?" he asked.

Simata, son of a Kiowa chief and a black woman, whom Luke Bouchard's workers had rescued from a murderous New Orleans group of Creoles, nodded acquiescence. "It took us about three months last year, Mr. Bouchard, and we ran into very bad heat and dust storms. By the time we reach Indian territory, the grass will be green and rich for grazing, and we'll miss the worst of the heat of July or August."

"I want to travel at a leisurely pace so that the cattle will be fattened by the time we get there. I want ours to be one of the first good herds to attract McCoy's buyers." He frowned as a sudden thought came to him. "But we took many more horses along on our *remuda* last year."

"You know we did not need them. You will see, we shall not use more than twenty fresh horses to round up the strays this time."

Lucien Edmond rose and stretched, looking up at the brightly moonlit sky. "There's no haze around the moon, so it'll be dry weather for a spell. And the first river we cross will be the San Antonio, which gave us no trouble at all last year."

"The Red River is the one to be feared. Perhaps this time, I shall go well ahead of you and find an easier place to ford."

Lucien Edmond's face sobered. "I don't want to see any men or horses drowned, not ever again. Manuel Rodriguez still mourns his brother Felipe, and many of our other vaqueros lost good friends last year. Out here, where the country is still so desolate, to lose a good friend stays with a man a very long time."

Simata nodded, and both men rose, silent and thoughtful as they prepared to turn in for the night.

At dawn of the next day, the vaqueros ate a hasty breakfast and rode out to drive the huge herd of lowing cattle north. Lucien Edmond had instructed the point riders to set no faster a pace than last year, when they had averaged five miles a day. He himself had supervised the choice of the lead steers, the most docile ones that would be the most likely to be followed by the rest of the herd.

As always, the vastness and desolate beauty of this country fascinated him. Yet he was thinking already of the years ahead, when there would be other ranches along this same trail with permanent barriers erected around each one, and when there would be conflict over the rights of water and of grazing land.

There was a camaraderie to this work unlike any other Lucien Edmond had known. There was endless monotony, of course, riding back to shout at a stray heifer or young steer, watching vigilantly until it had returned to its place in the long dust-raising processional, scanning the horizon for signs of other riders and anticipating what their presence might mean to the entire herd. The men were tested by the bone-wearying hours in the saddle, and by the sun beating down through the dry, sometimes oppressive air. Sometimes there was an unexpected diversion, such as the sinister sound of a coiled rattlesnake, hidden on a knoll near to which the unwary cattle approached. Then the vaqueros' nerves would be taut with the anxiety that one of the younger calves might come too close and be bitten. You could not risk a pistol shot to kill the rattler—it might cause a dangerous stampede in which far more cattle than one unfortunate calf could be lost. From Simata, Lucien Edmond Bouchard had learned to read the signs along a trail almost as well as the scout himself. The color of the mesquite, the chaparral, or the yucca, might signify drought and the need for reaching a creek or spring before a certain time. The sight of many hoofprints of mustangs might mean that an Indian hunting party was not far away, the time being indicated by the freshness of the droppings from their horses. Lucien Edmond also learned from Simata to identify certain types of poisonous shrubs and foliage, which might attract the cattle and cause agonizing death.

Yet, here on such a trail, despite his status as ranch boss, Lucien Edmond felt a spirit of kinship with his men, a unanimity of purpose and a sharing of friendship. Even the lowliest vaquero, who might go a week without saying more than a few words over the campfire at night, was as concerned with the safety of the herd as Lucien Edmond himself. It was a kind of selfless devotion to an arduous task that challenged a man's stamina and basic integrity. It was a healthful life, a life that reminded him of how the first settlers in this vast country must have lived. For him, it had its particular reward in the knowledge that these cattle would furnish food to thousands of people whom he would never see or know, people like himself with families, hopes, and aspirations. That was why he could understand his father's desire to go back to Windhaven Plantation, however late in life, to know once again the joy of tilling the earth and seeing it bear the fruit of his own labors.

It was Ramón Hernandez's task, each evening, to set up a temporary corral for the fifty horses in the *remuda*. Luis García and Miguel Locado helped him settle the geldings down for the night. In the morning, when the vaqueros selected their mounts for the day, they would hold a long rope several feet off the ground to keep the *remuda* in place until the vaqueros roped and saddled their horses. Back at Windhaven Range, Andy Haskins and Joe Duvray had worked closely with Ramón to select the strongest and most even-tempered geldings. Those horses would have to be able to endure the stress of rounding up strays, teaming up with their riders in the arduous task of roping young calves for branding. The horses selected for this drive had proved their mettle. They did not shy away from a bellowing steer or the sound of a pistol or rifle shot. As Ramón had told Lucien Edmond, all of them could stop short, practically sitting down at the moment when the lariat jerked tight around the running steer or calf and was then instantly snubbed tightly around the saddle horn. Yet, despite the customary practice of riding geldings on cattle drives, Ramón persisted in using his faithful little mare, Corita, whose valor and steadiness had long since been proved.

On the second evening out, Pablo Casares was still learning about his new chores as cook. The chuck wagon was a masterpiece of versatility and practicality, a veritable commissary on wheels. At its rear was a box for storing tin dishes, a Dutch oven, frying pan, kettle, and coffee pot. There were places for such standard staples as green-berry coffee, salt pork, cornmeal, flour, and beans. A folding leg had been attached to the chuck box lid so that it formed a table, when lowered, on which were prepared the breakfast, midday, and evening meals. Fixed securely in the front was a water barrel, with a convenient spigot running through the side of the wagon. And beneath the bed of the wagon was a cowhide sling for transporting dry wood, kindling, or buffalo chips so that a fire might be started swiftly and not delay the vaqueros in satisfying their hunger after their arduous work on the trail. In a box below the driver's seat, Pablo Casares had brought along axes, hammers, and spades, these last utensils a grim reminder that even on such a peaceful drive as this, fate might decree the need for digging graves for his fallen *compañeros*.

As he tidied up the chuck wagon, the middle-aged vaquero began to whistle "La Rasa," a popular Mexican tune. It was not so bad as he had feared, this cooking business for all his *compañeros*. And he had understood, even from their goodnatured taunts, that they approved of his efforts. It was enough to make a man feel wanted, to feel that he belonged.

Satisfied that everything was in readiness for the next morning, Pablo curled up in his bedroll outside the chuck wagon, and the gentle lowing of the resting cattle soon lulled him into a deep, satisfying sleep. One by one, the little campfires went out, the hum of voices died away, and there was only the soft silence of the calm Texas night.

Pablo was the first to rise at dawn. He shook the dew from the canvas which covered his kitchen-on-wheels, then built a fire with buffalo chips. When it was started and the smell of strong coffee rose from the pot, he hurried with his sourdough biscuits, and the beans and salt pork. Then, taking an iron skillet and hammer, he began to beat on it, bawling out, "*¡Vamanos, muchachos! ¡Pronto, para desayuno!*"

Lucien Edmond sat up and grinned at Simata. "There is a man who likes his new work," he chuckled. The Indian scout agreed, smiling, as they answered the new cook's imperious summons to breakfast.

Along the way, they bade good morning to the Franciscan friar, who was neatly rolling up the bedroll one of the vaqueros had given him. Seeing them, Friar Bartoloméo enthusiastically shouted, "Good morning, my sons! I've never slept so well, nor, alas," here he patted his stomach, "eaten so well. And the best of it is to be with so many warmhearted companions."

"Good morning to you, Friar Bartoloméo," Lucien Edmond returned the greeting. "I hope we have not set too hard a pace for you in our first days."

"No, not at all, my son. It's true that my old bones felt a bit sore when I rose from this comfortable blanket, but that's because I'm growing old. Besides, the smell of the coffee has already made me forget what few infirmities I may have. And you, Ramón." He turned to the young vaquero. "I cannot begin to thank you enough for the horse you picked to carry my ponderous weight. He is a fine, gentle animal and already we are friends. He will make my journey much easier, more even than my faithful old Caridad."

"If you return to us, padre, I promise you that Caridad will be fat and strong again. The vaqueros promised me they would give her better care than any of the other horses back at the ranch."

"That was kind of them, and I am glad, for Caridad's sake. But seriously, my son, already I can appreciate the kindness, thoughtfulness, and loyalty of all these men who have come along with this fine herd of cattle. Late last night, some of them asked me if I would not hear their confessions, and it touched me deeply to listen to what they considered their sins. I do not break the confidence of the confessional when I tell you that our dear Lord must have smiled, as I did, to listen to what they regarded as sins. Of these, perhaps only pride—which we are told is one of the seven deadly sins—is noticeable. Yet I, myself do not consider pride a sin if it is a quiet, assured knowledge that one has in the dignity of one's labors. I think, too, in view of my own lengthy travels, that when one lives under God's blue sky and is beset at all times by the elements of His blessed creation, he becomes a better man and is closer to Him who made us all."

"I, too, believe that, padre," Ramón Hernandez said quietly.

"Tomorrow is Sunday, Father," Lucien Edmond said. "We would all be grateful if you would say Mass for us."

Friar Bartoloméo Alicante's plump face glowed with pleasure. "I was just about to ask you if I might have that privilege. I still remember with deep gratitude what you men said to me back at the ranch, that they would build a chapel. I promise I will return there after I have visited the Creeks of whom you have told me, to say Mass and to ask God's blessing upon all of you. Yet these plains and these hills, these thickets of mesquite and the trees, and all that we see beyond, are part of His eternal chapel.

111

It is good to commune with Him in the midst of His handiwork."

"I will tell the men and we shall hear your Mass before we resume the drive tomorrow morning," Lucien Edmond promised. "Come along to breakfast now, Father."

"Gladly, my son. I fear that one of my own venal sins is my enjoyment of food, to which indulgence my corpulence is sad evidence!"

As they neared the line forming at the back of the chuck wagon, several of the vaqueros greeted the friar, and one said, "Padre, come up here and eat first, before we do. It's only right."

"Oh no, my son, but thank you for your thoughtfulness. Each of us will take his rightful turn. Today, I am simply a *compañero*, who asks no favors and who is ready to do his full share."

The next morning, at dawn, all the vaqueros rose and made themselves as tidy as they could, then knelt down in a circle in whose center the Franciscan friar stood to intone the mystic words of the Holy Mass.

On the afternoon of the seventh day out, Ramón Hernandez and his two companions rode at a leisurely pace around the unhobbled horses of the *remuda*, keeping them well to one side of the herd. Thus far, the weather had been ideal, with neither rain nor dust storms to harass the riders. Even the warm sun had not been too onerous. They had come thirty-eight miles already, and Lucien Edmond had only that morning remarked to Ramón how the Franciscan friar's presence among them appeared to be a good augury.

As trail boss, Lucien Edmond rode at the head of the herd, and turned in his saddle to wave to his point riders. It was about an hour before twilight, time to begin to slacken the pace. Simata had gone ahead to find a good camp site for the night, and Pablo Casares was beaming with satisfaction because one of the vaqueros had come upon a clump of wild onions and filled his sombrero with them. Beef and onions and thick gravy would be a hearty meal for men who had ridden all day.

As Lucien Edmond turned back, he saw, far to the northwest, two riders on black stallions. They were nearly a mile away; yet, even at that distance, it was obvious that they were riding south as if the devil were behind them. Lucien Edmond turned his gelding away from the head of the line and rode back toward Ramón Hernandez to point them out to the young Mexican. "Those horses won't last at that pace, Ramón. I wonder who they are and where they're going."

"Perhaps they're horse thieves. Simata's told me that many miles north of us, there are outlaws who steal horses as well as cattle, and they're even bold enough to try to steal from the Indians."

"Perhaps. Maybe they're heading for the Mexican border," Lucien Edmond agreed. "At any rate, they're certainly giving us a wide berth. If it were a band of men, I'd feel uneasy about the hacienda."

"It's well-guarded; don't worry, Lucien Edmond. But you're right about the way they're driving their horses. They won't last at that rate. They'll have to find other horses before much longer. Well, it's beginning to get dark now. *Con permiso*, I'll take the horses ahead and make a corral for them for the night."

CHAPTER TWELVE

The two men who rode south on black stallions had, until last month, been part of an inseparable quartet. They had been scouts, buffalo hunters, and skinners, employed by the army at Fort Griffin, which was set on a hill, overlooking the Clear Fork of the Brazos River. The fort had been near the village of the friendly Tonkawas, and it offered protection to early cattle drivers who sought protection from the marauding bands of roving Comanches and Kiowa Apaches.

All four men had come from Kansas and the two now dead had joined "God's Angry Man," John Brown, in his vigilante raids upon suspected pro-slavery families in that bloody time which had preceded the Civil War. All four had grown up on neighboring farms in western Kansas, and each had killed a man before he was sixteen. Joe Whitby and Rudy Morse had ridden with the notorious scourge of Kansas, William Clarke Quantrill, a former Kansas schoolteacher who had fled to Missouri to escape arrest for robbery, formed a guerrilla band, and returned to wreak death and rapine on the land that had given him birth. They had left Quantrill's ranks shortly after his raid on Lawrence, in which one hundred and fifty citizens had been killed, and the town burned and sacked, before Union cavalry could be summoned. The life of gambling, liquor, and women of easy virtue, plunder and the excitement of the kill, had appealed to them. But, after the Lawrence raid, Joe Whitby and Rudy Morse were sensible enough to realize Quantrill's days were numbered and they would be hanged without trial if they were ever caught.

So they had slipped away one night, shaved their beards and changed their names, and rejoined their boyhood companions, Jake Ellison and Marve Fenstrom, who had already come to Fort Griffin and been engaged as scouts. Unlike their friends, Whitby and Morse spoke no Indian dialect, but they were skilful hunters and the army needed meat. There were still vast herds of buffalo roaming the countryside near the fort, but Ellison and Fenstrom knew that certain terrains were dangerous because of the presence of hostile Kiowa Apaches and Comanches.

After the Civil War, all four of them stayed on at Fort Griffin. It was an easy life, and killing buffalo satisfied their bloodlust. All were outcasts from their families and had no ties. Besides, there were still wanted posters in several Kansas marshals' offices for Whitby and Morse, and older ones, now faded and almost illegible, for Ellison and Fenstrom, for murders committed over gambling or women during their adolescence.

As scouts and buffalo hunters, they were grudgingly respected by the soldiers, and when they needed women, they found the widowed squaws of the Tonkawa more than willing.

But the monotony of army life had begun to make all four men restless. They had heard that the Kansas Pacific Railroad had employed men like William F. Cody, the legendary "Buffalo Bill," to supply meat for the railroad laborers at the unheard-of salary of $500 a month.

Just a month before, in the new year of 1869, the four former Kansans had wandered into the little town of Griffin, which was almost entirely supported by buffalo hunters. They saw a plot of ground about four acres in size, covered with buffalo hides spread out to dry, as well as a large quantity piled up for shipment. Those hides were worth from $1 to $1.60 a piece. It was time, all four of them agreed, to strike out as a team and perhaps contract with some railroad company. Besides, there was talk of building the Santa Fe as far west as Dodge City, named after Fort Dodge, and there would soon be other railroads moving westward. That would mean the eventual obliteration of the buffalo herds which supported the Indians. It would pave the way for the invasion of cattlemen and thus develop more cities and towns to hold the broad expanses of territory safe from attack by hostiles.

Never before had the quartet from Kansas done such

far-sighted thinking about their future. Unfortunately, their lengthy discussion at the saloon was liberally dosed with several bottles of cheap whiskey. Shortly before midnight of that rainy February evening, the saloon keeper's pretty seventeen-year-old niece, knowing that business would be slack, came into the bar from her room at the back of the wooden frame building. After a steady diet of Tonkawa squaws, Beth Delson looked like a voluptuous houri out of a sultan's seraglio. Joe Whitby and Rudy Morse, drunker than their two companions, eyed her lustfully and muttered appreciative and clinical comments on her charms. When she departed, they noticed that she left the door partly open between the back of the saloon and the rooms beyond.

A few minutes later, when Marve Fenstrom and Jake Ellison ordered another bottle of whiskey, Joe and Rudy stealthily went down the narrow hallway as the saloonkeeper stood with his back to them, chatting with Jake and Marve. Rudy tried the knob of the farthest door to the left and found it open. Beth Delson wore only her cotton chemise. She was ready to climb into bed. Seeing the two men, she backed against the wall, pressing a hand against her mouth to stifle her scream of consternation.

They fell upon her and savagely violated her, clamping their calloused palms over her mouth to silence her cries. But her uncle, observing that the hallway door had been left open, came down the corridor about twenty minutes later. When he knocked at the door to his niece's room and heard a guttural oath, he flung it open and drew his sixshooter. Rudy Morse, who was watching his friend ravish the weeping girl for a second time, drew his pistol and fired first, killing the saloon-keeper instantly.

"Come on, you goddamn fool, let's get out of here," he panted to his rutting companion. "There'll be soldiers in here when they find out what's happened. Kill the little bitch—that way, she won't be able to point us out. Or do you want me to do it?"

Joe Whitby, lax with sated passion and his mind dulled by the whiskey he had imbibed, uncomprehendingly gazed up at his lanky friend. With a snarl of disgust, Rudy Morse reversed his pistol and, gripping it by the barrel, strode over to the bed and brutally brought the butt down crushing Beth's skull. "There, you stupid bastard," he panted, "now let's fan leather some and get the hell out of this mangy buffalo town. Marve 'n Jake'll be glad to shake its dust, too, I'm thinkin'. Get your breeches on. The little bitch is dead."

Closing the door, they stumbled back to the table where their two companions sat, and Rudy Morse leaned forward toward Jake and Marve and muttered, "We've all got to blow out of here fast. Had a little ruckus in the back room there."

Jake Ellison, thirty-eight, of medium height and wiry, with a straggly yellow beard and thick sideburns, scowled angrily. "What the hell do you mean, blow out of here fast? What have you got yourself into now? You're both drunker 'n a platoon on payday."

"Wasn't our fault," Joe Whitby began to whine, glancing nervously around the almost deserted saloon. "Little bitch put up a fight over her first pokin', and then the fellow behind the bar came into the room with his shooting iron, so we hadda kill 'em both."

"You stupid jackass!" Marve Fenstrom snarled. He was tall and heavyset, a year older than Jake, with a thick black beard and mustache. His slate-blue eyes narrowed as he leaned forward toward Joe Whitby. "We wuz talkin' about sashaying down to the railroad camp to hire ourselves out, but we weren't in no hurry. Now you've really gone and got us into a pack of trouble. Me 'n Jake could hear that shot, plain as day. Didn't seem to bother the galoots still swilling down this rotgut, though. They hardly perked up an ear. Well, what's done's done, I s'pose. Now you listen to some sense. Me 'n Jake'll go back into the fort and pick up the money we got stashed away, and we'll get your stuff, too. Next thing, we better git ourselves some good, fast horses. When Colonel Hartford finds out that purty little gal and the saloonkeeper got killed, he might just start putting two and two together."

"I told you, we couldn't help it," Joe Whitby protested as he reached for a half-empty bottle of whiskey.

Marve Fenstrom knocked it out of his hand to the floor with an angry oath. "You've had all you're going to get for a damn long time, Joe. Now let's get out of here. We'll leave one by one, so the galoots in here won't get

117

the wind up. You 'n Rudy go see if you can steal us four good horses, and meet us out beyond the flat."

Joe Whitby nodded, licked his lips, then shivered. He was rapidly sobering up. "Sure," he stammered, "I know jist where to find 'em too. Old Mr. McCready, you know, he's looking after Ben Sanderson's stable while Ben's away in Saint Louis visitin' his kinfolks, 'n he's poundin' his ear by now. Last time I looked in there, he had four jim-dandy black stallions."

"Well, you 'n Rudy go get them out then, and meet us in about an hour," Marve Fenstrom directed curtly. Glancing at Jake Ellison, he shrugged and muttered, "You know, we might just head for Mexico. Plenty of gals and tequila down there, and now they've got old Benito running the country, there ought to be easy pickin's in the little towns just over the border."

"I get your drift, Marve. I'd just as soon see Mexico as anything else around here," Ellison drawled.

An hour later, the four men met at the flat beyond the Brazos, Jake and Marve having collected their belongings and the money they had carefully concealed in their bedrolls. Marve Fenstrom had brought along his Sharps buffalo gun and tripod, as well as a bag of bulks and shells for making his own cartridges. Jake Ellison, who performed the work of skinner, had packed his knives and scrapers.

"Well, at least you got us good horses, I'll say that for you," Ellison exclaimed when he saw the four saddled black stallions. "We left our own mounts back at the fort. They're army property anyhow, so why add stealing from the army to the rest of the damages you jokers already got rung up against us. You know damn well we're all in this now. If Sheriff Colby takes it into his head to get up a posse, he'll bring back all four of us, and Jake 'n me won't have a chance to escape the rope. Damn, if you hadn't been so all-fired randy, we wouldn't have to change our plans this way."

"No use crying over spilled milk," Morse gruffly put in with a cynical shrug. "Anyhow, that bastard of a saloon-keeper deserved killing. Served the worst whiskey I ever poured down my throat and he charged for the slop like it was mountain dew."

"All right, all right, just mount up and let's head south," Marve Fenstrom snapped.

They had spent two days circling back on their trail so as to confuse any possible pursuers, and then headed toward the Colorado River Once across it, Jake and Marve reasoned that they would be fairly secure from any pursuers. By the evening of their fifth day out, they had reached the dusty high plain near Mineral Springs, where the land was barren and decorated only with clumps of mesquite, chaparral and wind-blown tumbleweeds. Here the soil was reddish-brown, with sparse, dry grass. They made camp for the night at the side of a little hill which served as a lookout post. Jake and Marve had taken turns watching for several hours while Joe and Rudy prepared their evening meal, but there was no sign of any posse.

But in the morning, when the hot sun began to beat down upon the sandy soil, Fenstrom swore under his breath. "We ought to have looked closer before we made camp. Look at the top of that hill. Injun burial mounds, no less. Good thing there weren't any redskins out last night, or we'd have been minus our scalps this morning, sure as you're born."

"Look," Whitby suddenly exclaimed, pointing toward the east. "Jeez, I never yet saw one of those. It's a white buffalo, so help me!"

A solitary white buffalo grazed about three hundred yards east of the Indian burial mounds. Jake and Marve stared, openmouthed, but Joe Whitby had already cocked his rifle, knelt down, and taken aim before either of them could stop him.

"What the hell do you think you're doing—it's bad luck!" Ellison cried out just as Whitby squeezed the trigger. The white buffalo's massive head lifted, then the great body quivered and slumped down to one side. Again it lifted its head, then lowered it and lay still.

"Against the wind, too," Whitby exulted.

Fenstrom strode toward him and backhanded him across the jaw, the rifle toppling from his hands as he fell heavily. "It isn't bad enough that we didn't see what we were camping near, you had to go and kill that white buffalo. I just pray to God Almighty there aren't any Injuns around until long after we've headed south. Let's get the hell out of here!"

Joe Whitby's whining tone was conciliatory. "I just thought we might get ourselves some meat before we crossed the Colorado."

Again Marve Fenstrom swore angrily. "Your cock got us all into a mess of trouble, and now your belly's gonna add to it. I'm sick of the sight of you!"

As Jake and Marve swiftly saddled their horses and mounted, Rudy Morse uttered a cry of terror. "Comin' there from the northwest! Looks like a dozen or more redskins—"

"Kiowa Apaches," Marve Fenstrom snarled. "When Joe pulled that trigger, he might as well have sent up a smoke signal. Come on, Jake, hit the leather and let's get out of here fast!"

Ellison glanced back over his shoulder and dug his spurs into the stallion's belly as he saw at least twenty braves, bending forward over the necks of their mustangs and urging them on, coming diagonally toward them to cut down the distance. Morse, his face ashen with fear, was buckling the cinch of his saddle straps, hurriedly mounting and swearing at his stallion as he smacked its hindquarters with the flat of his hand to urge it on. Whitby, petrified, hesitated a moment, seized his rifle and, not bothering to saddle up, mounted bareback and rode after his companions.

The angry war whoops of the braves, as they swiftly closed the distance, came to the ears of the fleeing men. Leading them was a stocky, middle-aged brave with war bonnet and paint tattoos of his clan on his chest, brandishing a feathered lance. Two of the braves just behind him raised their rifles and fired, and Rudy Morse leaned back in his saddle, dropped the reins, coughed blood from his lungs and toppled to the ground, as his black stallion, neighing wildly, raced on without its rider.

Marve and Jake, glancing back, spurred their stallions on to their fastest gallop. "Let's split up," Marve bawled to Jake. "You head southeast and I'll head southwest. Maybe we can shake them. Thank God we picked the fastest of these four horses!"

Joe Whitby had reloaded his rifle as he rode, panting

and cursing in his flight. Turning, he leveled the rifle quickly and took a shot. The young brave who had shot Rudy Morse pitched forward over the head of his mustang, then slowly toppled to the ground. A cry of rage rose from the chief, who gestured to his men to overtake the white-eyes.

Joe Whitby heard the whine of a bullet past his ear, and, crouching low, frantically reloaded his rifle. Suddenly his stallion stumbled into a gopher hole and threw him headlong to the ground where he lay, stunned and bruised. Jake and Marve had ridden off, pushing their horses to the utmost, and were now disappearing in the distance as the band of Kiowa Apaches circled round the dazed, bleeding buffalo hunter.

The chief dismounted, ran toward Joe Whitby and kicked away the latter's rifle as he tried wildly to retrieve it. Then he prodded the sharp tip of his lance against Joe Whitby's heaving chest.

"Oh Gawd, don't, don't please!" Joe Whitby's final whine was silenced as the chief thrust down the spear with all his might.

The Kiowa Apache leader turned to his men. "Tanipa has avenged the dishonor brought to our dead by these accursed white-eyes." He gestured with the bloodied spear toward the distant burial mounds. "Last year, when the cattle of the white-eyes came through our country, we attacked, and many of our bravest young warriors fell to their guns. So long as we live, we shall defend our sleeping comrades."

"They have killed the sacred white buffalo, O Tanipa," one of his braves angrily declared as he brandished an old musket. "There are two of them left. We shall catch them and put them to the torture stake."

"No. See, they have disappeared already. Their black horses are faster than our mustangs. It was the will of the Great Spirit to give us these two profaners of our sacred mounds as fitting sacrifice. That is what He has willed, and we shall not question it. Let us skin the sacred white buffalo and take the meat to our shaman. He will tell us what we are to do with it. But first, let us bury our warriors that the white-eyes killed."

They mounted and rode back toward the burial mounds with the body of their fallen brother.

On the fifteenth of March, Lucien Edmond Bouchard and his men were continuing the northward drive of Windhaven Range cattle toward their destined market. Though the weather was warm, the sky was gloomily overcast with hardly a hint of sun to brighten it.

Far to the south, at Windhaven Range, the vaqueros who had remained behind to guard the hacienda were in high spirits as they worked, along with Djamba and the other men, cutting down trees, trimming and pegging the logs to build the chapel. It was being set up to the southeast of the bunkhouse, framed by two large oak trees that would stand as sentinels to this crude but meaningful place of worship. Jubal, joyously barking, wagging his tail as one or another of the Mexican riders stopped to pat him, had appointed himself a kind of unofficial supervisor.

Inside the house, Sybella Forsden was chatting with Maxine Bouchard, while Celia and Felicidad, who was rapidly recovering from the snake bite, washed the breakfast dishes. The children, Carla and Hugo, who had already finished their breakfast, had gone out to watch the building of the chapel, and Maxine held little Edwina in her arms. Djamba had milked one of the cows at dawn, and strained some of the fresh milk into a baby's bottle, which Maxine tendered to the gurgling and cooing baby. Mara Hernandez had joined them for breakfast, while Maybelle Belcher was busy tidying up her own breakfast dishes in the little frame house near the creek. Henry Belcher, comfortably replete with griddle cakes, bacon, and two cups of strong coffee, was telling Tim and Connie that first they could help him plant some seeds in their mother's garden at the back of the house, and then go play with Carla and Hugo at the *hacienda*. . . .

Jake Ellison and Marve Fenstrom had separated temporarily, to elude the Indian pursuers, crossing the Colorado River at different points. Each man paused to rest his horse, then rode slowly toward an irregularly shaped hill just south of the river, so they might reunite. When Fenstrom saw the distant figure of his companion approaching, he lifted his buffalo gun high in the air and waved it, then chuckled with satisfaction as he saw Jake doff his sombrero and flourish it above his head. Spurring his horse, he rode on quickly toward the hill, where he was soon joined by his partner.

"That was too close for comfort, Jake," he wryly observed. "I guess they got both Joe and Rudy. Well, no sense stopping for funeral services, I'm thinking. Let's keep heading south."

"I'm all for that. But these horses are just about worn out. We'd better be thinking about finding some fresh mounts before we cross into Mexico."

"There's bound to be cattlemen driving their herds up Abilene way this time of year. That means there won't be many cowboys back at the ranches. If we locate one before we hit the border, there's got to be fresh horses."

"And women," Jake sniggered with a bawdy wink.

"I'm ready when you are, Marve. Shouldn't be any trouble, not with that Sharps you got. Put my buffalo knife up against the gizzard of some purty gal, it'll make her ready as a bitch in heat to accommodate a fella, I'm thinkin'."

Marve Fenstrom chuckled and nodded, then jerked on the reins of his weary stallion. "Look, Jake, over to the south of us. There's a big roundup heading north. Come on, let's get these horses moving. I want to see where that herd's tracks lead." And with an impatient oath, he dug his heels into the stallion's belly, forcing the poor animal to gallop on in the direction from which Lucien Edmond Bouchard, his vaqueros and his herd had come.

CHAPTER THIRTEEN

Not long after Jake Ellison and Marve Fenstrom had galloped past the cattle of Windhaven Range, the buffalo hunter's black stallion foundered, sinking to its knees and nearly pitching its rider over its head. As Fenstrom, swearing volubly, leaped clear of his fallen horse, it rolled over onto one side, uttered a pathetic snort, then died.

"Goddamn the luck," Fenstrom snarled. "All I was asking of this stupid critter was another forty miles. Hey, wait a bit." His face brightened. "What's that saying they have about an ill wind? If you and I were to ride into that ranch those fellows left behind them on just one horse, and tell them how we was out here on the desert dying of hunger and thirst, they'd for sure let us in."

"Not a bad idea, Marve," Jake Ellison agreed. "But I don't know if my horse can take the two of us, not for long, anyhow. I'd better let him rest a spell. Let's camp for the night."

"Smart thinking," Marve Fenstrom agreed.

Jake Ellison dismounted and unpacked his bedroll, as Fenstrom retrieved his belongings from the body of his fallen mount. After watering Ellison's horse, the two men ate a meager meal of jerky and hardtack—the only food supplies they had left—and then stretched out and wrapped themselves in blankets in an effort to protect themselves from the sudden chill of the night air.

The next morning, Marve and Jake both mounted the remaining horse, and rode slowly toward the southeast, coming upon the unmistakable tracks of the Bouchard herd. They stopped several times to rest the stallion and made an early twilight camp. The next day saw them advance only another fifteen miles, with frequent stops for the now faltering stallion. Having used up all their food and water the night before, they were relieved to come upon a shallow creek where they were able to fill their canteens, but only a handful of berries served as their evening meal.

And so, early in the morning of the tenth day of the Bouchard cattle drive, they came upon the valley and the expanse of verdant grazing land that marked Windhaven Range, and saw the hacienda in the distance.

"Here's where it is!" Marve Fenstrom exulted. "Now let's make this look right. Get down off your horse and lead it. Hell, it's only a couple of miles away. And if there's womenfolks as I 'spect there has to be, they'll sure take pity on a couple of poor buffalo hunters."

"I'm way ahead of you, Marve," Jake sniggered as he patted his buffalo knife, sheathed in a leather scabbard and fixed to his broad, black belt.

Marve Fenstrom gave him a crooked grin as he patted the long, heavy barrel of the buffalo gun.

"Maybe they'll have some cash stashed away there, too, Marve," Jake Ellison suggested greedily as he dismounted, and, grasping the reins of his weary stallion, began to walk toward the distant hacienda.

"I sure hope it's not that useless Johnny Reb money. You know lots of seceshers moved out around here when the war started. Well . . . whatever we find's gravy. Hell, I got a little over eight hundred bucks saved up from my army pay. How about you, Jake?"

"Nigh as much, Marve."

"All this time on the trail, I've been thinking about Joe and Rudy's humpin' that cute little saloon girl. A bit young for my taste, but that's the kind that bites and claws and scratches, and gives a man a real tussle. Now, it might just be our luck to find some sweet young stuff at that ranch. And I promise you we ain't gonna pay out no gold for our fun."

"Not hardly," Jake Ellison guffawed.

As they came closer to the ranch house, Marve Fenstrom scowled. "They've got a big stockade around the whole damn place," he complained to his partner. "Means we'll have to go to the gate and try to get somebody to let us in from the house. Can you see any cowboys around there?"

"Nary a one. Maybe they're out on the range. Or else . . . Hey wait, now I can make it out, they're building something out beyond that bunkhouse—see?"

"Yeah, I sure do," Fenstrom breathed, licking his lips with anticipation. "Now you and me, we won't make any fuss, we'll just go up to that gate and see if we can rouse somebody inside the house. Once we're inside, nobody's gonna come in unless he wants his head blasted off."

"That's the way to talk, Marve! But don't forget, we gotta get us some fresh horses."

"There's a corral there, stupid, can't you see it? Plenty of good horseflesh there for the picking. And listen, keep your eyes peeled—first thing you get inside, see if they've got any rifles or six-shooters. Grab onto them fast, understand?"

"Hell, Marve, you'd think I was a kid out of school," Ellison complained.

They had reached the gate of the stockade in front of the ranch house, and, after a quick whispered conference, Ellison clenched his fist and hammered at the gate, calling out, "Anybody t' home? We need help bad, you in there!"

Maxine Bouchard, who had been cradling little Edwina in her arms, rose from the living room couch. "Did you hear that, grandmother?" she asked Sybella.

"Yes, I did, Maxine dear. You stay here, I'll go see what it's about."

"Be careful. Maybe it's bandits again," Maxine ventured.

"I don't think so, dear. Besides, if there were a lot of riders, the vaqueros would have seen them.

"All right, but please be careful."

Sybella nodded, opened the ranch house door, and went out toward the gate. When she reached it, she called out, "Who is it?"

"Sorry to bother you, ma'am." Jake Ellison adopted his most apologetic tone as he winked at his companion. "My partner 'n me, we've had a bad time of it. Came all the way from Fort Griffin, chased by a band of murdering redskins. They shot my partner's horse out from under him. We've made it all this way with just the one, and he's about dead by now. Could we have something to eat, and maybe some water?"

126

"Of course. Wait, I'll let you in," Sybella called out.

As she opened the gate, Marve Fenstrom shouldered her aside, lifting his heavy buffalo gun and growling, "Now don't you let out a peep, ma'am, I wouldn't want to hurt you none. Let's go inside the house and talk a spell. Come on, Jake, never mind the horse. He's starting to heave, he won't last 'til sundown. All right, ma'am, in you go, nice and easylike."

Sybella Forsden glared at the two bearded, dust-covered buffalo hunters, then shrugged philosophically. "All right. I'll give you what you want, but I'll ask you to leave without causing any trouble. My granddaughter-in-law and her little baby are inside."

"And who else, ma'am?" Marve Fenstrom demanded as he marched behind Sybella, prodding her back with the muzzle of the Sharps.

"Only our cook and her helper, that's all. You know, we've plenty of cowhands around this ranch, and if they hear any suspicious noises, they're sure to come running, and they're well armed."

"I don't think you're going to call them, ma'am. Not unless you want that granddaughter-in-law of yours and her little brat to get in the way of some heavy lead," Marve Fenstrom gloated. "All right, Jake, go inside and see if you can find any guns."

Maxine Bouchard stood, petrified, her eyes widening with fear as the two desperadoes entered the living room, Jake closing and latching the door behind him. His beady eyes swept her up and down, and made a hot flush of shame color her cheeks as she watched white-haired Sybella, at Marve's direction, move over beside her and stand facing the two men.

"Take a good look around, Jake. Hey now." Fenstrom's eyes narrowed and glinted as he saw the Bouchard heirloom ruby ring on Maxine's finger, "That's something we can turn into good, hard cash. Take off that ring, sister, and hand it to me, nice and gentle. In case you don't know what this gun is, it's a Sharps, and I can bring down a buffalo bull at a thousand feet and kill him stone-cold dead with just one shot. So that gives you a pretty fair idea of what it could do close range, get me?"

"Don't—don't hurt grandmother or my baby—I—I'll give

you the ring," Maxine Bouchard faltered. Biting her lips, tears in her eyes as she adjusted Edwina in her arms, she began to pull at the ring.

"I'll take the baby, Maxine darling," Sybella offered.

"That's real cooperative, ma'am. Keep it up, and you'll be safe and sound when your menfolks get back from that cattle drive. Yeah, we saw them not quite a week ago, heading north with that big herd. All right, sister, now your grandmom's got the brat safe, get the ring off and hand it here," Fenstrom directed.

In the kitchen, Felicidad and Celia, having heard the unfamiliar sound of the male voices, stared wonderingly at each other. "I can't rightly make out what they're saying, but I don't like the sound of it, honey," the mulatto woman whispered to the pretty Mexican girl. "You better slip out the back door here and see if you can get help. Those men sound real nasty. Hurry up now, before they come snooping in here and find you."

"But if they have guns, Señora Celia, there is the little niña to think of, and the Señoras Maxine and Sybella," Felicidad whispered back. "Señora Sybella has a gun hidden in the hall closet, between the living room and the kitchen—she mentioned it the day after Señor Lucien Edmond left! I have an idea—the men are busy building the chapel, but I will bring Coraje in, and try to get the gun, too, and hide it behind me."

"Oh, child, you might get killed—my son wouldn't want you to run such a terrible risk, and I wouldn't either—oh, please don't, Felicidad. Just go get some of the men!"

"You will see, Coraje, my falcon, will scare them. He is very fierce when I tell him to be." Felicidad put a finger to her lips and hurried out the back door.

Jake Ellison had made a cursory search of the living room, overturning two chairs, and, drawing his skinning knife, slashed the upholstery to see if he could find any valuables hidden in it. "Nothing in here at all, Marve," he reported.

Marve Fenstrom had grabbed the ruby ring from Maxine's trembling hand. He held it up, grinning at his partner. "It's mighty purty, ain't it, Jake? Ought to get a good price for it across the border. Looks like a real stone. I knew a rich farmer's wife back in Kansas, had a ring something like this; claimed she paid a fortune for it. Now then, ma'am, how about some food? Jake, you take the old lady out to the kitchen and have that cock fix us up a mess of victuals. We're starved, you see, ma'am, been living on some jerky and berries last couple of days."

"I told you, you may have whatever you want, just don't hurt us," Sybella Forsden repeated. She held Edwina in both arms, and she stared at the glowering buffalo hunter.

Felicidad had gone to the little shed in which Coraje's cage was kept, and she opened it swiftly, extending a perch and talking soothingly to the falcon. "Come, Coraje, you must help us. There are wicked men in the house. I will take off your hood so you can see them. When we get in, and when I tell you *asalto*, you will attack them. You must do this for all of us, Coraje. That will more than pay us back for the love and care I have given you. Come now, *pequeño halcón*, show me that I have not made a mistake in naming you. You are strong and fierce and have much more courage than I do. I am so afraid for the Señoras Maxine and Sybella and for dear Señora Celia, who have all been so kind to me. And most of all, you must keep me safe so that my dear husband, Lucas, will come back to me when the drive is over. Come now!"

She removed the falcon's hood as she left the shed and, as it clung to the perch she carried, continued to talk to it in the gentle tone of voice to which it had become accustomed, stroking its proud head.

As she reached the door of the kitchen, she heard Jake's voice. "All right there, nigger gal, fix us up a mess of victuals and be quick about it. See this knife? It's sharper 'n anything you got in your kitchen here, so don't make me use it on you. And don't try to call for help. Say, didn't the old lady say you had a helper?"

"She—she went over to the Belcher house by the creek to help with the cooking there, s—señor," Celia stammered.

"Well, good for her, then she won't be sticking her nose in here. All right, hurry it up. Me'n Marve are fair starved!" Jake Ellison directed.

"I—I'll hurry, mister. Please don't hurt Miz Sybella," Celia begged as she began to cut slices of ham, then set the coffeepot on the stone oven.

"All right, then, you just bring the victuals out to the

129

living room on a tray, and we'll all be mighty cozy where everybody can see everybody else. I'll just wait here 'til you've got it ready, then we'll all go back and have a nice meal and maybe a little conversation. Like, for instance, where the menfolks keep their cash. Hell, with that many cattle going to market, they won't miss whatever we find here," Jake Ellison sniggered.

Sybella, who continued to hold the little baby in her arms, gave him a contemptuous look, but said nothing. Celia made a fire and began to heat the coffee, then cut slices of bread and generous wedges of a pecan pie. Arranging these on plates and putting them on a large copper tray, she poured out two cups of strong, black coffee, added these to the tray, and then walked carefully toward the living room. Jake Ellison, his skinning knife in hand, gestured to Sybella to follow her, and himself brought up the rear.

"Here's the chow, Marve. No trouble at all. These ladies are being real helpful," Jake grinned.

"Set it down on that table," the bearded buffalo hunter demanded as he drew up a chair and sat astride it, shifting the Sharps to his left hand as he held it upright. "Now, don't think because I'm sitting down, I can't level this here Sharps in a jiffy. Just don't any of you get the wrong idea, get me? All right, Jake, better get your share before I clean up everything—it looks damn good, I'll give you that, nigger gal."

Celia stood, waiting helplessly, clasping her hands and twisting her fingers in her growing anxiety over Felicidad's audacious plan.

The two men ate wolfishly, smacking their lips and making ribald comments about Maxine's attractiveness. She winced and closed her eyes, folded her hands in her lap, and sat motionless, trying to obliterate their presence and obscene humor.

"Let's have more coffee, nigger gal," Marve shouted as he banged his right fist on the table and made the plates and silverware clatter.

"Sure, mister, I'll go heat some more right now." Celia's voice cracked with the strain.

"Want me to go along with her, Marve?" Jake asked, preparing to rise from the table.

"Naw, I think she's got sense enough to know which side her bread's buttered on, Jake. Haven't you, nigger gal? If I hear anybody yelling for help out there, the first person gets blasted with this Sharps is you. Then I'll start on the others, and don't think I won't. Now get that coffee back here fast, if you know what's good for you!"

"I—I'm going to get it right now, mister," Celia stammered as she hurried down the hallway.

Jake Ellison chuckled. "Easy as pie. Hey, Marve, speaking of pie, don't eat it all up, save me some. You just took half my share."

"I'm hungrier, that's why. Anyhow, there's bound to be more 'n the nigger gal can get you some if you're still empty. Now shut up and finish your victuals."

Grumbling under his breath, Jake Ellison obeyed, keeping his skinning knife in his left hand and eyeing Maxine and Sybella.

Celia returned with the coffeepot and promptly filled both men's cups to the brim. It was at this moment that Felicidad crept into the kitchen, tiptoed quickly down the hallway, and cautiously opened the closet door. The Spencer carbine leaned against the wall, and she seized it with her left hand, hid it behind her back, and then moved toward the living room.

"Okay, nigger gal." Jake Ellison took a hearty swig of the hot coffee. "Just you go back and bring out more pie, see? Hey, who's this now—"

Marve Fenstrom goggled, stupefied for a moment by the sight of the slim, young Mexican girl with the yellow-eyed falcon perched on a stick, held in her right hand. Then, shoving back his chair, he began to rise from the table and bawled, "Get that goddamn hawk outta here, you lost your mind or somethin'?"

"*Asalto, Coraje!*" Felicidad hissed and swung her right arm forward. The falcon uttered a shrill scream, and then swooped directly at Marve Fenstrom's face. With a cry of fright, he flung up his arm, dropping the Sharps.

At the same moment, Felicidad tossed the carbine to Maxine Bouchard, crying out, "Shoot them, shoot them both, Señora Maxine!"

"Why you goddamn tricky little greaser, I'll fix you," Jake Ellison snarled as he lunged from the table, and,

131

shifting his skinning knife from left hand to right, tried to stab Felicidad.

Maxine Bouchard caught the carbine, lifted it, and pulled the trigger. Fenstrom uttered a cry of agonized surprise, still fighting off the falcon whose talons were raking his face. Then, as a dark red stain spread on the chest of his khaki shirt, he staggered forward and fell across the table. The falcon, with an angry cry, swooped above him, beating its wings.

Ellison uttered a roar of rage. Drawing back his hand, he was about to throw the skinning knife when Maxine turned, leveled the carbine, and pulled the trigger again. At the same moment, seeing her maneuver, he had moved to one side. He tried to take better aim with the knife, but it flew from his hand and sank into Sybella Forsden's right shoulder. Even as it left his hand, he staggered backward, crashed against the wall, slumped down to his knees and fell onto his side, then rolled over.

"Oh my God, oh my God!" Maxine burst into hysterical tears, the carbine dropping from her nerveless hands. "Grandmother, you're hurt, you're hurt!"

"It's only a flesh wound, Maxine. Thank God you had the presence of mind to use that carbine. Felicidad, you were so brave—I don't even want to think of what would have happened if they'd seen you hide that carbine behind your back," Sybella said in a voice that began to falter. Then she slumped onto the couch, bowing her head, and put her hand to her bleeding shoulder.

"Celia, hurry, get some hot water and some bandages. Grandmother, let me try to stop the bleeding." Maxine tore a strip from her skirt and bound it around Sybella's wound as a kind of tourniquet. Little Edwina, rudely jostled when Sybella, sinking back onto the couch, had laid her rather forcibly to one side, began to cry.

Djamba hurried in from the kitchen, having heard the shots. "Celia, what's happened, girl?" Then, seeing Sybella on the couch, pale, her head bowed, drawing irregular breaths as she fought to keep from fainting, he ran to her. "Mrs. Forsden, my God, what did they do to you?"

Celia was back now with hot water and bandages, and Djamba helped her sponge the wound and then bandage it carefully. On his knees, he stared up at the white-haired woman. "Are you feeling better now, Mrs. Forsden?" he asked hoarsely.

Sybella lifted her face and smiled wanly at him. Then she put a hand on his shoulder. "Yes, God bless you, Djamba. God bless all of you for being so loyal and quick-witted." Then, turning to look at Maxine, who was still sobbing wildly, she said softly, "The best thing Luke did for all of us was to make us take target practice back in New Orleans, before we came here. Maxine, I'm so proud of you, so very proud. You're a real Bouchard. And you, dear Felicidad, wait 'til Lucas hears what a clever, brave, and beautiful wife he's married." Then, exhausted from the loss of blood and the frenzied and violent drama which had just taken place, she fell back on the couch, unconscious.

"I'll have some of the hands take these animals out and bury them," Djamba muttered to Celia, who had hurried over to tend her beloved mistress. "She'll be all right. She's got more courage than any man here. I'm going to stay with her and look after her until she's better, Celia."

"Of course, Djamba. I want you to do that. And she would want it, too."

CHAPTER FOURTEEN

By noon of March 28, 1869, Lucien Edmond Bouchard and his vaqueros had driven the herd past the little town of San Marcos and forded the shallow waters of the peaceful San Antonio River. Simata had reported that the place where they had crossed so easily the previous spring was still accessible. It had been an orderly crossing, and the vaqueros had only a few strays to round up. After they had reached the opposite bank of the river, with a clear trail ahead and skies that held no dark hint of rain or storm to come, Lucien Edmond called a halt and Pablo Casares at once began to prepare a tasty midday meal for the hungry riders. Friar Bartoloméo Alicante was deeply touched when Manuel Rodriguez approached and asked him, "Padre, before you eat, the men have asked me to say that we would all like to thank the good Lord for our luck so far, and ask Him to keep us safe to Abilene."

"With the greatest pleasure, my son," the Franciscan friar responded. Then, once again, under the clear skies and amid the sound of the lowing of the herd, the vaqueros, Lucien Edmond and Ramón knelt down and received the benediction from their ecclesiastical *compañero*—for by now all of the men had accepted Friar Bartoloméo as a true friend, who, to their own good fortune, was empowered to communicate their hopes and prayers to the Almighty.

At exactly this time, on the east bank of the Leona River, three miles from the little town of Ugalde, Colonel James Tardish was assembling the troops of Fort Inge under his command. He had received orders from Washington to abandon the fort. Some of the settlers were greatly disturbed over this, fearing immediate Indian at-

134

tack, but Colonel Tardish had assured them that there would be ample protection from Camp Sabinal, which the army had established thirteen years previously on a site two miles west of the tiny town of Sabinal. Moreover, as he had already assured the townspeople, now that the Comanche stronghold near Fort Inge had been abandoned and the tribe and its feared chief, Sangrodo, apparently had sought refuge across the border, there was no great danger. The herds of buffalo had been disappearing also, and that in itself was a favorable sign that the settlers could expect a respite from Indian attack.

The abandonment of Fort Inge had been declared a military necessity, since the troops would be stationed closer to Indian territory, to protect the growing number of settlers who were heading toward the northwest. Yet the displacement of these soldiers, who had acted as a bulwark against marauding bands of Mexicans and Indians, would leave the land unprotected against unscrupulous land speculators—a possibility not at all envisioned by the war department.

At Ramón Hernandez's advice, Lucien Edmond Bouchard had saved the lead steer out of last year's drive to Abilene. His docility, and his placid following of the directions indicated by the point riders, had earned him the nickname of Corregidor, the corrector for those heifers and steers which would follow his lead. Six years old, with wrinkled, scaly horns, he had been one of the first to be gelded and trained to lead his fellows in the roundup, and then the drive. Much to the amusement of the other vaqueros, Lucien Edmond had arranged last summer for Corregidor to be taken back in style from Abilene, in one of the largest extra wagons allowing him time to graze and water when the men made camp for their three daily meals. And, once again, he led the milling, lowing, dust-raising herd across the San Antonio River. "If he leads us safely into Abilene the way he did last year," Lucien Edmond had remarked humorously to Ramón, "we'll save him for next year's drive, too."

Corregidor had proved his mettle in the terrifying stampede the year before, having run only a short distance and then, with seeming indifference, given up the headlong flight to nowhere. The swing riders had easily overtaken him, and, waving their sombreros, slickers, and neckerchiefs, directed him back to head the return of his straying companions.

With the first week of April, the grass seemed to grow greener and thicker as they moved steadily northward, and with that, too, the sun brightened noticeably and became more intense. The tail riders, who brought up the rear of the huge herd, steeped their neckerchiefs in water and tied them around their noses and mouths as a protection from the swirling dust raised by the cattle hooves. Well before twilight, Simata was sent ahead to find a suitable place to bed the cattle down and to make camp.

The Bouchard herd was strung out for about three-quarters of a mile in a kind of serpentine procession. For the most part, the cattle traveled in single file, or in twos and threes so that they might graze and meander. Even so, the vaqueros who flanked them and guided them from both front and rear were pleased with the progress thus far. They were averaging close to ten miles a day now. Familiarity with the trail and knowledge of good watering holes and suitable campsites seemed to ease this new drive. By now, too, Lucien Edmond had learned to avoid camp-sites near timber washouts or ravines. In the event of a stampede, such natural obstacles were dangerous; high and dry ground was chosen whenever possible. Cattle would lie better where insects were more easily blown away, and they were not likely to encounter streams, in case they panicked into a stampede.

As the red and purple of sunset tinted the sky, the vaqueros carefully and gradually worked the cattle into a more compact space, urging them toward the level ground selected for bedding. Since they had grazed and been watered during the day, they would stop, and many of them would lie down and chew their cuds. The others followed their example, and the vaqueros stayed with them until they made sure that every animal had room enough to rise and turn over without disturbing its neighbor. At the same time, they should not be bedded so loosely as to scatter the herd. In that case it would take too much time to ride around it, which would allow a steer time to dash for freedom. Some of the older vaqueros had told Ramón stories of their experiences in Mexico, when too casual an inspection of a bedded herd had led to the loss of many prize cattle. And, too, since Lucien Edmond believed that soon cattle buyers would pay for weight and prime condition, rather than so many dollars a head, he was determined to bring the entire herd into Abilene looking well-fed and well-watered. That way, the Chicago buyers would begin to recognize that the brand of WR would always stand for top quality.

That night, after they had made camp, Ramón conferred with his brother-in-law on the progress of the drive and the stamina of the horses in the *remuda*. "If we can keep this pace up, Lucien Edmond," he declared, "we should be in Abilene by the middle of June. And the cattle will be fat by the time they reach the good grazing land of Indian territory. We've been very lucky so far. I think it is because the padre is with us."

"I agree, Ramón. I'd like to get at least ten dollars a head for the herd. I want to make a sufficient profit to give all the men a good bonus, and to buy those Brahma bulls I talked about."

"You've told me how expensive they are, Lucien Edmond. As much as two thousand dollars, *¿no es verdad?*"

"That's right, Ramón. I'm going to see if I can get half a dozen shipped to Windhaven Range by fall. Then, by next spring, together with the Herefords we already have, we should really have the beginnings of a prize herd. Mark my words, in a few years the cattle owner who crossbreeds is going to make the most money. And there are certain to be more railroad lines to give us a choice of markets, maybe even to eliminate this three-month-long drive we expect to make every year."

"Do you mean, Lucien Edmond, that the railroads will extend their tracks as far south as we are?" Ramón asked.

"I'm sure of it. Think of all the work it'll save us, the hardships, the long months away from our loved ones, Ramón," Lucien Edmond exclaimed. "All we'll have to do is brand them in the chute, drive them down to a cattle pen near a railroad stop, and our work will be done. It's going to become a scientific business, raising beef on the hoof for the people who want good meat on the table all over the country, you wait and see, Ramón."

"It takes one's breath away to look ahead like that, Lucien Edmond. Every day, I give thanks to the good Lord that he guided Corita and me to find you. I never dreamed that I would have such a life as I now enjoy. And best of all, amigo, is my wonderful wife who is your sister. Sometimes I ask myself what I have done to deserve her."

"There's no reason why you should do that, Ramón. I've never seen her so happy, and there's no man better suited to be her husband, believe me."

Ramón's eyes glowed with pride. "When we go to San Antonio for supplies again, after the drive is over, I'm going to buy her and little Luke some presents. And perhaps presents for the next little *niño*—"

"She's going to have another baby? That's wonderful, Ramón! Maybe Friar Bartoloméo will be there to christen the child and to bless the chapel, even though he may decide to stay with the Creeks for a time, if he feels that he can be of service after he has visited them with us."

"That would be a very good thing. I, too, am eager to see Emataba and his people."

Lucien Edmond nodded and sighed. "You know, Ramón, history tells us that when the Spaniards drove out the Moors and the Jews, they began to fail as a world power. Who knows what might have happened if the white man had made peace with the Creeks and found that they could live side by side in friendship and unity? There's much we could have learned from them as they from us. Now, tell me, can we get along with the horses we've brought with us, or should we try to catch some of the wild mustangs I've seen along the trail?"

"Perhaps it would do no harm to break in another ten or so, Lucien Edmond. We've made good time thus far, and some of the vaqueros seem restless because there's so little work for them to do. Maybe tomorrow, if Simata sees any wild horses on the trail ahead, I'll take four or five of the men and go after them. And now, we'd best get some sleep so we can be up early and plan for that. *Buenas noches,* Lucien Edmond."

"And to you, Ramón."

Though they woke to an overcast sky the next morning, within an hour the sun's brightness eased the always present danger of a sudden thunderstorm that might terrify the herd. Shortly before noon, Simata rode back to report that he had seen about a dozen wild mustangs about a mile to the northeast. Ramón Hernandez volunteered to take six of the vaqueros to capture them, adding, "To reward Pablo for the fine way he has fed us on the trail, I myself will lasso and break in the best of the lot— it will be my present to him."

"That's sure to make him happy, Ramón," Lucien Edmond commented. "And it's time Henry Belcher had a new horse. He prides himself as a rider, so let's bring him back a good one."

"Understood!" the handsome young Mexican laughed as he touched the brim of his sombrero and then rode back toward the swing riders to ask for volunteers. One of these was Vittorio Salancár, Pablo Casares's best friend. Another was Sanchez Maderos, as well as Benito Aguilár and Miguel Dondero. Luis García and Jose Martinez, two veterans from the previous year's drive, completed the contingent, and rode ahead with Ramón in the direction which Simata had indicated.

"There they are!" Ramón exclaimed as he gestured toward a distant swirl of dust raised by the galloping mustangs' hooves. "This will be good practice for us all. Vittorio, you're the ketch hand of the ranch, let's see if you can prove your right to the job. ¡Adelante, hombres!"

The six vaqueros spurred their horses, three of them breaking to the left and three to the right with Ramón, as they sought to circle the fleeing mustangs. Ramón's eyes sparkled with pleasure at the exhilarating pace, a welcome diversion from the endless and tiring regimen of a day on the cattle drive. Giving Corita her head, he reached for his lariat and swiftly formed a wide noose, adjusting the honda, the eye at one end of the rope through which the other end is passed, to allow for a head catch. As the vaqueros neared the galloping mustangs, Ramón counted fourteen, all of them wild and none apparently ever broken to saddle, bit, and reins. Perhaps they had run away from some nomadic Indian corral, or, more likely in this part of the country, had never known what it was to lose their freedom.

Vittorio Salancár, racing his gelding at full gallop, had prepared his lariat with a small loop, which he used infallibly for a head catch while roping horses in the Wind-haven Range corral. He neared the leader, a magnificent black stallion, who threw up its head and snorted, its eyes rolling, as it caught sight of him. Its long legs seemed a blur in the still air as it raced madly, veering off to the right to outdistance its pursuer. Vittorio, with a tug on his gelding's reins, turned his own mount to follow, and again caught up to the black stallion. Whirling his lariat around in front of him toward the right, up over his head, he released it. As it went over the stallion's head it was turned in a way to cause it to flatten out, and the honda slid down the rope, taking up slack as it went. A cry of praise rose from the other vaqueros as they saw him ex-pertly jerk on the lariat, and the black stallion stopped in mid-flight, neatly roped around the neck, rearing on its hind legs and pawing at the air.

Vittorio quickly dismounted, with a gesture that or-dered his gelding to wait docilely for his return. Then, swiftly mounting the wild mustang, clamping his high-topped boots tightly against the mustang's flanks, he slackened the lasso and used it as reins to give the wild horse its full head.

Snorting wildly, the black mustang reared high in the air again, turning its head and baring its teeth as if defying its unwanted rider. The sturdy vaquero, holding his som-brero in his left hand, slapped it against the mustang's neck as he urged it, "Vamanos, amigo, I'm ready for you!"

The mustang began to buck, kicking in every direction, but Vittorio determinedly rode him bareback, nearly being thrown once but swiftly regaining his balance by tighten-ing the lasso around the furious mustang's neck.

Benito, Sanchez and Miguel had imitated Vittorio, though each successfully cast his lasso in his own particu-lar style. Miguel preferred the "blocker loop," which began like a straight overhead loop and whirled around the head to the left, then was flung over the horse's head. In the same movement, Miguel's hand and wrist gave a twist toward the left which left the honda on the side of the loop, opposite its position from which the throw was started. The vaquero's right hand kept pulling the rope after the loop had been thrown, letting it play out until it reached the mustang, an ideal throw at close range. Two of his compatriots favored the *mangana*, the throw of the lasso made by pointing the hand downward, dragging the loop forward and swinging it out so that it almost stood on edge. At first glance, it appeared that the racing wild mustangs stepped into the widening loop, and when the vaqueros drew up on their lassos, the mustangs were brought to a wrenching stop which taxed all the skill and strength of the horsemen, as well as the tactical agility of their own horses.

Ramón Hernandez, with his keen eye for horseflesh, had picked out a magnificent gray stallion. He let a piebald and a chestnut swerve off to the south beyond him, as he relentlessly pursued the gray. Behind him, the other vaqueros had dismounted and were riding their captive broncos, each showing off to his fellows. They demonstrated their skill and their endurance, parrying sudden kicks, bucks, and tosses while the infuriated wild horses strove with all their might to unseat their captors. The vaqueros' cries and exhortations rang out and echoed in that long stretch of isolated plain as, momentarily forgetting the arduous chores of the drive to Abilene, they savored this primitive duel between man and wild horse.

Corita whinnied, flattening her ears as she raced toward the fleeing gray stallion. Ramón slowly uncoiled his lasso, made his loop, tied the free end to the horn of his heavy saddle, and cast it out. It fell short and he swore under his breath as he retrieved and recoiled it. The stallion had gained a few yards in the race for freedom, but Ramón leaned to Corita and whispered into her ear, stroking her neck, and the gallant mare responded with an extra burst of speed that once again drew her up close behind the galloping mustang.

This time, Ramón's toss circled the head of the racing gray, and Ramón, using both hands, drew him to a snorting, raging halt. Leaping off Corita, he drew his knife in his left hand as he held the lasso in his right, and cut the end free from the saddle horn. The stallion, sensing its momentary advantage, lunged forward, but Ramón had swiftly looped the free end of his lasso between both hands and, running at full speed, leaped astride the stallion, then jerked on the loop to halt its flight.

As the other vaqueros watched, shouting encouragement

to the wrangler, the young Mexican seized the loop with both hands to use it as reins and gave the stallion its head.

With a bound, the magnificent gray galloped eastward, flattening its ears and ignoring its rider. Ramón gripped the loop tightly, his legs clamped solidly against the mustang's flanks, shouting words of praise, letting the mustang learn the sound of his voice.

Now the mustang turned in a circle, seeming to redouble its frenzied gallop, then suddenly stopped still, rearing and pawing the air with its front legs. Ramón had expected this maneuver, and locked his arms around the mustang's neck as he continued to talk to it, this time more soothingly. Again and again the superb gray stallion reared in the air, lunging out with its sharp hooves, but Ramón tenaciously clung to it, until at last, head drooping, snorting, it stood docilely, as if knowing that at last it had been conquered by one it could respect.

As the cheers of the vaqueros rose to acclaim Ramón's feat of horsemanship, the cloud of dust from the herd behind them came nearer. Now their amusement was at an end. There would be the work of saddling these new horses and hobbling them away from the rest of the *remuda*, perhaps spending an hour or so each day, as time allowed, to make them worthy of a vaquero's skills.

Ramón had christened his prize "Gray Devil," and when they made camp for supper that evening, he was the last to approach the chuck wagon where a weary Pablo Casares was doling out stew and biscuits, beans with molasses, and strong coffee.

"Have you a plateful left for a hungry man who has a horse to give you, amigo?" Ramón asked as he stepped out of the shadows and led the gray stallion, saddled, with reins and bit, for the astonished middle-aged vaquero-turned-cook to see.

"*¡Madre de Dios, es magnifico!*" Pablo Casares gasped. "But you're joking, a poor vaquero like me does not own such a horse."

"You do now, Pablo. It is our way of saying *gracias* for the way you have fed us and the sacrifice you have made in not riding point. Here, I will fasten Gray Devil to the back of your chuck wagon, and whenever you can spare a few minutes from your chores, get accustomed to him. He will not fight now, I promise."

The very next day, as if to rebuke the trail riders for their unexpected diversion, trouble threatened to mar the progress of the entire drive. The day had begun well, for the sky was cloudless. Lucien Edmond had wakened the men shortly before dawn to get a good start in this seemingly pleasant weather. They were reaching higher ground, with wider patches of grazing grass for the cattle. Simata, after a hasty breakfast, had ridden ahead for about two miles and returned to report that all was well. He had seen fresh buffalo tracks off to the northeast, but no sign of a herd.

Just before noontime, they reached a small, forked creek. Lucien Edmond, having been alerted to this supply of clear, fresh water, slowed the herd. Wise to the ways of the trail, he had instructed his vaqueros to divide the herd into small bunches and let each group drink. When a large herd of cattle hit water all at once, the leaders invariably were crowded out before they got enough water and those that came after them found only the muddy remains to drink. The cattle had begun to low and move more quickly, having smelled the water of the creek. Yet, even so, the winding procession remained orderly, thanks to the alertness of the swing and drag riders who patiently called out and gestured with their sombreros to keep the moving animals in a regular line.

Lucien Edmond nodded his satisfaction to Ramón as both men watched the cattle drink their fill, then go up onto the low bank beyond the creek, returning for more water as they wished. They were placid now.

The heat had become oppressive, and Lucien Edmond was not sorry to have paused for a daytime watering, rather than waiting until evening, as he usually did with the large herd. Half a mile away from the creek, the sky suddenly darkened and a gusty wind began to blow from the northeast, swirling the dust violently until the cattle were obscured in its clouds. Clumps of tumbleweed pummeled the vaqueros, who swiftly donned their neckerchiefs after dampening them with water from their canteens, and pulled their sombreros down as low as possible, to protect their eyes from the gritty dust.

There was a sudden clap of thunder, and a vivid bolt of lightning streaked the sky like a fiery dagger. Even placid Corregidor lifted his head and bawled, then turned and began to run toward the northwest. There was a thundering of hooves as the cattle behind him followed, panicked by the dust and by the sudden crash of thunder and the lightning.

Lucien Edmond and Ramón barked out orders. The vaqueros swiftly chose fresh horses out of the *remuda*, horses picked for their stolid temperaments and their ability to race alongside a milling, stampeding herd. Simata had reported that the ground was even, with no sudden gullies, wagon ruts, or gopher holes, and this was encouraging to the riders. In such swirling dust, galloping at full speed to overtake the herd and to guide it as best they could, the vaqueros had to rely entirely on the surefootedness of their mounts.

Twenty minutes later, as suddenly as it had begun, the dust storm ceased, and the sky brightened as if there had never been a storm. But by now most of the herd had plunged off to the northwest, with many strays veering in other directions as panic seized them and they found themselves separated from the main body of the herd.

Ramón uttered a cry of horror. "Look, Lucien Edmond, the buffalo whose tracks Simata found—hundreds of them —they'll attack the herd!"

"Yes, the cattle are running toward them!" Lucien Edmond exclaimed, shaking his head and drawing a long breath. "We'll have work to do. And we'll be lucky if we don't lose part of the herd."

"On the brighter side, Lucien Edmond," Ramón wryly observed, "we might kill a few buffalo and have plenty of fresh meat for the next few nights."

"Yes, but we certainly can't shoot them, that would only panic the herd more."

"Do you still have those metal lances Djamba made in New Orleans?" Ramón hazarded.

Lucien Edmond slapped his thigh with a boyish grin. "I'm sure Lucas brought a few of them along. I'd like you to go find him."

Urging Corita on to catch up to Lucas who was mounted on a sorrel gelding, the young Mexican quickly told him of his and Lucien Edmond's idea. Lucas nodded, turned his gelding, and rode off to find Simata. The two men rode back to one of the supply wagons, and each armed himself with one of the cast-iron spears Djamba had made from the wrought-iron railing of an abandoned New Orleans balcony. The lower halves of the arrow-shaped spears were enclosed in strong bamboo poles, the heft and balance of which made them ideal for hunting from horseback, as Simata's ancestors had done on these very plains.

By this time, most of the herd had turned toward the lumbering buffalo and some steers were mingling with them, to the dismay of the vaqueros who rode after them, shouting and waving their sombreros in a futile effort to head them off. Simata and Lucas spurred their geldings toward the stragglers of the buffalo herd, each approaching from one side. The young Indian chose a shaggy, humpbacked bull, and, overtaking it, clamped his legs against his gelding's flanks lifted the spear in both hands, and thrust downward with all his strength. The buffalo uttered a bellow of pain, stumbled, and then toppled onto its side and lay panting, dying from the thrust which had pierced the rib cage.

Lucas, emulating Simata, chose a smaller target, and, taking careful aim, thrust the point of the improvised spear into the animal's paunch. With a maddened roar, the wounded buffalo lunged to one side, and Lucas was barely able to wheel his gelding away from the charge of the infuriated beast. But he had inflicted a mortal wound. A few minutes later, the buffalo's front legs folded and its massive head lowered, then it rolled over onto one side and lay, kicking, in its death throes.

Fifteen of the vaqueros had joined Ramón, Lucien Edmond, Simata, and Lucas in pursuing the fleeing cattle, the others remaining behind to guard the chuck wagon and the wagons of supplies, as well as the *remuda* horses.

After two hours, the weary riders had managed to divert two-thirds of the herd away from the buffalo, and ten of the riders, wheeling their horses, directed the steers, cows, and heifers, with encouraging shouts and flourishes of their sombreros, back to the original line. The rest of the cattle, however, had merged with the buffalo herd, and it was a singular sight to watch Texas longhorns and short-horned Herefords trotting side by side with the shaggy wild animals of the plains.

"What a pity we can't drive some of those buffalo to Emataba's village," Lucien Edmond called to Ramón Hernandez.

"*Es verdad,* but first we'd better get back our own cattle to be sure we can drive *them,*" the young Mexican called back. "We may have to let them run until they're tired, and then perhaps we can rope one or two of the lead steers and bring them back. When the other cattle see that, they may follow. Look, even old Corregidor has joined the buffalo—he's a traitor, so we shall sell him at Abilene, along with the rest."

"I agree," Lucien Edmond chuckled. Then, in almost the same breath, he uttered a startled cry. "Look out, Ramón—that bull buffalo is charging you!"

From the left rear of the mixed herd of buffalo and cattle, a huge bull with curved horns had pawed the earth, snorted, then charged Corita. Ramón, hearing Lucien Edmond's warning, reined in his mare just in time to avoid her being gored. But the onrush of the huge beast carried it against Corita's hind legs and felled the gallant mare to the earth. Ramón just had time to leap free and to pull his Spencer carbine from its leather sheath, aim, and fire. The buffalo charged on a few paces, then suddenly crumpled and lay still.

As Ramón turned back, he uttered an agonized cry. "Corita, *querida,* you're hurt!" The mare lay on her side, uttering shrill screams of pain. One of her hind legs had been badly broken.

Ramón knelt next to her as tears coursed down his cheeks. He raised the carbine slowly, and, as Corita's last scream rang out above the thudding hooves of the fleeing cattle and buffalo, he squeezed the trigger.

He rose slowly, his head bowed, and Lucien Edmond halted his gelding beside the heartbroken young Mexican. "You loved her very much, Ramón. And she loved you, too."

"I would rather have had my own leg broken a thou-

146

sand times over, Lucien Edmond. Ten thousand devils out of hell, to lose such a brave, loyal companion! But you, you saved my life by calling to me—again I am in your debt."

"No, all of us are bound together on a drive like this, Ramón. We must help one another. Climb on my horse, we'll go back and pick up a mount for you from the *remuda*. Then we'll bring back the other vaqueros and see if we can round up our cattle. There are at least six hundred head missing from our herd."

Ramón Hernandez stared at the lifeless body of his little mare and then clambered up behind Lucien Edmond and circled the latter's waist with his arms. He slumped in dejection as they rode back toward the waiting group.

CHAPTER FIFTEEN

It took four days and nights of exhausting riding and roping to lure the rest of the Windhaven cattle away from the buffalo herd. And when, at last, the old bull leader of the buffalo had been driven off with the rest of his herd, Lucien Edmond tallied a loss of fifty-two of his own cattle. Some of the younger heifers and calves had been crushed to death in the stampeding rush of the buffalo, as they sought to evade their pursuers; the rest had simply veered off with some of the buffalo and disappeared.

It had been bone-wearying work, and the vaqueros had changed shifts throughout the day and night. Fortunately, none of the riders had been injured, and it was the Franciscan friar who, on the morning of the fifth day, gently proposed that the men of Windhaven Range give thanks to God for their good fortune in retrieving the cattle at so little cost. Ramón had chosen a sturdy chestnut gelding from the *remuda*, but his sorrowful face spoke eloquently of his grief over his faithful little mare's death.

Nine days later, Lucien Edmond, his men, and the reassembled and again orderly herd, reached the bank of the Colorado River. Remembering the quicksand which they had encountered last May, Lucien Edmond had sent Simata ahead to find a new fording. The half-Indian scout had selected a place some two miles east of their previous crossing, for the flurry of spring rains had swollen the river. Simata's judgment had been excellent. He had selected a bend in the river which proved shallow enough to permit the heavy supply wagons to ford it with no danger.

Even so, the crossing was not without incident. Three of the younger calves drowned, and Sebastiano Galvez's gelding lost its footing while scrambling up onto the opposite bank, throwing the vaquero and breaking its leg. Ramón Hernandez, who had ridden up to aid his *compañero,* stifled a cry of commiseration when he saw the vaquero draw his six-shooter and put a merciful end to the gelding's suffering. When they had completed the crossing to the opposite bank, Lucien Edmond rode up to his brother-in-law and patted him on the shoulder, signifying that he understood the reason for Ramón's distress.

Three miles beyond the Colorado River, Simata pointed out the little creek where, the year before, a thunderstorm had caused the stampede in which Pedro Tolivar had met his untimely death. And Lucien Edmond, remembering where Djamba and Lucas had dug the vaquero's grave, directed his riders toward that melancholy place and asked Friar Bartoloméo to say a prayer for Pedro's gentle soul. The jagged boulder which Lucien Edmond had placed there as a headstone marked the gravesite. After the friar had said his prayer—during which all the vaqueros removed their sombreros and stood with heads bowed in respectful silence—Lucien Edmond took a chisel and inscribed a cross and the date of its inscription upon the stone.

All the next day, Ramón Hernandez was somber and silent, and when they made camp that night, he said to Lucien Edmond, "Seeing Pedro's grave makes me remember all the dangers we faced last year, Lucien Edmond. But more than that, it was my selfishness that caused poor Corita's death."

"Why do you reproach yourself for such a thing, Ramón?"

"Because," the young Mexican stared unseeing beyond the cheerful campfire nearby, "as a vaquero I know very well that one does not take stallions or mares on a drive. And last year, as you know, I rode the piebald gelding you yourself named *Spots.* But I had missed Corita so much that I forgot the rule and brought her along this time—and she died because of it. We had shared so much together, and she was such a dear companion to me, that seeing Pedro's grave today brings all those memories back."

Lucien Edmond nodded. He put out his hand and gripped his brother-in-law's shoulder "I can understand that, Ramón," he said gently. "Corita saved your life at

149

Miero, and she brought you to find us. She brought you to a new and happy life, and I think—though I admit I have never asked myself whether animals have souls like humans—that she loved you and that she gladly would have given her life for yours. Perhaps that is the way you must think of what happened."

"You are kind to tell me this, Lucien Edmond. And it's true I loved her almost as much as if she were a person. Well then, if she gave her life for me, I must see to it that I'm worthy of that sacrifice." He rose abruptly and turned to look back in the direction from which they had come. "You know, I have a feeling about this drive. So far we have had no real dangers—we have not been attacked by Indians as we were last year, and we escaped the quicksand of the river. And, the good God be thanked, we have lost no men as we did last year, beginning with poor Pedro." He crossed himself quickly. "It's strange, Lucien Edmond, but I think I shall feel more at peace when we reach the village of Emataba. You know, the good padre wishes to spend time with Emataba's people. I hope he will come back with us after we have sold our cattle in Abilene."

"I'm sure that he will, Ramón. We shall leave him there when we reach the village, and by the time we have sold our cattle and are ready to come back, he will have had time enough to see if that is where he plans to remain as priest, friend, and counselor."

"He is a good man, Lucien Edmond. He has a heart for the oppressed, and he is indignant when justice is not done to those who are lowly and needy. Perhaps it is because all the people in the village where my father and I lived were simple and poor, that we longed for the comfort which a priest could bring us. Alas, a priest by himself could not stand against the cruel *ricos* who looked down upon us, as if we were worse than starving curs, begging for a scrap of food. Friar Bartoloméo would, I think, have stood against our oppressors—he is a courageous man to have defied the powerful *ricos* who run Santa Fe."

"I have the same feeling for him, Ramón. And I'm eager, too, to see Emataba again. If we've any luck with the weather, we should reach Mineral Springs in a few weeks, and after that it will be a swift journey to the Red

River and then on into Indian territory. That will be the worst part of our journey. We should be one of the first to bring a herd into Abilene this year."

"I have begun to think a little like you, Lucien Edmond." Ramón Hernandez began to unpack his bedroll. "You are already planning for the future, and you believe that the railroads will come down far south, so that we will not need all these vaqueros and all these long days and nights to drive our cattle to market. It sounds like a dream, almost too easy."

"No." Lucien Edmond shook his head gravely as he answered. "Even if it becomes more convenient, there will still be dangers. Perhaps there won't be Indians attacking us, but there may be neighboring ranchers who will fight us for grazing and water rights. Perhaps we shall all have to fence in our land and patrol our boundaries to make sure that no greedy neighbor tries to steal our cattle. There will always be men who are envious of their neighbors. But if we are united, those dangers will not destroy us, any more than an attack by Indians or bandits could."

"You have made me feel better tonight, Lucien Edmond. For that, *muchas gracias*. And in the morning, before breakfast, I shall ask Friar Bartoloméo to hear my confession. I have too much pride, and it is selfish pride."

"And I, for my part, Ramón, am very sure that Friar Bartoloméo will tell you that to take pride in one's work and in striving to improve oneself is surely not a sin. I would never call you selfish, nor would your *compañeros*. Certainly, my sister, Mara, would not. She came to me before we left Windhaven Range, Ramón, and told me how happy she is to be your wife—why, hombre—" this with a self-conscious little laugh, "she even told me to look after you and make sure that no harm came to you."

"She—she actually said that to you, Lucien Edmond?" Ramón asked.

Lucien Edmond Bouchard nodded. "When you first met Mara, you thought her proud, even insolent. The truth is, she was as lonely as you, uprooted from where she was born, the one suitor she was fond of back in Alabama dying before she could be married to him—and now she is more a Hernandez than a Bouchard. So don't reproach yourself, but go forward, and be confident and proud of what you've already accomplished, and what you will accomplish."

"God bless you for your words and for your kindness to me, Lucien Edmond. And now, let us go to sleep because there is much work to be done tomorrow."

The two men exchanged a look of deep understanding as, in the darkness of the warm night, they listened to the gentle lowing of the herd beyond them.

CHAPTER SIXTEEN

On May 20, Lucien Edmond and his vaqueros came within sight of the mighty Red River. Their journey had taken them over more than four hundred miles of barren desert, dry gullies, treacherous ravines and desolate, seemingly unending stretches, without sight of human habitation. Until now, aside from those two unknown riders who had been hurrying in the direction from which the cattle drive had come, they had seen no other human being.

They had skirted both San Marcos and Mineral Springs without stopping in either town. If they *had*, they might have learned that a month earlier, Congress had authorized Virginia, Mississippi, and their own state of Texas to submit their constitutions to popular vote for ratification, with the stipulation that these three secessionist states would be required to ratify the fifteenth amendment before admission to representation in the nation's government. Congress had created a board of Indian commissioners for the stated purpose of providing just and fair treatment for the tribes who had submitted to peaceful removal to reservations in stipulated territories.

And ten days before the Bouchard herd approached the Red River, the Central Pacific and Union Pacific railroads had met at Promontory Point in Utah, where one golden spike connected the Atlantic and the Pacific railroads, a symbolic ceremony that aroused a nationwide celebration. Then, just five days before, the National Woman Suffrage Association had been formed in New York with Elizabeth Cady Stanton as president, its objective being to seek suffrage through federal amendment.

Yet, because of this isolation and the vast emptiness of the land they crossed, the men of Windhaven Range were drawn together in a unanimity of purpose and of companionship. The choking dust, the sweltering sun, the sudden harsh gusts of wind, the endless riding, welded them into a finite, unique world in which all that mattered was their reliance on one another and their confidence in the success of this long trek to the north. What heartened them most was the uncomplaining presence of Friar Bartoloméo Alicante. They looked forward to his simple, devout blessing of every meal they shared on this arduous trail. At night, around the campfires, he would often walk from group to group, entering into conversations, relating stories of his experiences with the Indians. They observed among themselves his refusal to accept any special privileges that would place him above the others.

At times, when one or another of the vaqueros was troubled, the priest would reply in the language of a *compañero*, directly from the heart. Invariably, he would add with a smile, "My son, I am a sinner like yourself, and because God is infinitely compassionate, He has a special fondness for those who regret their sins and repent through good deeds thereafter. And I say that a man who has never sinned has never had to wrestle with temptation, and therefore may be even less saintly than the redeemed sinner. So you see, my son, there is hope for all of us."

When Simata returned from scouting the Red River, he reported that the waters were fordable and that he could see the occasional glint of a white sandbar here and there along a stretch that ran for some three hundred yards. The vaqueros were convinced that this good fortune could be attributed to the friar's prayers, and, indeed, the crossing was successful. Even so, since Lucien Edmond Bouchard had taken five hundred more head of cattle on the drive than last year, the crossing took nearly three days, from dawn until dusk. Many of the longhorns balked at the sight of so wide a river, and at times the riders were forced to cross back and forth several times before a reluctant steer, or cow, or heifer could be prodded across to the opposite bank, lowing or snorting its protest.

As he had done the previous year, Lucien Edmond let his men rest all of the next day and night. They needed to replenish their sorely taxed strength for the rest of the drive, which was well over four hundred miles, even though it would be through richer grazing land. Moreover, if they could make good time and compensate for the week they had lost, separating the cattle from the buffalo herd, he would be able to spend a day or two at the Creek reservation.

Lucien Edmond was looking forward to the reunion with Emataba and the blind old *windigo*, Equitaba. In his heart, he believed that Friar Bartoloméo would not scoff at the primitive mysticism of that sightless old man who yet could see into the future.

When he expressed to Ramón Hernandez once again, his eagerness to visit the little Creek village, the young Mexican concurred. "Last year, Emataba said his people were kept in the village and not given weapons for hunting, so it was like a prison for them I think that they will need the meat we bring them, perhaps very badly. It is a very good thing you do, amigo. And I am very glad the padre will be with us."

Here and there, between the long stretches of deep buffalo grass, the riders who had journeyed this way last year could see an occasional wagon-wheel rut, or the jumbled hoofprints of cattle, to mark the way they had come before. The grass was ample for the grazing needs of the now thoroughly placid herd. There were good campsites, too, and some of the vaqueros, who rode far ahead for the purpose so as not to frighten the herd with the sounds of rifle fire, were able to kill quail and rabbits. Pablo Casares was overjoyed with these welcome additions to the monotonous provender, and found pleasure in explaining in great detail to some of his interested *compañeros* which wild berries and vegetables to look for, so that he could make their stews more palatable.

As far as the eye could see to the north, east, and west, the plains extended, rising slightly higher as they moved farther north. The sky was almost an interminable azure, rich and often cloudless, adding to the seeming immensity of their solitary universe. And this, too, bound them together in their sharing of the hard work on the long trail.

To everyone's delight, Benito Aguilar had brought along an old, battered guitar which he had bought in Nuevo Laredo. At night, long after the campfires had been extinguished, he would walk along the edges of the resting herd, singing old Mexican songs, gentle lullabies, and love songs. His father had done that as a vaquero in Mexico, he had told Lucien Edmond, and it kept the cattle quiet. Besides, the sound of those old melodies, here in the silence of the night, seemed to make all of the vaqueros feel that they belonged together. The remembrance of those old songs which they had heard in their boyhood, back in Mexico, recalled to them memories of dark-eyed girls and bounteous family dinners, and the joyous freedom of riding the range for a *patrón* they had respected.

Sanchez Maderos, a stocky, good-natured man in his mid-thirties whose thick mustache with its long, drooping ends made his smile seem lugubrious, had constantly tried to cheer up Ramón Hernandez after Corita's death. Of cheerful disposition, he forever boasted to all who would listen how he would one day own a hacienda in his beloved Mexico. "Hombre," he told Ramón after they had crossed the Red River, "it will be easier for me when I drive my own cattle, *certamente.*"

"And why is that, Sanchez?" Ramón had baited him with an anticipatory smile.

"Why, because in Mexico, there are no big *rios* to cross."

"*Si, es verdad,* Sanchez, except for one thing," Ramón retorted with a straight face. "You have forgotten that the cattle will eat locoweed and you will lose them all. For whenever you speak, amigo, you spread the seeds of locoweed to all parts of the earth and they spring up behind you even before you begin your next sentence."

Sanchez Maderos looked crestfallen as he tugged at one end of his thick black mustache. Then he shrugged. "*No es importante.* And do you know why? Because I shall never be rich and I am really too lazy to run my own *estancia.*" Then, with a wry chuckle, he added, "All the same, if there were big rivers in Mexico, I could not squeeze the cattle as well as the Señor Lucien Edmond has done just now. He has learned much for a young man. He rode along with the other vaqueros to get the lead steers in, and he made sure that the other vaqueros swam their horses in the downstream side of the herd to keep the *ganados* from drifting. But you have taught him something, too—he loosened the cinches of his saddle, because horses swell up in swimming. And I saw also how he splashed water in his horse's face in the opposite direction he wanted him to go—*es muy intelligente.*"

"I thank you on behalf of Lucien Edmond, Sanchez," Ramón retorted. "When I tell him that you find him intelligent, I am sure that he will at least double your wages. And now, hombre, *por favor,* keep quiet and let us all get some sleep. Tomorrow our day of siesta is over, and we shall both have to work twice as hard to make up for our laziness."

And indeed, the next day found all the vaqueros urging on the herd with greater zest than ever, so that by the time they made camp for the night, they had covered nearly thirteen miles. As he had done the previous year, Lucien Edmond changed drag riders each day so that no vaquero could complain of constant riding in the wake of the swirling dust raised by the moving herd. Manuel Rodriguez, who had been one of the night riders the year before and sung gently to the cattle to quiet them after they had been bedded down, insisted on borrowing Benito Aguilar's guitar and resuming his function as the "night mother" of the herd. Both men quarreled amicably over this honor, until Lucien Edmond wisely decided that each man should alternate for the rest of the drive, and that on every second turn Manuel might borrow Benito's beloved guitar.

Sometimes, when he was unable to sleep, the portly Franciscan friar stayed on guard with either Manuel or Benito and often lifted his voice in some of the old Spanish songs. Much to the pleased surprise of the vaqueros, he had a pleasant and not too reedy baritone voice, and every now and again, when he had finished a song, one of the not-yet-sleeping vaqueros would call out softly, "*Bravo,* padre, *muy bueno!*"

As they neared the Creek village, Lucien Edmond Bouchard's spirits rose as he noticed the warmth and solidarity of friendship existing between his men. They were not so much workers or hired hands, as an integral part of Windhaven Range. More than ever, he could understand what both his father, Luke, and old Lucien had said about sharing labor so that it was not a matter of a superior in charge of inferiors, but rather a coming together of all workers as equals, in a common enterprise. Every man felt that he belonged, so he gave unstintingly of himself in work and devotion. And hard work could make a man go far. In this strong new nation, a man's accomplishments and progress were determined only by his own character, and unflinching ambition to do his very best.

On the last day of May, they came within sight of the Creek reservation off to the northwest, and Lucien Edmond, riding ahead with Simata, declared, "It's an hour before sunset, Simata, but if the men can hold out another hour, we can camp near the village and make a gift of cattle to Emataba and his people."

As they neared the small Indian village of tepees and wigwams, bordered on all sides by a waist-high, rickety wooden fence, they perceived that only a few tiny campfires had been lighted. Twilight had fallen nearly an hour before, and in the vague darkness of early evening, the reservation looked desolate and impoverished. It seemed to Lucien Edmond that there were even fewer dwellings than there had been last year, and he shook his head sympathetically as he murmured to Ramón, "Have the men cut a good bull out of the herd—yes, one of the Herefords —three heifers, and the rest cows and steers, and lead them through the gate. You and I and Friar Bartoloméo will visit with Emataba. Let Pablo prepare supper, and tell him to put on enough extra food to feed our friends. I'm certain those poor people in that bedraggled village have been starved all through the winter."

"Even though it's dark, I understand what you mean, Lucien Edmond," the young Mexican replied. "*¡Que lástima!* Are these, then, all that are left of the Creeks who were sent away from the land where your great-grandfather lived, Lucien Edmond?"

"No, Ramón, Emataba told me last year that there were several other reservations. Many of them are located near the fort so that the soldiers can supervise them easily and make sure the braves don't go on the warpath again." Lucien Edmond uttered a bitter little laugh. "I really don't think there is any danger of that. A generation ago, their spirit was broken when they were removed forcibly from the land of their birth and sent to this region, where it is cold in winter. Here the buffalo are already diminishing, because of the railroads and their slaughter by white hunters to provide food for the railroad workers. Joseph McCoy told me at Abilene that he himself shipped hundreds of buffalo to Chicago, where they were slaughtered and sold at the butcher shops, just as one sells steaks and roasts from our good Texas cattle. No, Ramón, all they have left are their bows and arrows and perhaps their lances. Their young men are growing older and dying off from lack of proper food, diseases which the white men spread among them, and, worst of all, from the despair of seeing their proud people treated like mangy curs one seeks to kick away and forget."

Lucien Edmond laughed bitterly again, then shrugged and smiled. "For tonight, at any rate, we shall give them a feast, and we shall make them feel that we respect what they once were and might now be if only men had learned to live together like brothers. I think Friar Bartoloméo will have great compassion for them, even though only a few of them know the Christian faith. I have told him the history of the Creeks and about my father and my great-grandfather, Lucien Bouchard, and he understands that in their way and in their method of worship, they, too, were taught there was one all-powerful God. Come now, choose your vaqueros and I'll go find Friar Bartoloméo."

Already the lowing of the cattle and the sounds of the vaqueros herding them had drawn the attention of the old men, women, and children in the village, and they were flocking toward the gate. As Lucien Edmond and Friar Bartoloméo approached it, they saw a tall, middle-aged brave emerge from the nearest and largest tepee. He was wrapped in a ceremonial blanket and he wore a feather headdress which proclaimed him *mico* of the tribe.

"We have come back again, Emataba," Lucien Edmond cheerfully called. "Will you allow your people to open the gate so we may drive in the cattle I have brought for you as a gift, to feed the old ones and the children?"

"I remember you well. You are Lucien Edmond Bouchard. Yes, since we met last year, I have thought often upon our meeting and of what you told me of your father and your great-grandfather, who lived with our people far to the south when the Creeks were strong and proud. I will open the gate, and you shall see for yourself how weak and poor we have become since the last time we met."

At his sign, the men, women, and children respectfully drew back, and he opened the gate and swung it far to the other side. Ramón, along with the other vaqueros, led the bull, the heifers, cows, and steers to the far end of the village, where there was a crudely contrived corral.

"This is Friar Bartoloméo Alicante, Emataba." Lucien Edmond gestured toward the smiling Franciscan. "He came from Santa Fe where the white-eyes drove him out because he showed too much kindness toward the Pueblo Indians. He has lived with other Indian tribes, though I do not think he speaks Creek."

"No, my son," Friar Bartoloméo shook his head, "but I know other Indian tongues and I am sure that if Emataba will let me spend a little time with one of his young braves who speaks English well, I shall learn enough to make myself understood. I know something of the history of the Creeks, and I have always admired them."

"Then you are more than welcome. You are a man of the white-eyes church, I can tell this from the crucifix you wear around your neck and your brown robe." Emataba extended his hand and the Franciscan friar heartily shook it.

"I'm in the service of Him whose children you are, as are all these men with whom I have come on the way to Abilene, Emataba," the friar gently replied.

"The last time the soldiers were here to bring our supplies, many weeks before your coming, they brought with them a man they called a minister. He spoke to us and told us of his God. Is He different from yours, Friar Bartoloméo?" Emataba led the two men to his tepee and motioned to them to enter.

They seated themselves, and Friar Bartoloméo gently shook his head. "He is no different from my God or yours, or those of the Navajo, the Apache, the Kiowa, and the Comanche. They give Him different names, it is true, and they worship Him in different ways, but He is all-knowing, all-powerful."

"Our God is called Ibofanaga, the Giver of Breath."

"And that is true also, for God created the world and

160

then made Adam and Eve in His own image. But who is to say that He did not also make men whose skins are red and black and brown and yellow? And when you lift your prayers to Him whom you call Ibofanaga, they are heard by Him as He hears mine and Lucien Edmond's and those of all good men."

"And so, all of us throughout the nation are brothers if this is so," Emataba mused aloud.

"Exactly, my son. Alas, it is only that men of little vision do not understand this universal truth. That is why we have wars—and bigotry, prejudice, suspicion, and hatred of one's neighbors—if they are different from us. But He did not plan the world that way."

"Yet when we pray to Him, our Ibofanaga, who you say is akin to your own God, why does He not take us out of this prison and give us back the good rich land where once we lived and raised our families?"

Friar Bartoloméo Alicante sighed deeply. "My son, you ask a question that men everywhere have always asked of Him. Why must good men die soon and evil ones persist in their wickedness? Why does He not restore you, and all the conquered peoples of the past, to what they once were? Yes, you may well ask that, and even a simple priest like myself has asked it in the stillness of the night. His ways are not always understood, and sometimes they may seem harsh to us who cannot understand. But believe this, Emataba, He who is almighty knows what wrongs were done to your people, just as He knows how many innocent and well-meaning people died by the persecution of others who believed themselves the chosen ones of God. I say to you, Emataba, that even though now you and your people are forgotten and given little food and little hope, He has not forgotten you. It may well be that one of your young braves will learn the ways of the white man and will come to honor. Then he may tell all his white neighbors of his proud Creek heritage. And perhaps this is the will of God."

Emataba sighed and shook his head. "You are a good man, Friar Bartoloméo. I understand what you tell me, but it does not give much comfort to my young men, who feel themselves prisoners in chains behind this wooden fence the white men have put up. Yes, the fence is old and falling down, and we can easily break through it. But then they would send soldiers to kill many of us and punish others. The old ones are resigned to their death. Indeed," he turned to Lucien Edmond, "since you visited us last year there are twenty-two names we no longer speak at our council fires. Most of them were old ones, it is true, but there were three young braves who sickened and had no will to live."

"That is why I have brought you a good bull and several heifers, so that you may breed cattle and have meat enough for those who need it most, Emataba. The cows will give milk for the children, and the steers can be killed for the good red meat that will nourish all of you," Lucien Edmond replied.

"I have no way of repaying you, my white brother, but my people will never forget your kindness. Nor will Ibofanaga, when he comes to judge us all," the tall *mico* gravely declared.

"There again you see proof that we all worship the same dear God," Friar Bartoloméo interposed. "We, too, Emataba, believe in the day of judgment, at which all who have ever lived upon this earth shall stand before Him, to await His pronouncement upon us. Then, Emataba, all wrongs will be righted, and those sinners who are not redeemed will be weighed in the balance and found wanting. That is what I believe, and it is this final justice which cheers me when I weep now for those who are wronged and oppressed. For our lives are but a tiny day in the eternal cycle of His vigilance over us. And this is why you must believe with all your heart that, in that final moment, the valor and goodness of your people will be known for what it was."

"There is wisdom in your words, and they give me new hope." Emataba rose, and Friar Bartoloméo and Lucien Edmond followed his example. "Will you and your men not eat the evening meal with us? It will be a good thing for my people to know that white men still think of us with kindness and bring us food when we are hungry."

"Willingly, Emataba," Lucien Edmond responded. "I have asked my cook to prepare extra food, so that there will be enough for everyone in your village. I shall have some of my men bring it in, and we shall have a fine supper to celebrate our meeting again."

"How many people are there in your village, Emataba?" Friar Bartoloméo asked.

"There are now about three hundred. And many of these will not be here if you come this way next year. They are old and tired, and the winter winds are cold and cruel to their weary bones."

"I have carried extra blankets in my wagons, Emataba, and my men will bring them to you, so that you may give them to those most in need," Lucien Edmond commented.

As the tall *mico* strode into the clearing before his tepee, a crowd of Creek villagers awaited him. There were women carrying their papooses on their backs in buffalo-hide slings, little children clinging to their mothers' doeskin skirts, wizened old men and women who stared curiously as the Franciscan friar and blond Lucien Edmond emerged.

Emataba raised his hand and spoke quickly in the Creek tongue. A murmur of pleasure and surprise rose from the crowd. Then they began to talk among themselves, some pointing at the friar and Lucien Edmond, as they made way for the two men.

Half an hour later, several of the vaqueros had carried the extra food, which Pablo Casares had prepared, into the reservation, along with stacks of blankets and several heavy bedrolls that Lucien Edmond had loaded in the supply wagons before he left Windhaven Range.

At Lucien Edmond's suggestion, the vaqueros took turns in sharing the feast, several of them eating with the friar and the young trail boss, while the others remained outside to keep watch over the resting herd. Then, in turn, those who had eaten went back to the cattle while others took their places, until all the vaqueros had entered the Creek village and met the grateful inhabitants.

Friar Bartoloméo blessed the food, and when he had finished his prayer, Emataba turned to Lucien Edmond and murmured, "Our old shaman, Equitaba, is still alive. Do you recall how he cast the sacred bones last year and foretold what would be for you?"

"I remember it well, and all of it came true, Emataba."

"That is good! I have had food sent to him, and when we have finished, after he has rested, he will throw the bones again. You will tell him what you have just said to me, and it will gladden him."

"I am eager to see him again, my brother," Lucien Edmond murmured back.

When they had finished eating and the vaqueros had returned to their posts outside the Creek village, Lucien Edmond turned to Friar Bartoloméo and said, "I ask your indulgence, Father. You know that I am a good Catholic, and yet, like all men, I am anxious about the future. What this blind old man read in the bones of animals last year, when I came to this village, foretold what happened so exactly that I could not explain it. Do not think that it's sacrilegious of me to wish to hear his words again."

Friar Bartoloméo shook his head. "I do not look upon it as sacrilege, my son. If it is true, as I steadfastly believe, that this Creek Ibofanaga is but another name for Him whom all of us venerate, then surely this shaman or *windigo,* the blessed man of every Indian tribe and its prophet, may stand in the same relation to them as I do as priest to my flock. I, too, am eager to hear his words."

Lucien Edmond pressed the hand of the smiling friar between his own and nodded to Emataba.

The hour had grown late. Even the young braves had gone back to their tepees and wigwams with the old people, and now only the *mico,* Ramón Hernandez, Lucien Edmond, and Friar Bartoloméo sat before the largest campfire, which had been lighted near the tepee of the *mico.* Emataba rose and walked slowly to a nearby tepee, bowed low before the opening, and said in the Creek tongue, "Come forth, wise old man of our tribe. Here, again, is our white brother for whom you cast the sacred bones a dozen full moons ago."

After a moment, there emerged a feeble, emaciated old man in his late seventies. His sparse hair was white, and his face wrinkled, yet he still carried himself with an air of profound dignity. He wore a cape of buffalo hide, the great horns of the bull being attached to a band encircling his forehead. In his bony, trembling hands he held a pouch made from the skin of a coyote. He stood for a moment, his face turned toward the fire, and then he said in a thin, cracked voice, "I remember the white-eyes who came to us last summer. Let him come before me, that I may read his face again."

"He walks the straight path as before, Equitaba," the *mico* replied. "He has brought food and blankets to our people; he has feasted with us, and he and his men have smoked the calumet of peace."

"I rejoice to hear this, O my *mico*. The friends of the once mighty Creeks are few indeed, and so the more to be valued. Let him come before me."

At these words, Lucien Edmond approached the blind old shaman, standing with his arms at his sides, and said in the Creek tongue, "I stand before you, Equitaba."

Slowly the old man extended his bony right hand to touch Lucien Edmond's face, his fingers tracing the forehead, the cheeks, chin and nose and lips. And last, as he had done before, with the delicateness of a feather, he touched Lucien Edmond's eyelids with his fingertips. "Yes, I see him again as I did then, stronger than before and wiser, too. He is truly our friend. For him I will cast the sacred bones."

Emataba hastened to the old man and gently helped him seat himself upon the ground, then carefully untied the rawhide drawstrings of the pouch and placed it between Equitaba's hands.

Lifting the pouch to the dark sky, Equitaba shook it three times, then cast it before him. The bones were those of an owl, a deer, and a coyote. Then, as all the others watched in spellbound silence, he groped toward them with his trembling fingers, to learn their position, patting each to ascertain its shape and the animal from which it came.

At last, lifting his blind face to the sky, he declared, "Now I remember what I foretold to this strong, straight-tongued white-eyes. Tell me, was it as I foretold?"

"It was, Equitaba." Lucien Edmond could not keep his voice from quivering with emotion. "All was as you foretold."

"Then hear me again, friend of the Creeks. Before you came to us, there was danger for your loved ones, yet you knew it not. It has passed. It is no more."

Lucien Edmond looked wonderingly at Ramón, who shook his head.

"Before you reach the end of this journey, there will be much danger from an enemy you do not expect. Be watchful; you will overcome it."

"I thank Equitaba for his warning," Lucien Edmond replied in Creek.

"The bones say more. They say that not long from this night, before the year is done and I go to the summons of Ibofanaga, you will be brought into a great peril which will touch one who is near and dear to you—and yet it, too, will pass without sorrow or death to any of you."

Once again Lucien Edmond and Ramón exchanged glances, as the old shaman lifted his right hand and intoned, "I see also that there will be others who will come to fight over the land from which these cattle come. Blood will be shed, but not yours, and you will hold your land and destroy the evil ones. And last, I see that there will be sorrow and death to yet another loved one, whose blood is like your own and who dwells far to the east of you. Yet this sorrow and this death will unite your blood with that of the Creeks. Once, long ago, there was such a bond of blood—do I speak the truth?"

"Lucien and Dimarte—yes, that is true!" Lucien Edmond exclaimed. "Yet how can it be?"

"That I do not know, white-eyes, friend of the Creeks, but the bones say it will be as I have said. And they say no more. I am tired now . . . I would sleep."

As the tall *mico* hurried toward the old man, Lucien Edmond helped him to lift Equitaba and gently led him back to his tepee, easing him down on the tattered blanket that served as his bed. Then, beckoning to Ramón, who had come forward with a thick new blanket, he gently covered the old man with it and murmured, "May my God and yours, your Ibofanaga, grant that there will always be friendship and understanding between us. Sleep well, wise shaman. My great-grandfather Lucien Bouchard respected the shaman of the Creeks of Econchate, and I, Lucien Edmond, descendant of his blood, respect you equally."

166

CHAPTER SEVENTEEN

By dawn the next morning Pablo Casares had already begun his preparations for breakfast, and the vaqueros, who smelled the aroma of strong coffee and bacon, had lined up before the chuck wagon. Lucien Edmond and Ramón had slept in their bedrolls outside the tepee of Emataba, and Friar Bartoloméo had slept on the other side of it. When Lucien Edmond and Ramón rose and packed their bedrolls, he was already up and waiting for them.

"My sons, if you've no objection, I should like to stay here with Emataba and his people. Then, after you've sold your cattle in Abilene, I shall return with you to bless the chapel which your men have built."

"I had hoped you would decide to stay with the Creeks for a time, Friar Bartoloméo," Lucien Edmond replied. "It would be a great comfort to them."

"And to me, also, my son," Friar Bartoloméo responded. "Even from the few hours I have spent in this village, I can see sickness of the flesh and of the spirit. The former can be healed with proper care and good food. The latter demands a will to live. From all you have told me about the Creeks, they have great courage. But when a man's freedom is taken away, even that courage is sorely tested. I will do what I can for them."

"If there were more men like you, Father, the Indians would not be herded like wild animals and penned up in an isolated prison such as this," Lucien Edmond declared indignantly. "It's a pity they can't go across the border into Mexico, where the Comanche chief, Sangrodo, dwells."

The Franciscan friar smiled and patted Lucien Edmond's shoulder. "My son, you would have made a good priest, but I fear that you would have been an outcast, like myself."

"Of course you are right, Friar Bartoloméo. Well then, I'll bid you farewell until we return. I cannot thank you enough for the spiritual comfort you have given to me, as well as to my vaqueros." With this, Lucien Edmond extended his hand. Friar Bartoloméo Alicante grasped it and shook it energetically.

"Go with God, my son. May you and your men have a safe and speedy journey. I promise you that by the time you return, I shall have learned enough of the Creek language to make myself understood, even to the children." With this, he made the sign of the cross over Lucien Edmond's bowed head.

Ramón Hernandez then took his leave of the Franciscan friar. "Padre, it has meant much to me to ride along with you," the young Mexican declared. "You have made all of us better men, and I speak for my *compañeros* when I thank you."

"You give me too much credit, my son. They are better men because they have within themselves that which makes them so. As for myself, I have profited from their companionship, and it is I who am the better man, through their friendship. Go with God, my son. I will pray for your wife and your little son, that you may return safely to them."

"*Gracias*, padre." Ramón bowed his head as the friar made the sign of the cross. Then, extending his hand, he added with a boyish smile, "All of us think that if you had not been a priest, padre, you would have made a *muy gran* vaquero."

Friar Bartoloméo Alicante burst into hearty laughter and shook his head. "Now that, my son, is the greatest compliment you and your men could have paid me. But to be a *gran* vaquero, I should have to shed much more weight than I have already done. You will see if they think as much when I ride back with you, after you have sold your cattle in Abilene. And I shall pray that your *patrón* will be given the just reward for his labors. *Vaya con Dios*, my son."

"And you, padre," Ramón said softly as he again shook the friar's hand.

168

Emataba and several of the younger braves had come to the gate to see Lucien Edmond and his men off. Luke's blond son mounted his gelding and turned to wave to the middle-aged *mico*, who returned it with a warm smile. Simata rode ahead as scout. Lucien Edmond followed and the point riders called out encouragement to the lead steers. Corregidor, having forgotten his earlier panic, ambled forward, his heavy body swinging from side to side in the inimitable gait of the Texas longhorn. Gradually the long, winding procession resumed. Clouds of dust rose behind them. Pablo Casares waved from the back of the chuck wagon to the friendly Creeks.

When they had disappeared from sight, his homely face broke into a grin as he contemplated the superb gray stallion that Ramón had captured, broken in and given to him as a gift. Since that time, the middle-aged vaquero had spent at least an hour every morning riding his new mount. By now, the stallion whinnied in recognition whenever it heard Pablo's voice.

"I will not call you Gray Devil any longer, amigo." He grinned at the stallion, which trotted docilely behind the chuck wagon, its reins tethered to a peg. "I must find a better name for you. We are friends now, and I am not so lonely. What should it be? Ah, I have it—*Fuerza Torda*— Gray Strength. You are gray and you are the strongest horse I have ever seen or ridden ¿comprende? Yes, even stronger than the black horse my own father gave me when I was a young man. Do you like your new name, amigo?"

The gray stallion tossed its head and whinnied, and Pablo Casares burst into delighted laughter. "*Bueno*, then that is what I shall call you from now on. After lunch, if Señor Lucien Edmond gives us a little time to rest, you and I will ride together again. And I will give you some sugar. Now, that is enough talking. I must get back to the driver's seat or the horses pulling this wagon may go off the trail and get us all lost. ¡Adios, Fuerza Torda, amigo!"

As twilight approached that day, Lucien Edmond conferred with Ramón and Lucas as they made their campfires and prepared for the evening meal.

"Ramón, you heard the words of the Creek shaman.

You remember, also, how his prophecies came true last year—about the child my wife Maxine would bear."

"Yes, Lucien Edmond, I remember. And he spoke again of a danger that threatened your loved ones which was already past. I have been asking myself if it could have had something to do with those two men we saw galloping south, soon after we started the drive."

"It may well be, Ramón. But if there were only two men, they could hardly attack our ranch by themselves. We can only pray that Equitaba's words are true, when he says that whatever danger there might have been has passed already. What concerns me most is his warning that we will be in danger before this journey ends."

"That must mean we will be attacked before we reach Abilene, Lucien Edmond."

"Yes, either by rustlers or bushwhackers. I'm sure it wouldn't be Indians. I know that Sangrodo's word has reached all of the tribes in Texas and that they respect it and know we are their friends."

"Then perhaps we should tell the vaqueros to make sure their guns are loaded and ready for action, and double the night guard. Indians might not attack at night, but rustlers and bushwhackers would choose that time above all others, thinking we were sleeping and off guard."

"You're right, Ramón. Lucas, pass the word among the men to make sure they have enough ammunition and that their rifles and six-shooters are fully loaded. Tell them that I want three times the normal number of men on guard tonight and every night until we reach Abilene. They can easily arrange their shifts so that no one loses too much sleep. We've been very lucky so far. I don't want to lose any men if I can possibly help it. And we'll do our best to keep the herd intact. With any luck, we should be in Abilene in two weeks, or three at the very most."

Lucas nodded. "I'll tell the men right away, Mr. Bouchard."

The Bouchard cattle drive had been delayed for two days by a sudden dust storm, which had been followed by a brief but violent thunderstorm. The men had had to round up fully five hundred stampeding cattle, but had

170

recovered virtually all of them. They were within thirty miles of Abilene now, and as the scorching sun began to sink in the west, Simata rode back, having located a good campsite for the night. It was a slightly elevated, broad, flat ledge to the northeast, with a good vantage point from which to watch in all directions in case of attack.

"Another two days and we'll be in Abilene. I'm surprised Joseph McCoy hasn't sent out a rider to meet us," Lucien Edmond worried.

"Mr. Sugg met us last year and told us that the market was waiting for our cattle," Ramón agreed.

"Perhaps there are other ranchers who are driving their herds to Abilene and McCoy's riders found them first. Or maybe they took a different trail," Simata suggested.

"Perhaps that's it." Lucien Edmond shrugged philosophically. "Remember last year, we didn't get to Abilene until September. And it's only June now."

"So far, the words of the Creek shaman have not come to pass," Ramón remarked.

"We haven't reached Abilene yet. We won't relax our vigilance, not for a moment, not until I get the gold to pay the vaqueros and the bank draft, Ramón. I'll stand duty myself tonight."

Lucien Edmond drew his Spencer rifle out of its scabbard, inspected and loaded it, then went off to the chuck wagon to get his supper.

It was Benito Aguilar's turn to serenade the drowsy herd with his battered guitar. He walked along the rows of cattle, strumming gentle chords, calling softly to them. Their peaceful lowing made him nod with satisfaction. *"Muy bueno,"* he said aloud. "You have given us a little trouble, amigos, but not too much. Ah, there you are, Corregidor. A disappointment awaits you, I'm afraid. No, you will not ride back in state this time, *pobrecito.* If you had not chased after the buffalo, you would have had another year of life, another chance to lead us back to this town where Señor Bouchard gets us the *dinero* we have earned by guarding you. Yes, Corregidor, we must say adiós when we reach Abilene. But it was a good life while it lasted, *¿no es verdad?"*

He had reached the head of the herd, and there was no vaquero within a hundred yards of him. The moon was hidden behind a cloud, and a soft but intense darkness had fallen on the sleeping camp. Just beyond him was a waist-high stretch of thick, green grass. As he turned to walk around to the other side, a lasso swept out and caught him around the throat. It was jerked tightly, viciously. Benito Aguilar dropped his guitar and clutched at his throat, his eyes bulging, fighting for breath. Another vicious jerk pulled his staggering body into the grass where a grinning, wiry half-breed crouched with two stocky cowboys who wore red bandannas wound around their mouths and noses. One of them, the leader, drew a hunting knife out of a leather scabbard and calmly dug it to the hilt in the vaquero's chest. Benito Aguilar kicked once, then lay still.

"Nice throw, Jasper," the man with the knife whispered to the half-breed. "Maybe you were born on the wrong side of an Injun blanket, but your white pappy sure taught you how to throw a lariat."

"My mother taught me how to cut the heart out of a white-eyes who called my father a squaw man, too, Mr. Reedy." The half-breed's eyes were dark and narrow with anger."

"Now, now, calm down, Jasper. No need to get touchy. See that herd? Three thousand head if I'm any judge. And it's all ours. Possession's nine points of the law when we drive 'em into Abilene. It was real smart of you to stash our horses in that canyon and have all the boys crawl on their bellies when we got close to this big herd."

"Indians have more brains than you give them credit for, Mr. Reedy," the half-breed whispered with a venomous look. "How many men have they got, do you figure?"

"Twenty, maybe twenty-five. I can see three guards from here and they've got Spencers. Well, we've got a couple ourselves. Crawl back and pass the word to the boys to be ready when I hoot like an owl three times. We'll come at 'em from this side. It'll stampede the cattle, but once we've killed their riders, we'll have all the time in the world to round up the herd and bring it into Abilene."

The half-breed began to crawl through the thick, tall, grass, to pass the leader's word on to the other ten members of the gang. Most of these men had come from Kansas, the rest from Missouri, and all of them were outlaws—army deserters, cattle rustlers, and murderers.

John Murriston crawled next to Jethro Reedy and whispered to him, "That's the biggest herd we've hit yet, Jethro. I hear they're paying nine dollars and over for prime cattle. We'll be able to take it easy after this one, I'm thinking."

"Maybe," the gang leader whispered in reply. "But that fellow McCoy might get the wind up this time. Last year you had two herds and different brands. Damned good thing you thought of faking those letters from the late owners of those herds, John."

Murriston, with more education than the other members of the gang, had posed as the owner of two herds after the Reedy gang murdered the ranchers and their men and driven their herds into Abilene.

"That's the value of an education, Jethro. But maybe this time we ought to try another market along the railroad."

"Could be. We can send the half-breed out to scout around and see if there's another place where they're buying cattle. First, though, we've got to get this herd."

"We will. Are you going to stampede it with gunshots and then charge?"

"Sure. At most, they'll have six riders standing night duty. We'll cut 'em down before they know what hit 'em, and the rest of our boys'll pick off the others as they wake up. It's nice 'n dark, John. That moon's doing us a favor, staying out of sight."

"Once we flush their guards, we can stay right here in the cover of the grass and pick them off as they come into range."

Jethro Reedy chuckled softly. "That's just the way I've got it figured, John. You and I will stay here, and the breed and the others will circle around to the left. Soon as I get Jasper's signal that the boys are ready, I'll start things off. There it is now . . ."

The soft hoot of an owl came faintly to his ears and he clapped his crony on the back. "There's a greaser comin' up to the head of the herd. Drop him, before he gets a chance to warn the others, and I'll get things under way."

With this, he cupped his left hand to his mouth and hooted three times. Then he raised his six-shooter above his head and fired.

Meanwhile, John Murriston took careful aim at the dark outline of a vaquero who was approaching the post which Benito Aguilar had occupied. Murriston squeezed the trigger, and his bullet grazed the shoulder of Sanchez Maderos. With a cry of alarm, Maderos dropped to one knee, leveled his Spencer carbine at the approximate area from which the bullet had come, and fired three times.

John Murriston uttered a strangled cry, stumbled to his feet, then sprawled on his face. One of the bullets had taken him through the cheek and come out from the back of his neck, a mortal wound.

Jethro Reedy fired two quick shots, but Sanchez Maderos, running in a zigzag pattern back toward his companions, was unhurt. As he ran, he bawled at the top of his voice, "*¡Cuidado, cuidado, guardarse de los ladrónes!*"

Jasper Harris and his dozen cronies, having heard their leader's signal, ran, crouching as they did so as to make themselves the most difficult possible targets. As they ran, they opened fire on the Bouchard camp from the eastern side. Lucien Edmond, who had been standing the first watch of the night with six vaqueros, knelt down at the side of one of the supply wagons, leveled his rifle, and fired repeatedly in the direction of the flashes of gunfire as he swung the barrel of his gun in a slow, searching arc. Screams of pain from two of the bushwhackers announced that at least some of his bullets had reached their mark. The half-breed went down with a wound in the groin, and lanky Caleb Masters, a Missouri horse thief and murderer, fell dead with a bullet in his heart.

Pablo Casares, hearing the first shots, seized his own carbine and leaped from the chuck wagon, sheltering himself behind one of the heavy wheels.

The cattle had begun to stir restlessly, even at the first hoot. Now they were in full flight, stampeding wildly in every direction as volleys of rifle fire filled the air. Ramón Hernandez, making sure that the *remuda* horses were securely hobbled, crawled under one of the wagons and, lying on his belly, kept his carbine ready to pick off any bushwhackers who came within range.

Jethro Reedy, having discovered that John Murriston was dead, swore under his breath and crawled over to where Benito Aguilar had dropped his rifle. He reached it just as Lucas, who had climbed on top of a wagon and stretched himself out lengthwise on the heavy canvas top, noticed his shadowy figure crawling toward the weapon. Carefully, Lucas took aim, then squeezed the trigger. Reedy screamed as the bullet broke his collarbone. He dropped the rifle and tried to run back to the cover of the thick grass. Once again Lucas took careful aim, and, as his second shot rang out, Reedy stiffened, his head bowed, then toppled to the ground.

"Never mind about the cattle, we'll round them up when we've beaten off the attack," Lucien Edmond called to Miguel Dondaro and Vittorio Salancár, who were about to mount their horses and ride after the fleeing cattle. "Get down off those horses, they'll pick you off like sitting ducks on a pond!" Even as he spoke, the whine of a rifle bullet, much too close for comfort, made Miguel Dondaro gasp and then, slapping his gelding on the rump, scurry for cover behind the wheels of one of the wagons.

But Vittorio Salancár was not quite so lucky. As he left his gelding, slapping it on the rump to drive it away, there was the sound of a rifle shot. Pablo's friend lifted his arms as if imploring a benediction, then fell backward and lay still. Lucas, having seen the flash of the rifle, swiftly shouldered his carbine and fired twice. There was a howl of agony as the unseen bushwhacker dropped his rifle, clutched at his belly, and rolled over and over, thrashing convulsively in his death throes.

The ten remaining bushwhackers had flanked the camp and moved stealthily toward the *remuda* and the chuck wagon at the very rear. Pablo Casares warily climbed out toward the driver's seat of the wagon, a six-shooter in each hand. He saw a dark shadow detach itself from the thick grass and move toward the whinnying *remuda* horses. Squinting down the barrel of his right-hand gun, he fired. The shadowlike figure halted, staggered back, and Pablo fired the gun in his other hand with deadly effect.

Ramón began to crawl forward on his belly just as two of the raiders broke from their hiding place and ran toward the *remuda*, intent on scattering the Bouchard horses. Swiftly sighting along the barrel of his Spencer, he brought one of them down with a clean shot through the head, just as the latter's companion turned to crouch and fire a Henry rifle at him. The bullet thudded against the wagon wheel a few inches away from Ramón. Before the bushwhacker could reload, the young Mexican had straightened and begun to run toward the attacker. At the same instant as the man shoved the cartridge into the breech and prepared to turn and fire, Ramón, wielding his useless Spencer like a club, smashed the butt against the bushwhacker's forehead and felled him without a sound.

Instinctively, the Mexican flung himself flat as a ragged volley of shots rang out. Pablo Casares emptied both his six-shooters at the flashes of gunfire in the humid night, and the youngest member of the gang, a nineteen-year-old horse thief, doubled up, both hands clamped to his belly, while calling hysterically for his mother with his dying breath. His older brother, who, at the age of twenty-three, boasted a dozen notches on the butt of his Starr .44, swore vehemently, dropped to one knee, and aimed his rifle at the chuck wagon. Before he could fire, the last bullet in Pablo Casares's right-hand six-shooter caught him squarely in the center of the forehead and he rolled over, an arm flung across his brother's body.

A middle-aged desperado with a price on his head for the robbery of a Sedalia bank and the cold-blooded murder of two of its clerks, whispered hoarsely to his four surviving companions, "Christ, they've about wiped us out, boys. We better get outa here. No chance to get that herd. They've got too much firepower."

"Let's get back to the horses. They must've got Jethro and John. Haven't heard any firing from their side since we started," muttered his fellow gunman, a short, red-haired man who was wanted for murder and horse stealing. "Let's get the hell out of here while we still can. See that coon on top of that wagon? Bet he's the one who's been picking off our buddies. I'll get that nigger son of a bitch if it's the last thing I do!"

He rose from his hiding place in the thick grass, leveled his rifle, and squeezed the trigger. Lucas uttered an agonized cry as the bullet tore through the fleshy part of his left arm but, seeing the powder flash, returned the fire. The gunman pitched backward into the grass without a word, a bloody hole in the center of his forehead.

The bushwhackers had had enough. The survivors turned and ran, bent over in the thick grass to hide from the marksmanship of the Bouchard riders.

Lucien Edmond had called to his men to hold their fire, since there had been no sound of attack since the last shot at Lucas. At his whispered instructions, Ramón Hernandez nodded; then he climbed into one of the supply wagons and improvised a torch by taking a cattle prod, wrapping torn strips of blanket around one end, and then touching a lucifer to the material. Cautiously, gripping the torch in his left hand and extending his arm from the wagon, the young Mexican brandished the glowing flare. But there was no answering volley from the thick grass, and now the moon had emerged to light up the scene.

"I think they've gone, Lucien Edmond," Ramón called.

"Señor, I've found one of these *ladrónes*, and he's still alive!" Manuel Rodriguez reported as, carbine in hand, he advanced slowly into the waist-high grass on the eastern side of the camp.

Lucien Edmond and Simata hurried toward the veteran vaquero, their Spencers cocked and ready. Lucas, still lying atop the wagon, gritting his teeth, had ripped off part of his shirt and was tying as tight a knot as he could just above the wound in his arm to serve as a tourniquet. Seeing the two men advance into the grass, he covered them with his carbine, his face contorted with pain and damp with sweat.

The half-breed, Jasper Harris, his hands trying to staunch the flow of blood from his wound, writhed and moaned as Simata and Lucien Edmond came up and stood beside Manuel Rodriguez. Rodriguez had already kicked away Harris's gun and pressed the muzzle of his own against the outlaw's chest, his face grim and vindictive. "Let me kill him, *patrón*. Such scum does not deserve to live," he growled.

"No, Manuel." Lucien Edmond shook his head. "We'll do what we can for him and take him into Abilene. A bush-

whacker like this is sure to be wanted by the authorities."
Then he turned to Simata. "Do what you can to bandage
the wound. He's lost a good deal of blood."

"I—I'd rather die—this—this way—you, you bastards," the
half-breed gasped. Then he tilted back his head, his teeth
bared in a rictus of intolerable agony, and emitted a piercing scream as a spasm of pain gripped him. Simata had
hurried back to the camp and taken a worn blanket from
the bedroll of one of the vaqueros. As he returned to kneel
beside the wounded half-breed, Jasper Harris gasped, "I
can't move—I'm done for—anyhow. I'd rather go this way
than with the rope—you bastards—if we'd had more guns
like yours, it'd have been different—goddamn you all to
hell, you lousy white-eyes—"

His head rose, his eyes glared in a last moment of defiance, and then he slumped to the ground.

"Perhaps it's just as well," Lucien Edmond declared.
"Now, let's see to our own men, Ramón."

But a sobbing cry had already drawn their attention
back toward the camp. Pablo Casares, seeing that the danger was past, had hurried from the chuck wagon and
come upon the body of his beloved friend, Vittorio Salancár. Kneeling, tears running down his weatherbeaten
cheeks, the middle-aged vaquero cradled his friend's head
in both of his trembling hands while he wept unashamedly.

They buried Benito Aguilar and Vittorio Salancár, while
Simata bandaged the wounds Lucas and Sanchez Maderos had sustained. Then the vaqueros, led by Ramón
and Lucien Edmond, mounted their horses and rode after
the stampeded herd.

This time, Pablo Casares insisted on accompanying
them. "You don't need a cook right now, Señor Bouchard.
You've lost one of the best vaqueros I ever knew, and I
ask only to take his place. You need every man for this
work. ¿Por favor?"

Lucien Edmond, tears welling up in his eyes, could only
nod and shake Pablo's hand in wordless compassion.

CHAPTER EIGHTEEN

It took three days and nights to round up the herd and move the frightened, exhausted cattle back into the procession to Abilene. When it was finally done, Lucas and Ramón made a hasty tally to determine their losses. The total herd now numbered 3,063, and thus, taking into consideration the ones lost to the buffalo herd and those given to the Creeks, it was estimated that 137 head had disappeared in the stampede.

Lucien Edmond decided to give his men an extra day of rest, for the harrowing attack by the bushwhackers and the grueling roundup had exhausted them. Moreover, a grief-stricken pall had settled over them because of the loss of Benito Aguilar and Vittorio Salancár. Pablo Casares was grim and silent. His face was drawn and haggard as he prepared the meals. The vaqueros did not try to cheer him with their usual banter, deeply sympathizing with his grief and having their own to sober them as well. Simata volunteered to leave after supper on their day of rest to ride ahead to Abilene, locate Joseph McCoy, and inform him that the Bouchard herd would arrive within two days.

Two days later the Indian scout returned to the drive, and his excited demeanor warmed Lucien Edmond's heart.

"The town has grown, Mr. Bouchard. The Drover's Cottage is open for business now, and there's another hotel besides, a couple of boardinghouses and four saloons. Ours will be the second herd to get there this season, Mr. McCoy told me. He said he expected to have as many as 150,000 head of cattle go through his pens this year. He's even had to wire east for more cars in order to handle the cattle load he's expecting."

"That's good news indeed, Simata. One more thing—

were you able to find out anything about the prices for cattle?"

"Yes, Mr. Bouchard. The buyer from Armour is already there—he bought the first herd, and he remembers you from last year. He says that if it's in prime condition, he's willing to go as high as $8.75 a head."

"Well," Lucien Edmond chuckled, "when he sees the crossbreeding I've done and the condition of the cattle, I think I can persuade him to up that price just a little. Our men deserve a bonus for the hardships they've suffered, and I mean to see that they get it. Good work, Simata. Now, go on over to the chuck wagon and ask Pablo to get you something to eat."

Late in the afternoon of June 21, 1869, Lucien Edmond Bouchard and his men drove their cattle down the dusty main street of Abilene and into the cattle pens that awaited them. As he rode at the head of the line, Lucien Edmond noticed a ramshackle livery stable on the western edge of the town and commented, "I think we'll spend two or three days here before heading back, Ramón. It might be a good idea to stable those mustangs and perhaps some of the overworked horses of the *remuda*, to freshen them up for the return journey."

"That's a good idea, Lucien Edmond. You know, poor Pablo is still mourning Vittorio. He doesn't even take any pleasure in riding Fuerza Torda. He's so terribly sad, and I'm worried about him."

"So am I, Ramón," Lucien Edmond admitted. "And I don't think any entertainment there may be in Abilene will cheer him up, either. He's not a drinking man, so I don't expect he'll waste his time in any of those four saloons."

"No, but many of the vaqueros will. Simata's already told them there are girls in some of them."

"I can imagine." Lucien Edmond frowned. "Well, I'm certainly not going to deny them the pleasure they've earned after this long, hard drive, but I hope you'll keep an eye on things and try to make sure they don't get robbed or drawn into a fight over those barroom butter-flies. You almost got killed in the saloon last year, and there weren't even any girls present. I don't want our men to risk their lives in a saloon brawl."

"I'll go with them, don't worry, Lucien Edmond. But

they're proud men, and they don't like to be insulted, as I was," Ramón replied with quiet dignity.

"I intend to help win respect for all our men, Ramón. I'll back them up if there's a showdown."

Ramón grinned. "Now you're talking like a real trail boss."

Ramón and Lucien Edmond made their way to the small frame building where the eastern and midwestern cattle buyers did business. It was only a few yards away from the cattle pens. As they approached, Lucien Edmond remarked, "Last year we had a few over twenty-six hundred head, and we lost two hundred and thirty-five. Now we've got close to thirty-one hundred, and we lost nearly as many. I'd say that's a fairly good average. The higher price this year will make up for our losses. Also, it took us about four months to get here last year, and this year we cut about ten or twelve days from that. We'd have done even better if it hadn't been for the stampedes. I think that the stamina of our cattle, due to the crossbreeding, is beginning to pay off."

"In spite of what we lost, most of the herd is in prime condition. There was plenty of good grazing, even though we did come to the best grazing land about two months ahead of last year's schedule."

"I'm glad we made the drive earlier, Ramón. It'll give us time to get those Brahmas and start early this fall in the sort of crossbreeding that will give us a really fine herd eventually. We can't rely any longer on mavericks and the wild longhorns we brushpop. The best cattle ranchers are going to be those who plan ahead, and I mean to be one of them."

Joseph McCoy came out of his office, looking the same as he had the year before. He wore rough, unblackened boots, a slouch hat, and wrinkled clothes. "Well, Mr. Bouchard, it's good to see you back again. That's a fine herd you've just let into my pens. I think you'll do a little better this year, money-wise. Have any trouble on the drive?"

"An attack by bushwhackers about thirty miles from here. The cattle were stampeded, or we'd have arrived at least four days ago."

Joseph McCoy scowled. "I've got my own suspicions

who that gang might be. Did you catch any of them alive?"

"There was only one survivor—a half-breed—and he died before we could get him to Abilene."

"A half-breed, eh? Wouldn't be surprised if that were Jasper Harris. That would be the Reedy gang. They had a slick-talking, well-educated fellow who acted as agent for some herds which we found out later were bush-whacked. You've done the state of Kansas a real service if you beat them off. I hope you killed them all."

"Including the half-breed, Mr. McCoy, there were eleven of them who didn't make it back to their horses," Lucien Edmond replied.

"Then you really smashed them for fair. Last I heard, they had about fifteen members—all of them with prices on their heads. By God, if we had a cattlemen's associa-tion with money in the bank, I'd vote you a reward for ridding the territory of those devils. Come on, now, Mr. Dade's waiting for you. As soon as he saw your cattle, he told me he'd stay up until midnight to do business with you."

Clapping Lucien Edmond on the back, Joseph McCoy led him to a little building where three buyers were wait-ing at a long table. Ed Dade, a genial, middle-aged man with a walrus mustache, rose and extended his hand. Lucien Edmond smiled as he shook it. "I'm glad to hear you're interested in my herd, Mr. Dade. You took all the cattle last year, and I hope you'll do the same this time."

"Not so fast there, Dade." A tall, gray-haired man spoke up. "You remember me, Mr. Bouchard. I'm Jack McCready, out of St. Louis. Last year I offered you top price on just a thousand head. This time, I might dicker with you for the whole herd. It's a fine lot you've brought in."

"Well, this is the sort of welcome a cattle rancher dreams about," Lucien Edmond chuckled. "I haven't made any advance decisions about to whom I'll sell my cattle, so long as I get the best possible price. And I expect it to be better than last year's."

"It is already. What about $8.75 a head, Mr. Bouchard?" Ed Dade proposed.

"I'll make it a dime more, but I reserve the privilege of cutting out the critters I don't fancy for my packing firm," Jack McCready countered.

"What do you say to that, Mr. Dade?" Lucien Edmond asked, turning to the Armour buyer.

Ed Dade took his gold watch out of his vest pocket and studied it with a scowl. He cleared his throat, glared at Jack McCready, and then responded, "Mr. Armour's instructed me to get as much top-quality beef as I can find, and I'm going to do just that. I'll take everything you've got and make it $8.90 a head. That suit you?"

"You've got a deal, Mr. Dade." Lucien Edmond shook the Chicago buyer's hand again.

"Have you written down your tally?" Ed Dade asked.

"Yes, sir. I have." Lucien Edmond took a folded slip of paper from his pocket and laid it on the table in front of the Chicago buyer. "I think it's accurate just about to the head, Mr. Dade. There's a total there of three thousand sixty-three."

Ed Dade scowled again, took out a pencil, and rapidly did some figuring. Looking up, he announced, "I make it $27,260.70, Mr. Bouchard. Last year you wanted enough of the price in gold to pay off your riders, and the rest in a draft. I imagine you'll want it the same way this year."

Lucien Edmond nodded. "Yes, Mr. Dade. And this year, I'm paying my riders forty dollars a month, with a hundred dollar bonus. We lost two men when we were bushwhacked just before we got here, so I've got a crew of twenty-seven."

"Let me do more figuring. You started out in March?"

Lucien Edmond again nodded. "I wanted to avoid the August and September heat and also get here before all the other ranchers with a good herd for you, Mr. Dade."

"Good thinking, Mr. Bouchard. From the looks of those cattle of yours—and I see some good Hereford breeding in them—you've had plenty of good grazing grass, even though you started early."

"Yes, and speaking of breeding, Mr. Dade, year after next I hope to bring you cattle that have been cross-bred with Brahmas. Then there won't be any worry about Texas fever."

183

"Yes, we know about that in Chicago. It sounds as if you know your business, Mr. Bouchard. Well now, back to these figures . . ." Once again Ed Dade concentrated on his figuring, then looked up. "I make it $4,320 in wages—that's at forty dollars a month for four months—times twenty-seven men, and another $2,700 dollars to take care of the bonus you promised them."

"That's the way I figure it, too, Mr. Dade."

"So you'll want $7,020 in cash—only I may have to give most of it to you in greenbacks this time. Northern money's coming out in greenbacks these days, but they're still as good as gold. In Abilene, the saloons and hotels will take the greenbacks just as gladly."

"Well, greenbacks don't weigh as much as all that gold would, so I'm agreeable," Lucien Edmond replied, laughing.

"Now, let's see," Ed Dade said, half to himself. "I'll give you $7,020, mostly in greenbacks and a little gold, and then a draft for $20,240.70. Is that satisfactory?"

"Indeed it is, Mr. Dade." Lucien Edmond's face shone with joy, for the price at which he had just agreed to sell his herd was about ten thousand dollars more than he had received the year before. Moreover, after deducting his losses from the stampedes, he had brought about four hundred more head of cattle to Abilene this year. But the key to this successful sale was the increase of nearly three dollars per head. No other fact could have so palpably convinced him of the wisdom of crossbreeding, proper feeding, and watering, to improve the quality of his cattle. The precept Luke had taught him, and which Luke, in turn, had been taught by old Lucien Bouchard, had served him well.

Joseph McCoy clapped him on the back again. "Hope you'll come back next year with an even bigger and better herd, Mr. Bouchard. Men like you justify all the hard work I put in to convince the Kansas Pacific they had a fortune here, if only they had the brains to realize it."

"I'm very much obliged to you, Mr. McCoy. By the way, I didn't meet your partner, Bill Sugg, on the trail this time."

"No, Bill took off for the Panhandle, because he heard there was a new rancher there who was doing pretty well.

Fact is, I'm expecting him and that herd here in about ten days. You know, I owe a lot to Bill. Right after the Civil War, when I was buying livestock for resale to the new packinghouses in Chicago, I found out from him that Baxter Springs was a nightmare for cattlemen. He'd bought a herd in Texas, driven it north, and then got it taken away from him when all those angry citizens and a band of bushwhackers started that business about Texas Fever contaminating Kansas and Missouri cattle. Some of those farmers even burned the grass, and a lot of swindlers bought herds with bad checks. Plenty of unsold cattle died—that was back in 1866."

"I'd heard of that. That's one reason we voted against trying Sedalia last year."

"Well, Mr. Bouchard, you have the right gut instinct. Bill knew about Sedalia that year, and that's why he tried Baxter Springs in '67. Well, after he told me what had happened, I figured we just had to have an open trail from the cattle country to a shipping point on the railroad. It's been my dream, and now it's coming true. There, I think Ed's got your draft written and he's counting the money and gold out of his cashbox. I've got rooms for you and your top hands at the Drover's Cottage. It's a pretty sight—remember when you came here last year, it hadn't been finished. But Abilene's been growing for sure!"

"Well, God willing, I'll be back next year, Mr. McCoy." Lucien Edmond turned back to the Chicago buyer and accepted the bank draft and a small box filled with greenbacks and gold coins. "Thank you, Mr. Dade. Not only on my behalf, but for all my men. I'll be able to tell them that their hard work paid off this year, and we'll all do better next year, mark my words."

"That's the spirit, Mr. Bouchard!" Ed Dade commented, rising from the table. "Well, how about some dinner? I'll stand treat. One of the boardinghouses has a Massachusetts farm woman running it who's the best cook anywhere in this country. Why Mrs. Talcott can take tough old steer beef and make it taste like a banquet."

"That's very kind of you, Mr. Dade. I'll be happy to accept your invitation." Lucien Edmond turned back to Joseph McCoy. "I'd like to put my vaqueros up at the boardinghouses if there's room for them."

185

"Plenty of room right now. You'll be staying a couple of days, I suppose?"

Lucien Edmond nodded. "Yes, a good two days. We had to chase cattle for about three days after the bushwhackers hit us. It came at the end of the drive, when my men were already tuckered out from all those weeks in the saddle."

"I'll take you over to the Drover's Cottage, Mr. Bouchard, but first you can put that draft in my safe."

"Yes. And now that Abilene's so much bigger than it was last year, I'm just wondering if we'll have any trouble. My top wrangler was drawn into that fight with Bud Larkin last year."

"That Mexican wrangler of yours was mighty handy with his carbine. Say, now that you've reminded me, did Larkin and his men come after you?"

"Yes, but we were lucky and beat them off. Just the same, I don't want to risk that again. We've already lost two good vaqueros and my men are still grieving for them."

"We'll have some law and order here in Abilene by next year, Mr. Bouchard. I'm working on it right now. Now, let me just slip this draft into my safe, then I'll show you what sort of accommodations we've got for good cattlemen like you."

Once installed in his room in the Drover's Cottage, Lucien Edmond Bouchard urged Ramón to call in the vaqueros, Simata and Lucas to receive their pay. Each man received $260, his wages for four months, and the hundred-dollar bonus. This done, Lucien Edmond and Ramón went down to supper with Joseph McCoy and Ed Dade in the large dining room of the boardinghouse. To Lucien Edmond's delight, Mrs. Edna Talcott, coloring with pleasure over the tributes paid to her culinary art by the young blond trail boss and his Mexican brother-in-law, agreed to provide supper for all the vaqueros.

Pablo Casares, quietly thanking Lucien Edmond for the wages and the bonus, did not partake of Mrs. Talcott's cooking. He walked slowly back to the chuck wagon, his face downcast, and gave the gray stallion tethered to the back of the wagon only a perfunctory pat. Somehow, the thought of sitting at a large dinner table with all his friends and being forced to talk—because he knew they were trying to help him out of the despair into which he had fallen after Vittorio's death—only served to make him feel more lonely and disconsolate than ever.

Besides, there was work to be done. Señor Bouchard was a very smart trail boss. Resting the chuck wagon horses and at least a dozen of those from the *remuda* which had been worked the hardest was an excellent idea. Then too, it would be wise to check into whatever supplies he might be able to buy in Abilene.

All of the horses had been put temporarily into the large corral near the cattle pens, but Ramón had already marked the ones for the livery stable simply by removing their saddles. *Bueno.* After he had taken the chuck wagon and Fuerza Torda to the stable, he would come back for the others. It would occupy him well enough through the night, and then he would go to sleep. Not in a room—he would feel too confined, too hemmed in with his sorrowful thoughts—but either in the chuck wagon or simply on a pile of straw in one of the empty stalls. Yes, that would do very well. As for the saloons, he had never liked tequila and he liked whiskey still less. The other vaqueros would be there to spend their money and to have their pleasures, and they deserved it after this long time on the trail and all the dangers. But he did not think he could bear watching them drink and joke and boast of their luck with the lovely señoritas.

With a melancholy sigh, Pablo Casares climbed into the driver's seat of the chuck wagon, clucked at the weary horses, and lightly flicked the reins to start them moving toward the stable, which was at the opposite end of the town. Glancing back, he could see the lights of kerosene lamps and lanterns in the windows of the saloons, the boardinghouses, and the hotels. Yes, there was life there, but poor Vittorio would never enjoy it again, never tease him about being a better point rider than he was a cook. When he got back to the ranch, he would write Vittorio's elder sister in Neuvo Laredo and tell her what had happened. He would explain how bravely her brother had died, defending the herd for a good, generous *patrón* who treated all men like equals.

There was a stretch of at least two hundred yards be-

187

tween the last saloon on the main street of Abilene and the ramshackle stable. As he neared it, he could see that it had been painted red, but the wood was not good and it would not last many years, not with hard rain and the winter snows. Still, he told himself, it was the only stable in town and surely its owner was doing well. Perhaps one day, when he was too old to ride on a drive, he would go back to Mexico with his savings and buy himself a stable. Horses were good to work with, and they were loyal and faithful. They did not trouble you with conversation when you felt like keeping silent. Even Fuerza Torda understood, prodding Pablo's arm with his nose and whinnying. Well, at least he had tried to avenge poor Vittorio's death. He knew that he had hit some of those accursed *ladrónes* with his six-shooters. Perhaps, in the beneficent justice of *Señor Dios,* one of his bullets might have hit the man who had killed his best friend. How he wished Friar Bartoloméo were here beside him, so that he could say all that was in his heart!

He drew on the reins as the chuck wagon pulled up before the stable. The doors were open, and as he leaned to his left to squint into the darkness, the muted glow of a lantern, hung just inside the entrance, showed the shadowy outline of stalls and, farther inside and to the left, a bale of hay with a pitchfork stuck into it at a slanting angle. Now, that was strange—that no one should be inside. That was no way to leave *caballos* for the night. Curious, he drew the horses to a halt, dismounted, and cautiously entered. There was no one inside the barn, and only two spavined mares in narrow stalls to his right. They tossed their heads and nickered softly as they perceived him.

"*¡Que pasa?*" He scowled, at a loss to know what to do next. It was very strange. Irresolute, he stood there a moment, his scowl deepening as he surveyed the nearly empty stable, then abruptly turned and walked back to the chuck wagon.

Beside the stable and toward the back of it was a cabin, constructed hardly a year ago, as he could tell from the border of upturned earth fringing its foundation and the newness of the logs and planks which formed it. He saw no light from the crudely shuttered windows, and, glancing uneasily back at the chuck wagon, moved toward the door to see if he could summon the occupants.

As he raised his fist to knock, he heard the muffled sounds of a woman's sobbing from the back of the cabin. The wagon's horses had heard it, too, lifted their heads and whinnied. Pablo Casares called out sharply, "*¿Quedarse aqui, comprende?*" and then strode along the side of the cabin nearest to the stable to investigate.

He stopped short as he saw, standing in the middle of a little yard with a low picket fence enclosing it, a slim, tall, black-haired woman in a blood-stained gingham dress. She held a spade, her head was bowed, and her shoulders shook with despairing sobs. Near her, lying on his back with his arms folded across his chest, was a brown-haired man in his early thirties, wearing dusty old boots without spurs, riding breeches, and a tattered brown jacket. His chest was wet with blood.

Pablo Casares stared as if hypnotized as the black-haired woman slowly straightened, uttered a muffled groan, and then, with a kind of agonized energy, dug the spade into the dry earth, lifted it, and wearily flung the crumbled dirt to one side.

"Señora—may I help you?" he said gently, not wanting to startle her.

The woman dropped the spade, turned, a hand to her mouth, her dark eyes wide with mingled hate and despair. "Do you want to kill me, too, the way you and your outlaw friends killed my husband, Brett?" she asked in a husky, trembling voice.

"*¡Pero no*, señora! I am Pablo Casares, and I have just come to Abilene with my *patrón* and his herd of cattle from Texas," he explained.

"Oh—I—I'm sorry—I—I didn't know—forgive me—oh, my God, my God!" She put her hands to her face and burst into helpless, racking sobs.

Pablo Casares vaulted over the little fence and approached her slowly, staring down at the dead man who lay near the partly-dug grave. "Please, señora, what has happened? Your husband—the stable was his? I was bringing my horses and I saw the doors open—"

The black-haired woman slowly lowered her hands, forcing herself with an indomitable will to face him. "Yes, it was his stable. We came here in March from Wichita Falls. Brett was so sure he could make a lot of money by opening a stable here in Abilene . . . because of Mr. McCoy's railroad market. I didn't want to come . . . not with our little children—I pleaded with him. There wasn't any school, there weren't really any people, not even any town to speak of . . . but he—oh, God, and now he's dead. I'm all alone and there's no one to help—"

Again she bowed her head, covered her face with her trembling hands, and gave herself up to the desolate anguish which possessed her. Pablo Casares compressed his lips, forcing back the tears that came to his eyes as he said hoarsely, "The *niños*—they didn't see—they're asleep?"

She nodded wordlessly, and her sobs redoubled.

"It is a good thing they did not see it. But how did it happen, señora?"

Once again she forced herself to look at him and to speak in a voice choked with tears. "About—about an hour ago, two men—two men came to the stable. Brett was eating supper in the house. He heard them calling. He ran out. There hadn't been much business, but he was sure there'd be lots of cattlemen and their riders coming in this summer. I—I suppose they wanted to buy horses—Brett had four there, but two of them are mares down with the spavins, you see."

"I know. I saw them, señora."

"I waited for him. I thought maybe this would be a good start. He'd brought those horses from Wichita Falls, and he always said he knew he could get a good price for them if he sold them to cowboys in from a drive. Well— I—of course I wasn't there—but then I heard loud voices and then there was the sound of two shots. I heard the horses galloping away, and when I came out—oh, God, why did it have to be like this, with nobody around to help us? What am I going to do? Oh, my God in heaven . . . what am I going to do?"

"Please, señora, I—I will help you. We will talk about that later. Will you let me—*por favor*, señora—will you permit me to do—to do what should be done?"

She nodded and then turned away, weeping softly as

Pablo Casares, casting aside his sombrero, took the spade and began to dig the grave. When he had finished, he said very gently, "How I wish we had the good padre here now to comfort you, señora. But you see, señora, I am a good *católico* and, if you will permit it, I will say what words I know so that *Señor Dios* will receive the soul of your *esposo.*"

He saw her dig her fingers into her palms and stiffen, and then heard her faint, husky murmur, "I—I would like that very much. God bless you."

Very gently, Pablo Casares eased the dead body into the grave, and then covered it with earth, patting it down firmly with his palms. On his knees, he clasped his hands and said aloud, "*Nuestro Señor Dios,* accept the soul of this good man, Brett—" he hesitated a moment, looking toward the woman.

"Strallis," she murmured back, and then, sobbing despondently, knelt down beside the grave, clasped her hands, and bowed her head.

"—this good man, Brett Strallis, murdered by cowards and thieves before he could make his peace with You. Be gentle with him, Señor, forgive him his sins and let him enter Paradise, if it be Your will. I pray You also to comfort his *esposa* and the *niños* and bless their lives with the memory of the good husband and father they have lost. I, Pablo Casares, ask this of you humbly. Amen."

He rose slowly, looking anxiously at the black-haired woman who knelt on the other side of the grave. After a long moment, she lifted her tearstained face and stammered, "Th—thank you. He—he would have liked that. You are very kind."

"I—I would like to help, Señora Strallis. But perhaps— forgive me if I ask such questions at such a time—did he have a family back in Wichita Falls?"

She shook her head. "No. His parents were killed by Indians when he was a boy. He went to school and worked for a farmer. And when he had a little money, he opened his own stable in Wichita Falls. You see—well, I—I'm what you might call a mail-order wife. I—I was an orphan in St. Louis, and then I went to work in a boardinghouse for a nasty old woman and—well, I couldn't stand it . . .

191

so I went to a marriage bureau. They had Brett's letter."

"I understand, Señora Strallis."

She slowly rose to her feet, a hand to her forehead, as if trying to remember the past. Pablo Casares approached her, blinking his eyes to clear them of the tears. "He—he sent for me—that was three years ago, and we had David and Jeremy. And then he had this idea about starting a stable in Abilene. He was so sure we'd make enough money to bring up the boys and have a good life, and then—oh, God—"

"Please, Señora Strallis, I didn't mean to hurt you, I didn't mean to ask questions that would make you cry—" Awkwardly, he put his arm around her shoulders. *Dios*, how young she was; she could not be more than twenty-three. She was even taller than he, and her disheveled, long, black hair suddenly reminded him of his faithless sweetheart, Concepción. He found himself trembling, and at once withdrew his arm.

To his dismay and embarrassment, the young widow suddenly clung to him, burying her face against his chest as she sobbed, "God bless you for being so kind. But—but I don't have any right to make you share my troubles."

Pablo Casares was trembling again and fighting his own tears. He patted her shoulder gently and said in a hoarse voice, "Señora Strallis, I have great troubles, too. My best amigo was killed by *ladrónes*, men like those who murdered your *esposo*. And because I know what sorrow death brings, I have much grief in my heart for you and the little *niños*. Please, Señora Strallis, forgive me if what I am going to say offends you. But if there is no one to care for or look after you— Could you think of bringing the *niños* and coming with me to my *patrón's* ranch—in Texas? He is a good, young man, Señora Strallis, with a family of his own. I know he will help you find a way to live and bring up the *niños*. And I myself, Pablo Casares, will look after you and the little ones all the way back there."

The words had tumbled out of him as if by compulsion. And now, fearful at his own audacity, he was silent, biting his lip and again awkwardly taking his hand from her quivering shoulder.

Her sobs had diminished as he spoke. Slowly, looking up

at him, a tremulous smile on her lips, she replied, "I think God Himself must have sent you, Pablo Casares. Yes, I will. I—I trust you, and my little boys will trust you too, I'm certain. My name is Kate Strallis."

CHAPTER NINETEEN

"Much obliged for the supper, Mr. Dade." Lucien Edmond Bouchard shook hands with the Chicago buyer. "And even more for taking my entire herd."

"My pleasure, young man. Well now, are you going to look for a little entertainment before you turn in for the night?" Ed Dade winked at Joseph McCoy, who grinned back at him.

"You mean the saloons?" Lucien Edmond chuckled. "Ramón and I will visit them just to make sure our vaqueros are being treated fairly. But I'm not a whiskey drinker myself and neither is Ramón. You see, my father was of French descent, and Frenchmen prefer wines."

"Well, I don't mind telling you I enjoy wine myself when I'm eating at the Palmer House back in Chicago." Ed Dade patted his considerable paunch and again took out his watch and eyed it. "But I don't think you'll find any wine being sold in Abilene in our lifetime—isn't that right, Joe?"

"These cowhands and cattlemen want something that kicks like a mule and does it right away. Corn whiskey is the tipple they'll ask for. Mr. Bouchard, we've got four saloons where we just had one last year. And that one, you recall, was in a plain old log hut. Now they're one-story frame affairs. Why, they've even got names printed on the plank just over the entrance—that's real progress in a year's time, Mr. Bouchard."

Lucien Edmond laughed heartily. "What I mark down as progress, Mr. McCoy," he volunteered, "is that this time you've got rooms for my riders. Ramón tells me a couple of them got in at your Drover's Cottage, while the rest are in the boardinghouses."

"I'm going to have a nightcap before I turn in. What

194

about you, Ed?" Joseph McCoy turned to the Chicago buyer.

"Not me." Ed Dade yawned. "I'm going to get a good night's sleep. I have to be up early tomorrow to supervise the loading of Mr. Bouchard's cattle into the cars headed for the stockyards back home."

"You mean the saloon girls we've got this year don't tempt you just a mite, Ed?" Joseph McCoy teased with a broad wink at Lucien Edmond.

"Don't rub it in," Ed Dade protested. "You know perfectly well I'm a married man. Only trouble with this job is, I spend three or four months out here buying up cattle for Mr. Armour, and my wife's started to complain that she doesn't remember what I look like by the time I get back home."

"Well, it's nice to know that some men still practice the old-fashioned virtues, even out here on the frontier," Joseph McCoy chuckled. "Good night to you, then. Come on, Mr. Bouchard, I'll show you around. You know, we're opening a general store here next month, and by next year, we might even have more than one, and a couple of hotels. The word's spread. You'll even find a few floozies hanging around our saloons this year."

"I just hope my riders don't get involved with them."

"Now, don't get me wrong, Mr. Bouchard. They're not bad girls. We've got about five now, mostly from St. Louis, though there's one, Sue Dambridge, came here from Topeka. Would you believe, she started life as a minister's daughter. Met up with some traveling drummer who sold her a bill of goods and got her kicked out of her home by her Bible-slinging old man."

"I feel sorry for her, having to live in a dreary, sunbaked place like this," Lucien Edmond began.

"Now, now," Joseph McCoy broke in, "Abilene's not all that bad. Sure, it's hot in summer, but it's hotter where you come from, Mr. Bouchard and you can't tell me it isn't."

"That I'll have to admit," Lucien Edmond agreed.

"I know we've got no law here, but some of the other fellows here and myself are going to incorporate this town, pass a couple of ordinances and build a jail. Next thing, we're going to post notices along all the roads leading into town to prevent cowhands from bringing firearms into our city limits. That way, you won't have any more trouble like your Mexican wrangler ran into last summer."

"And I shall be very glad of that, Señor McCoy," Ramón Hernandez added humorously.

"Say, I meant to ask you, Mr. Bouchard," Joe McCoy asked, "how'd you come up from Texas this time?"

"The same way we did last year, Mr. McCoy," Lucien Edmond responded. "First the San Antonio River, then the Colorado, then the Red River and up through Indian territory on to Abilene."

"That's what I figured. And last year, when you came by that way, didn't you find it sort of natural to cross the rivers where you did, and didn't you see some old hoof marks and maybe even the ruts of wagon wheels?"

"As a matter of fact, that's true, Mr. McCoy."

"Well, you know, that trail you took ought by rights to be called Black Beaver Trail. Black Beaver was an old Delaware scout, and he used that trail to guide Captain Marcy's expeditions, back in the gold rush days. Then, when the Civil War started, there was a Union colonel by the name of Emory who got trapped in Indian territory. Darned if old Black Beaver didn't use the same trail to help those soldiers escape to safety."

"That's most interesting."

"Nowadays, they're starting to call it the Chisholm Trail. That's after a half-breed Cherokee trader by the name of Jesse Chisholm. Four years ago, old Jesse hauled goods over that route south from Wichita, and came back with buffalo hides and some cattle. When he made the trek again, later that year and on into the next, he marked it plainly. Maybe your Indian scout caught some of those signs, and that's why he knew where to make camp and where to cross the rivers."

"Quite possible," Lucien Edmond agreed.

"Well, I take credit for the windup of that Chisholm Trail, from Wichita on here. You know, last winter, I mailed out circulars to every Texas cattleman I could get an address on—I had Bill Sugg go down to Austin and look at the record books. I told them all about Abilene being a darned good market without any swindling on the price or bad checks and such. Didn't you get one of my circulars?"

"No, but I meant to come here anyway, after the good deal I got last year."

"That Texas of yours is mighty big country. Can't expect mail to be delivered the way it is in places like where Ed Dade comes from." He paused at the first saloon. "Sure I can't buy you both a drink, boys?"

"No, thanks, Mr. McCoy," Lucien Edmond declined. "We're just going in to make sure our riders are having a good time and no trouble."

"Sure. Well now, in that case, I think I'll mosey back to the Drover's Cottage and make sure everything's ship-shape. Good night to you both. See you in the morning."

"Good night to you, Mr. McCoy, and thanks again. Just keep Abilene growing, we'll be back for sure next summer." Lucien Edmond Bouchard extended his hand and Joseph McCoy shook it heartily, then shook Ramón's, also.

"Well, Ramón, I don't hear any loud voices in this place, so I guess everything's all right. But let's go have a look, anyhow." His left hand grasping the barrel of his Spencer rifle and carrying it in a casual way, Lucien Edmond pushed open the door of the first saloon.

As Lucien Edmond entered, with Ramón beside him, he saw the same middle-aged bartender who had presided the year before over the earlier log-hut version of this drinking establishment. As before, he wore a black bowler hat. His pointed goatee was more prominent than ever, and his mustache thicker and with the upcurling tips heavily waxed. At the sight of Ramón Hernandez, he squinted nervously, cleared his throat, and called out, "Well now, gents, what'll it be?"

"Just a friendly visit this time," Lucien Edmond replied. "By the way, what are you charging for whiskey these days? And do you sell a full bottle?"

"Say, I remember that Mexican with you, mister," the bartender glowered. "He was in here last year and shot down one of Bud Larkin's pals. Used a carbine, too."

"It was a good thing he had that carbine, or he'd have been shot in the back. But you haven't answered my question." Lucien Edmond's tone was pleasant.

"Well," the bartender hedged, "we stocked up on whiskey this year, seeing what the trade was last. So I s'pose you could buy a bottle if you'd a mind to. Three bucks, mister, and it's still fifty cents a drink. But that's a good-sized glass I'm pouring. We don't aim to cheat cowhands here in Abilene."

"That's an excellent policy, and I compliment you for it." Lucien Edmond smiled. His eyes, as he spoke, swiftly studied the large room, furnished with six weather-beaten tables and rickety chairs. He recognized eight of his vaqueros, including Miguel Locado and Felipe Murcano at the one nearest the door. At the farthest table, José Martinez, Luis García, and Sebastiano Galvez sat, all of them ogling a pretty though thin chestnut-haired girl in a flouncy gingham dress, her pierced earlobes adorned with cheap brass earrings. She lounged against the bar, arching her back so that her small, high-perched breasts were shown off to their best advantage. A contemptuous little smile played on her mouth.

The other tables were occupied by cowhands and some of the residents of the town. They were engaged in playing poker, and there was a pile of greenbacks and coins on the center table, which was occupied by four men. One of them, a tall, freckle-faced cowboy with ornate chaps and jingling spurs, his wide-brimmed Stetson tilted back, was wrinkling his forehead as he studied his hand. He leaned back in his chair, shifting the cards, patting them at the edges. Then he turned them face down in his lap. With his left hand he reached for a greenback, shoved it to the center of the table and drawled, "I'll open with a five-spot, Mr. Wilson."

"You know the rules, Hank, pair of jacks or better opens the bid here," the dealer, a black-bearded, glowering little man, snapped back.

"Hell, Mr. Wilson, mebbe I never went to school, but I can read cards. None of your business what I got, 'ceptin' it's like you just said. Now, are we gonna play poker or are we gonna palaver, the way greasers and Injuns do?" This last remark was said in an insolently loud tone, and the young cowboy pulled the brim of his Stetson forward as he glared at the table where the three vaqueros sat.

Ramón frowned and whispered something to Lucien

Edmond, who nodded. Both men stood at the bar with their backs to it, watching the scene.

The middle-aged man at the young cowboy's left squinted at his hand, tucked it into a neat unit, then pushed a ten-dollar bill to the center of the table. "And up five," he observed with a soft snigger.

The cowboy shot him a scornful look, shrugged, then pushed another greenback forward. "I'll go along," he declared. "What about you, Mr. Wilson?"

"I'll stay," the dealer laconically declared as he tossed a ten-dollar bill to the center of the table beside the other stakes. "You, Mr. Carter?" This to the portly, nearly bald man at his left.

"I think I'll skip this hand. Been pretty bad ever since them Spiks sat down here."

Once again Ramón frowned and nudged Lucien Edmond, who nodded, his face grave.

"I know just what you mean, Mr Carter," the young cowboy drawled, purposely raising his voice and eyeing the vaqueros at the farthest table. "Seems like all of a sudden this town's overrun with them. I thought cowhands was white men in these here parts Can't say as I like greasers tryin' to peel little Sue raw with their dirty eyeballs."

At this insult, Luis García half-rose from his chair, but Lucien Edmond made a sign to him, then shook his head, and the vaquero settled back into his chair, muttering something to his companions.

"Come on over here, Sue honey," the cowboy called. "Bring me another drink while you're at it. Tell Ben to pour it up to the top of the glass, see? And I want a *clean* glass, one that ain't been handled by no dirty Mex, get me?"

At this, all three vaqueros rose, and the cowboy chuckled nastily. "Well now, seems like I riled them poor locoweed eaters, didn't I?" Then, shifting his cards to his left hand, he reached with his right hand to the holster at his right hip. "Any of you greasers want to call me out? Hell, I can take on all three of you at once and blow your brains out before you can even draw."

"Now, now, Hank," the bartender broke in uneasily, "don't go starting no trouble."

"You keep out of this. Sue, where's that whiskey?"

"I'll get it, Hank honey. Take it easy, please." The thin, chestnut-haired girl looked nervous as she hurried over to the plank counter which served as bar.

"Excuse me, but there's no need to call my men greasers," Lucien Edmond calmly broke in. The young cowboy whirled, his hand at the butt of his six-shooter, then drew his hand away as Lucien Edmond lifted the Spencer to waist-level, his left hand on the butt, right forefinger crooked around the trigger. "Well now, seems like you got the advantage over a poor cowboy, mister," he sneered. " 'Course, I can't stand up to a repeater like that."

"We don't need weapons to settle this at all, mister," Lucien Edmond retorted. "Just watch your tongue. These are my riders; they've been on a drive from Texas and they've worked hard. They're behaving themselves, and they're not insulting this young lady."

"Lady, hell!" the cowboy jeered. "Everybody knows Sue's just a plain ol' whore—ain't you, Sue honey?"

Her face turning scarlet, her lips compressed, the girl straightened. She was furious with indignation, yet cowed by the sight of the guns.

"That comment wasn't necessary, either," Lucien Edmond tersely declared. "I think you owe the young lady an apology."

"Say, just who the hell do you think you are, marching in here with a Spencer and telling us how we ought to talk and act, huh?"

"I came in to make sure my men are treated decently. They've money to pay for their drinks, they're quiet and behaving themselves, and there's no need to call them greasers," Lucien Edmond repeated calmly.

"Come on, Hank, you gonna play poker or chin all night?" the dealer demanded.

"You keep out of this, Mr. Wilson. What do you suggest we do, mister? Sure as hell I'm not gonna draw on you, not with that repeater pointing at my guts," the cowboy sneered.

"If you're man enough," Lucien Edmond instantly retorted, "you'll unbuckle your gunbelt and I'll give my wrangler the rifle, and we'll just step outside and discuss this with our fists."

"You're on, mister. You're a Texan, aren't you? Yeah, one of those goddamn Johnny Rebs. Me, I got no use for seceshers. Put in six months fighting you yellowbellies with the Fifth Kansas Volunteers."

"Let's see if you're as good with your fists as you are with your mouth," Lucien Edmond responded.

With an oath, the twenty-four-year-old cowboy unbuckled his belt and tossed it onto the table. He watched as Lucien Edmond handed Ramón his rifle, and then, as the latter turned to leave the saloon, he rushed forward and drove his right fist hard against the Texan's neck. There was a gasp of consternation and anger from the vaqueros as their boss stumbled forward and sprawled on the floor of the saloon.

"That's where all Johnny Rebs belong," the cowboy jeered, and then added, "Just tell your greaser friend to play it fair and not fill me full of lead. My gun's on the table, mister."

Lucien Edmond rose to one knee, shaking his head, groggy from the bruising, treacherous blow. "He won't shoot you. I see I made a mistake, turning my back on you. I thought we were going to discuss this outside, like gentlemen."

"Gentlemen? Hell, never heard tell of that breed around Abilene, mister. And you sure as hell ain't one, not a dirty sneaking secesher from Texas. Bet you never even wore one of them gray uniforms, either. Bet you bought your way out," the cowboy taunted.

Lucien Edmond got slowly to his feet, grimacing with pain. The cowboy, with a contemptuous laugh, moved forward, his right fist cocked. As he swung a looping blow at Lucien Edmond's jaw, the latter ducked and smashed his right fist with full force into his adversary's belly. With a groan, the cowboy stumbled back against the edge of a table, nearly upsetting it. "Why, you goddamn son of a bitch!" he panted. Lunging forward again, he aimed his spurred boot straight at Lucien Edmond's crotch.

Ramón, anticipating the cowboy's retaliation, had already cried out, "Watch out for a kick, Lucien Edmond!" But the latter had anticipated just such a move. Nimbly sidestepping to the right, he sent his right fist crashing against the cowboy's cheek and then drove his left into

201

his adversary's belly again. This time the cowboy reeled, stumbled, and sprawled on his back on the floor, a hand rubbing his belly, his face twisted with hate and pain.

"I—I'll get you for that, you lousy Texas Reb son of a bitch!" he gasped as he struggled to his feet.

Sue had scurried away from the bar to take refuge in a corner, where she stood with a hand over her mouth, her wide, frightened eyes fixed on the scene. The vaqueros cheered their young trail boss. "Finish him off, *patrón!* Keep after him, *hombre!*"

Now, slowly, warily, the cowboy moved toward Lucien Edmond. Then, suddenly lowering his head, he drove himself like a battering ram against Lucien Edmond's middle. Once again the rancher was ready for him, and, his strong hands gripping the cowboy's shoulders, he drew his right knee up sharply against his opponent's chin as the latter's forward momentum hurled both men against the counter of the bar, behind which the frightened bartender now ducked out of sight.

Pursuing his advantage as he righted himself, Lucien Edmond drove first his left and then his right fist against the cowboy's face and chin, sending him toppling back to crash against the edge of the table. A trickle of blood oozed from his swollen mouth as he straightened, his face contorted with pain and rage. Reaching behind, he seized a whiskey glass and smashed it against the edge of the table. Then, armed with the jagged shard, he came slowly toward Lucien Edmond. "Now I'm going to cut your goddam tripes out, Reb!" he snarled.

"Drop that now!" Ramón Hernandez angrily commanded.

But Lucien Edmond shook his head. "I can handle it, Ramón, don't interfere." His eyes fixed on the sharp sliver of glass, he shifted from foot to foot, awaiting his opponent's next charge. With a bellow of fury, the young cowboy lunged out with his right hand at Lucien Edmond's belly. Deftly sidestepping, the young trail boss launched a kick which connected with the cowboy's wrist, and with a yowl of pain, the latter dropped the shard to the floor and staggered back, rubbing his bruised wrist, and gasping convulsively.

Finally, in a last desperate assault, he hurled himself

once more at his antagonist, fists flying. Lucien Edmond returned blow for blow until, when the cowboy missed with a wildly flailing right hook, the Texan planted a vigorous uppercut on his opponent's jaw. Amid the exultant cries of the vaqueros, the cowboy was sent stumbling, this time missing the edge of the table and sprawling on his back on the dirty floor where he lay moaning, his head moving slowly from side to side, his eyes glazed.

"Now then, I suggest you apologize to my riders, mister." Lucien Edmond approached his fallen adversary and stood looking down at him.

"Better do it, Hank," the dealer advised. "You been beaten fair and square, no two ways about it. You hadn't ought to have shot off your mouth. Those Mexicans weren't giving anybody no trouble. Come on, let's get back to the game."

"All—all right. I take it back," the cowboy muttered sullenly as he propped himself up with one hand. He rubbed his jaw with his other hand, winced, tentatively clenched his teeth. "Ow, you hit like a mule, Johnny Reb. Guess I've had enough."

"I'm glad to hear that. And I hope you won't cause any more trouble for my riders. They're minding their own business, and I suggest you mind yours."

"Sure. Christ, my jaw feels like it's near broke. All right, I said it. Now I'm going to play some cards—all right, mister?"

"It's a matter of complete indifference to me what you do or don't do, so long as you don't bother my men. Come on, Ramón," Lucien Edmond said as he started for the saloon door.

Slowly the cowboy got to his feet wiping his bloody mouth on his sleeve. Unsteadily he made his way back to the card table, picked up his wide-brimmed Stetson, and made as though to put it on. Instead, he sent it skimming into Ramón's face as, in almost the same movement, he lunged for his gunbelt and began to draw the six-shooter.

Ramón stumbled back against the edge of the bar, righted himself, and, just as the six-shooter cleared the holster, fired two shots from the Spencer. The cowboy was flung back as if struck by an invisible hand, his face blank with surprise, his eyes wide. Then the light faded in them, he leaned back against the table, and slowly slid to the floor, rolled over, and lay still.

"Jeez, you done in Hank for sure." The dealer shook his head. "He was a damn fool to go for his gun. Guess he had it comin'. His trouble was, he never could forget the damn war."

Lucien Edmond had quickly turned at the sounds of the vaqueros' warning cries and Ramón's shots, and stood staring at the dead cowboy. He shook his head. "I didn't want that at all. But you saved my life, Ramón. What a pity he had to go on hating so long. None of us on either side really wanted a war."

At the back of the saloon, Sue had begun to sob hysterically. Lucien Edmond's face softened, and he walked back toward her. "I'm sorry, miss. I'm sorry he said what he did about you. Why don't you go back to your room now and have a good night's sleep and try to forget this?" Putting his hand into his pocket, he took out several gold pieces and thrust them into her trembling hand. "Here. That ought to be enough to take you home or wherever you want to go, to make a fresh start if you've a mind to." Then, nodding to Ramón, he left the hushed saloon.

CHAPTER TWENTY

After he buried Brett, Kate Strallis's husband, Pablo
Casares went back with the bereaved young widow to
her little house. He had realized at once how poor the
family was. The house was bare of all except necessities,
and it was obvious that Strallis had invested any money he
might have accumulated in setting up the stable in Abilene. Indeed, when Pablo gently asked Kate Strallis
whether there was any money she might take with her,
she told him, "I know that Brett put a few dollars away
under the sugar tin in the pantry. You see, Mr. Casares,
he had saved up about a hundred dollars, but he spent it
all on those new horses for the stable. He was so sure he
could sell them and double his money. And then—and then
those two horrible men—" and she burst into convulsive
sobs again, making Pablo feel awkward and helpless.

Pablo went into the sparsely furnished room where the
two children were sleeping. Kate recovered enough to follow him, and to force a warm smile to her lips as she
stood beside him. The older boy, David, slept in a crib.
"He's just two," she whispered, and the middle-aged
vaquero nodded silently, distressed because this room, like
all the others, spoke of the most elemental poverty and
self-denial. The crib was crude, and badly put together,
obviously homemade.

"Brett was very proud he could do things," Kate explained.

Pablo Casares stood, looking down at the baby, and a
sudden feeling of powerless rage enveloped him. It was
the same feeling he had when he came upon Vittorio's
body after the bushwhacker raid—a helpless, clawing, despairing rage against needless injustices to decent people.

That was why his voice was gruff when, leaving the

205

room with Kate, he muttered, "I think my *patrón* will begin the journey back to the ranch in two days more. It will give you time to pack. You have clothes, maybe some furniture you want to take with you? We have supply wagons, and there will be plenty of room for everything."

Kate Strallis uttered a poignant little laugh and said, "I haven't much to take, Mr. Casares. It won't even begin to fill one of your wagons. I've only got one other dress besides this. Neither of us had very many things except what we just couldn't do without. But then, I'm sort of used to it. I didn't have anything back in St. Louis, either. At least here I had Brett and then—then—the boys—" Once again she buried her face in her hands and her shoulders shook with her muffled sobs.

"You should try to get some sleep now, Señora Strallis," he told her. He almost found himself reaching out to put an arm around her shoulders, to let her know that he was there to help assuage her grief, but he restrained himself. He had no right to do that. Instead he said, as gently as he could, "I want to go out and put a marker on the grave. It will be in respect, Señora Strallis. Now you go to bed and sleep. And in the morning I will fix breakfast for you and the *niños*. You see, I am the cook on the chuck wagon for Señor Bouchard—he is the *patrón*. And I am a *good* cook, too, you will see."

She slowly dropped her hands from her tear-ravaged face and looked at him, then smiled faintly and nodded. "I'm sure you are, Mr. Casares. Thank you again for everything you have done. May God bless you."

"And you and the children too, señora," he responded, turning quickly and going out before she could see that his eyes were beginning to brim with tears.

He went back into the stable first, found two pieces of wood, and nailed them together in the form of a cross. Then, with a clasp knife, he carved the dead man's initials and the date of his death, and set the cross at the head of the freshly-dug grave. Next he knelt down, removing his sombrero, and prayed silently for a long time. When he finally rose, he turned and stared with surprise to find that Kate Strallis was standing near him.

"Señora Strallis, you—you should get some sleep now. Please."

"Yes, Mr. Casares. And you, too—there's room for you in the house."

"Oh no, señora, I'll sleep in the stable. I have a new horse, a gray stallion one of my *compañeros* caught for me before we came here, and he misses me when I am not there to tell him *buenas noches*."

"But you won't be comfortable there."

"Oh yes, señora, it will be fine. Please—you must not concern yourself about me. Why, the hay in your stable will be a softer bed than what I have in the bunk house back at the ranch." He forced a little, unconvincing laugh.

"Well, if—if you're sure—then, good night. I won't ever forget what you've done for me. Good night, Mr. Casares."

Twisting his sombrero between his calloused hands, Pablo Casares nodded, looking down at his dusty boots, as sheepish as a little boy might be when confronted by his teacher for some small misdemeanor. That was why he did not see her come quickly to him and put her hand on his shoulder. Suddenly he felt her lips brush his weather-beaten cheek. Then he uttered a stifled cry and stepped back, but already she was hurrying back into the house.

The moon was at full zenith now, and it lighted up the marker which stood at the head of the grave. He stared at it a moment, crossed himself, and then walked back into the stable.

Methodically, he made certain that the two strong chuck wagon horses were comfortable in their stalls, and that Fuerza Torda was settled in one nearby. He climbed back into the chuck wagon, opened a can of sugar, and returned with a handful which he offered to the gray mustang. It bobbed its head and nickered, then greedily licked up the sugar as Pablo Casares stroked its head and praised it in the soft tone he reserved especially for his new mount.

Then he closed the stable doors and, remembering where the pile of hay was, walked back through the darkness and stretched himself out on it, his hands under his head. He lay his sombrero beside him, and let his mind wander. Before he knew it he had begun to weep, not only for the unfortunate family he now sought to help, but also for his friend Vittorio and a little for the anguish which flirtatious Concepción had caused him so long ago. . . .

In the morning, true to his promise, Pablo used some of his chuck wagon supplies to prepare breakfast for Kate, the two children, and himself. There was little conversation between them, but he understood the constrained silence. It was a poignant moment when little David, pointing to him, turned to his mother and asked, "Dada come, mama?"

He glanced at the black-haired young woman, feeling himself an intruder. But Kate smiled, leaned over to kiss the little boy and murmured, "Not now, Davey sweetheart. He's gone away on a long trip. Now eat your breakfast like a good boy. If you do, Jeremy will finish his, you'll see."

After the meal was finished, Pablo cleaned and put away the few dishes, then turned to Kate Strallis. "Now I shall go see the *patrón* and tell him. I will find out when we are to go back, so you will have plenty of time to get ready, Señora Strallis."

"Yes. Thank you, Mr. Casares."

He hesitated, wanting to say something more, but not knowing exactly what. He fumbled with his sombrero for a moment, nodded, and left the little house.

Lucien Edmond had left the Drover's Cottage where he had slept later than usual. He was striding down the dusty street toward the boardinghouse to have breakfast when he saw Pablo Casares walking toward him from the other direction.

"*Buenos dias*, Señor Bouchard," Pablo greeted him.

"And to you, Pablo. I didn't see you last night. I'm sure you weren't in one of the saloons, though." Lucien Edmond smiled.

"Oh no, Señor Bouchard! The fact is—I wish to ask a great favor of you. I—I will pay for the inconvenience, that is understood. It would be a very kind thing if you would allow it—"

"What are you trying to tell me, Pablo? And there's no need to pay for a favor, hombre."

Pablo fidgeted, twisting his sombrero out of shape and staring at it as if he were seeing it for the first time. "Well, Señor Bouchard, last night, you remember I was going to take the chuck wagon horses and my Fuerza Torda to the stable. When I got there, the stable doors were open and

208

I heard a woman crying. She was behind the little house beside the stable. Her *esposo* had been killed by *cobardes* who took the horses without paying for them. When he asked them for his money, they shot him down like a dog. I—I buried him for her, and he left her with two *niños* and no money. She was an orphan herself and became his wife—how do you say it—through writing letters."

"Yes, a mail-order bride. I've heard of them in these frontier towns, Pablo. Now, what can I do to help?"

"I—I told her that perhaps if you took her back to the ranch, there might be some work for her to do. I do not like to think of her being alone here. She did not wish to come to Abilene. Her husband was sure that he would make *mucho dinero* by opening a stable, because of all the vaqueros who come here now with cattle and who need horses."

"Of course I'd be glad to help her."

Pablo's face was radiant. "I was sure you would say that, Señor Bouchard. You have a good heart. When will we head back to the ranch?"

"Well, it was so easy selling the herd and getting the money for it, Pablo, that we may as well pull out tomorrow morning, after breakfast."

"*Bueno!* I will tell Señora Strallis. Perhaps she can ride in one of the empty wagons?"

"Of course. And I'll have one of your *compañeros* drive it. You're such a good cook, Pablo, that I don't want you being a nursemaid to two little children when you should be cooking our meals on the way home," Lucien Edmond grinned.

Pablo Casares took a red bandanna out of his breeches pocket and blew his nose loudly to hide his emotion. "*Caramba,* I will be glad to go back to Texas, *patrón.* There is so much dust I don't know how anyone can live here."

"Nor do I, Pablo. I'm eager to see Windhaven Range again. Only this time, we'll go back on a different trail at the start, at least until we get to Indian territory. I got into a fight with a young cowboy last night at that saloon over there." He gestured with his thumb. "It was with fists, but when I was leaving, he went for his gun and Ramón had to shoot him. Remember what happened to us last year when Ramón had to kill that *pistolero*? Well, I don't want to take the chance of running into another ambush—though I don't think, in this case, we're going to have any future trouble. The cowboy was a loner, and he hated all Southerners."

"*Madre de Dios,* I would have liked to have watched you teach him a lesson, Señor Bouchard!" Pablo Casares smiled broadly.

"What you were doing was a lot more important, Pablo." Lucien Edmond's tone was serious. "Bring the lady and her children tomorrow, by all means, and I'll tell Ramón to assign one of the vaqueros to the wagon that'll take her back with us."

"*¡Gracias, gracias, patrón!*" Pablo's voice was joyous.

Ramón Hernandez had quickly explained to all the vaqueros the reason for Kate Strallis's presence on the return journey. Their reaction, to a man, was to praise their *compañero*. When Kate appeared, leading little David by one hand and carrying Jeremy in her other arm, two of the vaqueros sprang forward and urged her to let them take the children to the empty supply wagon in which she and they would ride. Moreover, all of the vaqueros vied for the honor of driving the wagon, until Ramón had to arbitrarily choose Sanchez Maderos.

Pablo Casares had acquired some sacks of beans and barrels of flour as well as two slabs of bacon, which would fill the gap in his supplies until the riders reached Wichita. When all was ready, Lucien Edmond rode to the head of the line and, turning in his saddle, called, "We're going to change our trail back, amigos. We'll go northeast from here for about twenty miles, and then gradually head southward. With luck, we should be able to cover about thirty miles a day. So with God's help, we ought to be back on Windhaven Range before the end of July. *¡Adelante!*"

Behind him, the mounted vaqueros raised their sombreros and cheered lustily, as Lucien Edmond turned to wave good-by to Joseph McCoy and Ed Dade, both of whom had come out to see them off and to wish them god-

speed and a safe return next summer. Pablo Casares, a
smile on his face, clucked at his horses and snapped the
reins to start them. "Now, mis caballos," he urged them,
"we must not lag behind even though we are at the end
of the line, ¿comprende? You have both been rested and
well-fed. Now we are going home, where you can rest
all through the long winter." He glanced back toward the
rear of the chuck wagon, where he could see his gray stallion trotting along, haltered to the peg near one of the
wheels. "When we get home, Fuerza Torda, I promise to
give you much exercise. Si, and if you are very good and
very gentle, I will let you have the honor of being ridden
by a beautiful señora."

Then he turned back, staring at the wagon just ahead
in which Kate Strallis and her two children rode. He
locked up at the blue sky and said aloud, "Gracias à
Dios!"

After two days on the trail it became evident that no
one was pursuing them, so Lucien Edmond's riders circled back to the southwest and then due south, in the
direction of Wichita. When they reached it, they acquired
more supplies, a task delegated to Pablo Casares who, as
cook, would know better than any other member of the
outfit what staples were needed for the return journey.

After he had finished dickering with the portly, bespectacled owner of the general store, the middle-aged
vaquero lingered at the counter, his businesslike demeanor
having suddenly deserted him. "Was there something else,
mister?" the owner asked. "How about some hard candy?"

Pablo Casares's face brightened and he vigorously
bobbed his head. "Si, si, señor! Candy for the niños, that
is a very good idea." Then again he stood irresolute and
embarrassed. "But there is something else—though I do
not know, señor, whether you would have such a thing.
It would be for a señorita—I mean a señora," he hastily
corrected himself.

The storeowner took off his glasses and squinted at the
vaquero. "I don't get your drift, mister. I carry all sorts of
merchandise here for the ladies, if that's what you're getting at."

"Would you have dresses, then?" Pablo Casares hazarded.

211

"Of course. Some of the latest styles, too. Just got a shipment in from the East a month ago. Step over this way, I'll be glad to show you. Something for your wife, maybe?"

Pablo emphatically shook his head. "Oh no, señor, it is not for my wife. It is—it is for a woman, a señora, who is going to work for my *patrón*, you understand." He stood looking at the rack of dresses which stood in a dusty corner of the store, framed by a pile of new brooms and, on the other side, garden hose, spades, and shovels. "I do not know what to choose, though, señor. They are all *muy atractivas.*"

"Tell you what, mister. I'll call my wife. She'll be able to help you." The storeowner walked over to a flight of narrow stairs ascending to the living quarters above and bawled, "Elsie! Elsie honey, can you come down? Got a customer who needs his mind made up."

In a few moments, a plump, dowdy woman in her midforties came down the stairs and Pablo gulped as she fixed an appraising stare on him. "This the gentleman, Horace?"

"That's right, Elsie. Says he needs some help picking out a dress for a lady in his outfit."

"I see. Well now, mister. How tall is she, and is she delicate or full-favored?"

Pablo swallowed hard. He lifted his right hand. "About this tall, señora. And she is *un poquita delgada.*"

"I don't hold with foreign languages, mister." The storeowner's wife sniffed disdainfully, giving her husband a withering look at which he noticeably quailed.

Pablo strove for a translation. "Well then, señora, she is not like you. I mean, she is—"

"Why don't you just say she's thin?" the storekeeper's wife interrupted, glaring at him.

Pablo Casares shuffled his feet and twisted his sombrero, wishing that he had not yielded to impulse. "I did not mean to give offense, señora," he stammered.

"Oh, very well. She's taller than I am and thinner, then. Now, what color do you think she'd favor? What's the color of her hair, mister?"

"Oh, that is easy. It is *negra*—black."

"Well then, this green dress—" the storekeeper's wife drew a bombazine dress, with full flounces to the sleeves, bodice and hems, from the rack. "This should fit her, just about."

"*Si*, it is very nice. Well, then, I will take that. Can you —would you please—put it in something?"

"Of course I'll wrap it. I declare, don't you think we're civilized here in Wichita, mister?" The storekeeper's wife bridled as she strode around to the back of the counter and, neatly folding the dress, wrapped it in brown paper and tied a string around it. "That'll be three dollars, mister."

"*Gracias,* señora. I thank you for your assistance." Pablo Casares was visibly sweating as he paid for his purchase and bowed low to the storekeeper's fuming wife. Then he clapped his hand to his forehead. "*Madre de Dios,* I almost forgot the candy!"

"Sure, mister," the storekeeper intervened, with a quickly whispered comment to his wife who sniffed loudly, then made her way back up the stairs. "Now, we've got some pepp'mint stick candy 'n some licorice."

"I—I—give me some of each, enough for two *niños,*" Pablo Casares stammered. When the purchase was completed and paid for, he thanked the amused storekeeper, then hurriedly beat a retreat to his chuck wagon.

Once again the riders had assembled to resume their homeward journey, and Pablo Casares hurried over to the wagon ahead of his. He had no wish to let Sanchez Maderos see what he was about to do, and so he scratched at the canvas at the back of the supply wagon and called softly, "Señora Strallis, *por favor,* I have something for you."

A moment later, the black-haired young widow drew aside the flaps and peered out. Then she smiled. "Oh, it's you, Mr. Casares. Is anything wrong?"

"Oh no, señora! I—I hope that you and the *niños* are comfortable?"

"Oh yes, thank you very much. Everything is fine."

"I—I—I have something for you here. I hope that you will not think me too bold—I meant only to please you— here! And—ah—here is some candy for the little ones."

213

Fumbling for words and very near to blushing, the middle-aged vaquero thrust the parcel and the bag of candy into Kate Strallis's hands, then turned to go.

"Oh please, don't go just yet! I want to see what it is." She began to unwrap the parcel, and then uttered a delighted little cry. "Oh, it's—it's just beautiful! You mean—you mean you bought it for me?"

"*Si,* señora. The wife of the storekeeper, she said it should fit you."

"I'm sure it will. Oh my goodness, this is the loveliest dress I've ever had—you shouldn't have—you're so good, so kind. Come over here, Mr. Casares."

Uncertainly, he moved forward. Kate Strallis leaned down, put her arms around his neck, and kissed him resoundingly on each cheek. "There! It's the very nicest present I ever had."

"I—I had better get back to my wagon, señora. They are all ready to go. I—I will make sure that you and the *niños* have plenty of good food and are comfortable. Sanchez Maderos is a good man—he is the one who drives your wagon."

"Yes, I know. You're all so very kind to me. I'll never forget it."

"And for now, *adios!*" Pablo Casares stammered, his heart beating like a trip-hammer and his face luminous with happiness.

CHAPTER TWENTY-ONE

Three days after they had left Wichita, the Bouchard riders crossed the Kansas border and entered Indian territory. It was now the last week of June. The warm sun and rain had thickened the pasturage. Best of all, from Pablo Casares's viewpoint, there was an abundance of wild onions, apples, and various types of tasty berries with which he could vary the monotony of the meals he served to the hungry riders. On the first night, he had served berry pies to the delighted vaqueros. After they had eaten, he slipped out, went to Kate Strallis's wagon, and offered her a small, individually baked pie which he had filled with especially juicy berries. If Sanchez Maderos noticed this, he said nothing about it to the others, for there was by now a tacit agreement among all the men to look the other way whenever Pablo and Kate were seen conversing.

On the next night, he brought her a bunch of wild flowers and, his sombrero held behind him, bashfully presented the bouquet. Kate Strallis, observing his sensitivity, gravely thanked him and did not embarrass him—as she sensed she had done over the episode of the dress in Wichita—by kissing him. Yet it was evident to all the riders, and to Ramón and Lucien Edmond in particular, that Pablo Casares had changed since their arrival in Abilene. Once again, he traded bantering quips with the vaqueros as he prepared their meals and served them, and frequently was heard at nightfall singing softly to himself, songs he had heard when he had been a young man in Nuevo Laredo. So, gradually, the men again began to poke fun at his culinary efforts, just as they had done before Vittorio had fallen victim to the bushwhacker raid. And he gave them back taunt for taunt, smiling widely, as if he savored his return to their good graces.

For that matter, there was a relaxed, happy atmosphere throughout the entire outfit. They had come over eight hundred miles, through rain, blazing sun, and dust, and the ever-present danger of ambush from unknown attackers. True, they had lost two of their own, and that memory would linger hard and long. But they had seen their young trail boss stand up to an even younger man when their race had been insulted, and this same boss had paid them high wages and a bonus. In addition, he was returning home with money he intended to put into improvements of the ranch, which was now their livelihood and their security.

There was also the unexpected presence of a young woman and two small children whom they were escorting, which at once conferred upon the humblest vaquero a re-doubled sense of vigilance and responsibility. Added to all this was the knowledge that the kindly Franciscan friar would return with them when they stopped at the little Creek village, and would bless the chapel which their *compañeros* had by now certainly finished building.

Vigilance was called for. Here in Indian territory, there were frequent patches of woods dotting the grassy bottomlands, any one of which could easily conceal a band of cattle rustlers. In the two drives they had made to Abilene, they had not been forced, as had other Texas ranchers, to buy their way through certain parts of Indian territory by giving a dozen or more head of their fattest cattle to the friendlier tribes in order to purchase an unharassed ride through tribal land. But Lucien Edmond, who saw no need to relax watchfulness, even now that the cattle had been sold, continued to double the night guard whenever they made camp.

Two days away from Emataba's village, however, Simata, who had been riding ahead about two miles, galloped back with a worried look on his face. "There's a small Indian village off to the northwest, Mr. Bouchard," he told Lucien Edmond. "It's been attacked, perhaps by Kiowas or wandering Comanches, and there are many dead bodies there."

"Do you know to what tribe the dead Indians belong, Simata?"

"I cannot be sure. I did not go into the village, wishing to hurry back to tell you of this."

"We shall ride that way, then," Lucien Edmond decided. "It is not far from Emataba's village, and if there are hostile Indians on the warpath, they may threaten his people, even though they are peaceful and live on a government reservation."

"That is what I was thinking myself, Mr. Bouchard," Simata admitted.

Lucien Edmond turned in his saddle and pointed in the direction from which Simata had come. "We'll head that way, amigos!" he called, and then rode on, with the young scout alongside him, detailing the way.

Half an hour later, Lucien Edmond reined in his horse and raised his right hand to halt his riders. They had come to a slightly higher stretch of grassy bottomland, with a clump of trees to the west and a little creek to the east. The sun had begun to set, and the hot dry air was acrid with the smell of smoke. As the riders drew up, they saw before them perhaps a dozen tepees and wigwams, toppled, some of them only charred wood and buffalo hide. With the smell of smoke, there rose the unmistakable smell of blood and death.

"My God!" Lucien Edmond Bouchard said in a low, shaken voice as he stared at the scene of carnage. "Kiowas, Mr. Bouchard," Simata muttered to him, shaking his head. "I count twenty braves and women—yes, and children, too." He dismounted, then hobbled his horse, which had begun to whinny and toss its head, baring its teeth at the smell. Slowly he moved forward into the silent camp. The only sound was the crackling of a charred lodgepole which obviously marked the dwelling of the leader of this group of nomadic Kiowas.

"These Kiowas were hunting, Mr. Bouchard." Simata turned back to the young trail boss. "They are not painted for war. They were after buffalo. See, over on that spit before the cooking fire? It is a haunch of buffalo. And beyond it is the skin, still bloody and not yet tanned."

"Do you think Comanche did this, Simata?" Lucien Edmond asked.

"I do not think so, Mr. Bouchard. I do not see arrows

217

in the bodies of the dead Kiowa braves, nor the wounds of lances. I see bullet holes. This was done by white men, Mr. Bouchard."

"How can you be sure, Simata?"

"Look over there, Mr. Bouchard, near those trees. There are the Kiowa horses. I do not know if they are all there, but if Comanche, or other tribes, had attacked here, they would have taken all the horses. And now look over here." Simata loped toward the little creek, then squatted down and pointed. "The tracks of horses, no more than five or six. These men, whoever they were, came upon this camp last night and killed all those here, perhaps took fresh horses and left the rest, then headed east. They stopped to burn this camp—perhaps to hide what they had done— I do not know."

Lucien Edmond's face hardened. "I wonder if it could have been those bushwhackers who got away after we wiped out the rest of their gang," he said, half-aloud.

Simata nodded. "It is very possible, Mr. Bouchard. They would have needed fresh horses to put distance between them and us, and perhaps also they feared that soldiers from the fort might ride after them. But these Kiowas had guns, too, I am certain. And I am sure, also, that these white men, whoever they were, stole the guns after they had killed everyone here."

"And yet it is said that Indians are more bloodthirsty than the white man," Lucien Edmond declared with scorn. "Wait—what was that? I heard something just now."

He held up his hand for silence, and there came the faint sound of a baby's cry, off to the rear of the Kiowa camp. Lucien Edmond dismounted and, accompanied by Simata, hurried in the direction of the sound.

The leader lay just inside his tepee, a tomahawk in his right hand and a bloody bullet hole in his forehead. Next to the tepee was a crude travois, a kind of sled. The Indians of the plains used it frequently to draw slaughtered game—or one of their own wounded companions—back to camp.

As Lucien Edmond and the scout reached the travois, the baby's cry was heard again, followed by a hiss. Simata, very warily, lifted the travois and let it fall to the other side. Lucien Edmond uttered a startled gasp. "It's a squaw and her papoose!"

She was young, not more than nineteen, with delicate features and black hair drawn into a single thick braid. She wore a doeskin petticoat and jacket. Her discarded moccasins lay nearby, and she clutched a little girl, no more than six months old, to her bosom as she stared with frightened defiance up at Simata and Lucien Edmond.

Simata spoke to her in Kiowa. "Do not be afraid. We are friends."

But she shook her head and clutched the baby even more tightly.

"At least she has lived among the Kiowas," Simata observed to Lucien Edmond. "Do you see, the sling which she wears on her back has the markings of this Kiowa tribe. It may be that she is Comanche, or even Sioux or Pawnee, but these Kiowas—perhaps the chief himself—captured her and forced her to take a Kiowa husband. I will try again. It is the remembrance of the horror she has seen and heard that keeps her silent."

Patiently, smiling, touching her gently on each cheek and then the forehead, Simata repeated in Kiowa, "Do not be afraid. I myself am of Kiowa blood. These white-eyes are good men who do not hate the Kiowas, and I work with them. I swear to you by the Great Spirit that we will do you no harm."

Slowly the Indian girl got to her feet, Simata gently helping her. She turned toward the largest tepee, and uttered a wail of anguish as she saw the body of the chief.

"All are dead except you," Simata gravely told her. "Tell me who did this, if you can."

Haltingly, her voice sweet and soft despite its unsteadiness, she replied in the Kiowa tongue. "They were white-eyes. They came upon us late last night as Pinikiswe ordered that we have a feast on the buffalo he himself had killed with his lance. They crept in upon us from the woods there—" She pointed with a slim hand toward the woods. "And they fired their guns and killed many before the men could get their weapons. I saw two men riding toward the site of our camp on our horses, and I was afraid, not for myself, but for Tisinqua, my Little Fawn. So I ran to the travois and hid us both under it. I did not dare to come out, because I did not know if the white-eyes had gone."

"Are you Kiowa, then?" Simata gently asked.

The young squaw shook her head. "I am Aiyuta Sioux. A year ago, this Kiowa chief and his warriors—there were many then—raided my father's village and stole me. The squaws beat me and made me do the hardest work in the camp until at last I could bear no more and agreed to be his squaw." She straightened proudly, looking down at her baby. "But I will bring up Little Fawn in the ways of the Sioux, who are gentle people and who fish and hunt and till the land, who do not kill others as the Kiowas do."

"I am sorry it is so, for I have told you that I am Kiowa, too." Simata tried to comfort her. "But it is a hard life. The buffalo are driven from the Great Plains and sometimes the Kiowas must live as best they can. What is your name?"

"I am called Elone. In my tribe it means Bright Star."

Simata translated for Lucien Edmond's benefit. "What shall we do with her and her child, Mr. Bouchard?"

"Perhaps Emataba will find a place for her in his village. There will be milk there for her little girl from the cows we gave him. And there is no hatred or desire for bloodshed among Emataba's people. They will be kind to her."

"It is a good thing." Simata turned back to Elone and explained Lucien Edmond's suggestion. She turned to look intently at Luke's blond son, and then nodded. "I have heard of the Creeks. My life was hard with the Kiowas, but now it is over. If Little Fawn will be safe there, I will go where you say."

CHAPTER TWENTY-TWO

As Lucien Edmond Bouchard's riders and wagons approached the fenced-in Creek reservation, the vaqueros could see that the occupants had already hurried to the gate to await their coming. Dismounting, Lucien Edmond tethered his horse to the ramshackle picket fence and walked toward the gate. Emataba awaited him, and beside the *mico,* beaming and making the sign of the cross, was Friar Bartoloméo Alicante.

"Welcome, my son," the Franciscan friar called. "The people here have eagerly awaited your return."

"It's good to see you again, Friar Bartoloméo," Lucien Edmond exclaimed. "We've brought some extra food for Emataba and his people."

The *mico* himself opened the gate and then came forward to shake hands with the young trail boss. "Welcome, my white brother! I rejoice to see that the danger which our venerable shaman foretold has passed from you as a cloud driven by the fierce wind across the sky." Then, gravely, he added, "The beloved old man has breathed his last. This, too, he foretold. It was swift and without pain, in his sleep three days after you and your men continued your journey to the north."

"My heart is heavy to hear such news, Emataba."

"He lived a long life and I think that for him death was welcome. He had seen the proud Creeks driven like a pack of mangy curs from their hunting ground to this lonely land where many of us believed Ibofanaga had abandoned us in His displeasure."

At these words, Lucien Edmond felt a sudden chill. He recalled how his father had told him the story of old Lucien and Nanakota, who had been first the "beloved man" of the Creeks of Econchate and then their *mico,* and who had welcomed death exactly as their shaman had foretold. After a moment, he replied, "We too have had our sorrows, Emataba. Two of our vaqueros were killed by men who tried to steal our cattle from us, soon after we left your village. And that, too, Equitaba had said would come to pass. Yet, to speak of happier things, I tell you that all of the men were eager to visit you before we finished our journey home."

"Thus sorrow can make the bonds of brotherhood even more binding," Emataba answered solemnly. "This good man who serves your God, my white brother, has walked among us and has begun to learn our language. He has helped brighten our lives, and we know already, from his lips, how he has tried to help our red brothers wherever he has gone. We should have known this without his telling us, seeing the love he has shown toward the sick and the old, and the young children who are, as yet, too innocent to know how Ibofanaga has turned his eyes from the Creek nation."

"Then you have learned their tongue, Friar Bartoloméo?" Lucien Edmond asked the Franciscan.

"Oh, not yet, my son, but Emataba has been kind enough to let me study with a young brave who speaks English nearly as well as I do. He is a good teacher and I wish to be a quick learner. I do not know enough yet to preach a sermon in Creek, or to say Mass, but I will do that one day, you will see."

Lucien Edmond turned to Ramón. "Have the vaqueros bring the food supplies into the village. And ask Simata to bring Elone and her baby."

Ramón nodded and went back to the riders and the wagons, while Lucien Edmond explained to the *mico*, "I am here also to ask a favor of you, Emataba. Shortly before we came to your village, we found a Kiowa camp which had been set upon, I am almost certain, by the same white men who attacked us and tried to steal our cattle. They killed all of the people there, except a young girl, whom the Kiowas themselves had captured from the Aiyuta Sioux. She had become the squaw of the chief and she bore him a daughter. They are the only survivors of that cruel slaughter. I told her of your village, and, since she believes that her own people are either dead or have moved far from the land where she was born, I told her that I would bring her here to live safely with the hospitable Creeks."

Emataba's smile was bitter as he nodded. "Already the holy man of your God has talked to me of the things which white men are taught about their Creator. He has told me that in the holy book in which are written the words of your God, there is the advice for a man of good heart to turn his other cheek if an enemy slaps him. Surely the Creek nation understands this teaching. Yes, my white brother, we will give this woman and her child refuge and share our food with them as you have shared yours with us."

"Thank you, Emataba. Even if others do not understand the wisdom of the Creeks, my men and I know very well that there is honor and kindness to be found here. I promise you that they and I will tell those dear to us, so that in turn they will tell those who come after us. It was so with my great-grandfather and with my father, and it will be so with me Emataba."

The tall *mico* stared at Lucien Edmond a moment, then gripped him by both shoulders and said in a low voice quivering with emotion, "We have not yet performed the ceremony that makes us blood brothers, but already I have called you my white brother. Now I know truly why I felt this from the first when you came to us last year."

"I would be proud to have us united in blood, as we are in spirit, Emataba."

"My heart is glad to hear you say this. And there is greater meaning to it now than ever before. Have you not brought to us a young squaw and her child, who alone survived the evil death brought on her village by white-eyes who in no way resemble you, our generous friend? And you bring her here at a time when the hearts of my people are heavy as they see another winter approaching, knowing there will not be enough food or blankets. Knowing that when the agent and the soldiers guarding him, as if he feared death at our weakened hands, come to visit us, they will see us only as a pack of wild dogs to be caged away from civilized men. That is what they have often said, though not in words so plain as mine."

Three of the vaqueros carried in the gifts of food which

Lucien Edmond had brought, and Ramón and Simata escorted Elone, carrying her baby, before the *mico*.

Emataba, spoke haltingly in the Kiowa tongue. "These men have told me what has been done to the people of your adopted village. Here, though you see the fence which declares that we are under the supervision of white-eyes soldiers, you will be safe from harm. You bring youth and life to us who have watched for many moons in the hope that the life of the Creek nation itself will not be extinguished. Be welcome, then, Elone, you and your child." Then, turning to one of the younger braves, he ordered, "Let her be taken to one of the tepees and see that she has blankets for herself and the child. Have one of the women bring food and milk for them both; they have traveled far this day."

"I thank the *mico* of the Creeks," Elone replied in her sweet clear voice, lowering her eyes before him as she spoke. Only the "beloved woman" of a tribe might look directly into the face of the chief.

"I shall be sorry to see your man of God leave us, my white brother," Emataba said as he turned to Lucien Edmond. "He has done much good here. He has lifted our spirits and he has helped us to understand that we are not yet forgotten by Him whom we call Ibofanaga and whom you and he know as God."

Lucien Edmond watched the receding figure of the friar, who accompanied Elone and her child to the far end of the reservation. "If I know what is in his heart, he will want to come back to you, perhaps to stay for a long time and to be of help to you. He has lived with many other Indian tribes since leaving Santa Fe. And you know that he was exiled from there because the white-eyes in power did not like his showing favor to the Pueblos."

"Yes, he has told me this. He has great courage, besides his love for all people. How strange it is that Ibofanaga has not put into this world more men like him and yourself so that all of us can live together in peace and in understanding."

Kate Strallis had climbed down from the wagon to stretch her legs and to let little David walk about and see the Creek village. On the journey there, Sanchez Maderos had done his best to inform her about the countryside and particularly about the little village. Kate had never seen an Indian before. In Wichita Falls, where her husband had been born, the citizens talked of Indian raids, but by the time she had come from St. Louis to marry him, all that she remembered were the gory tales told by the oldsters who lounged back in wicker chairs on the dusty porch of the town's only hotel. And in St. Louis, to be sure, she had never seen an Indian.

What struck her most was Lucien Edmond's friendly and unassuming demeanor as he moved among the people. When she saw the vaqueros carrying supplies of food into the village, and Sanchez Maderos told her of the gift of cattle which the *patrón* had left here before finishing his drive to Abilene, she turned to Pablo Casares and said softly, "What you told me about Mr. Bouchard is only the bare truth, Mr. Casares. How kind he is, how concerned for these unfortunate people! Why, they're not savages at all."

"That is very true, señora Strallis," the middle-aged vaquero nodded. "But you see, as a *niño* he was brought up by his father to believe that, since *los Indios* were the first in this country upon the land, what they did was only to defend their homes. The land was taken from them by men with guns who were greedy for it and the hunting on it. His great-grandfather came from France to live with the Creeks, and he became their friend and their blood brother. But not many white men would see things his way."

"I suppose not." She gave a nervous laugh, remembering the lurid stories of Indian massacres and tortures which had come to her ears in Wichita Falls. Then she asked, "If this territory ever becomes a state, Mr. Casares, what do you think will happen to these people?"

Pablo shrugged and shook his head. "Only *el Señor Dios* knows that, señora. Myself, I think maybe if there are settlers here, they will push *los Indios* out and take even this piece of land which has been given to them. Then, too, I think that those who are not yet on reservations will have to go where the buffalo are, and now that the railroads are coming into this country, the buffalo will go farther north until they are all killed off. Then I do not know what the Indians will eat."

"It's so sad. Those poor little children—and those huts or whatever they are in which they have to live. It must be dreadful when the winter comes."

"*Si*, señora Strallis. That is why my *patrón* has given them many blankets to help keep them warm. I think, so long as they are here, he will always try to help them— that is the sort of man he is."

Sanchez Maderos had walked ahead to chat with the men who had brought in the food supplies. Kate now turned to Pablo, put a hand on his arm, and said very softly, "I would like it if you would call me Kate, the way my friends do—the friends I had back in Wichita Falls."

He stared at her, his very soul in his eyes, and then, abashed at his own temerity, hastily responded in a low voice, "That is very kind. But I call you what I do out of respect for you—"

"Dear, thoughtful Pablo. You see, I would like to call you by your first name, too, because we are already such good friends. No one has ever done such kind things for me, or tried to make the children and me so comfortable."

"But—but—S—Señora Strallis—I—I mean, Kate, it is only what any man would do."

She was very close to him now, and her dark brown eyes were tender and questioning as they searched his weather-beaten face. "That's not true, Pablo," she said very gently. "Most men I know wouldn't have wanted to be involved, not with a woman who'd just lost her husband and had two little children. They'd be a hindrance."

"Oh no, Señora Strallis," he gasped, "you and the *niños* could never be that, *jamás!*"

Her smile was tremulous and she looked at him for a long moment. Then she patted his arm again and replied, "You're the most unselfish man I've ever known, Pablo. I hope one day you'll start to think of yourself a lot more." Then, as if afraid she had said too much, she turned to grasp David's hand and, shifting little Jeremy in her other arm, declared, "Oh, look, Davey, they're going to start cooking supper. Let's go see how the Indians do it, shall we, darling?"

Pablo Casares had never before worked so hard or so cheerfully. He had gone to Lucien Edmond a few minutes after his conversation with Kate Strallis and eagerly volunteered, "Señor Bouchard, with a little help I would willingly prepare dinner for *todos los Indios*. We need use only a little of what we have given them, and I will cook some of *their* food as well, so they do not think it is charity. It will be as if we took part in their fiesta, *¿sí?*"

And Lucien Edmond had clapped him on the back and said, "That's a marvelous idea, Pablo! Choose whatever men you need, and I'll tell Emataba. But I warn you, the squaws will watch you very carefully to see if a man can cook as well as they."

"Of that I have no fear!" Pablo's chest swelled like a pouter pigeon's. "I know now what I can do."

Pablo hummed a Mexican love song as he began to prepare beans with molasses and bacon. After setting water to boil for coffee, he hurried into the center of the village where the squaws had made their cooking fires. At his order, Paco Alvarez killed one of the steers and expertly began to butcher it. There were onions and herbs and potatoes, Pablo discovered to his delight, which the squaws eagerly offered to him. Soon the vaqueros of Windhaven Range sat side by side with the Creeks, eating with gusto and smiling at one another in a wordless spirit of amity and comradeship.

Not content with all this, Pablo walked through the village, a happy grin on his face, inquiring whether any of the vaqueros or Creeks wanted seconds. When a wizened old man, even older than Equitaba, held up his empty bowl, Pablo Casares burst into delighted laughter, bowed to the old man, and hurried back to the cooking pot to replenish the bowl. As he handed it back, he saw Kate staring at him, her soft lips wreathed in a smile. Overwhelmed with emotion, he turned on his heel and bawled to Paco Alvarez, "Hombre, they are starving here! There is still plenty of meat on that big steer's bones. Lazy one, do I have to tell you what to do when people are hungry?"

When all were full and the pleasant murmur of voices drifted over the village of the Creeks, Emataba rose and beckoned to Lucien Edmond to stand beside him. Holding up his right hand for silence, he spoke in Creek to his people. "Seldom in the history of the Creek nation has a *mico* said his thanks to a white-eyes for kindness done without seeking reward, for bravery and courage and honor which are not displayed to gain a cunning power over the Creeks. This man who stands beside me is such a man. In the days when the name of Econchate stood for the stronghold of the great *micos* Tunkamara and Nanakota, this man's father, and, before him, the grandfather of that good man, shared the bounty of earth and water and sky with their Creek brothers."

An awed stillness settled upon the villagers as they stared at their tall chief. "It will be said that we are no longer free, that this land is not where we would have come if the choice had been ours. Yes, that is true. But that is why we are grateful all the more, for the loyal friendship and the unselfish kindness of the white-eyes who, for the second year, has come to us to lighten our burdens. The soldiers who guard us bring us food and clothing, yes, but with the insolence that one shows in giving charity to beggars. This man alone is drawn to us because of the goodness in his heart and his belief that all men are brothers upon this land."

At these words, there was an approving murmur from the villagers. Emataba turned to Lucien Edmond Bouchard and spoke again. "Tonight, in having your men come among us, to sit side by side and to share food with us, you have done a good thing. I have never seen it happen before. It has given me new hope, as it has to even the oldest of my people. And so, I ask you to become my brother in blood as you have already shown yourself to be in spirit. Do you accept?"

"With deepest thanks and the hope that I may prove worthy of such an honor, Emataba," Lucien Edmond replied in the Creek tongue.

Emataba made a sign with his left hand, and a strong young brave came forward with a hunting knife and a rawhide thong. Emataba nodded to him, took the knife in his right hand, and grasped Lucien Edmond's left hand. Swiftly he made a slight nick to draw blood from the wrist, and then as swiftly cut his own left wrist. Next, extending his left arm with the palm upward, he gestured to Lucien Edmond to press his bleeding wrist against his own. When it was done, the young brave stepped forward to bind both arms with the rawhide thong.

"I, *mico* of the Creeks who were once of Alabama and are now of this land which is called Indian territory, say to all of you, my people who obey me as your chief, that Lucien Edmond Bouchard is from this moment forth brother of my blood. His blood flows into my veins as mine into his. We share each other's wisdom and courage and honor. So shall it be until that day when Ibofanaga summons us both for his all-knowing judgment. I, *mico*, have spoken."

The two men stood together in the moonlight, the only sound being the crackle of the campfires and the breathing of those nearest them. They stared into each other's eyes and Emataba's lips curved in a joyous smile. Lucien Edmond trembled suddenly, as if the very spirit of old Lucien Bouchard were there, invisible, to witness this communion.

In the morning, as Ramón Hernandez untethered the horses of the *remuda* and chose a docile gelding for Friar Bartoloméo Alicante, Emataba and Lucien Edmond said their farewells in the tepee of the *mico*. He had tendered Lucien Edmond the calumet of peace and friendship, and had remarked somewhat wryly, "Sometimes, when the agent wishes to show how generous he is to us, he brings a little tobacco for my old ones. This time, knowing that you would be with us again, I kept a little back so that we might smoke this pipe as brothers."

Lucien Edmond glanced at the faint scar on his left wrist, smiled, and nodded as he took the calumet and drew on it, then handed it back. "I shall never forget this honor, Emataba. And I shall not forget you or your people. If God grants that I come this way again next year, you may be sure that I will bring more heifers and at least another cow, as well as blankets and other things which your people will find useful."

"We shall be here, my brother, to await your coming. The soldiers see that we are peaceful and have no will to fight our oppression. But there is one thing which your man of God suggested while he was with us that brings new hope to me as *mico*, since by Creek law I must see that my people thrive, and are well in spirit as in body."

"And what is that, Emataba?"

"He told me, after his first day here, that when he

learned our language well enough, he thought that it would be good to start a school for the children. He would teach them English and perhaps a little Spanish, tell them stories and set them to work growing fruits and vegetables."

"That's a wonderful idea, Emataba. I can get seeds for you in San Antonio when I go there for supplies, which will be soon after I return to my ranch. Friar Bartoloméo can bring the seeds when he returns here, and the children can plant gardens. Thus, you will have more food for your people."

"Yes. And besides that, it will teach the children to be proud of their achievements, and in a way it will help restore their pride in being Creeks. Within a short year, my blood brother, you see how you have turned our sorrow into hope. And without hope, life has little meaning or flavor."

"For me as well, Emataba." Lucien Edmond took a last puff at the calumet and then gave it back to the *mico*.

"This time, I will not come with you to the gate. Now you are my blood brother, and you take with you part of me, as I who remain here keep part of you. Thus we shall not be separated from each other. And I will think of you and your men, and those who are dear to you, when you are back in your home."

"As I will think of you and all your people who did me such honor last night, Emataba. May Ibofanaga watch over you and yours always!"

Lucien Edmond left the tepee of the *mico*, went to his gelding and mounted it. He rode to the head of the line, and then, waving at the assembled villagers, gave the signal for the journey to begin.

CHAPTER TWENTY-THREE

The weather had turned sultry and oppressive two days after Lucien Edmond and his men left the Creek reservation. From time to time, there were ominous rumbles of thunder, and occasionally a jagged bolt of heat lightning zigzagged across the dull, gray sky. At noon one day, the group halted not only for the midday meal, but also because a sudden downpour made it almost impossible to see beyond the nearest rider. Hastily they drew off toward a clump of cedar trees. Half an hour later, the rain and the thunder stopped abruptly. The sun came out again, but the sticky, clinging heat fatigued the riders.

"We've made good time. There's no need to exhaust the men or the horses, Ramón," Lucien Edmond called from the head of the line to his Mexican brother-in-law. "And I'm sure Mrs. Strallis and her babies would be grateful for a more leisurely pace. It can't be comfortable for them, traveling in the back of that supply wagon. And it sure won't hurt to let Pablo and Sanchez bring up the wagons at their own pace. We can amble ahead and let our horses graze a bit."

"I agree, Lucien Edmond. It's just as well that we still have a few fresh horses in the *remuda*. We might need them before we get back home."

Pablo Casares had prepared a hasty meal, hampered by the drenching rain, but fortunately there had been enough *frijoles* and cooked bacon from the early breakfast to substitute for hot food. He had been able to make coffee, and this together with the *frijoles* and bacon, sufficed. Pablo saw to it that Kate Strallis was given a heaping plateful. Since some of the vaqueros had found wild apples the day before, Pablo cut them up, then mashed them into a kind of gruel to which he added sugar, water, and a spoonful of molasses. Both David and Jeremy found this quite palatable, and Kate Strallis went so far as to compliment the embarrassed vaquero for his thoughtfulness.

It seemed to Pablo that he had never been happier in all his life. He knew himself to be deeply in love with the black-haired young widow, but he knew that there was a world of difference between them, not only of nationality and very possibly religion, but also in terms of the economic side of such a union. True, Lucien Edmond paid generous wages, but Pablo questioned whether he could and should undertake the responsibility of a wife and two young children. Even more than this, Kate Strallis's simple dignity and candor led him to feel that she might be unhappy sharing the monotonous, often dreary, life of a vaquero. She should have a fine house and be near a town where there would be a school for her *niños*. As for him, he lived with his *compañeros*, which was all right for a single man who worked with the men and shared their hardships and pleasures; still, it would never do for her and the children.

Yet, when he had put away the supplies and the utensils and doused the fire, he smiled to himself, recalling her words of praise over a cobbler he had made. Then he frowned a little. Kate had looked just a little peaked and drawn. He would have to tell Sanchez to drive the horses more carefully, so that the wagon would not jostle her and the *niños* so much. There were so many miles yet to go before they would be home. No doubt Señor Bouchard would find a room for her and the children in the big ranch house, and that was as it should be.

After he tidied up the chuck wagon, he remembered his six-shooters under the tarpaulin just behind the driver's seat. It would be a good idea to reload them. He wasn't sure he had remembered to do so after the bushwhackers had ambushed them, just before they had reached Abilene with the cattle. Lifting up the edge of the canvas, he drew the guns out, and swore under his breath when he found that he had only reloaded one of them. To be sure, there was really no reason to worry. The cattle were gone. No rustlers or *ladrónes* in their right minds would attack a band of over twenty well-armed men. Just the same, it was always wise in this vast, empty country to have plenty of cartridges in one's guns in case of attack.

Por Dios, it was hot. It reminded him of Nuevo Laredo in the summer. Now that the sun was coming out, it would be worse than ever. He hoped that the señora and, especially, the *niños* were not suffering too much from the heat. It was good that the drive had started early this year. They would miss the heat of July and August, which was hard even for men like himself, who were accustomed to it. He loosened his belt a notch, trying to make himself more comfortable, then automatically put his right hand to his hip to make certain that his hunting knife was in its sheath. He took it out and lightly passed his left thumb over the blade, wincing to feel the sting of its bite. *Bueno*. It was still as sharp as ever. The other day he had seen a patch of wild onions and, grasping the little white bulbs in his left hand, wielded his knife like a scythe. It had sliced through the stems as if they had been paper!

When he heard Lucien Edmond call out, "*¡Adelante, amigos!*" he scrambled back into the driver's seat, picked up the reins, and clucked to his horses. They were good horses. They didn't try to start up until he told them to, not even when they heard the order to start the outfit forward. They deserved a little sugar this evening after he had made supper. Ahead of him, he saw the wagon in which Kate Strallis and her two children rode move jerkily forward, and he swore under his breath. What the devil was the matter with Sanchez, anyway? You started the horses gently, letting them start off at their own pace; you didn't make them lunge forward as if you were going to race one of your *compañeros* back to the ranch house. The señora would be holding the littlest one in her arms, with David sitting beside her, and the way that clumsy idiot Sanchez had made the wagon start must surely have startled her. He was going to have to tell Sanchez how to drive a wagon. Better yet, he would suggest that they change wagons until, of course, it was time for him to go to work with the meals.

The line of tall cedar trees extended much further than he remembered. Then he recalled that they were going home by a somewhat different route, just to be certain that there was no trouble from any *cobardes* who might be lying in wait for them. He saw Sanchez's wagon lurch forward again, then suddenly come to a jerky halt. Angrily, he reined in his own horses, swearing volubly. By all the saints, what was the matter with that stupid one?

"Amigo, the axle's slipped out," Sanchez called as he dismounted and hurried to the left rear wheel of the supply wagon. Kate Strallis drew aside the canvas flaps and peered out, her lovely face concerned. "What's wrong?" she called.

"Nothing much, señora. It will take only *un poco momento* to put the wheel back where it belongs. Do not disturb yourself."

Lucien Edmond and the vaqueros, as well as Ramón and his *remuda* of horses, had moved ahead. Looking back, Lucien Edmond reined in his gelding, wheeled it around, and galloped back toward the two wagons at the very end of the line. "What's the trouble here, Sanchez?" he asked.

"The axle, Señor Bouchard. It's all right; Pablo and I can put it back into place. You go ahead. No need to hold up on our account."

"Well, if you're sure it won't take too long. I'll send back two of the vaqueros to stand guard—there's no reason to take any unnecessary chances. If it takes longer than you think, Sanchez, fire your gun and we'll wait for you. Besides, with this heat, we're not going to exert ourselves or the horses."

"*Bueno,* Señor Bouchard. Pablo, you are as strong as an ox; come help me lift this axle while I steady the wheel," Sanchez Maderos urged.

Lucien Edmond Bouchard had gone back to his men, and now Paco Alvarez and Miguel Dondaro rode back as sentries for the two wagons. Little Jeremy had suddenly begun to cry, and Kate Strallis was busy soothing him, rocking him in her arms, while little David, thumb in his mouth, stared fretfully at his baby brother.

Lying on their bellies, hidden from view by the knee-high grass in an extended clump of cedar trees, four men watched the two wagons halt. They saw Lucien Edmond

234

ride back to them, then marked the return of the two vaqueros who would stand guard.

They were the survivors of the Reedy gang which had attacked Lucien Edmond's party thirty miles from Abilene, and they were in dire need of horses and weapons. Their leader, Ed Harschmer, lifted the butt of his Sharps rifle to his shoulder, then turned to whisper to the lean, sun-bronzed, younger man beside him. "Did you see what I just saw, Jack? That purty young filly in that first wagon there must be with some passel of settlers followin' that trail herd outfit up ahead."

"Yeah, Ed." Jack Castle drew his Starr .44 out of its holster, made sure it was loaded and primed for action, then leveled it at one of the mounted sentries. "Bet you five bucks those Mexican riders are from the same outfit we tackled with poor old Jethro."

"Wouldn't be surprised if you're right about that, Jack. Which means we sure as hell owe 'em something for what they did to our pals. Besides, we need horses 'n ammunition real bad. The horses we stole from that goddamn Injun village got plumb away from us," Ed Harschmer growled.

"Hell, I could'a told you that much, Ed. Only Injuns know how to break mustangs in so's they stay broke. And it was your idea to tackle those redskins, anyhow."

"Quit your grousin', you mangy Missouri sidewinder," Ed Harschmer scowled. "I recall you were the one who was so damn sure we could wipe out those redskins with no trouble 'n pick ourselves up a couple of their young squaws. Hell, there was only one good looker I saw out of the whole stinkin' bunch, 'n she got away, damn her ornery soul."

Jack Castle grimaced and mumbled something inaudible.

"Now listen and hear me good, Jack," Ed Harschmer insisted. "The soldiers out of that fort near that Injun reservation been out patrollin' ever since we hit those redskins. An' they're gonna catch up with us real soon unless we git ourselves more horses and guns mighty quick. So now's our chance. You just crawl back'n tell Pete 'n Donnie to come up here and get ready. We'll pick off those two sentries they got and grab their horses; then we'll have a try at snatchin' that young filly. Hell, she looks like she could take care of all four of us without battin' an eye." He uttered a soft, coarse snigger.

His younger companion nodded, then crawled back the dozen yards to where the two other survivors of the Reedy gang lay hidden. Soon the trio rejoined Ed Harschmer. The two were Donnie Claymore and Pete Arnoldson. Like Harschmer, they were armed with Sharps rifles.

"What's the word, Ed?" Donnie Claymore whispered.

"You'n Pete pick off those two Mexicans, then grab their horses. And make it fast!"

Donnie and Pete crawled forward a few yards, to the very fringe of the tall grass, and slowly aimed their rifles at Paco Alvarez and Miguel Dondaro while their cronies watched intently. Donnie pulled the trigger, and Paco Alvarez jerked in his saddle, his eyes wide, then slumped forward and toppled to the ground with a bullet in the center of his forehead. But Pete's shot, snapped off too quickly, only grazed Miguel Dondaro's shoulder.

With a cry of pain, the vaquero turned and fired his Spencer carbine into the tall grass, narrowly missing Ed Harschmer, and, enraged by the sight of his companion lying dead on the ground, spurred his gelding toward the clump of cedar trees, ignoring the danger in his furious desire for vengeance.

Pete rose from his cover, took quick aim, and fired. Miguel Dondaro cried out again as the bullet pierced his lung, but had the presence of mind and enough determination left to aim his carbine at his assailant and pull the trigger. The bullet grazed the bushwhacker's upper left arm, and the latter, drawing a pistol from his belt, fired at the vaquero and mortally wounded him. Miguel Dondaro dropped his carbine, both hands clutching his belly, then slid off his gelding, kicked convulsively, and lay still.

Donnie and Pete at once ran toward the snorting, rearing geldings, seizing their reins with one hand while they grabbed the Spencer carbines which the ambushed vaqueros had dropped, then leaped into the saddles and headed the geldings around the side of the two isolated wagons.

Pablo and Sanchez had just managed to fit the axle back

into its hub when the first shots rang out from behind the trees. "Get back! get back! Get your gun and protect the señora and the *niños*, imbecile!" Pablo Casares cried. Crouching low, he ran for the chuck wagon and scrambled into it, lying flat on his belly as he groped for his two six-shooters. As Pete and Donnie wheeled their stolen geldings and raced by the left side of the supply wagon, Pete, who had reloaded his rifle, leveled it and fired. He narrowly missed Sanchez, who, having retrieved his Spencer carbine, pulled the trigger twice. The bushwhacker dropped his Sharps, his head tilting back. Then he tumbled forward over the gelding's neck as it raced on, carrying his lifeless body until, at last, the corpse slid out of the saddle and sprawled on the ground.

With a furious oath, Donnie, seeing his companion fall, drew his six-shooter and aimed a snap shot at Sanchez, who cried out and clapped a hand to the bleeding wound from a bullet crease at the side of his neck. Seeing Sanchez drop his carbine, the mounted bushwhacker uttered a gleeful howl and rode toward Pablo's wagon, raising his reloaded Sharps to fire. But Pablo, whirling to meet his advance with one of the six-shooters in his right hand, fired twice. The second bullet took Donnie in the left side; his rifle dropped to the ground as he slumped forward over his horse's neck, the frightened animal galloping on toward the north.

Jack Castle and Ed Harschmer, nodding to each other ran out of the grass, crouching as low as they could to minimize the targets they presented. Castle, drawing his Starr .44 and firing almost without aim, whirled to meet Pablo Casares. The vaquero uttered an agonized yell as the bullet tore through the fleshy part of his right arm, causing him to drop his six-shooter. Lunging with his left hand, he groped for the other gun and, finding it, fired without taking time to aim. Jack Castle half-rose, then fell backward and rolled over onto his side, his eyes wide and staring in death. But Ed Harschmer had already torn open the rear flap of the lead wagon and was dragging Kate Strallis out, despite her frantic struggles and screams.

Panting, blinking his eyes to clear them of the haze of gunsmoke and sweltering heat, Pablo Casares lifted the six-shooter in his left hand and, taking careful aim, pulled the trigger. But the cartridge was defective and the weapon exploded. He cried out in pain, the useless gun falling to the ground, as Ed Harschmer lifted the struggling young widow in his arms and began to run with her for the cover of the trees.

Gritting his teeth against the pain, Pablo leaped down from the seat of the chuck wagon, stumbled, lost his balance, then righted himself. He began to run toward the lone bushwhacker, who looked back, grinning savagely, then called, "Tell your men I've got the filly, and I'll kill her if they come after me, greaser! I mean it!"

Kate Strallis, still screaming, kicked and clawed desperately at Ed Harschmer, but the bushwhacker, swearing under his breath at the distraction, tightened his hold on her and lurched on. By this time, the fusillade of shots had brought Lucien Edmond and his men riding back. Quickly assessing the situation, Lucien Edmond called out, "Don't take a chance and shoot, you might hit Mrs. Strallis! We'll get her away from him without endangering her!" Reluctantly the vaqueros lowered their guns, muttering to themselves, watching the bushwhacker stumble back toward the tall grass and the clump of cedar trees.

Pablo had left a trail of blood behind him. His smashed left hand was useless and his right arm was bleeding profusely. With a supreme effort, he thrust his right hand down and drew out his hunting knife. Glancing up at the sky, he murmured a silent prayer, then took the point of the knife between right thumb and forefinger and, drawing back his pain-racked arm, flung it with all his remaining strength.

Ed Harschmer stopped short with a grunt, turned slowly around, his eyes wide and uncomprehending. As Kate Strallis screamed, he suddenly dropped her to the ground, stumbled two steps forward, then fell full length into the grass.

A wild, exuberant shout of "¡Gran vaquero, gran vaquero!" burst from the mounted riders. Pablo Casares stumbled toward the young widow, who lay stunned by the abrupt fall. Slowly he knelt down, tears running down his dusty cheeks. "Did that animal hurt you, señora?" he asked in a hoarse voice.

"No, no, Mr. Casares, I—I'm all right. Oh, oh, the children—someone please see if they are all right—"

"Si, si, señora, I myself will make sure—" He tried to rise to his feet, but a sudden darkness claimed him. The pain and shock of his wounds carried him into oblivion, and he did not hear Kate Strallis's agonized cry, "Oh, he's hurt badly—please—please—someone take care of Mr. Casares—"

When Pablo came to, it was to find himself lying in the back of the supply wagon in which Kate Strallis and her two children rode. She stared down solicitously at him as he blinked his eyes. "¿Que pasa?—oh—I—now I remember—the niños—"

"Hush, Mr. Casares, you must rest. You lost a lot of blood. The children are fine, thanks to you. So am I. God bless you. You were so brave—those awful men might have killed you—and even though they hurt you so awfully, you —you still saved me—oh, God bless you!" Kate Strallis sobbed.

"No, señora," he whispered so faintly that she could scarcely hear. "It is the good God you must bless—He gave me the strength—"

"Hush," she murmured softly, her slim hand gently stroking his sweat-beaded forehead. "Just sleep and don't think about anything now. I'm going to help one of the other men with the cooking until your poor hands are well enough, Mr. Casares."

"Bueno, gracias," he murmured, and then sleep claimed him.

Twilight was falling as Lucien Edmond stood beside the graves of Miguel Dondaro and Paco Alvarez, listening to Friar Bartoloméo Alicante intone a prayer for the valiant dead.

CHAPTER TWENTY-FOUR

Shortly before noon on the twenty-second day of July, 1869, the riders and the wagons of Lucien Edmond Bouchard's outfit came within sight of the sprawling ranch house and the stockade which enclosed it and the bunkhouse. Young Lucas, riding his gelding up beside his trail boss, exclaimed, "Mr. Lucien Edmond, let me ride ahead and alert them!"

Lucien Edmond chuckled and nodded. "What you really want to do is to see your new wife, and I don't blame you, Lucas. By all means, go on ahead and tell your mother that we've got a lot of hungry men to feed. And, speaking of that, once you've let Felicidad know that you're safe and sound, you'd better give her some help. It's going to be hard work preparing all those extra meals after she's spent months just taking care of the family, and the vaqueros and workers who stayed behind."

"Sure I'll help her, Mr. Lucien Edmond! Thanks a lot!" Lucas grinned, then spurred his gelding and raced on toward the gate of the stockade, his face tensed in joyous impatience. As he neared the compound, he could see Joe Duvray and Andy Haskins, rifles in hand, standing guard just outside their dugouts. Beyond them, Dave, Frank, and Ned, the loyal blacks who had followed Luke from Windhaven Plantation, were teasing Jubal, who was barking joyously.

Maybelle Belcher had just left her own home to come to the ranch house and visit Sybella Forsden. As she saw Lucas riding toward her, waving his wide-brimmed sombrero and shouting in pure exuberance, "We're back, we're back now to stay!" she rang the handbell which she always carried to alert the occupants to open the gate for her. Dismounting, Lucas greeted her with a smile. "Now that's a right smart idea you've got there, Mrs. Belcher. Ring it good and loud. I can't wait to see Felicidad."

But the ringing of the bell had already brought Felicidad hurrying from the kitchen through the house, calling to Maxine and Sybella as well as to Celia, "They've come back—oh, it's Lucas!" and it was she who hurried out of the house to slip aside the bar which locked the gate of the stockade.

"¡Querido, mi esposo, mi corazón!" she cried, happy tears shining in her lustrous brown eyes as she flung herself into his arms.

"Honey, it feels like years that I've been away from you—have you been all right?" he inquired eagerly after their first long kiss.

"I'm just fine, especially now that you're back, Lucas." Felicidad sighed happily as she nestled in his arms.

"I'll open the gate wide for Mr. Lucien Edmond and his men, honey. Then you and I'd best get back to the kitchen. Your mother will need lots of help to prepare lunch. Oh, excuse me, Mrs. Belcher, I guess—"

Maybelle interrupted with a laugh. "You don't have to apologize to me, Lucas. If I were you, and I had a girl like Felicidad to come back to, I'd forget about a fat, old lady, too. And I tell you what, I'll help Celia fix lunch. Everybody's fine inside—and you've got a surprise awaiting you!"

"A surprise?" Lucas turned from Felicidad, holding her tightly in his arms, his eyes questioning.

"¡Si, mi esposo! You'll never guess—while you were away, all the men worked so hard to build our house that it's all finished and ready for us to move in!"

"That's wonderful! Say—is that it?" He had just seen the small frame house near the creek, not far from the Belcher house, surrounded by shady elm trees.

"Oh yes, yes, Lucas! And Mrs. Forsden has given us some furniture—a bed, and some chairs and a table—even some rugs for the floor. It is so beautiful, I could cry. While you were away I went there every day and said, 'Here is where my husband and I will have our meals, and here is where we will—we will—'" She blushed furiously.

By now, drawn by the excited conversation of the young couple and the ringing of Maybelle's bell, Celia,

Maxine, and Sybella, as well as Carla and Hugo, had hurried out of the house to greet Lucien Edmond. Maxine carried little Edwina in her arms, her eyes bright with happiness, and called out to her handsome husband as he dismounted, "Thank God you've come back to me, my dearest!"

Mara Hernandez, on her way to the creek for a bucket of water, had seen the mounted horsemen. Flinging the bucket away, she had hurried back to the house to get little Luke. Then, holding him in her arms, she ran back toward the ranch house, her face aglow.

Ramón saw her, quickly dismounted, and ran forward to meet her. "Mara, my sweet one, my beautiful *esposa!*"

"Oh Ramón, it's been so long; it's been so lonely without you! Oh, my darling!" She closed her eyes and surrendered to his kiss. Then she murmured, very low, for only him to hear, "I've kept my promise to you, my dearest."

"Your promise, *querida?*"

Mara nodded, her eyes teasing and tender, her lips soft and quivering. "I promised you that I'd give you a son to name after your father Jaime, Ramón. I know it'll be a son. Soon after you'd gone away, I knew I was going to bear your son."

"*¡Querida!* No man was ever luckier. I thank the good God for the happiness He has given me in you, my Mara!" He kissed her again, then said, "Let me hold my son, and let's go into the house and say hello to your wonderful grandmother."

Carla and Hugo had flung themselves at Lucien Edmond. Even as he held Maxine to him, kissing her tenderly, they were tugging at the legs of his breeches, impatient to be noticed. He laughed happily, released Maxine and turned to swoop each child up into his arms, in turn, and to hug and kiss them. Then he came toward Sybella, took her tenderly into his arms and kissed her on the cheek. "I'm glad to be home, grandmother." A sudden recollection seized him. "Was everything all right here while we were away?"

"Thanks to Felicidad it was, Lucien Edmond."

"What do you mean, grandmother?" he demanded anxiously.

"Two men broke into the house about a week after you'd left, Lucien Edmond. They were dreadful men. One of them had a gun and the other a knife, and they made Celia bring them food. But Felicidad went out to the shed to get the falcon, and when she came back, she picked up a carbine from the closet in the hall where I'd left it. She threw the falcon at the man with the gun and distracted him while she flung the carbine to Maxine. Your wife killed them both, Lucien Edmond."

"My God—what Equitaba prophesied *did* come true!" he cried, hoarsely. Then, his eyes narrowed with anxiety, grasping her by the arms, he demanded, "And no one was hurt? Tell me, grandmother!"

"Not really, Lucien Edmond. My gracious, you're terribly strong, and my shoulders are old and frail, you know," Sybella remonstrated with a smile.

"I'm sorry, grandmother—well? You haven't answered my question."

"Well, the man with the knife had thrown it, just as Maxine shot him. It grazed my shoulder, but it was nothing, just a scratch. Now don't look at me like that, Lucien Edmond. I'm perfectly all right. Stop making such a fuss over me and go tell your wife and Felicidad how brave you think they are to have outwitted those awful men."

After Ramón had led the *remuda* horses back into the corral and quartered in separate stalls the mustangs that they had captured on the plains, he and the vaqueros trundled their gear into the bunkhouse. Meanwhile, Pablo Casares, now fully recovered from his wounds, hesitantly ushered Kate Strallis and her two children into the ranch house living room to discuss her immediate future with Lucien Edmond and Maxine Bouchard.

Lucien Edmond began by asking the young widow about her background and education, in order to ascertain how he could best help her find employment. But it was Maxine who suddenly interrupted, after Kate had answered all his questions and begun to look dejected. "There's something you don't know, Lucien Edmond. Celia's been talking for the last month about wanting to visit Prissy in Sangrodo's stronghold and seeing her two grandchildren. Besides, she hasn't been looking too well lately, and I think a vacation like that would do her a world of good."

"I agree. And besides, I'd like to have news of Sangrodo and Catayuna," Lucien Edmond replied. "I can see what you're driving at, Maxine. We'll need another cook while Celia's away, won't we? Well, Mrs. Strallis, do you think you could help us out in the kitchen and still have time enough to care for your two fine boys?"

"Oh yes, I'm sure I could, Mr. Bouchard. I'm a very good cook. That was part of my job in the St. Louis boardinghouse. And you know that when Mr. Casares was hurt, I helped out with the cooking on the trail. And I enjoyed it, really I did!" Her face was lovely now, animated as it was by hope.

"Of course," he said slowly, "it wouldn't be just for our family here in the ranch house, Mrs. Strallis. You'd have to prepare meals for all the workers, three meals a day. Naturally, Felicidad would help you, and I'm sure that Pablo could spare an hour or two away from his duties on the range to do some of the kitchen chores. After all, he gave a pretty good account of himself as chuck wagon cook on our drive."

"Oh, yes," Kate Strallis agreed, leaning forward to emphasize the point. "He's a wonderful cook, for a man. And I can't begin to tell you how kind he was to the children and to me, Mrs. Bouchard."

Lucien Edmond exchanged a swift, knowing glance with his wife, then continued. "Well, then, that's settled. And when Celia comes back, maybe you can help her on a permanent basis. Your little boy, David, is growing very rapidly. He's already talking and walking, and from the looks of it he's going to be quite a man someday. What about Jeremy?"

"Oh, he's never been any trouble, Mr. Bouchard! He's a darling baby. As soon as he's fed, he goes right to sleep and never seems to get cranky. I'm sure I could manage the meals without having to worry about him."

"Now let's see about where you'll stay, Mrs. Strallis. Maxine, isn't there a small room at the back of the ranch house, just off the kitchen? I think if some of the men tidy it up, it would be large and comfortable enough for Mrs. Strallis and her children."

"Well, it's not really all that large, dear, but for the time being I think it would do nicely. We could have one of the vaqueros make a kind of playpen for David and a bassinet for Jeremy."

"Oh, Mrs. Bouchard, that won't be necessary, really!" Kate Strallis intervened. "You see, Brett—my—my husband—made those things for the babies, and I brought them along in the wagon."

"Why, then, everything seems to be working out very nicely, Mrs. Strallis. I'll tell Pablo to see what he can do about making you a suitable bed. I know there are some mattresses in the storage shed that should still be serviceable, and he could certainly make a frame to enclose one of them."

"I can't—I don't know how to thank you for your kindness, Mr. and Mrs. Bouchard." Kate Strallis's eyes were suspiciously bright. "I promise you I'll work very hard and earn my keep."

"I haven't the slightest doubt of that, Mrs. Strallis," Lucien Edmond said in a kindly tone. "And now, I think we're all ready for a bite of lunch. This time, you and the children will be our guests. We won't put you to work until you've had plenty of time to rest up from the long journey. I can imagine it wasn't too comfortable, riding all that way in a supply wagon."

"It was fine, Mr. Bouchard, really it was! Everyone looked after me so nicely, why, it was like a—a sort of excursion," Kate Strallis exclaimed.

Maxine Bouchard laughed. She was already quite entranced by the young widow's courage and sense of humor. "I think we shall all get along very nicely, Kate—if I may call you that. And speaking for my husband and myself, I hope you'll be very happy with us."

Kate Strallis rose, grateful tears glistening in her eyes. "I'm sure I will be, Mrs. Bouchard. And thank you too, Mr. Bouchard."

Felicidad entered the living room to announce that lunch was ready, and her sparkling eyes and happy smile indicated that all was well with her own little world here on Windhaven Range.

Friar Bartoloméo, at Lucien Edmond's invitation, sát at the head of the table and said grace. Even Carla and Hugo bowed their heads and remained silent during his brief but memorable prayer. "Bless, dear God, this food to our use and us to Thy loving service. May we give thanks for the reunion of loved ones with their families. We commend our lives and our endeavors to the veneration of Thine eternal truths. Amen."

Almost to his consternation, Pablo Casares had been invited by Lucien Edmond and his wife to enjoy luncheon with them. Self-effacing, he took no part in the conversation until prompted, but from time to time he glanced across the table at Kate Strallis, watching with bated breath as she fed little David and the baby, Jeremy.

When the meal was over, he insisted on carrying the plates to the kitchen, despite the good-natured chaffing which he received from Lucien Edmond and, indeed, from Celia herself, who tartly told him that she was not used to having a man invade her kitchen even if he *was* trying to be helpful. But Lucas, who was already helping to wash the dishes, grinned and clapped Pablo on the back, saying, "Don't you mind mama any, amigo. Her bark is a lot worse than her bite, and I ought to know."

"Now that's about enough of that, Lucas," Celia exclaimed, picking up a wooden spoon and pretending to brandish it at him. Djamba's handsome son burst into laughter, seized Felicidad, and kissed her resoundingly. "Before mama beats me to death, honey, I've just got to have one good kiss after all the time I've waited."

Pablo took it all in, grinning sheepishly, caught up in this aura of friendship and love which embraced the Bouchard family and all those associated with it. Finally, Celia turned to him saying, "Now see here, didn't I overhear Mr. Bouchard saying that you'd help that nice Mrs. Strallis get settled in her room? It's been cleaned out now, so why don't you go and make yourself useful for a change?" It was a suggestion which the vaquero was only too happy to follow.

Hurrying out to the supply wagon which had brought the young widow and her two children to Windhaven Range, Pablo unloaded the crib and the bassinet. Next, he hastened to the storage shed, chose the thickest mattress, and brought it into Kate's room. Then he went in search of Joe Duvray. He described what was needed, and within an hour the two men, working together, fashioned a box frame into which the mattress would fit exactly. Then, having found sheets and blankets, Pablo made the bed and smoothed it down. Finally, he went back to the living room to inform Kate that her room was ready.

"Why, it's absolutely wonderful, Pablo! Such a lovely bed, and you've put the crib and the bassinet in just the right places, too!" She turned to him with such a dazzling smile that he gulped and very nearly dropped his sombrero.

"I—I'm glad you like it S—Señora Strallis—" he began.

"My gracious, I told you to call me Kate. Or maybe you don't want to be my friend, is that it?"

"*Madre de Dios*," he broke out, unable to control his feelings any longer, "I hope one day to be more than that —I want to take care of you and the *niños* for always, I— *diablo*, what have I said—I haven't any right to say it— forgive me—"

As he blustered at himself, Kate Strallis touched his shoulder with her hand and said very softly, "You've said what's in your heart, and that's what a woman always wants to hear from a man."

"Then—then you are not angry with me? You forgive me for going too fast? I am only a stupid vaquero—"

Her hand moved to touch his mouth and she shook her head, her eyes soft and warm. "And you mustn't call yourself stupid, because it's not so at all. I should know. Who else would have done so much when I needed help, when I was tortured by Brett's horrible death and when I didn't know where to turn or what was going to happen to the children and to me? Who saved my life when that awful man pulled me out of the wagon, and didn't even think of his own wounds and pain? You, Pablo. Wait, don't say anything. It's too soon—you know about—how I feel. I can't think of anyone yet. But one day, when I do—because I'll want a father for David and Jeremy—I don't think I shall have to look very far."

"Oh, Kate, *¡mi corazón, mi querida linda!*" he gasped, almost beside himself, as if he had just been shown a blinding glimpse of paradise. Then, blinking his eyes, he took his bandanna out of his pocket and blew his nose hard. "You—you will want to rest now. I am keeping you from it—I—I will be back this evening—if you need anything—" And then, almost unable to speak, he turned and hurried out of the house and back to the chuck wagon, on the pretense of inspecting it from top to bottom.

Friar Bartoloméo Alicante, who confessed himself guilty of the sin of eating more than was good for him because of the savory excellence of the food which Felicidad and Celia had prepared, enjoyed a siesta until late afternoon. Then, greatly refreshed, he called for Lucas and Felicidad, and walked with them to their new house. On its threshold, he blessed the young couple and, opening the door and entering the house, blessed the latter, also. They knelt before him, holding hands, as he concluded his benediction with the words, "Be not afraid to speak of that which displeases you in your partner, for once differences are frankly brought into the open, they can be more easily dealt with. Be trusting and gentle with one another, for that is how love grows and magnifies itself throughout a lifetime. Strive always to turn to each other in your need, for this is the true sacrament of marriage in the eyes of Him who made us all. May God's countenance shine upon you to the end of your days and may your children know His love through your own for them. Amen."

Lucas and Felicidad echoed that last solemn word as a kind of pledge to each other as they turned to kiss, still holding hands.

"And now, my children, will you not hear the Mass with me? I go now to the chapel which these thoughtful and hardworking men built as a blessed place of worship, to say vespers. Let us go together and exalt Him in His infinite generosity to us who believe unwaveringly in His justice."

His face serene, Friar Bartoloméo Alicante walked toward the little chapel, where the entire Bouchard family, as well as all the vaqueros and workers, were assembled. Joe Duvray had built the altar out of cedar, staining it and polishing it until it glowed with a warm radiance, and he had fashioned a towering wooden cross above it.

His voice joyous, his face uplifted to the altar and the cross, the Franciscan friar intoned the holy litany as twilight fell upon the valley. When he had finished, all eyes fixed on him in reverent silence. He declared, "Blessed be those who come to worship in this house of God, which you have built with your own hands, in the spirit of love and praise to Him who is the hope and the love of this life and of the life everlasting. I, His humblest of servants, thank you in His holy name. Did he not say, 'Be still and know that I am God'? Verily, at this moment, when you thank Him in this His new house for His reward for your toil and labor, He is truly within your hearts. Go forth in your lives, sure that He is pleased with you, His faithful children."

CHAPTER TWENTY-FIVE

For Arabella Hunter, now entering the fifth month of her pregnancy, life had begun to take on a new and highly diverting savor. James had never been more attentive, even on their honeymoon, or at least so it seemed to the black-haired matron. Not only did he share the conjugal bed with what seemed even greater zest and affection for her, but his usually grave demeanor had altered drastically. Since that morning in March, when her announcement that she was with child had led him to a bout of what she had then regarded as scandalous love-making, he had behaved more like an impetuous young lover than a quiet, self-assured man of business. Now he appeared to have acquired a proud and possessive attitude toward her. His playful praises of her beauty and his satisfaction with what he teasingly called his "new Bella" made her blush as she had not done since she had been a young girl.

Often, as she sat in front of her mirror combing her still-luxuriant black hair, she would giggle to herself as she remembered what had caused this quite intoxicating transformation in her life. When she did, it was to recall with almost a kind of secret gratitude her flirtation with Durwood McCambridge. James had told her that the scoundrel had left Galveston. At times she wondered idly where this handsome adventurer was now plying his trade of flattering and wooing lonely or dissatisfied females. Yet, confronted with maternity at the age of forty-five, only to find that her husband was more in love with her now than he had been at the start, Arabella Hunter basked in the joys of being her own husband's adored consort.

Of much greater concern to her was the realization that she could not hide her condition from Melinda and Andrew indefinitely. The girl was now seventeen, and in some ways promised to be even more beautiful than her voluptuous mother. The boy, at fifteen, had begun to outgrow the sibling rivalry which had so exasperated his sister. Now he found pleasure in books and was even showing an interest in his father's business endeavors. James Hunter had, when time permitted, taken him on long walks and even fishing off a pier in the bay.

In order to conceal her pregnancy as much as possible, Arabella had had Mrs. Rosalyn Maybury, a garrulous seamstress, make her some full-fashioned dresses with long, flaring skirts and spacious bodices. These provided concealment while at the same time meeting the demands of the current modes of fashion. To be more comfortable in the always oppressive Galveston summer heat, Arabella dispensed with her stays, wearing only a camisole and drawers, and a single petticoat under her dress.

On this warm July afternoon, Andrew had gone fishing with his father. Melinda had been invited to lunch at the house of her best girl friend, Betsy Cornwall, whose father, now a practicing attorney with many important clients, had been a captain under Jeb Stuart during the Civil War. Arabella had some misgivings about Betsy Cornwall, since the blond minx, six months older than Melinda, was already tentatively engaged to be married and, in Arabella's private opinion, was much too outspoken about intimate matters.

Also, Arabella Hunter was aware that Melinda was beginning to display a growing interest in the opposite sex. She had already brought over a gawky, towheaded youth of seventeen for tea. She introduced him as "an absolute whiz in mathematics, mama, and he's been ever so helpful to me in figuring out some really awful homework problems Mrs. Starette assigns us."

To be sure, Arabella could find no fault with Lorne Whister. He was the only son of the city recorder of deeds and his mother was a patron of the arts and one of the leading luminaries in Galveston's social life. Yet, like every mother from time immemorial, Arabella sought to postpone the inevitable day when Melinda would leave the nest.

She had assumed that Melinda and Andrew would be

out most of the afternoon, giving her the rare luxury of an afternoon to herself. Since the marvels of pregnancy were beginning to preoccupy her with the sheer physical sensations of approaching motherhood, she looked forward with almost sensuous anticipation to a leisurely bath and then the massaging of her face and limbs with a very special cream which her talkative seamstress had insisted would make wrinkles disappear and flesh seem firm and youthful, once again.

She had taken her bath and was sitting, clad only in her wrapper and slippers, before her mirror, industriously applying the cream to her cheeks and chin. Disconsolately, she thought to herself that it would be wise to limit the amount she ate at meals. She had always had a healthy appetite, but because of the obvious girth which maternity was giving her, she wanted to keep her figure from growing even more extreme.

She leaned forward and contemplated a faint line in her forehead. Reaching for the jar of miraculous cream, she applied a generous dollop to the spot and began to rub it in energetically. She uttered a sigh of discontent. It wouldn't be long before she became really ungainly, and the thought of the next few months' intense humidity and heat from the bay was hardly a cheering prospect. But this was something which dear James could do nothing about; it was, eternally, a woman's sacred obligation, and it had been so ever since Eve had been driven out of the Garden of Eden. Somewhat wistfully, she glanced down at her swelling belly, and sighed again. Adoring as he was, James could hardly be expected to go on calling her his "concupiscent Venus" much longer—an endearment with which he had startled her last month in the throes of their marital ardors. The only consolation she could find at the moment was that, when this ordeal was at last concluded, she would regain her former hourilike contours.

Lost in her contemplation of her own image, Arabella did not hear Melinda enter the house. She had left the door of her bedroom slightly ajar, and her daughter interpreted that as a sign that her entry would not be unwelcome. Thus it was that Melinda, totally absorbed with the exciting news Betsy had just imparted to her, burst into her mother's bedroom and, without pausing for any ceremonial greeting, broke out with "Mama, Betsy's going to be married two weeks from today, isn't it the most thrilling news you ever heard?"

Startled by her daughter's unexpected return and boisterous entry, Arabella turned, the wrapper opening to disclose the telltale evidence of her condition. Melinda uttered a gasp, put her hand to her mouth, and stammered, "M—Mama—you're—oh my goodness gracious, and at your age, too!"

"How *dare* you come in here without knocking, you impertinent minx!" Arabella gasped, hastily fastening the wrapper and turning crimson. "And what did you dare to say just now, young lady? At my age *indeed!*"

"But you—you're going to have a baby, aren't you, mama?" Melinda asked in amazement.

"Good heavens! That is a most indelicate remark, Melinda. How in heavens' name—I mean—" she floundered.

"Oh, my goodness, mama, this isn't the Dark Ages, it's 1869. And anyhow, Betsy has sort of—well, you know—she's going to be married anyway, just like I told you, and—"

"Just *as* I told you, dear." Even in her flustered state, Arabella primly corrected her daughter's lapse in grammar. Then, aghast, she breathed, scandalized, "Do you mean to tell me that that Cornwall girl has been telling you about—about—*things?*"

"Of course she has, mama. She says she can't wait until she has her very own baby. Oh, my goodness, when I tell her—"

"You will do nothing of the sort, or else I'll use this hairbrush on your saucy backside, young lady!" Arabella interrupted, and put her hand on the very weapon of chastisement which, in a sense, had caused her own delicate condition. "Do you understand me?"

Abashed, Melinda lowered her eyes and a contrite and faint "Yes, mama," emerged from her quivering lips.

"Well, then, young lady, since the fat's in the fire, so to speak, it appears that I have been very remiss in my duties as your mother. It was from me you should have learned such matters, not from that Cornwall girl."

"But she's my very best friend, mama, and you know she's a lovely girl. You like her yourself." Melinda came to the defense of her best friend.

"That's true enough, but all the same, I'm shocked to think that she would be so bold. Decent girls just don't discuss such matters, dear. Oh well, yes, it's true, I—you're going to have a brother or a sister by late November, I should think, but if you tell Andrew, I shall certainly spank you until you won't be able to sit down for a week, and that's a promise."

"Oh, I won't, mama. I—I'm awfully sorry I was—I was so rude—but I came in to tell you that—"

"I know, that Betsy's getting married. High time, too, I should think, bold baggage that she is! Well, I suppose that means I shall have to get her a suitable wedding present. You'll help me choose it, of course, Melinda, since you know Betsy better than I do—as it certainly appears."

Melinda giggled, then came to her mother, put her arms around her and kissed her. "I love you a lot, mama. I hope you're not too mad. And I won't tell Andrew, cross my heart. Isn't it exciting, though? I mean, Betsy's asked me to be her best bridesmaid."

"That's very nice, dear. Just remember," Arabella could not restrain a bit of sarcasm, "you're a bridesmaid, not the matron of honor. My word, you're only seventeen and yet you're becoming as audacious as Betsy Cornwall. I'm going to have to watch you much more closely. And your father and I are going to have to discuss the possibility of marrying you off to a nice young man who will make you remember that you're a young lady at all times."

The man who had once unwittingly brought about the new complications in Arabella Hunter's life had himself entered upon a most grandiose project of his own. The day after his chance meeting with the land swindler who called himself Baron Rodrigo de Austencio, Durwood McCambridge visited his new partner's rooms in the Galvez Hotel in San Antonio and was introduced to Theobald Arnison. If he had had any misgivings about the future of his new partnership, Durwood McCambridge—or, to give him the name he had now adopted, Quentin Durwood—

254

was certain that this seedy old derelict was very likely the ultimate key to the success of their proposed venture.

Theobald Arnison was sixty-two, frail, with stooped shoulders, sparse white hair, and a straggly beard. His patched clothes were usually unkempt, and his voice was thin, cracked, and wavering most of the time. His watery blue eyes were myopic behind a pair of ill-fitting spectacles; his nose was bulbous, red, and thickly veined from his excessive tributes to Bacchus; and he had very few teeth left. At first glance, Quentin Durwood scowled and drew the baron to one side, muttering, "Is this old souse the man you're relying on for the Spanish land deeds?"

Norman Cantrell—who had urged Quentin Durwood to refer to him always as the baron and especially in mixed company—chuckled and nodded. "Haven't you ever heard of the old proverb that looks are deceiving, Quentin boy? Wait a bit. He hasn't had his morning ration yet. Give him a little time to mellow. Once he starts to spout, you'll feel like a pupil in the schoolroom. I told you, he used to work in a library as an historian and he knows more about old books than anybody else in Virginia—that's where he was born, by the way."

The baron opened a satchel and took out a bottle of corn whiskey at the sight of which old Theobald Arnison's eyes brightened. He poured out a generous glassful for the old man, who drank it down as if it were water, snorting and coughing, and then sat up straight as if it were a magic potion from the fountain of Ponce de León. Then, with what seemed an almost miraculous recovery, Theobald Arnison stood up, drew a deep breath, and began to pace about the room, declaiming historical dates and events with a loquacity and command of diction which made Quentin Durwood blink in amazement.

What was most impressive about this pathetic old man, and what most convinced Quentin Durwood that he and his two future associates stood on the verge of limitless wealth, was Theobald Arnison's smug, self-satisfied exhibition of samples of forged documents. Here was the very crux of the matter. If, as the baron claimed, the restoration of Texas to the union would probably not take place until the following spring, existing land titles could cer-

255

tainly be in doubt, in spite of the records kept in the land office in Austin.

What was more important, the population of this vast territory was extremely sparse. Except for El Paso and Presidio, most settlements lay east of the 98° longitude, from Henrietta to Junction and thence southwest to the Rio Grande at Del Rio, just west of Brackettville. Beyond this line to the west, the population was less than 100 persons per 1,000 square miles—the true cattleman's frontier. And below San Antonio to the Rio Grande and west of that line, there were only a few ranchers on unfenced land. In Theobald Arnison's opinion, most of that land, therefore, had originally been designated by a succession of Spanish kings to be given as rewards or bounties to able colonists, opportunistic military leaders, and mining administrators.

Spain, the old man went on (the whiskey having steadied his voice and given him a seemingly youthful energy), had always lusted for gold from the New World. Well, then, here were documents which would show, beyond any reasonable doubt, and even in a court of law—an uninformed and none-too-educated court at best in these days of the frontier—that the land on which present-day ranchers and farmers had settled did not, in fact, belong to them, but instead to the descendants of those who had rendered some inestimable service to the crown.

Glancing at the baron for permission, the former historian produced several rolls of parchment, yellowed with age and affixed with wax seals and ribbons. Inviting Quentin Durwood to approach and examine them for himself, Theobald Arnison pointed to one of the seals. "Do you see, young man? It says 'Yo el rey Felipe V.' He was the first Bourbon king of Spain and a grandson of the immortal Louis XIV."

"I see," Quentin Durwood dubiously admitted, though at the moment he did not quite see at all.

"Come now, you will need to keep your wits about you if you are to help bring off this coup which the baron has so ingeniously concocted."

Like a child wanting praise from a parent or teacher, Theobald Arnison cocked his head and eyed the gray-bearded land swindler, who saluted him with two fingers

256

pressed to his forehead and an indulgent nod. "You see, when Louis XIV accepted the Spanish throne for his grandson, he set off the War of the Spanish Succession. It dragged on from 1701 to 1714. This greatly reduced Spanish power. After that, our worthy royal benefactor was dominated by women and, ultimately, became mentally unbalanced. The power of Spain in this country may be said to have waned from the time he came to the throne. But no matter. What does matter is that he reigned about a century before the crowning of Ferdinand VII, under whose regime Spain lost all of its colonies on the North and South American mainland."

"History has never been one of my best subjects," Quentin Durwood admitted. "But if all this is going to help us make a fortune, I'll listen as long as your voice holds out, professor."

The old man beamed at this derisively flattering title. "And you will not have wasted your time, either, young man. Now, in the course of my studies, I acquired many sheets of this parchment. It can be treated with certain dyes and stains to make it look hundreds of years old. And after that—here, let me show you." He unrolled the document he had first put out for Quentin Durwood's inspection, and the young adventurer gasped. In a flowing script, written in Spanish (a language which Quentin Durwood read passably well) there was a description of a piece of land near Santa Fe. In it were references to certain peculiar geographic features, such as a broad, deep creek and, to mark another boundary line, a towering canyon.

"I begin to get your drift, professor," Quentin Durwood said with a satisfied sigh. "Of course, in a hundred or so years, those landmarks might change."

"Of course, of course, young man," Theobald Arnison retorted. "I made this one up out of my own head, when the baron first saved me from a most precarious situation and began to comprehend my true potential."

"What he's trying to say, Quentin," the suave land swindler explained with a broad wink, "is that here's where you come in, as I told you last night. You'll explore the southeastern part of Texas, where there aren't very many settlers to begin with. You'll make notes of what you see, and you will pay particular attention to landmarks that

257

can't possibly be missed. That, you see, will pinpoint the boundaries of the land we're going to grab. Oh, quite legally, because the document signed by Philip V will specify exactly those landmarks, and his royal grant will take precedence over any current claim. Don't forget, there aren't many lawyers in Texas and still fewer judges with enough acumen to start investigating that far back in time. Besides, we're not really going to run to the courts. We're going to show these documents to people already on the land, after, of course, you've been to the land office and found out to whom these properties currently belong. If they're sensible and believe Theobald's artistic creations, they'll oblige us by moving off the land. Then Theobald will forge a transfer of title in our favor, on behalf of the apologetic settler. We'll register that at the land office, and it will stand up for sure and forever."

"Marvelous!" Quentin Durwood chuckled with admiration. "That seal the professor affixed looks old enough to date back to when he says it does."

"That's why I've made him a full partner in our little enterprise. And if you're half as efficient and perspicacious as I think you are, Quentin, we'll wind up millionaires. I've already got a prospective buyer for some Texas property. He's a sheep rancher who presently lives not far from Taos, in New Mexico, and he's been running into a little trouble with some of the aristocratic Spanish families there. He's an outsider, you see, and they hate him because he's a Yankee, or, as they say, a gringo. Happens he married a rather brazen piece of baggage, the oldest daughter of one of those Spanish ranchers, who liked the cut of his jib and defied her father. Her father had other plans for bedding her—with a neighbor's son."

"I see. How much land do you figure this fellow will need?"

"He has about 2,000 sheep, so he'll need at least twice that many acres. His father-in-law will drive a hard bargain with him when he finally sells the land he's on, but then he bought it for a song just because of a mixup in the Taos land office deeds. That's another thing those Spanish ranchers won't forgive him for, and why they want him out of New Mexico. As I understand it, his father struck it rich in the gold rush of '49 and left him a fair amount in a San Francisco bank. He's a man something like yourself, Quentin boy, an adventurer who enjoyed everything from playing poker for high stakes, to breaking in a wild horse, to clerking in a store, if it brought him into contact with the ladies. From what he told me, he thought he'd visit New Mexico and see what life was like down there near the border. Then he met this hot-blooded filly and decided that the only way he could get her to bed was to marry her. Well, we needn't concern ourselves with his life story," he concluded, as he trailed off.

The baron eyed Theobald Arnison, who uttered a shrill cackle of laughter, then went on. "But you, Quentin, are going to be scouting around for a good piece of land that has enough grazing for all those sheep. Mind you, it's got to be land somebody is on already. We're not in the business of buying land ourselves and registering it with the recorder of deeds. As we progress, depending on your persuasive skill, we may decide to keep some of it for ourselves, hold it back and sell it a few years from now, when Texas really begins to get settled. But for now, I'm sure you'll find plenty of stupid farmers or ranchers who haven't been in Texas very long and don't know enough about the fine points of the law to prove that the professor's royal deed isn't authentic."

"My God," Quentin Durwood exclaimed, "I thought I was a sharp land speculator, baron, but I have to take my hat off to you. It was a sheer stroke of genius, finding the professor."

"Not precisely, Quentin." The baron permitted himself an indulgent laugh. "When I thought of this idea, I knew I was going to have to find someone who could do the paper work, so to speak. But finding Theobald was a stroke of pure *luck*. If I hadn't, I might still be looking for someone. I want you to get down to the Mexican border as soon as you can, and inspect the areas you think will be most advantageous for our little scheme. First off, you've got to find me some good land for this buyer I've just told you about. But don't stop there. Acquaint yourself with a good many other feasible sites for future takeover."

"I begin to wish that I had paid more attention to history in school," Quentin Durwood observed. "I think

I've got the general idea. . . . In other words, a grant signed by—who was that?—oh, yes, Ferdinand VII—wouldn't be nearly as convincing because we got the land away from him when he was on the throne. But this Bourbon king lived so far back that no Texan's going to know a thing about him, and those papers the professor's doctored up will look like the genuine article. The only question I've got is, how did this Philip V get to know so much about the shape and size of properties in Texas? You see, baron, up to now my game has been picking up pieces of land the owners have forgotten to pay their taxes on. Now that's cold hard fact, with a little bluff thrown in for good measure."

"And, as I'm sure you've already discovered, a good deal more dangerous than this new game, Quentin," the baron interposed. "To answer your question, there were surveyors, even in those early days. If memory serves me right, even George Washington got his start as a surveyor, and his father was a Virginia land speculator and iron-mine owner—isn't that right, professor?"

"Absolutely, baron." Theobald Arnison had taken off his spectacles and was polishing them with a torn and none-too-clean handkerchief.

"Well, then, Quentin," the baron pursued, "if I were in your place, I'd make a friend of someone who works in the land office in Austin. Entertain him lavishly, so far as your means permit. Then, when he trusts you, get him to show you the deeds of properties in the area which I've already indicated should be a fertile field for our endeavors. Copy the descriptions or, if that should make him the least bit suspicious, do your best to memorize them. The professor is quite adept at translating such descriptions into what we may call the romantic Spanish version. We will stay on here at the Galvez Hotel till you've done your homework."

"I'll leave tomorrow," Quentin Durwood promised, his face aglow with greedy anticipation.

The next morning, after a quick and scanty breakfast, Quentin Durwood was the first customer of the day at the Citizens' Bank of San Antonio, where he drew out $5,000 from his savings. Then, mounting a new roan gelding, he rode past the ruined mission of the Alamo with scarcely a glance at this memorial to Texas valor, and took the road toward Austin.

In his saddlebags, he had packed his best suit and hat, and sufficient accessories for a week's stay. Whatever else he might need could readily be purchased in Austin, and part of the money he had taken with him would be used to gain the favor of a corruptible land-office employee. He did not anticipate any difficulties in finding such a man. With land selling at fifty cents an acre, the clerks in that office must be paid the most meager of salaries. Whiskey and a complacent girl would work wonders in corroding the moral fiber of a man who probably could afford neither—at least as often as he might wish.

If he had any doubts at all, they were mainly those concerning the availability of an attractive woman who would be willing and able to play her part in his plan. Of course, saloon girls were always available, but experience had taught him that this particular type of easy-virtue female was seldom noteworthy for either beauty or intelligence. On the other hand, with a little coaching, some grooming, and enough money, it was amazing what changes could be wrought in the most ordinary of women. He had proved this in one instance. He recalled momentarily black-haired Arabella Hunter, with whom he had had the briefest of encounters in Galveston. Now, if he could find a female of her proportions and emotional uncertainty in Austin, the rest would be as easy as stealing candy from a baby.

Quentin Durwood made the eighty-two-mile journey from San Antonio to Austin in three days. He boarded his horse at a livery stable not far from Austin's best hotel, and there engaged the best available room. He ate dinner in an excellent restaurant across the street from the hotel, and then made a leisurely tour of the saloons. In the third, named the Longhorn, he found exactly what he was looking for.

Having ordered the best bar whiskey, he took his glass to an unoccupied table and sat down, studying the card-players, the cowboys, and various other citizens who occupied the tables around him. He had donned his best suit—an elegant frock coat and ornately cuffed trousers, with a ruffled silk shirt and a flowing cravat, decorated with a diamond stickpin. He became at once the focus of attention, whereupon he lifted his glass and toasted the other patrons. After a quick examination of this nattily dressed Easterner—for they rightly decided he must be one—the others turned back to their own devices and left him free to relax and await developments.

He had already noticed two dance-hall girls. One of them was already seated in the lap of a fat, well-dressed man in his early fifties, while the other stood behind one of the cowboys, her hands lightly caressing his shoulders. The girls were not particularly appetizing, and when the fat man suddenly pushed his girl off his lap, and she moved toward Quentin Durwood, he shook his head and smiled.

Then the narrow door opened and a tall, auburn-haired young woman entered. Quentin Durwood put down his glass and beckoned to her. She was perhaps twenty, wearing a sleazy, red calico dress which had obviously seen better days, but her face was striking and her figure still more so. She had an insolent face, with high-set cheekbones, and an aquiline nose with thin, sensuously flaring nostrils. Her mouth was small and supercilious, but ripe, with an arrogant curl which proclaimed its owner's belief that, despite her lowly social status, she was infinitely superior to most of the men in the saloon.

Quentin Durwood removed his hat and stood up to welcome her as she made her way past the other tables. "Good evening," he said pleasantly. "May I buy you a drink, Miss—Miss—?"

"Lily," she replied tersely as she seated herself. "Thanks, mister. Haven't seen you here before."

"No, it's my first visit to Austin, Lily. My name's Quentin Durwood. I'm from the East, and I represent a very influential and wealthy man who traces his lineage back to the grandees of Spain. I'm here to acquire some land for him, you see."

The auburn-haired young woman eyed him suspiciously, then shrugged. "I don't know what all those fancy words mean, mister, but if you're looking for a good time, maybe you and I can have one."

"That was what I had in mind, Lily," he chuckled. "Shall I buy a bottle or will a glass suffice?"

"I don't know what that last means, Mister Quentin—say, that's a crazy name, that one is—but Jim, who runs this saloon, doesn't much like fancy dudes to hog a table all to themselves and just buy a glass of whiskey, if you get my meaning."

"I do indeed, and I'm grateful for your advice. Here." Quentin Durwood took out his wallet and handed the redhead a ten-dollar bill. "Why don't you buy the bottle and keep the change?"

"Say, you're a real sport. Thanks a heap. I'll be right back—now don't you go away," she said with an arch smile, rising from her chair and leaning forward so that he could observe the thrusting pear-shaped globes of her ample bosom.

"I haven't any intention of going away without you, Lily," he chuckled again.

She gave him a bawdy wink, walked over to the bar, whispered to the ruddy-faced Irish bartender, and came back with a bottle of whiskey and a second glass. Quentin Durwood watched her with amused interest. She certainly had possibilities and he was remembering that he had been continent for longer than he cared to remember. It would do no harm to begin his plan by bedding her.

She calmly poured out a surprisingly large shot, lifted the glass, and saying curtly, "Here's mud in your eye!" she downed the drink nearly at a gulp. His eyes widened with surprise and admiration. "I sort of needed that, Mr. Quentin." She felt the need to explain. "It's been a rough couple of weeks in this crummy town. If it isn't cowboys stepping all over your feet when you're dancing, it's slobs like that fat old Abner Whitman, over at that table there." She jerked her thumb in the direction of the man who had just pushed the other girl off his lap. "He's an old skinflint; always wants more time with a girl than he pays for, and he's no good in bed, anyway. What about you? At least you're young enough."

Quentin Durwood tilted back his head and burst into hearty laughter. Such candor was refreshing after his many encounters with vapid, married women whose conscience got the better of them once they had finally succumbed to his virility. When he stopped laughing, he leaned across the table and said in a low voice, "You'll be able to answer that question yourself in short order, Lily girl. In fact, if you're as good as I think, you'll be glad you walked through that door. Now, what do you charge for your, shall we say . . . companionship?"

The redhead gave him a bold, appraising look. "Let's get one thing straight, Mr. Quentin. Just because I put out doesn't mean I don't choose whom I go to bed with, understand? Of course, when a girl gets on her uppers, sometimes she doesn't always have much choice—like with that slob, Abner Whitman. But once was enough. He may be an upstanding citizen and all that—he runs a general store on Harris, in case you didn't know—but he's got bad teeth and bad breath and I don't think he's taken a bath in three years."

"I took one just this evening before I went to dinner, Lily. And my teeth ought to pass muster." He bared them, and Lily giggled. "But you haven't answered my question yet. What's the tariff?"

"Well, the bottle of whiskey was four dollars, and you said I was to keep the change, that's six, isn't it? Well, that'll pay for all night if you want me that long. I sort of like the way you talk, even if I don't understand all your fancy words, Mr. Quentin."

"What would you say, Lily, if I put you up at my hotel, paid you a hundred dollars a week for as long as I care to have you around, and a nice little bonus if you get friendly with someone who's going to be very important to me?"

Her gray-green eyes narrowed as she stared at him silently for a moment. Then, suspiciously, she demanded, "You're not putting me on now, are you, Mr. Quentin?"

Glancing around to make sure that no one was watching him, Quentin Durwood again took out his wallet, extracted five twenty-dollar bills from it, replaced his wallet in his trousers pocket, then held up the bills. The redhead gasped and reached for them, but he pulled back his hand. "When you've earned them, Lily girl. And I think you saw just now there's plenty more where that came from. Now, since we've paid for the bottle, I assume we can take it along with us to make the evening more companionable."

"You want me to go with you right now?" She rose slowly, sinuously, letting him see her svelte, lithe body as the thin calico hugged its contours.

"Do you have to tell the man who owns this place about our transaction, Lily?" he inquired.

"Nope. I work when I feel like it, but as it happens, tonight's your lucky night because I'm behind in my rent and old Mrs. Stillman said she was going to put me out if I didn't come up with the green stuff by tomorrow. Joe and Max will see me when they see me, that's all. Hell, they get a cut of all the whiskey I sell and from the dances, and they even get a cut when I take a fellow to my room, so I don't owe them anything. Only," this with a sly wink and crafty smile, "they're not going to learn a thing about this little deal of ours, honey, not from little Lily, if you get my meaning. Let's go." She shoved the cork back into the bottle, pressed it down firmly with her thumb, grasped it by the neck, and walked slowly toward the door of the saloon. Quentin Durwood followed her, a broad smile on his face.

An hour later, as they lay side by side on the bed, the redhead sighed languorously and playfully tweaked the hairs on his sturdy chest. "That was the best poke I've got since I came to Austin from New Orleans six months ago, Quentin, honey," she confided.

"I enjoyed it too, Lily," he smiled as, his left hand still cupping one of her superbly firm breasts, he ran his right palm down the inside of her thigh. "But I'm curious, why would you have left New Orleans to come to this dusty town? From what I've heard that city is a mecca for ladies of the night."

She giggled, sliding her hand slowly down his flat, muscular belly. "If you're trying to say that I'd have made more money in New Orleans than here, you're perfectly right. Only thing is, I worked for a madam who had herself a nigger sweet man. One night he got himself all likkered up and came into my room and tried to rape me. Well, my daddy used to own slaves, and I just wasn't having any. I let him have it with a hatpin, and I guess I did him in, so I had to run. Madam Bella had powerful connections. Anyhow, one of daddy's kinfolks moved to Austin just before the war started, so I thought I'd look her up 'cause she was the only kin I had left—daddy and mama both died the last year of the war. But it turned out that Cousin Hettie wanted to take real good advantage of me and make me do all the household chores and pay me nothing. 'Sides which, her old husband figured if I was living in their house, I owed him bed rights." She shrugged. "So I figured I might as well get paid for it as be taken advantage of like that. But that's enough about me . . . now, honey, why don't you tell me all about this deal you've got in mind—you know, about that important man you're supposed to meet and I'm supposed to be real nice to?"

By now, her slim hand had reached his reawakened manhood. Quentin Durwood emitted a hoarse chuckle as he mounted her. "Later, Lily honey, much later," he breathed.

CHAPTER TWENTY-SIX

Lily Mellers—such was her infatuation with her new client that she had revealed her actual surname to him—had found Quentin Durwood the most physically satisfying lover she had known since she had begun to sell her favors at the age of sixteen. To be sure, the sight of his well-filled wallet and the promise of a semi-permanent liaison at a price beyond her wildest reckoning had aided her in bringing more than feigned passion to her professional technique. Yet his curly hair and twinkling blue eyes, his almost boyish air and regular features, had made their first night together something more than perfunctory, as had his thirty-two-year-old male vigor. Nonetheless, for all her admiration of him and her determination to retain his interest as long as possible, Lily Mellers was wise enough in the ways of men to sense that he was something of a rogue and an adventurer. And once he had divested himself of his clothing and come to bed with her, she was sure of it.

His brown hair and his crisp Van Dyke seemed genuine enough, but when he had quitted her and gone to light the candle, she had noticed that his body hair was much darker. The discrepancy could be significant, but she had no intention of pointing this out to him; that would mean the end of their relationship. But her instincts told her to be cautious with him and to think over twice whatever proposition he was likely to put to her. As for Quentin Durwood himself, as soon as he had lit the candle, he had been aware of his blunder. But he reasoned that a mere whore with Lily's sketchy and unimpressive background would hardly bother herself about such details so long as she was well paid for her efforts. Nor did he intend to show himself unclad to the settlers whom he intended to fleece. Also, he was remembering what Lily had told him about having killed a man back in New Orleans. If she should show moral scruples enough to balk at entertaining one of the Austin land clerks, he would have only to remind her that, although what she was now doing was not outside the law, she would assuredly be accountable to the law for what she had already done, if he chose to inform on her.

Just to keep on her good side, however, he behaved like a *grand seigneur* the next morning by ordering breakfast served in the room they shared, and tucked a twenty-dollar bill into the bodice of her calico dress after they had finished a sumptuous repast. "That's just for spending money, Lily," he told her with a genial grin. "Now, as soon as you've tidied up and feel like seeing what the world looks like in broad daylight, we're going to the best dressmaker in Austin and get you dolled up. You see, this friend of mine has a weakness for lovely ladies, and that's exactly what you're going to be."

"Oh, Quentin, you're so good to me!" She wound her arms around him, glued herself to him and gave him a far from professional kiss. For, if Lily Mellers had a weakness, it was decidedly in favor of being dressed like a lady of fashion, so that she could not be mistaken for what she really was. Already her suspicions about her tall, handsome client were receding, simply because no man to date had treated her so generously.

An hour later, Quentin Durwood escorted her down the street to a middle-aged seamstress who displayed homemade dresses in the window of her shop. He allowed her to purchase two bombazine dresses with flounces, high bodices, and widely flaring skirts, one blue and one green.

Lily Mellers had decided that she would balk at her new benefactor's scheme only short of murder. She watched him, her eyes wide with fascination, as he took out his wallet with a flourish and paid cash for the two dresses, then ordered, "Burn that calico dress, Mrs. Eady. And now, can you outfit my charming fiancée in some coquettish unmentionables?"

"My dear sir!" the middle-aged spinster gasped, turning a furious crimson, much to Lily Mellers' sly amusement. "That is a matter which only this charming young lady and

268

myself should discuss, and certainly never in the presence of a gentleman. If you will be kind enough to withdraw from the shop until we have finished coming to an understanding concerning the rest of her attire, I should be most grateful to you."

"I can deny you nothing, fair lady," Quentin Durwood blithely declared as, winking at the outraged spinster, he put on his hat and walked outside. Left to her own resources, Lily Mellers promptly acquired several pairs of lace-trimmed drawers and camisoles, a new pair of stays, some stockings, and a pair of elegant ladies' ankle-length boots with mother-of-pearl buttons. Then, opening the door of the shop, she called, somewhat apprehensively in view of her extravagance, "Quentin, dear, I'm ready now."

To her delight, he paid the total bill—which amounted to $147—without a murmur. She wore the green bombazine, and when she saw herself in the mirror, she breathed, "It's sort of like having a fairy godmother, just like in a dream!"

"Except I can hardly be your godmother, my dear Lily," he retorted, which comment drew another stifled gasp from the spinster. It was by far the best sale she had made in weeks, which somewhat mollified her indignation over Quentin Durwood's highly outrageous remarks.

He told Lily to go back to the hotel and wait for him, and sent her an admiring glance as she went down the street. There was no doubt that fine plumage made fine birds. In that green bombazine she was wearing, Quentin would never have recognized the trollop from the Longhorn. Nor would a land-office clerk, who probably not able to afford the Longhorn's brand of entertainment in the first place.

He bought himself a couple of good cigars at a nearby tobacco shop, then slowly sauntered toward the land office. It was just about time for lunch, he estimated, and he would have a chance to size up the employees as they came out of the office. There was no hurry at all. He had already learned that overanxiety and impatience bred suspicion, and could as easily scotch a deal as finalize one.

No, he would simply mark his man, come back again in a day or two and invite him to dinner, and then gradually put Lily to work. He would make himself a crony of the fellow, so that their meetings would seem natural and spontaneous. After he had acquired all the information he needed, there would be long days of riding under the hot sun, making lengthy notes about the landmarks of the terrain, and then the long ride back to San Antonio.

Remembering last night's activities, for a moment he entertained the notion of having Lily accompany him. Then he dismissed the idea. She couldn't be expected to ride horseback, not all that long way, and rough it the way he'd have to. But one thing was certain. Before he left Austin, he'd get his money's worth out of Lily Mellers.

Quentin Durwood seated himself on a bench, on the edge of the little park across the street from the land office, and watched the people coming in and going out. One of his principal assets had always been the ability to size up a person at first glance, and thus far his instincts had been right most of the time. There was a tall, sun-bronzed rancher wearing a broad sombrero and chaps, with two guns in his belt, talking earnestly to a fat little man with a walrus mustache and exaggeratedly long sideburns. Now a couple came out of the land office, a gray-haired man who looked like a farmer and his fat, dowdy, blond wife. Most likely nesters, the Texas term for farmers whom the big ranchers were beginning to dislike because they were always making a fuss about cattle trampling their crops. German, too, by the looks of that pair. For a time, he amused himself by making up backgrounds and histories for these people, fancifully theorizing on why they were buying land and where they were buying it. Then he slowly got up from the bench as he noticed a short, heavy-set, straggly bearded man in his late forties or early fifties. The man's clothes were rumpled, and he wore thick spectacles. A pencil stub was stuck behind one ear. There couldn't be any doubt that here was a man who worked in that office and was busy all day, figuring out tracts and parcels of land and registering the deeds to them.

Durwood watched the man come across the street to the park, stop in his tracks as a mounted cowhand galloped past him, and heard him utter an irritated curse at the thoughtless rider. As the man approached him, Quentin Durwood slowly rose and commented, "Some selfish people just don't care about the rights of others, do they, mister?"

"You're sure as hell right about that, friend. Say, you're dressed right smart for a hot day in these parts. You must be an Eastern dude by the looks of you."

"Now you know, that's absolutely right. Just about my first day in town, too. I was seeing the sights; took a little walk and found this park. Say, my stomach tells me it's about lunchtime."

"That's what mine tells me too, mister. I'm Tobias Jennings. What might your monicker be?"

"Quentin Durwood, Mr. Jennings. Glad to meet you." He offered his hand, and the stocky man shook it. "Say, maybe you know a place around here where a man could get a decent lunch? I'd be grateful if you'd show me the way, and I'd like to stand treat. When a man's a stranger in town, it's always good to have a friend."

"Why, Mr. Durwood, that's mighty neighborly of you. And I think I'll just take you up on your offer." Tobias Jennings grinned, a little sourly. "I tell you, I can stand a little friendliness today, after the morning I've had. These damn settlers coming in and ranchers wanting to stake their claims on land, and half of them haven't even marked their boundaries yet. You know, you've gotta check your property before you can buy it, Mr. Durwood, and you've gotta be accurate, too. And then you get a silly argument from some old fool who hasn't even taken the trouble to figure out how many acres he wants to buy. It can waste a morning."

"It must be a dull and dreary job, and I'll bet it doesn't pay too much, Mr. Jennings," Quentin Durwood suggested.

Tobias Jennings snorted. "You'd be right as rain to make a bet like that and you'd win, Mr. Durwood. I'm just about fed up with it, if you want to know the truth. Came over here from Houston right after the war. They needed men in this land office and I'd done some surveying work. I clerked in the recorder of deeds office back in Houston, and of course the war just about put me out of business. So when I had this offer and my wife, Rachel, came down with spotted fever and passed on, I figured I might as well try to do this new government up here

271

some good." He shook his head disgustedly, and tugged at his wispy, graying beard. "But this town is just about dead."

"You have my sincere condolences for your great loss, Mr. Jennings," Quentin Durwood murmured. Then, adopting the air of a man of the world to an equal, he hinted, "You mean there aren't any diversions here in Austin? Wine, women, and song and such? Seems to me that a man like you, in the prime of life and a widower, to boot, would have himself a time."

"Hah! Now that's a real pipe dream, Mr. Durwood. You ever seen some of the chippies they got in those saloons and dance halls near Harris Street? A man would have to be plumb loco to go there for his pleasure. And on my wages, I've all I can do to keep body and soul together. As for fancy girls, I haven't seen one yet. I don't make enough to get hitched to a decent woman—and I haven't seen many of those around town, either."

Quentin Durwood was already congratulating himself for his acumen in approaching Tobias Jennings. He was convinced that if he had interviewed every one of the clerks employed in the land office, he couldn't have found a more logical candidate. "That's really a shame, Mr. Jennings. But maybe your luck will change. You know, it's interesting that you work at the land office. I'm here representing a big Eastern syndicate. I'd like to look over some of the available land and see if it meets with their specifications."

"Well, you've come to the right place to do that. I'm assistant chief clerk, so maybe I can help. We've got plenty of land in Texas to sell, Mr. Durwood, and that's a fact."

"Fine, fine! But you see, being new here, I was hoping to find a man who's honest and reliable, and who knows the land business. You could be of great help to me, and I'd certainly be willing to pay handsomely for your assistance."

From the quick, interested look in Tobias Jennings's pale-blue eyes, Quentin Durwood knew that he was on the right track. "Well, it's my duty as a public servant to give you information, Mr. Durwood," Jennings replied

272

with a certain wary dignity. "You understand, I couldn't take a bribe, not for doing my duty."

"Please don't get me wrong, Mr. Jennings, I wouldn't think of offering a bribe to a man of your integrity. What I mean is, seeing as how you've had so little entertainment the past few years, I might be able to provide some. Ah, is this the place you'd recommend for lunch, Mr. Jennings?"

They had arrived at a little restaurant about three blocks from Quentin Durwood's hotel. The assistant chief clerk nodded. "Best chili and stew in town, and Ed Williams uses only the best beef he can get. Thank God beef's cheap. I'll bet they're paying a fancy price for it back where you come from, eh, Mr. Durwood?"

"Why don't you call me Quentin and I'll call you Tobias? I feel as if we're old friends already." Quentin Durwood slapped the stocky clerk on the back as he opened the restaurant door and gestured for his new friend to enter.

The chili was better than Quentin Durwood had expected, and, wanting to replenish his energies for the night ahead with Lily, he ordered a dish of *arroz con pollo* that was even more delicious. Expansively, he invited his newly found friend to order the same dish. Tobias Jennings looked longingly at the heaped plate set before his host, and plucked at his beard again, torn with indecision. "Well, I don't generally eat a big lunch, Quentin. But that sure looks mighty good. Tell you the truth, I've been skimping on my meals lately. My pay's a mite overdue, so I've had to take it easy."

"Then by all means enjoy it as my treat, Tobias!" Durwood heartily urged, beckoning to the Irish girl who served tables. "A large plate of this delicacy for my good friend here, my fine colleen!"

The girl tittered, put a hand over her mouth, glanced back at her glowering employer, who had put his head through the little open window of the kitchen, then nodded and hurried back to place the order.

"Mighty generous of you, Quentin, and I appreciate it a lot."

"Think nothing of it. It's not every day a newcomer to

a strange town meets a good friend like you, Tobias."

When the chicken with rice was placed before Jennings, he licked his lips, then dug in with gusto while Durwood leaned back and lit a cigar, beckoning to the girl to bring him coffee. When at last his guest had finished, he ventured, "Perhaps we could have supper this evening, Tobias. I'd like to talk to you about the land situation. I realize you're an expert, and of course I'd pay you for your time. After all, I don't expect a man to talk shop after hours."

"Now, that really won't be necessary, Quentin. Not after this fine lunch. Haven't much to do with my evenings, anyway, and I'd be glad for your company, to tell you the truth."

"Fine. I'm staying at the Hotel Coronado, in room 206, Tobias. When do you finish work?"

"Depends, Quentin. If we have as many people filing claims this afternoon as we did this morning, I might be there until close to six o'clock. Good gosh, I'd best be getting back, I'm a little late already."

"Well, Tobias, for a man of your status in that office—after all, you *are* the assistant chief clerk—I should say you could take a few minutes extra. Here, take a cigar with you. Shall I expect you, then, a little after six?"

"I'm not putting you out now, am I?" Tobias Jennings rose from the table, belched, then looked apologetic. "Excuse me, Quentin, but that was a damn good feed, if you get my meaning. Much obliged." He patted his paunch and grinned sheepishly. "It'll be all I can do to keep from falling asleep this afternoon, after all I've eaten. Thanks again. Room 206, you said?"

"That's right. Here, might as well take another cigar too. You'll have one to smoke this afternoon when you take a breather, and one for tonight at supper."

Jennings nodded, pocketed the second cigar, belched again, and then waved his hand to his generous host. Quentin Durwood nodded and returned the greeting with a wave of his hand, and then turned to pay the young waitress. "A superb lunch, my lovely colleen," he complimented her. "Be sure to tell the chef how much we enjoyed his exemplary cuisine."

"Huh, mister? I don't catch you," the girl faltered,

stepping back in some concern at his exuberant manner.

"Forgive me, my sweet, but this fine lunch has put me in a poetic mood, you see. What's the tariff?"

"It'll be a dollar six bits, mister."

"Here." Quentin Durwood flung down a ten-dollar bill on the table. "Keep two bits for yourself, and bring me back eight dollars, agreed?"

The girl, bedazzled by such an extravagant tip—for the customers of this little restaurant seldom if ever acknowledged her services—dropped him an awkward curtsy as she hurried away to obtain change for the bill. The owner of the restaurant stuck his head through the window again and called out, "Much obliged, mister. Glad you liked it. Come in again real soon."

"You may be sure I will." Quentin Durwood tipped his hat to the bemused Irish girl, gave the restaurant proprietor an affable nod, and then went back to his hotel. Before going upstairs to his room, he stopped at the desk to engage the room next to his, and then, whistling a cheerful tune, knocked at the door of his room.

It was opened by Lily, who promptly flung her arms around his neck and kissed him zestfully. "Oh, Quentin," she glowed with excitement, "I just can't believe you let me buy all these fancy duds!"

"But you see I did, Lily." He patted her bottom, and then pinched it slyly. "Lock the door, my dear. And you can take off your things right now and keep them fresh and unwrinkled for tonight."

"Whatever are you talking about, Quentin?" she giggled.

He strode to the window and drew the shutters, and calmly began to undress. "I shall have to forego my enjoyment of you tonight, my sweet, but the sacrifice will be easier to make if I enjoy you now."

"You mean—you want me right now? In broad daylight?" Lily gasped, coloring hotly.

"Now I've really seen the seventh wonder of the world," Quentin Durwood chuckled as he finished undressing and stood only in his drawers. "A trollop blushing—you must have good breeding in you from somewhere back, Lily girl. Now come on, can't you see I'm pining for you?"

"My goodness, you've certainly got lots of surprises up your sleeve, Quentin." Lily Mellers sighed in resignation as she pulled her dress over her head and sinuously wriggled out of it. He took it from her, shook it out, then hung it on one of several nails in a little cubicle which served as closet. He watched with undisguised admiration as she divested herself of her camisole, stays and finally her drawers, standing before him in the piquant near-nudity of long white stockings high on her thighs, held up by ribboned garters, and her button-on boots.

"That's the way I like you!" he said hoarsely as he moved to her, his fingers digging into her resilient buttocks and pulling her up against him. "You've brought me good luck, you sweet red-haired bitch."

"Say, wait a minute, Quentin, you don't have to get nasty with me. Didn't I treat you right last night and now look at this—"

"Shut up and listen to me, honey," he interrupted, his fingers increasing their pressure till she winced and gasped with discomfort. "Before I go out to supper tonight, you're going to move into the next room. I've just taken it, understand?"

"Sure, but why—" she began.

"I told you to shut up and listen. Now, last night I told you about a big, fat bonus for being nice to a very important man. Well, I just met him. We had lunch together, as a matter of fact, and we're going to supper tonight. He's got lots of information that I need, and he's a lonely widower. I'll admit, Lily, he's not as young and handsome as I am, but I'll say that he's less revolting than that Abner Whitman you pointed out to me last night."

"Oh." Lily Mellers' shoulders slumped and she frowned. "You want me to get him in bed, is that it?"

"Good girl, you're catching on fast! Now I'll give you a little advice. He works in the land office, doesn't have much money to spend on a good time, and when I mentioned the dance halls and the saloons, he turned up his nose at the chippies. At least he's got good taste. So you're going to be—let's see now—" Quentin Durwood looked up at the ceiling, scowled, and reflected a moment. "You're going to be my ward."

"Your what?" she echoed, mystified, automatically beginning to caress his resurgent maleness, which was pressing against her through his drawers.

"My ward," he patiently explained. "It's a legal term that means I'm in charge of you. Let's suppose you're an orphan—"

"Well, that's true enough, Quentin. But why—"

"Let me finish. You were married at an early age. Your husband was wounded seriously in one of the last battles of the war, but lingered on for a couple of years before he died. After his death, I took you under my wing. That'll explain why you're not a virgin when Tobias Jennings—remember that name, because he's the man who's going to be very helpful to me—starts showing a desire for your voluptuous charms."

"Hey, there you go again with all those fancy words," Lily Mellers complained. "Come on to bed, honey, you can explain to me later, hum? Oh my, are you ever ready!"

"Take your hand away until I finish." Quentin Durwood's voice was thick and slurred, as his hands moved up to cup Lily Mellers's swelling, naked breasts. "There, that's better. Tonight, when Tobias Jennings starts to love you up, you're not going to use any of those cute little tricks you're trying on me, you understand? You see, you're a genteel young widow, forced by dire circumstance to be my ward. You're trying hard to lead a righteous life, but because you acquired a taste for a man during your ill-fated marriage, you can't help your natural instincts. But of course you fight against them."

"Whatever are you trying to tell me, Quentin? Come on, be a sport, give it to a girl. It's mean to keep me waiting like this," Lily pouted.

Quentin Durwood's eyes narrowed. He stepped back and slapped Lily Mellers viciously across her left jaw and cheek. She uttered a frightened cry and stumbled backward, putting a hand to the reddened splotch on her face and stammering, "What did you go and do that for?"

"I want you to pay particular attention to what I say and not to forget it, that's why. I'll go over it once again and I'll try to use words you can understand, Lily. All right?"

Thoroughly cowed by this time, she nodded.

"All right, then As I started to tell you, Tobias Jennings is a widower. He's close to fifty, if I'm any judge. He lost his wife at the end of the war, he can't afford a regular bed partner from his choice of chippies, and he doesn't really want that sort, anyhow. Understand so far?"

She nodded, her eyes fixed on his suddenly taut, inimical face.

"Good! So, as I told you, you got married at about fifteen, probably to a fine, Southern gentleman who got wounded in the war and died a year or so later. Let's say I was his business agent, that's how I got to know you. I took you under my wing; you haven't any money of your own—"

"God knows that's true enough," she interjected with a bitter little laugh.

He glared at her, then went on, "I have to take you along on business trips, naturally. I travel a good deal, you see. Now the point is this, Lily. The only man you ever had in bed was your husband, and you've tried to be a good girl ever since. But you've got an itch between your legs and you just have to satisfy it every so often. So of course when this fine upstanding widower starts trying to seduce you, you're going to pretend to be a girl who doesn't know what he's got on his mind and in his pants—can you understand that sort of language?"

"Sure. When you put it like that, it's easy. Every floozy knows how to play that game. Hell, Madam Bella sold me as a virgin at least twenty times, the nasty old bitch," Lily Mellers observed angrily.

"Now we're getting somewhere. That's why I say, no whore's tricks. You can flutter your eyelids all you want, say that you really mustn't and you shouldn't, but he's so big and strong you just can't help yourself. You know what to do and say. All right?"

"Sure."

"That's my good girl. And just as I promised, there'll be a nice big greenback when you've sent him home happy and proud over bedding such a high-society young widow." Then he chuckled, "And now, Lily, get into bed and see how many tricks you can show me that I haven't seen before."

Despite his admonition to Lily Mellers, Quentin Durwood actually had no intention of allowing the fish to take the bait the first time it was dangled. Instead, after he had entertained Tobias Jennings at the most expensive restaurant in town and treated the bespectacled land clerk to wild duck and wine, he invited his grateful guest back to the hotel to meet his "ward." Lily Mellers had moved into the adjoining room and wore her blue bombazine dress. At his instruction, when he knocked at her door and she opened it, she curtsied awkwardly though prettily upon being introduced to Jennings, and offered the ingenuous news that she had been occupying herself reading the Bible, which was her favorite book. "I didn't mean to disturb you, my dear," Quentin Durwood apologized, turning to Jennings, who was staring at Lily Mellers with a fatuous expression on his homely face. "Perhaps tomorrow evening, Lily, you would do us the honor of dining with us."

"It'd be my pleasure, Mr. Durwood. It's nice to meet you, Mr. Jennings," Lily replied sweetly, dropping the land clerk another curtsy.

Quentin bade her a flowery good night, which she returned to him and Jennings as she slowly closed the door. Tucking the land clerk's arm in his, Durwood led him back to his own room and poured a glass of the best whiskey he had been able to buy in Austin. "She's a shy, sweet girl, Tobias," he explained. "As I was telling you, she was married at quite a tender age—they do things like that down South, you know. And then the tragedy of losing her husband—I'm afraid it's made her somewhat retiring. But I could tell she's taken a fancy to you."

"Go on with you, Quentin." Jennings laughed self-consciously and took a hearty swig of his whiskey. "How could a lovely young lady like that take any notice of an old stick-in-the-mud like me?"

"You underestimate yourself, Tobias. Here, have some more whiskey. And here's a cigar to go with it. Lean back and enjoy yourself, man. Take my word—and I've had plenty of experience with the ladies—when a girl like Lily has been exposed to grief and bereavement, she's looking for a mature protector. And the fact that you yourself are a widower will make you all the more desirable in her eyes, believe me."

"You—you really think so?" Jennings leaned forward, his eyes glistening behind the thick lenses.

"I do indeed, Tobias. Don't forget, she's already been married, so she knows the ways of a man and a maid, if you take my meaning." Quentin Durwood gave his guest a meaningful wink. "Tomorrow night, after supper, I'll leave the two of you alone to talk over your sorrowful experiences. I'm sure it will be a great comfort to Lily to talk to a man who, in spite of having lost his beloved wife, is making a name for himself in Austin. Why, Tobias, you're responsible for one of the most important functions in this entire state."

"Oh, no, you're giving me too much credit. I'm just trying to do my job, that's all."

"Don't be so modest. On the other hand, that note of modesty is exactly what will convince my charming, shy ward that you're a man to be trusted. You're totally unselfish, Tobias. Be tender toward her. Mark my words, she'll take to you in good time the way that duck we had for supper tonight took to water. Shall we say supper tomorrow night at about six-thirty at the same place?"

"Sure—I mean, only, it ought to be my treat the next time—"

"Nonsense! I won't hear of it, Tobias. I know your circumstances and I appreciate them. And besides, I told you I work for a big Eastern syndicate, with lots of money to spend. You see, they're thinking of bringing a railroad down toward the border. That'll help the cattlemen no end. So your supper tonight and the one tomorrow night will go on their tab. Don't give it a second thought."

"Gosh—thanks, Quentin." Tobias Jennings got to his feet, puffing at his cigar, his face flushed from the good food and drink he had consumed. "I'd best be going now. Would you give my regards to Miss Lily?"

"Of course I will. And, you know something, Tobias? I'll bet that before we meet tomorrow night, she'll have told me how happy she was to meet a man of your sterling character. Good night, old friend."

After Jennings left the hotel, Quentin visited Lily and,

to her wide-eyed delight, presented her with a hundred dollars for her first week of service and an additional fifty dollars to reward her for her adept performance in the role of young, widowed ingenue. "I've decided to string Tobias Jennings along until the end of the week, my dear," he told her. "You really pulled it off magnificently. I'm pleasantly surprised you did so well without too many rehearsals. Now then, tomorrow night, I'll leave you two together for a bit, and you'll tell him your sad story. I've decided not to let the three of us have supper together—it'll whet his appetite all the more. If he tries to get fresh—and I don't think he will right away—tell him how masterful he is but that you really aren't ready yet, because you're still in mourning. He'll respect your sentiments, and it'll make him want you more than ever if I know my man." Then, as an afterthought, he added, "To play up to your sad story, Lily, I'm going back to that seamstress in the morning and buy you a black dress. It'll be as daring as our present styles permit. It's been my observation that black, especially on redheads, makes their curves and skin all the more alluring. And in spite of his advanced age, I think I can assure you that Tobias Jennings will give you quite a tussle in bed when the occasion presents itself."

The very next evening, true to his word, after having provided Tobias with another sumptuous repast and plenty of wine with which to wash it down, Durwood led the land clerk to Lily's room. This time, Jennings's face wore an even more fatuous expression when he beheld the red-haired young woman, in a black gown with puffed sleeves and flounced skirt. Durwood had imaginatively altered the gown by snipping away a V-shaped portion of the bodice so that just a hint of the cleft of Lily's high-perched bosom was visible. Throughout their restrained conversation, Lily had all she could do to keep from giggling when she noticed that his eyes invariably and hypnotically returned to that display of smooth, satiny skin.

By Saturday evening, on Tobias Jennings's fourth visit to the Hotel Coronado, he dared a clumsy kiss. Lily's slim fingers gently pushed him away, but not too firmly, as she turned her face toward the shuttered window. "Please, Tobias dear, I—I like you a lot. But you have to give a girl time. I still miss my darling Claude. You—you do remind me of him a little, though."

It was all Jennings could do to keep from asking his considered and devoted friend to arrange another rendez-vous for him. Durwood, well aware of Jennings's increasing lust for the red-haired dancehall girl, anticipated him by proposing that on the following Tuesday evening he and Lily dine alone together. "I've some business which will take me out of town for a day or so, Tobias," he explained. "Besides, I've a feeling that my ward is smitten with you—she's told me so, in fact."

"You—you mean it, Quentin? Gosh, she—she's beautiful! I can't wait to see her again—do you really think I've got a chance with her?"

"Didn't she as much as tell you that herself, Tobias?" Quentin clapped the land clerk on the shoulder and grinned knowingly. "Didn't she tell you that you remind her of her adored and departed husband, Claude? He was an older man, not unlike you, Tobias. So my advice is that when you are alone with Lily, be fatherly, tender, protective. You'll see how well it works, I assure you."

"And you're sure—I mean—after all, she is your ward, Quentin. I—I wouldn't want to take unfair advantage of her—" the land clerk faltered.

"Nonsense! I told Lily long before we came to Austin that it's high time she turned her back on the past and looked to the future. And right now, Tobias, you're her future."

"That's just wonderful! I'll never be able to thank you for all you've done—you're a real friend—"

"That's what friends are for, Tobias. Now, there's just one little thing. You remember, I told you I'm working for this big syndicate. When I come back from my little trip, I'll want to sit down and tell you what I've got in mind."

"Sure, whatever you want—that's as long as it's legal, of course."

"Of course it'll be legal. My firm is famous for its ethics and honesty, Tobias. Well, I might as well tell you here and now what I'm after. I told you we might want to build a railroad down toward the Mexican border to pick up the cattle that all those ranchers are popping out of the brush. Right now, they have to go up to Abilene with the Kansas Pacific. My syndicate thinks it can put the KP out of business by backing their own line. I'll want to see what land is available down, say, near Ugalde. And of course, some other tracts, as well."

Jennings looked doubtful for a moment. "I can't very well let you go through all the records, Quentin, you know that." Then he brightened. "But of course, now that I know what you've got in mind, I could copy some of the descriptions of the holdings in that area. As I recall, a couple of them have already been sold. 'Course, I suppose you could dicker with the present owners, and if your syndicate paid enough, they might consider selling."

"Now you've hit it on the head, Tobias. The moment I laid eyes on you, I told myself that here was a man with vision. All right, then." Again he clapped Jennings on the back. "Now you be here, dressed up in your very best and ready to take Lily to dinner, next Tuesday. I ought to be back Thursday morning at the latest. By then if you haven't made her forget poor old Claude, you're not the man I think you are, Tobias."

Quentin Durwood spent most of Sunday and Monday enjoying Lily Mellers's grateful and not entirely professional embraces. On Tuesday morning, he went down to the telegraph office and sent off a wire to the baron at the latter's hotel in San Antonio, a cryptic and brief message which indicated that he had taken the first important step toward the realization of their scheme which, though he had no way of knowing it, was to embroil Lucien Edmond Bouchard and imperil Windhaven Range itself. . . .

CHAPTER TWENTY-SEVEN

Quentin Durwood did not leave Austin on business, as he had told Tobias Jennings he would. After sending off the wire to the baron, he took a room under an assumed name in a small hotel at the other end of town, and locked himself up with a bottle of the best whiskey he could buy and several books on the history of Spain and its colonization of the New World, that had been given to him by "professor", Theobald Arnison. It was his intention to acquire as much knowledge as he could about the baron's favorite subject which, combined with his natural glibness and disarming manner, might better impress the settlers whom he intended to defraud. He had no doubt that Lily Mellers would fill in very ably in his absence.

Indeed, things went off almost exactly as he had calculated. Jennings, after having bathed and trimmed his beard, presented himself at the Hotel Coronado on Tuesday evening, and escorted Lily Mellers to the restaurant where Durwood had taken him on the two previous occasions. He did not even grumble over the cost of the elaborate meal with wine which he himself ordered, having remembered his young host's munificence. Though it cost him almost every penny he had brought with him, he had no reason to regret this unaccustomed extravagance.

Once again, Lily wore the black bombazine dress. This time, however, she had left off her stays and petticoat, wearing only the thinnest camisole and lace-trimmed drawers beneath. Hence, the dress adhered all the more suggestively to her lithe figure, and, just as before, Jennings found himself unable to take his eyes from the satiny expanse of tempting flesh which the bodice disclosed.

Lily, relishing this game, acted with a coyness and feigned shyness that would have done credit to Eleanora

284

Duse (who was ten years old at the time and who was to make her debut four years later as Juliet). She allowed him to escort her back to her room, and there lingered, the door partly closed between them as he hoarsely pleaded, "Please, Miss Lily ma'am, I just want to talk some with you. I'm a lonely man—Mr. Durwood must have told you how I lost my Rachel. I've been pining for a chance to talk to some nice, decent woman, Miss Lily, and you're the first I've seen in this backwoods town, honest you are."

"Well, just for a few minutes, then. It really isn't proper, Mr. Jennings. I mean, we—we'd be all alone—"

"Oh, Miss Lily, I know how to act like a gentleman, honest I do!" he earnestly assured her.

"All right." She seemed to hesitate a moment, and then held the door open for him to hurry in, closed it, and, as he stood with his back to her, stealthily turned the key in the lock.

Demurely, Lily Mellers went back to her chair by the table at the window and picked up the Bible. Jennings stood, hat in hand, twisting it nervously. With a sweet smile, she looked up and murmured, "I'm so awfully lonely, Mr. Jennings, I turn to the Good Book whenever I can."

"I know. I—I don't mean to break in on your feelings, Miss Lily, but I—well, I—I'm terribly lonely, like I said, and I was hoping—well, maybe that you like me a little?"

"Yes, I do. I shouldn't; it's still too soon after poor Claude. But I do need someone to lean on. Mr. Durwood, you—understand, takes care of—of the money I have to live on, but he's not kinfolk, you know."

"Sure, I—I understand, Miss Lily." He was perspiring now, and twisting his hat more rapidly than ever. "You're a real fine woman no two ways about it. I—well, I'd sort of like to be—well. like kinfolk to you, if you'd let me. That is, if you think you could care just a little for me—"

She gave him a sweet smile and sent him a long look from under her curly lashes. "You're very sweet, Mr. Jennings. Why don't you put your hat down and make yourself comfortable?" She rose from the chair and went over to the settee to the left of the door, seated herself and patted the place beside her. "Maybe you'd like to sit by me and talk a bit, Mr. Jennings?"

He gulped, nodded, put his hat on the table and then awkwardly moved toward her, seating himself not too close, not wanting to offend what he took to be her tender sensibilities. Lily had, at Durwood's suggestion, purchased a little jar of scented ointment, which she had diligently massaged into her slim neck and satiny chest. That scent now reached Tobias's nostrils, and it soon began to have an effect on his already inflamed senses. Before he could restrain his impulses, he had clumsily circled her waist with his left arm and, leaning toward her, gave her a noisy buss on the cheek.

"Oh, Mr. Jennings—Tobias—you—you really shouldn't—" she murmured faintly, regarding him with an innocent, wide-eyed expression which only served to intensify his by now almost uncontrollable desire for her.

"Please, Miss Lily, I know I ain't a rich man, but I've got a steady job at the land office, and anybody in town'll tell you I don't really have any bad habits. Like going out with chippies—I shouldn't have said that—no offense meant—it's only—"

"You poor dear," Lily cooed, "I do believe you're trying to tell me you're in love with me."

"Oh yes, Miss Lily ma'am, I surely am! You don't know how much I think about you nights—I'd be so proud—I'd be so grateful—couldn't you—I mean—" he babbled.

Despite her secret amusement over his pathetically earnest attempts to woo her and yet not let her believe that he was bent solely on getting her to bed, Lily felt a certain sentimental pity for this straggly bearded, middle-aged widower. And so, not unaware that her capitulation would bring her a tangible reward, she finally whispered, "Tobias, I—I can't hold you off any longer. You're so nice to me, and you do remind me of poor, dear Claude so much. And, just like Mr. Durwood says, I ought to forget about the past and start living some. So—so if you really want me—would you please blow out the candle? And then I'll get into bed and then—and then, Tobias dear, you can come to me. But please be gentle, I'm not—I'm not used to it yet—you understand."

He was trembling violently as he stumbled up from the

settee, went over to the glass lamp and blew the candle out. Then he stood, licking his lips and straining his ears as he heard the rustle of Lily Mellers's dress being drawn from her tall, shapely body. A few moments more, and he heard the telltale creak of the bed which signified that she had climbed into it. Then, his fingers all thumbs, he divested himself of everything except his drawers and socks and stumbled through the darkness, groping for the edge of the bed until at last he found it. The touch of her cool hand on his made his teeth chatter as he gasped, "Oh, Miss Lily, I'll be nice to you, I swear I will! Oh, you darling, you love, you!"

If truth be told, her self-sacrifice did not provide Lily with erotic ecstasy. Tobias was short of breath, overly stout, and the youthful warmth and lithe contours of her naked body totally undid his staying powers. Nonetheless, for him it was a journey into paradise itself, and his effusive, rhapsodic praises of her, combined with his contrite declarations that he had never meant to take advantage of her, made Lily not at all sorry that she had played the role she had.

Knowing how important it was to keep Jennings a cooperative ally of her generous patron, she pretended to be overcome by the land clerk's virility, while at the same time whispering, "Oh, Tobias dear, what must you think of me now?" with an effectively timed sob which appealed to his noblest instincts. Instantly abashed, Tobias mumbled an apology and hastily got out of bed, groping for his clothes. "I—I hope you aren't mad at me, Miss Lily. I—I just couldn't help myself—"

"I know, dear. It was wrong of me to lead you on the way I did. But—but I'm really not sorry, Tobias, honest I'm not. Maybe—maybe sometime again, when we get to know each other better—I didn't mean for this to happen quite so soon. But—but it was wonderful just the same!"

Quentin Durwood moved back into his room at the Hotel Coronado on Thursday morning, and closeted himself with Lily Mellers to receive a full report on the events of Tuesday night. Hugely satisfied, he rewarded her again with another sizable banknote, took her to lunch, and then to the seamstress, to buy a pair of fashionable gloves, a parasol, and a garishly decorated wide-brimmed hat

which she had always wanted. He spent most of the afternoon in bed with her. When it was nearly time for the
land office to close, he took his leave of her, and had a
carriage drive him to Jennings's place of employment.
Seated on the park bench from which he had first selected
his dupe, he saw the land clerk emerge from the adobe
building, and whistled to him from across the street.

"I'm back, as you see, Tobias. How have you been?"

"Well, Quentin, very well. I—er—I want to marry Miss
Lily. She's your ward, which makes you her guardian, so
I guess I have to ask you for permission, don't I?"

Durwood had not been prepared for this unexpected
development. But his quick mind agilely considering the
pros and cons, he saw his advantage and took it. "That's
true, Tobias, I do have to pass judgment on any request
for my ward's hand in marriage. But I don't think you
have anything to worry about. Am I to take it that you
and Lily have come to an understanding?"

The portly widower flushed and looked down at his
feet, thoroughly uncomfortable. "Well, not exactly, but
you see, Quentin—"

"You sly old dog, you!" Durwood nudged him in the
ribs and winked. "So you finally overcame Lily's grief,
did you? I knew you had it in you, I knew it all the time.
Well, since that's the way matters stand, I don't know
why I should stand in the way of two fine people's happiness. Now then, have you been able to investigate the
matter we discussed earlier?"

"Oh, yes, I didn't forget that at all, Quentin. It was a
slow day today, so I had a chance to do some copying,
just like you wanted. Here." He put his hand into the
inner pocket of his dusty coat, took out a sheaf of papers,
and handed them to the Easterner. "There's one pretty big
spread near Carrizo Springs. Belongs to a fellow named
Lucien Edmond Bouchard. And last week, a German
couple bought 4,000 acres about three miles west of Mr.
Bouchard's holdings. Now, farther west and along that
border of the Nueces River, there's plenty of land, all
the way past Ugalde. I wasn't sure just how much land
your syndicate was interested in, so maybe I've got a lot
more descriptions here than you'll need—"

"No, the more the better, Tobias. You see, when the

288

syndicate decides to back that railroad I told you about, they'll want to have a pretty clear picture of what they'll have to go through. Now, in some cases, they may approach ranchers who are established already on the land and try to buy them out. Of course, I'll get my orders from the East as to what they want. My job is to give them just this information which you've so kindly provided."

"It wasn't too much trouble, not really, Quentin. Gosh, when I think what a friend you've been to me and how you've put me in the way of meeting and—and falling in love with—Miss Lily, it's not much to do for a friend at all," Jennings protested.

"Nonsense, you've done me a good turn. I was going to ask you, though, Tobias, are you at all familiar with that region down by the border?"

"A little," the land clerk admitted. "What do you want to know about it?"

Remembering the baron's instructions to find land that would be suitable for sheep raising, Durwood pursued, "Is there much grazing in the region?"

"In certain places, yes. This fellow Bouchard is in a kind of valley, and the grazing isn't bad at all. Farther west, you get into brush and dry country, though I suppose cattle could manage. But you see, Quentin, the ranchers drive their cattle to Abilene these days, and there's plenty of good grass in Indian territory. And in the fall and winter, I'd say there's enough in that border region to keep the cattle alive.

"I see. Well, this has been most helpful. By the way, Tobias, I'm going to have to go back East with these reports, once I copy them into a presentable form for my employers, you understand."

"Sure. Will you be coming back? And what about Miss Lily?"

Quentin Durwood shrugged philosophically, and put his hand on Jennings's shoulder. "I know it's been a short acquaintance, Tobias, but I feel I can trust you like an old friend. I think you'd be good for her. Go ahead and marry her with my blessing, if she'll have you."

"Do you—do you really mean that, Quentin?" The land clerk's face was radiant.

"Of course, I mean it. I'll leave her here at the hotel, and she'll have money enough for her necessities until you two can set the happy date."

"Gosh, that's mighty generous of you—and you can trust me with Miss Lily. I respect her, Quentin, 'cause I want to marry her so much."

"Of course you do, and that's why I'm going to go back East alone. Now you have a good supper, go home and rest. Remember, I advise you to be gentle and take it slow and easy with Lily."

"Sure, I'll do just what you say. Will I be seeing you again, do you think?"

"It's possible, Tobias. If the syndicate hires me to buy any of this land or to try to get the present owners to sell it, then of course I'll have to come back here to record the deeds, won't I? And by the time I come back, I expect to find the two of you settled down in domestic bliss."

The two men shook hands, and Quentin Durwood watched the land clerk walk back across the street. Then he chuckled to himself and, seeing a carriage for hire moving toward him, beckoned to the driver. Half an hour later, he was in Lily Mellers's room again and startling her with the abrupt statement as he entered, "Well, Lily girl, I'm going to pack and take off tomorrow morning. I've work to do. Tobias has been very helpful."

"You mean—you're finished with me?" she asked.

"That's right, Lily. I'll be doing a lot of horseback riding, and somehow I don't think we could rough it together too well. But cheer up, I've good news for you. I met Tobias just now as he was leaving the land office, and he asked my permission to marry you."

"He did—he did *what?*" Lily couldn't believe her ears.

"That's right, honey. He wants to make an honest woman out of you. And I told him yes. I gave my permission—you see, you being my ward makes me your guardian. And a guardian has to give permission when somebody wants to marry his ward. So that's exactly what I did. Now, if you're a smart girl, you'll wait for Tobias to come calling."

"But—"

"Just listen. I'm going to give you two hundred dollars more. That way, you can stay on here until Tobias comes calling. And I'd advise you to accept him without too much delay. You wouldn't want him to find out where you really came from."

"My God!" the tall redhead was staggered by the sudden prospect.

"Of course, he's not a rich man, but at least he loves you. And you won't have to go selling yourself for six dollars a night anymore. Yes, Lily, all things considered, it was a lucky evening for both of us when you walked into the Longhorn." He took out his wallet, removed a sheaf of bills, and tossed them on the table. Then, with his inimitable grin, he added softly, "If you feel like displaying your gratitude, honey, you can make my last night in Austin a happy one by servicing me in your best professional manner. Don't look so unhappy—just tell yourself it'll be for the last time."

Quentin Durwood went to the stable where he had quartered his gelding, saddled it, and rode out of Austin early the next morning, heading directly for San Antonio. Three days later, he went to the baron's room in the Galvez Hotel and delivered the sheaf of papers which Tobias Jennings had given him.

"This is really excellent, Quentin," the suave land-grabber chuckled as he perused the descriptions. "Now, as you know, your next step will be to make a journey into that region—I trust you made copies for yourself of these holdings?"

"Of course I did. Just the essentials, of course—I didn't put down every single detail."

"That's right, you won't need all that yet. So you'll go down there, take in the lay of the land and see what sort of settlers are on some of the plots we may be interested in. Now this one," as the baron scanned the description of Windhaven Range, "is a really juicy tract. One of these days we might just have old Theobald concoct a land grant to dispossess this fellow Bouchard. This clerk you befriended in Austin was kind enough to write down the names of the present owners of some of the properties. Good work, Quentin."

"You want me to pay special attention to landmarks so the professor can go to work?"

"Exactly. By the way, you might take a look at this land which your accommodating friend has listed as being next to the Bouchard ranch. It might just do for my increasingly impatient client in Taos. Yes, I think it might just be ideal for him. Now, you see just how we can turn a neat profit, Quentin. These four thousand acres cost—" the baron squinted at Tobias Jennings's cramped handwriting "—Ludwig Engelhardt all of two thousand dollars, and once we oust Herr Engelhardt, I'll sell the land to my New Mexico client for a little more than twice as much. That's a profit of three thousand dollars over the bona fide sales price at the land office, Quentin—but of course, for us, it'll represent a clear five thousand."

"That's the sort of profit I like to think about, baron."

"Well, you've a little work to do first. Head for the border area, take plenty of time to be sure of the topography so that Theobald can't possibly make any mistakes. Then he'll go to work, and you'll go back with an official document from Philip V and be prepared to oust any present settlers."

"It couldn't be clearer, baron. Now it'll take me about a week to reach that territory and another week back. Say two weeks charting the terrain?"

"Yes, I'd figured about that. So you should be back here around the first week of May, give or take a few days. Then, a week or two after that, you'll be ready to get us our first profitable grant and it'll be the start of our fortune, split three ways."

"I'll head there this afternoon," Durwood promised as he shook hands with the baron. Then, turning to Theobald Arnison, he waved his hand and declared, "Now you keep well, professor. I want to be proud of you when I get back."

Durwood stabled his horse and bought a fresh and sturdier black gelding. After providing himself with food enough for his journey and packing it into his saddlebags, he rode out of San Antonio late that afternoon and headed in the direction of Windhaven Range.

While on the trail, he made extensive notes of certain portions of land which he believed might be of future interest to the baron. Within a week, he came in view of the stockade which circled the ranch house, bunkhouse, and the new chapel of Windhaven Range, and shrewdly appraised it. Then, turning his gelding westward, he galloped toward the spread that Ludwig Engelhardt had purchased. He arrived there on the evening of the eighth day after his departure, dismounted, tied his horse to the trunk of an oak tree, and approached the log cabin which the new German owner had constructed. As he did so, the door opened and Quentin Durwood blinked with surprise. He recognized the stocky, gray-haired man who had come out of the Austin land office the day when he had met Tobias Jennings.

"Good evening," he greeted the surly looking German.

"*Was wollen Sie herein?*" the man suspiciously demanded. He held a Sharps rifle as he glowered at Durwood.

"I'm sorry if I alarmed you—my name's Quentin Durwood."

"*Ich bin* Ludwig Engelhardt. What do you want here?"

At this moment, there appeared in the doorway the fat, bedraggled, blond matron who had accompanied the German out of the Austin land office. "*Was ist los,* Ludi?" she asked in a whining voice.

"It does not concern you, Minna. Go back inside." He turned to glare at her, and she swiftly retreated, closing the door behind her. "Well? What do you want of me?"

"I'm making a survey for the state government, Mr. Engelhardt," Durwood glibly lied, "and I wanted to ask you what you're going to do with this four thousand acres you've just bought."

"I do not think it is any of your business. I have paid hard cash for the land; my Minna and I have worked hard all our lives."

"I didn't mean any offense, Mr. Engelhardt. Your neighbor, Mr. Bouchard, over to the east, is raising cattle."

"*Ach so!* I know that. Well, not that it is any of your business, but I will farm some of this land with fruits and vegetables, and some for cattle. Minna and I came from Germany to St. Louis before the *verdammt Krieg,* and we have come here to start a new life, away from people who want slaves and to break away from this country to which we came to gain *Freiheit.*"

"Thank you, Herr Engelhardt." Durwood smiled and

inclined his head in mock thanks. "Let me wish you and your wife every success here. You do not have your cattle yet, or your workers?"

"*Nein, nicht jetzt,*" the stolid German growled, his blue eyes narrowing suspiciously. "I have bought some Herefords, they are being shipped now from St. Louis. And *meinen Arbeiteren,* I have hired them from Mexico to meet the cattle at Corpus Christi and drive them here. It will be by next *monat,* I think. Now that is all I have to tell, and that is already too much."

"So you and your wife are here all by yourselves, Herr Engelhardt? It must be a very lonely life, with no one here to work with you."

"You ask too many questions, young man. I do not think your people in Austin need to know so much. I have two fine *Sohnen,* and they help me build *dieses Kleine Haus.* They have gone to visit *mein Bruder* in Sacramento, but this summer they will be back to help with the work. And now, *gute Nacht!*" With this, Ludwig Engelhardt made a jerky, forward gesture with his rifle as if to suggest that Quentin Durwood should not wait upon the order of his going, then stepped back into the house, slammed the door, and shoved home the plank which served as bolt.

The young Easterner chuckled softly to himself, then went back to his horse, mounted it and rode due west. He camped that night not far from the ruins of what had once been the stronghold of Sangrodo, and by the light of the campfire, made extensive notes on what he had seen and been told. Here, indeed, was the place the baron would want to send his Taos client—he was sure of it. But this grumpy German was going to be a hard nut to crack. He probably wouldn't go for the Spanish land-grant business. Durwood frowned, mulling over the plan of action which the baron would have him take if Engelhardt refused to be intimidated by the sight of the fraudulent parchment. It would mean killing Engelhardt's fat old wife, too. As for the Mexican workers, they would be loyal to whoever paid them. He would simply have to make sure that they were not in the vicinity when he did what he would most likely have to do. And of course it should be done soon—before the German's two sons returned to help their father with the farming and the cattle.

For the next two weeks, Durwood wrote lengthy and graphic descriptions of the physical contours of the stretches of land between Carrizo Springs and the Cañon de Ugalde. Then, as he began his return journey to San Antonio for his conference with the baron, he took equally extensive notes on the terrain which lay north of this border country. By the time he concluded his surveying, he had matched each of Tobias Jennings's legal declarations of land sold and land already chartered and available to prospective purchasers.

It was on the second day of May, 1869, that he entered San Antonio and, after stabling his weary horse and removing his saddlebags, he went directly to the Galvez Hotel and engaged a room for himself. Once he had unpacked his saddlebags and freshened up after his hot, dusty, and monotonous journey, he went to the baron's room and knocked. He was immediately admitted by the baron himself.

"Welcome back, Quentin! I was expecting you, as a matter of fact. Sit down and have a drink. You look bone-tired. Here, Theobald, make yourself useful and pour Quentin a tall glass of our best whiskey."

"At once, at once." The frail old man brightened, eyeing his employer with an almost pleading expression.

"And one for yourself, of course. You deserve it. You've kept out of mischief and saloons for most of the month, and it's been rather tedious waiting for our young associate to return with the data you'll need, Theobald." The baron nodded indulgently. Theobald at once filled a glass for himself and brought a second glass to Quentin. Then he seated himself, took a hearty swig of his drink, and waited expectantly.

The baron sat at a table and spent the next twenty minutes examining the notes which Durwood had made. Then he looked up, his eyes glistening with greedy pleasure. "This is absolutely marvelous, Quentin! You've done your work very well. My congratulations! Theobald won't have any trouble producing the most convincing royal land grant anyone has ever seen in this part of the country! And you come at a most opportune time, I might add. I just had a wire from my client in Taos. You'll be meeting him in due course, so you may as well know his name. It's Andrew Moultrie. Also, I'll give you one piece of very good advice, friend to friend. When you meet his wife, Anna, just forget your philandering ways. Not that she isn't a hot-blooded Spanish filly with eyes for any capable man, but Moultrie's an insanely jealous husband. In one of his letters, he casually mentioned that he'd nearly horsewhipped a vaquero to death for flirting with Anna. Also, he's a crack shot and he knows how to use a saber and a rapier."

"A word to the wise is generally sufficient, baron. Right now, I'm more interested in replenishing my bank account."

"Spoken like a true land speculator, Quentin," the baron joked. "Theobald, now you may pour me a glass of that whiskey and we'll drink a toast to our young friend."

The elderly historian hurried over to the table and, with a trembling hand, uncorked the bottle of corn whiskey, poured a glass, and brought it to the baron, who lifted it in a toast. "To our first client, Andrew Moultrie, and the money he's going to pay us for his new property!" Then, after they had drunk the toast, he turned to Arnison and ordered, "Now then, Theobald, you may have just another half glassful, no more and no less. After that, get to work on the royal grant which will eventually transfer Ludwig Engelhardt's four thousand acres to Andrew Moultrie."

Turning to Quentin, he added, "Of course, I didn't expect you to get a specimen of Engelhardt's handwriting, though it would have been very useful. Now, here's the way it's going to work. Give Theobald about a week, and then you'll take the royal deed down to this German. Let's hope that he's amenable to reason. If he isn't, you know what you have to do."

The young Easterner's face hardened, and he nodded.

"Good. I'm glad you don't have a queasy stomach."

"I've never had any problems with my stomach, baron. And I didn't particularly care for Herr Engelhardt's inhospitable greeting."

"That's the kind of talk I like to hear. Once you're done, Theobald will prepare a transfer of deed, showing that the *late* Herr Engelhardt, prior to his untimely death or disappearance—however you may arrange it—decided to transfer his acreage to us. Then you will file that deed with your helpful friend at the Austin land office, along with the bill of sale which you and I will prepare after we've had Moultrie's cash on the barrelhead. See how simple it all is, Quentin?"

"You don't have to sell me any more, baron. But how do I represent myself to these settlers?"

"That's easy. Theobald will draw up a letter from Madrid, which I'll sign as the Baron Rodrigo de Austencio. It will appoint you my official agent. The letter will state unequivocally that I am the last surviving descendant of the noble family to whom His Majesty Philip V granted this good Texas soil as a reward for their valorous deeds performed for the well-being of his realm."

Quentin Durwood shook his head in admiration. "My God, baron, if I were Herr Engelhardt, I'd already be packing up."

"Well, for his sake, let us hope he is of the same opinion. And now I'm going to send Theobald to an early bed so that he'll be fresh as a daisy in the morning. Perhaps you and I can take a tour of San Antonio and see what it has to offer in the way of nocturnal entertainment, Quentin."

"After just about a month in the saddle, without a woman to comfort me, I couldn't think of a better remedy for boredom," the young Easterner chuckled.

CHAPTER TWENTY-EIGHT

The first shadows of twilight began to darken the beds of reeds and the branches of pecan trees along the winding Nueces River. A lone horseman on a black gelding, wearing elegant riding breeches and black boots, dismounted and led his horse toward an oak tree which stood atop a high, grassy knoll. He glanced up at the cloudy sky, a scowl on his handsome features as he heard the ominous rumble of distant thunder. Far to the east, he could barely make out the vague outline of a large, wooden stockade. About half a mile to the west stood a log cabin. A faint wisp of smoke rose from the brick chimney. It was quiet except for that first warning roll of thunder, and the whirring of a swarm of blowflies which suddenly appeared, mingled with the chirping calls of night birds.

The rider wore a pair of white doeskin gloves. In each hip pocket he carried a small, single-shot derringer with mother-of-pearl handle. He turned slowly now, in a circle, squinting at the darkening horizon, and his tensely drawn features relaxed only when he detected no other sign of human life.

It was the seventeenth of May. Armed with the rolled parchment, the wax seal of which bore the royal Spanish crest of Philip V, and which had taken Theobald Arnison almost ten days to fabricate, Quentin Durwood had consumed a week in reaching the vicinity of Windhaven Range.

The vaqueros and the cattle expected by the German had not yet arrived, to Durwood's great relief. This was going to be child's play, even if the surly, dull-witted old fool resisted when confronted by this spurious grant. The forged document declared that this parcel of land had, over a century ago, been awarded to the forebears of the

298

noble Baron Rodrigo de Austencio in return for invaluable services rendered to the monarchy. With no workers around to come to the German's aid, Durwood would have ample time to search the cabin for a letter, or perhaps a diary or other papers, which would bear the actual signature of Ludwig Engelhardt. Then the professor could easily duplicate it on a bill of sale and quit-claim, which would be filed in Austin and stand as incontrovertible proof that Engelhardt had legally transferred his holdings to the baron.

The German had been busy. At least two acres west of the cabin had been plowed for farming. Durwood could just make out, in the gathering dusk, the upright shafts of a hand plow. There were also waist-high wooden stakes around one side of the plowed land, the beginnings of a fence which would shelter the produce from the cattle when they arrived. Yes, there was grass enough for sheep, not that it mattered one whit to Durwood. Once this Moultrie fellow had turned over his five thousand dollars, all Quentin would be concerned about was the division of the spoils. In fact, he had already made a mental note to tell the baron that his share ought to be a little more than a third, considering that he might have to dispose of the German and his wife permanently.

No one was going to see what happened tonight, and it was highly unlikely that the man's two sons would discover their father and mother, once the latters' bodies were safely interred. The new owner, this fellow Moultrie, would, of course, know nothing of their whereabouts. In a state as vast as Texas, anything could and did happen.

He was ready now, and he might as well get it over and done with. It was a shame that Lily Mellers wouldn't be on hand to solace him after this night's work. But once he got back to San Antonio, there would be other women. It was a large town, and there were women like that black-haired beauty he'd met in Galveston. A decent woman wouldn't know all the tricks that Lily did, but the fun of breaking her in would be compensation.

Quentin Durwood smiled to himself as he opened his saddlebag and took out the impressive-looking roll of parchment. He furtively patted each hip pocket. The derringers didn't show. The only risk would be if that stupid German came at him with a rifle. But since he would appear unarmed, Quentin doubted that Engelhardt would try to shoot him down in cold blood. There were times when the prevailing code of weapons was entirely on his side. He hesitated only a moment, then knocked loudly at the door.

"Was ist los, wer ist da?" he heard the man call out. "It's Quentin Durwood, Herr Engelhardt. I'm here on official business—I'm sorry to disturb you without warning like this, but it's very urgent. Please let me in," he called back.

Straining his ears, he thought he heard a whispered conversation between the man and his fat, dowdy wife, and then there was the sound of the heavy wooden plank which served as bolt being drawn aside and thudding to the floor. Engelhardt opened the door quickly, and stood framed in the flickering light of a lantern set on the mantelpiece, his rifle in his hands, the barrel pointing at Durwood's middle. "The *Mensch* from Austin, *hein*—It's you again? Well, *was in der Teufel* do you want?"

"May I come in and talk to you and your wife for a minute, Herr Engelhardt? This is very serious business, I'm afraid, and I can't discuss it standing here in the dark, with a gun pointed at me. As you see, I haven't any weapons." Durwood, the parchment still tucked under his left arm, extended his gloved hands, palms up, to verify his statement.

Engelhardt stared hard at him for a moment, then lowered the barrel of his rifle and grunted. "All right. I kick you out if you make trouble, *verstehen Sie?* Come in. *Meine Frau* Minna and I, we were going to have our supper just now. She did not cook enough for a guest, but you can have a cup of coffee, if you want."

"Thank you, Herr Engelhardt. Good evening, Frau Engelhardt." Durwood smiled at the middle-aged blond matron who sat at a crude trestle table on which, incongruously enough, a fine linen tablecloth had been spread. To the left of the cabin were bunk beds, and on the other side was an old mahogany chest of drawers with a chair flanking each side of it. The floor was made of split logs with the faces rough and uneven. In the fireplace an iron pot hung from a hook, and a small wood fire crackled under it.

The woman stared hostilely at him. Then, seeing her husband's quick nod, she slowly got to her feet, went to a crudely made wooden sideboard on which pewter plates and cups were set, took a cup and filled it from the dented coffee pot beside her. She shoved the cup toward Durwood, who, at Engelhardt's curt invitation, had seated himself on a rickety wooden stool. "Thank you, Frau Engelhardt." Durwood smiled, but she gave him only a faint grunt in return and watched her husband seat himself at the other end of the table.

Engelhardt sat stiffly, glaring at the Easterner, his rifle gripped in his right hand with the butt pressed against the floor. With his left hand he picked up a pewter spoon and dipped it into the bowl of stew which his wife had already set before him. He took a tentative taste, smacked his lips, and downed the spoonful. Replacing the spoon in the bowl, he growled, "All right, get on with your business, young man. What has made you come all this way from Austin to bother us God-fearing people while we are having supper by ourselves?"

"I'm afraid I have bad news for you, Herr Engelhardt."

The stocky middle-aged settler glared at Quentin Durwood, the pudgy fingers of his right hand tightening around the barrel of the rifle until the knuckles were white. Leaning forward, he demanded, *"Was ist los, das Sie sagen?"*

Durwood lifted the beribboned, carefully rolled and sealed parchment and held it up for the scowling German to see. "You see, Herr Engelhardt," he explained, "when I first visited you, I worked for the land office in Austin. Since then, however, I've been employed by the last surviving member of an old, noble, Spanish family. His name is the Baron Rodrigo de Austencio. And this piece of paper, Herr Engelhardt, is a royal deed, signed by His Majesty Philip V of Spain."

"What has all this to do with me?"

"Everything, I'm afraid, Herr Engelhardt. This document is the original land grant for the acres which you supposedly bought in Austin."

"*Was sagen Sie? Sie sind verruckt!*" Engelhardt half-rose from the table, his face twisted with anger, then thudded the butt of his rifle down against the floor to emphasize his outburst.

"I'm afraid it's all very legal, Herr Engelhardt. It's true that this grant was signed over a hundred and fifty years ago, but it still takes precedence over your transaction in Austin. I will read it to you, and you will see how it desscribes the land you have here. Why, it even tells about that group of oak trees just at the edge of the creek, about a hundred yards west of here."

"That's a *verdammt* lie, do you hear me? For this place I have paid two thousand dollars to the man in the office in Austin, *verstehen Sie?* This is my land, and you have no business here. *Gehen heraus.* I will throw you out myself!" The thick veins in his neck swelled as he scowled at Durwood. Engelhardt lifted the rifle in his right hand, and at that moment, coolly and without a flicker of expression on his face, Durwood dipped his gloved right hand toward the rear pocket of his breeches, drew out the derringer, and pulled the trigger.

Minna Engelhardt uttered a shriek and clapped her hands to her cheeks, her eyes huge and staring as she saw her husband slowly look down at the tiny bleeding hole in his shirt, then pitch forward over the table, the rifle dropping to the floor.

"Murderer! *Mein Gott,* you have murdered him!" In her hysterical grief, she rose from the chair and stooped to retrieve the fallen rifle, but Durwood's other hand had already drawn out the second derringer. "No hard feelings, Frau Engelhardt," he observed as, leveling the derringer at the back of her head, he pulled the trigger.

The stillness of death was in the cabin now. He stood there a long moment, assuring himself that both were dead, then calmly stepped around the woman's sprawled body, picked up the rifle, and examined it critically. Opening the breech, he saw the cartridges, then slammed the breech shut and whistled softly to himself. "I gave him just a little too much time for comfort."

Then, laying the rifle on the stool, he moved to the head of the table, grasped the German's inert body, with his arms around the latter's chest, and began to drag it toward the door. He let the corpse drop as he turned to pull open the door, then stooped again, took hold of Engelhardt, and dragged him outside. When he reached the border of the little creek—that, too, had been included in Theobald Arnison's description—he stopped. Leaving the body, he went back to the cabin and, grasping Minna Engelhardt's wrist, dragged her out to lie beside her husband.

There was a spade in the garden plot. He went to get it and then began to dig. It took nearly an hour to dig two graves, smooth them over with earth, and break off some branches from a nearby oak tree to disguise them. When he finished, he thrust the space back into the earth where it had been, and walked slowly back to the cabin. Methodically, he ransacked the Engelhardts' possessions until he found what he had been looking for—a Bible with Ludwig Engelhardt's own signature boldly and clearly inscribed on the flyleaf. Then, picking up the parchment from the table, he went back to his gelding, put both parchment and Bible into the saddlebag and fastened it, mounted, and rode north toward San Antonio.

"There you are, Mr. Moultrie, your title to the four thousand acres as agreed." Immaculately dressed in a fawn-colored frock coat, with cambric shirt and flowing cravat into which he had thrust a pearl-headed stickpin, the baron handed his client a neatly folded sheet of paper from the Austin land office. It had been signed by Tobias Jennings, in his official post as assistant chief clerk, and it declared that as of the twenty-ninth of May 1869, the tract of land originally purchased by one Ludwig Engelhardt and subsequently deeded over to the baron, had been transferred to the ownership of Andrew Moultrie.

The very night of his cold-blooded murder of the Engelhardts and the interment of their bodies, Durwood had ridden back to San Antonio at full speed, stopping only briefly for food and drink. Arnison, using the dead man's signature from the Bible flyleaf, had drawn up a quitclaim naming the baron as purchaser; next, he had prepared a transfer of title, and Durwood had ridden to Austin to have these two ingeniously forged documents officially recorded. On the day that he had started for Austin, the baron had sent a wire to bring the Scotsman to San Antonio. Now the transfer had been completed and five thousand dollars in banknotes had been paid.

"I congratulate you on your purchase, Mr. Moultrie," the baron added, signaling Theobald to fill glasses with whiskey all around. "Your holdings will increase in value once this Eastern syndicate in which I have a not inconsiderable investment begins its survey and which will ultimately bring the railroad down through Texas and perhaps as far as your land."

Andrew Moultrie was thirty-seven, six feet two inches tall, rangy, and rawboned. His dark-brown hair was unruly and he wore a short, neatly clipped beard and trimmed sideburns. His features were angular, his dark-blue eyes widely spaced on either side of a hawklike nose, and his cheekbones were slanting and high-set. His mouth was firm and incisive. So sun-bronzed was his skin that at first glance he might have been taken for an Indian, but the pleasant brogue of his speech proclaimed him a Scot. He accepted the glass of whiskey with a gracious nod to old Theobald Arnison, lifted it and clinked it against the baron's glass. "You're a man of business after my own heart, baron. Aye, I'm indebted to you. It's a right comfortable spread you've sold me, plenty of room for my sheep and far enough away from my unfriendly in-laws so that Anna and I can really start to enjoy our lives."

"I must warn you, of course, Mr. Moultrie," the baron interposed, "that you and your lovely bride will find conditions somewhat primitive. Quentin tells me that the German couple who were gracious enough to recognize the validity of the royal grant had built only a rather rough log cabin. They started a garden and did a little plowing, but that's about all. They were expecting some cattle, but I'm sure they canceled those arrangements when they decided to sell. You see, sir, I was interested only in claiming my just inheritance, and I saw to it that the Engelhardts had a fair price so that they did not suffer." He sent a meaningful glance to Durwood, who suppressed a cynical smile of amusement.

"I'm glad to hear that you did fairly by the settlers, baron," the tall Scot replied. "I'm as ready as any man alive to drive a hard bargain, but I never cheat folks. To be sure, there are those in Taos who'll say that, as a gringo, I shouldn't have been allowed to buy land near these high-flown Spanish aristocrats. But once I met my Anna, I knew that here was my fate and fortune, and thanks to you, it's all worked out very well."

"It's always gratifying to have a customer satisfied with a transaction, Mr. Moultrie." The baron gave the Scot a ceremonious little bow, then took a swig of his whiskey.

"And as for roughing it, Anna and I won't mind at all," Moultrie went on. "I'll send off a wire to Ramón Guitterez—he's my foreman—and he'll arrange to ship the sheep and come himself with five good men. Once we've started the sheep grazing there will be time enough for the men to help me build a better house. Yes, it'll be an exciting sort of adventure, almost like starting married life all over again. Gentlemen, I drink to my wife, to a courageous and beautiful helpmate!"

Quentin Durwood, the baron, and Theobald Arnison lifted their glasses and politely echoed the toast.

"What neighbors do I have adjoining my land, baron?" Andrew Moultrie then asked.

"Only one to the east, Mr. Moultrie," the baron promptly responded. "It's a fellow by the name of Lucien Edmond Bouchard. He has some eight thousand acres just a few miles east of you, and he raises cattle."

Andrew Moultrie frowned and studied his half-empty glass. "Well, it can't be helped," he finally said, his Scottish burr more vibrant than ever, a characteristic when he was preoccupied with serious matters. "After all, with the creek and the Nueces River, there's water enough for the two of us, I'm thinking It is true that sheep eat the grass down to the very roots, but then that'll be on my acres and not his. And I won't expect his cattle to come trespassing on my land. We'll get along. I'm sure of it."

"Of course you will, Mr. Moultrie. From what I've heard, Bouchard's a reasonable man. And you're right about the water. Well then, you'll be setting off at once to take over your new holdings, I suppose?" the baron inquired.

Andrew Moultrie nodded. "I'm going to the telegraph office now and send that wire. Ramón Guitterez will inform Anna, and she'll come on ahead of the workers and the sheep. Oh, aye, it'll be a lonely life until she comes there, but then the best things in life are worth waiting for, don't you agree?"

"Always." The baron permitted himself a smug little smile as he lifted his glass again to his client, then finished his whiskey.

Eight days after Quentin Durwood had ridden back from the Engelhardt cabin to San Antonio, six vaqueros skirted Windhaven Range to drive four hundred head of cattle toward the ranch of their new *patrón*. They had ridden up from Nuevo Laredo to await the arrival of the steamboat, *Tensaw Belle*, at Corpus Christi. August Freylinghausen, the St. Louis factor with whom Ludwig Engelhardt had arranged to purchase prime cows, heifers, and a dozen pedigreed bulls, himself had escorted them all the way to this desolate Texas port. The overland journey had been without incident, but the vaqueros had been in no hurry, and they had taken nearly a week longer than had Lucien Edmond and his father, Luke, to transport their wagons, their families, and workers to the verdant valley.

It was midday and the sun was pitiless as Enrique Poteros, whom Ludwig Engelhardt had chosen as foreman, reined in his horses, a puzzled look on his swarthy thickly mustached face. "¿Donde esta nuestro patrón, amigos?" he anxiously demanded as the other riders came alongside him. "There is no one out in the fields. Perhaps he and his señora are in the cabin. I will ride ahead and look. Keep the cattle quiet. It has been a very long journey. Indeed, I think I shall ask the *patrón* for more *dinero*."

So saying, he dismounted and strode toward the cabin. When he emerged, he had taken off his sombrero and was scratching his head, a worried look on his face. "It is very strange, amigos. They are not there. There is no sign of them. *Nada*."

"What shall we do, Enrique?" his best friend, Diego Subarca, a small, pockmarked man in his late thirties, asked.

"I don't know, Diego. But I think we will wait a little. We have been paid the *dinero* to bring the cattle here

306

and then to work for the *patrón*. There is nothing else to do."

"Perhaps, if he and his *mujer* have gone away for good, we can keep the cattle and go back to Mexico," Diego suggested.

Poteros shot him a piercing glance, then chuckled softly to himself. "We are not *ladrónes*. We will wait. But, *certamente*, if he and his señora do not come back at all, then we shall have to think of something. *¿No es verdad,* Diego?"

The six men waited two days for the return of Ludwig Engelhardt and his wife, Minna. By then, their food supplies were nearly gone and they were restless. The loneliness, the merciless sun, their growing feeling that there was more money due them than had been paid at the outset, at last induced all five to demand of Poteros that they take the cattle and go back across the border, where they could easily sell the herd and divide the proceeds. Indeed, Diego Subarca volunteered that he had heard of a friendly Comanche village whose chief might be willing to buy one of the bulls and some of the heifers. And when his *compañeros* protested that notion because everyone knew that the Comanches and the Mexicans had been age-old enemies, Diego had shrugged and said, "That may be, but not this chief. He has *una esposa Mejicana,* and he is at peace. And then as we go back to Nuevo Laredo, there are many little villages where the people will pay *mucho dinero* to have such fine cattle as these. *¡Vamanos,* hombres!"

CHAPTER TWENTY-NINE

Andrew Moultrie left San Antonio with the recorded deed to his new land, and rode to the border town of Del Rio. There, after a day or two spent in the local *cantina*, he hired six Mexican laborers who had formerly been peons for a despotic *hacendado*. Of the six, who sometimes hired themselves out as *pistoleros*, one had formerly been a skilled carpenter and was clearly respected by his five compatriots. His name was Jorge Maduro and he was affectionately called El Borrachón because of his fondness for tequila.

"When you and your amigos have finished a house for my *esposo* and myself, Jorge," the Scotsman announced, "I'll see that you have all the tequila you want, enough to drown yourself in if you've a mind to. *¿Comprende?*"

Jorge Maduro, a heavyset man in his late thirties and nearly as tall as his new *patrón*, grinned wolfishly and fingered the drooping ends of his thick mustache. "*Si, patrón, comprendo bueno*. I have not forgotten how to build—if there is the wood to work with. The *patrón* has arranged for this?"

"Yes, Jorge. On my way here, I stopped at Brackettville. There's a man there with a load of timber to sell. It was an order for some Easterner who lost all his money in a poker game in San Antonio and got himself shot by saying the dealer had marked the cards."

Jorge shook his head and grinned again. "That was *muy estúpido*, unless he was a better *pistolero* than the dealer."

"Well, obviously he wasn't, Jorge. Now, this lumberman's name is John Bramson. Here, you'll show him this bill of sale and he'll turn the lumber and the wagons over to you. Your men will ride to my land near Carrizo

Springs and start work at once. I'll go with you, of course."

"*Bueno*. It will be good to do honest work and make *dinero* like this without having to worry about the soldiers." Maduro grinned again, barring crooked, yellowing teeth. "You understand, my friends and I are neither thieves nor murderers, but we have learned to use guns when there's a need for our services. Still, now that the Juaristas are in power, they do not look kindly on our taking the law into our own hands."

"You're right: you'll be doing honest work. But I don't want you and your friends to get out of practice with your pistols, Jorge. I'll be bringing sheep onto my land, and my neighbor to the east is a cattle rancher."

Jorge pursed his lips, and then whistled softly. "I begin to understand. Cattle and sheep do not mix well."

"I know that. But I'm not looking for trouble; I just want to stay one step ahead of it. My neighbor can always put up fences to keep his cattle off my land. Now then, we'll leave in the morning. Here." He tossed a gold piece onto the table. "See that your friends have what tequila they want—but not too much. I want you all sober and ready to ride at dawn."

"No need to fear, *patrón*. And when do the sheep arrive?"

Moultrie lifted his own glass of tequila to salute his new foreman, and took a moderate swig. "From Taos to my ranch is over six hundred miles, Jorge. My own vaqueros have already started the flock. They should be there sometime in July. My wife will come by stagecoach, accompanied by one of my most trusted men, from Taos to El Paso, and from there on to San Antonio. I'll ride up and bring her back. So we have work to do, hombre."

"*Bueno*. I think we will enjoy working for you, senor." Jorge held out his hand and Moultrie shook it, smiling.

Six days later, Moultrie rode ahead of the heavy wagons, filled with lumber and driven by his six new workers, toward the log cabin which Ludwig Engelhardt had built. He had made himself a map of the land, after receiving his recorded copy of the title, and observed the terrain with satisfaction. "There'll be water enough for the sheep,

309

Jorge, and there's plenty of pasturage off to the north and west. I want you and your men to start putting together the house as quickly as you can. My wife will join me by the first week in July, and I'll see that you have a bonus, all of you, if you've got the place ready for her by then."

"That is scarcely more than three weeks, *patrón*," the heavyset Mexican complained. "But since we have nothing else to do and you promise us more *dinero,* we will do the best we can."

"Good! I don't ask more than that from any man, even myself," the tall Scot chuckled. Tying the reins of his gelding to the trunk of a nearby tree, he strode toward the cabin with Jorge Maduro at his side, while the five wagon drivers halted their horses, unharnessed them, and led them to a clump of oak trees to be tethered for the night. They had brought tools and sufficient food for ten days, their new employer having promised that more supplies would arrive from San Antonio before their own provisions ran out.

Andrew Moultrie had sold his land in Taos for $8,000, representing a profit of nearly $6,000, thanks to an error which had been made by a clerk in the Taos land office, both in the evaluation of the land itself and in the number of acres which the Scot had actually acquired at the time of his purchase. His haughty, arrogant brother-in-law, Miguel Soldarado, who had never forgiven Moultrie for having wooed and won his younger sister, repurchased the land from him and told him with a sneer, "If you had remained here, Moultrie, I should have had to kill you one day. So, for the salvation of my soul, I do not regret giving you all these Yankee dollars to be rid of you. But if I learn that you have not made Anna happy, I will seek you out and end this unsavory marriage. You are a gringo adventurer, a man who causes trouble and violence wherever he goes. How she could have fallen in love with you is beyond my comprehension—but since she has, heed my warning."

Moultrie had only smiled and remained silent. He had come to Taos in the spring of 1868, his wallet lined with banknotes, thanks to an unbelievable streak of luck in a poker game in San Francisco. His father's legacy, deposited in a solvent San Francisco bank, had been nearly $75,000, and the tall, enterprising Scot believed that whatever he attempted would turn out successfully. He had tried many things in his youth, working one summer with a horse breeder and savoring the danger and excitement of breaking in wild mustangs and gentling them. He had even spent a year clerking in a San Francisco general store, wanting to size up customers and persuade them to buy more than they intended through his own personable tactics. From that experience alone he had learned merchandising enough to know what supplies should cost and what price they should bring. This knowledge had aided him in his own dealings as a sheep rancher. His father had been seventy-three when he died, just six months before Moultrie decided to abandon California in favor of the still insular, Old World Spanish culture of New Mexico.

From the very first, Andrew had been made to feel like an outcast. The Spanish families were determined to keep the aura of the Old World, aristocratic way of life as a barrier to any union with this vulgar, new United States. To be sure, Moultrie had found traces of that in California, particularly in Los Angeles and Monterey. But in Taos the oldest and most influential families clung to their heritage with a doubly intense zeal—perhaps exactly because they saw only too well how weak their homeland had become as a world power, and how most of Spain's colonies were Hispanic no longer. It was as if they had resolved to maintain the bastion of blue-blooded superiority that would exclude all gringos.

But when he had seen the lovely young Doña Anna de Soldarado and her plump, talkative *duenna*, Doña Josefa, step out of a carriage to visit a dressmaker's shop, he had been smitten with an irrational desire for her. He had been staying at an inn, and the proprietor had listened to his description of this vivid, brown-eyed, black-haired Circe who had appeared to him as if in a vision, and then replied, "I will say only that you have good taste, Señor Moultrie. But to seek a romance with Doña Anna de Soldarado would be the act of a young fool who is ready to throw his life away. Her family is one of the oldest in Taos, and her father's land was granted to his father

311

before him by a great Spanish king. The Soldarados are proud people, and they resent gringos who come to trade with them, to fleece them of their money and to try to mingle with them as if they were equals."

But Moultrie hadn't heeded that friendly warning. Instead, riding frequently near the Soldarado hacienda, he had seen a pretty young maid leave it one afternoon and hurry to meet a young footman who worked in the equally elegant house nearby. Intercepting the girl, Andrew had exerted all his charm and, using the considerable Spanish he already knew, told her that he had fallen madly in love with her young mistress and that he would pay her well if she could possibly arrange a secret meeting between them.

Pretty Rosa Loringar, eighteen and herself enamored of the Rosario's pompous, handsome young footman, had sympathized with this tall, handsome *gringo*. Besides, she knew very well that Doña Anna had been in a vile mood lately. This was due to her father's announcement that he planned to marry her to Don Carlos de Amaduro, the son of one of his best friends. So she willingly conveyed Andrew Moultrie's message to the startled Doña Anna who, willing to seize any hope of escaping an odious union, agreed to meet the Scot one evening when her parents would be away from the estate.

Anna de Soldarado dressed herself like a maidservant in peasant blouse, red cotton skirt, and thonged *huaraches*. She wound a bright green *chal* over the lower part of her face to disguise herself. Then, bribing Rosa not to betray her to Doña Josefa, who was taking an overlong siesta, she slipped out of the house to meet her unknown cavalier.

It was the very challenge which her aristocratic upbringing presented to him, and to all that he represented, which obsessed Andrew Moultrie. He was determined to win her. He recognized her as the kind of woman who, secure in her own narcissistic virginity, amused herself with men both of her own status and, even more daring, with those beneath her station. When he took her in his arms for the first time, however, and kissed her passionately on the mouth—despite her initial resistance—he felt her respond to him and knew there was latent passion in her such as he had never known before. Finally, when she told him of her father's insistence that she marry a man she detested and begged him to help her escape it, he had eloped with Anna de Soldarado to Santa Fe, where a kindly old priest had made them man and wife.

When the newlyweds returned to Taos, there had been a stormy scene between Anna's father and his new gringo son-in-law. Don Sebastián de Soldarado had denounced Moultrie as a cowardly opportunist who had sought to gain a fortune by compromising his daughter, and threatened to have the marriage annulled. But the tall Scot, undaunted by the blustering of the angry white-haired nobleman, had calmly produced the certificate of marriage and declared, "Your daughter is a Catholic as you are, Don Sebastián. And I am not unaware of the strictures of that faith. The marriage was performed by a Dominican priest and is on record in Santa Fe. You cannot annul it because it has already been consummated."

His face drained of color, his lips compressed, Anna's father had clutched the edge of his desk for support, reeling from the shock of this brazen defiance by a detested gringo. At last he had been able to say, "So be it. But if you think to have gained entrance into the family of de Soldarado, if you believe that you have earned a dowry, I shall disillusion you at once. From this moment forth, I no longer recognize my daughter as my flesh and blood. Not one penny shall you have of my estate, no more than shall the issue between yourself and my traitorous offspring. And if you will now kindly take yourself from my house, I shall be obliged to you."

Moultrie had turned his back on the trembling old man and left. A week later, Anna's former fiancé, goaded to perhaps his first display of manhood by his raging parents, had challenged the hated gringo to a duel. He had come upon Andrew and Anna, drawn off his glove, and slapped the Scot across the cheek, demanding satisfaction for the shame and degradation which Moultrie had inflicted on Anna.

Moultrie had accepted the challenge. He had chosen dueling pistols at twenty paces, and when his fat, whey-faced opponent missed him with his first shot, Andrew contemptuously turned his pistol toward the ground and

313

fired it. Then he remarked, "Go back to your mama and papa and tell them you have behaved creditably, señor. The next time you interfere with Anna and me, I will not spare you."

Andrew visited the Taos land office shortly thereafter and, shrewdly taking the measure of an uninformed clerk, had acquired a coveted stretch of land for a pittance. He had bought sheep, had his workers build him a hacienda, only to find that he and his beautiful, black-haired wife had begun their new lives in an atmosphere of hatred. Only Rosa, the friendly little maid who had served as go-between for these rebellious lovers, had gone to work for them and fulfilled the duties of both maid and cook.

But after a year, Anna began to chafe in her new domain. Her ambitious and frugal husband did not believe in the trappings of luxury to which she had been accustomed since her childhood. For him, money was to be used not for gewgaws, but for investment in land, sheep, and workers. He did not shower her with gifts of jewelry and fine clothing, and in time, since she was still a petulant and spoiled young woman, she spitefully sought to test his love through flirtations. Thus it was that the Baron Rodrigo de Austencio had heard of the episode in which Andrew Moultrie had almost whipped to death a young vaquero who dared not only lift his eyes to Anna Moultrie, but actually had been caught embracing her. What the baron had not been told was the sequel to that story. His face red and twisted with jealous rage Moultrie had declared, "If ever again you act like a *puta*, I'll use this whip on you, Anna. You'll never need any other man but me so long as you live—and don't forget it, *querida.*"

So it was that Anna learned that it would be hazardous to test her husband's patience further. That was why she had pleaded with him to buy land far from Taos, where the two of them could be free at last of the baleful hatred of her parents, her own brother, and her family's friends. That, indeed, was what had prompted Moultrie to engage the baron to negotiate for land that would be far enough from Taos and yet in the same climatic region so that his beautiful, impetuous young wife would feel herself not too-far-removed from her parents whom, despite her defiance of them, she still sincerely loved.

Andrew Moultrie himself set an example for his six new workers, putting pegged planks into place, hammering nails, impervious to the blistering sun and the dry, sometimes furnacelike wind which prevailed through the month of June. Their pride refused to let this domineering, hard-driving gringo outdo them. The house was finished only a day after the three weeks which Moultrie had hoped it would take. And on that day, the audacious Scot, true to his word, paid each and every man a bonus to reward them for their efforts.

The discovery that their gringo *patrón's* promise was not an empty one earned their loyalty, as did their admiration for his forceful and well-calculated planning. Periodically, wagons of food supplies and more tools arrived from San Antonio. Moultrie had engaged a capable factor in that town to act for him. With the supplies came furniture, rugs, and even artistic bric-a-brac for the house in which Anna Moultrie would reign. Late in the afternoon of the day the house was completed, Andrew winked at his workers, took a spade, and dug into the ground near the crude cabin which the Engelhardts had once occupied. He uncovered six bottles of the finest tequila and declared, "There's a bottle for each of you, amigos. And I've one in my own saddlebag so that we may drink together to celebrate a job well done. Tomorrow, I ride to San Antonio to bring back *mi esposa*. While I'm gone, I suggest you build a bunkhouse for yourselves. You, Jorge, as top hand shall have the cabin. You'll know how to put it into shape for your own comfort, I'm certain."

"Is my husband happy to see me again?" Anna Moultrie asked teasingly as she watched her wiry, gray-haired escort lift her baggage down from the stagecoach at the San Antonio office of the line.

Andrew Moultrie grinned and nodded. "I'll admit you surprise me, *querida*. And that's why I'm not going to kiss you, not here in the street where everyone will see us. Not when you're dressed like a man."

315

Anna wore a black sombrero with a string tied under her pert chin, a cambric shirt and black trousers, and new boots with jingling spurs. Over her shoulder was a poncho such as a matador might wear when he entered the bull-ring. Her dark-brown eyes flashed coquettishly as she turned to Ramón Guitterez and laughingly asked, "Tio Ramón, my husband doesn't recognize me. But it was you yourself who suggested this disguise."

Ramón Guitterez had been a peon for twenty years in the house of Anna de Soldarado's father. He had watched her grow from infancy to a stunning, sultry beauty, and he had secretly approved of her courage in defying her father's choice of mate. When she and Andrew Moultrie had eloped, he had left her father's service and volunteered to serve her. Since he had worked with sheep as a stripling and Anna's father had later put him in charge of the tannery, Moultrie had promptly engaged him as supervisor of the flock he intended to move from Taos to his new ranch. It would be Ramón Guitterez's responsibility to oversee the shepherds driving the flock toward the Nueces River, to supervise the raising and breeding of the flock, and to take charge of the shearing operation. For it was Andrew Moultrie's intention to sell not only the wool, but also the sheep themselves as meat on the hoof, just as beef was being sold to the Midwestern and Eastern markets. What he had seen in New Mexico of the indifferent way in which the large sheep ranchers had been resigned to low profits and disproportionately high operational costs made him impatient to try his own hand in a new locale.

"Well, Ramón, was it your idea that my Anna change herself into a *caballero?*" Andrew Moultrie demanded, laughing.

"It is true, Señor Moultrie, that I did not think it wise that so beautiful a señora ride in a stagecoach with only an old man like myself to protect her. Fortunately, the good God was kind on our journey. There were no *bandidos* or *Indios* along the way."

"But I wouldn't have let them stop me from coming to you, *mi corazón*," Anna purred as, glancing quickly up and down the street, she pressed herself against her hus-

316

band and gave him a stinging kiss on the mouth, then stepped back with a mocking little smile. "There, that will have to do, Señor Moultrie, until we reach our new home. And I hope that it is comfortable. You don't know what it's like to be crowded into a bumpy stagecoach for days and days on end!"

As Jorge Maduro came out of the cabin to help with the cooking of the evening meal, he let out a shout that brought his five companions hurrying from the fire they had started in a little ditch near a cottonwood tree. "It's the *patrón, compañeros!*" he called, energetically waving his sombrero at the three distant riders who were approaching rapidly, a small cloud of dust rising behind them in the hot, evening air.

"Don't forget to tell him about those two young gringos who came here last week asking for their father and mother," Jesús Moreno, a short, squat man with a purplish knife scar on the left side of his jaw, reminded him.

"*Estúpido,* of course I'll tell him. But I don't understand, the *patrón* said he'd bring his *mujer--caramba,* he *has* brought her, and she's dressed like a vaquero!"

"By all the saints, I wish the *patrón* had thought of bringing some *putas* along to keep us company in this accursed, lonely place," Moreno grumbled.

Maduro shot him a withering glance. "Best keep that to yourself, amigo. And Señor Moultrie won't like it if you look too much at his *mujer.* He's quick with a gun, that one, and he knows how to use it. Why, he could have been a *gran pistolero* if he'd chosen to be, instead of bringing sheep here." Then, raising his voice, he called to the others, "Make more tortillas and bacon and beans, they'll be hungry after this long ride!"

Then, removing his sombrero, Maduro hurried up to his employer, who was just dismounting, and took the reins of his horse. "Welcome home, Señor Moultrie!"

"*Gracias,* Jorge. This is my wife, Señora Moultrie." Andrew helped his wife off her horse, and held her tightly against him for a long moment while he glanced around at the six *pistoleros;* then at last he released her. "Well, *querida,* what do you think of your new home?"

317

Anna Moultrie untied the chin string of her black sombrero, struck the brim against her thigh as a man might to clear it of the dust, and made a wry face. "It's not like my father's hacienda. But I suppose it will do."

"Come now, *mi corazón*," he chuckled, "it's only temporary, until I have made my fortune here. Then I'll build you the finest hacienda you've ever seen, and that's a promise. Besides, you won't find bare floors and walls inside. I've had some pretty things shipped from San Antonio just for your sake." Ramón Guiterrez had dismounted, and one of the vaqueros came forward with a companionable nod to take the reins of his horse and tether it to a branch of a cottonwood tree. Andrew turned to Maduro. "The sheep aren't here yet, I see. I'd sort of hoped the drivers would have made better time. Well, next week for sure. I suppose everything's gone well? Any news of our neighbor to the east?"

"No, Señor Moultrie. But last week two young gringos rode up here. They were very angry when I told them that their father and mother did not own this land any longer and that you did. At first they called me a liar, but my *compañeros* told them that I did not lie and that you had bought the land from their father."

"I see." Andrew Moultrie scowled and rubbed his knuckles against his chin as he thought for a moment. "Well, I did buy it, though I got it through a man who bought it from their father. What did they finally do or say, Jorge?"

"They said they would ride to the land office in Austin and find out for themselves. They asked me if I knew where their father and mother had gone. I could not tell them anything because of course I did not know. One of them, who called himself Hans Engelhardt, said it was strange that his father and mother had left no word for his brother and him, that it was not like them at all. But we had our guns with us, Señor Moultrie, and so at last they rode off."

"Well, to be truthful with you, Jorge, I don't know where the Engelhardts went, either. But my deed to the land has been recorded in Austin, and so far as I'm concerned it's mine now, to do with as I wish. At any rate, you and your men have done very well. And now, if you'll fix us some supper, my wife and I will be grateful."

"I have already told the men to prepare more food, señor, for you and your *esposa*," Jorge Maduro replied.

CHAPTER THIRTY

"I had a feeling we'd have trouble with those damn sheep, Joe," Andy Haskins declared with irritation as, rising in his saddle and tightening the reins to halt his black gelding, he scowled at the sight of a dozen ewes and lambs placidly grazing a few feet across the western boundary of Windhaven Range.

"Mr. Bouchard's been back a week now, and he says he's been meaning to visit his new neighbor. We better head for the ranch house and let him know what's happening, so he can get this straightened out without any trouble," Joe Duvray responded. Then, waving his sombrero and shouting, he drove the sheep, plaintively bleating, back to Andrew Moultrie's land. "Skedaddle now, and don't come back! You've got plenty of grass in your own pasture without eating up all of ours!"

"Something like that could start a range war, I'm thinking," Haskins mused as the two young Southerners turned their mounts and headed back to the ranch house.

It was true that Lucien Edmond Bouchard had intended to pay a formal visit to meet his new neighbor. But he had been preoccupied, not only with his plan to bring in Brahmas, but also with arrangements for Celia's journey to Sangrodo's stronghold, to visit her daughter, Prissy. Djamba had naturally volunteered to go with his still-slightly-ailing wife, now that Kate Strallis had so willingly and efficiently stepped in as Celia's kitchen replacement. Indeed, only last night Kate had been in charge of the supper for the vaqueros in the bunkhouse as well as that for the Bouchard family, and her culinary efforts had been pronounced a huge success.

Since the trip across the border was not without potential danger, Lucien Edmond had assigned Carl, Dave, and Frank, all armed with Spencer carbines and plenty of ammunition, to ride along. Then, at the last moment, Lucas had decided that he wanted to accompany his mother, and had persuaded Felicidad to make the trip with him. So Lucas had driven the wagon in which his mother and Felicidad rode, the food supplies for the seven of them being carried in the back.

Lucien Edmond had been chatting with Maxine when Andy and Joe knocked at the front door of the ranch house. Excusing himself, Lucien Edmond strode to the door and opened it.

"We've got trouble with our new neighbor, I'm afraid, Mr. Bouchard." Haskins's face was grave. "Joe and I, we just drove about a dozen of these sheep back where they belong. But not until they'd made a pretty wide stretch of grazing land out of our own good grass."

"Thanks for telling me, Andy. I've been meaning to call on our new neighbor, and this is as good a time as any. It's a couple hours before supper, and I ought to be back by then, Maxine dear."

"I do hope there won't be any trouble, darling," she responded. "Maybe it would be a good idea to invite him here for supper some evening, so we can all get to know one another better. It's such a huge country, I guess maybe I wasn't prepared to have someone living so close by, so soon."

"I wasn't either, to be truthful, Maxine dear," Lucien Edmond chuckled as he picked up his Spencer from the corner, where it had been leaning, and followed Andy and Joe out to the corral to get his horse.

"Something mighty funny about that fellow next to us, Mr. Bouchard," Andy scowled, and scratched his ear. "About two months before you got back from the drive, we saw a cabin out there. We didn't think much of it, and there weren't any sheep or cattle, so we didn't pay much attention. But I sort of recall seeing a man and a woman there. Now, as Joe and I told you last week, there's a big frame house and Mexicans who look like *pistoleros* to me. And now there's all those sheep."

"Well, let's hope we can clear up the mystery with a little friendly conversation, Andy," Lucien Edmond replied.

321

As the three men dismounted, Jorge Maduro came out of the log cabin, his spurs jingling and his right hand near his holstered gun. "What do you want, señores?" he called in an unfriendly voice.

"My name's Lucien Edmond Bouchard, and I'd like to have a talk with the man who owns this spread," Lucien Edmond said with a pleasant smile. "These are my two hands, Andy Haskins and Joe Duvray. They help me run Windhaven Range, east of you."

The stocky Mexican gave Lucien Edmond a surly look as he brought his left hand up to smooth the drooping ends of his heavy, black mustache. "I'll go see if the *patrón* wants to see you. If he doesn't, you can talk to me as top hand, or to Ramón Guitterez, the *patrón's* foreman."

"If you don't mind, I'd rather see your boss."

Maduro shrugged, turned to his friend Jesús Moreno who had come up beside him, and growled, "Hold the horses for the señores. I don't think the *patrón* wants to be disturbed. And keep your mouth shut, *¿comprende?*"

"*Sí*, Jorge. Señores, I will take the reins, and you will wait here till my amigo comes back," Moreno told the trio.

In the living room of the frame house, Anna Moultrie was standing, hands on her lissome hips, angrily confronting her glowering husband. "You call this a house, *mi amor?*" Her endearment was sarcastic. "*Por todos los santos*, old Ramón had a better house back in Taos when he worked for my padre. You promised me we would be happy here and that I should have all the comforts of the beautiful hacienda where I was born."

"Now that's enough of that, Anna." Andrew Moultrie's face was flushed with anger. "I told you we had to get started. This is going to be our way of life for a few years. You're close enough to go back to your folks whenever you've a mind to, you know that. And besides, I brought in rugs and chairs and a table, and there's a fine bed—"

"Oh yes, my adored husband," she interrupted sarcastically, "a fine bed to which you come late at night, stinking of those sheep and thinking not of me, but of your plans for building a shearing pen and a tannery and all the other stupid things which a peon thinks about, not a rich gringo!"

322

"Now it's finally out, isn't it, Anna?" He uttered a mirthless little laugh. "You were so grateful when I came to take you away from that fat *novio* of yours, I really thought you loved me. The truth of it is, Anna, you've roving eyes for any man who looks good to you. Yes, even a stable boy or a vaquero, like that Jaime Sabonaro I caught you with."

"And now you're putting all the blame on me, aren't you? You didn't have to beat that poor boy. It was cruel and heartless, and I don't think I shall ever forgive you for it. Oh yes, you love me, but you're a jealous, blindly selfish man. And what's more, you think more of your sheep than of me!" Anna tilted back her head and arched her shoulders to thrust out the high-perched globes of her magnificent bosom, her warm, olive skin coloring with her spiteful fury. She wore a red cotton blouse and a matching *rebozo*, and the black trousers and boots in which she had ridden from San Antonio. Lithe and quivering with anger, she had never been more beautiful. Andrew clamped his teeth together. He could not help staring at what she had intended so brazenly to display.

Finally he burst out, "I told you before, what I should have done was take that whip to you, and I'll do it yet if you keep this up. Look at you, showing your *tetas* in that thin peasant blouse, which only a kitchen maid would be bold enough to wear. And trousers and boots, pretending to be a man."

"Well, and why not?" she boldly defied him. "You have a dozen men here, and I am the only woman. You spend more time with them and your sheep than with me. Is it any wonder, Andrew, that I spend my time riding horseback and perhaps even wishing I hadn't met you?"

"Instead, you'd be bedded with that mama's boy Carlos de Amaduro. And he probably wouldn't even know what to do with you in bed."

For answer, she stepped forward and, compressing her lips, slapped him with all her might across the cheek.

Andrew Moultrie chuckled, and then, to her horrified astonishment, returned the slap. She stumbled back, a hand at her bruised cheek, her dark-brown eyes wide and flaming with hatred. "Since you want to play the man, remember that you don't slap a man without getting slapped back or worse. If you didn't like it, suppose you change your outfit for a suitable dress. God knows I bought enough for you in San Antonio," he taunted.

She stood there, her bosom heaving, her fingers curved like talons, as if she wished to spring on him and claw him. Then, mastering herself, choking back a sob, she turned away and was about to leave the room when there was a loud knock on the door.

"Stay where you are, my love," Andrew ordered. "I think we've our first company. And as my wife, I expect you to be hostess and to welcome newcomers to this our happy house."

"*¡Cobarde!*" she hissed, turning to face him, drawing a deep breath and then standing with her arms at her sides and forcing an impassive look to her flushed, lovely face.

"Well, what is it, Jorge?" Moultrie demanded as he opened the door.

"I am sorry if I have disturbed the señor and the señora." Maduro bowed his head, taking off his sombrero. As he did so, he sent a covert glance at the beautiful young woman, who, quite conscious of his lecherous admiration, stiffened and began to regard with studied indifference the stuffed sofa against the nearest wall.

"What have you to tell me, Jorge?" Moultrie pursued. "If it's about those three men I see out there, bring them in, by all means. Even though twilight's approaching, the sun is still murderously hot in August."

"*Al punto, Señor Patrón.*" Again, Jorge made a respectful bow, then hurried back to Lucien Edmond and the young Southerners. "Señor Moultrie will see you. Jesús will keep your horses ready. It would be best if you do not take too much time. The señor has a lovely *esposa,* and it will soon be time for their evening meal."

His arrogance made Andy Haskins glance quizzically at Joe Duvray, who put a finger to his lips and shook his head. Jorge escorted them to the door and then stepped back, a sneering grin on his swarthy face.

"That's all right, Jorge," Andrew Moultrie called. "I can handle this. Go back and make sure that the men have all the food they need. And a little tequila, but not too much, you understand me? I want you to lose your nickname now that you are working for me."

"The *Señor Patrón* is pleased to make a good joke," Jorge Maduro sniggered, put his sombrero back on, and trudged back to his fellows.

"Now then, gentlemen, what may I do for you? This is my wife, Anna Moultrie. I am Andrew Moultrie." The Scotsman confronted his three visitors, his booted feet planted widely apart in an attitude of hostile defiance.

"My name is Lucien Edmond Bouchard. Delighted to make your acquaintance, Mrs. Moultrie." Lucien Edmond inclined his head. Anna Moultrie eyed him, and a faint smile curved her full red lips before she turned slightly away, as if not in the least interested in her husband's visitors. "And I'd like you to meet Andy Haskins and Joe Duvray, two of my top hands at Windhaven Range. We're neighbors, Mr. Moultrie, and Andy and Joe here tell me that somehow a few of your sheep have been grazing on our grass."

"It's a free range, isn't it?"

"Not exactly. I'll admit that we've had this part of the state pretty much to ourselves the last year or so." Lucien Edmond tried his best to be affable. "But you see, the problem is your sheep. If you had cattle, now, it would be a different matter. Then your riders and mine, at roundup time, would simply separate the herds according to their brands. But sheep, sir, as I'm sure you know, leave very little grass once they've grazed. And it takes a good season or more to grow it, even with the heat we have out here."

"I'd say that's your problem, not mine, Mr. Bouchard," Moultrie drawled. "If you're worried about your cattle, why don't you put up some sort of a fence?"

"I might ask you the same question, Mr. Moultrie. Suppose, as my first act as your neighbor, I offer to share the cost of such a fence with you? In that way, it'll serve us both."

"Mr. Bouchard, I have an old shepherd in charge of five men who tend the flock. He's been handling sheep for almost forty years and he knows his business. And in the main, my flock has stayed within my boundaries. If once in a while a few of my sheep wander over onto your land, I can hardly be blamed for that, can I? I've work to do here, a good deal of building, because I want to

325

drive the sheep to market, and I want to have them shorn here and sell their wool."

"And I wish you every success in your venture, Mr. Moultrie. But I'm sure you wouldn't want my cattle grazing on your grass, any more than I want your sheep grazing on mine. And up to now, thanks to the good crew I have, my cattle have stayed at least a mile away from the boundary. I'm sure your men have noticed the markers my workers put up some time ago."

"To be sure we have. But it's not all that much of a problem. I told you, once in a while sheep will stray, just as your cattle are bound to. I don't think there's much more to discuss on the subject, really, Mr. Bouchard. You've caught me at a rather inopportune time. And we hadn't planned on inviting guests to supper—though of course in good time I'm sure my wife and I will issue a formal invitation." The words were polite, but the tone was so insolently cutting that Lucien Edmond flushed and strove to control his temper.

"I must apologize, then, for disturbing you and your lovely wife, Mr. Moultrie. By the way, before I go, I'd like to ask a question if I may?"

"Ask it," Moultrie curtly responded.

"Andy and Joe tell me that this cabin to the west of your house was built quite some time ago, and they recall seeing a man and a woman here." He turned to the two Southerners. "To the best of your recollection, boys, were the two you saw the same as you see in this room now?"

"No, sir, to tell the truth, I don't think they were," Andy Haskins responded, and Joe Duvray nodded confirmation.

"Now, that's about enough, Bouchard." Andrew Moultrie took a step forward, his eyes glittering and narrowed. "If you're implying that there's anything illegal about my being here, let me assure you that this land was originally awarded by a royal Spanish grant to a noble family. The last surviving descendant of that family bought it from Ludwig and Minna Engelhardt. And since I happened to contact him quite some time ago in my eagerness to find new land on which to conduct my venture, he was kind enough to sell his legacy to me at a very fair price. Now, if you don't mind, I'm rather tired of answering questions."

"I see. Well, I bid your and your wife a pleasant good evening, Mr. Moultrie," Lucien Edmond said, then turned on his heel and left the house.

"It was good of you, señores, not to take too much of Señor Moultrie's time," Jorge Maduro sneered as he watched Lucien Edmond, Andy, and Joe walk toward him. "Jesús, amigo, give them back their horses. We have no quarrel with you, señores, but you see, Señor Moultrie pays us well to protect his land. There are *bandidos* and *Indios* in this country. And sometimes there are men who wish to steal someone else's land."

"Why, you—" Andy Haskins began, but Lucien Edmond gripped his elbow and shook his head, and the one-armed Southerner subsided as he took the reins of his horse and mounted.

Moultrie's workers grouped together to watch them ride off. Once they were out of earshot, Andy turned to his employer. "Mr. Bouchard, I've got a funny feeling there's something fishy about that Moultrie character. First time I heard about any Spanish royal land grants."

"Oh, they were common enough centuries ago, Andy," Bouchard explained. "But I'm not sure how some of them might stand up in a court of law. You see, Texas was on the Confederate side in the war, and the state hasn't yet been formally readmitted to the Union. That means that there's certain to be plenty of land speculation and even swindling, because in the excitement of the war, some of the original records might have been altered or lost. You know," he continued soberly, "it wouldn't do any harm to ride to the Austin land office and have a talk with the chief recorder of deeds. Of course, if this transfer of title is legal, we're stuck with Mr. Moultrie."

"Looks to me, Mr. Bouchard, like he and that purty young wife of his aren't getting along too well out here. I shouldn't wonder, with those shepherds they've got and those *pistoleros* all over the place," Joe Duvray asserted.

"Well, Joe, a domestic spat is something I have no intention of getting into," Lucien Edmond chuckled. "But I'll agree she's a real beauty, with Spanish blood in her. And he's a rawboned Scot if I ever saw one. My guess is they met in New Mexico. Yes, that would surely account for the sheep. From what I've heard, when the Spanish colonists christened that territory Nuevo Mexico, it was in the hope that they might discover untold resources of gold, copper, and silver. But so far, all they've really produced has been sheep, and the market isn't too good for that commodity just yet. Beef is what the Midwest and the East want, and that's what we're going to continue to bring them."

"Would you mind if I rode over to Austin, Mr. Bouchard, and had a look-see about that title this Mr. Moultrie's talking about?" Duvray spoke up.

"No, that wouldn't be a bad idea at all. We've got plenty of time to take things easy, now that we've sold our cattle. Yes, by all means, start whenever you want. Oh, since you'll be passing through San Antonio on your way, there's no reason why you coudn't do a few errands for me which I'd much appreciate. I want to get off a wire about those Brahmas. And you might just pick up a few more supplies on your way back."

"Be glad to, Mr. Bouchard, be glad to."

Andrew Moultrie waited until he saw through the crudely shuttered living room window that his three visitors had retrieved their horses and set off for Windhaven Range. Then he turned to confront his fuming wife. "And now, *mi paloma*, let's go back to where we were when these gentlemen interrupted our discussion. Or, as the French might say, *revenons à nos moutons*— aye, that's not a bad play on words, seeing as how you were accusing me of preferring sheep to you."

"Well, it's true, Andrew! And you accuse me also of playing the man instead of being a woman—you might have been considerate enough to have brought along a maid for me. Instead, I have a potbellied iron stove and you wish me to cook your meals as if I were the daughter of a peon rather than of one of the noblest ranchers in all New Mexico!"

"Why," he gave her a crooked grin, "that alone should prove how faithful I am to you. I am sure that if you'd brought along Rosa, you would be accusing me of infidelity."

Again Anna's cheeks colored, and her eyes blazed with

328

scorn. "Oh, I know that you had many women before we met. But that I do not hold against you. It is the nature of a man, and I would not have thought much of you if you had come to me knowing nothing of *amor*."

"Well now, my fine señora," he mocked her, "if I were not a gentleman—even if I am a gringo—I might remind you that on our wedding night you showed far more eagerness to be between the sheets with me than was seemly in the virgin daughter of a nobleman."

"You are forgetting that I had lived with sheep so much of my life that even from watching the rams mount the ewes, I could not have been completely ignorant of such things. Of course I knew how babies were made before I wedded you. There are girls even in convents, my fine husband, who know that much."

His eyes narrowed with a sudden anger as he came slowly toward her. "Then what I ought to have done is to have given you a child, Anna. Then perhaps I wouldn't have to be jealous of you. Every time you see a man that attracts you, you stare at him with those bold eyes of yours. Yes, and you arch your hips and you shove out your *tetas* for everyone to see. Just as you did with that fellow Bouchard—don't think I didn't notice."

"And you blame me now for not having given you a son? That is what is at the heart of all this, Andrew, I was eighteen when I married you three years ago. And you cannot deny that I have been your wife whenever you wished it. Have you thought that the fault may not be mine?"

"You Spanish bitch, you teasing slut!" he snarled, almost white with rage, as he slapped her viciously across the mouth.

Anna Moultrie stiffened, drew herself up with patrician dignity, touched the back of her hand to her bleeding lips, and glanced at it as if mildly curious.

"I have come to expect that of you," she said wearily. "But I would remind you that is not the pay you give a cook, Señor Moultrie. I shall go to my room, and if you wish supper, cook it for yourself or else have your *pistoleros* feed you." She went out of the room, slamming the door behind her. Andrew Moultrie stood staring after her, his fists clenched, his chest heaving. Then, after he had mastered himself, he strode out of the house and toward the cooking fires which Jorge Maduro and Jesús Moreno had lighted.

CHAPTER THIRTY-ONE

The Wednesday of the week following Lucien Edmond Bouchard's first call upon his new neighbor was a day of curiously variable weather. At dawn, the bold red ball of the sun seemed to indicate a typically blazing Texas day without respite from the unrelenting heat. Shortly before noon, however, the sky suddenly darkened, and there were bolts of heat lightning to the west and north, followed by an hour of raging wind that flattened the grass, first from one side and then another. Then, by mid afternoon, the sun seemed to have disappeared entirely behind ominous clouds, and from time to time came the distant rumble of thunder.

After the cattle drive had been completed, Lucien Edmond Bouchard and Ramón Hernandez estimated that, not including the Hereford stock which had been held back for crossbreeding, there were roughly five or six hundred longhorns on the range. Many of these were mavericks which had meandered across the Rio Grande, wild cattle belonging to the first man who could brand them. "It will be the nucleus of a good herd, Ramón," Lucien Edmond had predicted. "The Brahmas should be here by the end of next month. We've agreed on the price, and I had Joe Duvray arrange to send the draft to the supplier when he stopped in San Antonio. We should be able to count on between four and seven hundred calves by early next year. And even though we may have a much smaller herd to take to Abilene, it'll be of prime quality. The market price is going to be a good deal higher then, too, so we'll do reasonably well. Besides, we're building for the future. We've made a wonderful start, and the money has been invested wisely."

"What worries me is the stubborn sheep rancher you've

331

got next to you, Lucien Edmond," Ramón commented. "From what you've told me about the way he recieved you, he sounds like a man who can cause trouble. He wants his own way and he seems to resent anyone who keeps him from having it."

Lucien Edmond shrugged philosophically. "I'm willing to give a little if he will, Ramón. I offered to go halves on the cost of fencing the western boundary. It would be a tedious job, and besides, even with good, strong, wooden fences, cattle could break through if they stampeded in force. One of these days, though, as this state develops, you're going to see less and less of the limitless range we first settlers have enjoyed."

Late that afternoon, Lucien Edmond and Ramón rode out along the western stretch of Windhaven Range, accompanied by the vaqueros Pablo Toldanos and Sanchez Maderos. The wind and the thunder had frightened some of the grazing cattle, and Lucien Edmond reined in his gelding and pointed, with a worried exclamation. "Sanchez, Pablo, I can see about a dozen head at the end of our boundary. They'll be crossing over into our neighbor's land. See if you can drive them back."

"Sí, señor," Sanchez nodded. Then, gesturing to Pablo, he galloped toward the distant longhorns.

Ramón turned to his brother-in-law. "Let's hope they turn them back before they start grazing on Señor Moultrie's land. I have a bad feeling about that one, Lucien Edmond."

"I'm beginning to share your feeling, Ramón. And there's unhappiness in that house, too. That beautiful Spanish wife of his didn't seem to be enchanted with her new home or with her husband, either. In fact, when I walked in there, I had the feeling that I was interrupting a family quarrel."

"If she's one of those high-flown daughters of an old Spanish family, Señor Moultrie will either have to tame her or give her up," Ramón commented, shaking his head at the prospect. Then he brightened as he thought of his own, formerly tempestuous and headstrong, young wife. "I should be willing to bet that she misses the luxury of her own hacienda. It must be a very lonely life for her here."

"I've no interest in the squabbles Mr. Moultrie and his wife may have, Ramón, only in what he's like as a neighbor," Lucien Edmond declared. "The men who held my horse and Andy's and Joe's weren't vaqueros, they were armed guards—what you call *pistoleros*. I asked myself why a rancher would need those, unless he's anticipating an attack—which certainly would never come from my men and me—or intends to be my enemy. And why should he want to be that, when he doesn't even know me? If he's handled sheep before, and it's obvious that he has, he certainly knows that the grazing habits of sheep and cattle are vastly different."

"I don't know, Lucien Edmond. But, as you say, it is strange that he'd hire *pistoleros*—look there, Sanchez and Pablo are turning our cattle back—*diablo*, they're being shot at!"

The sound of pistol shots reached their ears. Jesús Moreno and Jorge Maduro, having seen Lucien Edmond Bouchard's two vaqueros ride across the boundary line, shouting and waving their sombreros to head the straying animals back toward Windhaven Range, had drawn old Belgian pistols and fired at both riders. Sanchez Maderos clapped a hand to his shoulder, a startled look on his face as he stared at the grinning Moreno.

"That's just a warning, amigo!" the scar-faced *pistolero* shouted. "I'll kill you if you come on this land again!"

"*Cabrón, estúpido*, are you mad?" Maderos shouted back, staring at his blood-smeared hand. The bullet had only creased his shoulder, but he was thunderstruck at the *pistolero*'s vicious act. "Didn't you see we were only getting our cattle back so they wouldn't graze on your land? We didn't shoot at any of you when your accursed sheep came over on ours!"

"You've had your warning, now get back where you belong!" Maduro snarled, raising his pistol and leveling it at Sanchez's head.

With an indignant cry, the wounded vaquero spurred his horse back toward Lucien Edmond and Ramón Hernandez, who waited, their faces tense with anxiety and anger over what they had just seen.

"He's a madman, Señor Bouchard," Sanchez panted.

"He shot me—and Pablo and I had just got those stupid cattle to come back home, too! Why did he do it?"

"That, Sanchez, is what I intend to find out. Are you wounded badly?"

"No, it's only a scratch. But never in the world did I think a *compañero* would shoot at me for what I did," Maderos declared, looking back with a furious scowl at the two mocking *pistoleros,* who waved their arms in taunting derision and then sauntered back to the house.

"Look at them," Pablo Toldanos panted, "going back to boast about shooting at unarmed men."

"The next time, Pablo," Lucien Edmond said quietly, his lips tight and thin with anger, "when you ride out on the range, you'll carry your weapons, both of you. That's an order. I'm the last man in the world to want a bloody quarrel with a neighbor, but I'm not going to stand by and see my workers shot at. Now get back to the house, Sanchez, and have your wound looked after. I don't like the looks of all that blood you're losing."

"*Si* Señor Bouchard. *Madre de Dios,* if I'd had my gun with me, I'd have made that scar-faced idiot laugh on the other side of his mouth! I'm sorry, *Señor Patrón.*"

"There's no need to apologize." Lucien Edmond patted his Spencer at the side of his saddle. "Ramón and I should have followed you there, and maybe we could have stopped those fools from firing at you."

"I wonder that you didn't shoot him down, Lucien Edmond," Ramón muttered, turning back to send a last angry look at the receding figures of the *pistoleros* who were now at the door of the house.

"That was my first impulse, Ramón. But if I'd killed one or both of them, then there really would have been war between Mr. Moultrie and myself. There would have been no chance for explanations, or to find out if we can appease his apparent grievance against us. Tomorrow morning, after breakfast, I'll call on him myself, and alone. Let's go back, Ramón."

The sky was cloudless, showing no sign of the previous day's capricious weather, and the heat made Lucien Edmond's shirt cling to his wiry body as he rode toward the Moultrie ranch. He had insisted on going alone, though

Andy and Joe, as well as Simata, had urged him earnestly to let them come along as protection against the swaggering *pistoleros*. But Lucien Edmond had shaken his head and, patting his rifle, remarked wryly, "This is more effective than their pistols, but I pray I won't have to use it and that they'll see that I'm coming alone and in peace."

Nevertheless, the Indian scout and the two young Southerners saddled their horses about five minutes after he had ridden out, and followed him at a distance, armed and ready to give aid if the need arose.

Lucien Edmond tugged his sombrero down to shield his eyes from the scorching sun. He paused a moment at the last boundary marker which separated his range from that of Andrew Moultrie's and then, with a silent prayer, urged his gelding forward.

Far to the west, he could see the sheep and the five Mexican shepherds moving among them, one of them stooping to lift a baby lamb which had fallen and was in danger of being trampled As he neared the log cabin, Jorge Maduro emerged, his hand already edging toward his holster, and, at a signal from his other hand, the other five *pistoleros* advanced, warily eyeing Lucien Edmond.

"*Momento, por favor, gringo.*" The *pistolero*'s tone was contemptuous. "Our *patrón* does not wish visitors. I have no orders to let you pass."

"But I have business with your *patrón*," Lucien Edmond retorted, "and I think you know why. You shot at my riders yesterday when all they were trying to do was turn back some of our cattle so they wouldn't eat your *patrón*'s grass. If you had done the same with your sheep, there wouldn't have been any need for this visit of mine. I can assure you that my men would not have shot at your riders or shepherds."

"All this talk on a hot day, gringo, makes me very tired, *¿comprende?* Now I think it would be very wise to turn your horse around and go back to your ranch. And so do my men."

"I want no trouble with you, hombre." Lucien Edmond curbed his rising annoyance. "But to show you that I have no harmful intentions toward your *patrón*, I will get off my horse and ask one of you to be good enough to tell him that I wish to talk with him."

Jorge Maduro shook his head, with a nasty grin that bared his decaying teeth. "I told you before, gringo, that it is too hot to stand here under the sun and argue. I have my orders. And if you do not go back, you will be trespassing on our *patrón*'s land and we shall have to shoot you, I'm afraid."

Lucien Edmond heard the sinister clicking as the other *pistoleros* drew out their guns and cocked them. Undaunted, he held the reins of his gelding loosely and declared, "You see that I have a rifle, and I have not reached for it. I will not reach for it. If you shoot me, you'll be killing me in cold blood and I do not think your *patrón* has told you to do that."

With this, suddenly leaning forward and tightening his grip on the reins, he raced his gelding forward, wheeling it, first to one side, then to the other, to avoid being an easy target. Jorge Maduro swore aloud, "The devil take that damned gringo! Shoot him down, amigos!"

Jesús Moreno leveled his six-shooter and fired, but the bullet sped harmlessly to the right of Lucien Edmond Bouchard, who had wheeled his horse again and was rapidly approaching the house. At that moment, Anna Moultrie came out onto the veranda, dressed in a black sombrero, trousers, and boots, and carrying a rifle. "Stop it, you *cobardes!* Let him come here, I order it!"

Maduro held up his hand. "Do what the señora says, amigos. There will be another time for this gringo when he will not be so lucky."

"I do not think that the *patrón* would like to know that his *mujer* lets a gringo go with her into the house when he is away on business," Pedro Bustamente, a tall, rangy *pistolero* in his late twenties, suggested slyly, with a snigger.

"Of course he would not, Pedro," Maduro chuckled, "but you will not tell him. I am top hand here, do not forget it, amigo. Our orders are to obey the señora when the *patrón* is away; it is all very simple. To be sure, if the *patrón* should come to me and ask if his *mujer* has behaved as a proper wife should, that is another matter. And perhaps to our advantage, eh, amigo?"

His cronies burst into knowing laughter and slowly went back to their guard posts, watching as the beautiful young woman gestured to Lucien Edmond to enter the house.

"I am glad I saw you through the window, Señor Bouchard." Anna Moultrie's English diction had the soft, graceful nuance of a Castilian accent. "Those peons are animals, always looking for a fight. *Mi esposo* hired them in Del Rio, and I assure you they were not of my choosing."

"Thank you for preventing any violence, Señora Moultrie," Lucien Edmond graciously replied, inclining his head. Seeing this, Anna's large, dark-brown eyes grew warm with pleasure, and a faint smile curved her mouth. "I was hoping to find your husband here. Actually, that *pistolero* who appears to be the leader, or else his companion with the scar, shot at one of my riders yesterday. Thank God the wound was slight, but it was uncalled for. My men were simply trying to drive back stray cattle which had wandered onto your husband's land."

"I understand, Señor Bouchard. Do sit down." He seated himself on the settee while Anna crossed to a chair near a small writing desk and sat, turning to him and leaning forward with attentive interest. "Yes, I heard the shots, and I'm very sorry for what happened. But my husband left for San Antonio late last night." She rose abruptly, and paced back and forth, not bothering to remove her sombrero. Suddenly she stopped and faced him. "I am from Taos, Señor Bouchard. My great-grandfather was one of the first settlers of noble lineage there."

"I understand," Lucien Edmond said noncommittally, watching the vibrant young woman who confronted him. "But you, see, Señora Moultrie, I have no quarrel at all with your husband. It's true that he's raising sheep and I'm raising cattle, but I suggested to him that we put up a fence between us so there won't be any cause for future misunderstanding. And yet he's taken offense at this and apparently told his *pistoleros* to shoot at my riders if they cross over onto his land. That's what I want to avoid at all costs. We're neighbors, and I'd much prefer that we be friends, as well."

"And I should like that too, Señor Bouchard," Anna said quickly, sending him another swift, warm look and a dazzling smile. Then, as if her face were a kaleidoscope

337

which constantly changed, her features took on an aloof and impersonal cast as she declared, "You see, Señor Bouchard, my father and my brother hated Andrew, said he was only a fortune hunter." Her smile was scornful now and she uttered a little laugh. "They were wrong, of course. He had inherited money enough, but what he did was to come upon me at a most difficult time. My father had betrothed me to a man I detested, a weakling, a fool. And Andrew saved me from him—so I thought. I was romantic, he was strong and new, and different from all the men of Taos."

"I have no wish to pry into your life, Señora Moultrie," Lucien Edmond interposed gently.

Anna Moultrie turned her back to him, struggling for composure. When again she turned to face him, her face was bland, as if she stood aside to comment on herself as a third person. "You are not prying, Señor Bouchard. I thought he loved me very dearly, as I did him. But he has two obsessions—and one is to prove to my father and my brother, and all those other noble families who are forced to graze stupid sheep and pretend it is a great thing, that he is better than any of them. And the other obsession— he is the last of his line, Señor Bouchard, and he desperately wishes for a son. A son I haven't given him."

Lucien Edmond fidgeted on the settee, his face coloring at this unexpectedly candid revelation. He was about to speak, when Anna Moultrie went on. "We lived not far from my father's ranch, you see, Señor Bouchard. And when a year had passed and he saw that I had not given him a child, he became angry with me. Angry and jealous. And then the next year was worse—a vaquero was helping me to mount my horse because it had become frightened over a noise, and Andrew saw me slip from the saddle and thought he saw me kissing the vaquero." She turned away now, her eyes tragic, her voice suddenly distant, "Poor Jaime. He was so young, only a few years older than I. I'm sure he loved me, but he meant no harm. I'd fallen into his arms, and he forgot himself and kissed me—" Then again she turned to face Lucien Edmond, her eyes blazing. "Andrew took a whip to Jaime until he was practically dead, using the butt of the whip against the poor young man's head when his rage became ungovernable.

338

All my love for him vanished after that, but I could not leave him. He had married me in the Catholic Church, and so you see—"

Lucien Edmond rose from the settee, embarrassed at being made an unwitting party to such a secret. "Please, Señora Moultrie—"

"But I want to help you understand what drives my husband so, Señor Bouchard. Because I have not given him what he wants, now all his thought is for this land and those accursed sheep. *Dios,* sometimes I think I hear their bleating in my sleep!"

He waited for her to regain her composure, and yet he could not help but be troubled by her provocative, bold beauty, accentuated by her mannish attire. At last, diplomatically, he put in, "Señora, perhaps you can do me a great service by clearing up a mystery which has puzzled my riders and me."

She was breathing quickly, now, her bosom swelling against the thin blouse. Mastering herself, she nodded. "I will tell you what I can, señor, but my husband does not tell me everything about his affairs, you must understand."

"Of course. Did he mention to you how he happened to buy this land in Texas and move you so far away from your home in Taos?" ....

Anna Moultrie nursed her chin and frowned, as she sought to recollect. "All I know is that he told me he had met a Spanish nobleman who held grants on some of the Texas land near the Rio Grande, and that he was going to San Antonio to buy a new ranch for us. That's truly all I know, señor."

"You see," Lucien Edmond pursued, "two of my riders thought they saw a man and a woman in that cabin near your house, while my vaqueros and I were away driving our cattle to Abilene. They were almost certain that those two persons were not you and your husband, Señora Moultrie."

"I know even less about that, Señor Bouchard. Wait— *momento*—I did hear him tell Ramón Guitterez that this baron—whose name I truly do not know—owned a royal deed to land on which others had settled wrongfully. But I myself saw no one here when I rode with my husband

339

from San Antonio—only the *pistoleros* and our shepherds."

"I see. Thank you for your help, Señora Moultrie." Lucien Edmond rose, hesitating a moment. "Can you tell me when your husband will be back? I really must have it out with him on this matter. My men would never shoot at his unless, of course, they were attacking us. By the same token, I cannot have my riders shot at when they are performing the work expected of them and bringing back stray cattle."

"I know how you must feel." She moved closer to him, touching his arm. "He will be back in a fortnight, Señor Bouchard. I—I myself will tell him what you have said."

"Yes," Lucien Edmond responded in a doubtful tone, "but I should much prefer to be my own spokesman in this matter, Señora Moultrie. He must be made to see that unless he controls his *pistoleros,* someone may be seriously hurt or even killed. And that must not happen. Can you—is it too much to ask that you have one of your men ride to my ranch to tell me when you husband has returned, so that I may talk with him?"

"Yes, I think I can do that for you, Señor Bouchard." Anna had not moved away, and now looked up into his face, her lips parted and moist, her eyes warm and inviting. "You know, señor, you are only the second Yankee I have known. There's strength in you like that I thought I saw in my Andrew. Only with him, there's cruelty, also. I do not feel that you are cruel." Her hand moved slowly up his arm, and Lucien Edmond crimsoned with embarrassment at this sign of intimacy, stepped back, and stammered, "I—I apologize for having disturbed you, Señora Moultrie. With your leave, I'll ride back now."

"But there's no need to go so soon, really. I—I am very lonely here. You know that I cannot lower myself by talking to the *pistoleros—Dios,* they are nothing more than peons, and some of them were once *bandidos,* I know. Please stay a while, señor—tell me how you are called?" She cocked her head, an engaging little smile curving the corners of her mouth, her eyes dancing and inviting in their intent warmth.

"My name is Lucien Edmond Bouchard, Señora Moultrie. I am married and I have three children," he said gravely.

He was not prepared for her response. Without warning, uttering a choking little sob, she had pressed her face against his chest, her arms circling him, as she gasped, "You have children, you are *muy hombre!* Oh, Lucien Edmond, I know I am not barren—Andrew accuses me of that. He would destroy me! It is he whose seed cannot create life; I am certain of it. Will you not—could you not—prove that I am like any other young woman who can conceive? He will never know—it will save our marriage—don't you find me *agradable*, Lucien Edmond?"

He could feel the thrust of her breasts against his chest, the tension of her fingertips feverishly pressing into his back, the pressure of her thighs against his own. For a giddy instant desire swirled in him, nearly overwhelming him. His hands had gripped her shoulders, and then with an effort he reached behind him to unlock the grip of her arms and to say hoarsely, "Yes, Señora Moultrie, you are very desirable, very beautiful. But I, too, am a Catholic, and I would not break my marriage vows or betray an unknowing husband. Please forgive me if I hurt you by saying this—I must say it. I sympathize with you deeply in your unhappiness—that is all I can do, Señora Moultrie."

She stood, disconsolate, lost, and covering her face with her hands, burst into hysterical sobs as Lucien Edmond, trembling with nervous reaction, bowed to her, turned on his heel, and left the house. As he closed the door, he could hear the muffled sounds of Anna Moultrie's poignant weeping.

CHAPTER THIRTY-TWO

It was on Monday in the last week of August that Joe Duvray reined in the two sturdy horses which had drawn his supply wagon from San Antonio. He stopped in front of the gate and leaped down with an exultant shout to be welcomed by his best friend, Andy Haskins. Three days earlier, Djamba, Celia, Felicidad, and Lucas, and the three black workers who had served as their armed escort, had returned from their visit to Sangrodo's stronghold. The visit had greatly helped Celia regain her spirits as well as her health, for she had brought back the joyous news that Prissy was again with child by her Comanche husband, Jicinte. Her other news, which had delighted Lucien Edmond, was that Sangrodo's beautiful and courageous wife, Catayuna, would bear a child by October and, if the child were a son as she devoutly prayed, she intended to name it Desyagata, which in Comanche meant "he who is loved."

"It took you long enough, you old sidewinder." Andy joyously and energetically shook hands with his Southern comrade-at-arms. They had been inseparable during the war in which Andy had lost his right arm. They were bound together not only by their friendship and their rustic backgrounds in the days of peace which had preceded the Civil War, but also by their loyalty to Lucien Edmond's father, who had hired them in New Orleans and given a new purpose and meaning to their uprooted lives.

"I figured to be here sooner, Andy." Joe grinned back at his friend. "Only you forget I had some things to do for Mr. Bouchard. So don't hold me up, I've got news he'll be mighty interested in. Hey, that reminds me, any more trouble with that sheep outfit west of us?"

"Haven't heard anything, Joe. Some of the vaqueros

have been riding the boundary line out there, so's our cattle won't mosey over onto that fellow's grass.

"That's good." Joe uttered a sigh of relief. "I've been worrying about it all the way to Austin and San Antonio and back, and I still think we're going to have trouble. Anyway, time for chinnin' with you later; right now I gotta go see Mr. Bouchard."

Lucien Edmond Bouchard, who had been playing with Carla and Hugo and not forgetting little Edwina, had heard the two Southerners' joyous greeting, and came out of the house to open the gate of the stockade. "Joe, I'm glad you're back!" he exclaimed as they vigorously shook hands. "Come on into the living room and rest a spell. I'll have Kate rustle up something for you to eat, and something nice and cool to drink."

"Much obliged, Mr. Bouchard. Whew, it sure was hot on the trail, and I think I ate about a ton of dust." Joe dusted off his trousers and the top of his boots, then followed Lucien Edmond back into the living room.

Maxine welcomed him with a smile, and Carla and Hugo ran to hug him. Joe Duvray was a great favorite with the Bouchard children. He had made Carla and Hugo each a whistle, the use of which gift Maxine had to regulate. The children had discovered that Jubal always came running to the whistle, barking furiously, and the resulting clamor sometimes disturbed Maxine's siesta.

Lucien Edmond seated himself beside his beautiful wife, his arm around her. He waited attentively for the young Southerner to discuss the success of his mission.

"Well, now, Mr. Bouchard," Joe began, "first off, I took that note of yours to the man at the bank in San Antonio and he said for me to tell you that he'd sent off the draft for those Brahmas."

"That's fine, Joe. And what happened at Austin?"

"You know, Mr. Bouchard," a serious look came over Joe Duvray's genial features, "it's a funny thing. I went right to the land office, just like you told me to, and when the fellows there weren't too busy, I asked one of them if he could help me look up the titles on some land that was near the stretch I'm working on."

"What did you find out, Joe?"

"Fellow I talked to was one of the top clerks there,

name of Tobias Jennings. Right friendly fellow, too. I guess maybe he was feeling good because he'd just got himself married—that's what he told me, anyhow." Joe chuckled. Lucien Edmond nodded, waiting for him to go on, and shushed Carla and Hugo, who had begun to interrupt by asking if their friend Joe had brought them back any presents.

"I sure did, you two rapscallions." Joe turned to grin at them. "There's some hard candy in the wagon and a doll for you, Carla honey. Now you'll just have to wait until I finish telling your daddy what he wants to hear, and then I'll go and unload the wagon, see?" Then, turning back to his employer, he went on. "I gave him your name, Mr. Bouchard, and I told him you had the stretch near the Nueces right by Carrizo Springs. I said that somebody's moved in right next door to us, and was raising sheep, which worried us a little, because sheep and cattle just don't get along."

"Did he tell you who'd owned that spread before Moultrie bought it?" Lucien Edmond demanded.

"He sure did, Mr. Bouchard. And that's what I was leading up to; what a funny thing it was. You see, I got into that office a little after lunchtime, and this fellow Jennings told me that just that morning, he'd had another visit from two brothers by the name of Hans and Heinrich Engelhardt. They were mighty upset, Mr. Bouchard, and it wasn't the first time they'd been there, either. They claim their pappy bought that land fair and square, and intended for them to come out and help him work it after they finished up in Sacramento. Only when they got to the land, they couldn't find either their pappy or their mammy, and those ornery *pistoleros* that fellow Moultrie's got working for him told them they didn't know anything about it and to get off the land if they knew what was good for them."

"Then the Engelhardts must have been the two people you and Andy saw while I was on the drive, Joe," Lucien Edmond said slowly.

"That's the way I've got it figured, Mr. Bouchard. But there's something else, and that's why I think there's something plumb loco going on, if you ask me. You see, when I asked this fellow Jennings how Moultrie came to buy

344

that land away from Mr. Engelhardt, he said that some
fellow who worked for a Spanish nobleman brought in
a quitclaim signed by Engelhardt which showed that he'd
sold the land to this fellow. Let's see, it was a funny
name, so I wrote it down on this scrap of paper." Duvray
fumbled in the pocket of his shirt, took out a scrap of
paper, squinted at it, and then got up and went over to
hand it to his boss.

"Baron Rodrigo de Austencio," Lucien Edmond read
aloud.

"Yes, sir, Mr. Bouchard, that's the one. Now here's the
real crazy thing about it. After I'd got all this information
you wanted, I rode back to San Antonio to get the supplies and to buy me a couple of horses and a wagon to
fetch them back in. Well, damned—'scuse me, Mrs. Bouchard ma'am—doggone if I didn't see some wanted posters
in the marshal's office. And one of them, plain as day, had
that name I just gave you, Mr. Bouchard. When I saw it,
I asked the marshal if I could have the posters to bring
back to you, and he had some extras so he gave them to
me. Here they are."

Lucien Edmond took the folded posters from Joe,
opened them, and then frowned, deep in thought. "It
seems there's a $500 reward on this baron and on a Quen-
tin Durwood, who apparently set up offices in San Antonio
and swindled quite a few honest people out of hard cash
by selling them land that wasn't theirs to sell. I'm beginning to put two and two together now, Joe."

"Do you think all this involves that new neighbor of
ours, dear?" Maxine asked her husband.

"I'm afraid it does. You see, Maxine, when I visited Mrs.
Moultrie about two weeks ago, she told me that her
husband had acquired that land from a man who called
himself a baron. And Mr. Moultrie ought to be back from
San Antonio any day now. When he gets here, Joe, you
and I are going to pay him a visit and find out what's at
the bottom of this entire affair."

An hour before twilight of the same day a lone rider,
whipping his mare to a thundering gallop, approached
Windhaven Range from the west. Simata and Andy Haskins, who had been riding the range that afternoon, headed

their horses back from the north to intercept him. As he neared them, they saw a wiry, gray-haired man, his gaunt, sun-bronzed face creased with anxiety and his eyes suspiciously wet with tears.

"Take me to your *patrón*, amigos!" he panted. Simata and Andy Haskins, exchanging a mystified look, rode back with him toward the stockade. Chet and Ned hurried to open the gate and admit the three riders. "I come from Señora Anna," the exhausted rider gasped as he dismounted. "I am Ramón Guitterez. I must see Señor Bouchard!"

"I'll take you to him, Mr. Guitterez," Haskins volunteered. "Chet, Ned, take care of his mare, she's winded bad." Indeed, the mare was snorting, foam drooling from her mouth, and her flanks were glossy with lather.

"I know, señores, *el Señor Dios* forgive me for my cruelty to that *pobrecita*, but it is of the greatest importance that I talk to your *patrón*." Ramón Guitterez distractedly glanced back in the direction from which he had come. "*Por favor*, every minute that I stand talking to you, he—I must see Señor Bouchard now!"

Lucien Edmond had heard the sound of voices and, opening the door of the ranch house, came out onto the veranda, followed by Sybella. "I am Lucien Edmond Bouchard, señor. How can I be of help to you?"

Guitterez hurried forward, twisting his gnarled fingers in his anxiety. "Thank God I've found you, Señor Bouchard! Señora Anna wished to send me to tell you that the *patrón*—her *esposo*—returned two days ago. But he—that one is a devil out of hell, Señor Bouchard, and when he heard her telling me to come here, he said he would have me beaten—I, Ramón Guitterez, who for so many years was like a godfather to that *niña linda*." He stopped his face working with his overpowering emotions.

"But you've come now, Ramón—why?" Lucien Edmond gently prompted.

"Because, Señor Bouchard, when I heard her cries and saw him beating her with his whip—*si*, as he did to poor Jaime—I could not stand there and let it be done. I could not think of myself, only of her, Señor Bouchard."

"My God! I've got to help her. Andy, go get Joe Duvray. I want Mr. Moultrie to hear what Joe found out in San

346

Antonio. Hurry, and tell him to bring his rifle—I'll take mine."

"May God bless you, Señor Bouchard." Ramón Guitterez's voice cracked and he bowed his head, unable to speak.

"The *pistoleros* did not try to stop you when you rode here?" Lucien Edmond demanded.

"No, Señor Bouchard. And I do not think they will shoot at you if I bring you and your vaquero back—they, too, heard how my poor *niña* screamed under that madman's whip," Guitterez replied.

Sybella, who had been listening in silence, now interrupted. "Lucien Edmond," she interposed, "that poor soul will need a woman to look after her. You'd best take Felicidad with you. She'll be able to speak to her in her own language, too, and that might soothe her."

"Grandmother, that's a splendid idea. Andy, saddle a horse for Felicidad, and I'll go ask her to ride along with us. Come to think of it, when Moultrie's *pistoleros* see a woman with us, it may prevent bloodshed." Hastily, Lucien Edmond strode back to the kitchen, quickly informed Felicidad what had occurred and, with a solicitous gasp, she nodded and followed him back to the veranda.

Joe Duvray came hurrying from the bunkhouse, where he had been chatting with some of the vaqueros, loaded rifle in hand. Simata, anticipating what must be done next, had already gone to the corral and brought out the two horses for Lucien Edmond and Joe to ride. Andy Haskins followed, leading a horse for Felicidad. "Andy and I should go, too, Mr. Bouchard," the Indian scout volunteered.

"No, Simata, but thank you for the offer. With Felicidad along—and I am so grateful to grandmother for having suggested it—I feel certain that Moultrie's men will think twice before firing on us. Besides, I'll be in the lead, and if they should fire, I'll draw it so that no one else is exposed to needless risks." Lucien Edmond mounted his gelding. He took the reins in his left hand, holding his rifle in his right, and made certain that it was fully loaded. Ramón Guitterez was about to mount his mare, but Simata shook his head. "You have ridden her too hard. I'll bring you a fresh horse."

347

In a few moments he returned with a sturdy chestnut gelding, bridled and saddled, and the old Mexican thanked him effusively as he mounted the horse.

The three men and Felicidad rode at a gallop toward the west, oblivious to the magnificent panorama of the Texas sky at dusk. They approached Moultrie's land, rode hard past the log cabin, and as they neared the house, they could see the six *pistoleros* crowded together, muttering among themselves, near the side of the house. From a window, the light of a lantern cast an eerie glow against the soft, gathering darkness. There were the sounds of a man's angry voice, a voice straining with frenzy and almost breaking, accompanied by the hoarse, agonized sobs of a woman.

"He will kill her, the monster," Ramón Guitterez groaned as Lucien Edmond shoved open the door and strode inside, his rifle ready, with Joe and Felicidad behind him. The old Mexican turned away, his hands to his face, his shoulders heaving at the sight. Anna Moultrie lay sprawled on the rug before the settee, her blouse ripped to shreds, and her black sombrero, with its chin strap torn off, balanced at an angle against the wall, where it had been thrown. Naked to the waist, her hands covering her face, she lay on her side, the smooth, warm, olive skin of her back, shoulders, and sides savagely welted by the short-handled, rawhide whip which Andrew Moultrie still gripped in his right hand. He stood staring down at her, his face contorted and red in his violent rage. The large vein in his temple stood out, visibly throbbing.

"Put down that whip, Mr. Moultrie!" Lucien Edmond's voice shook with anger and disgust. "Do you want to kill your wife?"

For a moment it was as if the tall Scot had not heard him. Then he turned slowly, a crafty smile on his thin lips, deceptively calm. "I didn't hear you knock, Mr. Bouchard. Isn't it customary for a gentleman to do so before he breaks in on a family argument?" His voice was soft and sly, with a strong hint of the Scottish brogue.

"I don't think you would have heard me knock, considering what you were doing to that unfortunate woman," Lucien Edmond retorted.

"Oh, I see. It's Ramón who brought you here, isn't it?

That meddling old fool! For your information, Mr. Bouchard, so far as I understand, a man has the right to thrash his wife for indiscretions or disobedience as long as he doesn't kill her. And I assure you I had no intention of killing her. She's had this lesson coming for some time."

Felicidad, her hand to her mouth, her eyes wide with horror at the scene, now burst out, "¡Que monstruosidad! What sort of man are you to let your wife lie there in pain? Joe, out of pity, help me lift her to the settee!"

The young Southerner shot Andrew Moultrie a contemptuous look as he crossed over to the sprawled woman. He and Felicidad carefully lifted her onto the settee, easing her down. Felicidad uttered a sob as Anna Moultrie groaned and bit her lips in pain.

"Now, sir," Lucien Edmond began, "I won't argue with you over the moral or legal right of what you've done—though I feel like taking away that whip and using it on you—but my real reason for coming is that my hand, Joe Duvray, got back from San Antonio a few days ago and he learned some very interesting things there about this ranch of yours."

Andrew Moultrie tightened his lips and glared at Lucien Edmond. "Might I inquire what he learned?" he drawled, moving slowly toward a small writing desk and standing with his back to it. His eyes were fixed on Lucien Edmond, then slid to Joe Duvray.

"You'd better tell him yourself, Joe," Lucien Edmond said to the Southerner.

"Sure, Mr. Bouchard. Well, Mr. Moultrie, it's like this. I was running some errands for Mr. Bouchard, and while I was there I did some checking at the Austin land office. The clerk who handled the transaction for you, Mr. Moultrie, says that Ludwig Engelhardt's sons had been in there, pestering him about what happened to their folks. They wouldn't take no for an answer, either. They didn't believe their father would sell his land—not when he'd bought cattle and hired vaqueros to drive the herd all the way from Corpus Christi."

"I don't see how this concerns me, gentlemen. I paid a factor in San Antonio for this property after he showed me, not only a royal land grant, but also the quitclaim which Mr. Engelhardt gave him. That's proof that the owner received the land from Mr. Engelhardt quite properly and legally, and in turn sold it to me."

"On the surface, that would appear to be correct, Mr. Moultrie. However, when Joe went back to San Antonio, he found wanted posters for a Baron Rodrigo de Austencio and his accomplice. They're charged with land swindling, using the dodge of forged royal grants. It would appear that you've been fleeced, Mr. Moultrie. That so-called baron is no more a nobleman than I am. This land actually belongs to Ludwig Engelhardt's two sons—if, as I expect, he and his wife met with foul play at the hands of the 'baron' and his accomplice."

"Then let the law prove that, Mr. Bouchard," Moultrie retorted, "because I, for one, am not going to take your word. And if that's all you came to tell me, sir, I ask that you and your hand leave my house at once, along with that girl. Oh, don't worry. I've finished teaching Anna her lesson, at least for the time being. I commend you for your gallantry, Mr. Bouchard, but it's greatly misplaced, I assure you. She's a barren, treacherous, and unfaithful bitch!"

"You—you lie, Andrew Moultrie," Anna stammered, trying to lift herself on one elbow, her face haggard and swollen with tears. Her lips were raw from where her teeth had scored them as she had tried to endure the savage lashes of the whip without crying out for mercy. "He's—He's been to San Antonio himself, and he—he knows all about—about the baron."

"Shut your mouth, or I'll shut it for you for good, you whore!" Moultrie shouted. At the same time, thrusting his right hand behind him to the drawer of the little writing desk and yanking it open, he drew out a six-shooter and, whirling to one side, pulled the trigger.

Felicidad, who had been crouching beside the settee whispering soothing words to Anna, had seen Moultrie's sudden gesture. She cried out "*¡Guardese—cuidado, señores!*" But her cry came too late. Joe Duvray uttered a cry of pain as the bullet found its mark in his upper right thigh. Taken by surprise, he dropped his rifle and, at the same instant, Andrew Moultrie turned to level the six-shooter at Lucien Edmond.

Lucien Edmond flattened himself on the floor and, lifting his rifle, pulled the trigger. Moultrie jerked back hard against the edge of the writing desk, his gun lifting toward the ceiling, his blue eyes huge with shock. Then, without a word, he slumped down, rolled over onto his side and lay still, the gun slipping from his nerveless fingers.

Lucien Edmond turned to Anna Moultrie. "I'm sorry, Mrs. Moultrie," he said. "I meant to injure him, not kill him." Then he called, "Mr. Guitterez, come in here and help me with her."

Ramón Guitterez hurried in and turned to stare at the lifeless body of Andrew Moultrie. Then, very gently, he knelt down beside the settee and murmured, *"Pobrecita,* it is over now. You are free of him forever."

"Is there any salve or ointment to rub on those welts?" Felicidad asked. Lucien Edmond blanched as he noticed again the cruel, purple marks which had been left by the whip.

"Si, I'll get some." Ramón Guitterez hesitated a moment. Then he turned and hastened out of the house, returning a few minutes later with the ointment. "This will help her, I am sure," he declared, holding out a jar of sour-smelling grayish ointment.

"I will do it, *por favor,"* Felicidad volunteered. "I am a woman—I will cause her less pain than you, señor."

"Gracias," Ramón assented, surreptitiously wiping his eyes with his sleeve as he watched the young Mexican girl rub the ointment on Anna Moultrie's wounds. "May the devil burn his soul in hell forever," he muttered. "My *linda niña* will have those scars for the rest of her life! I am glad that you killed him, Señor Bouchard. If you hadn't, I would have done it myself!" Then he turned to Felicidad. "It is kind of you to look after my Anna—the good God will bless you for it, as I do."

"De nada, señor. She is young and strong, and it will soon be as if nothing had happened. Already she feels a little better," Felicidad said softly, as she turned back to Anna.

Meanwhile, Lucien Edmond hurried over to Joe Duvray, and was trying to stanch the blood oozing from the bullet hole in his thigh. He had torn off part of his shirt and bound it above the wound, and was trying to tie another tourniquet below it. "You won't be able to ride for a while, Joe," he declared, shaking his head ruefully. "I should have fired when he drew that six-shooter out of the desk. But I didn't want to kill him, as God is my witness."

"Hell, Mr. Bouchard, if ever there was a mangy cur who needed killing, it was that one. Anyway, it's a clean wound, and the bullet came out without touching the bone. It'll be sore and stiff for a couple of weeks." Joe grinned wanly. "I think I can ride back to the ranch, though, and once I get there Andy can patch me up. Hell, Mr. Bouchard, if this was a war we'd be doing that for each other. What's going to happen to Mrs. Moultrie, though?"

Ramón Guitterez finally rose from his place by the settee and, taking off his poncho, gently laid it over Anna's naked back. "I will stay with her, Señor Bouchard. There's something else I will tell you. Before I came to your *rancho,* I had been listening for a while, until I could bear no more when that one—" he contemptuously jerked his thumb toward Andrew Moultrie's corpse—"was beating her. He knew that he had been swindled by that man. He found out in San Antonio, when he went there to buy some things for the ranch. And he hated her because she did not give him a son—"

"I know, Ramón," Lucien Edmond murmured. "She had already told me that."

"And I'm sure the fault was his. He was jealous, and hated by her family in Taos. He wanted to bring her here and treat her as if she were a slave. *Pobrecita!*" Ramón sighed and shook his head. "We'd best bury him quickly. Then I will take her back to Taos. She still loves her father and brother, and when they hear what that one did to her they will be happy to take her back, I know."

"What about the *pistoleros?*"

Ramón Guitterez shrugged. "Once they know their *patrón* is dead, they will run away like the dogs they are. Even *cobardes* like them have some manhood left. I think that if it had gone on much longer, they themselves would have stopped him from beating her."

"You'll stay with her tonight, then, and look after her?" Lucien Edmond asked. The old man nodded.

Joe Duvray had leaned back against the settee, wincing with pain as he tried to test his leg. Lucien Edmond and

Ramón Guitterez lifted Andrew Moultrie's body and carried it outside. Jorge Maduro, his eyes wide with concern, was waiting for them. Acting as spokesman for the other *pistoleros*, he asked "Ramón, *¿que pasa?*"

Ramón turned to him. "Señor Moultrie nearly killed the señora. When we made him stop beating her and Señor Bouchard told him that he had found out that this land actually belonged to someone else, the *patrón* took his gun and shot the vaquero who came with us. Señor Bouchard had to kill him to save his own life. I will take the señora back to Taos with me, so there is no more work here for you and your men."

Maduro swore under his breath. Then he shrugged, and went back to tell his fellows what he had just learned.

"It would be well to bury him near the creek," Ramón Guitterez panted as the two men paused for a minute. "Over there, by the oak tree. It's as good a place as any." Lucien Edmond nodded. "I will bring a spade, Señor Bouchard."

Ramón sighed, then walked slowly toward a little storage shed, and returned with a spade which he handed to Lucien Edmond. The latter began to dig, and soon his shirt was plastered to his body with sweat. The night air was uncomfortably humid and still. From the nearby creek, there could be heard the croaking of frogs and the twittering of night birds. The moon was half-hidden behind a thick cloud, and the branches of the oak trees filtered its light, making weird patterns on the ground. Ramón Guitterez glanced down at the face of the dead man, who lay nearby, and then hastily crossed himself, mumbling a prayer.

"I've hit something here." Lucien Edmond scooped out a spadeful of moist earth. Then he recoiled. "There are bodies here. My God, now I know what happened to the Engelhardts!"

"May the holy saints watch over us!" Ramón Guitterez quavered, again crossing himself and forcing himself to peer down into the uncovered grave.

Gritting his teeth, Lucien Edmond carefully scooped away the earth to reveal the bodies of Ludwig and Minna Engelhardt. Then he straightened. "They were murdered. I can see the bullet holes."

353

"Did—*he* do it, Señor Bouchard?" the old Mexican gasped.

"No, I don't think so," Lucien Edmond said slowly. "Those posters about the baron and his accomplice suggest that those two men took Moultrie in. And, in his grief because his wife did not give him a child, and his realization that he had been tricked and did not own this land, he was driven to the breaking point. I think that if we can find those two men, we'll find these poor people's murderers. I'll cover them up again, and dig a new grave."

When he had finished his grisly work, Lucien Edmond went back to the house, Ramón Guitterez hurrying ahead to see his young mistress. Then Lucien Edmond and Felicidad urged Joe Duvray to put his arms around their shoulders and helped him to hobble back to his horse. Both men and the young Mexican girl rode back toward Windhaven Range, silent and brooding as the terrible events of this strange night drove all other thoughts from their minds.

CHAPTER THIRTY-THREE

All through the month of June, 1869, Quentin Durwood and the baron had thrived in their cunning endeavors to intimidate honest settlers into giving up their land. Two immigrant Dutch families who had purchased their spreads in Austin and who had begun to farm along stretches of cleared land about twenty miles west of the Cañon de Ugalde, had accepted Theobald Arnison's forged documents with only a plaintive jeremiad. Their tracts had amounted to about a thousand acres each, and the baron had ingeniously resold them for $2,500 each—five times what the original purchasers had paid for them. During the last week of June, however, Durwood had visited a stubborn Irish farmer named Patrick Gilligan, a widower in his forties with two sons, aged thirteen and seventeen. Gilligan had, in February of the same year, bought 2,000 acres about 40 miles north of the Dutch settlers' properties, and he and his sons had already started their crops—corn, barley, and rye—as well as breeding a small herd of about fifty cattle.

When Durwood had shown him the awesome parchment with its fraudulent seal, Gilligan laughed aloud. "Man, d'you take me for an idiot? You've the look of a spalpeen about you, Mr. Durwood, and so has this pretty piece of paper with its nice little ribbon. Be off with you now, before Dugal and Billy and I lay a stick about your shoulders, man!"

Durwood, having already noticed that the two sons were assiduously working in the fields, had taken out one of his derringers and shot Gilligan to death. Then, reloading, he had gone out to the fields and, after engaging the youths in a brief conversation, calmly shot them both down, buried them alongside their father, and ridden back to San Antonio. The land had been quickly resold, with the usual forged quitclaim registered at Austin, to a middle-aged couple from San Francisco who had originally been farmers in Ohio.

But by the time Durwood registered this last quitclaim, which purported to reflect Patrick Gilligan's wish to transfer his land to the Baron Rodrigo de Austencio, Hans and Heinrich Engelhardt had visited the Austin land office to demand that the officials there investigate the mysterious disappearance of their parents. Tobias Jennings, who had married Lily Mellers just two weeks after Durwood had given his permission, had finally begun to sense that all was not as it seemed.

"Now look here, Quentin," he had told the Easterner, "you've done me a real good turn by letting me marry Lily, and I won't ever forget that. Just the same, I don't like what's been going on at the office, with those two young Engelhardt boys talking about swindling and murder and such like. Now, mind you, these quitclaims you've been filing look to be perfectly proper. Just the same, I think you ought to tell the baron to hold off a spell, until this Engelhardt business can be straightened out."

When Durwood reported the result of his interview with Jennings, the baron had chuckled and declared, "It's always wise to be just one step ahead of the game, Quentin boy. We've been in San Antonio long enough, and I have a mind to change our base of operations, anyway. I've picked out Laredo. Conveniently, it's far enough away from here, with not too many families settled in the area, and we might just open our own land office in that border town."

"There's still plenty of property down along the Nueces River, baron," Quentin Durwood had reminded him.

"True enough, my boy, and there's one tract in particular I've got my eye on—you remember that 8,000-acre spread near the Engelhardts' property? The one that's owned by this Bouchard fellow? You yourself told me that when you rode over to talk to the Engelhardts, you saw how much Bouchard's built up his spread—all that cattle and plenty of water and grazing grass. Well, I might have a prospective buyer, come early fall. I've been corresponding with a fellow in Richmond, a die-hard Johnny Reb. He and his family were smart enough to transfer some of their cotton profits before the war into gold they put away in an English bank. They don't like what's going on with the Carpetbaggers and the Scalawags down South, and they'd like to do some farming in a nice warm climate that'll remind them of home. Well, Quentin, that Bouchard spread will be just perfect for them."

"So you mean to relocate to Laredo. Well, I've no objection. God knows it's close enough to Mexico so that if anything goes wrong, we can save our hides by saddling up and riding."

"Now, now, Quentin boy, that's not the right attitude for a partner of mine to take. Nothing's going to go wrong. You're forgetting there's still no organized law and order here in Texas, and the towns are so far apart that no one's going to come looking for us in Laredo. Besides, I've already arranged to transfer our funds from the Citizens Bank to the Laredo Commercial Bank. And not by courier, either." He drew out a bulging wallet. "Yankee greenbacks, enough to stake our temporary headquarters near the border and to give us the prospect of gracious living south of the border, just in case it comes to that, Quentin."

"Well, that's sensible enough," Durwood admitted grudgingly. "Do we go after more land once we're down in Laredo?"

"Of course, of course. But on a smaller scale. We'll bide our time, I'll change my title—that's easy enough for old Theobald to handle—and this time we won't bother going all the way to Austin to record the deeds. Don't you think Theobald can forge a quitclaim and show that it's been recorded as easily as he can whip up a royal land grant from the eighteenth century?"

"I suppose he can."

"Certainly he can. It's July now. Well, this client of mine in Richmond won't be ready to pack up and move out here until some time in September. So you go on with a few small deals in your usual persuasive manner, Quentin, and then toward the end of August you'll be ready to oust this fellow Bouchard. I think I can sell those 8,000 acres of his with all the improvements on them for about

$15,000, and when that's done, we'll slip over the border and enjoy some high living in the land of señoritas and tequila."

By the middle of July, the baron had opened an office just off the main street of Laredo with a sign that read *Land Ventures Corporation*, and had changed his name to the Conde Juan de Castlemar. Durwood had then embarked on a survey of properties around Kingsville and Alice, towns about sixty miles from Corpus Christi. Most of this land was unsettled, barren, sandy, and desolate, but the new "conde" had assured him that there were many Mexican aristocrats coming into Laredo to escape the stern rule of the Juaristas. They would be eager to buy American land and set themselves up as wealthy ranchers. Many of them had brought their peons with them and would thus try to resume the arrogant, tyrannical way of life they had enjoyed before Benito Juárez had come to power.

By early August Durwood, working with Theobald Arnison, had detailed a dozen tracts of land. The flowery words with which they were described in no way indicated the actual barrenness of the terrain. And the Conde Juan de Castlemar, exerting all of his eloquence and charm, had actually managed to palm off three of these tracts to wealthy Mexican refugees for a total profit of $9,500.

"There's not the slightest danger in transactions like this, Quentin," the land swindler had reassured his partner. "First of all, that land around Corpus Christi doesn't legally belong to anybody, as yet. I'm sure that if you went back to Austin and had your friend Jennings look up the records, you'd find that no one so far has put in a claim for anything we're offering. Once they get there and take over their property, is it our fault if the land is hardly good for anything? There's worse looking land where they come from, believe me. And you haven't been called upon to persuade any recalcitrant settlers this time, so your conscience can be perfectly clear."

To be sure, one of the gullible Mexican purchasers, José Salinas, had ridden back to Laredo a week after he had moved onto his land. He had been furious, but was pacified when the conde told him, "Patience, hombre. It is true that it will take a little time to farm some of those acres. But if you want to know the truth, I've just found out that there are reports of silver ore in that area. If you have your workers start digging, I wouldn't be surprised if one day you thanked me for the fortune I've made available to you by selling you this land."

By the last week of August, the erstwhile Norman Cantrell was ready to proceed with his biggest coup, the fraudulent acquisition of Windhaven Range. All that week, Theobald Arnison had been toiling diligently over a parchment, locked in his room and denied his daily ration of whiskey until his work was completed.

"Now then, Quentin here's how we're going to work it. There are plenty of vaqueros on that Bouchard spread, so you can't think of handling this the way you did the Engelhardt affair. What you'll do is convince this Bouchard fellow that the royal grant takes precedence over the Austin deed, but that since your client—myself, of course—is a reasonable man, I'll accept a modest settlement—say $10,000. And, of course, when Bouchard pays you that and you give him this document, you'll tell him that never again can there be any question about the ownership of that land.'"

"But I thought you intended to sell the Bouchard spread to that Richmond client of yours," his partner objected.

The grey-bearded land swindler shook his head, an indulgent smile on his thin lips. "Quentin boy, there are times when I find myself wondering if you have any imagination. You're too used to thinking on a small scale, that's your trouble. To answer your question, I'll just find something else for my Richmond client. We could always palm off another big piece of desert land around Alice, and tell that trusting Johnny Reb there's bound to be a rich silver ore deposit on his property."

"You think this fellow Bouchard will go for the royal grant, baron—I mean, count?"

"It's worth a try, anyhow, Quentin. I don't expect you, as I said before, to eliminate all those vaqueros. But he's French from the sound of his name, and I'm gambling he knows enough about how French kings granted land

359

to settlers in Louisiana to get the notion that our pretty little piece of paper from the Spanish Court might be the real thing."

"All right, I'll take it to him as soon as Theobald gets it ready."

"That's the way I like to hear my partner talk. Confidence, Quentin, is half the battle. Stand your ground. Point out, as part of the authenticity of Theobald's deed, how accurate the description is of the creek and the river that borders his spread. And the valley. You know by now how to talk so it'll impress a man, I'm sure."

"Of course I do." Quentin Durwood was annoyed by the tone of his older-associate. "But suppose Bouchard isn't impressed enough to pay out the money for the Spanish deed?"

Norman Cantrell sighed wearily, reached for the whiskey decanter, and poured himself a generous measure. He eyed the glass a moment, then took a fastidious sip, and smacked his lips. "I thought, Quentin, when we first met in that restaurant, that you were a clever rogue who knew when to bluff. Tell him that we'll institute a suit to recover his land. And, if he still won't give in, then you can pay a visit to Andrew Moultrie and offer him Bouchard's spread for the same amount. I happen to know how much he has on deposit in a San Francisco bank. By the way, speaking of San Francisco, some amusing news came in on the Laredo telegraph last month. Would you believe that there were street riots against Chinese laborers? They've been bringing coolies in, and the upstanding white citizens of San Francisco don't like it one little bit. Of course not, because coolies can work for a few pennies a week." His face hardened and his eyes narrowed. "The point, my dear boy, is that you're working for considerably more than a few pennies. Take care I don't have to replace you with cheaper labor."

The blood rushed to Durwood's face and he opened his mouth to speak, then checked himself. Finally, he shrugged. "At times, count, your needling gets under my skin. Just don't forget who it was that earned you that big stack of greenbacks you took out of the Citizens Bank and brought along. And by the way, I haven't seen any of those greenbacks yet. It's about time you gave me a substantial advance on my share of the enterprise."

"Very well. I'll give you $2,000 now, and when you come back with the news that you've either bluffed Bouchard or induced Moultrie to buy the Bouchard spread, I'll settle up in full, and that's a promise."

"Good!" Durwood strode to the whiskey decanter, poured himself half a glassful, and downed it almost in a single swig.

At this moment, there was a timid knock on the locked door of the room in which Theobald Arnison had been closeted, and the land swindler went swiftly to the door and unlocked it. "Here it is, I've finished it. It's one of the finest pieces of work I've ever done," the old man quavered. His eyes were fixed on the whiskey decanter. "Please, can I have just a small glass now? I'm dying of thirst."

"Theobald," the count chuckled, "you can finish off the decanter and get roaring drunk, as far as I'm concerned. Quentin, I suggest you leave tomorrow morning."

It was a journey of a little over three days on horseback from Laredo to Carrizo Springs. Quentin Durwood took nearly four. He had dressed with particular care in order to impress Lucien Edmond Bouchard as a representative of a descendant of old Spanish nobility. He wore a fuchsia-colored taffeta coat and white silk vest, plum-colored satin riding breeches, and new white, calfskin boots. To complete the outfit—which in truth could have been worn by a Spanish nobleman—he had added a short-brimmed white sombrero with a black velvet chin strap. Cantrell had remarked, just before Durwood's departure, that if this elegant raiment did not convince Bouchard that his young partner truly represented a grandee of Old Spain, then assuredly Andrew Moultrie's Spanish-blooded wife would approve of it. Perhaps she could sway her ambitious husband into coveting the Bouchard spread enough to buy it.

He had brought the two mother-of-pearl-handled derringers with him, but this time it was more for self-defense. Brash though he was, Durwood had no desire to risk his own skin when the odds were so enormously against him. He reined in his horse before the gate of the stockade at Windhaven Range, and dismounted quickly when he saw Andy Haskins and Joe Duvray emerge from their dugout, carrying Spencers. "I'm unarmed, gentlemen," he called out loudly. "I've come to see Mr. Bouchard."

The two young Southerners exchanged a speculative look, then advanced toward the dapper Easterner. "I'll take your horse, mister," Haskins volunteered. "My pal Joe will take you in to see Mr. Bouchard."

"Thank you, gentlemen. I've a matter of important business, and I've ridden in all the way from Laredo."

Andy took the horse's reins, and led it toward the corral, while Joe pushed open the unlocked gate. Jubal, lolling on his side near the veranda of the ranch house, sprang to his feet and began to bark noisily, ready to attack if the newcomer proved to be an enemy. "That'll do, Jubal boy." Joe made a downward gesture with his left hand. "This way, mister. Now you just stay here and I'll go find Mr. Bouchard for you. What's your name, anyhow?"

"Quentin Durwood. I'm an agent for the Conde Juan de Castlemar." The Easterner drew himself up to his full height. Then, almost unconsciously, he patted the long, deep, and specially tailored pocket of his frock coat in which the fraudulent royal grant was lodged.

"All right, Mr. Durwood, I'll go tell Mr. Bouchard right off," Joe agreed. He knocked at the front door, then opened it and closed it behind him quickly, making sure that the visitor did not follow him.

Lucien Edmond was in the living room with Maxine and the children. He looked up as he saw his employee come slowly forward, sombrero in hand. "What is it, Joe?"

"Didn't mean to disturb you, Mr. Bouchard. You've got a visitor. A real interesting visitor, too."

"How's that?"

Joe Duvray advanced a few steps toward Lucien Edmond, lowered his voice, and said in a confidential tone, "Remember those wanted posters I brought back from San Antonio? Well, Mr. Bouchard, guess who's just come to see you on important business—those were his very words. Mr. Quentin Durwood, no less."

Lucien Edmond rose to his feet, saying to Carla and

Hugo, "Why don't you both go to the kitchen and see if Kate has some cookies she can give you?"

"Only not too many for either one of you," Maxine added as she rose, lifting Edwina into her arms, and following the children to the kitchen. Lucien Edmond turned to Joe. "Let him come in, by all means. I've kept that poster and it's in the desk in my room, the first to the left down the hall, Joe. I'd appreciate it if you'd get it and keep it handy."

"I get your drift, Mr. Bouchard" Joe grinned broadly. Then, stepping to the door, he opened it. "Mr. Bouchard will see you now, Mr. Durwood."

Quentin Durwood walked confidently into the house and held out his right hand to Lucien Edmond Bouchard who, after an almost imperceptible hesitation, shook it. "It's a pleasure to meet you at last, Mr. Bouchard. I've heard a great deal about your ranch."

"I'm flattered, Mr. Durwood. I'm told you've important business to discuss with me. Are you by any chance wanting to sell me Brahmas?"

The Easterner looked mystified and Lucien Edmond hurried to explain, "That's a species of cattle originally imported from India, Mr. Durwood. There's such an uproar about Spanish fever that a good many people up north don't want to buy Texas cattle. Brahmas, you see, are not affected by the tick which sickens the longhorn down here."

"Oh—oh, yes, I see." Durwood had been taken aback, but now recovered himself. "The fact is, Mr. Bouchard, I may have some rather unpleasant news for you. I understand that you acquired your property at the Austin land office."

"One slight correction, Mr. Durwood. My father bought it, and then transferred it to me when he left Texas to return to his birthplace in Alabama."

"I see. Well, at any rate, you assume that you have clear title to this land."

"Naturally. The transfer from my father was duly recorded in Austin, as is customary."

Quentin Durwood shook his head, a doleful expression on his face. Slowly he reached for the parchment, drew it out with an impressive flourish, and then eyed Lucien

Edmond. "As you may or may not know, Mr. Bouchard, a good deal of the borderland in the southeastern part of this country was originally held by the Spanish. The monarchs of Spain often awarded grants of land to those who had done them a service, such as opening up new trading posts or extending the Spanish dominion, sometimes by military control."

"I am reasonably familiar with Spanish history, Mr. Durwood. Would you get to the point, sir?"

"Of course, of course." Durwood untied the ribbon, opened the parchment, and held it up for Lucien Edmond to see. "His Majesty Philip V bestowed a certain tract of land in the year 1731 to the noble family of the Conde de Castlemar. I represent, Mr. Bouchard, the last surviving descendant of that patrician family, his excellency Juan de Castlemar, Count of Aragon and of Navarre. If you will be so good as to read it, you will observe that it describes almost exactly many of the physical landmarks of this property, which you believe to be yours."

"Now that's most interesting, Mr. Durwood. May I see it, if you please?"

"By all means, Mr. Bouchard."

Joe Duvray had returned and entered the living room, standing just inside the door. Lucien Edmond studied the unrolled parchment for a moment, and then turned to the young Southerner. "I think, Joe, you may have a document which Mr. Durwood will find even more absorbing than this one. Would you let me have it, please?"

"Sure, Mr. Bouchard." Joe grinned as he ambled toward his employer and handed him, neatly folded, the poster which he had procured in the marshal's office in San Antonio.

Lucien Edmond carefully rerolled the parchment, tucked it under his left arm, and then handed Durwood the folded poster. "I'd be obliged if you'd look at that, Mr. Durwood."

"If you wish. I don't really know what you're driving at, Mr. Bouchard, but—oh well—" he unfolded it, then uttered a startled gasp, and the poster dropped from his limp hands.

"I think, Mr. Durwood," Lucien Edmond suggested,

"you'll find that piece of paper somewhat more authentic than the one you've just handed me."

"This is a dreadful mistake—I assure you I have credentials—" Durwood blustered.

Lucien Edmond's face was grave. "I wonder what credentials you or your partner, who, under the name of the Baron Rodrigo de Austencio—I suspect he is the same gentlemen you now call the Conde de Castlemar—showed the unfortunate Mr. and Mrs. Ludwig Engelhardt."

"What do you mean—I don't know who they are—"

"Look out, Mr. Bouchard, he's reaching for his back pocket—" Joe called out, but Lucien Edmond had already seen Durwood's stealthy maneuver and stepped forward suddenly, gripping the Easterner's wrists and forcing them behind his back and upward until the land swindler uttered a cry of pain and crouched forward to relieve the agonizing tension. Duvray moved behind him and swiftly retrieved the two derringers, holding them up. "Here's what he was reaching for, Mr. Bouchard."

Lucien Edmond released a shaken and pale Quentin Durwood. "You see, Mr. Durwood, we happen to know a little more than you think. Andrew Moultrie, my neighbor to the west, who, by the way, is now deceased, bought his land from your partner, who was then known as the baron. Moultrie shot at Joe here, when he and I called to ask your client if he would be good enough to put up some sort of fencing, so that my cattle and his sheep wouldn't stray and ruin the grazing land. He drew a gun on me and I had to kill him in self-defense. But you see, Mr. Durwood, when I buried him, I uncovered the bodies of the Engelhardts. They had bullet holes in them. So it appears that you and your partner will be wanted on charges of murder, also."

At these words, Quentin Durwood turned and bolted from the living room, flinging open the front door and running as hard as he could toward the open gate. Joe Duvray emitted a piercing whistle. As Durwood ran like one possessed past the stockade, a lariat thrown with unerring aim by Andy Haskins halted him in mid-flight, pinning his arms to his sides and bringing him up short.

"That was as good as an admission, Mr. Durwood."

Lucien Edmond Bouchard approached the panting, now visibly terrified Easterner. "You know, we could hang you out of hand and claim the reward." His lips quivered with the hint of a smile which he tried to suppress. Durwood took him at his word. He sank down on his knees and began to babble. "No, for God's sake, I want a fair trial! I had to do it, he—the baron—yes, he's the same one, his name's really Norman Cantrell! If you catch him, you'll catch the real murderer! For God's sake, give me a chance!"

"Where is your friend of many titles, Mr. Durwood?" Lucien Edmond demanded.

"In Laredo, Mr. Bouchard, that's the God's truth! I can take you to him. I'll cooperate; maybe they'll let me off with a prison sentence—I had to do it—he made me—" Durwood burst into hysterical sobs.

"All right, Durwood, we'll ride to Laredo this afternoon. Joe, you and Andy will go along with me, if you're willing."

"I wouldn't miss the fun for anything, Mr. Bouchard," Joe chuckled as he dragged on the lariat. "Come on, stand up, you sniveling excuse for a man. I'm going to put you in the storage shed for a spell, until we're ready to leave. You're going to be real hot in those fancy clothes, I'm thinking. But that's your problem. Come along now!"

Early in the morning of the fourth day after their departure, Lucien Edmond Bouchard rode down the dusty main street of Laredo, with Andy Haskins and Joe Duvray behind him, on either side of their prisoner. Quentin Durwood, haggard, dirty stubble covering his face, rode with his hands bound behind his back, the reins of his gelding gripped in Joe Duvray's left hand. As they neared the sheriff's office, Durwood again broke down. "For God's sake, don't take me to see Cantrell; he'll kill me for sure! I'll testify against him, I'll do anything to save my neck—please, Mr. Bouchard, for God's sake, give me a chance!"

"You'll have a fair trial, and if there's a jury system in Laredo you'll be judged by your peers," Lucien Edmond called back without turning his head. "But speaking of testifying, I might tell you that when I examined the bodies of Ludwig and Minna Engelhardt, their wounds were caused by a very small-caliber bullet—the kind, in fact, that might come from those pretty derringers of yours."

"Oh God!" Durwood groaned, bowing his head. All hope fled. Then, knowing himself to be irretrievably lost, he began a profane and hysterical denunciation of his partner to which the three men paid not the slightest heed.

Dismounting in front of the sheriff's office, Lucien Edmond entered the building and laid the wanted poster from San Antonio down in front of a thin, tired-looking man in his late forties, who sat in a rickety straight-backed chair reading the *Laredo Gazette*. Seeing Lucien Edmond enter, he yawned and blinked his eyes, straightening up. "You got business with me, son?"

"I've got the man whose picture is on this poster from San Antonio, Sheriff. He's outside. He's probably guilty of at least two murders."

"Well, I'll be hornswoggled!" The sheriff came to life, surreptitiously rubbing a dirty sleeve on his tin-plated badge to polish it. "Let's see that poster you got—land swindling, huh? But you said murder, mister."

"I did, and the man's practically confessed to it. He was carrying these derringers." Lucien Edmond laid them on the table. "The man and woman who had bought the land near my spread were shot and killed, and when I uncovered their graves, I found that their wounds were made by bullets as small as these."

"I'm Bill Gatesby, mister—mister—"

"Lucien Edmond Bouchard, Sheriff Gatesby. This man came to my ranch four days ago and showed me a document which was supposed to be a royal Spanish land grant, proving that my property was originally awarded to a Spanish nobleman. My prisoner is the partner of this so-called nobleman, and he has an office in your town. There's a poster out on him, too, and here it is." Lucien Edmond produced the other poster, unfolded it and showed it to the lawman.

"You particular about who collects the reward on this character?" Sheriff Gatesby asked, his voice suddenly eager.

"Of course not. I just want to see justice done."

"Well, Mr. Bouchard, I'll tell you, a sheriff's pay in a

367

town like this isn't near what it ought to be. Not when you consider cowboy drunks and Mexican *pistoleros* trying to blow each other's heads off on a Saturday night. So, if you've no objection, and bein' as I'm the law here, I might as well mosey along with you and pick up this here baron whatever-his-name."

"Do you have a judge in town, Sheriff Gatesby?"

"Well, we have a traveling one, you might say. Name of Henry Horkner, and he rides this circuit every other month. Happens he's due here in about ten days."

"Then I'll bring Durwood in and you can put him in your jail."

"I'll do just that. Then we'll go over and pick up this baron. Sure glad you came to town, Mr. Bouchard. Now, I'm gonna have to wire San Antonio just to make sure everything's done right and proper, understand?"

"Of course, I'd expect you to do that, sheriff. Now, if you'll excuse me a minute, I'll bring in your prisoner." Going outside, Lucien Edmond gestured to Joe and Andy, who helped Durwood down from his saddle and marched him roughly into the sheriff's office. "This is Quentin Durwood, Sheriff Gatesby."

"Well now, Mr. Bouchard, you sure got him hog-tied for fair. Might as well cut him loose, he ain't going nowhere, 'cept straight into a cell. Got a couple empty this morning, so he can take his choice." Sheriff Gatesby emitted a dry cackle which passed for laughter. Joe Duvray cut the cords from Quentin Durwood's wrists with his clasp knife.

"Come along, mister," the sheriff prompted, drawing his pistol. "Nice and easy, now."

His shoulders slumped, his head bowed, Quentin Durwood allowed himself to be led to the back and locked into a cell. Sheriff Gatesby returned, opened a drawer in the desk and tossed the keys into it, then holstered his gun and turned to Lucien Edmond Bouchard.

"Where do we find this other critter, Mr. Bouchard?"

"He's got an office with a sign reading *Land Ventures Corporation* just off the main street, Sheriff Gatesby."

"Sure, I know where that is. My stars alive, why I never would have thought that nice, polite old feller was in cahoots with that fancy dude you just brought in. Just goes to show you can't tell by appearances. Well, it's only a short way up the street and then turn north. My mare's in the stable, so I'll just meander over there with you."

"As you like, Sheriff Gatesby." Lucien Edmond smiled at the unassuming manner of the lawman. "Joe, why don't you tie Durwood's horse to that post, and yours and Andy's, too? I'll take care of mine."

A few minutes later, the four men turned off the main street toward a single-story, frame building which housed a saloon and the office of the man whom Lucien Edmond Bouchard had described to his two companions as the would-be baron of Texas.

As they neared the door, Lucien Edmond turned to Sheriff Gatesby. "My two men, Joe and Andy here, are armed, as you see. I left my rifle in its saddle sheath. What I'd like to do, Sheriff Gatesby, with your permission, is talk to this man and tell him that we've caught his partner. Maybe he'll say something that'll convince you he's the brains behind this clever swindling enterprise."

"You sound as if you might have been brung up to be a lawyer, sonny," Sheriff Gatesby chuckled dryly. "I'll back your play. I'll stand just behind you. Anyhow, those Spencers are mighty convincing arguments, better'n my handgun. Go ahead, I'll be right behind you fellows."

Norman Cantrell, seated at his desk, had been talking to Theobald Arnison. "I don't know what's keeping Quentin, but I'm getting a little edgy. We ought to have heard from him by now. There was time for him to see Bouchard and, if that didn't work, go sell Moultrie a bill of goods."

"I know, I know. But I tell you, Mr. Cantrell, that grant I made for the Bouchard tract was the finest piece of work I've ever done, I—Mr. Cantrell, somebody's coming—four men—"

"Perhaps some new clients, Theobald. Damn you, I told you never to call me by that name, didn't I? I'm the Count Juan de Castlemar, and don't you forget it."

Lucien Edmond Bouchard opened the door and walked in, with Joe and Andy close behind him and Sheriff Gatesby standing in the doorway, a quizzical expression on his wrinkled, weather-beaten face.

"Good morning, gentlemen. I trust you've come to inquire about some good Texas land?" Cantrell bestowed his most urbane smile on the group.

Lucien Edmond stepped to the front of Cantrell's desk, his eyes cold and his lips tightening as he replied, "Your partner, a certain Mr. Quentin Durwood, tried to sell me a royal deed to my own land. My name is Lucien Edmond Bouchard."

"Ah yes, that's right, Mr. Bouchard. You see, I happen to be the last survivor of an old and very noble Spanish family, the de Castlemars. Oh, let me present Mr. Theobald Arnison, a most erudite historian. He has been of invaluable assistance to me in tracing the titles of much of this Texas land, which was originally under Spanish rule."

"And I suppose he traced the Englehardts' land back to a similar royal grant," Lucien Edmond countered. "And then, when the Engelhardts wouldn't budge, your other associate killed them at your order. You see, Andrew Moultrie is dead. He tried to kill me and I had to shoot him in self-defense. And when I buried him, I uncovered the graves of Ludwig and Minna Engelhardt. Each of them had been killed with a small-caliber bullet. Your partner, Quentin Durwood, is in the Laredo jail, and I gave Sheriff Gatesby his derringers. I'm sure that when he's brought to trial, it can be proved that derringers were used to kill those unfortunate people. And you, sir, are the partner who gave him the order to persuade stubborn settlers who wouldn't accept what are most likely forged deeds."

Cantrell's features contorted as his suave mask vanished. He suddenly lunged for the drawer of his desk. As he did so, Lucien Edmond leaned forward, and with all his might slammed his palms hard against the edges of the drawer.

"Ahhrrr! You've broken my wrist—oh God—it hurts—it hurts—ease up, for God's sake!" Cantrell yelled, slipping down from his chair onto his knees, his face tilting back and convulsed in agony.

"All right, I'll ease up, but if that hand of yours comes out with a gun, Joe and Andy will cut you down. Is that understood?" Lucien Edmond demanded.

"Yes, yes, for God's sake, anything—oh my wrist— you've really broken it—please—"

Lucien Edmond let go of the drawer and stepped back. "Very slowly, take your hand out of the drawer and lift both hands as high as you can," he ordered.

Sweat bathing his contorted face, groaning, Cantrell gingerly withdrew his right hand, fingers splayed and dangling, and then, as Joe Duvray stepped forward with the rifle leveled and snapped, "Higher than that, mister!" forced himself to lift both arms above his head, swaying on his feet. Old Theobald Arnison, his mouth agape, had flattened himself against the wall and was whimpering with terror.

Exactly two weeks from that morning, under a gray and cloudy sky, Durwood McCambridge, alias Quentin Durwood, and Norman Cantrell, alias the Baron Rodrigo de Austencio and more lately, the Conde Juan de Castlemar, stood side by side on a gallows in the town square and dropped through the trap at the same fateful moment. Theobald Arnison, who had given evidence before Judge Horkner which had helped link both swindlers to the crime of double murder, was sentenced to five years in the Laredo jail. That night, using a sheet from his bunk, he hanged himself from the bars of his cell.

CHAPTER THIRTY-FOUR

Two hundred years before, there had been an Indian town at the point where the Allegheny and Monongahela Rivers joined to form the mighty Ohio. Nearly a hundred years after that, the ambitious French colonists built Fort Duquesne, and four years later it was rebuilt and renamed Fort Pitt by the British. In 1760, the village around the fort was settled, and grew with the increase in trade and traffic after the opening of the Northwest Territory. Now it had become a bustling city, with its thriving industries iron and coal mining. Meat-packing and glassmaking also flourished. It was named Pittsburgh after Fort Pitt, the bastion which had valiantly defied the might of the combined Indian horde that had launched itself against the hated white-eyes. The town had drawn men of vision like the Scottish immigrant Andrew Carnegie, who was to turn pig iron into steel, the strongest substance that the world had known until now.

Yet, for all its growth and wealth, this sprawling city was no stranger to squalor, poverty, and disease. Along the mud flats of the triangle of rivers, run-down shacks and huts housed many who toiled for paltry wages, whose children were badly clothed and poorly nourished, and often succumbed, as did their parents, to what in New Orleans would have been called "river fever". The summer of 1869 had been unnaturally hot and humid and there had been sporadic epidemics of this deadly malaise and a new ailment which young, erudite doctors called diphtheria.

The epidemic had not been limited to the slums. It had spread even to the elegant mansions along Castleton Drive, and during the last week of August, George Hardesty was dying from it. Now fifty-seven and only two months earlier elevated to the presidency of the Bessemer Iron Works, he lay in bed, gasping for breath, in a private room of Pittsburgh General Hospital. When he had been admitted, he had asked feebly that Dr. Ben Wilson be assigned to him, rather than the hospital's pompous, bearded director, Dr. Elmer Drawley.

Two years before, George Hardesty had taken umbrage at the young Quaker's insistence that a clinic be established for the poor and needy, and had compelled Dr. Drawley to discharge him. Then, stricken by a heart attack, he had, in his fear of death, summoned to his elegant house the very man he had once branded as a dangerous radical. Ben Wilson had put him on a strict diet, shown him how to make peace with his tyrannized, thirty-six-year-old wife, Cora, and his frail, sensitive, ten-year-old son, Daniel. George Hardesty had recovered and, to express his gratitude, endowed a new hospital on Melvin Road, to be named the George Hardesty General Hospital. Ben Wilson was appointed chief of staff. Now George insisted that the Quaker physician attend him at the very hospital from which he had arranged to have him ousted two years before. His request stemmed from a kind of superstition, a belief that the man who had saved him once could again effect a miraculous cure. Now that he had come to show a gruff tenderness to Cora and Daniel, which he had never before displayed, Hardesty was even more afraid of death than ever. Life had suddenly become too rich and rewarding to abandon.

For Laurette Douglas, the only child of Maybelle Williamson and the unscrupulous Mark Bouchard, the summer of 1869 was hectic and oppressive. Not only was the weather sultry and humid—even the breezes off Lake Michigan did not alleviate it—but little Howard, now a year old, was fretfully cutting a tooth. The three-year-old twins, Arthur and Kenneth, had summer colds, and she and their young nurse had their hands full. Then, to cap matters, Charles had decided to sell their house on Prairie Avenue and to move to a much larger house on Dearborn, near Division Street. It was true that he'd been able to aquire the house—with its spacious, fenced-in yard it would of course be ideal for the children—and land for

373

the very modest cost of $4,000 dollars. Just the same, moving had been the last thing in the world she'd wanted.

Still, now that it was over, as were the twins' colds and little Howard's nerve-racking crying, Laurette had to admit that Charles had got a real bargain in the house. It was ever so much roomier, and of course, socially, it was a step up the ladder. There were many prominent families in the neighborhood, people you read about in the newspaper. The nice, gray-haired woman next door, for instance, turned out to be the wife of the city treasurer. The afternoon before, Mrs. Benderson had been saying that prolonged heat could be dangerous to a city built primarily of wood. Indeed, there had been a few fires in the Bridgeport slum area last month. But the dreary skies and hazy moon at night promised rain very soon, and that would be a blessing.

Laurette was going to market this Friday afternoon. One nice thing about the new neighborhood, she had discovered, was that the greengrocer and butcher shops were side by side, with attractive and economically priced offerings. Even though Charles was doing exceptionally well at the department store, she believed in economizing.

Never once had Laurette regretted marrying Charles Douglas, the enterprising young store clerk from Tuscaloosa. His success in the booming city of Chicago had proved indisputably his merchandising abilities, and the fact that he was a Southerner had in no way stopped him from adapting to the post-war commercial boom. In addition, his absorption with business had never caused him to neglect his roles as her faithful husband and devoted lover.

Laurette entered the butcher shop first and was about to call a greeting to Stanley Harshman, the good-natured German proprietor, when she stopped suddenly, her green eyes widening with disbelief. No—it couldn't be. Not that dreadful Carrie Melton, who had spread such lies about Charles that she'd taken a horsewhip to the young trollop right in the bank where Charles had his account.

And the hussy was wearing a silk dress that must have cost a fortune, too! Laurette was about to turn on her heel and walk out of the butcher shop when suddenly her worst fears were realized.

"Oh, my, it's Mrs. Douglas, isn't it?" came Carrie's sweetly unctuous voice.

Laurette stiffened, her slim fingers driving into her gloved palms. When you were well bred, you showed it by not descending to the level of a creature like Carrie Melton. And now that idiot of a butcher had to go and call, loud enough for everybody to hear, "I'll just be a minute, Mrs. Douglas. I've got a standing rib roast set aside for you—the minute I saw it, I put your name on it."

There was no hope for it. Laurette turned slowly back, a sickly smile on her lovely face. "Th—thank you, Mr. Harshman," she managed. Then, to the chestnut-haired, expensively dressed young woman, "How do you do, M— Miss Melton is it?"

Carrie giggled, shook her head until the artificial berries sewn around the rim of her modish hat—a hat Laurette had, earlier that week, stared at longingly in the window of a department store—seemed to dance. "Oh, my goodness, not anymore, Mrs. Douglas," she beamed. "It's Mrs. Dalton Haines now. Would you believe it, dear old Dalton married me anyway—in spite of—well, no sense mentioning our little difference after all this time, is there, dearie?"

Laurette could cheerfully have killed her for that "dearie." But before she could recover, Carrie Melton Haines sweetly added. "You know, we're neighbors now. Fact is, our house is across the street and just north of yours. Oh my goodness, we'll have to get together some evening, won't we?"

Dr. Ben Wilson had visited George Hardesty this stiflingly hot morning in the last week of August, and seen at once that the diphtheria was advancing rapidly. Worst of all were the complications caused by a heart that had already been overtaxed, even though the industrialist had tried to mend his ways these past two years. Ben Wilson prescribed what medicine he could, knowing that even cutting into the patient's trachea to restore breathing, a drastic measure used as a last resort in such cases, would not save him. The shock to the nervous system, the advance of the dread disease, the patient's age, and his already laboring heart and irregular pulse pronounced the final sentence on the man who had once been his implacable enemy and then his unexpected benefactor.

"Can—can you s—save m—me, Doc—Doctor—W—Wilson —can you—" George Hardesty panted, his eyes wide and glazed as he tried to turn his head toward the earnest, kindly face of the only man he was certain could.

Wilson, now thirty-five, his brown hair still unruly as ever, bent closer to the dying man. "You mustn't try to talk, Mr. Hardesty. I've told the nurse to give you a mild sedative to help you sleep. You must relax, try to give your body a chance." Even as he spoke these comforting words, Ben Wilson knew they could provide only a spiritual placebo. "I'm going to the clinic now—the clinic you made possible two years ago with your kindness and your generosity. But I promise I'll be back this afternoon and I'll do all I can."

"G—God bl—bless you—" Hardesty gasped.

Ben Wilson patted his shoulder. "Close your eyes and rest now. Try to sleep. The sedation will be good for you. And I promise I'll be back."

He beckoned to the nurse, and then left the room, where Dr. Drawley waited impatiently for him.

"Well, Dr. Wilson?"

"There's very little chance. He'll sleep now, and if worse comes to worst I'll try a tracheotomy. His trachea's already affected, as you've seen for yourself."

"It's extremely dangerous."

"There's nothing else. He's got a bad heart. He was overweight for ten years or more before I first took charge of him, and although his general health has improved since then, the diphtheria has already put excessive strain on his vital organs. If he were younger, there might be a chance."

"It's a pity. He's been a great philanthropist to the medical profession. He has absolute faith in you—and so do I."

"Thank you, Dr. Drawley. I'm going over to the clinic now, but I'll be back this afternoon, just as early as I can."

"I'll watch him myself until you get back, Dr. Wilson."

The sanctimonious respect with which the director of Pittsburgh General treated the man he had once berated and discharged was not lost on the soft-spoken, tall

376

Quaker. Yet in his sincere faith, which held that a benevolent God would soften the wrath of the bitterest enemy, Ben had forgotten long ago the humiliation Dr. Drawley had inflicted on him once. He said, with a gentle smile, "Thank you, Dr. Drawley. Then he'll be in good hands, I'm sure. As soon as I return, I'll see you in your office. Good-by now."

Outside the doors of Pittsburgh General, Ben Wilson hailed a passing carriage and told the driver to take him to the George Hardesty General Hospital. He leaned back in his seat with a sigh, passed his hand through his thick, light-brown hair, and then smiled as he remembered the way Fleurette still teased him about the wayward curl that fell over one side of his forehead. His lean face might have been called homely by a casual observer and his chin a trifle sharp—Fleurette had always cited this as proof of his innate stubbornness, and remembering that, he smiled again. But his quiet demeanor, the brown eyes which could be quizzical, or compassionate, or aglow with zeal in his work to help the poor, belied that disparagement. He closed his eyes for a minute, envisioning Fleurette's sweet face, her dancing green eyes when she teased him about working so hard that he had no time to remember that he was both a father and her lover.

How kind God had been to him, when, as a medical corpsman, he had been wounded in battle. Captured by Confederates, he had been treated with consideration, and they had accepted his word that he would not try to escape. Without that, he might have been sent to Libby Prison and perhaps died, as many prisoners did, of disease or malnutrition. Instead, a gentle, copper-haired angel had helped him convalesce, and urged him to continue his medical studies so that he might ease the suffering and misery of the needy. Though she had been two years older than he, even now she was still as young and beautiful as the day he had first seen her bend over his cot and ask him if he felt better. She had given him his strong son Thomas and a daughter, Sybella, named after her own wonderful mother.

As the carriage drew up in front of the hospital Ben Wilson frowned, remembering that he had not yet been able to keep his promise to Fleurette. George Hardesty's

377

endowment of this new hospital and his own appointment as director of it had kept him from carrying out that promise. But once this dreadful epidemic was checked, he would take Fleurette and the children to Texas and meet her mother for the first time. He knew from her letters that she must be a magnificent woman. Yes, God willing, he would take Fleurette to visit Windhaven Range very soon.

Her work at the clinic, which she had insisted on pursuing, was tiring her, he had noticed lately. He hadn't liked her color the night before when she got home. True, they had Molly O'Brien working for them now as the children's nurse. Cora Hardesty, once her husband had recovered from his heart attack, had spoken to Ben privately, suggesting that the presence of the pretty Irish maid in the mansion was too much of a temptation for her lusty husband, and so Molly had come to work for the Wilsons. She was an absolute jewel with the children, and a good cook, too. She also helped relieve Fleurette of some of the household chores. Just the same, he was going to speak to Fleurette this evening at supper and suggest that she not go back to the clinic until the cooler fall weather. By then, the epidemic would surely be on the wane.

He paid the driver, then went into the hospital. In his office, his head nurse, Emma Persky, was waiting. She was a tall, angular-faced woman in her late forties whose bustling efficiency and brusque manner of speaking hid her selfless dedication to her patients. "Good morning, doctor," she greeted him before he could speak. "We've three new diphtheria cases this morning. I've had them isolated in the special ward."

"Thank you, nurse. I'll get to them at once. How's old Mr. Bromberg?" He was referring to an elderly German who had taken a job as a hod carrier after his wife's recent death, and had injured his leg so badly that it was necessary to amputate it. Ben had performed the operation himself, despite the man's heartrending pleas to save the leg so that he could go on working to earn money for his three children.

"Badly, I'm afraid. He seems to be in a state of shock, doctor. And his pulse is very weak."

"Then I'll see him first. Oh, by the way, is my wife still on duty?" Fleurette usually spent three hours in the clinic every morning and, when she could find time away from the children and her household chores, at least two afternoons a week.

"She left for home about half an hour ago, doctor. She had a rather bad headache, she said. I didn't like her color, if you want the truth."

"I noticed the same thing last night. I'm going to have to speak to her about taking a good, long rest. It's wonderful how she's helped, but she doesn't spare herself—she never did. Well now, let's go see Mr. Bromberg."

About an hour later, Dieter Bromberg was dead. He had suffered congestive heart failure, despite all Ben Wilson's frantic efforts to save him. As Nurse Persky solemnly drew a sheet over the flaccid, thickly bearded face, Ben put one hand on the bedrail and wearily leaned there for a moment. "Those poor children; what will become of them?" he murmured.

"Charity, I daresay, Dr. Wilson," Emma Persky tartly offered.

"Destined to grow up in an orphanage with little food and less affection, and then perhaps jobs in the coal mines or the factories. It's a cheerless prospect. May God in His infinite mercy grant them a better fate." He sighed heavily, shook his head, and straightened. "Now we'll go to the diphtheria ward, nurse."

By four P.M., Ben Wilson had done all he could, both in the clinical ward and in the special isolation ward reserved for the victims of this devastating epidemic. Many such patients were crowded into Pittsburgh General also, and countless others had died in their hovels and shacks along the riverbanks. He hurried back to Pittsburgh General and went directly to Dr. Drawley's office.

"He's very low, Dr. Wilson." The white-haired director pursed his lips and shrugged. "I don't think he'll last through the night."

"Then the fever has progressed? Is he cyanotic?"

Dr. Elmer Drawley nodded. "About half an hour ago he began to show signs of cyanosis. At least, he seems to be in no pain."

"Then there's only one chance: to perform a trache-

379

otomy and remove the false membrane. With your permission, I'll order surgery."

"You may as well try that. What a pity to lose such a benefactor!" Dr. Drawley looked piously sad.

Ben Wilson glanced at him sharply, but did not speak, and went directly to the head nurse's office. In a few minutes, George Hardesty, breathing stertorously, was lifted onto a stretcher by four young interns and carried to the operating room.

An hour later, Dr. Ben Wilson left the operating room and bathed his haggard, sweating face in a basin of cool water which one of the nurses had thoughtfully provided. Then he slumped into a chair and closed his eyes, utterly exhausted. To his surprise, the industrialist's pulse had remained relatively steady through the operation. At least Hardesty would not die of suffocation. But tonight would witness the crisis, and determine whether that corpulent body with its aging, slightly enlarged heart could withstand the postoperative shock.

Half an hour later, Ben hailed a carriage and was driven to his house. As he dismounted, Molly O'Brien came out to meet him, wringing her hands. "Oh, Dr. Wilson, it's the missus! She's awful sick. She had a dreadful headache, and I put some cold cloths on her head, and then she started to vomit, and then—"

"My God, it sounds like—Molly, run after that cab and tell him to wait. I'm going to take Fleurette to the hospital at once!"

First glancing into the room where little Thomas was playing in his crib and baby Sybella lay cooing in her bassinet, he hurried into the bedroom and uttered a cry of anguish. Fleurette lay sprawled on the bed, a hand over her head, moaning feebly. Already he could see the fateful bluish tinge. The virulent bacillus had struck her with ferocious speed and was threatening her very life.

He stooped to lift her in his arms, his lips trembling, tears welling up in his eyes, and then hurried outside. Molly had intercepted the driver, and Ben Wilson carefully lifted his half-conscious wife into the back of the cab, then called, "Hardesty General, as fast as you can get those horses of yours to go—it's my wife, she may be dying!"

Emma Persky came out of her office to meet him as he carried Fleurette in. For once, her usual stern demeanor deserted her. "Oh, no, Dr. Wilson, not your wife? Oh, poor Mrs. Wilson—is it diphtheria?"

He nodded grimly. "It's the fastest-moving attack I've seen yet, Nurse Persky. I'm going to have to do a tracheotomy. Please get the interns and the nurses ready."

"Don't you think you ought to let Dr. Martin take over for you, Dr. Wilson? You look pale as a ghost, and I know you're tired—"

"No, no, I must do it. She's my wife, my beloved—she trusts me. It was she who helped me gain what skill I have, and I pray to God it will be good enough to save her now, when she needs me!"

He steeled himself to think of Fleurette as just another patient who was in dire need of this operation, so that his fingers would not tremble or his hand falter. Expertly, carefully, he made the incision, clearing away the false membrane, and suturing the wound, while the nurses and interns around him, awed by his almost unnatural calm, swiftly responded to his every gesture or terse order.

"Oh, Dr. Wilson, you were just wonderful—I know she'll live now; she just has to!" young Sally Caswell, a pretty, brown-haired nurse who, rumor had it, was engaged to Dr. Thaddeus Martin, exclaimed as four interns carried Fleurette, on a stretcher, to her room.

"I pray God she will, Sally. Bless you for your words. All we can do now is pray." Ben walked out of the operating room, slumped into a chair and bowed his head, covering his face with his hands. Suddenly all the fatigue of the long, sweltering day had drained his strength.

He must have fallen asleep, for the next thing he knew, a hand was gently shaking his shoulders. Then there was a muffled voice he could not at once identify saying, "Oh, Dr. Wilson, please—please wake up—oh dear God in heaven!"

He blinked his eyes and straightened. As consciousness returned, he felt an overpowering fatigue which made it almost impossible for him to move. "Nurse Persky—what is it—" his voice was hollow, halting.

Her homely face was swollen with tears, and her long bony fingers twisted this way and that in agitation as she

381

faced him. "It's—I wish I didn't have to tell you—I don't believe it—it should never have happened—she was so young—it's—it's your wife, Dr. W—Wilson—"

He was galvanized, springing up from his seat. "Fleurette—has she taken a turn for the worse? Take me to her, nurse!"

"Please—it—you can't—oh my God, my God, why did it have to happen to her, Dr. Wilson?" Now Emma was sobbing distractedly, and a sudden, terrible chill made his heart nearly stop beating. He forced himself to speak. "Tell me—please, this isn't like you—take a grip on yourself, Nurse Persky—what's happened?"

With a supreme effort, the head nurse forced herself to speak. "It was her heart, Dr. Wilson. Just a few minutes ago, I went in to see how she was. Of course, she hadn't come out of the anesthesia, but she looked so peaceful, I thought she was sleeping—and then—then I took her pulse—she's dead, Dr. Wilson, I wish to God I hadn't been the one to have to tell you this dreadful news!"

He closed his eyes and swayed a moment. Then a fit of trembling seized him. After a long moment, he said hoarsely, "You mustn't blame yourself. At least, if it was God's will to take her, He spared her pain. Diphtheria is a frightful death."

"Shall I—do you want me to—" Emma Persky no longer tried to halt the flow of tears.

Dr. Ben Wilson shook his head. "No. God bless you and thank you. I—I'll go to her now."

Straightening his shoulders, his eyes unseeing, he walked down the corridor to Fleurette's room and entered. He saw the lovely sheen of her copper-red hair spread out against the white pillow. Her face was serene, her eyes closed. With a professional detachment, he walked to the bed and first felt her pulse and then her heart. How could it have been? She was only thirty-seven, with never the slightest indication of any heart trouble. There hadn't been too much anesthetic, her pulse and heart had been steady during the operation and he knew it had been effective. Medically, she should have survived. And yet she was gone.

He sank down on his knees by the bed and prayed. It was the gentle Quaker prayer, at once a eulogy and a benediction, a profession of deep gratitude to Him who noted something as minuscule as the flight of a sparrow, as well as agonized thanks for having been permitted to share even a short five years with this woman who had been wife, mother, lover, and helpmate, and joyful inspiration to all his waking days.

He could see her now bending over him in the bed in her friend's Richmond home, which during the war had been converted into a hospital. He could remember their talks as he convalesced. There had been, since she had not been of his faith, a simple civil ceremony to unite them in war-torn Richmond. And then they had gone back to his home in Pittsburgh, and she had asked of her own accord that they be married at a Quaker meeting.

How well he remembered. A group of deacons had visited one night and questioned both him and Fleurette to make certain that this union was yearned for by both, and without covetousness. Then, two months after they had announced their intention to take their vows at a meeting of the Society of Friends on Eccles Avenue, they had held hands, and each, in turn, repeated the vow that would make them one. Next the pastor had read the vow, word for word. And after the meeting, all those present had come forward to wish them joy and fulfillment.

To the Quakers, all of life was a sacrament, and so a wedding, even a death, required no special and independent ritual. The faith was profoundly gentle and tender.

Ben rose now and moved to Fleurette, bent and kissed her forehead and murmured, "Sleep, my dearest darling. May the inner light of Almighty God cherish you and comfort the children and me through the years ahead."

He stood in the congregation. When the hour-long service was over, he was comforted, though his face had been wet with tears from the time it began. From the floor, many members of the congregation spoke their praise of Fleurette Wilson, who had touched their lives with her kindness, helped their children, given good counsel to their wives, unstintingly dedicated herself—as did her husband—to helping the poor, the sick, and the disconsolate.

Pastor Arthur Maris, a printer by trade whose myopic

383

eyes squinted through thick spectacles and whose stooped shoulders stamped his profession upon him, approached, and took Ben by the hand. "All of us are the poorer without her, Dr. Wilson. But I know that you will go on with your life as she would have wished."

"Yes, Pastor Maris. But first I have a mission. Rather, I must keep a promise I made to her once and could not keep. I must be the one to tell her mother and to bring our children to that woman who gave her birth."

"And then you'll return to Pittsburgh?"

"I'm not sure, Pastor Maris. Perhaps after that I shall go where I am most needed. This city was my birthplace and has been my home. But if, as I believe, there was divine purpose in ending her life when she was still so very young, it may be that my own life is to be changed. Wherever I go, I shall fulfill the Hippocratic Oath I took when I was certified as a physician. You see, Pastor Maris, this city has many good doctors. But Fleurette's mother lives in Texas, where there are still so few people and so vast a land. It may be that I shall be needed there much more than I am here."

"God will show you the way, and may His grace be with you always."

"And with you, Pastor Maris. Good-by, and thank you."

"God's inner light be with you always, Dr. Wilson. When will you leave for Texas?"

Dr. Ben Wilson smiled sadly. "Tomorrow, Pastor Maris. I must go to the hospital now and see to one of my patients who, through God's will, has made a marvelous recovery. You see, Pastor Maris, though he is not of our persuasion, he was first my persecutor and then my benefactor. And each end of that pole touched and changed my life."

He shook hands a last time with the kindly pastor, then walked out of the meeting house and hailed a cab to take him to Pittsburgh General. He had another farewell to undertake. George Hardesty was out of danger and would live.

Simata had seen the wagon coming from the east, following the trail which Luke and Lucien Edmond Bouchard had taken four years ago, when they had first come

384

to Windhaven Range. It was the day after Lucien Edmond, Joe Duvray, and Andy Haskins had ridden to Laredo with Quentin Durwood as their prisoner. Lucas had kissed his lovely young bride, Felicidad, after they shared breakfast in their new house, and came out to take his turn riding to the western boundary and then circling north to make sure all was well. He, too, spied the lumbering wagon, and called to Simata, "More settlers moving in, looks like, Simata! Or maybe it's the Engelhardt boys come back to take over their poor pappy's property."

Simata peered, cupping his left hand over his eyes to shield them from the already oppressive sun, then shook his head. "I do not think so, Lucas. They are coming closer now—I see the driver of the horses, and beside him a man who has two little children with him."

"Wonder who they are, then? They must have come all the way from Corpus Christi," Lucas remarked. "They're turning this way. Let's go saddle up and meet them!"

A few minutes later Simata and Lucas trotted their geldings toward the heavy wagon, and Lucas called out to the driver, "Where are you bound for, mister?"

"This the Bouchard place?" the lanky young Texan drew on the reins to slow his horses.

"Yes, it is."

"Sure glad to hear that, mister," the driver grinned. "It's a long way from Corpus Christi and it's been hotter than the devil's own griddle all the way. Well, I brought a fellow who's traveled a lot farther than I have, all the way from Pittsburgh—isn't that so, Dr. Wilson?"

Holding little Sybella in his arms, and with young Thomas huddling beside him, tugging at his father's trouser leg for attention, the tall Quaker nodded. "That's right. I've come to visit Fleurette's mother, Sybella, and to bring her grandchildren to her."

"Lord Amighty," Lucas exclaimed, "you sure have been traveling a spell, Dr. Wilson! Miz Sybella's just fine. I swear, I don't know how she takes this heat and all the work there is to do keeping up the big house, but she's got more energy than all of us put together. Simata will escort you. I'll go on ahead and tell her and Miz Bouchard you're coming!" Then, nodding to Simata, he spurred his gelding and rode back toward the stockade.

In the living room, Sybella Forsden and Maxine Bouchard had been amusing Carla and Hugo, and discussing the singular turn of events which had taken Lucien Edmond to Laredo. When Lucas knocked at the front door, Maxine hurried to open it. "Why, Lucas, is anything wrong? Lucien Edmond certainly can't be back yet—"

"No, ma'am, not hardly. Miz Sybella, you've got a real special visitor. Came all the way from Pittsburgh—"

Before Lucas could finish, white-haired Sybella had risen from the couch with a joyous cry. "It's Fleurette and Ben and the children—oh, how wonderful—I've wanted to see them for so long, and I thought they were coming last year!"

"Yes, ma'am. Only—" Lucas hesitated a moment, then finished, "only I didn't see Miz Fleurette. Of course, she might be in the back of the wagon. They came overland from Corpus Christi, and a trip like that in that heavy old wagon would tucker a woman out. I don't mean you, Miz Sybella," he hastily added with a sheepish grin.

"Go along with you, Lucas!" Sybella laughed. "Just bring them all in here. Maxine dear, would you go ask Kate to get some cool milk for the children and tell her maybe the Wilsons would like an early lunch after their long journey."

"Of course, grandmother!" Maxine turned to kiss Sybella on the cheek, gave her a little hug, then hurried off to the kitchen.

The wagon stopped before the open gate of the stockade, and Lucas helped little Thomas down, then reached up to take the baby from Ben Wilson's arms.

Ben turned to the young driver. "I'm very grateful, Eddie. You're a wonderful driver and you must have picked out the easiest trail there was to give my children and me so few bumps along the way."

"Hell, Dr. Wilson, begging your pardon, it was the least I could do. You made it real interesting for me, talking about things the way you did. I've never been to a real big city like Pittsburgh, but you sure gave me a clear picture of what goes on back East." The driver reached down to extend his hand, and Ben shook it warmly. "Well, guess I'll be unloading the supplies you've got left and then heading back to Corpus Christi."

Ben Wilson turned to Lucas. "This is Eddie Gentry. He tells me he's a pretty good cowhand, too, but he's had some bad luck. It seems he was hired by a Mexican who'd bought some ranchland near Corpus Christi, only the land turned out to be practically desert and so his employer discharged him. His bad luck was my good fortune, because I was able to hire him to drive the children and me to see their grandmother."

Lucas nodded sympathetically, then said, "I'll give you a hand with those supplies, Mr. Gentry."

"Thanks a lot. Yup, just like Dr. Wilson was saying, I'd been taken on as a temporary hand by an outfit near Laredo, and my boss decided to sell out and go to California. Then I met this Mexican fellow who asked if I wanted a job and said he'd bought a big piece of land near Alice. Well, I needed the money, but I did try to tell him that I didn't see how he was going to bring up any cattle around that God-forsaken place. Then—well, he found out, too." He turned back to Ben Wilson. "By rights I'll leave the wagon here, too. You paid for it, Dr. Wilson. But I'd sure appreciate the loan of one of those horses. Think I'll change my mind and mosey back to Laredo—I was thinking of signing on as a hand with that steamboat captain, only I'm not so sure he needs any help. Yep, I think I'll go back to Laredo and try my luck."

"Eddie, why don't you let me talk to Mr. Bouchard and see if there might not be a job for you here? It's a big ranch, and maybe he'd have a spot for you."

"Sure, Dr. Wilson," Lucas put in with enthusiasm. "Fact is, we lost a couple of vaqueros to bushwhackers on this last cattle drive. You wait till Mr. Lucien Edmond gets back, or maybe you can talk to his brother-in-law, Ramón Hernandez."

"Say now, that's downright friendly of you, mister," the young cowboy beamed. "And after that stretch in Alice, I'd sure like to pull leather on a range like this. It's a beauty!"

"All right, Thomas, we'll go see your grandmother." The tall Quaker stooped down and spoke to his little son.

"Does mama know we here?" the curly-haired little boy asked plaintively.

Ben Wilson nodded, fighting the tears. "Yes, Thomas.

She's in heaven watching over us. Now let's go see your grandmother. She won't believe what a big, strong boy you are. Come along now."

Sybella Forsden had already come out onto the porch and, seeing Ben, hurried forward with a joyous cry. "Oh, Ben, Ben dear, I've prayed so long to see you and Fleurette—and these are my grandchildren—"

"Yes." He stiffened his shoulders with an effort, his face worn and dusty from the long trek across the barren lowlands. "This is our daughter, whom we named after you, mother. She has Fleurette's red hair."

"Oh the darling! Let me hold her!" Sybella's eyes filled with tears of joy as she tenderly lifted the little girl from Ben's arms. ""Yes, and Fleurette's eyes, too!" she murmured wonderingly. Then, blinking her eyes quickly, she looked down at Thomas. "My gracious, isn't he big for his age! Such a fine, strong young man—and he's going to grow up to be just as fine a man as his father, I just know it! Thomas, I'm your grandmother!"

"Gwandmama," the little boy echoed with a faint lisp. Then, stricken with a sudden shyness, he huddled against his father's leg and turned his face away.

Sybella looked out to where Lucas and young Eddie Gentry were unloading the supplies from the wagon. "Ben, where's Fleurette? Was the trip too much for her? Did you come overland all the way from Corpus Christi? I know how hard a journey it was—Ben—your face—"

He bit his lips, his eyes meeting hers, and then he murmured softly, "She's dead, mother."

"Oh, God, oh, no—how, Ben—how did it happen?"

He glanced down at Thomas and patted the boy's curly head. "I'd best tell you when we're alone. You see, I finally kept the promise she'd made in her letters—that you'd see your grandchildren as soon as we could."

"Oh, my God—oh, Ben—Ben my heart goes out to you—and you came all this way from Pittsburgh with those two little children—come in, please, don't stand out here in the hot sun!" Sybella reached into the pocket of her dress for a handkerchief and blew her nose vigorously.

Ben followed his mother-in-law into the living room, and Maxine Bouchard, who had just returned from the kitchen, came forward to greet him. Seeing Sybella Fors-

den's anguished look, she sensed at once that something
was wrong and withheld a question until, once they had
been seated with Sybella tenderly cradling her namesake
grandchild in her arms and little Thomas seated tightly
against his father and hugging him, the white-haired ma-
triarch gently suggested, "Perhaps Thomas would like to
go to the kitchen for a nice cool glass of milk and a
cookie."

At this, the curly-headed boy nodded his head vigorously and clapped his hands together. "Then I'll take you,
darling." Sybella turned to give Maxine the baby girl,
came over to Thomas, gravely took his hand, and declared,
"Such a big, strong, young man can probably eat more
than one cookie, don't you think so, Thomas?"

"Yes, Gwandmama," he retorted. Sybella turned to
flash Ben a warm, compassionate look, and then led the
little boy to the kitchen. "Kate dear, this is Fleurette's son,
my grandchild. Keep him with you a little, and I told
him all about your fabulous cookies."

"I'll do that, Mrs. Forsden. Well now, Thomas, here's
a nice, tall glass of milk to make you strong," Kate coaxed
the little boy, holding it out to him. "And see, here's a
plate of cookies. Let's see how many you can eat, but
slowly now, dear."

Sybella nodded with satisfaction, patted Thomas's head,
and then went back to the living room.

"There was diphtheria, an epidemic of it, you see,
mother," Ben explained, his eyes searching the white-
haired woman's face as if to find some solace there. "Even
after little Sybella was born, Fleurette insisted on spending some time at my clinic. I'm convinced that's where she
caught the disease—it's terribly contagious and we haven't
been able to isolate it. Well, I had to do a tracheotomy,
but the operation went well. I didn't even think—but her
heart stopped. She was so young, so vital, so dear to me—
and how dear to you I can only guess, mother. Somehow,
I failed her."

"No, Ben, she trusted you with her life. She wrote me
often how happy you'd made her, how you'd fulfilled her
as a woman, how you respected her and let her know
what she meant to you in your work. Yes, it was a short
life you two had together, but a wonderful one. And

389

above all, never reproach yourself. I know something of your Quaker faith, you see. She'll never be dead for you. She'll live in Thomas, and in my namesake—and I know that it was *your* generous and thoughtful wish in naming the little girl after me." Sybella smiled down at the sleeping baby in Maxine's arms, put out her hand, and gently touched the copper curls. "She'll be a beauty like her mother. And she'll have your gentleness and kindness, Ben. No child could have a greater legacy than what you and Fleurette have given them both."

He could not speak and continued to stare at her, unashamed of the tears that now flowed.

Gently she asked, "What will you do now, Ben?"

With an obvious effort, he forced himself to speak. "Go on being a doctor, of course. But I don't think I'll go back to Pittsburgh, mother. At least, not for a while. I only wish I'd been able to bring Fleurette out to see you before this—"

"I know, Ben. Don't torture yourself, dear. Now all you must think of doing is resting after that long journey. And Maxine and I will look after Thomas and the baby."

He looked up at the ceiling, striving to gain composure. "It's a strange thing, mother, but everything was arranged for us. You see, there was an important man in Pittsburgh. I'd saved him from a heart attack after he'd had me discharged from the hospital where I worked because I wanted to have a clinic for people who couldn't afford medical attention. And then, as if he wanted to make it up to me, he put me in charge of a new hospital he'd endowed and built. Then he came down with diphtheria, and I operated on him and was sure he would die because his physical condition was very bad. And when I came home, it was to find Fleurette stricken—"

"We cannot always know God's ways, Ben. At least she didn't suffer?"

"No, I thank God for that," he responded. "And then, when this man was out of danger, he took a pad of paper and a pencil and asked me how my wife was—and I had to tell him. Then he wanted to know what I planned to do. When he heard I was coming to Texas with the children, he wrote orders to have the nurse get in touch with his secretary and arrange the rail and steamboat trans-

390

portation as far as Corpus Christi. He had her send a wire to Corpus Christi, too, to the mayor, and actually had the mayor buy a wagon and outfit it with supplies. And he told the mayor to be on the lookout for someone who could drive the children and me out here—that reminds me, mother."

"Yes, Ben?"

"It was a very friendly young cowhand—I think that's what you call them here—who was out of a job and was waiting there when I got off the steamboat. He said he'd be willing to drive me here, and he took wonderful care of us. I wonder—I haven't the right to ask it—but I wonder if there couldn't be some sort of a job here for him, with the cattle and horses and such."

"I'm sure there can be, Ben. Lucien Edmond's in Laredo. He should be back in a few days. We'll talk to him about it."

Lucien Edmond Bouchard gripped Ben Wilson's hand and shook it warmly. "I'm sorry I wasn't here to welcome you to Windhaven Range. We had a little trouble with a would-be land-grabber who was posing as Spanish nobility and wanted to take over this place. But no matter. Now, grandmother told me about this cowboy who met you at Corpus Christi and drove you and the children here. I saw him out in the corral this morning when I rode in, and without knowing anything about him, I liked the way he has with horses. So I've offered him a job as one of my riders."

"That was kind of you, Lucien Edmond."

"I need good men. I lost a few on this last drive to Abilene. Grandmother says you're not sure about going back to Pittsburgh."

Ben Wilson nodded. "There are capable doctors to take my place at the clinic, and the work's going well there. Besides, after—after what happened, I've a feeling I'd like to start all over again, somewhere where there's even more need for a doctor's skill and services than in a big place like Pittsburgh."

"I may know of such a spot," Lucien Edmond replied. "Have you any prejudice against Indians?"

"Prejudice? You're forgetting I'm a Quaker. The shoe

has always been on the other foot, if you've read your history." He smiled faintly. "Usually it's the other people who are prejudiced against us. And besides, the Indians were the first settlers in this country. From all I've been able to learn, and certainly from what Fleurette told me about your father and your great-grandfather, they had a rich, strong civilization before we began to corrupt them. It was the white man who brought them all the advantages of our so-called progressive society, like diseases and indiscriminate slaughter, and the dishonest treaties that stripped them of their land."

"I'm glad you feel that way, Ben. You see, I met the chief of the Creeks in Indian territory and I came to know him pretty well. He's got about two hundred men, women, and children on that reservation, entirely dependent upon a slipshod government agent who doesn't really care whether their rations arrive on time. There's a fort that supervises them from a distance, and the soldiers make them feel like penned-in animals. Their chief, Emataba, speaks English well, and so do several of his braves. He's been able to keep up their morale and give them courage, but he can't do a thing when sickness strikes them, after a bad winter or a drought when they haven't been able to do any hunting. Of course, the only weapons they have are their lances and bows and arrows. The soldiers won't allow them to keep guns."

"It's tragic. But it seems to me that, as this part of the country expands and more settlers come to it, the Indians will be pushed farther and farther away, into still less desirable regions. Maybe that's one way of exterminating them without having it on one's conscience."

Lucien Edmond abruptly rose from the couch, his eyes sparkling with interest. "Perhaps you'd consider spending a little time in their village, Ben, if that's the way you feel. You'd be useful, and you'd be busy, I guarantee you that. We gave them a good bull, and some heifers and cows, so they'd have meat and milk, and I plan to send them, several times a year, what food I can, along with blankets and things like that to make their life a little easier. But they don't have a doctor. And their medicine man is dead."

"I think I'd like that. But the children—"

"That's no problem. You know that grandmother's tickled pink to have Thomas and Sybella here with her. You can leave them here, they'll be cared for just as dearly as—I'm sorry—I didn't mean—"

"That's all right, Lucien Edmond." Ben smiled and gripped his brother-in-law's hand. "I can cope with it now. And Fleurette would want me to be useful." Then, more gravely, "In a way, I'd hate to be away from Thomas. I've tried to help him understand why Fleurette isn't here, but it's hard."

"You leave that to Maxine and grandmother, Ben. Besides, Carla and Hugo are very sensible children for their age, and I'm sure they'll make Thomas feel at home. And I'll have Joe or Andy whittle him some new toys. He'll be so absorbed with all that he won't have time to miss you too much."

"God bless you, Lucien Edmond. Now then, how do I get to this Creek village?"

"I'm afraid it'll have to be by horseback and it's a long ride. A good six hundred miles, maybe more. Of course, I'll send a couple of vaqueros with you. With winter only a couple of months away, it's going to be much colder than it gets down here near the border. I want to send more blankets along anyway, and some potatoes and produce we've been able to raise for ourselves."

"Fine! I'll leave whenever the riders are ready."

"There's a man there I want you to meet—a Franciscan, Friar Bartoloméo Alicante. It's true he's a Catholic, as I am, but he has such compassion for, and understanding of, all people that you and he will hit it off at once. And I think maybe he'll be of help to you, as well as you to him."

Ben Wilson nodded. "It will be a challenge, Lucien Edmond. I'm grateful to you for suggesting it. Right now I need a new purpose, one where I can be wanted and needed. Now I'll go have a chat with Thomas and tell him all about the Indians." He uttered a rueful little laugh, "I'd better not make it *too* colorful, or the next thing I know he'll be insisting I take him with me."

CHAPTER THIRTY-FIVE

It had been a halcyon summer for Luke Bouchard at Windhaven Plantation. His only real fear had been that Laure might find the comparatively sedate and regularized life too monotonous for her taste, after the glitter and excitement of New Orleans. More than that, he had been worried that the twenty-five-year difference in their ages, combined with the placid life of a gentleman farmer's wife, might make her restless and, in time, regret her decision to come to the red-brick château on the Alabama River. She had known the demanding challenge of helping to run the bank. Now, she had to settle for a life of domesticity in which little Lucien and Paul required increasingly more of her attention, as did the smooth running of the household of which she had insisted on taking almost complete charge.

Yet he had been very pleasantly surprised to find his gloomy apprehensions completely unfounded. Not only was Laure enthusiastic about all the affairs of the plantation, but she had made friends with his white and black workers alike, showing not the slightest partiality to any particular one and yet genuinely interested in all, their families and their welfare. Even Buford Phelps was impressed when she stopped to talk about politics and the still-tangled problems of readjustment which the North was imposing upon the South. She also complimented him on the flourishing yield from the garden he had planted. Luke had encouraged him, understanding that a man gives his best when he is given a free hand to carry out his own ideas with only token supervision.

Once again there was a demand for cotton, though the price wavered between twelve and thirteen cents a pound —a low price when one considered the prewar prices. Yet

Luke Bouchard had no intention of devoting his combined acreage solely to that crop, which had originally been the South's making, and then its ruin. Crops of vegetables and fruits were now thriving in the rich soil. From the hundred head of cattle, Luke had been able to sell milk and cream to the new dairy near Montgomery. Some of the cattle had been slaughtered and brought a good price from the local butchers, since the meat was of prime quality.

By now, all of Luke's black workers, who had purchased their original fifty acres and agreed to be full and equal partners with him in this new enterprise, had resold their land to him. In return, Luke had drawn up contracts guaranteeing them not only steady wages but also a percentage of the gross profits to which all their efforts contributed.

Finally, if Luke Bouchard, beginning a new life as he was at the age of fifty-three, had worried that his twenty-eight-year-old wife must eventually see in him an aging man who was more father than lover, he had been ecstatically disabused of such a notion. Many an afternoon, he and Laure saddled horses and rode out along the fringes of the six hundred and forty acres. And often, especially at twilight, they stopped by the side of the towering bluff where old Lucien and Dimarte lay buried. There, to Luke's delight, Laure would often signal to him to dismount and tether his horse and hers to a tree, and then take him by the hand and lead him to a secluded little glade, hidden from view by cedar and cypress trees, where they caressed.

It was a bucolic life, in many ways similar to that of those early days when life had been serene and uncomplicated, when old Lucien Bouchard had shared his profits with the Creeks and found life good and rewarding. Yet Luke, for all the joy which this new life brought him, did not deceive himself over the bitter facts that were the aftermath of reconstruction.

Although the Ku Klux Klan had been officially outlawed, it had disbanded only perfunctorily. It still hounded the radical Northern Republican puppets, the Scalawags and Carpetbaggers who, the Klan believed, had scourged the conquered South by foisting "black equality" upon reputable and honorable whites. Perhaps worst of all, Congress had failed to act on the amnesty question the year before, so that men who had genuinely opposed secession in 1860, then cooperated with the Confederacy only as far as their honest convictions would permit, and were now fully willing to accept Reconstruction, had not yet been exempted from the stringencies of the Fourteenth Amendment. In Luke's opinion, if the amnesty question had been settled, loyal and decent men who knew the workings of state goverment could be returned to office, and they could sensibly banish the dread specter of the Klan for all time. As it was, these loyal whites were denied a chance to form a permanent Republican organization in Alabama, and thus Carpetbaggers and Scalawags controlled that national party in the South as they had done since 1867. The Klan had accomplished, in part, one of its scurrilous purposes. Blacks, terrorized by its nocturnal raids and violent reprisals, were not yet sufficiently organized to demand concessions from the whites as the price for their votes.

Finally, the balance between native sons and newcomers had been permanently upset after the presidential election of the previous year, when the Scalawags received strength from many prominent Alabama Democrats who, concluding that political survival necessitated a change in their affiliations, had swallowed the bitter pill of condemnation by their neighbors and defected to the Republican party.

Most prominent among these men of ability who had defected was Lewis E. Parsons, who had served as provisional governor of Alabama in 1865, and then been elected United States senator, only to be refused his seat by a vindictive Congress. The year before, he had led the Alabama delegation to the Democratic National Convention and actively campaigned for Horatio Seymour. During the current summer, he spoke frequently at gatherings in eastern Alabama, endorsing the course of Governor Smith and urging Alabamians to free their state from the Carpetbaggers who misrepresented them. From authoritative sources, Luke had heard that Parsons was preparing to endorse the Republican party and blame the Democrats for all the evils resulting from the war. That action, Luke knew, would infuriate the underground members of the

Klan and doubtless cause them to threaten once again all those who believed in the equality of white and black.

Remembering how Hurley Parmenter, the Lowndesboro storekeeper, had, as a prominent member of the Klan, kidnapped Marius Thornton and threatened him with death by fire, Luke had been particularly vigilant in recent months. He sent some of his most trusted and loyal workers into town to buy supplies, and in the course of their conversation with the storekeepers, they learned how the wind was blowing—whether there was any rumor that the Klan continued to function actively. Even now, in the last week of July, Luke had not heard of a single visit by any of these cowardly night riders against any black or white dwelling in the vicinity. Yet, perhaps because life was going so smoothly and he found himself enjoying what amounted to a glorious second honeymoon with a lovely young woman, he had the sense that this might only be the calm before some, as yet unsuspected, but gathering, storm.

Mitzi Vourlay, who had come to Windhaven Plantation with Laure as nursemaid to little Lucien and Paul, had conscientiously devoted herself to the two children. Part of this, to be sure, was her awareness of her feelings for Luke Bouchard. As Mitzi observed the deepening love between her mistress and Luke, she experienced pangs of envy. Yet, without Laure's aid, she had unknowingly met someone whom she respected and admired. Often, when Dan Munroe drove to the little town of Lowndesboro to buy provisions for the plantation, Mitzi accompanied him, with a list of necessities to be had from the general store.

Just ten days after Laure and Mitzi arrived at Windhaven Plantation, Mitzi had gone on just such an errand. When she entered the store, a tall man in his late forties emerged from the back room and greeted her. "Good morning, miss. How may I serve you?"

Mitzi, always sympathetic toward the handicapped, immediately noticed that the left sleeve of his cambric shirt was rolled up and tied just below his shoulder. He wore a cravat, neatly pressed gray trousers, and his quiet courtesy at once reminded her of Luke Bouchard. She gave him the list of supplies, and watched with growing admiration as, despite his handicap, he moved swiftly from section to section, picking out the items.

As she was paying for the supplies, he startled her by suddenly saying in French, "*C'est un grand plaisir pour moi de servir une si belle demoiselle.*"

"*Monsieur parle français avec un accent parfait, vraiment!*" she exclaimed.

With a gentle smile he informed her, still in her native tongue, "My wife, you see, was French, from Rouen."

"And I, monsieur, my parents were born in Cannes. *Moi*, my name is Mitzi Vourlay."

Still in French he replied, "And I am Dalbert Sattersfield, *à vôtre service.*"

Dan Munroe came into the store to collect the supplies and carry them out to the wagon. But Mitzi Vourlay lingered, enchanted to have found someone who could speak her native tongue so fluently. She found his features as appealing as his manners. His neatly trimmed black hair was gray at the temples, and his slightly graying side-burns emphasized the sensitivity of his face. He had high cheekbones, with firm jaws and chin, but his mouth had a frank, almost sensuous fullness to it. His nose was sharply aquiline, his eyes a warm blue. He wore neither mustache nor beard and, though he was an inch under six feet in height, to petite Mitzi he seemed as tall and distinguished as Luke Bouchard.

"I should like to meet your wife, Monsieur Sattersfield," she commented eagerly.

Dalbert Sattersfield looked down at the counter, then quietly responded, "Alas, Mademoiselle Vourlay, I regret that is not possible. She died four years ago, of pneumonia."

"Oh, forgive me, I didn't know—"

"Of course not, Mademoiselle Vourlay." He smiled sadly. "I lost my arm at Gettysburg, and I would have gladly lost both of them if I could have saved Odile."

Impulsively, the black-haired young woman put out her hand to touch his. "I am so sorry, Monsieur Sattersfield. Perhaps—perhaps you might like to meet my mistress, Madame Bouchard; and Monsieur Luke Bouchard. I will ask them to invite you *pour le dîner* some evening. We are at Windhaven Plantation, *vous savez.*"

"You do me too much honor, Mademoiselle Vourlay. I am only a humble storekeeper."

"You mustn't say such a thing." Again Mitzi's impulsive and generous nature asserted itself. "When I tell my mistress what a fine gentleman you are and how reasonable the prices are at your store, I know she will want to meet you and so will her husband. Besides," she said with a roguish little smile, "I know it will be good for your business. I will tell Madame Bouchard that from now on we should do all our—*comment dit-on*—buying here."

"You are most kind, Mademoiselle Vourlay." Then, to Mitzi's delight, he had taken her hand, brought it to his lips, and kissed it as he might that of a princess, and then come around the counter to hold the door open for her and to wish her good-day.

Mitzi Vourlay kept her promise. When she returned, she excitedly described Dalbert Sattersfield to Laure Bouchard in such glowing terms that the golden-haired young woman tapped her on the cheek playfully and replied, "Of course I'll invite Mr. Sattersfield here for supper. Now confess, you little minx, that it's not just because you feel sorry for his having lost his wife, and his arm in the war, or the fine quality of merchandise and modest prices which concern you. Do you know what I think, *ma petite?* I think that here may be the man who will win that silly heart of yours."

Mitzi blushed furiously and protested. But, a week later, when Sattersfield came to supper at Laure's own invitation, it was quite obvious that the soubrette hung on the storekeeper's every word and constantly urged him to take a second helping, observing that he was much too thin.

Luke, delighted and amused at Mitzi's obvious interest in Sattersfield, welcomed the opportunity to make an ally in Lowndesboro. After he and his guest retired to the study for brandy and cigars, Luke remarked, "Mr. Sattersfield, it was a pleasure meeting you, and I much appreciate your kindness toward Miss Vourlay. I'm very pleased, too, with the way you handled my wife's order, and I assure you that I'll be a steady customer. Now then, you can do me a service, if you will."

"It would be my pleasure, Mr. Bouchard."

"I know that you acquired the store after the death of Hurley Parmenter. You may or may not know that he was one of the leaders of the bands of rabble-rousers who are called the Ku Klux Klan."

"I have been told that, sir."

"Then you know what atrocities those men are committing in the name of saving the war-torn South."

"I do, Mr. Bouchard, and I have absolutely no sympathy with their actions. I myself had a plantation in Tuskegee, not a large one, with about fifteen slaves, but I manumitted them before the Emancipation Proclamation. My father was of the same persuasion, except that he did not dare do that openly."

"I understand. My own grandfather detested the concept of slavery, as I do myself. But what I'm getting at, Mr. Sattersfield, is that it would be very valuable to me if you would keep your eyes and ears open in town and let me know if you hear of any news—even rumors, sir— of the existence of those bigoted and vicious men who take the law into their own hands. You see, some time ago my foreman, Marius Thornton, was kidnapped by the Klan and was told that they would burn him if I did not join their ranks. My men drove them off, and I've heard and seen nothing of them since. But I know that with the political turmoil which exists, they have appeared in other parts of this state, even though they've been outlawed."

"I've heard of that too, sir. At the moment, there's nothing I can tell you as far as Lowndesboro's concerned, but I promise to get word to you if I do hear anything."

CHAPTER THIRTY-SIX

Besides his concern over the possibility that the Klan would reappear to seek reprisal against him for the death of their leader, Luke Bouchard kept to himself the uneasy feeling that a ghost he thought forever laid to rest might return to imperil the harmonious existence on Windhaven Plantation. He had, of course, maintained a regular correspondence with Jason Barntry, who was now in charge of the Brunton and Associate Bank. At Laure's suggestion, he had written to Barntry that Laure and he authorized and, indeed, requested that the name of the bank now be changed to Brunton and Barntry. It was a tangible reward for Jason Barntry's unswerving loyalty and banking acumen, which had made the institution, founded in the days of old Lucien Bouchard, one of the strongest and most solvent financial houses in New Orleans.

Barntry had written to Luke about Henri Cournier's visit to the bank, when the Creole had withdrawn all of his dead brother's money and the contents of the latter's safe deposit box. For Luke, who had not known that Armand Cournier had a brother, this news had been troubling. Barntry wrote that Henri had just returned from Haiti, and that he had come to New Orleans after having received the news of his brother's death. Luke could only speculate as to whether Henri Cournier was obsessed, as Armand had been, with the desire for vengeance against the Bouchards.

Luke Bouchard had read enough history and philosophy to know that happiness tends to lull a man's apprehensions in the face of unsuspected dangers, whereas actual adversities sharpen his wits and forearm him against future contingencies. It was not easy to forget the almost demented hatred which suave Armand Cournier had displayed. Thus, Jason Barntry's letter had aroused Luke's wariness. The existence of another Cournier might well mean a continuation of the irrational but deadly feud. It was possible that Henri believed, as had Armand, that it had been Jean de Bouchard (old Lucien's brother) who had called the Courniers' grandfather out in a duel to avenge his honor and cripple him for life. Clinging to this belief, Armand had sworn to bring down all those who bore the hated name of Bouchard. Naturally, Luke reasoned, if Henri was Armand's brother, the former would surely be aware of the family feud and might even seek to continue it. For that reason, as soon as he received Barntry's letter, Luke had told his workers to exercise more than usual vigilance, particularly at night, and to keep their weapons at the ready. Dan Munroe had volunteered to patrol at night to make sure that there were no prowlers lurking near the red-brick château.

But it was the first week of August, 1869, and so far there had been no word of Henri Cournier. Luke had concluded at last that Armand's older brother had gone back to his plantation in Haiti, having learned the truth about the duel and decided that there was no point in pursuing this nearly century-old animosity.

His work in the fields, his frequent trips to Montgomery, and, above all, his happy marriage, had kept him from making a trip to New Orleans to see Jason Barntry. Besides, Barntry's regular, monthly reports of deposits, investments, and profits obviated any real need for such a visit. Moreover, summer was not the ideal time to spend in New Orleans, for there was always the ever-present danger of yellow fever. Yet this morning, at breakfast, he had promised Laure that, with the first cool days of fall, they would both spend a week or two in New Orleans as a kind of vacation. "Besides, my darling, it's time you bought yourself some new dresses and gowns. I've been thinking that we should have a homecoming party for our friends and neighbors, and it's been rather long delayed."

"That would be wonderful, Luke!" she exclaimed, rising from the table and coming into his arms to give him a lingering kiss. "But I can see right through you, you're so transparent. You think that I'm bored to tears as the mistress of a plantation and that I miss the excitement and the glitter of New Orleans. To tell you the truth, at first I thought I might miss them just a little—but I don't. It's exciting to be with you, and I find I'm not nearly so sophisticated as I once thought I was. It's so peaceful here, with these friendly people who are like family working with us and for us and sharing our lives."

"You've made me very happy, Laure, beyond my fondest hopes. I promise you I'll try never to grow dull and really old—you won't let me, I know that," Luke told her with a happy little laugh as he kissed her. They stood, locked in each other's arms, oblivious, for the moment, to everything else around them. Hannah Atbury, who had come out of the kitchen to ask Laure a question about supper, retreated discreetly. "It does my heart good to see Mr. Luke and Miz Laure so happy with each other. Never thought when those awful Ku Klux Klaners took Phineas and me out and whipped us that we'd ever live to see folks so happy and peaceful again. Thank the Lord God for all His blessings!"

Hannah's husband, Phineas Atbury, had gone out toward the dock that morning. He had never quite recovered his strength from the flogging he had received from the Klan; still there was a faint breeze near the river, and the warm sunlight buoyed his spirits. He had heard the shrill whistle of the *Alabama Belle* a few minutes earlier, and, in his post as steward, was anxious to collect any mail there might be. Marius Thornton had also hurried out of the little house he shared with Clementine. With him came two black workers who would help unload some of the supplies which Luke had ordered from Mobile—garden tools, seed, and egg crates. Clementine had suggested to Luke that she raise hens and chickens to add eggs and fryers to Windhaven Plantation's trade in Montgomery and Lowndesboro. Luke had approved of the idea.

Marius beamed with ill-concealed joy as he caught up with Phineas and put an arm around his shoulders. "Take it easy now, Phineas. Sun's hot today in spite of that breeze, and I've got two strong men with me to cart off the goods Mr. Luke ordered."

"I'll just get the mail and bring it to Mr. Luke. What makes you so chipper this morning, boy?" Phineas asked.

Marius burst into hearty laughter. "Well, you'd feel

mighty chipper, too, if you'd just found out you were going to have another baby by Christmas."

Phineas stopped and turned to look at Marius, a broad smile on his face. "Well, I never! Guess you've got a right to be smiling. All right, now, the steamboat's just about at the dock. You go on ahead and do all the hard work. Me, I'll bring the most important thing there is, the letters for Mr. Luke."

"All right, I'll let you feel good this morning. Wouldn't want to rile even my worst enemy after news like Clementine just gave me!" Marius chuckled as he gestured to his two companions to quicken their pace toward the dock and be ready to take the unloaded cargo from the stevedores.

Captain Horace Tenby came down the gangplank and stepped out on the landing dock. He shook hands with Marius and then with Phineas. "I've got a couple of letters for Mr. Bouchard, Phineas," he greeted the old steward. "You're looking a mite better."

"*Feeling* a mite better too, Captain Tenby," Phineas replied. "Just like old times. Everything's just fine now, captain. Thanks for the letters and good luck to you."

"And to you, Phineas. Soon as I unload the rest of my cargo up at Montgomery, I'll be coming back this way. Marius, you figure you'll have anything ready for Mobile?"

"I'll ask Mr. Luke. We just might have a load of melons and the rest of that cotton. The June weather wasn't too good for it; that's why it's a mite late this year."

"Then I'll be sure to stop. Give Mr. Luke and his wife my best; don't forget now." Horace Tenby smiled and touched his cap, then went back up the gangplank.

"I'll hurry back with these letters. They look mighty important, all the way from New Orleans," Phineas Atbury commented to the young foreman. Marius, despite his authority over the other workers, did his full share of the toting and carrying of the various boxes and crates the stevedores had just set down on the dock.

When he reached the château, Phineas went directly into Luke Bouchard's study, to find the latter sitting at his writing desk. His employer was finishing a letter to Lucien Edmond, and he turned to greet Phineas. "I see you've brought the mail. That was very thoughtful, Phineas. Thank you."

The old man straightened his shoulders and proudly, gratefully replied, "That's my job here, Mr. Luke. When I can't do my job no more, you'd best kick me off this place."

Luke Bouchard shook his head as he rose to take the letters from the steward's hand. "That'll never happen in my lifetime, Phineas. You and Hannah mean a great deal to me. Without your courage and your wife's writing me in New Orleans, I might never have been able to get back grandfather's wonderful home. And the men and women who are your friends, Phineas, have become my finest workers."

There were tears in Phineas Atbury's eyes which he tried to conceal by blinking rapidly and coughing. Then he grumbled, "That old steamboat sure raised a mess of smoke comin' down the river, Mr. Luke. Must've got in my nose and eyes. But it's mighty nice for you to say such things to me. Hannah 'n me, we couldn't never find anyone nicer to work for, nor that sweet lady, Miz Laure."

"Thank you, Phineas. I'll tell Laure what you said. It'll make her very happy. Now then, did Captain Tenby say he was going to stop here on the way back from Montgomery?"

"He sure did, Mr. Luke. Marius told him you'd prob'ly have cotton 'n maybe melons and stuff like that for him."

"That's right. Good. If you like, Phineas, I'll entrust you with this letter for Texas. Captain Tenby can take it along when he stops back in a few days."

"I'll take right good care of it; you can depend on it. Mornin' to you, Mr. Luke," Phineas beamed again, nodded and took the letter, then slowly left the study.

Luke watched him go, and shook his head in compassion. Poor old man. His spirit had been just about broken by the brutal flogging those cowards had given him. One of these days, Luke thought to himself, he'd have Dr. Medbury come down from Montgomery and look Phineas over. And he'd have a private word with Hannah and tell her to try to fatten her husband up. Phineas was much too thin these days.

There were three letters, one from Sybella, another from Jason Barntry which would be the report of the bank's July business, and a third with an official seal on the back of the envelope which showed it to be from the city hall in New Orleans. He closed the door of his study, put the other two letters to one side and, seating himself, swiftly opened the New Orleans letter. As he read it he began to frown, his lips tightening incisively. It was as if the vague presentiment, lurking in the back of his mind, had inevitably led to this crystallization of his worst fears.

July 22, 1869

Dear Mr. Bouchard:

First may I extend my heartfelt thanks for the unexpected and beautiful gift you sent to me last Christmas. The matched dueling pistols in their red velvet case are indeed collector's items, and because they have a particular significance for both of us, you know that I shall cherish them as a mark of the deep friendship I bear you.

My apologies are more than in order for the lateness of this acknowledgment of receipt, but the honest fact is that political events in this city have been so swiftly moving and so drastic as to compel my full attention. Indeed, it was my real wish to visit you and your beautiful wife to express my thanks in person and to see the magnificent château where your illustrious grandfather began his new life of such lofty purpose and noble aim as to demand the admiration of every citizen who believes in justice and equality.

I know these sound like high-flown words, and perhaps there is a tinge of bitterness in my use of them. What I am getting at, my dear friend, is that I am being deposed from office as deputy chief of the civil guards. The Carpetbaggers from the North have spread their poison, and they have incited many influential and wealthy citizens to demand my ouster on the grounds that as a Southerner who had naturally been loyal to the Confederacy—though in no way did I take up arms or act seditiously toward the present conquerors—I do not deserve to hold public office. By the time this letter reaches you, I shall have retired, though I am not quite fifty. I have been toying with the idea of going to California and seeing if I could be of service there in a growing young territory where law and order are certainly required.

Now, to the serious point. I was proud to be your second in that duel against Armand Cournier, whom I regarded as one of the most dangerous scoundrels of our city. But you may not know—as I did not until only about two months ago—that a brother survived him. That brother is Henri Cournier, and from what information I have been able to gather in this short time, I begin to believe that he may be an even more dangerous and unmitigated rogue than the man who broke the dueling code against you.

As the sole survivor of the Cournier family and the next of blood kin, Henri Cournier naturally received through probate court order his brother's estate and fortune. He is presently residing at Three Oaks, just as Armand Cournier did. My agents have reported that several disreputable men have been visiting, and two have been identified as former members of that vicious and unprincipled hoodlum gang who call themselves the Ku Klux Klan. Lately, we have had reports of depredations against white Republicans in this state, as well as in Georgia and eastern Alabama. Just last week, my agents arrested, and were forced to kill when their prisoner put up armed resistance, a man who was smuggling cases of repeating rifles destined for the leader of a Georgia Klan group.

My object in telling you all this is not to alarm you, but to urge you to maintain the utmost vigilance. I remember well what you told me of Armand Cournier's warped desire to avenge himself on the Bouchard family. Understand me, I have no proof that Henri Cournier contemplates any resumption of harm and malfeasance toward you or any other members of your family, but knowing the breed, I urge you to be on your constant guard.

My successor in this office will be one of those

407

*Radical Republicans who profited, ironically enough,
by smuggling contraband during the late hostilities.
I have already given him the dossier on Henri
Cournier and his known associates, but I very much
doubt that he will take any action. I say this because one of my loyal agents, just last night, came
to my house to tell me that he had seen my successor
and Henri Cournier going to the opera. You may
draw your own conclusions.*

*I wish you and your family every happiness and
joy. If I am successful in finding a post that suits
me in California, I shall let you hear from me. Till
then, may God be with you.*

Your friend,

Arthur Traylor

As he put down the letter, Luke Bouchard felt a sudden
chill and noticed that his hands were trembling. It begins
all over again, he thought. Evil that I thought was buried
in the past, with the death of one man, may now be dis-
interred. Are the living, then, not content to let the dead
rest and with them all the misunderstandings and hatreds
which can shadow an otherwise honorable man's life?

He rose from his desk, his hands clasped behind him,
his face grave and lined with anxiety. To face a man on
the dueling ground, though by nature and conviction he
did not hold with killing, was one thing. At least it was
direct and forthright, and, although it went against all
dictates of conscience, it had the sanction of the law. But
how could one fortify oneself against nameless fears,
secret and insidious plots which the rational mind could
only grudgingly accept as pure conjecture and even fan-
tasy? Could one set a twenty-four hour armed guard
around Windhaven Plantation and yet be sure that so
ruthless and cunning an enemy might not find some way
to breach even such a wall of sentries? The thought which
most tormented him was the question of how far Henri
Cournier's baleful influence might be spread and whether,
indeed, the thwarted vengeance of Armand Cournier
might be revived with even greater malevolence against

the other members of the Bouchard family. What did Henri Cournier know of his family? Did he know that Lucien Edmond was in Texas, or that Laurette, who had been a Bouchard before her marriage to Charles Douglas, was in Chicago, or Fleurette in Pittsburgh? Thus he, Luke Bouchard, was left without a clue as to where and when and how this new enemy might strike.

Restlessly he paced the study, and then stopped suddenly, remembering. Fate had its strange coincidences and, somehow, in the overall pattern, they seemed inseparably linked. The pathetic letter from Hannah Atbury addressed to John Brunton had led him to realize his dream of regaining Windhaven Plantation—but also it had brought in its wake the abduction and near death of his foreman, in a plot that had been fomented by Armand Cournier. Now another unexpected letter informed him that yet another Cournier was alive and involved in dark conspiracies, conspiracies that could involve not only Windhaven Plantation, but perhaps Windhaven Range, also.

As he stood staring at the letter on the desk, his thoughts, now honed by the fear of danger to his loved ones, brought him a new recollection almost forgotten. Early in February, about ten days after Laure's arrival from New Orleans, his workers had brought in from the fields the old conjure woman, Ellen, who had been mercilessly whipped by Klansmen in Attisburg. She had dragged herself all those agonizing miles to seek refuge. And when he had stood at her bedside, she had told him that she had seen a dark cloud coming down over little ones dear to him.

Little ones dear to him—little Lucien and baby Paul. . . . Now he remembered it all clearly. Of course the vengeance would be directed at him, first, and what better way to effect it than to endanger the lives of those children who would be his heirs?

His mind whirling with all the chaotic thoughts which this letter from New Orleans had evoked, Luke Bouchard sank down on his knees, bowed his head, and clasped his hands. He prayed to his Creator as old Lucien Bouchard himself might have prayed, not to ease his life by ridding him of this unforeseen danger, but rather to give him the courage and the skill to anticipate and defeat it. When he had finished, he left the château, saddled his horse, and rode to the conjure woman's cabin.

Ellen had recovered from the Klan's beating within a few weeks, although she would bear the scars of that whipping to her grave. Her stamina and courage had amazed Luke, and he had ordered a small cabin built for her on the northeastern edge of his acreage. Luke knew that Hannah and Mary spent much time with her during those early weeks, and they had expressed amazement at the speed of her determined recovery. As soon as she could walk about, she had started her own garden, and Luke had made a special point of selling some of the melons that she raised and bringing her the proceeds. When she had thrown up her hands and protested that never in all her life had she had money of her own, Luke had promised to bank the money in her name and assured her that whenever she wished to spend it, she had only to ask him for it.

Now, as he approached the cabin, Luke saw Ellen, protected from the sun by a wide-brimmed straw hat, kneeling before the melon plants. She crooned to herself as she tended the small gourds. She saw his shadow fall beside her and looked up, then smiled and started to rise.

"No, no, Ellen, don't tire yourself, please," he said gently, touching her shoulder. "I'm very glad to see you're feeling better."

"I sure am, Mr. Bouchard, feelin' mighty spry for my old bones, yessir!" She nodded vigorously.

Luke knelt down beside her, his face grave, and took her hands in his. "Ellen, do you remember the night you came here to us?"

Her smile faded; she shivered and her eyes rolled nearly to the whites as she muttered, "Can't never forget that night, Mr. Bouchard. My back still give me misery some nights, yessir."

"I'll have Hannah get you some more healing salve. And you mustn't work so hard in this hot sun, either. Promise me you won't. You've earned your keep, Ellen, and I'm grateful for what you've done, to come here and warn us about those wicked men."

"It was my bounden duty, sir. It sho' was. You're awful

410

kind to old Ellen. God goin' t' bless you for that, you'll see."

"I pray that He will, and you, too, Ellen. Now try to remember what it was you said when I talked to you that night, after you'd been put to bed and your hurts cared for. Do you remember saying that you saw a dark cloud coming down over little ones dear to me?"

Again she shivered, again her eyes rolled almost to the whites as she nodded, then clutched his hand in both of hers. "That's right! I'se seen it agin in my dream, not just once, but three, maybe four, times since I come here, Mr. Bouchard."

"I wanted to be sure, Ellen. And then, I remember your saying that one of the little ones would run and the other would be swallowed up by the cloud and carried off."

"That's right agin!" The white-haired woman nodded, her bony fingers gripping his hand with unexpected strength. "Every time I had that dream, Mr. Bouchard sir, I seen that cloud movin' west and then there's a big rainbow and the cloud is gone. That's the truth, I seen it plain as day."

He stood, staring at her for a long moment, then nodded solemnly. "God bless you for telling me, Ellen. I'm not sure yet what it means, but I think I'm beginning to understand it for the first time."

"But you done forgot the most 'portant part, Mr. Bouchard!" Ellen exclaimed, again clutching at his hand with all her strength. "You has to give them little ones a sign, a mark so's you'll see 'em again and keep 'em close to you. That way, when the dark cloud grabs one, you're goin' t' find him at the rainbow. Don't forget that, please, sir!"

He put his other hand against hers and nodded, smiling. "I won't forget. And thank you again, Ellen. Now, promise me you'll rest. I'll ask Hannah to bring you some good soup with plenty of meat in it tonight, and more of that salve. And, you know what? I'm sending some of your best melons down to Mobile when the steamboat comes back this way, and you'll have more money in the bank to spend on whatever you want."

"God bless you for bein' kind, Mr. Bouchard, God bless you!" Impulsively, before he could prevent it, she had bowed her head and kissed his hand.

411

Luke Bouchard was deeply moved as he took his leave of her. Looking up, he saw the tall bluff fronting the river, and he stared at it, Ellen's words still ringing in his ears. "Mark them both, give them a sign so you will find them again."

The talisman. The talisman of Sangrodo. The great turquoise with its mysterious, smoky light in the very center, the talisman which had saved his life from that drunkard's bullet on his way back to New Orleans.

He looked up at the blue sky, and murmured to himself, "God has sent me this sign through the lips of the old conjure woman. This is not superstition, but rather a divine sign of how He has answered my prayer."

He crossed himself again, his lips moving silently. Then, mounting his horse, he rode toward the bluff. Tethering the horse to a tree, he ascended on foot by the same path he had so often taken to commune with old Lucien and Dimarte.

When he came to the site of their graves, Luke knelt down and prayed again. Then he spoke to old Lucien. "Once again, through your spirit, Grandfather, I am shown the way. When I brought the talisman of the Comanche chief to you, I could not know that I was meant to take it back, this time to safeguard the Bouchard name. I will return it to you, grandfather. From the heart of this stone, a symbol of the valor of the noblest of Comanches, who would have been proud to call you brother as did the mighty Creeks, I will have a jeweler cut but two tiny pieces. They will contain the heart of this symbol, and your great-grandsons, Lucien and Paul, shall wear them as symbolic talismans. Understand my momentary desecration of your grave, grandfather, and know that it pays new homage to all that you dreamed and worked for. And you, beloved woman, may your sweet spirit hover over the dark cloud which that frail old woman saw in her dream, and bring the light of the rainbow, as she foretold."

He bent his head and for a moment knelt in silence. Then, remembering where he had buried the turquoise, he unearthed it, smoothed the upturned earth back into place, turned, and went back down the path to where his horse was waiting.

So lost had he been in the mystic aura at the top of the

towering bluff that he did not even glance across the winding river. If he had, he would have seen two horsemen, one with a telescope leveled at the top of the last resting place of old Lucien Bouchard and his gentle Dimarte.

CHAPTER THIRTY-SEVEN

The man with the telescope chuckled, then handed it to his companion. "Take a look for yourself, Jack, just so's you'll recognize the son of a bitch when we get our orders," he said.

His companion, a short, heavyset man in his late thirties with an unkempt black beard and a porcine face, grunted assent and squinted through the telescope. "Yup, Arnie, I see him plain as day. Pretty good-sized fellow—looks like he might be able to handle hisself."

"We don't run up against him, that's Mr. C.'s orders, savvy?" Arnie Grimes sharply countered, pulling the telescope out of his companion's hand. "We're gittin' paid to do what he wants, and the pay's too damn good fer you to mess things up, you hear me?"

"Sure, sure, Arnie, don't get mad, now." The black-bearded man pacified him with a wheedling tone and a sly grin.

"What we do next is head down to Mobile. Mr. C. will be waiting for us there, just like he wrote. We tell him how we've been watchin' the house and the land, and how many niggers and such this Bouchard's got workin' fer him, and then we'll get our orders."

"Just like you say, Arnie. So we better get back to Attisburg, pack up our stuff, and get that *Alabama Belle* down to Mobile. It went on up to Montgomery this morning, so it'll be due back down there in about a week, I figger."

"That's right. For once, Jack Stallman, you're showin' some brains. Let's just hope for your sake you don't fergit to use 'em when the time comes."

"Aw, Arnie, you oughtn't to talk to me like that; it makes me feel bad," the fat man whined.

With a contemptuous laugh, Grimes wheeled his horse

and headed downriver. They found a point shallow enough to allow them to cross over to the eastern bank, then made their way to Attisburg.

Arnie Grimes was thirty, the bastard son of a poor, white sharecropper from Marion County. His father had actually been an indentured bondservant working for a wealthy plantation owner. His mother had been the pretty, youngest daughter of the town blacksmith. She had been all too willing to trade her virginity for the comforts of living in a handsomely furnished house, sleeping in her own bed, and eating meals the like of which she had never before enjoyed. When the plantation owner had tired of her and replaced her with one of her own sisters, Arnie's mother had begged her lover to make some provision for her future. She was only mildly jealous about her sister's replacing her. What frightened her was that there was no other situation for her in town, and her widowed father had already informed her that, since the plantation owner had no further need of her, he himself meant to have her fulfill the duties of his wife, who had died from overwork and too many pregnancies.

The plantation owner had not been a cruel man. He had torn up Hamer Grimes's indenture, sectioned off one of the least productive parts of his acreage, and ordered his former bondservant to work a portion of it as a sharecropper, the rest of that comparatively barren land being worked by black slaves. And he had ordered Grimes to take Mattie Yarborough as his woman, with or without benefit of clergy, as Grimes preferred.

Hamer Grimes had been so poor and dependent on his former master's bounty that he had not saved enough hard cash even to pay a minister's fee. Hence Mattie never received her marriage certificate. Arnie was born the next year, and Mattie died from childbirth fever a week after that. The embittered sharecropper replaced her with a black slave who brought Arnie up as if he were her own.

By the time the Civil War began, both the plantation owner and Hamer Grimes were dead. Arnie and his elderly and ailing surrogate mother continued to work the land for bare subsistence. When Reconstruction began, the land was sold to emancipated blacks, and Arnie Grimes was left homeless and orphaned, the black woman having died on the day that Robert E. Lee surrendered at Appomattox. Grimes moved to Attisburg, where he found work with an elderly cooper. There, too, he was initiated into the Ku Klux Klan. He brought to that secret society his own rage against the wealthy and the blacks—the wealthy, because his father had filled him with stories of the plantation owner's callous indifference to the poor whites, and the blacks, because Arnie had long brooded over being treated no better than they were. He had been a member of Hurley Parmenter's klavern. And he had been one of those who had helped abduct Marius Thornton.

After Parmenter's death and the official outlawing of the Klan, Arnie Grimes had gone back to Attisburg, this time to work as a clerk to a storeowner. It was there that Henri Cournier had found him. And it was to be Arnie who would become the instrument of Henri Cournier's avowed vengeance against Luke Bouchard.

Arnie Grimes glowered over his mug of rum and turned to scowl at the old grandfather clock on the wall of the squalid tavern. A quarter-inch over six feet in height, he had his mother's wiry, rawboned physique. His dirty, sun-bleached brown hair was gathered in a thick Indianlike braid at the nape of his neck and fell below his shoulder blades. His bushy beard and gaunt features, with deep-set eyes and hawklike nose, made him look like a traveling Baptist preacher who toured the circuit of provincial Southern villages, prophesying the imminent end of the world. Across the table, his companion eyed him nervously and tried to lighten his sullen mood. "Aw, Arnie, the steamboat's always late from N'Awleans. He's not gonna run out on us."

"That slick Frog had better not try a trick like that with Arnie Grimes, I'm telling you, Jack." Grimes bared his snaggly, decaying teeth in a twisted smile. "I'll tell you straight, I don't fancy that high 'n mighty Creole one God-damn bit. Thinks 'cause he's got money he can lord it over honest folks like us." He grinned again, this time slyly. "But he pays good, and what he's got in mind's likely to be good sport for both of us, Jack, so I'll put up with his snotty ways for now."

"I wonder why he's so keen to know what this Bouchard

feller's doin' all the time? Hell, Arnie, we've been campin' out along the river the last couple of months."

"He'll tell us when he gets here. Wait—that's him now! Now you just mind your manners, Jack, and lemme do all the talkin', see? I'm the one he hired first off, so that means he knows who's got the real brains."

Jack Stallman grumbled under his breath, gave his companion a spiteful look, then suddenly grinned from ear to ear as he rose from the table to greet the dapper Creole. Henri Cournier wore an elegant frock coat, cut in the very latest style, a long, stylish cravat, and a black silk hat. Although the weather had been ferociously humid in New Orleans, he looked cool and composed.

"Gentlemen, I'm glad to find you both here. Now, Arnie, have you drawn up the report I'm paying you for?" he asked without the slightest acknowledgment of the fat man as he seated himself at the table and snapped his fingers at the proprietor. "Your best rum—not the swill you usually serve in this filthy place, my good man." His tone of voice was cutting and arrogant.

The proprietor, a retired steamboat captain, saw at a glance that swift service would be far more profitable than an acrimonious reply. Accordingly, he nodded his head, hurried back, and returned with a mug of excellent Cuban rum, then stood waiting for approval.

Henri Cournier, arching his eyebrows, lifted the mug and took a tentative sip, a quizzical expression on his bearded face. "Not too bad. Now you may leave us."

The tavern keeper backed away, inclining his head. Cournier gripped the ivory knob of his walking stick with both hands and leaned forward. "Now then, sir, what have you learned about Luke Bouchard in the time that you've been spying on him?" he demanded of Grimes.

"Well, he's got two brats. I know, 'cause I've seen that yellow-haired wife of his take one of them for a walk and a fancy black-haired piece hold the other in her arms and walk alongside Bouchard's wife."

"That's most interesting," Cournier murmured, his eyes glinting with a malevolent light. "Now, as to the workers he's got on the land, how many would you say are there?"

"Like you told us, we've been watching everything that goes on around that big brick house of his for almost nine weeks now. Jack and me counted about a dozen, and mebbe half again as many womenfolk. We may be a couple of men off, but I don't rightly think so."

"Mmm." The dapper Creole shifted in his chair, frowning. "Do they seem to go into that big house of his much, did you notice?"

"Not a lot, Mr. C. Mostly, they've got their own cabins out there. Now, as to how many's in that house, I know there's an old nigger who opens the door, and Jack saw a nigger woman come out of the back—she must be the cook or something like that. He was way over on the creek side, using that there glass you gave us. Lots of times, we both seen a tall young nigger talkin' to that Bouchard feller. And once I seen that same nigger with a neat, high-yaller gal holdin' a baby in her arms. You know somepin', Mr. C.? Jack 'n me figgered Bouchard lets them live in that big house of his, damned if he don't. Now you *know* that's not right."

Henri Cournier picked up his mug of rum and sipped it fastidiously, then set it down again, hawked, and spat on the puncheon floor. "The first sip deceived me. This is really vile stuff, but it'll have to do. Now then, to business. Mr. Grimes, I've learned from reading my dead brother's correspondence that you were under the command of the late, lamented Hurley Parmenter."

Arnie Grimes gave him a crooked grin and a nod. "Right on the button, Mr. C. Nuttin' I like better than to put on that white sheet and scare hell out of those goddamn niggers who strut 'round thinkin' they're the equal of us white folks—why, by God, next thing you know, they'll be trying to *poke* our white women, yessir, our wives 'n daughters, 'n say it's their right under the law 'cause Abe the Ape set 'em free."

"I am convinced of the honesty of your sentiments, Mr. Grimes," Cournier retorted. "Now listen to me very carefully, both of you. I think it would be wise for you, Mr. Grimes, to engage another man as sturdy as your friend here to help in this affair."

"That's easy. I got a friend in Attisburg, name of Casey Meldrun, taller 'n I am, used to do some fist-fightin' fer hard cash. Knows how to handle hisself and keep his mouth shut, too, Mr. C."

The grimace on Cournier's face reflected his distaste for Grimes's shortening of his surname. He did not, however, deign to comment upon it, and continued, "If you're sure he can be trusted and will help, by all means engage him. Tell him that he'll be paid what your friend is getting. Now, let me tell you a bit more than you already know."

"I'm listenin' real good, Mr. C.," Arnie Grimes chuckled, then nudged Jack Stallman in the ribs and muttered, "Pay attention now, this is important, see?"

Again the grimace flickered over the Creole's face. Yet his voice showed no disdain, but rather a fierce, though controlled, intensity. "My grandfather, gentlemen, was left a cripple for life by the great-uncle of this Luke Bouchard whom I have had you keep under such constant surveillance. My own brother, a man of vision and rare intelligence, died at Luke Bouchard's hand in a duel which was forced upon him. Being an honorable man, he had no choice but to accept it—and Bouchard shot him down by firing a split second before the call to fire."

"Now that's downright scummy, that is, Mr. C.," Grimes spoke up. "I'd want to kill a son of a bitch like that myself, if he did that to my brother."

"Now, now, Mr. Grimes, restrain yourself. I don't want him killed. He has much on his conscience, and he's a learned, well-read man. Such a man, gentlemen, suffers much more when disaster strikes him than if a quick and merciful death puts an end to his agonies—you follow me, I hope?"

Arnie Grimes nodded, only half-understanding the Creole's rhetoric.

"Excellent!" Henri Cournier leaned back in his chair, a wry smile signifying that he was pleased with the way his henchmen were reacting. "I may tell you also that a cousin of my brother and myself, a gentleman of exquisite good taste who was well known in New Orleans, committed suicide because, when he sought to win the hand of Luke Bouchard's stepsister, this infernal meddler had the gall to accuse him of being a scoundrel, a gambler, and a liar. Because there were many armed slaves nearby, our poor cousin could not respond with a challenge of honor—and he loved Bouchard's stepsister so much that her loss crazed him into taking his own life. So you see, gentlemen, I have ample reason to hate Luke Bouchard."

"I'd say you have and then some, Mr. C.!" Arnie Grimes volunteered with a vigorous nod of his head. Jack Stallman chimed in, "Yessiree, me, I wouldn't have let him live this long if I'd been you, Mr. C."

"But you're not, Mr. Stallman, and I'll thank you to remember it," the bearded Creole tartly replied. "Mr. Grimes appears to understand how much more savory my vengeance will be if we allow Bouchard to live but to suffer irreparable loss. He brought shame upon the name which my grandfather handed down to us. He shall know shame, as well, in addition to that loss."

The two conspirators exchanged an uneasy glance, not following Henri Cournier's high-sounding drift. The latter leaned forward again, eager to clarify and simplify that objective. "Would you not think, gentlemen, that if a man were to lose his older son and to have his beautiful young wife ravaged and used, he would suffer much more than if he were to have a bullet put through his heart?"

"Sure he would, Mr. C.," Arnie Grimes agreed. "Now, sir, you might jist tell us what you mean by what you said about that purty wife of his—that's a word I ain't never heard before."

Henri Cournier looked around to make sure that no one but his two henchmen could hear him. Then he murmured, "I mean, gentlemen, that she is to be taken, her clothes ripped from her, and used the way you might use a whore in one of our New Orleans houses of pleasure. Do you understand that now?"

An unholy light glowed in Grimes's narrowed brown eyes. "You mean, you want us to really lay her, Mr. C.?"

Cournier almost shuddered. "That's it precisely. But that's actually the second and less important part of what you're to do. I want that older child taken from its parents. I want it brought to me in New Orleans."

"You—you're not going to kill the brat, are you?" Grimes asked hesitantly. Even for such a conscienceless rogue, such a thought was a stumbling block.

"Of course not! I am not a murderer, gentlemen, I simply seek to avenge the honor of our family name. No, that child will be adopted by a family in my employ and taken

420

across the plains to a distant place where he will never be found again by his father. Thus, as you can well imagine, throughout the rest of his life Bouchard will know nothing but agony and torture, wondering what has become of his firstborn, who might have otherwise inherited his name, his wealth, his land, and the fine house in which, up to now, he has been permitted to lead an untroubled existence."

"By God, Mr. C., I gotta hand it to you!" Arnie Grimes burst out. "Damned if I ever heard a neater way of payin' back a cowardly son of a bitch like that, damned if I did!"

There was a small smile of triumph on Cournier's compressed lips. "Now, as to the details, gentlemen. From your reports, it appears that Bouchard makes several trips a month to Montgomery and stays for a day or two. Obviously, it's to your advantage to have him away from that house of his. Also, make certain that the workers are in the fields. You must think of a way to gain entrance to the house without arousing suspicion. For example, Mr. Grimes, you might drive a wagon up and say that you have supplies that were ordered from Attisburg by Mr. Bouchard himself. The elderly black servant you've already mentioned would undoubtedly let you in—or at least open the door. I leave it to your ingenuity and skill to go on from there. You will take Mrs. Bouchard and abuse her—but do not harm her permanently in any way. A woman, gentlemen, is not a frail and delicate porcelain vase that shatters if it is bruised. Ah no." His lips curved in a sadistic smile. "I know myself of a very fashionable and dignified young woman, of excellent family background, who discovered that she did not die if a whip was used on her pampered white flesh nor if a manservant flung her down on the bed and used her—if you follow my meaning."

"I follow it real good, Mr. C." Grimes sniggered and winked at the dapper Creole. Jack Stallman licked his lips, belched, and nodded.

"One of you, at the very outset, will find the room in which these children are kept and will take the older boy. See to it that the fastest horses you can obtain are harnessed to the wagon. Once you've accomplished all this, let the man who takes the child go first, so as to outdistance any possible pursuers. Is that clear so far?" Satisfied by

421

Arnie Grimes's quick nod, he went on. "I think it would be well if the man who takes the child travels to New Orleans with a woman. It will seem as if the child is theirs."

"That's easy, Mr. C. Casey Meldrun has got a gal that's been pesterin' him to marry her for a coon's age, and she'd jump at the chance to go along as his wife, figgerin' he'd make it legallike once they got the brat to New Orleans."

"Very good, Mr. Grimes! You're beginning to show the sort of imagination I admire," the bearded Creole chuckled. "And you may tell this Casey that when he brings the child to me, I shall pay him $2,000."

Grimes gave a low whistle, and shook his head in admiration. "Old Casey'll take that brat all the way west hisself fer that sorta cash, Mr. C."

"No, he will not do that at all," Cournier interposed sharply. "I already have a loving pair trained for that assignment. Besides, once the Bouchard child is reported stolen, and if by some mischance this friend of yours should be described to the authorities, it would not be well for him to continue the journey with the child. Also, let me point out that he should make most careful arrangements to reach Mobile, and thence New Orleans. First of all, dress the child in different clothes, that's the first thing to do. Then I should suggest changing the color of the boy's hair. Finally, I should recommend not boarding any boat from here to Mobile, but rather going on horseback down there and then taking the ferry across to the dock, where the steamboat for New Orleans lies at anchor. It's true that it will take more time on horseback than by boat, but my guess is that Luke Bouchard would ask river captains if they saw a child answering the description of his missing son aboard any of their vessels."

"That's smart, that is, Mr. C.; it sure is!" Arnie enthused.

"The steamboat from Mobile to New Orleans, gentlemen, is usually the same one going and coming; it does not continue a journey up the Alabama River to Montgomery and then back to Mobile. Once your friend and his female companion reach Mobile, they may board the boat without much danger. They will then bring the child to the address I have written on this card." Taking out his wallet, he handed Grimes a card, then laid down several greenbacks in front of each man. "That's a kind of bonus, just to make sure that both of you give me your undivided loyalty."

"What about us, after it's all over, Mr. C.?" Grimes wanted to know.

Cournier frowned, lost in thought for a moment. Then he leaned forward and declared, "My feeling is that it would be wise for both of you to remain in Attisburg, as if absolutely nothing had happened. There should be no reason for Bouchard to suspect you. Even if he does, due to some unfortunate accident—which I trust you will see does not occur—" (this, in a tone of veiled warning and with narrowed eyes) "he can prove nothing. If, of course, he then becomes troublesome, and you have to defend yourselves against him, I cannot ask you to give up your lives."

"I gotcha, Mr. C., yessiree," Grimes smirked. "Why, if this Bouchard feller comes in, spoutin' off 'bout my bein' the cause of pesterin' his wife 'n takin' away his brat, I'll tell him he can go plumb to hell 'cause I ain't never seen him afore in my life. And then, should he git downright bothersome, I'll just slip my knife into his gizzard."

"That, of course, Mr. Grimes, would be only as a last resort, if you are forced to defend yourself to save your own life, you understand," Cournier retorted with a crafty smile. "Now both of you have it clear, I trust?" Seeing them both nod, he concluded. "There is no hurry in this matter. I have waited many months to pay Luke Bouchard back for his crimes against my family. Let it take a week, two weeks, a month even, so long as it is done neatly, without a trace of suspicion that would carry back to me. Or, of course, gentlemen, to you."

He rose abruptly, his face calm, and replaced his silk hat in the manner of a New Orleans dandy about to depart for an evening of pleasure. "I shall take the next steamboat to New Orleans. I suggest gentlemen, that you return to your posts and await the moment you consider best for the swift performance of your deeds. As soon as your friend and his female companion bring the child to me, I shall be in communication with you and reward you as I promised at the beginning of our acquaintance. Gentlemen, I bid you good-day."

CHAPTER THIRTY-EIGHT,

"Look there, Jack, that Bouchard feller's gittin' on the *Alabama Belle*. An' he's goin' upriver, jist like we wanted!" Arnie Grimes whispered to his companion. The two men huddled in a copse of mulberry bushes, high on the bank of the Alabama River across from the Windhaven wharf. "You go git on your horse and ride to Attisburg, 'n tell Casey to load up the wagon and harness up those three fast hosses we bought in Millersville. When it gets dark tonight, that'll be the best time. Sure as you're born, those niggers and white trash Bouchard's got workin' fer him in the fields'll be back in their cabins, and we'll jist walk into that big, fancy brick house easy as you please!"

"You gonna stay here a mite, Arnie?" Jack Stallman demanded as he began to crawl backward, toward the two horses tethered to an oak tree far behind the mulberry bushes.

"Just a spell, Jack. Now you git goin'. I jist wanna make sure that Bouchard feller don't change his mind and stay to home tonight! Wait until I get hold of that there yaller-haired bitch of his, won't I make her holler!" Arnie Grimes exulted.

"Hey now, Arnie, that's no fair—ain't I your partner, ain't I doin' my share of what Mr. C. asked us t' do? Why can't I give her a good, hard poke, too?" Jack Stallman asked.

" 'Cause I'm the one Mr. C. came all the way from N'Awleans to work this here deal out with, Jack, so you do jist like I tell you to if you want to git your money. Hell, you can buy all the fancy whores you've a mind to when you git your share."

"All right, I'm goin'," Stallman grumbled as he rose,

424

ran to his horse, mounted it, and then galloped back down-river.

Arnie Grimes squinted through the old telescope and grinned as he saw the tall figure of Luke Bouchard ascend the gangplank. His smile widened as he observed that young Marius Thornton was also making the journey to Montgomery. He waited until the stevedores had hauled up the gangplank, saw the waters churning as the paddle-wheels began to move, and chuckled as the *Alabama Belle* emitted its shrill blast to mark its departure. Then he got to his feet, mounted his horse, and rode in the direction Stallman had taken.

Luke Bouchard stood at the rail, waving good-bye to Laure, who held little Paul in her arms, while Lucien tugged impatiently at her skirt. Turning to Marius Thornton, he commented, "When we finish our business in town, I'm going to ask Dr. Medbury to come back with me and look old Phineas over. He's still quite weak and he seems to get thinner all the time."

"That's true, Mr. Bouchard," the handsome young foreman agreed. Clementine had come down to the wharf to see him off, carrying little Jasper in her arms. He paused to wave good-by to her and to blow her a kiss, then chuckled. "Guess I'll be a pappy again before the year's over, Mr. Bouchard. When I was in New Orleans, I never thought I'd live to see the day, especially that day you saved me from those riled-up Creoles." Then his face sobered as he added, "And I wouldn't be here today, either, if you hadn't come for me when the Klan dragged me off to the woods."

"You can forget the past, Marius; the future lies ahead for you—for all of us, I pray God," Luke answered. Even as he said those words, he sensed the irony of them. This long month of tense vigilance against the lurking menace of Henri Cournier had made him more somber than was his wont. Even Laure had begun to tease him about turning into an old sobersides again, and, though he had more than adequately silenced her wifely censure in the conjugal bed, he could not put aside his growing uneasiness.

Ten days ago, he had returned from Montgomery with

two gold chains, in the center of which hung an exquisitely chiseled triangular chip from the great turquoise stone which Sangrodo had given to him. Each of those chips had the sky-blue radiance of the stone itself; yet in the center of each was a greenish glow. He had placed the chains around his sons' necks, and when Laure, puzzled by this singular gift, had asked its meaning, he had explained, "Why, my dearest, it's only natural that a father should want his sons to have the same good luck he did. Sangrodo's talisman brought me to you, and you in turn gave birth to our sons and heirs, who will carry on the Bouchard name in the years to come. So what more appropriate gift could there be than for Lucien and Paul to wear a part of that good luck charm?" The answer had satisfied her, for he had taken great pains all through these worrisome weeks to keep her in ignorance of Arthur Traylor's warning.

As the *Alabama Belle* moved around the bend of the river and the château momentarily disappeared from view, he turned to Marius and said, "I want you to come to Lawyer Danforth's office with me when we get to Montgomery and witness my will."

"Mr. Bouchard, folks make a will when they think they're going to die, and you've got lots of long years before you have to bother worrying about that, I'd say," Marius responded, a worried look on his handsome face.

"No one has a covenant with God as to the time of His summons, Marius," was Luke's solemn answer. Then, with a reassuring smile, he clapped Marius on the back and added, "It's just good business to provide for unforeseen contingencies. When you get older, you'll understand that. And, by the way, I've added a clause which will leave you and Clementine, as well as Jasper and his brother or sister, as the case may be, fifty acres of Windhaven Plantation and a percentage of the net cash holdings of my estate. It's little enough reward for your magnificent work as my foreman."

"All I can say, Mr. Bouchard, is Clemmie and me don't ever want to find out about that clause."

Luke gripped Marius Thornton's hand and smiled into his foreman's eyes. "Thank you for your friendship and your loyalty, Marius. But, practically speaking, I'm just about twice your age, so in the general scheme of things you're likelier to outlive me than I am you. And now, let's go have a visit with Captain Tenby."

Twilight had fallen on the river, and the sounds of bullfrogs and night birds mingled with the gentle wash of waters along the sandy banks. The pale crescent of a September moon edged upward from the east, its faint light still too distant and weak to touch the top of he towering bluff. An owl stirred in the branches of a tall tree, uttering one sleepy hoot and then another, and, after a pause, still another.

Now here was another sound, the crisp and regular beat of horses' hooves and a creaking and rattling sound accompanying the first, as a wagon, filled with barrels and pulled by three black horses, came down the old Indian trail.

The verdant acres of Windhaven Plantation were set nearly a quarter of a mile behind the majestic château. As the wagon skirted the towering bluff and came toward the stately edifice, Arnie Grimes shifted the reins to his left hand, softly calling, "Whoa!" to his three horses, and fumbled for the telescope. He leveled it quickly at the fields beyond. Then he grunted with satisfaction. The workers had gone back into their cabins, and at this moment he could see no one working in the fields or, far to one side, in the fenced-in section which enclosed Luke's small, but prime quality, herd.

Without looking back, he called out, "We're in luck, boys. They've quit work for the day and nobody's seen us. Now you stay down on your bellies until I git up to the house, and then I'll knock at the door while you slip out and get ready to come in with me, once that old nigger opens up, understand?"

Jack Stallman and Casey Meldrun, the latter a gangling, buck-toothed farmer's son in his mid-twenties, called assent. But Jack Stallman, seized by a sudden thought, anxiously asked, "Hey, Arnie, don'tcha think we oughta cover our faces up so's nobody'll recognize us?"

"Naw," Arnie Grimes retorted, "they ain't never seen us before and ain't likely to see us again. Casey, you'll be on your way to N'Awleans with the brat and Janie, and me 'n Jack'll hide out in Attisburg until Mr. C. sends for us

427

to pay us off. Now we're gittin' close, so be ready to git down and follow me in!"

But Jack Stallman had still another worry. "What about the wagon? You gonna leave it here? It's got *Attisburg Livery* painted on the side."

This time Arnie Grimes pulled on the reins to halt the horses, scowling as he pondered this last-minute suggestion. Then he chuckled and nodded, "Fer once, Jack, yer usin' yet brain 'stead 'a yer fat gut. Tell you what. Casey, you unhitch the fastest hoss so's you kin ride like hell back downriver with the brat. Me 'n Jack'll drive the wagon back to Attisburg. So's we kin git the most speed outa them two other hosses, we kin dump off the barrels—hell, they're all empty, anyhow! Now in we go, so be ready!"

He had driven the wagon to the front entrance of the château. Leaping down from the wagon, Grimes secured the reins to a tall post set into the ground about fifty feet from the door, then advanced toward the entrance with a confident swagger.

Catlike, Meldrun straightened, put one hand on the side of the open wagon, and vaulted down to the ground, reaching out his hand to steady the panting fat man's descent. Then both men crouched and ran toward the side of the entrance with its stone steps, flattened themselves against the wall, and waited as Grimes lifted his right hand, grasped the brass knocker, and struck three times.

Old Phineas Atbury, calling, "Just a minute, I'm comin' —now who can that be this time o' day?" drew back the bolt and opened the door only a few inches so that he could peer out. "What you want, mister?"

"Didn't mean to bother you none when your white folks most likely are gettin' ready for supper," Grimes grinned, "but I got me here some supplies Mr. Bouchard ordered. Should I bring the barrels in?"

"No, sir!" Phineas shook his head. "Mister Bouchard didn't tell me nuthin' 'bout no supplies—hey, what you doin'—Lord have mercy, don't stick me with that knife, please, mister!" Grimes had suddenly drawn his clasp knife and put the blade to Phineas's throat.

"Jist keep yer mouth shut, nigger, and open that door

real wide now—that's better! C'mon boys!" Grimes beckoned with his other hand to his two cronies.

Phineas perceived the wagon beyond, just as he backed away, his hands held above his shoulders. Then his gaze fixed on the sharp knife. The point just grazed his Adam's apple. "Please don't cut me, mister," he pleaded.

For answer, Grimes reached into his back trousers' pocket for an old pistol, reversed it and gripped it by the barrel as, with a vicious swipe, he brought the heavy butt down on Phineas Atbury's skull. The old steward slumped to the floor with a feeble moan and lay still.

"That does for him. Don't think I killed the old coon, but he'll sleep long enough for us to be done with our business and gone. Now let's go find the brat. When we do, you grab him, Casey, and get the hell out of here. Pick up Janie and go down to Mobile jist like you wuz told, understand?"

"I got it straight, Arnie. Don't worry; I'll handle it good. Hell," Meldrun sniggered, "when I told Janie I was bringing a kid down to its granddaddy and that I'd hitch up with her if she'd come along to take care of it, she couldn't wait to get started."

"Never mind that. Let's go down this hall," Grimes whispered, jabbing his thumb toward the south wing of the house.

At this moment Laure, having peered through the shutters to see the wagon stop in front of the château and the three men descend from it, opened her door. She was about to go out into the hall, but stepped back, stifled a cry of alarm and tried to retreat back into her room.

Grimes let out a whoop of bawdy laughter. "Yer the one I'm after, honey!" Before she could close the door, he flung his weight against it and entered. Gripping the handle of the knife and thrusting it out in front of him, he growled, "You jist let out one peep, honey, and I'll cut your throat!"

"What—what do you want—for God's sake, who are you?" Laure gasped, shuddering with revulsion at her unkempt, shabbily clad assailant. "Please—don't hurt the children—"

"Never you mind about them. You do what I want, my

boys won't touch 'em. Now you're gonna be real obligin' to me, honey." Savoring her trembling fear of him, he eyed her from head to toe, his mouth broadening in a lewd, knowing smile. "Yer made jist the way I like a fancy bitch," he muttered thickly.

Mitzi Vourlay, in the adjoining room, had been cradling little Paul in her arms and humming an old Creole lullaby to the black-haired baby. Little Lucien was playing in his crib. Suddenly Mitzi stopped humming, having overheard the voices, and opened her door cautiously just in time to see Jack Stallman and Casey Meldrun move toward her. "Hey, there's the kid!" Casey exclaimed.

"Naw, you dummy, that's the baby—it's got black hair, anyhow, and you was told to grab the older one!" Jack reproved him.

Mitzi uttered a terrified cry, but Jack Stallman, his agility belying his bulk, clapped his left palm over her mouth and pointed his pistol at her head as he snarled, "Try that again, girlie, you won't have time to say your prayers! Bet the other kid's in the room, Casey—go git him!"

Mitzi's eyes rolled frantically, and she tried to speak, but Stallman pressed the muzzle of the pistol against her forehead, and shook his head. "Better keep your mouth shut, girlie. I'd hate to kill a purty piece like you!"

Casey had entered the room; he saw little Lucien in his crib, reached down, lifted the boy up and ran out of the room. Mitzi could not suppress an agonized cry, but Stallman brutally pressed his palm against her mouth and forced her to move backward, the pistol still pressed against her forehead. "Git back in there, sister! I mean it now! You 'n me, we're gonna stay here, nice and peaceful-like, until the boys have finished their job. Be smart, you and the brat won't get hurt. Otherwise—" He did not finish, but Mitzi, pale and trembling, needed no further explanation. Eyes huge and blurred with tears, she stared at him with horror. "All right, if I take my hand away, you gonna promise not to yell? Good—" She had faintly nodded. "Then sit down on that chair and don't open your mouth, not even once, get me sister?"

After she had obeyed, he moved back, the pistol still trained at her head. He glanced nervously at the open door, waiting for Arnie to carry out the last part of Henri Cournier's odious vengeance.

Laure stood, helpless, and she did not speak, reading in the narrowed, blazing eyes of her assailant what he intended. She could not suppress a convulsive trembling. She swallowed hard but straightened her slim shoulders, striving almost hysterically to maintain an attitude of utter calm and contemptuous dignity, her only defenses during this violent episode.

"Proud 'n mighty, ain't you, honey-gal?" Grimes's gaze lingered over the green-eyed beauty. "Think I'm low white trash, not good enough for your sort, don'tcha?"

A shudder of loathing and hatred crossed Laure's exquisite face. Finally, fighting for self-possession, she forced herself to speak with relative calm. "I'm not concerned for myself. But if you harm my children, my husband will hunt you down and kill you."

"Fine talk!" Grimes scoffed, idly tracing the sharp point of his clasp knife over the bodice of her simple, green cotton dress. "Don't worry, your brats ain't gonna be hurt, that much I'll tell you—and that's all. Now let's get down to cases, honey. I'll bet, under your skin, that nice purty soft skin, yer dyin' to find out what it's gonna be like when a real man beds you. Ain't that right, honey?"

Laure did not speak. She closed her eyes and clenched her fists at her sides. She was like a statue, but the quickened rise and fall of her breasts betrayed her fear.

With a lecherous snigger, Grimes reached out his left hand and grabbed the high-necked bodice. Then he drew it out slightly so that the knife would not mar the satiny flesh of his victim. Next he slashed downward, and the fabric shirred with a soft sound as the dress was laid open to the woman's belly. Under it, she wore only a camisole and drawers, and because the weather had been oppressively humid, no stockings and only thong sandals. Grimes sucked in his breath as he saw the hard darts of her nipples prod against the thin camisole. Then, his left hand clutching the torn dress, he yanked downward; it draped her ankles. Laure swayed, sinking her teeth into her lower lip, her eyes shut tightly.

Her passiveness infuriated Grimes. Keeping a tight grip on his knife, he backhanded her across the left cheek. She staggered a little with a stifled cry of pain and surprise, then righted herself. "Don't treat me like I wuz dirt, you hoity-toity bitch, you! I know lots more about you 'n you think, honey. You usta work in a whore house in N'Awleans 'fore you got yourself hitched, so don't put on no airs with me," he snarled.

Her continued silence goaded him to fury. Brutally, the fingers of his left hand twisted around the bodice of the thin camisole and ripped the garment off, leaving Laure Bouchard naked to the waist and clad only in her drawers and sandals. Again he sucked in his breath at the unveiling of her proud breasts, the tawny sheen of her skin, the smooth contours of her belly. Then, his lips twisting in a vicious smile, he hissed, "Now you jist step outta them drawers nice and easy, honey, and we'll have ourselves a time!"

A sudden crimson flooded Laure's bruised cheek. Stiffening, she opened her eyes and hollowly retorted, "I won't help you. Do what you want, but I'll never help you!"

Again he hit her, this time making her stumble, lose her balance, and sink to the floor on one knee, supporting herself only with her right palm. She looked up at him, fearful now at his savage, unleashed rage, and her only thought was that she must not die, because she wanted to live for Luke. Instantly he bent toward her, the knife upraised. "Take them goddamn drawers off, I said, or I'll cut your tits so's yer fine hubby won't like 'em much afterward—hear me, bitch?"

He made a stabbing gesture with the knife and this time Laure cried out in a choked voice, "No, no, don't do that—I'll do what you want."

"That's a lot better, honey," he jeered, stepping back and lowering the knife. "Git on with it then, I ain't got all night—not that I wouldn't like to stay here all that time and show you I'm a better man than your hubby'll ever be!"

Awkwardly, Laure got to her feet and then, closing her eyes again and shuddering violently, forced her slim fingers to lower the lace-trimmed drawers.

Only Arnie Grimes's awareness that further prolongation of his cruel sport might endanger the success of the enterprise, stopped him from subjecting Laure to new, depraved acts of surrender before the ultimate degradation. Unbuttoning his trousers with his left hand to liberate his ferociously swollen manhood, he seized her by the wrist and dragged her over to the wide bed, shoving her brutally onto it. "Get down there, bitch. Stretch out on your back and git ready for a real man," he boasted.

When she had silently complied, again closing her eyes to blot out the sight of his gaunt, lust-contorted face, Grimes fell upon her and pitilessly ravished her. The mercilessly harsh and rapid act of copulation drew involuntary gasps and moans from the agonized young woman, who endured her martyrdom with heroic self-control until her fingernails drew blood from her palms as she lay beneath his violent thrusts.

With a hoarse bellow of triumph, he vented his seed into her, and then clambered off the bed. "There now! Damn shame I gotta leave you after jist this one time to get acquainted, honey, but I got other things to do. Too bad—yer not stretched—jist the kind we like. Guess that says somethin' about your husband, too." He guffawed. "Now then, you better not go yellin' fer the niggers in the fields fer a while, 'cause I got other friends 'a mine waitin' 'round the house and they might not be happy if you wuz to start makin' a fuss. 'Sides which, if they'd get a gander at you, they'd like as not have themselves some fun, like we just did. Mebbe I'll see you again, honey, when I got more time!"

Closing his clasp knife and pocketing it, and buttoning his trousers, Arnie Grimes hawked and spat at Laure's shuddering, ravaged body, and then hurried out of the bedroom.

An arm over her forehead, Laure burst into racking sobs. After what seemed an eternity, she raised herself feebly, slid from the bed, and walked toward her closet, fumbling for a robe. She drew several long quivering breaths, closing her eyes and leaning her head against the wall, until the fit of nausea and almost overwhelming blackness began to recede. Then, with a supreme effort, she forced herself to walk out of her bedroom and to the room on her right.

By then, Jack Stallman had joined Arnie, and the two men had whipped the two black horses to draw the wagon, empty now of its barrels, in the direction of Attisburg.

Mitzi sat slumped in a chair, hugging little Paul to her, and sobbing wildly. Through tear-blurred eyes, she saw her golden-haired mistress in the doorway and sprang to her feet. *"Oh, mon Dieu, les sales brutes vous ont fait mal!"*

"Mitzi, don't think about me. Give me little Paul. Go to the fields and ask Dan Munroe to ride to Montgomery and bring back my husband. Hurry, I beg of you!"

CHAPTER THIRTY-NINE

It was nearly dawn on Saturday when Luke Bouchard and Dan Munroe rode up to the red-brick château, their horses exhausted and lathered. Dan had changed horses in Montgomery, for he forced his gelding, at full gallop, to cover the more than forty miles from Windhaven in four hours.

Luke dismounted and, his face lined with deep anxiety, entered the house to be met by the weeping Hannah.

"Thank God you're here at last, Mr. Bouchard sir," she sobbed, wringing her hands. "Miz Laure, she's the bravest woman I ever saw—but, God protect us all, those awful men took little Lucien away!"

"Where is my wife, Hannah?" Luke panted, and then, seeing the domestic break down and lift her skirt to mop her tear-filled eyes, gently put his arm around her. "There, there, don't cry, Hannah. Did anyone see the men?"

"No sir, only Miz Laure 'n Miss Mitzi. One of the men made Mitzi stay in the room with the babies, and she said another man took Lucien away. Oh God, and they hit poor Phineas on the head and hurt him bad!"

Torn between his compassion for the weeping black woman and his own agonized concern over Laure, Luke stood irresolute, his eyes bloodshot and his face haggard from the exhaustion of the long ride home. "Sit down, and try to rest, Hannah," he urged her at last, his voice hoarse with fatigue and grief, striving to soothe her as best he could. "I'll go see Laure now—is she in her room?"

"Yes sir. Oh Lord, what did poor little Lucien do? Why'd You let those wicked men take him away from us?" Hannah slumped into a chair and gave in to anguished sobs. Luke strode to Laure's bedroom, knocked, and entered. Laure lay in bed, the sheets drawn up over her, and Mitzi,

435

dabbing her tear-swollen eyes with a lace handkerchief, was beside her.

"My poor darling—Dan got to me and I came back as fast as I could! Are you hurt, my dearest?" Luke exclaimed hoarsely.

Laure's face was pale and drawn, and as she lay, her head propped up by two pillows, she slowly lifted her arms out to him. With a sob, Luke embraced her tenderly, stroking her long, golden hair. "My sweet, my love, my heart's own, thank God you weren't killed—don't talk about it—you must rest, my dear one—" Luke slowly rose, looking at Mitzi. "Come outside, *ma petite*, and tell me. I don't want to distress Laure." Then, turning back to his young wife, he assured her, "I'll come right back and stay with you; I swear it, Laure."

Gently closing the door, Luke turned to Mitzi in the hallway. "Now, tell me all you can. Dan found me at the hotel. Mitzi, please, I know it's been a terrible ordeal for you, but you've got to try to remember everything!"

"*Mon Dieu,* I won't ever forget it," Mitzi began, her voice breaking. She stopped to dab at her eyes again and to blow her nose, while Luke waited. "I—I was in the room with the *bébés*. Then I heard voices, and I opened the door and there was a horrible man, *Monsieur* Luke, *très gros, avec une loupe sur le nez.*"

"A wart on his nose, a fat man—he should be easy to find. Go on," Luke ordered tersely.

"Oh, yes, but it was not he, *Monsieur* Luke, who took little Lucien; it was a younger man, very tall. But the fat one made me sit in the chair and pointed a gun and told me I must keep very quiet. And then—then when it was over—I heard Madame move around in her room and she came out and told me to bring Dan to her at once! Oh, *c'était incroyable, vicieuse!* There—there was another man, *Monsieur* Luke—he—he—"

Luke felt a blind fury seize him. He shuddered with the murderous rage that welled up in him. "You needn't tell me—I can guess, *pauvre petite.* Now then, go back and comfort your mistress, and I'll go see to poor Phineas. Hannah told me that one of the men bludgeoned him with a gun. Poor old man; I pray to God he's not seriously hurt.

As soon as I've talked to him—if I can—I'll come back to Laure. Be sure you tell her that, *petite*."

Mitzi nodded and went back into Laure's room, while Luke went back to the foyer of the château, where Hannah still sat, huddled in her chair, weeping bitterly.

"Hannah, may I see Phineas?" he gently asked.

"Reckon so, sir. Mary's with him now, doin' the best she can."

"I know. If this hadn't happened, I'd have brought back a doctor from Montgomery to look Phineas over and make him strong and well again," he told her. Hannah at last controlled her weeping, rose, and led him to one of the small guest rooms at the end of the north wing of the château, where Phineas had been taken. Luke entered, nodded to Mary, who was sitting beside the elderly black man's bed, and then bent over his hired hand, who appeared to be asleep. "How is he, Mary?" he whispered.

"Little while ago, Mister Bouchard, he done woke up and talked just a little. I tol' him he had to rest and not try to talk, the old fool." There was tender pity in Mary's epithet, and Luke smiled understandingly. Drawing up a stool, he seated himself beside the old man, and watched carefully. The sound of voices seemed to waken Phineas. He blinked his eyes and slowly turned his head. Luke noticed that Mary had applied a bandage, and that there was an obvious swelling beneath it, left by the butt of the gun. Gently, he said, "Phineas, it's Luke Bouchard. Can you hear me?"

"Yes—yessir—I can—" the old man faltered in a faint voice.

"Now I'm not going to disturb you long, and I want you to get all the sleep you can. I left a note for Marius in Montgomery and told him to ride back later this morning and to see if he couldn't bring Dr. Medbury out here to look you over. But it's very important that you help me all you can right now. Because the men who hurt you and broke into the house have gained a lot of time over us, and we've got to try to find them."

"Yessir—I'll try all I can—when that man hit me with his gun, I don't remember nothin' after that—"

"Of course you wouldn't," Luke reassured him. "But

437

maybe, just before he hit you, you might have seen something that will tell me who those men were. Try to think, please!"

"Don't rightly remember—it all happened so fast—wait a minute, Mr. Bouchard—I do remember somethin'—"

"Take your time, Phineas, don't tire yourself. Don't try to move, just rest, and when you can, tell me what it is you remember," Luke urged.

"Man knocked at the door, an' when I opened it, he said he was bringin' supplies you done ordered. I tol' him I didn't know nuthin' about no such supplies, 'n next thing I know, he puts a knife to my neck 'n makes me open the door so's he 'n his friends can get inside. That's when he done hit me, Mr. Bouchard—"

"Yes, I understand. But you were saying—"

"Yessir—I did take a peek outside, 'n there was a wagon Had a lot of barrels in it, I remember."

"Yes, a wagon with barrels. Is there anything else?"

"Yessir—now it comes back to me, clear as day—on the side of that wagon, it said *Attisburg Liv'ry*, that's what it said!" In his eagerness, Phineas Atbury had tried to lift his head, his eyes wide and beseeching.

"It said *Attisburg Livery*, is that right?" Seeing the old man nod feebly, Luke bent to touch his shoulder and murmur, "Thank you, Phineas. You're going to be all right. You let Mary take care of you, and here's Hannah to stay with you. Go to sleep. You've helped, much more than you know."

He went to Hannah then, whispered a few words to her, and then left the room. Dan Munroe was waiting in the foyer, hat in hand, in his dusty boots and sweat-drenched shirt. "Did you find out anything, Mr. Bouchard, sir?" he queried anxiously.

"Yes, Dan. The men who stole my elder son and abused my wife came here in a wagon from Attisburg, I'm convinced. And I have the description of two of them. Now I'm going to see if Laure will tell me about the other man."

"I want to go with you, Mr. Bouchard. I want to lay my hands on those men and tear 'em to pieces!" Dan Munroe exclaimed.

"No, Dan, you've ridden all night long, and you're falling asleep on your feet."

"So are you, Mr Bouchard, and you know it's not much more 'n an hour's ride to Attisburg on a fresh horse."

"I know, but you've already ridden eight hours, and you're exhausted, man!" Luke tried to dissuade him.

"Listen, Mr. Bouchard, no offense meant, but when you came here last year after what happened to Phineas and Hannah, me 'n some of the others was just about ready to pull out and let the Klan pester some other poor niggers. You gave us all a chance for a decent life, and you treated us like we was your own family. Mr. Bouchard, I'm goin' t' ride with you, whether you want me or not! And you can fire me right now if you like, I'm still going!"

Luke Bouchard could not hide his tears as he went to the wiry, middle-aged black, gripped his hand and shook it. "All right, I'll admit I can use some help. There were three of them, and like as not, if they went back to Attisburg, they'll have friends. We'll go well armed, Dan. But first, you're going to lie down for an hour, I insist on that. Get yourself a drink of whiskey and relax. I'll go back to my wife—and may God bless you, your wife, and your children for what you've done."

They rode into the little town of Attisburg two and a half hours later, each armed with a Spencer repeating rifle. It was somewhat after nine o'clock in the morning, and the principal street of the town was deserted. There was a small general store, a blacksmith's shop, and, farther down, a false-front frame building where weatherbeaten signs announced the places of business of a combination barber-doctor, a lawyer, and a job printer. Across from the building and at the end of the street was a livery stable. Luke gestured to Dan, who nodded, and both men rode quickly toward the stable, then circled the back.

"Mr. Bouchard, there's the wagon—see how it's painted, jist like old Phineas said?" Dan whispered.

"Yes. But the stable's locked and there's no one around. Let's try the general store."

"I'm right with you, Mr. Bouchard. You say your wife told you who the man was who—" Dan coughed and lowered his eyes, not finishing the sentence out of respect for his employer's suffering.

"Yes, she gave me an excellent description of that filthy

coward, Dan. And Mitzi described the other two men. Let's go to the store now."

They mounted their horses and rode back down the street, halting at the small general store. Tethering the horses to a post in front of the store, they slowly moved toward the door. Through its dirty glass panels, they could see a bearded, gray-haired man with rolled-up shirtsleeves held in place by thick rubber bands. He was methodically wielding a broom over the puncheon floor. Dan knocked on the glass and gestured impatiently.

The gray-bearded man straightened, scowled, then moved to the door and in a whiny voice berated them. "No sense yer fussin', I don't open up fer an hour yet."

"You better open the door, mister," Munroe called, "or we'll break it down!" He lifted his rifle so that the proprietor could see it.

"Hold on now, don't do that," the whiny voice croaked with alarm. "I'll let you in. Never saw nobody so eager to buy vittles or such this early of a Saturday mornin'!"

Mumbling to himself, he drew back the bolt and stepped back as Dan pushed on in, followed by Luke Bouchard.

"You gonna rob me, you fellas?" the proprietor whined. "Ain't hardly worth your while, nohow, I—"

Luke had seen the sudden movement of a dingy cloth drape which covered the narrow entrance to the back of the store, and shouldered the proprietor aside as he exclaimed, "Come on, Dan, let's see who's in the back there. They've been listening!"

Pulling the curtain to one side, he saw two men, their backs to him, in the act of opening the back door, and called out: "Stop where you are, or I'll shoot you down!"

"Why, mister, what's the matter with you? We didn't do anything. You got a helluva lotta nerve bustin' in here this way when Mr. Jedediah Thompson tells you this store don't open for an hour yet."

Luke's knuckles whitened as he gripped his Spencer, holding it at hip level. This was the man whom Laure had described. And the other, sweating, his fat jowls quaking with fear, fit Mitzi Vourlay's description perfectly, even to the wart on his nose.

"I'll tell you why I'm here." Luke kept his voice level, fighting against the black rage which surged through him.

"Yesterday evening, you two men paid an uninvited visit to my house, near Lowndesboro. One of you kidnapped my elder son, Lucien; the other violated my wife."

"Now see here, mister, whoever you are, we never saw you before in all our life." The gaunt-faced man made a fine show of indignation. "I work for Mr. Thompson, see, mister, and my friend Jack here came by to keep me company. What right have you got, comin' in here with guns and accusin' us when we don't even know who you are?"

"My name is Luke Bouchard, and my wife, Laure, described the man who raped her. She was perfectly calm and rational, and she made no mistake in her description. You, you cowardly, filthy animal, did it. And your friend with the wart on his nose," Luke glared contemptuously at Stallman, who shot his crony a terrified, piteous glance. "You were the one who held my children's nurse at gunpoint so that a third man might kidnap my son Lucien."

"So you say, Mr. Bouchard or whatever your name is," Arnie Grimes sneered, thrusting his hands in his pockets and teetering back and forth on his heels. "Yer wife might jist be makin' it all up. And anyhow, I got friends'll swear on a Bible that Jack 'n me was playin' cards all night long, right here in Attisburg. You better be ready to prove a tall yarn like that, Mr. Bouchard, or Jack 'n me'll take you before the law and swear out a warrant fer ruinin' our good name!"

It was all Luke Bouchard could do to keep from emptying his rifle into the taunting, unkempt, bearded man who defied him. Conquering that impulse, he turned to Dan Munroe. "Maybe if you put a bullet through each of his kneecaps, Dan, you'd help him change his alibi."

Munroe eyed Luke Bouchard, and caught the almost imperceptible wink which accompanied this callous order. He grunted an assent, then slowly raised his rifle and aimed it at Grimes's right knee. Then, emphatically, he cocked the trigger so that its crisp click was distinctly heard.

"Hey now, wait jist a minute." Grimes put up both his hands, palms outward, backing up against the door. "If you're so all-fired sure that me 'n Jack did what you claim we did, you better git the law in here. We gotta right to a fair trial, and don't fergit it!"

"You want a trial. Very well, I'll give you one. Dan, take my rifle and stand back. You," pointing to the trembling fat man, "back over there to the corner and keep your hands up. If Dan sees you try for a gun, he'll kill you."

"Now what the hell's all this about?" Grimes jeered.

"I'm going to thrash you until you confess what you did to my wife, you filthy scum!" Luke Bouchard hissed between his teeth.

"Oh sure, and if I beat the hell out of you like I'm gonna, your nigger friend over there blows my head off. A fair fight, hell!" Grimes mockingly rejoined.

"I give you my word he won't shoot you. You see, I'm going to kill you myself, with my bare hands." Luke's voice was deadly calm.

"Big talk, Mr. Bouchard! But I'll jist take you up on that offer. All my life my pa 'n me, we been put down by fancy rich folks like you. Now's my chance to git back at someone as high 'n mighty as you are. Naw, you won't kill me, Mr. Bouchard. I been fightin' niggers 'n rivermen since I was a kid, and I can't 'member losin' a fight yet. Come on, if you've got the guts!" He crouched, clenching his fists, a mocking sneer warping his thin, cruel mouth. Then, with a bellow, he charged forward, trying to butt Luke in the belly and knock the wind out of him.

Luke stood his ground and swiftly brought up his right knee. It collided smartly with Grimes's jaw and the antagonist staggered back, a surprised look on his face. "Oh, so you want to fight dirty, do you? That's jist fine with me; that's the sorta fightin' I like best," he snarled and shot out his right fist. Luke ducked and drove his left fist into the pit of Grimes's belly. Once again Grimes stumbled back, his eyes squinting and blazing with pain and hate. Suddenly he lunged for a rickety chair near the door, lifted it and threw it at Luke Bouchard.

Luke dodged, the chair grazed his right shoulder, and he stumbled. In an instant, Grimes was on him, flailing away, and he gained a momentary advantage when one of his vicious jabs made Luke groan and sink down onto one knee. With a roar Arnie Grimes bent over him and dug his fingers into his adversary's neck. Dan Munroe gasped and moved a step forward, but Jack Stallman held out his hand and yelled, "He promised you wouldn't shoot if

Arnie beat him. You nigger bastard, don't you use those guns!"

Luke Bouchard's hands gripped Arnie Grimes's wiry wrists as he tried to break the stranglehold. Then, as he felt his senses swimming, he clenched his right fist and struck forward and upward with all his might into Grimes's groin.

He connected and Grimes screamed and released his hold, clapping both hands to his crotch and bending over, his ugly face hideous with its contorted agony. Unsteadily rising to his feet, Luke seized him in turn by the neck and, exerting all his strength, lunged forward to smash his opponent against the wall.

Stunned, agonized, Grimes curved his fingers like talons and tried to gouge out Luke's eyes, but the latter bowed his head and butted Grimes's chest as his own fingers dug into the scrawny neck of the rapist.

"Awrggh—wait—wait—got sumpin' to—to—say—urfff—awghh—lemme be—" Arnie Grimes gasped.

"Well, say your piece and be quick about it! You were the one, weren't you?" Luke hissed, his face a mask of fury, his eyes blazing.

"If—if you kill me," Grimes wheezed painfully, "you'll never see that brat of yours again."

"So it *was* you, and your two friends!" Luke panted, without lessening his grip, pinning his gasping adversary against the wall and pressing his right knee against Grimes's already tortured groin.

"You want your brat back, don't you, Bouchard? But you won't find him here, no sirree—lemme talk, damn you—God, you've got me in the nuts and I can't hardly breathe—"

"Well? Quick now! Where's my son?"

Grimes emitted a raucous sound. "Like I said, he ain't here. We packed him off with a new father and mother—they're bound for the West, so if you want to git your brat back, Bouchard, you better lemme go and start chasin' after him, see?"

That confession, that taunt, that vicious mockery, drove away Luke's already waning conscience. A now-primitive man who fought for his young and to avenge the dishonoring of his wife, he saw and knew only that hideous face before him, heard only the boastful admission of those heinous crimes. With an almost demented cry, he dragged Grimes forward, then smashed him back against the wall again. This time his strong, lean fingers tightened inexorably, as he turned his face this way and that to avoid his opponent's last feeble attempts to gouge out his eyes. Only when he felt Grimes's body go limp and saw the blackening of that twisted, repulsive face, did he release his hold and step back, panting, his eyes fixed on the inert body at his feet.

"My God," Jack Stallman breathed, "You've killed him! You've killed Arnie Grimes, mister!"

Drawing in great gulps of air, tottering, Luke gradually regained control of himself. He turned slowly toward the cringing fat man. "I think I can kill you, too," he muttered, and walked slowly forward.

"No, oh Jesus, don't let him, nigger—please I didn't touch your wife, I swear on a Bible, I never did, 'n I didn't take your kid, either, God's my witness—" Jack Stallman wailed as he held up his hands in front of his face as if to ward off a blow.

"Tell me where my boy is, if you want to live!"

"But I can't," Stallman whined. "Mr. C. never said exactly where he meant for the kid to be taken—that's the truth—I wouldn't lie to you now, honest!"

Luke Bouchard stopped, his eyes widening. "You said Mr. C., didn't you? By any chance, would it be Henri Cournier?"

"Yes, yes, sure; he's a Frog from N'Awleans. He came here to Attisburg to see Arnie and cook up this whole business. He paid good, mister—I never seen so much money before in all my life. I'm jist a poor feller tryin' to earn my daily bread, honest. I wouldn'ta harmed your wife, not me, mister!"

Luke Bouchard turned away, sick with mingled anguish and contempt.

"Oh my God." Jack Stallman's voice cracked in desperation. "Don't kill me! Gimme a chance, mister. I'm not mean like that Arnie Grimes."

Slowly, Luke's self-control gained the upper hand as Dan Munroe watched him anxiously. At last he turned to the cowering fat man and demanded, "Are you ready to

444

swear it was a man called Henri Cournier who hired the three of you to steal my son and shame my wife?"

"Sure, mister, I'll sure swear to that! It wuz Arnie 'n me met him down in a tavern in Mobile last month. I heard him plain as I'm hearin' you tell us wut it wuz he wanted us to do. 'N the kid wuz to be brought to this Froggie—we all called him Mr. C.—in N'Awleans. That's the truth, so help me God, mister!" Stallman pleaded.

"Get some rope and tie him up, Dan. I can't stand the sight of him," Luke Bouchard decreed. "We'll take him to Montgomery on Monday and let him make that confession in front of the sheriff. It's the evidence I need, and perhaps it will lead me to my son."

"Yessir, I'll do it right off. But we'll need another horse if we're gonna ride him back, Mr. Bouchard," Dan prompted.

"Then we'll find one in that stable, even if we have to break in. I'll leave money to pay for the horse and any damages. Hurry, Dan, make sure he can't get loose. I want to get back to Laurel"

CHAPTER FORTY

If Casey Meldrun had followed the orders which Arnie Grimes had transmitted to him from Henri Cournier, Luke Bouchard would certainly have reached New Orleans ahead of him. But Meldrun could think of nothing but the $2,000 which he had been promised as soon as he delivered young Lucien Bouchard to Henri Cournier. Moreover, he had inadvertently allowed Janie Norton to learn that he was coming into a good deal of money. He had bragged of this in order to overcome her scruples about trying to preserve her virginity until she was, to quote her, "Yer right and proper wife, Casey honey." And when she had teased him, saying that he was only making the story up so as to enjoy her without benefit of clergy, he had told her, "Hell, Janie, I can prove it. All I hafta do is git to N'Awleans with the kid 'n turn him over to a rich fella, and he'll hand over the cash and no arguments."

In return, Janie Norton had bargained with him. "All right, then, Casey honey. Then you'n me's gonna git to N'Awleans jist as quick as we kin. An' when I see that feller hand you over all that money, then I'll go to bed with you."

It was true that Casey Meldrun did not really want to marry Janie Norton. On the other hand, though she had almost driven him away by her constant urging that she would make him the happiest man alive once he put the ring on her finger, the promise of her young body and the sensual fervor which she imparted with the kisses and fumbling caresses she grudgingly granted, had driven him wild to possess her—at almost any price. Thus it was that when she wheedled out of him the essentials of the project which was to earn him such a large sum—which to both the impoverished lovers represented very nearly the riches

446

of Croesus—it was Janie who set about convincing him that even the best-laid plans could go astray.

"Jist 'sposin' yer pals Jack 'n Arnie beat you down to N'Awleans, Casey," she told him. "They were the ones let you in on this, 'n they could be the ones who might jist talk this rich fella into payin' 'em most of your share, 'cause they wuz the ones who picked you, don't you see? But if we git there first with the kid, you'll get your money all the quicker. Ain't that so, honey?" Then, slyly, an arm around his waist and pressing herself up against him, she murmured huskily, "Jist think what fun we can have, stoppin' at one of those fancy hotels I heard nasty old Mr. Dougherty tell his wife about, and be all by ourselves in a nice big bed. Wouldn't you like that, honey?"

Casey Meldrun's perseverance had little chance against Janie's wiles. So, as soon as he had seized little Lucien from his crib, mounted his horse, and ridden back to Attisburg, he had set about preparing for an immediate journey to Mobile and thence to New Orleans. First, having blindfolded the terrified little boy and tied his hands behind his back, he had locked him in a closet in his dead father's dilapidated farmhouse, and then gone to fetch Janie Norton. She had collected and crushed some red berries, and, after straining them carefully, set to work at once rubbing the mixture into little Lucien's hair, in order to dye it. Then they had undressed the tearful and frightened child, replacing his clothes with a nightshirt.

Finally, knowing that Casey had almost no money, Janie had waited until her miserly employer and his sharp-tongued wife were sound asleep, crept into their bedroom, and rummaged through a chest of drawers until she found a cache of over a hundred dollars in greenbacks. This she appropriated, and then left the farmhouse forever, eager to begin an exciting new life with the man of her choice.

Finally, she had won Meldrun's admiration by showing that she was an even better conspirator than he was. After she had finished disguising little Lucien, she said with a crafty smile playing about her full red lips, "Honey, there's a steamboat stoppin' tomorrow afternoon down at the dock at Cloris, 'n that's only ten miles from here. We can be on it, down in Mobile by Sunday morning. An' I remember I heard old Mr. Dougherty say there's a steamboat leavin' from Mobile every Sunday evening at six sharp. Don't you see, Casey honey? We kin be there early Monday, and you kin collect all that wonderful money. And then you and I kin rent the swellest room they got in that spiffy hotel. I'll make it up to you, honey, I promise, honest and true I will!"

Accordingly, a young couple with a red-haired little boy (over whose mouth Janie Norton had slyly pressed her palm to prevent him from crying when they ascended the gangplank) boarded the *Tombigbee Star* and arrived at Mobile a little after three o'clock Sunday afternoon, and bought passage on the *Princess,* which departed promptly, at six o'clock that evening, for New Orleans.

When they disembarked, Janie again proved to be the more practical of the two, hurrying ahead of Casey to hail a cab and to beckon imperiously to her intended husband. It was she, also, who directed the driver to Henri Cournier's gambling house. Fifteen minutes later, both of them awed by the luxurious furnishings of red velvet and green baize of stuffed ottomans, magnificent tables with cherry-wood and teakwood chairs, they stood somewhat apprehensively in an antechamber while an insolent uniformed doorman bade them wait until he could determine whether Monsieur Cournier would waste his time on such as them.

But when Cournier emerged from his private office, the disdainful look on his autocratic face was instantly replaced by one of utter incredulity. Hastily waving away the doorman, he beckoned to Meldrun and, in a hoarse whisper, urged, "Step this way, and please be quick!"

Meldrun flashed Janie a triumphant glance, bobbed his head, and followed the dapper Creole into his luxurious private office. Cournier closed and locked the door, waving the young couple to a seat. He did not sit himself, however, but approached them, his eyes fixed on little Lucien Bouchard. Janie had managed to calm the boy somewhat by telling him stories and assuring him that he was being taken to see his grandmother. That last fabrication had been a pure stroke of luck on Janie's part. Luke had several times in the past told little Lucien about white-haired Sybella, far away in Texas, and promised that one day he should see her.

"That is the older Bouchard child?" Cournier demanded in a voice that throbbed with excitement.

"Yes sir, that's the one," Casey Meldrun grinned.

"You, sir, I presume, were the one whom Arnie Grimes engaged for this purpose?" the Creole demanded.

"That's right. We made good time, if I say so myself." Janie, who was holding little Lucien on her lap, gave him an irritated nudge to remind him that it was she who had altered the original plans.

Cournier's eyes narrowed. "How long ago did this removal take place, mister—mister—?"

"Casey Meldrun, that's my name. Do you mean, when did I grab the kid?"

A pained expression appeared on Henri Cournier's face. "Yes, that's what I mean. Two weeks ago, I presume?"

"Oh, no, nuttin' like that, Mr. C. Arnie 'n Jack 'n me, we got into the Bouchard house Friday evening."

"Incredible!" Cournier gasped. "Then you must have taken the steamboat to Mobile and changed there the same day of your arrival." Then, his lips tightening, he exclaimed angrily, "But weren't you told to avoid the steamboats, that the riverboat captains might have had the news of the child's abduction and been on the lookout for him? You took an unnecessary risk, and it was extremely stupid—"

"Excuse me, Mr. C.," Janie Norton piped up, "it happened so fast from what Casey told me, there wouldn't have been time to spread any news. I was the one, anyhow, who made Casey come here jist as quick as he could. You see, I knew where the riverboat was stoppin' on Saturday, and the folks I worked for been to N'Awleans lotsa times. They knew about the steamboat leavin' Mobile on Sunday evenin'."

"I see." Henri Cournier frowned. "Was there any trouble with the child on the riverboat to Mobile? Did the captain or any of his hands ask you any questions?"

"No sir," Janie Norton declared. "Casey here jist paid the money for a cabin, and nobody bothered us nohow. That's a fact!"

Henri Cournier's grim features relaxed, and he permitted himself a slight smile. "Well then, in that case, young

449

lady, I must congratulate you on your ingenuity. At least, you carried out the other orders I'd given Mr. Grimes, concerning the change of clothing and the color of the child's hair. Now, to business." Briskly, he walked back to his desk, opened a drawer, took out a sheaf of banknotes, and counted out two thousand dollars.

Meldrun, grinning like a schoolboy singled out by his teacher for scholastic prowess, ambled forward to take the money and to pocket it hastily. "Much obliged, Mr. C. If you've got any other jobs I can handle, jist say the word."

"Thank you, Mr. Meldrun. As it happens, other arrangements have already been made for the transfer of the child out of this city, and because of your zeal—for which I suspect your attractive companion has been mainly responsible—I shall have to carry them out immediately. Do you plan to stay in New Orleans long?"

Meldrun eyed Janie, who nodded. Then he turned back to Cournier. "Well, Mr. C., we was sorta figgerin' on gettin' hitched."

"It'd be such a wonderful place for a honeymoon, you see." Janie felt it incumbent upon herself to explain.

Henri Cournier's brows knitted in thought and he stroked his pointed beard before replying.

"There's always the chance that someone may have seen you and reported it to the child's parents. And they would assume that the child's abductors would head for New Orleans. So I think the wisest course would be to put you up at Three Oaks, my estate some miles upriver from here." He favored them with a seemingly benign smile. "As it happens, I have a minister staying with me as my houseguest, and he is about to marry two of my most loyal employees. He could easily be persuaded to make it a double wedding."

"Aw, Casey, wouldn't that be somethin' swell!" Janie excitedly grabbed Casey's arm, her eyes sparkling.

"Sure—well, yeah, I—I guess so," the prospective bridegroom half-heartedly assented.

"Then I think you should spend at least a week as my guests—oh, there are diversions at my mansion so that you won't be bored, Mr. Meldrun. I have a private gaming room—if you play cards, sir—or if your fancy is the dice,

450

you'll find ample distraction. That is, of course, if you can manage to tear yourself away from your lovely bride."

"Sure!" Casey's face brightened. "Me 'n my ol' pappy used to play cards. Only we didn't play for money."

"I assure you, Mr. Meldrun, that you will be able to indulge your sporting instincts to the fullest in my gaming room. Then I take it the matter's settled." He struck a silver handbell on his desk, and then went to the door and unlocked it to admit the liveried doorman. "Arrange for a carriage to take my two friends to Three Oaks, Joseph."

"Very good, Mr. Cournier. It'll be here in a few minutes."

"Thank you." Henri Cournier closed the door, then went back to the young couple. "Give me the boy," he ordered. As Janie rose and lifted little Lucien, the child began to cry, "Want my daddy! Where daddy?"

"Never mind that, young man," Cournier said with an ironic smile as he firmly grasped the now struggling little boy. "You're about to have a new father and mother. And you'll grow up in a bright new country. You're fortunate, if you only knew it. Alabama is an extremely dreary state, with little future. It's in the West that the real future of our country lies. Oh, I believe that the carriage is ready, Mr. Meldrun and Miss—?"

"Janie Norton, Mr. C., 'n it's been real nice meetin' a gentleman like you." Then, seeing that Casey Meldrun had walked ahead of her to the door, she nodded briskly to Henri Cournier and hurried after him, exclaiming, "Wait fer me, Casey honey!"

CHAPTER FORTY-ONE

That same night, Henri Cournier, immaculately dressed in beige frock coat and trousers, a red carnation pinned to the buttonhole of his coat lapel, stood behind Roger Benson and Amy Harrison while a bespectacled, sanctimonious Church of England minister performed the marriage ceremony.

It would have been difficult to recognize Amy Harrison as the poised and lovely young woman whom Henri Cournier had kept waiting in the antechamber of the old Amberley mansion seven months before. Despair, shame, and suffering marked her cameolike features. Her eyes were red and swollen from incessant weeping, and as she stood beside Cournier's valet, she shivered perceptibly whenever his arm brushed hers.

In a dull, lifeless voice, she responded affirmatively to the minister's questions, and when Benson, with a suggestive smirk and wink, slipped the ring on her finger, she closed her eyes, and tried her best to stifle a heartrending sob. Swiftly, leaning toward her, Benson hissed, "Just you try any of your fine lady's tricks now, Amy, I'll take the hide off you—you know I will! Now stand up straight and when the reverend pronounces us man and wife, give me a nice, sweet, wifely kiss!"

The fateful words were at last pronounced, and the minister beamed and nodded to Cournier as Benson turned to his abashed bride, drew her to him, and crushed her sensitive, trembling mouth with a lustful kiss. Obediently, her arms went around him, and she submitted, shaken though she was by shudders of the deepest revulsion.

"It was a beautiful ceremony, Reverend Henshaw," Henri Cournier purred as he came forward. "My congratulations to you both, Roger and Amy." From an imported leather wallet, he extracted a hundred-dollar bill and tendered it to the bespectacled minister, who thanked him and began to exclaim on the obvious devotion of the couple he had just joined in wedlock, wishing them every blissful happiness which the holy sacrament of matrimony augured.

Businesslike, the dapper Creole then turned to his valet. "I'm very much afraid, Roger, that you won't have any time for a honeymoon. On the other hand, the journey you and your beautiful bride are about to undertake will give you the utmost privacy. Ah yes, I wish I myself might embark on such a trip! Think of it, Roger, the two of you sharing the majesty of open country and the stars and sky, and a romantic moon at night to light your conjugal bed!"

"We have to leave right now, Mr. Cournier?" Benson asked in disappointment.

"Within the hour. The wagon I bought is waiting outside, and I had it fully provisioned this afternoon. Now attend me, Roger. In order to avoid any possible detection, you will set out from here and head northwest. It's true that you'll go through some unpleasant swamp country, but it's negotiable. That course will take you through Indian territory, and you should go on to Wichita. At that point, you may abandon the wagon—sell it or do whatever you choose with it—and take the stagecoach on to California. Here is an envelope with sufficient funds to give you and your charming bride as much comfort as one can buy on so tedious a journey. But console yourself, Roger, I know that with your imagination and with the inspiration which Amy is certain to accord you, you won't have time to think of the tedium."

"I follow you, Mr. Cournier. Come along, Amy, you've got to change your clothes " Taking Amy Harrison Benson by the wrist, digging his dirty fingernails into her sensitive flesh until she winced with pain, Roger Benson led the unfortunate young woman out of the room.

Half an hour after Amy had been married to the sadistic valet, Casey Meldrum and Janie Norton stood before the bespectacled minister and were joined together in holy wedlock. Henri Cournier did not preside, as he had on the previous occasion. He was occupied with seeing Benson off to the West with little Lucien Bouchard. Kegs of water and barrels of food and other supplies had been loaded into the wagon, but there was ample room for a little trundle bed for the child, and another, adequate enough for the bridal couple. Her face downcast and wet with tears, wearing a cheap, calico dress, a simple bonnet, and sturdy shoes, Amy clambered into the back of the wagon, Cournier handing the child up to her.

"Your brother's debt is herewith canceled, my dear," he told her. "You understand why you were obliged to marry my faithful valet. Of course, I shall miss him a good deal. But in this way, a child disguised as Lucien will have been traveling in the company of a devoted young couple and will arouse no suspicion. That, I may add, is another reason why Roger will not board any train with you and the child; there is far less likelihood of any official search being made along stagecoach lines."

Amy did not speak. She was too crushed by her situation. More than that, the methodical and cruel physical coercion to which Benson had subjected her over the months had broken her spirit. She had not been told the identity of the child, only that Cournier was carrying out a promise to convey the child to its new home.

Nor did she need Cournier's parting advice. "I'm sure you understand, my dear Amy, that it would be futile, as well as painful, for you to attempt to run away from your husband. Reconcile yourself. This may well inaugurate a new life for you as a frontier wife. If you please my valet, your marriage will be decidedly less stormy. Who knows, you may even come to fall in love with him. And now I bid you adieu." He bowed obsequiously in the best Gallic manner.

Then he went to Benson, who was gathering the reins in the driver's seat and testing them to see how the four-horse team responded. "I have taken the liberty of drawing a map, Roger," he told his valet. "If you will follow it, you will avoid some of the worst spots. I have calculated that it is roughly seven hundred and fifty miles to Wichita. If you average from fifteen to twenty miles a day—as you should unless you stop overly long to enjoy your conjugal rights—you should arrive at Wichita in early November. You will then proceed by stagecoach to San Francisco, where I have a dear friend who will arrange a job for you. He is a widower, very rich, and has been barren through two marriages. Thus he will have a sturdy little son to bear his name and inherit, eventually, his fortune."

Benson nodded, then glanced toward the back of the wagon and grinned wolfishly. "One question, Mr. Cournier. Do I have to stay married to that bitch? I'm starting to get tired of her."

"That, Roger, is because you're more of a gourmand than a gourmet at the banquet of love. I fear that you tried to glut yourself too quickly with the fastidious Miss Harrison. As a consequence, she is probably even more tired of you than you of her. Well, to answer your question, since you are leaving my service to take employment with another, I leave you to your own devices. I'm sure you're ingenious enough by now to do what you please."

Benson smiled craftily. "She might just get bitten by a snake. I hear tell there's lots of rattlers out where we're going, Mr. Cournier. Well, it's been nice working for you. Want to shake hands?"

"Just one time, Roger, since you are now a free man. Now understand me, I don't care what you do with your bride, but I care very much what happens to that child. If I find that you haven't carried out my orders, I'll have you tracked down and it won't be pleasant when you're found."

"Mr. Cournier, you know I wouldn't do a thing like that!" Benson protested.

"What I am thinking of, Roger, is that your materialistic nature might tempt you to return the boy to Luke Bouchard who, I should imagine, would gratefully pay you a great deal more money than I am paying you for undertaking this commission for me."

"No, sir, not me, I wouldn't double-cross you, Mr. Cournier!" There was sincerity in Benson's avowal. He had already observed many of the Creole's cunning enterprises and himself witnessed the agonizing atonement which had been exacted from a disloyal servant.

"Just in case the idea should enter your head, Roger, let me tell you that I have three trusted men who live near the Bouchard estate and who would, if they saw you attempting to return the boy, kill you.

"You'd best be getting a head start," he went on. "After all, you'll want to get clear of the swamps in time for your wedding night, Roger. Remember, when you get to San Francisco, you go to the house of Gerald Masterson and give him the letter of introduction with which I've already provided you." With this, Cournier went back into the luxurious mansion, and Benson, with another baleful glance toward the back of the wagon, started the horses forward.

Henri Cournier returned to the newly wedded couple and offered them a wedding supper of pheasant, champagne, and other delicacies which neither Meldrun nor his young wife Janie had even dreamed existed. Meldrun drank considerably more champagne than was good for him and, instead of retiring to the guest room which the Creole had put at his disposal, there to consummate his nuptials, insisted on whiling away the night in the gaming room.

At first it seemed he could not lose. But, as midnight neared, he began a losing streak which so terrified him that he made the fatal error of doubling his bets. An hour later, he had lost not only his $2,000 but was in debt to Cournier for the sum of five times that amount.

Half-drunk, sick at heart with the realization that his dream of a honeymoon in gaudy New Orleans had vanished, he numbly followed Cournier to the latter's office. There he learned, as in a far more tragic way poor Amy Harrison already had, that the suave Creole was pitilessly inflexible when money was owed to him.

"Obviously, Mr. Meldrun, you are penniless and have no resources from which to draw enough to meet your honorable debt to me," Cournier declared. "The game was honest; you yourself were enthusiastic with your winnings the first several hours, and so I do not expect you to complain that you were cheated."

Meldrun stared at him, then shook his head and slumped in his chair, utterly crushed by the turn of events.

"I will give you a chance to wipe out your debt, Mr. Meldrun. Since you were the one who brought the Bouchard boy to me, I owe you some small consideration. You shall have a position as a hostler in my stables. Your background on a farm suggests that you would be efficient at such a task. And it may be that from time to time, when I have assured myself that you are sufficiently responsible to be entrusted with them, I shall commission you to carry out more important duties for me. Now, sir, the hour is extremely late; I shall seek my bed, and you have a wife waiting for you."

Casey Meldrun's wedding night was catastrophic. Seeing his hangdog mood and quickly observing that he was intoxicated, Janie began to upbraid him with shrill invectives. "You stupid bastard," she raged, "that's a fine way to start off a marriage! You haven't got a dime left to your name, and I ain't neither! A stable boy, that's all you're gonna be for that Mr. Cournier. And how do you think we're gonna live in a big city like N'Awleans, you answer me that, Casey Meldrun!"

When he tried, half-heartedly, to embrace her, she sprang out of bed like a young tigress and hissed, "Oh, no you don't, mister! I told you I'd be real sweet to you if you got that money. Oh sure, you got it, and now it's all gone. Well, I'm gone, too, as far as sharin' the same bed with you. You know what I'm gonna do right now? I'm gonna go ask Mr. Cournier if he can find me something to do so's I don't starve!"

Whereupon, deaf to his entreaties, Janie Meldrun dressed, stormed out of the room, and demanded that one of the servants take her to Henri Cournier.

Amused, wearing only a velvet dressing gown as he smoked a last cigar and enjoyed a nightcap of fine Spanish brandy, the Creole listened patiently to her tirade. When she finished he soothed her, praising her youthful, ripening charms, flattering her by declaring that from the first moment he had met her and Casey, he had known that it was she who had the real intelligence and imagination. "Janie, you could be a wealthy young woman if you'd let me take charge of you," he promised.

"What do I have to do?" she demanded suspiciously.

He shrugged diffidently. "Why, no more than you'd have done tonight had you not driven that misguided young man from your bed, my dear. There are wealthy

457

men in New Orleans who would pay a great deal of money to make love to you. You would have fine clothes, jewels, a carriage of your own, and servants."

Janie's first reaction was to turn scarlet, but as he expounded on the alluring prospects which a young *demimondaine* could enjoy if she exchanged monogamy for a life of hedonism, she forgot her virginal scruples and began to hang on his every word.

He poured a glass of brandy for her, and, through lowered eyelids, watched her sip it hesitantly, cough, recover, and then finally down it. She looked up at him boldly. "If you really mean what you just said, Mr. Cournier, I shouldn't mind giving it a try. 'Course, I'll have to learn what I'm s'pose to do so's I can make all that money."

"That's quite simple, my dear." He rose from his desk and came toward her with a patronizing smile. "In my finest house of pleasure, the madam, Mademoiselle Stephanie, is a teacher who has taken raw country girls and turned them into fashionable belles, sought by the most important and wealthiest men in New Orleans. A week with her, my dear Janie, and a man like Casey Meldrun will be merely dirt under your pretty feet."

Janie rose from her chair, swaying prettily against him. She looked up at him, and asked coyly, "You really think so, Mr. Cournier? You wouldn't fool a girl like me, wouldja?"

"Of course I wouldn't, my dear. On the other hand," his left arm slipped gently around her waist, "since I own several such establishments which cater to discriminating clients, I make it an invariable rule to determine for myself the qualifications of any applicant."

Janie did not understand these elegant words, but when Cournier expertly cupped her rounded, dimpled chin and his thin lips lingeringly and knowingly merged with hers, she understood very well indeed what was expected of her. Indeed, it might well be said that, having swiftly weighed both Henri Cournier and Casey Meldrun in her scale of values, she became ardently eager to prove that, compared with the exciting and lucrative life the former proposed to offer her, the farmer's son was decidedly found wanting.

458

CHAPTER FORTY-TWO

Luke Bouchard and Dan Munroe rode back to Windhaven Plantation with Jack Stallman riding between them, his wrists tied tightly behind his back. When they arrived at the red-brick château, the two led Stallman to a tool shed and locked him in. "You won't suffocate," Luke told him coldly. "There's an outlet in the ceiling which will give you enough air to breathe. On Monday, we'll take you to Montgomery and turn you over to the county sheriff. If Phineas Atbury dies, you will stand trial for murder, in addition to the crimes of abusing my wife and abducting my son!"

"For God's sake, Mr. Bouchard," Stallman sniveled, "I swear I never touched your wife, I swear it! And it was Casey Meldrun took your kid. All I did was keep that purty li'l black-haired gal from yellin' her head off when Casey was grabbin' the kid. I don't want to hang, Mr. Bouchard, please. I'll do whatever you say, just don't let them hang me."

"Are you ready, then, to sign a confession as to what your two cohorts did? And further, will you, under oath, name the man who was behind this abominable scheme?" Luke demanded.

"Sure, sure, I'll do it, I'll do it! Just take me to the sheriff, Mr. Bouchard, I'll swear it on a Bible. Just like you said it was; we called him Mr. C. 'cause we couldn't say his fancy French name. But when you told me what it was, I recognized it right off. He was the one that did all this, that had us do it—honest to God he was, Mr. Bouchard!"

"Very well, then: I'll see that food and drink are sent to you and you'll be reasonably comfortable until Monday morning."

"Thank'ee," Stallman whimpered, slumping down to sit

on the floor, then wincing at the constriction of his bonds. "Cain't you ease these ropes some? My arms are sore and it hurts even to breathe. I give you my word I won't try to get away, Mr. Bouchard."

"All right, Dan, loosen the rope a bit, but make sure he can't get free. I need Mr. Stallman's confession to prove my case against Henri Cournier."

Dan Munroe quickly complied and then shut and locked the door of the tool shed. Turning to Luke, he asked, "Are you gonna have the sheriff send a warrant down to N'Awleans for that Cournier fellow, Mr. Bouchard?"

Luke's face was worn with exhaustion, but his eyes brightened now with a white-hot anger. "I have never believed in taking the law into my own hands, Dan. But at this moment, all I can think of is the loss of little Lucien, taken God knows where across rugged country, in oppressively hot weather, by ruffians who know nothing of how a young child should be cared for. I can think of nothing but the way that filthy animal, Arnie Grimes, besmirched Laure and gloated, like the lecherous beast he is, in subjecting her to his vile lust. But these people were only tools of the man whose brother tried by every means he knew to take Windhaven Plantation from my family and me, to corrupt my half-brother and turn him against us all, to use as his instrument the daughter of a heartless girl who changed the course of my grandfather's life."

Dan listened to him, his mouth hanging open with amazement as he began to comprehend the enormity of the crimes committed against his benevolent employer. Luke nodded as if to emphasize the import of his words as, in a low voice quivering with emotion, he continued, "Not content with all that, when I came back from Texas to aid Laure in running her husband's bank, the brother of this same man secretly tried to gain control through buying up shares of stock. Failing that, he insulted her and challenged me to a duel, during which he fired before the signal to fire had been given."

Luke paused, striving to control his blazing anger, then went on. "No, Dan, this matter concerns Henri Cournier and me most personally. When he heard of his brother's death, ignoring the news that Armand Cournier had been shot down by my second for having violated the dueling code, he proceeded to resume an old family feud which in itself had been based on deceit. I mean to go to New Orleans and confront him with Jack Stallman's confession. My lawyer, Jedidiah Danforth, will make a copy, and that confession should force Cournier to admit his guilt in this atrocious business. I will offer him the choice between an honorable duel or his arrest and conviction for rape and kidnapping and, if poor Phineas should not recover from that blow, for murder, as well!"

With this, Luke Bouchard shook hands with his loyal black worker and gently urged, "And now, Dan, you ought to get some sleep. You've been on horseback for the better part of a day and Katie'll never forgive me for demanding so much of you."

"No sir, Mr. Bouchard, Katie's real proud I could help you. We cain't never pay you back enough for all you done for us. But you're the one needs sleep bad, Mr. Bouchard."

"I'll get some, just as soon as I've seen to my wife. Thank you again, with all my heart, Dan. You'd better ask one of the men to stand guard around that tool shed, just in case our fat friend changes his mind about cooperating."

Luke went directly into the house and to Laure's room, only to find, to his pleasant surprise, that Marius Thornton had brought Dr. Jonas Medbury with him, in accordance with the urgent note Luke had left for his foreman. Dr. Medbury was a small, plump man in his early sixties, his gruff manner hiding an almost sentimental affection for his patients.

"Dr. Medbury, it was very good of you to come, sir," Luke exclaimed. "How is my wife?"

"Resting comfortably, Mr. Bouchard. I gave her something to make her sleep. Physically, she hasn't been seriously hurt. Your Miss Vourlay told me the details—abominable, sir. Whoever did that was a filthy blackguard whom I should personally like to lynch!"

"It's odd that you should say that, Dr. Medbury," Luke observed. "Her assailant died of strangulation this morning, after he had confessed and even boasted of his exploits."

"Good, sir. Admirable! That will save us decent citizens

the cost of keeping the rogue fed until he swings from the end of a rope!" the doctor fiercely exclaimed.

Laure was sleeping, and Luke bent down to kiss her cheek and forehead tenderly, and then beckoned to the doctor, who followed him out of the bedroom. "I fear the inevitable consequences of that brute's attack uopn her," he anxiously murmured.

"I am happy to assure you that you should have no real concern over that, Mr. Bouchard," Jonas Medbury assured him. "That very competent young lady who acts as nurse-maid to your children saw to it that, shall we say, necessary precautions were taken. And I myself, upon thorough examination, effected a cleansing which should certainly prevent possible conception."

"Bless you, Dr. Medbury. Have you seen to poor Phineas?"

"A mild concussion only, Mr. Bouchard. Fortunately, the rogue who struck him did not choose a part of the skull where a vigorous blow might have meant death. Within a week or two at most, he should be active again. It's true that he's somewhat feeble, and I've recommended to his wife that she give him as much nourishing broth, good butter, cheese, and milk as he can consume."

"I'd be grateful, Dr. Medbury, if you'd come back next week to see to both your patients," Luke told him with a warm smile. "And please accept this as your fee. You rode a good distance and, I'd say, well after office hours."

"Oh, Mr. Bouchard, that's far too much!"

"Not nearly enough for what your services are worth to me and to my peace of mind, and mostly to poor Laure's. Thank you again for coming, and please, before you go, let Hannah prepare some food for you. Your horse needs resting, and you've traveled a good distance as it is."

On Monday morning, Dan Munroe and Luke Bouchard, with Jack Stallman between them, rode to Montgomery. There, in the office of the county sheriff, the profusely sweating fat man made a long-winded confession, citing the meeting with Henri Cournier in Mobile, even quoting to the best of his memory the Creole's remarks as they concerned the fate of little Lucien and Laure.

Leaving the prisoner to be remanded to the county jail,

Luke and Dan went to Jedidiah Danforth's office, where the attorney's clerk prepared a neat copy of the confession, the original of which was to remain in the lawyer's files.

That done, Luke and Dan headed back to Windhaven Plantation, having learned that the *Alabama Belle* would arrive late that evening in Montgomery and be ready to return downriver by the following noon. "I'll catch her at the wharf, Dan, and go on to New Orleans. Marius can carry on quite ably with the crops and the cattle, and after all, you men know your work and are doing it admirably," Luke commented.

They reached the château shortly after suppertime, and Luke went directly to his wife's room. Mitzi was with her, holding little Paul in her arms, and Laure gently stroked the boy's black curls.

"Are you feeling better, my dearest?" Luke asked as he came to the bed and bent down to kiss her cheek. But Laure uttered a soft little laugh, cupped his face in her hands, and kissed him on the mouth. "Why, Mr. Bouchard sir," she murmured, "I should think that a husband who has given his wife two children would hardly be the sort to content himself with such an unfeeling peck. Now kiss me properly, or I'll begin to think you were what I first called you when we met at the Union House!"

"Oh, my dear one, my sweet love," Luke exclaimed as his arms enfolded Laure's supple body and he kissed her eagerly. Mitzi could not suppress a sentimental sniff.

At last Luke straightened, drew a deep breath, and declared, "By rights, my darling, I should stay. But I have to go to New Orleans. I've found out who it was that had this done to you and who arranged for little Lucien to be taken from us."

"Who could it be, Luke? I thought that Armand Cournier was the only enemy you'd ever had, and he died as he deserved," Laure replied.

"I prayed myself that with his death that ancient enmity would be erased forever. But Armand had an older brother, Henri. The brother had a plantation in Haiti, and when news reached him of Armand's death, he returned to claim his inheritance. Jason Barntry wrote me about that."

"But you never told me," Laure reproached him softly.

463

"There was no need to. It would only have worried you. No, I asked myself, too, whether this brother, whose existence I hadn't even known about until Jason's letter arrived, would be content to let matters rest. Also, to protect us against the other eventuality, I had my men stand armed guard as much as was practical. And after all these months, when I heard nothing more from Jason, I began to believe that all danger was past. Then Arthur Traylor, who, as you remember, seconded me in the duel with Armand Cournier, wrote to tell me that he was being ousted from his post as deputy chief of the civil guard and warned me that Henri was apparently involved with evil associates, just as his brother had been."

"It sounds like a nightmare, my darling. But it doesn't matter what happened to me—I want little Lucien so! Oh God, Luke," she raised herself on the pillow, "it must be so frightening for the poor child! Who knows where they've taken him or whether they even bothered to feed or clothe him, or—oh, my God—they may even beat him!"

"I know, I know, dear. Don't fret yourself." Luke gently grasped Laure's shoulders and eased her back down on her pillow. Then he kissed her again and said, "And it's because we both know the agony that our innocent little son must be suffering that I must go to New Orleans and face Cournier. Let us hope not only that I can bring back our boy, but that I can finally put an end to this hatred. I don't know how long it will take, Laure, I must warn you. But I swear that I won't return until I've found our son."

Laure's eyes filled with tears and she nodded, then held out her arms to him. And Mitzi, holding back her own tears, silently tiptoed out of the room.

CHAPTER FORTY-THREE

Carrying a valise and an overnight bag, Luke Bouchard walked down the gangplank of the *Princess* shortly before noon on Friday, September 17, 1869. A cab took him first to the city hall, where he asked to see the new deputy chief of the civil guard. After an hour's waiting, he was at last ushered into the presence of a prissy man in his early fifties, with pince-nez and a fussy little mustache.

"Well, sir, state your business; I'm already late for a luncheon appointment at Antoine's," the deputy chief demanded.

"My apologies, Mr. Diedeman. But I believe the matter urgent enough to wish to consult you before I took any further action."

"Well, sir, get to the point!" Arnold Diedeman made an impatient gesture.

"Your predecessor, Arthur Traylor, was my second in a duel with Armand Cournier, a notorious gambler and speculator, among other things, and an associate of the equally notorious Pierre Lourat."

"That is ancient history, sir. I believe you said your name is Luke Bouchard? Well, Mr. Bouchard, Mr. Traylor departed for California some weeks ago, and what he and you did in the past, officially or unofficially, is none of my concern. I do wish you would hurry with this, sir."

"I'll be brief, then, Mr. Diedeman. A week ago, three men broke into my house near Lowndesboro, raped my wife, and kidnapped my older son. The man who abducted the boy has not yet been found. The man who ravished my wife is dead, after having confessed in front of witnesses that he indeed was her assailant. And the third man, Mr. Diedeman, is at present in the Montgomery County jail. He has already made a full confession which

465

involves not only those two associates of his, but Henri Cournier, the brother of Armand. I have brought along a notarized copy of that confession; the original, of course, is with my lawyer and will be used in civil proceedings against the prisoner."

With this, opening his valise, Luke took out the copy, unfolded it, and laid it before Diedeman.

"What do you expect me to do with this?" The deputy chief adjusted his pince-nez, and stared accusingly at his unwelcome visitor.

"I had thought, Mr. Diedeman, that you, as the foremost law officer in New Orleans, would wish to issue a warrant for the arrest of Henri Cournier."

"Oh, you did, did you, Mr. Bouchard? Let me tell you that this apparent crime—and I have only this copy of a so-called confession and your own word as to its veracity—took place in a different state. I can hardly arrest a man in Louisiana and take him to stand trial in Alabama. Be reasonable, Mr. Bouchard. It seems to me that your logical course would be to initiate civil action against him from your own point of venue."

"I see. I am sorry to have taken up your time, Mr. Diedeman. I should hate to think that you would miss your luncheon at Antoine's," Luke said as he rose and left the pompous little man's office.

On the street, he hailed another cab and, with the air of a man of the world bent on pleasure, asked, "I've heard that a Monsieur Henri Cournier has some of the finest houses of pleasure and gambling between here and New York. Do you, by any chance, know of these?"

"All New Orleans knows Henri Cournier, monsieur," the driver, a genial, gray-haired Creole, volunteered. "Generally, a gentleman visits the *maisons de luxe* in the evening."

"And I shall certainly do that. But at the moment, *mon ami*, I have a desire to try my skill at baccarat."

"Ah, in that case, monsieur would be well advised to visit the Bon Jeu."

"It is certainly appropriately named," Luke chuckled.

"Assuredly, monsieur. Shall I take you there now?"

"Would this famous gentleman be there at this time of day, do you think?"

"Of a certainty. It is his favorite house of chance, and I myself have driven him there many a time. He takes his luncheon, you see, in his office. There is a little restaurant around the corner which has the most magnificent and authentic gumbo one can find anywhere in our beautiful city."

"And I am hungry, too," Luke observed. "Perhaps, if I spend enough money at the Bon Jeu, Monsieur Cournier will offer me some of this superlative gumbo. Drive me there, and we shall see what we shall see!"

The elegantly uniformed doorman at the Bon Jeu held open the door for the impeccably dressed patron and, as was customary, wished him, *"Bonne chance!"*

"Let us hope that your prediction is correct, *mon ami,*" Luke retorted. "Is Monsieur Henri Cournier in this establishment?"

"Mais oui; he is in his office. Shall I tell him that you wish to see him, monsieur? If you will give me your name—"

Luke had turned away for a moment to look into the luxuriously furnished waiting room to his left, and had perceived, going down the velvet-carpeted corridor, a pretty young girl dressed in a fashionable white silk gown in the act of entering a room halfway down. "Why, there's Viviane Legros, I met her at the opera last night!" Luke exclaimed, rushing forward. Then, before the doorman could halt him, he strode swiftly down the hall and, putting his hand to the knob of the door, flung it open.

Luke stared at a man with a waxed mustache and neatly pointed Vandyke. He wore a red silk waistcoat and white silk trousers, a yellow silk cravat with a diamond stickpin, and was dipping a silver spoon into a bowl of Creole gumbo, while his left arm circled the waist of the young woman who stood beside him, her right hand gently stroking the back of his neck. At the sight of Luke Bouchard, he dropped the spoon into the bowl and at the same moment the young woman gasped and moved to one side. "By what right, sir, do you break into my office unannounced?" His voice was dry and querulous.

"By every right, if your name is Henri Cournier," Luke solemnly replied. He had dropped his overnight bag beside the open door, and now opened his valise and drew

467

out the copy of Jack Stallman's confession. He tossed the valise beside the bag and advanced slowly toward the desk behind which Cournier sat.

"But all New Orleans knows my name, monsieur. How do you presume to say that this gives *you* the right to disturb me when, as you can plainly see, I take my *déjeuner*? No, don't go, Janie, I'll get rid of this fellow presently."

"Indeed, I'd like her to stay, Monsieur Cournier, to be witness," Luke interposed.

"You begin to mystify as well as annoy me, monsieur. State your name and your business. I can only assume that you came here to try your luck with the cards, the dice, or the wheel. Maurice, who ought to have stopped you outside, could easily have led you to the game of your preference without this uncalled-for interruption."

"I should not say that it was uncalled for, Monsieur Cournier. You see, my name is Luke Bouchard."

The blond girl uttered a startled gasp and recoiled, a hand to her mouth, staring at Luke as if she had just seen a ghost. From Henri Cournier, there came a malicious chuckle. "So at last we meet. I've been interested in knowing what you really look like. And you say you have the right to march into my establishment and to disturb me in my private office?"

"I am here, Cournier, to accuse you of having caused the rape of my wife and the kidnapping of my older son, Lucien."

"*Mon Dieu!*" Henri Cournier leaned back, laughed softly, and responded, "And now, besides being a meddler and a boor, you are guilty of slander, Monsieur Bouchard. On what proof do you base this outrageously absurd accusation?"

"On the confession of your henchman, Jack Stallman, Monsieur Cournier. I have it here—a copy, since I took care to leave the original with my lawyer in Montgomery. Besides that, I have the dying statement of Arnie Grimes, the man who molested my wife."

Cournier turned pale, and put his fingers to the tips of his mustache, nervously twisting them. "These are names which mean nothing to me, Monsieur Bouchard," he said at last.

"They should, Monsieur Cournier. If you care to read this confession, you will see that Jack Stallman gives many interesting details concerning your conversation with him and Arnie Grimes in a certain tavern in Mobile. According to him, it was you who proposed that my wife be shamed and used, her clothes ripped from her, and then treated as if she were one of the whores in your pleasure houses. But most interesting of all, Monsieur Cournier, is the fact that Stallman, to save his fat neck from the gallows, named your third accomplice who carried off my son Lucien—Casey Meldrun."

"Casey—oh, my God!" Janie cried.

"Shut your mouth, you stupid country bitch!" Cournier snarled. Springing from his chair, he turned to the wall behind him, on which two superb French rapiers with basket guards were hung. Swiftly disengaging the lower one, he moved, catlike, around the side of his desk and advanced toward Luke. "Very well, Monsieur Luke Bouchard. I will admit that your evidence is sufficient to cause me some small concern. However, it will never reach any court of law. I shall kill you, and Maurice and Janie here will testify that you broke into my office, that you tried to have me tear up one of your gambling IOUs. When I refused, you tried to kill me. Naturally, I had to defend myself."

"But, Henri, darling—" Janie gasped.

Cournier was at her right, and, without taking his eyes off Luke, clenched his left fist and struck out viciously. With a cry of pain, the woman staggered back and sprawled on her side, then began to weep hysterically. "Now, Monsieur Bouchard, stand still. I shall make it swift. A single thrust to the heart, although it's much more than you deserve for the shame and dishonor you've brought to the Cournier family."

With this Henri lunged, the long, deadly blade of steel aimed at Luke Bouchard's chest. But Luke leaped to one side and, swiftly glancing around him, saw a chair and seized it. As Cournier lunged again, Luke parried the thrust with his improvised shield, shoving his assailant backward. Then he sprang toward the other side of the desk, having seen the other rapier in place on the wall rack.

469

"I admire your agility, Monsieur Bouchard, but it will hardly help you. I'm a master with the rapier, and I shall not content myself with a single thrust to your heart. I shall wound you many times, so that you begin to feel a little of the pain and agony you Bouchards have made us suffer!"

With that, he lunged again. Luke was able at the last moment to deflect the glittering blade by swinging the chair sideways and dashing the rapier to one side. Having taken his opponent off-balance for an instant, Luke took full advantage of it. With a bound, he was at the rack and had drawn the paired weapon free.

"Bravo!" Henri Cournier taunted him, lifting his own rapier straight above him in the traditional salute of one duelist to another. "I confess I do not mind a fair fight when the odds are all in my favor. *En garde!*"

Janie Meldrun had regained her footing, gingerly rubbing the bruise on her jaw and cheekbone which Cournier's fist had so savagely and unexpectedly inflicted. She cowered back now, both palms pressed against the wall to the left side of the desk, her eyes huge, her bosom heaving as she watched this bizarre scene.

Lazily, Cournier extended his blade in a straight line, and Luke touched the tip of his rapier to it. But, in the classical feint from that position, the Creole lunged upward at Luke's throat. The Alabamian parried clumsily, and Cournier laughed, his eyes glittering with hatred. "You know the rudiments, *mon ami,* but that is all you know. Now, let us see how you parry—this!" His blade had dropped, almost to the floor, then suddenly risen in a wide arc, only to flicker downward and thrust with sinister purpose toward Luke's chest. But Luke lunged to one side, and the blade went harmlessly past. At the same instant, his short thrust drew blood from Cournier's upper left arm.

With an annoyed exclamation, the Creole stepped back, glancing at his arm. "*Touché,* but only a scratch. It will be the only victory you will take to your grave, Bouchard."

Again he lunged with deadly intent and once more only a clumsy parry deflected the blade from Luke's heart. Yet the point of the rapier, shoved downward, grazed Luke's left side and drew blood in turn.

"There, you see!" Cournier triumphantly crowed. "And now, I think I shall put an inch of this good French steel into your belly. Oh, it won't be fatal, but there will be many others—*alors!*"

Once again from the *en garde* position, his narrowed eyes measuring his opponent, the Creole made a wide flourish with the shining rapier, advanced his right knee, and lunged. This time, Luke's parry was not in time, and an exultant laugh broke from his opponent's thin lips as the point of his rapier embedded itself a full inch, to the right of Luke Bouchard's navel.

Janie Meldrun uttered a scream as she saw Luke stagger back, his face contorted with pain. "Don't kill him, please don't kill him, Henri, I can't stand to see it!" she wailed.

"I told you I should take some time with this murderer," Henri rebuked her. Then again he lunged. This time, his reflexes slowed by the throbbing pain of that last wound, Luke Bouchard was unable to parry it completely. Janie cried out again as she saw Cournier's rapier tip gouge his opponent's left side along the rib cage. Bright red blood spurted from the wound.

"A few more, and you'll be begging me to kill you," the Creole laughed. Then, dropping into the *en garde* position once more, he made his blade dance to the left and to the right, taunting his weakened adversary. "Come on, what do you fear? Is my swordsmanship too much for you, murderer of my poor brother?"

Goaded by pain and blind, unreasoning hate, Luke flung himself forward, waving his rapier above his head and then thrusting. Taken by surprise at his opponent's renewed and unexpected burst of energy, Cournier moved back, not noticing that he was at the very edge of his huge desk. As he moved back again, preparing to lunge, Luke thrust home.

The rapier dropped from Cournier's hand, his eyes dropped and became aware of Luke's rapier buried deeply in his abdomen; then he clapped a trembling hand to the bleeding wound. Luke Bouchard swiftly wrenched out the rapier and stared at the Creole, whose face was ashen and whose eyes, dilated and glazed, seemed to Luke to stare at him almost quizzically. "May God forgive me for taking a human life," Luke said, his voice shaking, "but your death will end, for all time, the evil you have done to me and mine—and, God alone knows, to countless others." Then, tightening his lips, he thrust the rapier into Henri Cournier's heart.

"Oh, Mr. Bouchard, you're hurt bad—" Janie Meldrun babbled as she stumbled toward Luke.

With a great effort, he turned to her. "You called out when I said Casey Meldrun's name—do you know him?"

"Mr. Bouchard, he's my husband—oh, I've got to get a doctor for you—"

"Wait—tell me—he was the one who took my son, wasn't he?"

"Yes, sure, I—I was his girl—we got married—and then he lost all the money Mr. Cournier gave him fer stealing your kid. But I swear I don't know where they took him, Mr. Bouchard. All I did was help Casey git to N'Awleans 'cause I wanted to marry him so bad. Honest, I didn't have anything to do with stealin' your kid!"

Luke was panting, and a giddy weakness had begun to take hold of him as he groped his way to the desk. He leaned against it, head bowed, trembling now with reaction to his own pain. Cournier, his eyes wide and staring in death, was bent across his desk, the rapier protruding from his chest. Slowly, the lifeless body began to sink and then fell with a thud to the velvet-covered floor.

CHAPTER FORTY-FOUR

By the last day of September, Roger Benson had driven his team across the Sabine River and was nearing the little town of Kilgore. Using Henri Cournier's map, he had avoided the worst of the swamps and lowlands, but the desolate terrain through which the indicated trail took him had badly frayed his nerves. He had filled his water kegs at the river, and as he returned with the last one, a sinister rattling sound made him stop in his tracks, his heart pounding wildly. Coiled on a rock near a clump of mesquite lay a huge rattlesnake, flicking out its narrow, pointed tongue. Cautiously reaching for the revolver holstered at his right hip, the burly valet drew it and fired. The snake began to thrash, unwinding its hideous coils, and Benson fired again and again, uttering a strident oath in his terror, until at last the snake's convulsions ended.

Little Lucien Bouchard began to cry, frightened by the sounds of the shots, and Amy, cuddling him in her arms, her calico dress torn and the faded marks of the whip visible on her bared chest, shoulders, and neck, cried out, "For God's sake, won't we ever get out of this horrible country?"

"Shut your mouth, you bitch! I wish I'd never laid eyes on you!" Benson snarled as, giving the dead snake a wide berth, he lifted the last keg with effort and trundled it back to the wagon. "The worst is over now, Amy, but I swear, if you keep squallin' and you can't keep that brat quiet any better'n you do, I'll leave you out here with that dead rattler for company!"

"I wish you would," she muttered under her breath, closing her eyes and shuddering.

Each day had been agony, but each night had been hell itself. Alone with this girl whom he had so sadistically subjugated, Benson had unleashed all of his depraved carnal cravings. He had whipped her brutally the first night on the trail, when her inept attempts at cooking his supper had infuriated him. She no longer tried to resist or even to protest when his carnal fantasies compelled her to endure unnatural uses of her body at which even a whore in the lowliest New Orleans crib would have rebelled. At times she had thought of killing him, or at least herself, but he had shrewdly made certain that at no time was she within reach of his revolver and the fine new Spencer repeating rifle with which Cournier had provided him. To make doubly certain, he saw to it that at night both weapons were unloaded and the ammunition kept in his trouser pockets.

Climbing back into the driver's seat, he turned to glower at her. "It's a couple of hours till sundown, so we'll make camp after I've covered five or six more miles. Hell, the further we can go each day, the sooner we'll get to Wichita. This goddamn wagon is just as uncomfortable for me as it is for you, and don't forget it, bitch!"

Although President Grant had, in April of this year, approved the act of Congress which created the Board of Indian Commissioners, the Kiowas and Comanches were not ready yet to trust the United States government. In the fall of 1865, these two mighty Indian nations, as well as the Kiowa Apaches, had signed a treaty near the mouth of the Little Arkansas, the site of Wichita. The tribes had agreed to occupy a reservation in southwestern Oklahoma. But the government had failed to live up to the terms of the treaty. A few months later, a new pact was signed at a council on Medicine Lodge Creek, seventy miles south of Fort Larned. The three tribes were officially confederated and agreed to move to their reservation—a move which symbolically marked the end of freedom and independence for them.

Perhaps a third of the Comanches settled on the land assigned in Oklahoma, but it was not easy. The government had made no preparations for them and there was little game in the region. By the summer of 1868, the beginning of the end was already in sight. Lucien Edmond Bouchard had realized it when he had met with

Emataba, *mico* of the Creeks. If the Indians lived on the reservation, they found little food. If they remained away, they were set upon by federal troops.

President Grant, yielding to the petitions of fairminded citizens, decided to appoint to this new board Quakers who would regulate the future lives of submissive Indian tribes. Laurie Tatum had, just at the time that Roger Benson began his wagon trek toward Wichita, become the Kiowa and Comanche agent at Fort Sill. Kindness and honesty, Tatum was sure, would solve the Indian problem. And yet two-thirds of all the Comanches did not come to the new reservation, and Tatum could scarcely provide for those who *had* accepted their fate.

It was for that reason that many offshoots of the Comanche nation broke apart and wandered in their nomadic, almost desperate quests to find campsites where there would be game. Such a band was that of the fearsome Penateka Comanche, who ravaged the southern region of Texas.

One humid September evening, as Roger Benson drew his horses to a halt and began to make camp for the night, a band of twenty war-painted Penateka Comanches galloped past the little hamlet of Longview and headed south. One of their scouts thought that he had seen buffalo tracks near the Sabine River. Kiminanto, chief of the war party, had overcome the objection of his braves in following so isolated a trail. "We have not had fresh meat for a week," he rebuked them. "Our squaws and our children go hungry, and they wait in our stronghold. If there is even a deer or a few rabbits, at least they will have some meat for the fire. Come, we ride!"

The scout had seen Benson's campfire, and galloped back to tell Kiminanto. "White-eyes, one wagon, four horses," he had excitedly reported.

"It is good. The white-eyes will have food, and he will have a gun. We shall take the wagon to our stronghold, it will have many uses," the chief declared. His braves raised their lances and uttered the fearsome war cry, a prolonged ululation which had been the last sound that many a would-be white settler in southern Texas had heard before a whizzing arrow or a hurtling lance had obliterated his senses forever.

"Ride swiftly! If there is but one white-eyes, he must not be allowed to kill Comanche warriors!" Kiminanto ordered. Then, drawing his old Sharps from its rawhide sheath, he loaded it, and rode forward on his mustang at the head of the band.

Roger Benson stood, hands on his hips, his eyes fixed on the young woman who crouched over the iron pot under which he had built a small fire. "Christ, you still haven't learned how to fill a man's belly right and proper!" he snarled and kicked her brutally in the hip with the toe of his heavy boot.

Amy uttered a stifled groan, righted herself, and began to stir the contents of the pot in an effort to satisfy him. His lips curved in a cruel, anticipatory smile. "You jist wait till I get you to bed tonight, honey. You haven't shown enough respect 'n love for your hubby lately, but we'll fix that tonight, see if we don't. Now hurry up, I'm fair starved! Wait until I get to San Francisco and have me some of those crabs and some good wine, just like Mr. Cournier does. Come on, come on, I don't want to waste too much time eatin', we got other things to do tonight, haven't we, Amy?"

But Amy was staring, transfixed, at the group of horsemen who suddenly appeared out of the twilight and circled around them.

"What's the matter with you? Didn't you hear me? I said—oh—Jesus—aaaahhhh!" A feathered arrow lodged in Benson's throat, and he fell to the ground, his hands scrabbling at the shaft, his feet kicking sporadically, until, with a gurgling moan he lay still.

Amy could not move. She remained crouched in front of the pot, her hand frozen to the long spoon. A young Comanche brave rode swiftly toward her, lifted his lance, and plunged it into her heart. It was swift, it was merciful, and as blackness claimed her, there was time, perhaps, for an infinitesimal prayer of gratitude.

The Comanche reined in their mustangs, waving their lances and bows, shouting in jubilation at their victory. Kiminanto himself dismounted, strode to the wagon, and peered inside. Then he drew back, his face twisted with surprise and called, "*t taat tual* [a little boy!]"

Michanido, his war chief, clambered onto the driver's

seat and looked inside for himself, then crawled to little Lucien, who was crying in terror at the sight of the half-naked, painted Comanches.

"Bring him out, that we may see him," Kiminanto ordered.

The war chief seized little Lucien, laughing with amusement as the boy tried to strike out at him with his fists, and leaped down to the ground, then carried him to the fire which Benson had prepared. He called, "There is something strange here, Kiminanto!"

"What is it that you see?" The Comanche leader peered at the boy.

"This, about his neck. It is turquoise."

"Yes! I have seen it before—but it was then part of a great stone, the stone of a great chief who killed many white-eyes soldiers after they had slain his people," Kiminanto exclaimed.

"But how can it be, Kiminanto, that a man-child of the white-eyes would wear a piece of the stone of Sangrodo?"

"That I do not know, Kiminanto, but we are Comanches, wanderers like the mighty Sangrodo and his tribe. He will know what to do with this white-eyes man-child. You will take him there, Michanido. The other braves and I will take the food, the wagon, and the weapons back to our stronghold."

"It is far from here but I will do your bidding, my chief."

"All Comanches know where the mighty Sangrodo holds his camp now, so that the white-eyes soldiers will not seek him out for having conquered their brothers. It is across the Rio Grande, near the village of Maxtime. Saguardti, give him your horse, it is fresher and faster than his own. Ride, ride, Michanido, and tell Sangrodo that we of the Penateka send him this man-child who wears a piece of his stone to show that we are his brothers as we have always been and shall be!"

CHAPTER FORTY-FIVE

Luke Bouchard had fainted from loss of blood after his duel with Henri Cournier. Janie Meldrun, piecing together what she had heard in that violent confrontation, at last understood that Luke had been the aggrieved one rather than the guilty party. She had rushed out of Cournier's office, urged the doorman to go across the street and bring Dr. Jules Raimond and then summon the civil guard. That action had undoubtedly saved Luke's life, for he was bleeding profusely when the Creole doctor hurried in and bent over him. Swiftly the physician stanched the bleeding, and then commanded, "It will be necessary to take him at once to the hospital. Before you call the civil guard, get some of the men who work here to carry him—very gently, *entendez-vous*—to a carriage. Take him to the Hôpital des Veuves. I shall accompany him."

Twenty minutes later, Luke was carried gingerly to a bed in the old hospital. Dr. Raimond made a full examination of his wounds, and at last announced himself satisfied that the bleeding had stopped. He gave orders that the patient be watched carefully and get plenty of rest.

When Janie Meldrun told what she had seen and heard to the three officers of the civil guard who had come in response to Maurice's call, she was taken with them to the city hall to make a formal deposition. The new deputy chief, remembering Luke Bouchard's demands upon him, had testily begun to try to shake her story. "I tell you, young lady, this very man entered my office and accused Monsieur Cournier of absolutely incredible crimes. How can I be sure that what you are telling me is the truth, that he did not go there for the express purpose of murdering that worthy gentleman?"

"Because I heard Mr. Cournier laugh and tell Mr. Bouchard that, yes, he'd arranged for all those things, but that he was going to kill Mr. Bouchard so it wouldn't matter whether he knew, that's what," Janie had insisted. And so, at last, the deputy chief was satisfied, albeit grudgingly, that it had been a fair fight and that Luke Bouchard was innocent of any charge of murder.

There had been a mild thunderstorm over Carrizo Springs at noon of the day on which Luke Bouchard had at last put an end to the peril which had threatened Windhaven for so many years. After lunch, however, the sun came out, and soon it shone brightly on the ranch house, the chapel, and the lands surrounding them.

Kate Strallis had finished washing and putting away the dishes, and, seeing that little Jeremy had fallen asleep, yielded at last to little David's plea to go for a walk. He could not as yet express that wish in words, but the lovely young widow understood his signs—especially the tugging at her skirt, which signified his eagerness to accompany her outdoors. His favorite place was near the creek, where he would clap his hands in delight at the sound of the birds or the croaking of frogs hidden in the tall reeds which lined the bank.

Little Carla had volunteered to stay with Jeremy during his nap, so Kate lifted David into her arms and crooned to him, "Yes, mama's big boy will have his walk right now."

She left the kitchen and circled the house, Jubal trotting after her, barking and wagging his tail, coming up to her and rubbing his muzzle against her leg. She reached down to pat his head, and he licked her hand. "See the good doggie, Davey?" she said to her little son, who nodded and linked his arms around her neck. She laughed joyously, kissed him, then opened the door of the stockade and went out toward the creek.

Pablo Casares had decided to spend this rainy morning making a little flute for David. Its sounds would imitate the birdcalls which so delighted the boy. He had just about finished it, and decided that he would try it down at the creek to see if its playing might draw some of the birds and thus prove he had done his work well.

He whistled softly to himself as he walked slowly out of

479

the stockade, and then stopped, his eyes widening with pleasure. Beyond him, he saw Kate walking slowly. She was wearing the dress he had bought for her in Wichita. There was a lump in his throat, and he looked up at the blue sky and blinked his eyes, then took out his handkerchief and vigorously blew his nose. "You're an old fool, Pablo Casares," he scolded himself. "She is young and *muy linda*, how can she care for an old vaquero like you? Oh, *si*, she has said that she thinks very much of you, but that is because she is a good woman; she is polite, and she speaks so well. She has love in her heart, but it is for her *niños*. *Madre de Dios*, it is time you went back to Neuvo Laredo and found yourself a *mujer* who is as ugly and old and wrinkled as you. Such a one would make a wife fit for a vaquero like you, hombre."

He quickened his step to catch up with her. Kate had not yet seen him, and now stooped to put little David down. He walked a few steps, then sank to all fours and began to crawl toward the bank of the creek.

Pablo put the little flute to his lips and blew it experimentally. Ah, it was good, there was the call of the night dove, almost as if the dove were there! David would like this very much. And when the other one was a little older, he, Pablo, would make another flute just like this one. It was never wise to let one child be favored over another.

Now he was only a few feet away from Kate, and again he put the flute to his lips and blew, more loudly. She whirled, and uttered a soft laugh of recognition and pleasure. "It's you, Pablo—my goodness, I thought it was a dove, I really did! How clever of you!"

"It is nothing señora. I have made it for the little one."

"How very kind of you, Pablo. But didn't I tell you to call me Kate? You keep on calling me señora all the time."

"I—it is a habit with me, out of respect, you see," he fumbled, shifting uncomfortably from foot to foot like an errant child.

"But you know, if you keep calling me that, you will make me angry. And I do not—"

"Wait, do not move—" Pablo interrupted her in an agonized whisper. "Move away to my right, quickly!"

Her eyes widened, but she obeyed, her eyes fixing on

480

his face. The little boy had moved forward on all fours toward an oval-shaped rock in front of which was a wide, shallow hollow in the moist ground. Against the base of that rock was a huge scorpion.

"Do not call out; do not startle the boy; be very still!" Pablo whispered as he began to tiptoe in a semicircle to his left.

David had stopped, seeing the scorpion, and was about three feet away from the deadly creature. It was eight inches long, with a long, curved tail at whose end was its poisonous stinger. Two young calves had already died from scorpion bites the past summer, and although the poison rarely killed a man, it would surely kill a child.

David uttered a happy little laugh and inched forward, extending his right hand toward the scorpion. Drawing a deep breath, crouching, Pablo now moved behind the rock and suddenly flung himself upon it. David uttered a startled cry and looked back tearfully at his mother who, a hand at her mouth and pale as death, was watching helplessly.

As he fell upon the rock, Pablo had reached out with his hands to push away the little boy. The fall had stunned him and he lay for a moment, panting hard.

Kate ran toward David, picked him up, sobbing with relief, covering him with kisses, and then turned to the vaquero. "Are you hurt? Oh, Pablo darling, speak to me, are you hurt?"

"*Es n—nada*—I think I have killed it. Wait, I will get up now and see," he gasped, the hard rock having momentarily knocked the wind out of him. He righted himself, and laughed exultantly. "*Bueno!* The rock has crushed Señor Alacrán!" Then, to show her, he warily extended his booted foot and forced the rock upward. The scorpion had been crushed to a pulpy mass but still quivered, and Pablo hastily forced the rock down again upon it to hide the sight.

Kate, tears running down her cheeks, had set David on the ground and was running toward him. To his astonishment, she flung her arms around his neck and began to kiss him, half-laughing, half-crying, "Oh, Pablo, Pablo, what more do I have to do to tell you that I care for you very much, that I want you? Now you've saved my David, and you still won't call me Kate, no, nor even kiss me. How can I make you understand?"

He was trembling now, and he felt his own tears mingle with hers as, with a joy that left him speechless, he held her tightly to him and gave her back kiss for kiss.

Dr. Raimond had insisted that Luke Bouchard convalesce in the Hôpital des Veuves for at least two weeks. So, despite Luke's protests, the kindly but determined nuns who served as nurses compelled him to submit to long days and nights of total inactivity. These made him fume with impatience because of the time wasted in his quest to find his kidnapped son.

When at last Dr. Raimond pronounced him fit, Luke demanded, "I know that I *feel* fine, Dr. Raimond, but I want to know if I can travel."

"That'll depend, Monsieur Bouchard," the doctor replied, "on how strenuous a journey you mean to undertake."

"Will my wounds reopen or will there be any danger if I ride on horseback for, shall we say, a week or so?"

Dr. Raimond pursed his lips and frowned. "No, but I should not recommend it. The fact is, Monsieur Bouchard, you've lost a great deal of blood. I would not tempt fate or gamble on your mature age by too long a journey."

"I shall have to take my chances, Dr. Raimond. I must go to Texas. My little son was kidnapped from me and the man who arranged it sent him West with a companion in his hire. My oldest son is in Texas, and it's just possible he may be able to help me trace my little boy."

"I understand, Monsieur Bouchard," the doctor replied. "But if you must make such a trip, get plenty of rest and good food along the way. And may God be with you and may He return your son to you!"

"Amen to that, and my deepest thanks for your skill in keeping me alive to carry out that wish, Dr. Raimond."

The day after leaving the hospital, Luke Bouchard boarded the steamboat *William Wallace*, which he and his family had once taken from New Orleans to Corpus Christi on their way to Windhaven Range, and which he had taken alone when he returned to New Orleans from Texas. Bearded Captain McMurtrie did not recognize Luke at first. There were more passengers on this trip than he had taken aboard the past six months. But after the steamboat had cleared port in New Orleans and headed down the gulf, Luke went up to the captain's deck and introduced himself. "By all that's holy, it's been a long time since I last clapped eyes on you, man!" the old captain exclaimed as he gripped Luke's hand and shook it warmly. "Aye, now I remember well. You were telling me then your poor wife, peace to her gentle soul, was killed by bandits, and you were going back to New Orleans—yes, it comes back to me—and then on to Alabama."

"You've a remarkable memory, Captain McMurtrie," Luke smiled. "And I'm still in Alabama. My oldest son, Lucien Edmond, has been most successful with the ranch near Carrizo Springs." His face grew grave as he turned to watch the distant wharf recede and saw the seemingly limitless stretch of the calm waters of the gulf. "I spent some time in New Orleans, and I married the widow of my dearest friend and went back to Alabama. But, you see, Captain, the little boy she bore me was kidnapped and sent West. I'm on my way to see my son Lucien Edmond in the hope that I can find my little abducted son."

"And you'll make that long trek all by yourself on horseback from Corpus Christi? That's a hardship I wouldn't wish on anyone. Corpus Christi indeed—without any sacrilege—" here the bearded captain crossed himself devoutly— "I don't think our Dear Lord would want His body to founder in that dreary hellhole of a port. Now, Mr. Bouchard, come to my cabin and I'll drink a tot of rum with you to the hope you'll be bringing back your little boy on my good old ship!"

Luke arrived in Corpus Christi on the eighth of October and, after spending half a day trying to buy a horse, at last succeeded in obtaining a somewhat restive brown mare, for which the owner charged him an exorbitant price. The rest of the day was spent in providing himself with supplies—cooking utensils and a rifle for the long journey ahead. He awoke at dawn in the wretched little

483

hotel near the wharf, paid his bill, and, without bothering to stop for breakfast, mounted his mare and rode off toward the west.

It had taken twelve days in that hot July of 1865 for the Bouchards to travel from the barren port of Corpus Christi to the fertile valley of Windhaven Range. But they had been encumbered by wagons and delayed by a bandit attack. After the first few days of his journey, Luke's wiry body became inured to the physical exertion, as did his spirit to the seemingly endless monotony of riding through uninhabited land. The driving, plus the torturing knowledge that his little son was in the hands of conscienceless rogues who had carried him to God-alone-knew-what destination, goaded him on. He even begrudged the time it took to prepare a simple meal, or the hours wasted in sleeping; and each day he arose at dawn—often before it—to water his horse, and then mount it and travel on.

There were agonizing moments for Luke Bouchard whenever his mind dwelt on little Lucien. What if, through neglect, improper feeding, carelessness—even the brutality of the kidnappers—his son were to die? How could he console Laure? And how could he console himself? Alone for seemingly endless days and nights, with only his mare for company, Luke was tortured again and again by that possibility. His only recourse at such times was to kneel, clasp his hands, and pray to a just and merciful God to spare little Lucien. "Thou who has marked even the flight of the sparrow," he prayed one night, his voice hoarse with emotion, "look down upon this innocent child, stretch out Thine hand to him, and shield him from misplaced vengeance. Oh God, if I have offended Thee, I earnestly beseech Thee to punish me. But please, most merciful Lord, please spare my child!"

Even the recalcitrant mare seemed to sense Luke's dogged will, and agony-driven anxiety, for it became docile and obedient enough after the first day. Though she was strong, he knew the terrain well enough not to push the steed beyond its abilities. If the horse should drop under him, or break its leg in some gopher hole, there would be no chance of replacing her. Just as four years ago, there were still almost no settlers along the trail.

By noon of October 17, 1869, Luke Bouchard rose in his saddle with an exultant shout as he saw the circle of the stockade which surrounded Windhaven Range.

"Come on, *amiga*," he said, patting the brown mare's neck, "we're nearly home. Then you'll have all the water, oats, and sugar you want. You've earned them. Now, one last gallop and we're there!"

The mare pricked up her ears and responded at once to the gentle nudge of his boots. He could see the dugout where Andy Haskins and Joe Duvray were quartered for sentry duty against attack. He could also see new houses beyond the stockade, which had not been there when he had gone back to New Orleans. They were the houses of his daughter Mara and her husband, Ramón Hernandez, and of Lucas and Felicidad.

He glimpsed someone coming toward him now on horseback—it was Simata, the Indian scout. Luke cried out and waved his sombrero, and Simata quickened his gelding's pace and galloped to meet him.

"Mr. Bouchard! We'd hoped you'd come here! How good it is to see you again, my friend." The Indian held out his hand and Luke clasped it with both of his, feeling tears well up in his eyes.

"Lucien Edmond's at home?" he demanded.

"Yes, Mr. Bouchard. And your friend Sangrodo is here with Catayuna and her newborn son."

"Sangrodo, Catayuna—oh, this is good news indeed! Hurry, Simata, I can hardly wait to see them again after all this time!"

The two men galloped toward the open gate of the stockade. Luke dismounted, scarcely feeling the bone-weariness of his long journey. Then the door of the ranch house opened, and Sybella came out holding a little blond boy in her arms. Beside her stood Lucien Edmond and Maxine.

"Lucien—oh God—oh God, I thank you!" Luke Bouchard sobbed aloud as he sank to his knees, clasped his hands and looked up at the sky. Then, hardly believing his eyes, he rose to his feet and ran toward Sybella. "Mother, dearest mother—and my little Lucien, my son—but how—it's like a dream—"

"No, my son, it is the will of our dear God," a gentle voice interrupted.

Luke turned to see a plump, nearly bald Franciscan friar. And beside him, tall and proud, stood Sangrodo, the Comanche chief. Catayuna, in doeskin, holding a tiny baby in her arms, stood beside her husband.

Lucien Edmond came forward and embraced his father. "Father, how wonderful to have you here! Your wire from the hospital, which that good doctor sent to me at San Antonio, arrived a week before I had to go there for supplies. So I knew that little Lucien had been kidnapped. But you see, father, the man and the woman who had taken Lucien from New Orleans were attacked by a band of Penateka Comanches. They were killed, but their chief recognized the stone of Sangrodo about Lucien's neck. He sent his war chief to Sangrodo's stronghold with the child to ask what should be done with him. Recognizing that bit of the talisman, Sangrodo in his wisdom knew that it must belong to a Bouchard, and so he brought Lucien safely home to me just last night."

"Yes, it is indeed the will of our dear God." Luke Bouchard's voice broke with emotion. He turned to the Franciscan friar. "Will you hear my confession, Father, and then how I rejoice at God's great kindness and His pity for a sinner?"

"Yes, assuredly, my son."

"Father, this is Friar Bartoloméo Alicante," Lucien Edmond interrupted, an arm around Luke's shoulders. "He has lived with many of the Indian tribes and came to us this spring. Our vaqueros built this chapel so that they might worship here. Friar Bartoloméo asked that we take him on the drive to Abilene, so that he might visit the Creek village in Indian territory—it is the reservation to which those Creeks whom you loved had been sent. And now he's come back to us, to dedicate our chapel."

"Then let me be one of the first worshipers," Luke said humbly. He held his little son in his arms. Little Lucien put out his hands to tug at his father's beard, and Luke laughed through his tears.

Then he turned to the Franciscan friar. "You have the same feeling of brotherhood with the Indians that my grandfather, my son Lucien Edmond, and I have always had, Father."

"Yes, my son. But now my services are no longer needed at the Creek village. There is a young doctor there, Dr. Ben Wilson. He has been there only a few weeks, but already he has helped cure many of the sick. He cured the little baby of that poor girl, Elone, who had been captured by a tribe whose people were killed by wicked men. She fled to the Creek village, and Emataba gave her shelter. I think, though it is much too soon, that Elone will one day console that good man for his great loss."

"Ben Wilson in Indian territory?" Luke echoed wonderingly. "But why—"

"Father, Fleurette died of diphtheria in Pittsburgh. Ben came here, sick with his grief—as we all are—" Lucien Edmond paused and bit his lips.

"My lovely little sister," Luke murmured sadly, "so gentle, so selfless, with such a gift of love!"

"Ben told us she didn't suffer, father. He operated on her, but her heart stopped. There was no pain. We have his children with us now, Thomas and baby Sybella."

Luke Bouchard sobbed unashamedly. Then he turned to Sangrodo and Catayuna, holding out his hands, and the Comanche chief and the beautiful Mexican woman clasped them in wordless communion. Luke at last controlled the tears that blinded him. Kissing his little son again, he turned and said, "Lucien Edmond, you are the patrón of Windhaven Range, so it is you who give the orders here. Will you then summon all your vaqueros to the chapel, so that all of us may give thanks to Him who guides our lives and gives us courage against the deadliest of perils?"

"Gladly, father." Lucien Edmond's voice was unsteady as he turned to Simata. "Simata, bring Ramón and Mara, and the Belchers. And Kate and her boys, too—soon Friar Bartoloméo will be marrying her to Pablo Casares."

Half an hour later, in the crowded chapel, the Franciscan friar stood before the altar, his voice joyous as he asked benediction. "O dearly beloved God of our fathers, hear our voices raised to Thee in praise of Thy goodness. Truly this day Thou hast shown Thy mercy and kindness upon this family, bound in love and in faith. Here is Thy house, built out of the wilderness, verily, in the same way that Elijah the prophet sought to venerate Thee, built by good men from another land who worship Thee as do all the people of this Thy bounteous earth. Accept it, O dear Lord, with our humility and our unending devotion and belief in Thee. Didst Thou not say, 'Suffer the little children to come unto Me, for theirs is the kingdom of Heaven'?"

Then he turned to the breathless worshipers and said gently, "Let us pray."

Luke Bouchard, cradling his son in his arms, raised his eyes to the altar and said softly, "Thou hast given me back my son, as Thou didst unto Abraham. With Thy blessing, if it be Thy Will, I shall go back to her who bore Lucien and Paul, and there I shall build a chapel, too, in Thine eternal homage."

Dear Reader:

The Pinnacle Books editors strive to select and produce books that are exciting, entertaining and readable . . . no matter what the category. From time to time we will attempt to discover what you, the reader, think about a particular book.

Now that you've finished reading *Windhaven's Peril,* we'd like to find out what you liked, or didn't like, about this story in particular and the Windhaven Saga in general. We'll share your opinions with the author and discuss them as we plan future books. This will result in books that you will find more to your liking. As in fine art and good cooking, a matter of taste is involved; and for you, of course, it is *your* taste that is most important to you. For Marie de Jourlet, and the Pinnacle editors, it is not the critics' reviews and awards that have been most rewarding, it is the unending stream of readers' mail. Here is where we discover what readers like, what they *feel* about a story, and what they find memorable. So, do help us in becoming a little better in providing you with the kind of stories you like. Here's how . . .

WIN BOOKS . . . AND $200! Please fill out the following pages and mail them as indicated. Every week, for twelve weeks following publication, the editors will choose, at random, a reader's name from all the questionnaires received. The twelve lucky readers will receive $25 worth of paperbacks *and* become an official entry in our 1979 Pinnacle Books Reader Sweepstakes.

The winner of this sweepstakes drawing will receive a Grand Prize of $200, the inclusion of their name in a forthcoming Pinnacle Book (as a special acknowledgment, possibly even as a character!), and several other local prizes to be announced to each initial winner. As a further inducement to send in your questionniare *now,* we will also send the first 25 replies received a free book by return mail! Here's a chance to talk to the author and editor, voice your opinions, and win some great prizes, too!

—The Editors

Subject to all federal, state, and local restrictions; void where prohibited by law.

READER SURVEY

NOTE: Please feel free to expand on any of these questions on a separate page, or to express yourself on any aspect of your thoughts on reading . . . but do be sure to include this entire questionnaire with any such letters.

1. Are you glad you bought this book, and did it live up to your expectations?

2. What was it about this book that induced you to buy it?
   (A. The title_____) (B. The author's name_____)
   (C. A friend's recommendation_____)
   (D. The cover art_____)
   (E. The cover description_____)
   (F. Subject matter_____) (G. Advertisement_____)
   (H. Heard author on TV or radio_____)
   (I. Read a previous book by author_____ . . .
   which one? _____)
   (J. Bookstore display_____)
   (K. Other? _____)

3. What is the book you read just before this one?

   And how would you rate it with *Windhaven's Peril?* _____

4. What is the very next book you plan to read?

   How did you decide on that? _____

5. Where did you buy *Windhaven's Peril?* _____

(Name and address of store, please):

_____

_____

6. Where do you buy the majority of your paper-backs? _____

7. What seems to be the major factor that persuades you to buy a certain book?

_____

8. How many books do you buy each month?

_____

9. Do you ever write letters to the author or pub-lisher . . . and why? _____

_____

10. About how many hours a week do you spend reading books? _____ How many hours a week watching television? _____

11. What other spare-time activity do you enjoy most? _____ For how many hours a week? _____

12. Which magazines do you read regularly? . . . in order of your preference _____,

_____, _____,

_____

13. Of your favorite magazine, what is it that you like best about it? _____

_____

14. What is your favorite television show of the past year or so? _____

15. What is your favorite motion picture of the past year or so? _____

16. What is the most disappointing television show you've seen lately? _____

17. What is the most disappointing motion picture you've seen lately? _____

18. What is the most disappointing book you've read lately? _____

19. Are there authors that you like so well that you read *all* their books? _____
Who are they? _____

20. And can you explain *why* you like their books so much? _____
_____
_____

21. Which particular books by these authors do you like best? _____
_____

22. Did you read Taylor Caldwell's *Captains and Kings*?_____ Did you watch it on television?_____
Which did you do first? _____

23. Did you read John Jakes' *The Bastard*? _____
Did you watch it on TV?_____ Which first?_____
Have you read any of the other books in John Jakes' Bicentennial Series? _____
What do you think of them? _____

24. Did you read James Michener's *Centennial*?_____
Did you watch it on TV?_____ Which first?_____

25. Did you read Irwin Shaw's *Rich Man, Poor Man*? _____ Did you watch it on TV? _____
Which first? _____

26. Of all the recent books you've read, or films you've seen, are there any that you would compare in any way to *Windhaven's Peril*? ____

27. Have you read any books by Patricia Matthews? ____ Which ones? _____

28. Have you read any other books in the Windhaven Saga, by Marie de Jourlet? ____ Which ones? _____
Did you read them in the order they were published? ____

29. Have you read any books by Gloria Vitanza Basile* or Michãela Morgan†?
*The House of Lions ____   †Madelaina ____
*Appassionato ____   †Zanzara ____

30. Which one did you like best, and why? _____
_____
_____

31. In the Windhaven books, which character did you find most fascinating? _____
Most likeable? ____ Most exciting? ____ Least interesting? ____ Which one did you identify with most? _____

32. Do you think any of Marie de Jourlet's characters were based on real historical figures? If so, who reminded you of whom? _____
_____

Would you like more involvement of historical characters? _____
_____

33. Rank the following descriptions of *Windhaven's Peril* as you feel they are best defined:

	Excellent	Okay	Poor
A. A sense of reality	____	____	____
B. Suspense	____	____	____
C. Intrigue	____	____	____
D. Sexuality	____	____	____
E. Violence	____	____	____
F. Romance	____	____	____
G. History	____	____	____
H. Characterization	____	____	____
I. Scenes, events	____	____	____
J. Pace, readability	____	____	____
K. Dialogue	____	____	____
L. Style	____	____	____
M. Values	____	____	____

34. Do you have a favorite classic whose main character(s) you would like to see continued in a sequel? ____ In a movie? ____ Which classic(s)? _____
_____

35. Have you read the sequel to *Wuthering Heights*, entitled *Return to Wuthering Heights*, by Anna L'Estrange? ____ Would you like to see the movie? ____

36. Would you be interested in reading a sequel to *Jane Eyre*? ____ *Madame Bovary*? ____ *Moll Flanders*? ____

37. What, in your opinion, is the best or most vivid scene in *Windhaven's Peril*? _____
_____

38. Did you find any errors or other upsetting things in this book? _____
_____

39. What do you do with your paperbacks after you've read them? _____
_____

40. Do you buy paperbacks in any of the following categories, and approximately how many do you buy in a year?

   A. Contemporary fiction   _____

   B. Historical romance   _____

   C. Family saga   _____

   D. Romance (like Harlequin)   _____

   E. Romantic suspense   _____

   F. Gothic romance   _____

   G. Occult novels   _____

   H. War novels   _____

   I. Action/adventure novels   _____

   J. "Bestsellers"   _____

   K. Science fiction   _____

   L. Mystery   _____

   M. Westerns   _____

   N. Nonfiction   _____

   O. Biography   _____

   P. How-To books   _____

   Q. Other _____

41. And, lastly, some profile data on *you* the reader . . .

A. Age: 12–16_____ 17–20_____ 21–30_____
31–40_____ 41–50_____ 51–60_____
61 or over_____

B. Occupation: _____

C. Education level; check last grade completed:
10_____ 11_____ 12_____ Freshman_____
Sophomore_____ Junior_____ Senior_____
Graduate School_____, plus any specialized
schooling _____

D. Your average annual gross income: Under
$10,000_____ $10,000–$15,000_____
$15,000–$20,000_____ $20,000–
$30,000_____ $30,000–$50,000_____
Above $50,000_____

E. Did you read a lot as a child?_____ Do you
recall your favorite childhood novel? _____
_____

F. Do you find yourself reading more or less
than you did five years ago?_____

G. Do you read hardcover books?_____ How
often?_____ If so, are they books that you
buy?_____ borrow?_____ or trade?_____ Or
other?_____

H. Does the imprint (Pinnacle, Avon, Bantam,
etc.) make any difference to you when considering a paperback purchase? _____

I. Have you ever bought paperbacks by mail
directly from the publisher?_____ And do you
like to buy books that way? _____

J. Would you be interested in buying paperbacks via a book club or subscription pro-
gram?_____ And, in your opinion, what would
be the best reasons for doing so? _____
_____ . . . the problems in
doing so? _____

K. Is there something that you'd like to see
writers or publishers do for you as a reader
of paperbacks? _____

_____

*THANK YOU FOR TAKING THE TIME TO REPLY
TO THIS, THE FIRST PUBLIC READER SURVEY
IN PAPERBACK HISTORY!*

NAME _____ PHONE _____
ADDRESS _____
CITY _____ STATE _____ ZIP _____

Please return this questionnaire to:

The Editors; Survey Dept. (WS)
Pinnacle Books, Inc.
2029 Century Park East
Los Angeles, CA 90067